About the Author

Meg Hutchinson left school at fifteen and didn't return to education until she was thirty-three, when she entered Teacher Training College and studied for her degree in the evenings. Ever since she was a child, she has loved telling stories and writing 'compositions'. She lived for sixty years in Wednesbury, where her parents and grandparents spent all their lives, but now has a quiet little cottage in Shropshire where she can indulge her passion for storytelling.

Also by Meg Hutchinson

Abel's Daughter
A Handful of Silver
No Place of Angels
A Promise Given
Bitter Seed
A Love Forbidden
Pit Bank Wench
Child of Sin
No Place for a Woman
The Judas Touch

Writing as Margaret Astbury

The Hitch-Hiker

For the Sake of Her Child

and

No Place of Angels

Meg Hutchinson

WH S

First published as two separate volumes:
For the Sake of Her Child © 1996 Meg Hutchinson
First published in Great Britain in 1996 by Hodder & Stoughton
First published in paperback in 1997 by Hodder & Stoughton
A division of Hodder Headline
A Coronet paperback

No Place of Angels © Meg Hutchinson
First published in 1998 by Hodder & Stoughton
First published in paperback in 1998 by Hodder & Stoughton
A division of Hodder Headline
A Coronet paperback

This paperback omnibus edition published for
WHSmith PLC 2001

A Coronet paperback

2 4 6 8 10 9 7 5 3 1

Hodder and Stoughton
A division of Hodder Headline
338 Euston Road
London NW1 3BH

A CIP catalogue record for this title
is available from the British Library.

ISBN 0 340 82315 1

Printed and bound in Great Britain by
Clays Ltd, St Ives plc

WHSmith PLC
Greenbridge Road
Swindon SN3 3LD
www.whsmith.co.uk

For the Sake of Her Child

Meg Hutchinson

WH S

For my parents. With my very deep love and gratitude for a truly wonderful childhood.

Prologue

'Shit!' George Walker swore vehemently, feeling the sharp stone bite into the ball of his right foot. ''Ang on,' he called to Ben Corns who, hands in pockets and head down against the cold April morning, was picking his way along the narrow path that was a short cut from the drab back-to-back houses of Lea Brook to Brinson's steel foundry. 'Summat in me shoe.' George hopped on one foot while rearranging the layer of cardboard he had cut and fitted to the inside of his shoes the night before, to cover holes that stretched from side to side.

'Summat in thee shoe?' Ben sniffed, too cold to take his hand from his jacket pocket to wipe away the drip festooning the end of his nose. 'Well, whatever it is, it ain't no sole. Thee wants to tek them to old Harris an' get 'im to put a bottom on 'em.'

'Oh, ar?' George shoved his bare foot back into the shoe only prayer was holding together, wiggling it around, trying to slide the cardboard insole to a more comfortable position. 'An' what do I pay 'im with? John Harris is a good cobbler but he ain't no saint. You can't pay, then he don't mend. Like I says, he don't do nothin' for love.'

Ben sniffed harder, his top lip curling back towards his nose in an effort to dislodge the enlarging drip.

'So 'is missis tells my Kate. He only meks the effort on a Saturday night, an' 'er 'as to buy 'im an extra quart of Old Best afore he can rise to that – and at best it's over in two minutes. 'Er reckons as 'er don't know why 'er bothers, 'er would get more pleasure from drinking the quart o' Best 'erself!'

Their laughter rang out in the sharp cold dawn, sending a cloud of startled crows shooting into the air.

George stared after them for a moment, watching the effortless way they lifted clear of the dismal smoke-blackened buildings.

Wednesbury . . . He glanced behind him at the untidy strangle of decaying houses that was his end of the dirty little Midlands town. Christ, no wonder they called it the Black Country!

'George . . . hey, George!'

Ben Corns's call broke into George's thoughts, something in the tone telling him to hurry up.

'What's up?' He hobbled along, his right foot held awkwardly sideways; the cardboard was precious thin, every stone threatening to pierce it through. This damp would see it off soon enough and that meant sparks from pouring steel under feet as good as bare.

'What's up?' he asked again, catching up with Ben who was staring down at the grey-black water of Millfield Pool.

Millfield Pool had once been a shaft of the Bluefly Coalmine; it had flooded following an underground explosion that had taken nine men with it, among them George's own father. There were folk in the Brook said Millfield Pool was haunted, that the calls and cries of the trapped men could still be heard on summer nights, but that was claptrap – old women's talk. George didn't cotton to such daftness. Nevertheless his eyes found a way of drifting away from the slatey mouth of the dead mine.

'Down theer. Look, George.' Ben pointed towards a mantle of green weed that circled the pool. 'Look theer in them weeds.'

George didn't want to look. He didn't believe in no tales of hauntings – bloody silly old women with nowt better to do than talk such daftness! – yet still he didn't want to look into the waters that had swallowed his father; waters that had added a thousandfold to the misery of an already poverty-stricken existence. In his earliest years he'd had to finish school at dinnertime to spend the rest of the day, and much of the night, running and fetching for anyone who would pay a penny; then at nine years old start working dawn to the early hours, doing anything that would add a few coppers to his mother's earnings from skivvying up at The Lodge. He could likely have earned more if he'd gone to the mine but his mother would have none of it. It had taken one, she told him, it wouldn't have another. So it had gone on until they could manage no longer and he had taken work at Brinson's.

'George . . . oh, bloody 'ell!'

Ben grabbed his arm, causing him to bring his right sole down hard on the ground. He winced, not knowing if it were caused by the sudden jab of pain through his foot or from the sight of black cloth being spread by the breeze ruffling the calm surface of the water.

'Oh, Christ, it's 'er . . . it's Mary Carter!'

Ben's work-grimed fingernails pressed through the thin cloth of George's jacket, the drip on the end of his nose jiggling as he looked up at his friend who was a clear six inches taller than himself.

'Don't you talk so muttonheaded.' George shook off the hand with its mute demand and looked again at that patch of black. 'I'll tell thee summat, Ben Corns, you've got Mary Carter on the brain. Didn't Beth Haywood say as how the wench buggered off wi' a bloke from around 'Ampton way?'

The drip jiggled precariously with the shaking of Ben's head. 'Mary Carter wouldn't buggar off wi' nobody. I'm tellin' thee, George, somebody 'as done for 'er.'

'Done for 'er?' George echoed the words scathingly. 'More like somebody's done *to* 'er. Probably copped for a babby and took off rather than face the music, not that you can blame 'er for that, knowing the Lea Brook . . .'

''Er weren't 'avin' no babby.' Ben grabbed his elbow. ''Er wouldn't look at a man after 'er Jed was took an' you know it. I'm tellin' yer, George that's 'er down theer an' if you'm so sure it ain't then you won't be agen goin' an' 'avin' a look.'

A push to George's elbow added to the challenge, but George hung back, reluctant to accept, for fear of going near the water that terrified him.

'That ain't anythin' other than some old rags.' He shook his friend's hand from his elbow. 'Kids likely throwed 'em in.'

Ben sniffed loudly but unsuccessfully.

'Well, if they'm just old rags you won't mind goin' an' provin' it.'

The challenge was unmistakable: refuse it and George would be the laughing stock of the foundry for weeks to come; accept it and he risked worsening the nightmares he still suffered from, of men drowning in Millfield Pool.

'If we am late we'll get quartered,' George countered, hoping the reminder they would lose pay if they were a minute late arriving at Brinson's would deter Ben from challenging him further. But his ploy fell on deaf ears. Ben was determined to see if his supposition was right.

'Go on,' he urged, 'whatever it is down theer, it can't eat yer.'

Unwilling to lose face before the men at the foundry . . . because hear of it they would, Ben was too fond of a good story to let the pleasure of telling it go by . . . George slithered down the shallow bank that gave on to the edge of the pool, feeling the scree of coal chippings shredding the cardboard from his soles.

'Can yer reach it?' Ben asked, as close to George's rear as a dog after a bitch in heat.

Gritting his teeth, George stretched out a hand and grabbed the slime-covered cloth.

'It's 'eavy,' he muttered, heaving at the sodden mass, 'you'll 'ave to give me a hand.'

Together they freed the floating cloth from its anchor of weed.

'Oh, Christ!' Ben breathed as a wreath of brown hair appeared on the grey water. 'Oh, Christ . . .'

Detaching itself from his nose, the pearly dewdrop fell on to the swollen, blotched face of Mary Carter.

Anna Bradly sat on one of the two wooden chairs that, together with a scrubbed wooden table, almost filled the tiny kitchen. Her feet, bare below the cotton of her blue print dress, rested on the drab hearth.

How long had it been? Leaning her head sideways, she let it rest against the rough brick of the wall. Light from the oil lamp on the mantelpiece caught the movement of her rich auburn hair. How long since Mary Carter had been pulled drowned from Millfield Pool . . . how long since the accusations had started?

Mary Carter had come twice a week to this house since Anna's mother had died in childbirth ten years ago. Mondays were given over to washing. The fire already lit beneath the brick-lined copper before she arrived, she would hang her shawl on the nail behind the kitchen door and go straight into the poky wash-house. Anna had been allowed to watch as she ladled heavy buckets of steaming water into the round wooden washtub and sometimes Mary let her help cut thin slices of yellow scrubbing soap and drop them like dusty curls in among the wash.

Thursday Mary baked.

Anna breathed deeply, remembering the smell of freshly baked bread and sugar-topped cinnamon cake. This had been her favourite day. A half-burned coal settled further into its glowing bed, sending flakes of grey ash falling into the hearth.

Anna looked back across the years since her mother's death. Standing on a chair beside a table white from years of scrubbing, she would pour the liquid yeast and sugar mixture into the huge earthenware bowl of fluffy white flour after Mary had said the devil had been raised.

'Does yeast and sugar really raise the devil?'

She remembered the smile on Mary's face as she answered, but even more clearly remembered the answer she had never understood.

'There's more than yeast and sugar can raise that one.'

Only now could she see just how true that was.

The coals settled again and Anna stared into the depths of the fire, hypnotised. Oh, the devil had been raised all right! Only not in a cup of yeast and sugar water.

It had been on a Friday morning. Two men crossing the fields to work had seen the floating mass of clothes caught in the reeds; they had pulled the body on to the narrow path skirting the water-filled mine shaft . . . the body of Mary Carter.

'Death from misadventure' had been the Coroner's report but people hereabouts had called it murder, a murder they accused Anna's father of committing. That had been three years ago and not one of them had set foot in this house since.

At thirteen Anna had taken on the running of it, watching the taunts and jibes turn her father from a quiet man to a morose, withdrawn shadow.

He had murdered Mary Carter, they said, because she'd refused his advances. She would have nothing to do with his filthy suggestions so he had forced himself on her, then, knocking her senseless, thrown her into Millfield Pool.

Anna closed her eyes. Her father was innocent, that much she knew. Mary Carter had always arrived at the house after he had left for work and had long gone home before he returned. How could he have murdered her?

The hollow echo of the old tin bucket rattling across the cobbled yard woke Anna. The low fire now gave little light, and for a moment she could not make out the shape looming in the doorway as the door was thrown back on its hinges.

'Where are you, you bloody bitch?'

The harsh shout rang in the silence. Her father was drunk again. This had become the pattern of his life: trying to sink his pain at the bottom of a pint tankard.

'Where are you . . . you lying, stinking bitch?'

Stumbling forward, he half-fell across the table, sending the cups she had set out for tomorrow's breakfast crashing to the floor. Anna stood up, reaching for the oil lamp, turning the wick a little higher. She would help him to bed as she had done so many times; once there he would sleep off the beer.

'There you are, Mary Carter!'

He had pushed himself upright. Eyes glazed with alcohol and hatred stared at Anna. Her hand fell away from the lamp; he had called her by that name before, always when the accusations had been flying thick and his drinking heavy.

'No . . . it's me, Father . . . Anna.' She didn't move, watching the swaying of his head as he continued to stare at her.

'Do you know what you've done to me, Mary Carter?' The question was thick and slurred. 'Do you know what I've gone through because of you? The lies and insults I've suffered. Do you, you cow, *do* you?'

'Father.' Anna spoke softly, carefully. She had never seen him this bad before. 'Father, it's me, Anna . . . Mary has gone home.'

'Do you know what they are saying down there, those bastards!' He banged a heavy fist on the table, setting the knives dancing a crazy jig. 'I'll tell you what they're saying: they are saying I screwed you, forced you when you said no, then knocked you senseless and threw you into the pool.'

Swaying, he moved around the table, dim light filtering through the open door, turning him into frightening solidity. His hands hung at his sides, his head lolled tipsily forward on his neck. 'But that's not true, Mary Carter, and you know it. Screwed you? – Pah! – Christ knows I never laid a finger on you.'

Across the short distance Anna could smell the beery fumes

exhaled with each breath. Something must have happened, someone in The Collier must have baited him more than usual for him to have drunk himself into such a state. Nervously she stepped forward, bare feet soundless on the flagged floor.

'C'mon, Father, I'll help you upstairs.'

His eyes continued to stare. Locked on her face, they did not see her, but what they did see contorted his expression to a twisted mask of bitterness. He moved slowly, head thrust forward, feet shuffling on the stone floor and Anna wanted to cry out but was afraid. If she remained calm he would recognise her and that terrible look would be gone from his face.

'No, by God, I never laid a finger on you. Was that why you did it? Was that why you told your cronies that every time you came to this house I made you lie with me? Was that pretence to cover the fact that I never did?'

He came closer. The dull yellow pool of light cast by the oil lamp flickered over his face, touching the long smear of blood on his left cheek, paling before the glitter of his almost transparent blue eyes.

'And why didn't I, did you tell them that, Mary Carter? Did you tell them Jos Bradly takes no whore?'

Anna clutched her hands tightly, pressing them against her sides as her father took another swaying step towards her. She had thought to help him to bed but now instinct told her to get to her own room. He would shout and swear for a few hours, smash a few dishes, but she could clear up in the morning. Right now she was safer out of his sight, for in his drink-fuddled mind he was seeing not her but Mary Carter.

'For months I've taken the brickbats,' he began again, but this time he didn't shout. His words were little more than a whisper, almost as if he were talking to himself. 'For months they've pointed the finger at me, accusing me of that which I never thought to do. Well, now I've changed my mind. I've taken the insults so I might just as well take the pleasure.'

For the first time in her life Anna was afraid of her father.

He would never harm her in his normal state. But tonight he was not normal, he was in drink. And there was worse than that wrong with him; the long months of mental torment since Mary's death, months of being a social outcast, treated like a leper by those who had called themselves his friends, had at last broken him.

Heart thumping, she stepped sideways. The light from the lamp, what little there was of it, was shining into his eyes. If she moved slowly, chances were he would not notice.

But she was wrong. One hand shot out, grasping the hair tied at the back of her neck and at the same time wrenching her forward, her scream muffled by the rough material of his jacket.

'You can go, Mary.' Above her head the words came out in a quiet sing-song voice. 'You can go, but this time it will be the truth you'll tell those bastards.'

Pulling back her head, Anna's anguished cries did not register on his fevered mind. Wiping his free hand across his face, mixing blood and sweat together, Joseph Bradly swore with the soft vehemence of one who has waited long for vengeance. Then, grasping the neckline of the cotton dress, he ripped it violently downward, tearing the cheap thin material to the hem.

For a moment he stared at the creamy skin above Anna's bodice then that garment too was torn away, his hand leaving a smear of blood across her breast.

'This is what you've talked of so often to your dirty-minded women friends, you filthy, bloody bitch! That you were crucifying a man didn't matter to you, did it? Well, now you're going to pay.'

'Father . . . please, Father, it's me, Anna. Father, please . . .'

Anna's screams died as a blow to the side of her head sent her spinning to the floor and the blackness of nightmare began. A nightmare that would stay with her for the rest of her life.

His weight pinning her to the floor, he dragged away her underclothes, freeing his own body as he did so. Then, with one knee forcing her legs apart, he drove deeply into her. Each thrust was like a red hot knife but Anna was already beyond pain. Her mind closed to what was happening to her body, she did not cry out. Eyes closed too, she waited while her father vented his rage and passion.

At last it was over and with a low grunt he rolled away from her.

Anna lay still, his sweat drying cold on her bare skin. Above her the yellow flame flickered a warning of the lamp's need for oil but she did not move. How long she lay there she could never later remember but at last, limbs as numbed as her mind, she pushed herself to her feet.

Her dress lay half under the snoring man stretched on the floor and there she left it. Pulling the remnants of her underwear about her, she walked slowly upstairs.

Moonlight silvered the tiny room that had been hers from birth, but Anna saw none of its magic. In a trance-like state she filled the bowl on the wash stand from its matching jug, unaware of the icy sting as she plunged her hands into the water, lifting palmsful to her face. For long seconds she threw the water over a face almost as cold, then stripping off her torn garments, reached for the thick greyish bar of soap. Again and again she scrubbed herself, covering every inch of her body, ignoring the sting of carbolic where the violence of his entry had lacerated her. She scrubbed her breasts, washing away the smear of blood; scrubbed her stomach where the flesh felt sticky; and still she scrubbed, trying to wash away the smell of his breath from her nostrils, the touch of his sweat-soaked flesh, the memory of what he had done to her.

Silver light turned a cold grey before Anna finally slipped a clean white calico nightdress over her frozen body. Her hair, still wet from the merciless scrubbing, dripped spots of icy water on to the front. In the small mirror hanging from a nail on her bedroom wall she watched them spread and join, forming a smear, the way the blood from her father's hand had smeared her breast. It was only then, hands blue with cold covering her face, that she sank into a heap on the bare wooden boards and cried: the desperate, hopeless crying of a soul doomed to everlasting torment.

The same grey light paling to opalescent pearl fingered past the undrawn curtains of the tired kitchen. The last embers of the fire had long settled and the lamp gave no more light. Groaning from the stiffness of his cold limbs, Joseph Bradly stood up. Shaking the last clouds of alcohol from his brain and remembering. That whore Mary Carter had got what she deserved. From now on the insinuations of the townspeople would carry some truth at last. Satisfaction in the grim set of his mouth, he reached for the poker, stabbing ash from the grate with hard jerky movements. Now she would have something to talk about, the bloody bitch. It was this last thought that halted his assault on the cold cinders. Mary Carter was dead! He had seen her bloated corpse laid on the path by Millfield Pool. He couldn't have been with her last night, it could not have been her, but he had . . .

Turning from the grate, he saw in the faint blush of morning the heap of torn blue cotton where he had lain. He reached for it, the iron poker dropping loudly to the stone hearth. He knew this dress. He had seen delight spread across the face of the child he had bought it for. Lifting the cloth to his face, he could smell the faint scent, as if the pattern of cornflowers gave off a living perfume . . . and then he knew. Last night he had not wreaked vengeance on Mary Carter. Last night he had raped his own daughter.

Chapter One

The long climb up Church Hill seemed neverending. Glancing at the black, smoke-grimed walls of the ancient Parish Church that crowned it, Anna thought it still seemed as far away as when she began the trudge up Ethelfleda Terrace.

Back aching with the effort of freeing every step from mud that threatened to suck her down, swollen mound of a stomach making her lean awkwardly back, she willed herself on.

Pulling her foot from the squelching earth, she gripped the basket she was carrying, forcing the bamboo handle painfully into the flesh of her palm. But the pain went unnoticed, hidden beneath the breath-snatching agony that suddenly lanced through her.

Clutching at the nearest gate, Anna leaned heavily against it, her breath coming in short frightened gasps.

It had started, she thought through the pain. The long hopeless months of waiting were about to end. The child that had been set inside her with so much pain and bitterness was about to enter the world, about to begin a life that would be led the same way, could only continue in the malice and hatred that had been her lot since the finding of Mary Carter's body.

One hand gripping the grey splintered wood of the garden gate, Anna gasped, waiting for the pain that flared through her to diminish. Drawing in a long ragged breath, she lifted her head, glancing along the path of beaten earth that led to the door of the house. But though the curtain at the window twitched, no one emerged to help her.

She was Jos Bradly's daughter, his whore. No decent woman in Wednesbury would be seen helping her.

Sweat bathing her face, Anna pushed herself upright. She had to climb the hill. She must get home or give birth like some animal in the hedge.

Stopping every few yards, panting against the recurring stabs of pain, she dragged on to the house that once had held so much happiness for her, the house where her mother had loved and cherished her for the first seven years of her life.

Pushing open the door that gave on to the kitchen, she stumbled inside, grabbing the edge of the table that almost filled the little room, fighting the red hot spasms that threatened to cut her in two.

'Mother . . .' she moaned softly into the emptiness. 'Mother, help me . . . help me.'

But her mother could not help her. Her mother had died ten years before, died in the agony Anna was suffering now, the boy she had carried dying with her.

Letting the basket fall to the table, Anna breathed hard. She must fight the pain. She was alone and would be until past her usual bedtime. Only then did her father return to the house that had become his prison and her penitentiary.

Trying to keep her breathing calm and even, she took an enamel basin from the shabby wooden dresser. She was placing the eggs she had bought into it when fresh searing pain ripped through her, jarring every nerve with searing, brutal agony. The eggs jerked in her hands, splashing the front of her with oozing stickiness.

Anna gazed at her dress, the terror she had known once before returning with stark clarity.

Her stomach had been covered in the same slimy mess when he had finally lifted himself off her.

'No! No, mother, no!'

The cry was dragged from her as she rubbed at her dress in a vain attempt to wipe it clean.

• • •

It was too early to go back.

Jos Bradly walked out of the yard of the steel foundry in silence; no friendly wave acknowledged his going, no voice called a goodnight.

Shoving his hands deep into his pockets, he walked quickly in the direction of Church Hill. This was the wrong way, he told himself, he had never gone home before ten since . . .

He closed his eyes, momentarily trying to shut out the scene that never left him.

He never went back to the house until he knew she would be in bed, until she would not have to look at the man who had raped her. And he would not see, at least in the flesh, the hurt and fear in his daughter's eyes.

But tonight, try as he might to tell himself he must not return, his steps carried him home.

He could see from the gate that the door to the kitchen was wide open. Suddenly sick with new fear, Jos ran up the narrow path.

She was there, a crumpled heap on the kitchen floor, her red-gold hair covering her face – a face he did not need to see to know it was crumpled with pain.

'Anna! Anna, my little wench!'

Blood draining from his face, he stepped towards her then turned back to the open door.

Clear of the house he began to run, streaking away down the hill as if Gabriel's Hounds were already snapping at his heels.

'Will yer come, Polly?'

He fell into the tiny house that was one of a ribbon of tumbledown dwellings edging Trouse Lane.

'Say yer'll come? There's none other I can ask. I don't want none o' they touchin' 'er.'

Polly Shipton twisted round on her stool, her withered left leg dragging on the bare flagstones. She had wondered where he would turn when the girl's time came. Well, now she knew.

She looked up at the face she had known since childhood, a face smeared by tears mixed with the dirt of the steel foundry. Was it true what they said of him? Had he murdered one woman and then raped a young girl, and that girl his own daughter?

Polly sighed. She didn't have the answers and was never likely to have them.

'Please, Polly . . . yer must come.' At his sides, Jos's hands balled into fists. 'Anna, my little wench, 'er was on the floor. I . . . I couldn't . . . I don't know how!'

Shoving herself from the stool with her sound right leg, Polly reached for the heavy woollen shawl hanging on a nail in the scullery door. She pulled it close as she followed Joseph Bradly past the mocking eyes of the quickly gathered women – women who took care to keep their opinions in their mouths until he had passed.

Hobbling painfully, Polly kept her own head high. From this day on she would be as much an outcast in the town as the man she was following. No matter. Whatever else he might be, he was now a man sharing his daughter's agony, and the fact that she would be ostracised and ignored for helping either of them was of no consequence compared to a young girl's pain.

'It be all right, Anna.'

Pushing past Jos into the kitchen, she bent over the girl huddled on the stone floor.

'It'll be all right, me wench. Polly Shipton 'as come to be with you, Polly will take care of you. Come on now, there's a good wench, let's 'ave you upstairs.'

Hair plastered to her cheeks with sweat, Anna lifted her head and Polly saw the look of terror in her eyes as Jos Bradly bent to take his daughter in his arms.

'No . . . o . . . o!'

The scream filled the tiny kitchen and Polly Shipton knew she need go no further to find the father of the child struggling to enter the world.

* * *

Standing beside the wooden crib, Anna stared at the son she had borne a month ago, hearing in her mind the taunts and sneers that met her whenever she ventured out of the house.

She tucked the blanket closer around the sleeping child.

It had grown into something of a sport; women gathering in twos and threes as she approached, calling after her from the safety of their married respectability.

'That father o' 'er's . . .'

Words emerged from the shadows of her mind like silent wraiths.

'. . . 'e be bloody jailbait. 'Ow come the bobbies ain't fetched 'im afore now?'

They passed their taunts from one to the other, each woman raising her voice, ensuring Anna could hear.

'Ar, why ain't they? 'E killed Mary Carter, we all knows that, an' 'e be the one who 'as fathered that babby. That by blow belongs to Jos Bradly as sure as there be a God in 'eaven.'

'You didn't hear them, did you, sweetheart?'

Anna stroked a finger across her son's downy head.

'You didn't hear what they said or realise what they think, and you never will my precious . . . you never will.'

But those women had been partly right. Anna sat on her bed, one hand resting on the crib that her father had made for her own birth.

The child now sleeping in it was Jos Bradly's, in that they had been correct, but the rest of their accusations bore no truth. There was no God in heaven. She looked at the sleeping child, her heart filling with pain at what she knew was in store for him as he grew.

No, there was no God in heaven. Had there been she would not have been raped.

Rising from the bed, she lifted the child from the crib, a wild surge of love and sorrow sweeping through her as the tiny body touched her own.

'They have judged him too,' she murmured, her mouth against the tiny head, 'my father and yours. They have all judged him and, right or wrong, he will pay their price. All the years of his life will not wash away the sin of which he is guilty, even though he would have suffered death before committing it had he been sober.'

In her arms the tiny face crumpled, one arm freeing itself from the swaddling blanket, and Anna rocked gently back and forth, her lips touching her son's face, soothing away his complaining cry.

'Shhh,' she whispered, folding one finger into his clutching palm. 'Shhh, no one will hurt you. No one in this town will ever call lies and filth after you.'

But as she lifted the tiny hand to her mouth, Anna knew they would.

Anna placed the wicker laundry basket in a small hollow to shield it from the wind, checking the blanket that covered the child inside.

'You will be warm there,' she murmured, 'but Polly will be cross if she learns I brought you with me. You see, neither of us ought to be out of the house. We can't go into a shop or into anyone else's house until I have been churched.' Not that anyone in Wednesbury would have me inside their gate, much less their house, she thought. She gazed across the heath towards Ocker Bank. But if she were not churched, her son would be even more of an outcast for who would so much as glance at a child whose mother had not asked God to forgive the sin of conceiving it, whether in wedlock or out of it? But why? Anna thought. Why be forced to beg forgiveness for a sin which she had played no part in committing?

No, she had no desire to go to the Parish Church, no desire to pass the women who would be standing with shawls draped over their heads, tongues wagging, as they watched her walk alone. But she knew she would do it, for the sake of her son.

If only her mother had not died. If only . . . Anna looked into the distance where the glow of furnace fires turned the sky scarlet. There were not enough 'if onlys', not enough to give her back her life.

Beside her the baby snuffled and Anna bent to check that his face was free of the knitted blanket. Of all the people in Wednesbury, Polly alone had stood by her; Polly Shipton who had taught her so much yet had refused to tell of the herbs that would cause the child to leave her body before its time was due.

'You will come to know Polly Shipton.' Anna smiled at the sleeping child. 'She will teach you about flowers and herbs as she taught me. Look.'

Snapping a dandelion at the base of its stalk, she held the golden head over the basket.

'These can be made into soup or a drink.'

Suddenly Anna was six years old again, her tiny hands clutching Polly's skirts as they walked across the heath just beyond the town.

'Not just the flower, me wench, take the root an' all.'

Anna's mouth curved in a smile as she remembered.

'What will we make?' she had asked, running from one golden cushion of flowers to another, eager to grab them all at once. Polly had halted in her task of gathering the gleaming crop.

'Well, if you take them from the earth properly we can make several things. But you go snatchin' the 'eads off 'em an' we won't be makin' a lot of anythin' for they dandelions will be no use.'

She had hesitated then in her own task of gathering the delicate white flowers of the elder and had sat beside Anna, spreading her dark skirts on the green of the heath, and taught her to make chains from the white and purple clover. Anna draped them proudly about her neck to show her father.

She had chattered all the way back to Polly's house, dancing into the kitchen and watching excitedly as she gathered an assortment of pots and pans.

'You wash them flowers.'

Polly had stood her on an old wooden chair at the scullery sink.

'And mind you scrub all the soil off the roots.'

Anna twisted the flower she held in her hands, reliving the gentler days of the past.

Polly had kept an eye on the washing while herself drying the plants on a piece of cloth then together they laid them in the oven to roast before grinding the dried roots to make herbal tea.

'Now then.'

Polly had taken the cloud of white flowers from her basket, spreading them across the kitchen table.

'We be goin' to make these into creams and lotions that will keep that pretty skin of yours soft an' fresh, spite o' the muck that spews from them factory chimneys.'

'Like this?'

Anna had taken a sprig of white flowers, trying to make it stay on her face without holding it.

'No, not like that.'

Polly laughed, scooping up several handfuls of flower heads and dropping them into a pan of water bubbling over the fire.

'We 'ave to boil them first.'

'Like taties in a broth?'

Anna held out a tiny hand filled with fragrant snowy blossom.

'Yes, me little wench.'

Polly took the offering, dropping it beside her own in the pan.

'Just like taties in a broth.'

Now Anna sank to the ground beside her sleeping son, a wealth of loving memories in her head.

'She also taught me how to make wine from berries,' she

whispered, touching the tiny hand that had pushed from beneath the covers. 'But you watch out, young man. It makes your nose tingle. And besides, not all plants are so kind as elder flowers.'

'It won't 'urt after a minute or so.'

Anna heard the words across the years and saw again the crippled woman bend over her as she cried at the pain of a nettle sting.

'Let Polly show you 'ow to chase away that nasty old sting.'

Followed by a tearful Anna, she had gone into her tiny garden, selecting a broad leaf from a plant growing at the base of a tree heavy with apples and rubbing it over the white blisters erupting along Anna's fingers, spreading the soothing juice over the skin.

'There you be, me little love, it'll be better now.'

Then she had picked an apple from the tree, giving it to Anna before taking her indoors where she had nursed her on her knee while the apple was slowly eaten.

'Polly taught me so much,' Anna whispered, stroking a finger across the soft cheek of her child. 'She taught me what was good and what was bad. And what will you be taught, my darling? What will the bastard son of Jos Bradly be taught?'

'You must go, me wench.' Polly Shipton looked at the pale face of the young girl dressed in a plain brown dress, red-gold hair braided and tied with a ribbon. 'You must be brave for the sake of the child.'

For the sake of her child. Anna took the shawl the older woman held out to her. Everything she had lived through, the taunts and jibes she had endured, had been for the sake of the child, but how much more could she stand?

'I would come with you but you know the child mustn't leave the house until you've bin churched an' I can't leave him 'ere in the house alone.'

No, the baby could not be allowed outside his place of birth until she sought the atonement of God, the God whom her

Sunday school teachers had taught protected and loved. But where had his protection been the night she had been raped? And where his love?

Anna walked slowly from the house that stood in the lee of the smoke-blackened church, thankful that the distance at least was small. Behind her women stood beside their garden gates, their eyes as well as their criticisms on her. Passing beneath the lych gate, Anna turned from the path leading to the church door, following the worn turf to the spot where her mother lay buried. 'Sacred to the memory of Leah Ruth, beloved wife of Joseph Bradly', she read, tears blurring her vision.

'He didn't mean it, Mother,' she whispered, 'he didn't mean it.'

'Have you a covering for your head?'

The robed figure of a priest she did not recognise stood beside the pew where Anna knelt in the empty church.

She felt for the shawl, only to realise it was gone.

'You should have your head covered when you enter the house of God.' The priest did not bother to disguise the irritation in his voice. His rest between the end of Sunday school classes and the beginning of evening service was being disturbed by the churching of a girl who did not deserve the holy mercy.

Anna remained silent. Father James did not demand she cover her head before entering the church, but then this was not Father James.

'Oh, well!' The priest sighed audibly. 'We will carry on. Only next time be sure and cover your head.'

The service would be short, Polly had assured her, but to Anna, listening to words she had never heard before and giving the responses urged on her by the priest, it seemed to go on for ever.

And then it was over and the priest was gone, leaving her alone in the church. To the right of the altar steps stood a life-size replica of Christ, one hand reaching out; to the left, a figure of the Virgin cradling her infant son. Anna gazed at it and wept.

Back in the house Polly Shipton held out a cup of tea to the young girl whose hands trembled like leaves in the wind. One ordeal was over but there was a lifetime of others ahead, one of them being the christening of the child that lay sleeping in a laundry basket beneath the window of the tiny living room. Who beside herself would stand godparent to a bastard? Two godfathers and one godmother were the church's requirements for a boy child. Polly sipped the strong hot tea she had poured for herself. Where in Wednesbury could there be found two men to stand godfather to the offspring of a rapist and his daughter?

She sipped again, feeling the liquid hot against her throat. The answer was plain – nowhere.

Anna tucked the baby inside her shawl, then passed the knotted corners over her head.

'We are going to buy you some milk,' she crooned softly to the tiny face peeping up from the folds. 'Yes, some milk. You'll like that, won't you?'

Picking up her basket, she slipped the handle over one arm, cradling her son to her with the other. Once out of the house she held him close against her, shielding him from the breeze and from the hostile stares of the women who drew their skirts closer to their legs as she passed, as if proximity to a sinner would somehow contaminate them.

She had not been right into the town since the birth of the child, Polly bringing the few things they needed on her daily visits. Cripple Polly. Anna held her son tight. What would have happened had that woman not stood by her?

Reaching the bottom of Church Hill, Anna crossed over Trouse Lane, turning into Meeting Street. This way she could avoid the High Bullen with its shopping women.

She was on her way home, milk and butter tucked into her basket, when she passed a group of them chatting outside

Tedd's wet fish shop. Anna felt her heart jump as they stared, then closed around her as she drew level.

'Well, if it ain't Jos Bradly's whore.' A dark-haired woman with a front tooth missing grabbed the shawl that held the baby. 'An' this must be the bastard he's fathered.'

Instinctively Anna stepped back but a second woman stood firm against her.

'Maybe it is, maybe it ain't,' the second woman said. 'Depends on 'ow many men 'er's had beside 'er own father.'

'Well, let's 'ave a look then.' The gap-toothed woman grabbed at the shawl, pulling it from the sleeping baby.

'Let's see what sort of kid a father and 'is daughter mek.'

'Don't touch him!' Anna flared, snatching the shawl from the woman's grasp. 'Don't you dare put your dirty hands on him.'

'Ooh, you hear that, Liza?' The third member of the trio wiped a hand across her nose. 'You've got dirty hands.'

'You should be careful who you call dirty!' The gap in her teeth looming wide, the woman snatched at Anna's hair, dragging her head back painfully. 'A bloody whore like you!' The woman's eyes gleamed with a captor's delight over her helpless prey. 'We don't like your sort, an' we ain't 'avin' you here.'

The woman pitched her forward, throwing her against a wall. Dazed by the force of the impact, Anna stumbled away, clumps of mud and stones finding their mark as she went.

'Don't go comin' down 'ere,' the woman who had grabbed her head shouted after her. 'You bring your spawn this way again an' you'll be sorry. Get out of Wednesbury, you bloody whore, and tek your by blow with you . . .'

Somehow she managed to reach home, though Anna never remembered how.

'Lad is all right,' Polly said when she called later. 'He's teken no harm and you will be all right as well in an hour or so.' But she stayed the whole day nevertheless, seeing to the baby and preparing a hot meal.

'Little 'un is sleepin'.' Polly eventually reached for her coat, hanging from a peg at the back of the sitting-room door. 'An' you should be too. Get yourself a few hours afore 'e wakes for next feed. Jos's meal is ready in the oven, you 'ave nothing to do.'

Anna watched her friend limp away down the hill, then climbed the stairs to her room. Her father would make no call on her. Coming home as late as possible, he would take his meal to his bedroom and be gone at first light next morning. He could go on like that while the months of summer held but what would he do when the ground was frozen hard? Anna stared listlessly at the whitewashed wall. Her father could not be out of house and home for the rest of his life, but neither could he decently be in it or suspicion of them would fester, father and daughter, the evil minds of some seeing them living as man and wife.

'But it's not true,' Anna cried softly. 'My father is not like that, he would never harm me, it's just not true.' Neither was it true that he had killed Mary Carter, she thought hopelessly, but they believed he had and would go on believing it, the same as they would go on believing she was her own father's whore.

'It doesn't stop.'

Eyes brimming with unshed tears, Anna looked at Polly Shipton who sat beside the kitchen table, her crippled leg in its high laced boot jutting out beneath her black skirts.

'I don't think it will ever stop. Every time I take him out of the house there are filthy insults and people throwing stones.'

'It be bad for you, me wench, but it be new to folk yet. Give them a year or two and they'll get used to seein' you with the child. Give them time and they will forget how he was got, find summat new for their tongues to wag on.'

But Polly knew they would not forget and neither would they ever allow Anna to forget. She was a branded woman and one who would never know peace or real friendship in the town again. Strange, she thought, watching her cross to the child sleeping in its basket beneath the window. The working-class people of Wednesbury would endure poverty, they would pull together in hardship, but immorality among their own they would not countenance. Their eyes became closed to the real rights or wrongs of a case and, victim or not, there would be no place in this town anymore for Anna Bradly.

'No, they will not forget, Mother Polly.' Unconsciously Anna used her childhood name for the woman. 'No matter what else may happen they will not forget, and as long as I am here they will not let him forget. But I can't let my child pay for what happened. He and I should not have to bear the brunt of what my father has done.'

Polly sat quietly. The girl had not finished; there was more yet to be said.

'I cannot stay here.' Anna kept her eyes on her baby. 'If he is to have any life at all, I must go.'

'Go?' Polly asked sharply. 'But where? You 'ave no kin as I be knowin' of.'

'No, I have no kin other than my father,' she answered dully.

'Then where would you go, wench? You can't just pick the lad up and leave. You must 'ave shelter for 'im.'

'I have thought of that.' Anna reached into the basket, one finger fondling the baby's cheek. 'I have thought of it night after night, of his life and my father's. What will they be worth with me here? They both have little on which to build a future, but with me gone, at least they stand a chance.'

'Leave the child behind?' Polly looked at the girl she had helped to rear, the girl she had loved as her own, and saw the anguish in her face. 'Is that what you really want?'

'No,' Anna cried. 'I want *him*, I want my *son*, but I cannot condemn him to a lifetime of taunts, I love him too much for that. I love him too much to keep him.'

'Have you said anything of this to Jos?'

Bending over the child as it stirred in its sleep, Anna murmured softly, soothing it before answering.

'No, I have said nothing to my father. If I tell him what I feel, I know he will be the one to leave. But it would be hard for him to start again. Trying to find work would be difficult enough, but to leave behind all that he had with my mother . . . no, I cannot do that to him.'

'But you will be leaving all you have,' Polly said gently. 'All that you love in the world. Will you be able to do it, Anna wench?'

'Oh, help me, Mother Polly!'

Anna ran to the cripple woman, sinking to her knees and burying her face in her lap, choking on her sobs.

'Help me . . . take my son and care for him . . . love him for me, Mother Polly . . . love him for me.'

'Ar, I'll tek 'im for you, me little wench, an' I'll love 'im for you too.' Polly stroked the red-gold head pressed against her knee. 'I'll love 'im as I love you.'

Mother Polly would take her son, she would care for him and raise him as she had raised the motherless child of Jos Bradly. She would find the first tooth, hear the first words; she would feel the tiny arms about her neck, she would soothe and comfort . . .

'But he's mine . . . mine!'

Almost blinded by tears, Anna pulled open a drawer in the chest set against her bedroom wall, taking out her few belongings and placing them one by one in the shabby carpet bag standing open on the bed. Then she paused as a gleam of pink showed in the sallow light of the oil lamp.

Holding it in her fingers, she looked at the shiny strip of ribbon, one diamond-shaped piece of paper glued to its centre.

Peter! Her mind flashed back across the years. She had been eight years old and Peter a grown-up thirteen, already earning his living. They had spent their childhood together, he indulging her childish games, always there, always protecting; even helping with the Sunday School outing because she had cried until he said yes.

Anna walked slowly to the crib, holding out the shiny ribbon as if the sleeping child could see it.

'You would have liked Peter,' she murmured, half to herself and half to the child. 'And you would have liked the Sunday School outings: riding on long low carts all done up with flowers and ribbons, the horses with ribbons in their manes and tails, the sugar buns and lemonade. You would have climbed the trees and most likely fallen into the stream . . .'

Peter had fallen into the stream. Anna left off speaking, the rest of her memories for herself alone. Peter, his brown hair shining in the sun, trousers rolled to his knees, laughing at her as he tried to catch one of the tiny fish. She had demanded a tiddler to take home in a jar, and he, unable as always to refuse her, had waded into the water. That was when she had seen the pretty orange butterfly and wandered off after it. When he could not see her and she had not answered his call, Peter had panicked and in scrambling too quickly from the stream, slipped and fallen back into the water.

He had found her downstream and persuaded her a dead butterfly would be of no use. She had tried her usual childish ploy of tears but he had not given way.

'Let the poor little thing be.'

Anna felt the tears in her throat as she remembered the tender way he had dried her eyes.

'I will give you something that can't die.'

He had taken her by the hand, matching his longer stride to her short one, leading her to where he had left his coat on the river bank. And from the pocket he had taken a pink ribbon with one diamond-shaped piece of paper at its centre.

'One day, Anna,' he had said, 'you will have a whole string of diamonds.'

Now crossing to the window of her cramped bedroom, she looked out through her tears, over the darkened town to where the steeple of the church rose like a pointing black finger.

Those had been his words as he tied the ribbon about her neck, but Peter had died from meningitis and she had died inside the night her father raped her. There would be no more diamonds in her life.

Anna pulled the slip of ribbon through her fingers as memories of yesterday ran through her mind. Then she turned back to her son. Tenderly lifting the tiny head, she slipped the ribbon about his neck. The people of Wednesbury had claimed one innocent victim, they would not have two.

Lifting the child from the crib, Anna held its tiny body close to hers. Peter had always protected her just as she must now protect her son. She would do that the only way she knew how. He must not suffer because of her. To keep him safe she had to leave him, give him into the care of Mother Polly even though it meant breaking her own heart.

Kissing the tiny face snuffling after her breast, Anna felt as if the world were shattering around her. This would be the last time she would hold him, the last time she would tell him of her love for him, for when morning came she would have to leave this house, leave everything in the world she loved. She would do it for the sake of her child.

Chapter Two

A thin drizzle of cold rain dripped from a weeping sky as Anna stepped out of the train. She had wanted to stay in the closed security of the third-class compartment but the little money she had saved so carefully from the weekly allowance her father left on the kitchen table every Friday morning would only buy her so many miles, and a courteous conductor punching a neat round hole in her ticket had said those miles were up.

The carpet bag no weight in her hand, she shivered against a wind which drove freezing spots of water against her thin body, using its superior strength in an effort to force her out of the strange town she had just entered.

Coseley. She read the name on a board fastened against the grimy brickwork of the little platform. However far the two shillings and six pence she had paid for her train ticket had carried her, it wasn't far enough to escape the smoke and dirt of factory chimneys.

Anna lifted her eyes, half-closing them against wind-blown flurries of rain, and squinted up at chimneys rising dark and menacing in a drowned sky. She had changed one industrial town for another, but at least in this one nobody would know her.

The sudden scream of a steam whistle startled her and her fingers clutched convulsively around the handles of her bag, before her shoulders slumped in relief. It was only the hooter of one of the factories, signalling the end of a shift.

Suddenly the empty street was filled with people. Women and young girls seemed to pour from every side alley, their wooden clogs clattering on the shining wet cobblestones.

'Excuse me!' Anna reached out, touching the arm of a woman hurrying past.

'Aye?' she demanded.

'Could you tell me, please . . . is there someone around here who . . . who takes paying guests?'

'Paying guests!' The woman shook off Anna's hand impatiently, her face frowning in the circle of her black woollen shawl. 'Not as I knows of.'

'But there must be.' Panic coloured Anna's reply. She was in a strange town and already it was getting dark; she had to find a room somewhere.

'Must be?' Again the woman echoed Anna's words before her own. 'Then yer must find it for yerself, I have my man's meal to get. If I stand 'ere talkin' to yer much longer the men's shift will be finishin' and 'im comin' home to an empty table.'

She pulled the shawl tighter with an indignant tug, holding each corner in hands pushed beneath heavy breasts, and turned on her way, long black skirts swinging around urgent feet.

Anna stood and watched her disappear down the long street. In the distance the lamplighter came slowly towards her, lighting each street lamp in turn; behind her the clanging bell of a laden trolley bus sang its strident song. And then, as suddenly as it had filled, the street was empty.

A trickle of rain slid over the brim of Anna's cheap straw hat, slithering down her neck, soaking into the high collar of her blouse.

From a distance a train sounding its readiness to depart seemed to taunt her, to say it could carry her home.

'You won't.' Anna's defiant whisper banished the temptation. 'Nothing will take me back there, I'd rather die first.'

'Are yer lost?'

Anna twisted sharply, startled by the question. On the

pavement stood a girl of about her own age, pulling a thick shawl protectively over her mousy hair.

'I've been watching you from in there.' The mousy head gave a small backward toss.

'There', Anna saw, was a small, ill-lit shop, its tiny window filled with an Aladdin's Cave assortment. Huge pink hams, plate-sized pies, sausages and black puddings, jostled for space against brightly coloured packets and boxes.

'I was just gettin' some barley for me mam, she's settin' tomorrow's dinner on the fire.' The girl's face broke into a rueful grin. 'Forget 'er 'ead, me mam would, if it wasn't tied on. She's bin in Bella Castleton's twice today an' still forgot the barley.'

'It's easy to forget,' Anna replied, wishing the words held some truth for her. Forgetting was a luxury and this life held no promise of luxury for Anna Bradly.

'It is for me mam, and so it ought to be – she's practised all 'er life.' The girl's laughter pealed out, ringing off a long row of identical small houses joined in homage at the foot of majestic mills. Houses where lamps were fast being lit in the windows. The sight hurt and Anna felt frightened and alone. Soon curtains would be drawn, Coseley would close its eyes, and she would still be on the street.

'Where did you want to get to?' The rain didn't seem to bother the girl. 'I 'aven't seen you round these parts afore, 'ave I . . . you got relations in Coseley?'

So many questions and Anna did not want to answer any of them, but reticence would not find her shelter.

'No, I'm a stranger here. I was hoping to find a place to stay. A . . . a guest house.'

The wind bit through the thin cloth of her old green coat and she pulled the lapels together across her throat.

'Do you know where I can find one?'

'Eee, wench, there's nowt like that in Coseley, we don't get visitors as such 'ere. You should 'ave gone into Birmingham.

Like as not you would find plenty o' them guest 'ouses there. Birmingham's a big town.'

'Thank you.' The reply trembled on lips white with cold. Anna hitched the carpet bag more comfortably in her frozen fingers. She had better go back to the railway station. At least there would be a fire in the waiting room. Perhaps they might let her sit in there until morning.

'You'll not get a train to Birmingham tonight, wench.' The girl still stood before her, raindrops like crystal freckles on her pert young face. 'But if it's nowt grand you're after, you could always try Maggie Fellen.'

'Maggie Fellen?' Anna tried to keep the hope out of her voice. 'Can you tell me how to find her?'

'I'll do better than that, I'll take you to her. She lives just against our house. C'mon, let's get in out of this rain or we'll both be growin' flippers!'

The sound of Anna's worn shoes was lost beneath the clatter of wooden clogs as the girl guided her along a street of grey, effacing sameness, turning left along a narrow alley to emerge into another street that could have been the first one for the long rows of tiny houses were an exact match, their doors leading straight off the narrow footpath, windows half-shrouded in lace curtains.

''Ere we are, number seventy-six, that's our 'ouse, and Maggie Fellen is seventy-eight. The number of 'er 'ouse, I mean, not Maggie.' The happy laughter broke out again and in a pool of waxy yellow light from a street lamp the girl's eyes twinkled roguishly. 'She'd 'ave my guts for fiddle strings if she 'eard me say she was seventy-eight. She's a mite particular is Maggie Fellen, and not just about her age either.'

Pushing open a door which Anna noted had been left off the latch, the girl stood aside.

'I'll 'ave to give me mam the barley before I go round next door. She'll be wonderin' what kept me as it is.' One eye closed in a wink. 'I can always tell 'er Bella Castleton kept me natterin', and that's not a hundred miles from the truth.

But come in with me, me mam likes meetin' folks. She can natter almost as good as Bella Castleton. If ever they 'ave a competition for who can talk longest and say least, I reckon they two would 'ave a rare battle.' She waved Anna across the whitewashed step. 'Go on, wench, get you in afore the rain soaks the mat.'

Leading the way along a short, narrow passage, the girl called over her shoulder, 'Me mam will be in 'ere.'

After the harsh grey streets,the kitchen of number seventy-six seemed to shout with colour. Anna blinked against the yellowness of the gas mantle, aided in its fight against the shadows by a brass oil lamp crowned with a fluted white opalescent glass shade. On one wall a wooden dresser displayed a proud collection of blue and white willow pattern china, while another was taken up by the fireplace. Baking ovens polished to the brilliance of jet, bowels filled with crimson coals, glowed a welcome.

Putting the blue paper bag of barley down on a table white from constant scrubbing, the girl pulled Anna forward.

'Mam, I'm tekin' 'er round to Maggie . . . Mrs Fellen's. She's lookin' for a room. I found 'er in front of Castleton's shop.'

'I bet 'er found you afore you was lost, wench, knowin' my girl.' The woman's plump face creased into a wide smile. 'But come yer in, now yer 'ere . . . eee, but you be sodden through.'

Shooing a sleepy marmalade cat from a chair next to the fire, the girl's mother drew Anna to it.

'Sit yerself down, wench, and tek off them wet shoes. You'll be tekin' that influenza if we don't get you out o' them wet things, and soon.'

Already filling a brown earthenware teapot from a huge iron kettle steaming quietly to itself, she called, 'Get a fresh cup, Essie, then go and ask Maggie Fellen to step round. If she can't find wench a room then we'll have to squeeze her in with us somehow, for she can't be out there no more tonight.'

Stirring sugar into the cup she filled with fresh-brewed tea, the woman offered it to Anna, brown eyes studying her pale tired face. The girl had gone through torment and not long ago, judging by the look in those eyes. It wouldn't take much more to break her.

'Our Essie is a good wench but a little empty-headed at times.' She smiled as Anna took the mug, sipping the hot liquid immediately. 'She fair rushed off without sayin' your name.'

'It's Anna . . . Anna Bradly, Mrs . . .' She broke off awkwardly. She had followed this woman's daughter into their home and not thought of asking their name.

'I'm afraid I'm empty-headed too sometimes. You see, I didn't ask her name either.'

'It's lost no brass, wench.'

Reaching into a drawer of the dresser, the woman pulled out a length of clean white huckaback, passing it to Anna to use to wipe the droplets of rain from her face.

'That one is Hester, my first. And I'm Mary, Mary Cresswell.'

'How do you do, Mrs Cresswell?' Anna answered politely, but her face had long since lost the ability to smile. 'Hester did find me standing outside the shop. I had just got off the train and was looking for a room. I had thought to find a guest house somewhere in the town.'

'Not this one, Anna.' The name was already comfortable on Mary Cresswell's lips; there was something she liked about the thin, frightened-looking girl lost in the depths of her old chair.

'Coseley is hardly grand enough for that sort o' thing, nobody stops by here longer than they 'ave to.'

She was interrupted by Hester pushing aside the floor-length red chenille curtain that hung across the door to keep out draughts. She was followed by a woman who looked to be in her late thirties. Rich brown hair drawn into a flat knot at the back of her head gave a sharp, almost severe look to her well-shaped features. The obligatory shawl covered her shoulder. Beneath it a snow-white apron reached almost to the hem of the skirts that touched her clogs.

'You asked me to come, Mary.'

The words were for her neighbour but the woman's steady grey eyes remained on Anna. Already she had taken in the soggy straw bonnet, well-worn green coat and carpet bag.

'Aye, Maggie.' Mary Cresswell reached for another cup while her daughter took off her wet shawl and shook it before hanging it behind the scullery door.

'This 'ere is Anna Bradly and she's lookin' fer a place to stay.'

'Oh, aye!' Maggie Fellen took the mug held out to her. 'And what's that to me?'

'Well, I knew you 'ad a room that's empty since . . .' Hester coloured violently and looked to her mother for help.

'Hester told her there might be a chance of your lettin' her come to you. It was a kindness on my girl's part to a wench not knowin' her whereabouts.'

'A kindness to a stranger is one thing,' Maggie Fellen returned in clipped tones, 'bringin' me a lodger is something else again. I have no mind for tekin' in lodgers, especially one I've never clapped eyes on afore.'

'I know that as surely as yourself even if it seems my wench did not. But since you're 'ere, sit yourself and drink your tea. There's no brass charged for sittin'.'

The pale grey eyes stayed on Anna's face as Maggie Fellen drew up a straight-backed wooden chair and sat beside the table, one hand curved about her mug. Anna dropped her own glance to the steam beginning to rise as her coat dried in the fire's heat.

'Will you be in Coseley long, Miss Bradly?'

The woman did not call her 'Anna' as Hester's mother had done. But the tea and the fire had warmed away some of her desperation and Anna looked at her levelly.

'I can't say yes or no to that yet, Mrs Fellen. It depends upon whether or not I can find work here.'

'Where did you work afore?'

It took Anna by surprise. She had not thought to be questioned about her background. Sipping her tea, she gained a little time, then, meeting the grey gaze with complete candour, answered, 'I kept house for my father. I have done for three years, ever since I was thirteen. My mother died when I was six and my father did not marry again.'

'And what about your father now? Who will look to him now you 'ave up and left him?'

Anna could feel the tears gathering in her throat but banished them determinedly from her eyes. Her voice quiet and steady, she spoke the one lie she had worked out in the train.

'My father is dead, Mrs Fellen.'

'Eee, you poor wench!' Mary Cresswell leaned forward, patting Anna's knee with a podgy hand. 'No wonder your little face looks as if it's been drawn through a needle's eye. You be such a skinny one, all eyes.'

'It's not easy to bear losin' a loved one.' Maggie's grey eyes dropped and for a moment only the fire spoke, crackling out its own questions, spitting back its own replies.

'So, the tape being cut, you be off and running?' Maggie Fellen commented, then took a long sip of tea.

Behind her mother's chair Hester fidgeted, uncertain what to make of the exchange.

'Not running, Mrs Fellen.' Anna was suddenly dignified beyond her years. 'There was nothing left for me in Wednesbury, nothing to hold me except the unhappiness of losing my family. I had to start on my own, find a way of earning my living. It . . . it seemed a good idea to find fresh ground on which to do it.'

'Well, y'ave got spunk, wench, I'll give you that.' Mary Cresswell heaved her over-proportioned frame out of the chair she had settled in and picked up the bag of barley, emptying it into an iron saucepan, then stirring the contents with a long-handled spoon.

'A fresh start canna do you great harm and I don't see anything against you mekin' one in Coseley. As for work, our Hester can tek yer on up to Rewcastle's Mill when you've a mind. They'll set you on up there all right.'

Leaning sideways, Anna placed her empty mug on the table.

'Thank you, Mrs Cresswell. You and Hester have both been very kind.'

'Kind nothing!' The large woman blustered, giving the stewpot an unnecessary stir. 'Isn't that what the good Lord placed us on this earth for? My mother taught her brood to do people a good turn whenever the chance was given, and if you couldn't do them a good turn, then you shouldn't do them a bad one. It's a rule that's always stood me in good stead. Help others and the Lord will help you.'

Leaving the spoon in the pot, she turned, hands resting on ample hips, mouth a straight line.

'So what say you, Maggie Fellen? Do you find the wench a place, 'cos if not I do. And that bein' so, she'd best be off in scullery and get them wet things off.'

'She can 'ave the room.' Maggie Fellen rose, pulling the shawl across her breasts. 'But if she proves to be carryin' then either you or the Lord better find her a place, Mary Cresswell, for I'll have none of that in my house.'

'Carryin'!' Hester's mother laughed. 'She don't look strong enough to be carryin' 'erself, let alone a babe. Look at 'er, she's as thin as a stick.'

'Aye.' At the door, Maggie held the chenille curtain aside. 'And you should know better than to let that fool you, Mary Cresswell. When a body is expecting, they're thin afore they get fat.'

'You need have no fears, Mrs Fellen.' Anna's cheeks were scarlet. 'I am not expecting, but if you feel that I will be a nuisance then I would rather not come with you. If Mrs Cresswell could just let me stay here tonight, I will find some other place tomorrow.'

The grey eyes flicked back to Anna standing in front of the fire, the old carpet bag in her hand, and for the briefest second they held admiration.

Here's a girl I can trust, Maggie Fellen thought, and suddenly she did. A smile lifting her thin mouth, she held out a hand.

'Come on, wench, let's get you home and Hester can come and help you settle if she's a mind.'

Chapter Three

Anna climbed into the train carriage. The long buttoned skirt of her green coat refused to stretch and she had to lift the hem, displaying a little of her shapely calf above black sidebutton boots.

Catching the ticket collector's appreciative grin, she blushed, settling quickly into a window seat and fumbling in her bag for the fare. The carriage filled slowly, mostly with women with children at their skirts, heavy baskets unwieldy on their arms, but eventually it was full and lurched forward, rattling alarmingly over the noisy points.

It would take almost an hour to run from Birmingham to Coseley, stopping at every tiny village along the way, but Anna didn't mind. She had come to enjoy this monthly excursion to the large steel town.

'Did yer have a good day, Mrs Dalby? Where did yer pigeons come in last race, Bert, or has yer missis put them in a pie yet?'

The conductor, a short red-faced man, had a word for each passenger as he made his way slowly along the narrow aisle. As he clipped her return ticket, he smiled at Anna. He had seen her several times; come to live over at Coseley so he'd been told, and she looked a right bonny wench. Pity she never smiled.

'You likin' Birmingham, me wench?' he asked as she slipped her ticket into the bag resting on her knees.

Anna glanced back at him, green eyes clear beneath her straw hat.

'I do,' she nodded, 'but I prefer Coseley. People there are not in such a rush.'

'I know what you mean, wench.' He pushed back his boater with its navy blue band, scratching a finger along his receding hairline. 'I find meself wonderin' what them there folk do with all the time they saves, rushin' from pillar to post all day.'

'It's certain we'll never see you rushin',' a woman in another compartment called good-naturedly. 'I reckon we shall all see the Second Coming 'fore ever we see you break into a sweat.'

Pulling the boater back into place, the conductor moved on, a grin splitting his florid face.

'Now then, you just behave. You don't want for me to tell your man the high jinks you gets up to in Birmingham.'

A storm of laughter greeted his remark and Anna turned her eyes to the window. Trees dressed in the green of late-summer; fields, having given their bounty, waiting for the plough. Between the towns the countryside had a quiet beauty she never tired of looking at.

The fields around Wednesbury would be green, their skirts of grass looking even more beautiful swirling around buildings dark with the soot of foundries and the dirt of coal mines. Would her son be out among that greenery, up on the heath where she had carried him in a laundry basket? Polly Shipton could not carry him and her father would be working and there was no one else. I had to go, she sobbed inwardly, I had to leave, it was the only way to protect you. But I love you, my darling . . . I love you so much.

The train grumbled to a halt and a woman on the seat beside her gathered her several hessian shopping bags, calling a cheery goodnight as she stepped down. People here were so friendly.

Anna watched the hedges dance away as the train pulled itself onward. People had been friendly enough in Wednesbury until . . . She closed her eyes, feeling the familiar surge of pain, that remembering her home and son always brought. Then, lifting her lids, she swallowed hard. That was in the past; her home was here now with Maggie.

It didn't seem like six months since Maggie Fellen had taken her in, giving her the room that had been her son's until he had left his job at Rewcastle's to try his hand in America.

Maggie herself never talked of him, as she never asked questions of Anna. From the start she had respected her privacy, asking no more than she had that night in Mary Cresswell's kitchen, and now the liking they had for each other was more than just respect; Anna knew she loved fierce, outspoken Maggie, and though her landlady might never say it, she had a strong feeling her love was returned. Perhaps in time Anna might be able to bring herself to tell her what had happened to drive her away from home. But not now, not yet, it was still too raw.

How greatly her life had changed. Anna's body rocked with the motion of the train. A home with Maggie, a job at Rewcastle's, and two pounds a week – a fortune. She felt like a queen every Friday when she drew her wages from the office and watched the clerk enter the amount in the huge ledger, and later smiled at Maggie's grateful, 'Eee, wench, that's too much,' as she slipped one of those pounds into the painted tea caddy on the mantelshelf.

The other pound was her own and she had known from the first what she intended doing with it. The second pay day she had asked about a bank, saying she felt she ought to save some of her money. But there was no bank in Coseley, so if she couldn't keep her brass under the bed like other folk, Maggie told her, then she would have to traipse all the way into Birmingham.

But it hadn't been a bank so much as a Post Office that Anna wanted and that had not taken long to find. Her letter was already written. Slipping a ten-shilling note into the envelope she had sealed it, placed a stamp on one corner and dropped it into the post-box.

She had addressed it to 'Polly Shipton, care of Siverter's

shop'. The letter had conveyed little more than her thanks for the woman's help. The money, Anna wrote, was to help with the child, for she knew Polly would have the rearing of him. Adding that she would send two pounds every month, she had signed the letter simply 'Anna'. She made no mention of her father, nor did she give an address.

She had not dared to look back at her baby because on doing so she could never have left him, but neither could she stay with him, living with the finger of scorn always pointing at her and thus at him. It was better this way. He would grow up never knowing her but she would carry him in her heart until they buried her.

'Coseley . . . this is where you get off, wench.'

A touch on her shoulder brought Anna out of her reverie.

'Thank you. I was day dreaming.'

Clutching her bag, she scrambled up from the slatted wooden seat and called her own shy goodnights to the few people left on the train. Holding her skirt, she watched her feet, pretending not to see the hand the conductor held out to help her down from the high step. He swung himself back aboard.

'Be seein' you, take care now.'

The train trundled away, trailing a cloud of grit-filled smoke behind it. Anna watched for several moments then turned to cross the street. Maggie would have the tea brewed and the Saturday night meal of sausages and mash would be ready and waiting.

'Oh!' Anna gasped as her foot twisted on an uneven cobblestone, almost throwing her off balance.

'Steady, girl.'

The street lamps had not yet been lit and the greyness of dusk had masked the figure that stepped towards her. Tall and hatless, a man reached for her.

'No . . . oo!' Anna's scream ripped through the silence. Even now the thought of a man's hand touching her set a flood of panic welling up in her. Intent on escape from the shadowy form, she began to run but tripped, falling to her knees.

'I told thee to go steady.'

The voice was quiet and this time its owner made no move towards her, offered no hand as she scrambled to her feet.

'Is tha hurt?'

Anna brushed a hand across her coat in embarrassment. Fancy falling down like that, and screaming too. It was a wonder every house in Coseley hadn't thrown wide its doors.

'No, I'm all right, thank you.'

'Then hadn't tha better do that on path? If carter comes round corner, tha'll be right in way and he might not be too wide awake, especially if he's called in Black Bull as he usually does.'

'Yes . . . I . . . yes.'

Still not lifting her eyes to the man beside her, Anna stepped forward then lurched again as her right foot came down unexpectedly flat on the cobbled surface. The heel of her right boot had torn completely away.

'Damn!' she swore, not quite beneath her breath.

'Twisted your ankle?'

'No.' Anna turned, searching the road behind her. 'It's my heel, it's come off.'

'Must have been as you got off that train. You stepped down a mite sharp.'

'I'll go back and look. It must be in the grass somewhere.'

This man had seen her react as the conductor had offered her his hand. Did that mean he had been watching her . . . waiting for her, perhaps? Anna's heart missed a beat. Had he watched her before, got to know she took a monthly ride to Birmingham and was here now waiting for her to come back?

'You stand on path, I'll go find tha heel.'

Anna watched him bend then straighten up, holding up a hand in triumph before rejoining her. She had been given a chance to run, either to the nearest house or into Bella Castleton's shop, and she had done neither.

Without knowing why she had waited for the tall angular man to find her broken heel, waited for him to come back across the road and stand beside her.

'Thank you.' She looked up into a finely drawn, clean-shaven face. Despite the shadows she could see it was not the face of a young man.

Hair she guessed to be dark drooped softly over a wide forehead and somehow Anna felt pleased it was not plastered with the brilliantine that seemed so much in favour with the men at Rewcastle's. Beneath thick brows a pair of eyes whose colour she did not even try to guess regarded her solemnly.

'If tha lets me have that boot, I could have this back on in no time.' He tossed the offending heel in the air, catching it as he spoke.

'That's all right, thank you. No doubt Maggie will know a cobbler somewhere. You . . . you've gone to enough trouble on my account as it is, Mr . . .'

She had not meant to ask his name and was glad the gloom of late-evening hid the sudden flush that flooded her cheeks.

'No trouble, lass, and the name is Edward, Edward Royce. And yours is Anna Bradly, tha's the lass as lives with Maggie Fellen.'

'How did you know?'

He smiled. The accusation in her tone seemed to amuse him.

'In a small place like Coseley a man gets to know many things, Miss Bradly. Besides it's not often we get a lass coming to settle here. Why, half of the ones we have already would give their eye teeth to be shot of the place.'

'Maybe.' Anna held out a hand, aware as she hadn't been before of her lack of gloves. 'I must be going, Mr Royce. Thank you again for finding my heel.'

Circling once more in the air, the heel came down again

in the wide palm of Edward Royce's hand, his fingers closing firmly over it.

'I live just at the back of Maggie Fellen's place, in Slater Street. We could walk along together. Unless, of course, you object?'

She did object, and yet perversely she didn't. After that first offer of a steadying hand he had made no move to touch her, keeping a distance of several feet between them as they talked yet.

'I . . . I have no objection, Mr Royce.'

Anna gave way to the part of her which said she was in no danger from this man.

Keeping pace with her awkward up-and-down step, Edward Royce walked beside her. He could smell the faint aroma of violets from her, so different from the chemical smells of the steel works or the cheap scrubbing soap that was the perfume of most of the women of Coseley, and wondered as he had a hundred times about the circumstances that had brought this girl here.

'I haven't seen you at Rewcastle's.' Aware of the silence between them, Anna tried to break it.

'An' tha won't if I can help it.' He caught the upward tilt of her head. 'Oh, I've nothing against Rewcastle's, their mills find work for most of the folk in Coseley, but not for me. I prefer things the way they are, I like to be my own man.'

'Nice evening.' Across the street the lamplighter lifted his long pole to the street lamp, turning on the gas and watching until the flickering mantle glowed a steady yellow.

'It is that.' Edward Royce lifted a hand in acknowledgement, the same wide smile coming readily to his face. 'Tell tha wife I'm askin' after her.'

'I will, lad, goodnight to yer.' Pole across his shoulder, the lamplighter moved on into the night. Anna watched him go. In this small community everyone seemed to know everyone else so it was little surprise the man walking beside her had known her name and with whom she lodged. They had reached number seventy-eight Roker Street and Anna asked again for her heel. She would not invite him in; it wasn't right to ask a stranger into Maggie's house.

'Why don't you go in and take off that boot? Tell Maggie Edward Royce is offering to mend it for thee.'

He lifted the heel, holding it between thumb and finger.

'If she raises an objection then I'll give thee this back and say no more . . . go on.' He pushed open the door that was as ever on the latch, catching the scent of violets once again as Anna whisked inside.

Chapter Four

'Well, what did he say?' Hester Cresswell wrapped a metal soup ladle, pushed it into a tea chest then stared across the packing benches at Anna.

'Go on, Anna, tell!'

'I've already told you half a dozen times.' Her green eyes smiled though her mouth did not yet remember how. 'It'll be no different if I tell it another half dozen.'

'I know, but Rachel wants to hear you tell it.'

'Eee, Hester Cresswell, I do not! You be tellin' lies.' Rachel Orme's huge brown eyes swivelled towards Anna. 'I was just interested, that's all, Anna. It's none o' my business if Edward Royce waits for you at the bottom of the road.'

'Waits for me?' Anna stopped, the ladle she was about to wrap held in her hand. 'What do you mean, Rachel?'

The girl's lower lip trembled slightly and she bent to the job of nailing a lid to a filled tea chest.

'Everyone knows, all Rewcastle's is talkin' of it. Every Saturday night Edward Royce waits for the Birmingham train. And for what? Nobody else goin' there . . . the only one from Coseley goes into Birmingham is you, and it was you he spoke to and walked home on Saturday, Anna Bradly, you can't deny that.'

No, she couldn't. Anna wrapped the ladle, her fingers moving automatically.

The man had walked with her as far as Maggie's door, but as for waiting for her at the street's end . . . he couldn't have.

'Eee, Anna, you ain't cross, are yer?' the girl twittered nervously as Anna dropped the wrapped ladle into the half-full tea chest and reached for another. Hester Cresswell let her mouth run away with her sometimes.

'What's to be cross about, Rachel? It's no secret after all.'

Anna's fingers resumed their customary swiftness and she was glad of a valid reason for not meeting the other girl's stare.

'The heel broke off my shoe when I came out of the station and Mr Royce very kindly found it for me, that's all.'

'Oh no it isn't!' Hester joined in. 'Tell it all, Anna Bradly, about how he walked you home.'

'You make it sound like one of those tuppenny romances Bella Castleton has in her shop.' Anna kept her eyes on her work.

'Ar . . . lovely,' Rachel sighed, a ladle forgotten in her hand. 'Lovely.'

'Well, it was nothing like that, and I hope you haven't been giving the rest of the girls the wrong idea, Hester.'

'Me! I haven't given anybody the wrong idea. Besides, you should know by this time they don't need any coaching. They can all have ideas quite nicely for themselves.'

'Well, they've certainly grabbed the stick by the wrong end this time if they think Mr Royce was waiting for me. I . . . I've never seen him before so why should he wait for me?'

'Well, he's seen *you* afore!' A little way along the line of women and girls engaged at the packing benches, the voice of Ella Barnes chipped in.

'Our Davy often goes down to Royce's workshop after tea, says he likes to talk to somebody that doesn't work for Rewcastle's. Makes a bit of a change for him. Well, any road, he was down there the other night, and accordin' to 'im Edward Royce could talk of nowt save you, Anna.'

Aware of a row of interested faces she stooped to pull a fresh sheaf of wrapping paper from a shelf that ran beneath the long benches. Edward Royce had talked of her? But why? For what reason?

'In that case, he and your Davy must be very short of topics for conversation!' She dropped the paper heavily on to the bench, slitting the string binding with a sharp flick of her knife.

'They wasna short last Monday by sounds of it,' Ella retorted quickly. Then seeing the colour sweep into the other girl's cheeks, added maliciously, 'Our Davy says if he didn't know Edward Royce better, he could swear as 'ow that man was sweet on you, Anna Bradly.'

'We can all understand your Davy sayin' that – he's puddled, poor sod, like the rest o' the Barneses.' Hester flew to Anna's defence, tiny golden flecks of anger sparkling in her hazel eyes. 'If all you've got to say is the drivel that brother o' yours spouts, then you'd best keep your mouth closed.'

'You mind your tongue, Essie Cresswell, or there's them that'll mind it for yer!' Ella Barnes's freckles seemed to join into a brown mass. 'Always 'ad too bloody much of a bob on yourself, you 'ave, though God only knows why. Y'ave never 'ad no more than one pair o' bloomers to your name, an' them none too clean neither!'

'That'll cost three-halfpence.' Eli Curran, foreman of the packing shops, declared as a ladle flew from Hester's hand, barely missing Ella Barnes. 'You should wait till shift finishes and break one another's heads outside. That way it's none o' my business and won't cost you yer hard-earned brass.'

'Serves you right, Essie Cresswell.'

'And you better put a sock in it an' all!' Eli turned a sharp look on Ella. The Barneses were trouble and well known for it, but he was having no ructions in his department.

'If I report you to the office, you'll be docked tuppence for stirring. You knows old man Rewcastle will have no arguments between 'is workers.'

'Then go on an' tell 'im, Eli Curran. We all know 'ow much you enjoys that,' the girl spat viciously.

'The same as you know I need give 'im no reason for sacking anybody.'

A buzz of speculation sped from mouth to mouth and the girl's face paled, anger draining away with the same speed it had risen.

'Now I suggest the lot of you get stuck in. This order is for dispatch tonight and if it doesn't go out the gaffer'll not wait for me to give anybody the sack – he'll do it 'imself. And like as not, he won't stop at one.'

'Phew!' Rachel released a long breath as Eli walked away. 'I reckon you got off light there, Ella. I really expected Eli to tell you to draw your pay.'

'So did I.' Ella Barnes wiped a hand across her face, leaving a grimy smear across one cheek. 'Either it's my lucky day or 'is missis spread 'er legs last night.'

'If you want it to go on being your lucky day, you'll shut your mouth now or I'll shut it for you!' Along the bench one of the older women looked at Ella Barnes, hands not needing the help of eyes to do the work of packing kitchen implements. 'Yer has a nasty tongue, Ella Barnes, and if I hear any more on it I'll gi' you what yer mother or father should o' given yer long since.'

A sullen look settled over Ella's face but she knew better than to argue with any of the older women. Like her mother their tempers were unreliable and their vengeance could be swift.

'Well, it's no surprise if Edward Royce is setting his cap at you, Anna,' a woman lifted a sallow smile. Her own youth stolen by perpetual pregnancy, she recognised the shyness of the young girl who had come to settle in Coseley.

'You make a fair picture. I saw hair just that colour in a painting once when my dad took me with 'im to old man Rewcastle's house. I peeked round the door 'fore my dad caught me and clipped my ear. Ooh, it was lovely that painting, but no more than yourself, Anna wench. Yer skin looks as clear and fragile as me mam's best china cup, and that 'air . . . 'ow do you manage to keep it looking so shiny in a place like the mill?'

'I've been wondering that an' all.' Rachel's candid brown stare fixed on Anna. 'Is it something you buy in Birmingham?'

'No,' she replied hastily, not wanting the conversation steered towards her trips to town and glad also of the chance of escaping the subject of Edward Royce. 'I just use my own cream for my face and make a rinse up for my hair. It takes all the hard soap scum out of it once I've washed it.'

'You makes yer own?' The older woman's enquiring eyes looked too large for her pinched face. 'I reckon I'd like to try some of it.' A sudden smile brightened her tired face and she patted her already swollen stomach. 'But I don't need to gi' my man any encouragement.'

'Where did yer learn to make them things?' asked Ella Barnes, forgetting her sullenness.

'At home.' The words were out before Anna really thought of what she was saying and the twist of pain that followed them brought a tiny furrow to her forehead. It still hurt to think of home.

'Did yer mam teach yer then?'

'No,' Anna answered, methodically wrapping each kitchen implement in a sheet of paper before placing it in the tea chest that stood half-full beside her. 'Mother Shipton taught me. She was a woman who lived alone.'

Curtains of memory opening, Anna gazed across the chasm separating her from the years of her childhood. She had been so happy then, with a mother who adored her, a father who doted on them both, and Polly Shipton, the woman the other children were so afraid of, the woman they said was a witch.

But Anna, despite her tender years, had recognised the loneliness of a woman who had lost the love of her life and tried to fill the gap by making herbal medicines for an ungrateful town. She had spent many long summer afternoons out in the fields and on the hills, helping gather herbs and plants then carrying the wicker basket back to the cottage, watching and learning as Polly brewed her lotions and tonics. She had been so safe in her own tiny world . . . a world that had been shattered the night her father had raped her.

'Did she tell you of anything that can shift freckles?'

'I don't know if they can be shifted, Ella, but she used to make a face wash that some of the girls in Wednesbury swore by. They said it certainly seemed to fade their freckles.'

Anna caught the girl's hopeful look; that covering of dark brown freckles was responsible for much of Ella Barnes's sour outlook. Feeling a surge of pity for the girl, she offered, 'I will make you some up, if you like, but mind, I can't promise it will work.'

'Oh, would you, Anna?' Ella Barnes looked almost happy. 'Eee, I'd be that grateful.'

The hooter blared its message. The female shift had ended. The women reached for their shawls hanging from nails driven into the walls either side of the packing benches, clogs beating a tattoo as they hurried their several ways. In an hour the men's shift would finish and a hot meal would be expected on the table.

Anna and Hester followed, the soles of Anna's boots almost soundless on the rough cobbles of the mill yard. She was glad the conversation stayed on face creams and hair rinses until they reached number seventy-eight.

'And what did you say?'

The meal of ham and salad and crusty bread finished, Maggie Fellen reached for the empty plates, carrying them into the scullery to be washed in hot water drawn from the huge black kettle.

'I told them it was nonsense, they were reading too many of those tuppenny romances they buy from Bella Castleton.'

Anna refilled the kettle from the single brass tap, carrying it back to the kitchen and setting it on the gleaming black range where the heat from the fire would have it ready boiled for supper.

'Then you be a fool,' Maggie told her bluntly as she returned to the scullery, picking up a rough huckaback cotton towel and beginning to dry the crockery. 'Why else do you think Edward Royce waited for the Birmingham train, and why else do you think he mended that boot and brought it back 'imself?'

'I don't think he was purposely waiting for the train.' Anna carried the dried plates and pots to the kitchen, giving each its own position on a wooden dresser such as every house in Roker Street seemed to possess. 'And as for my boot, he was just being helpful.'

'Oh, aye! He was being helpful, all right.' Maggie followed her, drying her hands on her long white apron. 'Only question is, who was he helping? You or 'imself?'

'Now what is that supposed to mean?' Picking up a plate only to replace it in its former position, Anna avoided that penetrating grey stare. The subject of Edward Royce, and the reason for his actions of late, embarrassed her.

'How on earth can his cobbling my boot be of any help to him? You told me he would take no payment for doing it.'

'True he would accept no brass for his efforts but that doesn't mean he has no intention of being rewarded for them.'

Picking up the cushion cover she was crocheting, Maggie settled beside the fire that burned winter and summer, her fingers moving deftly.

'And if you hadn't run upstairs swift as a scalded cat the minute yer 'eard 'is voice the followin' afternoon, when he brought yer boot to the door, yer would know that for yerself.'

Turning to the window Anna straightened a curtain, her nerves suddenly taut. Beyond the sky was a vast canvas of purple, blue and red. The sun was dying, its passing marked in breath-taking splendour.

Behind her, fingers idle for a moment, Maggie Fellen watched the girl she had taken into her home. Red-gold hair touched by the colour of the evening sky gleamed like some precious setting for the pearl of her skin. Pale green blouse and dark skirt following the curves of her body, the girl had a waist a man could span with his hands and no help from whalebone either.

'He's set his cap at you, wench.' Maggie bent to her crocheting, her own hair burnished by the light that slid past Anna. 'And you could do worse than take Edward Royce for a husband.'

'Maggie!' Exasperated, Anna swung round. 'I have no intention of marrying anybody. I'm happy the way I am, living here with you. I don't want to be married, and even if I did, that man would not be Edward Royce.'

'Maybe, maybe.' Maggie's fingers worked the cream cotton about the crochet needle. 'But what a woman fancies she wants isna always what she gets. And like I say, you could do worse.'

They were interrupted by Hester coming in the back way through the scullery.

'Mrs Fellen, me mam says to tell you she is 'avin' Kate over to do the cups and would you and Anna like to come round?'

'I thought Kate said she was finished with the cups?'

The crochet hook rested in Maggie's lap.

'Oh, aye, that's what she said. But like me mam says, when brass is short, yer'll do most things to feed kids.'

'Ar, your mam's right there, Essie.' Folding her needlework and putting it away in a raffia basket, Maggie walked to the door that closed off the narrow stairs from the kitchen. 'Thank 'er for me, will you, wench, an' say as 'ow I'll be round in a minute. I must tidy meself up a bit first.'

Anna waited for the door closing behind Maggie.

'What on earth is doing the cups . . . and who is Kate?'

'Kate O'Keefe,' Hester whispered back. 'She's Irish, lives over the other side of Coseley. Has about six kids an' none of them working. Times were bad in Ireland, they reckon, that's why they came here for her man to get a job in steel mills, but from look of the kids it don't seem they are much better off. Poor little buggers! Their arses hangin' out of their trousers an' a half-starved look on them most o' the time.'

'But what are the cups?' Anna heard the sound of Maggie coming downstairs and rushed to ask the question of Hester.

'Kate reads the tea leaves, she can tell your fortune from your cup.' Hester's explanation ended abruptly. It didn't do to be talking about other people's private lives when Maggie Fellen was around.

Reaching for her shawl, the older woman glanced coolly at Anna.

'Well, now you knows who Kate O'Keefe is, you might as well meet her for yourself. An' bring your brass. Kate 'as a good 'eart but also six mouths to feed besides her man.'

Mary Cresswell's kitchen was in its usual state of cheery chaos. Fire chased the shadows of early-evening, playing them over the blue and white willow pattern china that was Mary's pride and joy. Beside the hearth the black kettle sang its favourite song.

Billy, a year younger than Hester, had followed his usual pattern, going out as soon as he had finished his meal. Knowing that pattern, Anna's heart gave an unwanted twist. He would be with Edward Royce, she knew, in the tiny workshop Edward had told her had been left to him by his father, a master cutler, a true craftsman who had seen to it his son followed in his steps.

Traces of the five-year-old twins were everywhere; a picture book half hidden by a yellow jumper, shoes on the hearth, lined like a miniature guard of honour. Anna would have liked to cuddle them, loving their mischief, but tonight their mother had them out of the way, tucked up in bed. William Cresswell, Mary's husband, was out the back, flying his pigeons.

'Take off your shawl, Maggie. Kate will be here shortly. Anna, sit yourself down, wench. I'll just brew the tea.' Mary Cresswell turned to the dresser. Tonight was to be something of a social evening, calling for the use of her beloved wedding china. Setting the pretty cups and saucers on the snowy cloth, Hester gave Anna a covert look, eyes sparkling with merriment. She found the whole business a bit of a joke and her glance said so but her mouth remained sensibly closed. One wrong word and she would be out through the scullery door, her mother's clog following.

As if on cue Kate O'Keefe arrived as the hissing water bubbled into the painted teapot, sending out the fragrant essence of scalded tea.

'Is it bein' in ye are, Mary Cresswell?'

'Aye, Kate. Come you in, wench.'

'Sure and a foine evenin' it's bein'.' The full figure of Kate O'Keefe pushed aside the chenille curtain placed against the draught and stood poised in the doorway like an avenging angel.

Anna stared at the two perfectly round spots painted on her cheeks, at the black hair pulled into a knot on the nape of her neck. Eyes sharp and dark as a raven's wing swept the room beneath brows so straight they might have been drawn with a pencil and ruler.

'Evening, Kate. The little ones and your man are all well?'

'They are, Maggie Fellen, an' thanks be to Jesus.'

Pulling a chair to the table, the twinkle gone from her eyes, Hester offered, 'Would you like to sit here, Mrs O'Keefe . . . can I hang up your shawl?'

Giving the shawl to Hester, the woman beamed, heavy black skirts rustling as she lowered herself on to the chair.

'It's a deal of growin' ye've done, Essie Cresswell, since last oi came here. Who knows . . . perhaps the cup will be tellin' how long ye still have beneath your mother's roof?'

'Oh, Mrs O'Keefe, I haven't a lad yet.'

'Maybe not but nothing can be hidden from the cup. Itself will be tellin' me how far off the one is, an' all yer blushin' will alter it not a jot, Essie Cresswell.'

Mary's indulgent smile was turned to her daughter whose

looks were hers of years before. Cup or no cup, it wouldn't be long before some lad took her off to be his wife.

'Will you be startin' now, Kate?' Mary nursed the teapot in her large hands.

'Aye, that oi will, Mary Cresswell, as soon as one o' ye has the good sense to be introducin' me to this colleen.'

Across the table the dark eyes lanced into Anna as if already scanning her very soul and she felt a shiver run through her as she looked at the woman, perched like some huge bird of prey on the edge of her chair.

'You knows well who wench is,' Maggie answered, her voice a mite sharp. 'You visits too many houses in Coseley not to know, but I'll tell you all the same. She's Anna Bradly. She came from . . .'

'Sure an' there's no need of ye tellin' me anything more,' Kate O'Keefe cut in quickly. 'The cups will be doing that, and tellin' where she'll be goin' to, Maggie Fellen.'

'Going to?' There was more than a little fear in Maggie's tight reply. She hadn't realised how much Anna had come to mean in her life; the thought of her leaving brought cold fear.

'A body can swirl the tea and move the leaves,' Kate O'Keefe's soft Irish brogue filled the tiny kitchen, 'but they will find their own resting place, Maggie Fellen. They will say what they have to say and nothing can be changing that.'

Silence settled while Mary filled her precious cups with tea, holding the room in enchanted silence until the contents were drunk.

'Who'll be after bein' the first?' Kate pushed aside her own cup. 'Will it be yerself, Mary Cresswell?'

'There be not much of a fortune left for me, I be thinkin'.' Mary's loud laughter burst out. 'What bit is left can hang fire a while longer. Read the others first, Kate.'

'Then oi'll be taking Essie's cup. Pass it here, girl.'

Hands red and rough from constant work fastened about the dainty cup and Kate turned it slowly, peering into it.

'There be a lad for thee, Essie, but he be a ways off. Ye'll walk out of God's house with a foine man and work together well. The leaves say ye have a good life spread afore ye with all the comfort ye could ever want, but it's not near. Ye must be patient, Essie Cresswell, but rest assured that which the leaves promise will be given.'

'Is it a lad I knows?' Gold flecks shone like sequins in Hester's excited eyes.

'No, ye'll not be knowin' him, nor is he in Coseley. He waits on ye a long ways from this house.'

Kate replaced the cup in its saucer.

'Now what of ye, Maggie Fellen? Have ye any wish to be knowin' the future?'

Maggie smiled, a tight smile that found no echo in her slate-coloured eyes.

'Like Mary, most of my life is done, Kate, and there can be no change around the corner for me. But it can do no harm to hear you say as much.'

William Cresswell's soft encouraging calls to his pigeons wafted in through the half-open scullery door as the women watched Kate perform her ritual, turning Maggie's cup slowly between her rough hands.

'Ye have lost two men,' the soft brogue began at last, 'each to their own God. One who followed after wealth ye will see again in this life but once only. The other waits for ye beyond the veil . . .'

Despite lengthening shadows Anna saw Maggie's lips blanch and the hands resting in her lap curl about each other.

'. . . but ye be wrong in thinking life holds no change.' Kate hesitated, drawing in a long breath. 'Ye thought the Good Lord was after denyin' ye the daughter of yer heart but the girl ye desired for so long is yet to come . . .'

'Me havin' another child . . . now I know the cup is wrong.' Maggie laughed bitterly. 'My man has been gone many years and I've no thought to tekin' another.'

'The child will come,' Kate went on resolutely, ignoring the interruption. 'Though not of yer body, it will be the daughter of yer soul. Yours will be the carin' of it and ye will live to see the growin' of it.'

'Andrew?' Maggie asked softly, hope chasing disbelief from her voice.

'No, the child will not come from that direction but from one who will become as close to ye, an' it is not so far off. Within a twelve month ye will know. Ye are not to end yer days here in Coseley. The leaves tell of a foine house and a comfort ye never dreamed of, but some of yer heart will be here where much of yer days were spent in sorrow and where some still wait on ye. There will be hard times afore there be soft, Maggie Fellen, but better times are planned for ye.'

Putting the cup upright on its saucer, Kate turned a beady glance to the silent figure of Anna.

'An' what of ye, Anna Bradly?'

The voice had not risen yet Anna recognised the challenge. Kate O'Keefe's eyes passed behind her own, looking into the secret corners of her mind, probing, seeking, and Anna could not free herself from those black needle points.

'Oh, go on, Anna,' Hester urged, insensitive to the other girl's reticence. 'It canna do yer any harm.'

'Anna will not be tekin' a reading if she's no mind for it,' Maggie said quickly, recognising that something more than shyness held Anna back.

'But it's only a bit o' fun, Mrs Fellen, nobody teks any notice really.'

'So ye think it's a bit o' fun, do ye, Essie Cresswell?' Kate's bird-like glance swivelled to Hester. 'Then think on this: a month afore ye see yer twentieth year ye will take yer leave of Rewcastle's Mill. Ye will be mistress in yer own place and answerable to one only, and that one will be female. When this happens, come ye round to Kate O'Keefe's and tell her that no notice need be teken of what she sees in the cups.'

Beyond the door William Cresswell called coaxingly, tempting his pigeons from the sky, shooing them gently into their white-painted loft.

In the warm kitchen the fire whispered softly and in its glow Kate's black hair took on a darker shade. Her eyes, already brilliant, glowed like burning coals.

'Well?' She returned to Anna. 'Is yourself wantin' to hear what the cup has to tell or is it leavin' now Kate O'Keefe will be doin'?'

'What do I have to do?' Anna asked the question while every fibre spoke against it. Kate O'Keefe held some strange power; her black eyes seemed capable of passing through the barrier of flesh and travelling into the mind itself.

Kate's mouth curved in a tiny movement of triumph.

'Swirl the dregs in yer cup three times, slowly to the left. Turn it upside down into the saucer, then using yer right hand, pass it to me.'

Doing as Kate instructed, Anna handed it to her.

'You has no need, me wench.' Maggie saw the shaking of the small hand. 'Life will bring only what it holds, whether you hears the cup or whether you don't.'

'I . . . I do want to hear, Maggie.' It was half true. 'I would like to know what Kate can see for me.'

'You know your own way!' Maggie leaned back in her chair. She had said her piece and was done.

'Tap the bottom of the cup three toimes with yer marriage finger. That way ye chase tears that have no need of shedding.'

Kate waited solemnly until it was done then waited a while longer as Mary held a taper of paper to the fire, lifting it to the iron bracket fastened to the wall behind the table. The gas mantle began to glow and Mary turned up the light, filling the room with an eerie yellowish tinge. The taper thrown into the fire, Kate lifted Anna's cup and began to turn it.

'Holy Mother of God!' she swore, lifting her eyes to the girl facing her across the table.

She knows! The thought ran through Anna. Oh God, she knows, I can see it in her eyes!

'Yer've had yer troubles, mavourneen,' Kate's brogue thickened, 'an' they're not after bein' over yet. There be tears in yer cup . . .'

Tipping the cup sideways she watched the minute dribbles of milky tea hang against the rim then shook her crow-like head as most slipped obstinately back inside. She straightened it, peering once more into its depths.

'. . . an' it's refusin' to be dried, so they are. It's spillin' many more yer'll be, girl, for ye are not to be havin' an easy life, Anna Bradly, though there will be those to argue different. Toil and tears are the price ye'll pay . . . toil and tears.'

'But there must be something else, Mrs O'Keefe?'

'Shh!' Mary's sharp hiss silenced her daughter. Kate's eyes remained on the cup she was slowly twisting in her hands.

'Yer stay here will be short.' Kate's voice was hypnotic. She seemed almost to be in a trance, eyes glued to the mass of dark brown leaves. 'Ye're thinking never to wed but ye will. The man who will put the ring on yer finger is close by, but the man who will encircle yer heart is not in this land. There will be children . . .'

Kate paused and Anna's heart leaped again.

Instinctively she felt this woman knew of the son she had borne and of his fathering. She badly wanted to break the spell that seemed to bind her, to run out of Mary's kitchen and lock herself in her own little room in Maggie's house. But she couldn't, she could only brace herself as Kate lifted that piercing glance to her face.

'. . . one who is to grow with ye and one who will not.'

She had said *will* not *is*, thought Anna, clenching her teeth until they hurt. She knows one is born already . . . one who can never grow with me.

Kate's eyes softened, recognising the fear in the girl who was little more than a child herself. There was none would learn from Kate O'Keefe that she had already borne a child, one conceived from rape.

'There will be a parting that ye'll take hard, and deceit that will be as a smack in the gob.' Kate dropped her glance to the cup as relief shone in Anna's green gaze. They understood each other, a rough old Irish woman and a girl who had already been scarred by life. 'But from that parting ye will become yer own woman. The lives of many will be bound to yer own. Ye will have the carrying of them for it's yer back their fortunes will ride upon. Ye will work all the days of yer life, Anna Bradly, but that life will prove to be a great one, bejesus. Aye, a great one to be sure.'

Chapter Five

The train wheels clicked over the points with monotonous regularity but Anna didn't hear. She had posted two pounds to Polly as usual then wandered aimlessly around Birmingham until it was time to get the train home, and all the time one thought had whirled in her brain. Would he be there . . . would Edward Royce be at the end of the street tonight? The nearer the train carried her to Coseley, the more the thought pounded, refusing every effort of her will to dismiss it.

With a brief nod of goodnight to the passengers in her compartment, Anna stepped hesitantly on to the platform. The evening breeze carried back a steamy grey cloud of smoke as the engine pulled away down the track. She couldn't leave the station in case he was there, but at the same time, she told herself sharply, she couldn't stay here, jumping at every shadow like a startled deer.

Anna gripped her bag, her boots making little sound on the wooden platform as she made her way towards the street. If Edward Royce *was* there, and if he *did* speak to her, she would tell him flatly his attentions were uncalled for and unwelcome.

In the event she did neither. Emerging from the entrance to the tiny station, Anna felt colour surge to her cheeks and her tongue cling helplessly to the roof of her mouth.

'Good evening, Miss Bradly.' Edward Royce caught the scent of violets. 'I was waiting until tha came.'

The moon passing behind a cloud left the long street in

darkness before them. Roker Street suddenly seemed at the ends of the earth.

'Billy Cresswell said you would be away to Birmingham today but if he hadna I would still have bin here, just as I am every Saturday.'

He doesn't wear clogs as all the others do. Anna found herself consciously listening to the softer tap of leather. Nor does he cover his head with a flat cap.

'If tha are annoyed by my cheek, Miss Bradly, then I'll tell tha goodnight here. It's not my intention to cause tha any worry.'

Anna looked up then, catching the set of his jaw by the light of the re-emerging moon, seeing his mouth, straight and tense.

'I . . . I'm not worried, Mr Royce, but I am confused. Why should you wait for me?'

'I've asked myself that question many times. Why should I wait for thee when I would wait for no other lass in Coseley?'

They turned into the alley that led to Roker Street, its narrowness forcing them to walk closer beside each other, and Anna felt the brush of his arm against her own.

'I only know I must come.' They passed from the alley and Edward took a sideways step, widening the space between them. 'P'raps it's the thought of tha walking alone.'

'I don't think you should worry about me, Mr Royce.'

Anna stopped in front of number seventy-eight, painfully aware that no curtains hid her from the prying eyes of Roker Street. 'But it was kind of you and I thank you.' Her hand was already on the door.

'Miss Bradly, can I . . . do you think . . .?' He sounded suddenly awkward, like a schoolboy searching for the proper words. 'Would tha object to my calling on you tomorrow?'

Anna was stunned. This was the last thing she had expected and the last thing she wanted.

'I . . . I'm sorry, Mr Royce,' she stammered, pushing open

the door and swiftly stepping inside the house. 'I . . . I'm afraid my Sundays are always spent with Maggie.'

Anna carried the plates to the scullery, washed and dried them then returned them to the kitchen, placing them back on the dresser. Thoughts of Edward Royce's confession that he had purposely waited for her claimed her concentration so she didn't hear Maggie say she had a headache and was going to lie down.

'What?' Anna was still vague as Maggie opened the door leading on to the stairs.

'Eee! I don't know where yer've bin all morning, wench, but I do know as it's not here.' Maggie lifted her heavy black skirts from around her feet. 'I said, I'm not coming with yer today.'

'But we always go to the moor together on Sundays.' Anna turned from the dresser, the memory of her last words to Edward Royce rushing back to her.

'Aye, I knows that, but you'll have to manage on your own this afternoon. I have a head as thick as a mill chimney.' Maggie set a foot on the bare wood of the stairs that over the years she had scrubbed almost white. 'You can call me when you gets back.'

'I'm sorry.' Anna crossed to the foot of the staircase, guilty that her mind had been elsewhere. 'I didn't realise you were feeling bad, I'll stay here with you.'

'What good do you expect that will do? I be no babby as needs to be fussed on.' Maggie continued on up the stairs, her clogs loud against the wood. 'Besides, I thought you needed them herbs an' things for to mek creams for them wenches up at the mill?'

'I do.'

'Well, you'll not get them sitting here the rest of the day.'

Anna's eyes watched her straight back.

'They will have to wait . . . I would rather stay here with you.'

At the head of the stairs Maggie stopped, turning a questioning look at the girl below.

'Did you promise?'

'Yes,' Anna answered reluctantly, remembering Ella Barnes's freckles. 'But . . .'

'No buts, wench, a promise is a promise. If you're not going to keep it then you shouldn't mek it in the first place.' Maggie turned away into her own room. 'Wake me when you gets home.'

It was the first time Anna had come to the moors alone. On every side green space rolled before her to join the blue of the horizon. At each step insects hummed, flying up from the sun-warmed grass, settling again to their labour as she passed. Anna breathed deeply, loving the fresh clean air, the feel of the sun on her face. It was a different, lovely world. The words of a hymn her father and mother had often sung with her touched her memory and as she knelt to pick rosebay willow herb, butterfly orchid and delicately perfumed sweet briar, she sang softly: 'All things bright and beautiful . . .'

'I could help with that if tha let me?'

She had heard no one approach, the soft springy turf muffling the sound of footsteps. Taken by surprise, she gasped then twisted about to squint at the tall figure outlined against the sky.

'I . . . I've finished.' Scrambling to her feet, Anna brushed grass from her skirt with one hand, clinging to her canework basket with the other.

'Tha hasn't picked many.' Edward Royce passed a glance over the basket. 'Judging by the way the women at Rewcastle's are tekin' to those creams and lotions tha makes, I doubt that will be enough.'

'So you've heard about that too!' Anna's voice was tart. 'It appears you hear a good deal about me, Mr Royce.'

'Aye, I do.'

'Billy Cresswell, I suppose?'

'True enough he tells me of tha doings.'

'Billy Cresswell talks too much.'

'The lad thinks tha's something special.' Without asking, Edward took the basket, turning away towards a clump of newly awakening evening primrose, picking some with careful, precise movements. 'An' he's not alone in that.'

'Mr Royce . . .'

His words had unsettled Anna. Unsure of the feelings stirring inside her, she was nervous.

'Mr Royce . . .'

'Look, Anna lass . . .' Squatting on his haunches, Edward Royce turned his head towards her.

His hair had fallen across his brow. Anna saw how the sunlight burnished it. It was almost the colour of her mother's wooden chest, the same rich mahogany.

'It's true I like thee more than somewhat but tha need have no fear I'll push myself on thee. I'm no sprig of a lad that thinks every lass should fall flat on her face just because he looks at her.'

The same light caught his eyes, deepening them to the blueness of hyacinths, bringing a fresh batch of tiny lines to their corners as he screwed them up against the glare.

'I waited for thee purposely last night but my seeing tha here this afternoon is accidental. I come here sometimes when I need to think a thing out . . . I must say, I was surprised to see thee on this part of moor.'

'I don't usually come this far but today . . .'

'And where's Maggie?' he interrupted. 'I thought that tha always came up on to moor together?'

Narrowed against the sun, his eyes seemed to accuse her and his hands rested idly against his knees, waiting for her answer. They were strong hands, the fingers long with white half moons showing at the base of nails that were surprisingly clean. His wrists and forearms below the rolled sleeves of a striped cambric shirt were covered with short fine hairs that glistened in the sun.

'She . . . she wasn't feeling too well.' Suddenly conscious she was staring, Anna pulled her glance away to the line of houses in the distance. 'I really should be getting back to her.'

'Then it's as well I did come across thee.' He turned back to the business of collecting plants. 'Two pairs of hands can do most jobs quicker than one.'

He was right, of course and if she didn't fill the basket it would mean her having to come to the moor again one evening after work.

'Thank you, Mr Royce.' With a shy whisper, Anna bent to pull the fragrant plants.

'Phew!' Half an hour later Edward Royce flopped to the ground, rolling on to his back, eyelids closed. 'It's warm work, is that. I need five minutes before I tackle the walk back.'

Anna stared at him. He stretched a good six feet. He had said very little as they had worked and not once had he attempted to touch her. It would do no harm to sit just for a few minutes.

The basket between them, she sat down. Pulling up her knees, skirts tucked around her ankles, she gazed out over a forest of mill stacks rising above terraces of tiny two-up, two-down houses.

So like Wednesbury. There too factory chimneys dominated a skyline regularly turned to blood red as furnaces were opened to receive offerings of pig iron or to spew out molten steel. And there, as in Coseley, there was no way out, no employment other than the foundries and mills. That was what her son would grow up to, that was his future. And what of hers? It could only be the same hard work and little besides, despite what Kate O'Keefe had read in her tea cup. A bee hummed loudly, investigating the contents of the basket; beyond, in the distance, a lark rose from the grass, filling the sky with song. Somewhere there was a beautiful world but its doors were closed against the likes of Anna Bradly.

'Coseley is a small place, Anna . . .'

He had not asked to use her Christian name but neither

was sitting on the moors alone with him conventional. What the women of Wednesbury would have had to say about such 'carryings on' didn't bear thinking of.

'. . . but I would tek it against the big cities any day.' His eyes were still closed against the sky.

'Billy Cresswell told Maggie you had been to London.'

'It's true, I took my cutlery design and entered it in an international trade fair. When it took first place in its class I wrote to the King asking his permission to call it "King's Choice".'

'You wrote to the King?' Anna was more astounded than impressed.

Edward drew up one knee, resting his other foot across it. The buttons of his shirt opened just below the throat, showing the same covering of short glistening hairs. Anna quickly diverted her glance as his head turned and his blue eyes looked up at her.

'I wrote to Buckingham Palace. Whether the King will get to see my letter or whether it will be read by one of those aides he has is anybody's guess. They might even have thrown it away.'

'Oh, they wouldn't do that.'

Anna meant to look at his face but somehow her eyes were drawn to the line of hairs below his throat. Blushing, confused by her own feelings, she turned her attention to the basket, re-arranging the collection of plants.

'Mebbe not.' He sat up, his gaze on their small world of Coseley.

'I have the workshop my father bought when he moved here from Sheffield. It was he taught me the making of cutlery; he was a fine cutler and made sure I learned his skills. He would brook no shoddy workmanship. He also left me the house I was born in. That might be counted little enough by some folk but it's enough for me. I am my own master and as long as I can, I will keep it that way. I want no bending and scraping to ironmasters like

Rewcastle. Seems to be better to be your own man, for either way brings the likes of me no riches.' He wondered how to continue.

He had been aware of this slight girl with the head of red-gold hair since shortly after Maggie Fellen had taken her in and had long realised that he wanted Anna Bradly for his wife.

'What I'm tryin' to say, Anna, is this. Has tha any objection to my callin' on thee?'

You could do worse than tek Edward Royce for a husband. Maggie's words echoed in her mind. If she were walking out with Edward it would put an end to the way the lads at the mill looked at her, the whistles as she passed and the sniggers when they thought she was out of hearing. Yes, she could do worse than accept Edward, but would he still want her once he knew her past?

'Edward.' She hesitated. Maggie had listened to her story and at the end had shaken her head and said Anna had been in the way of the devil's temper that night, that Maggie Fellen would not be the one to continue his evil by throwing her out so long as she kept a decent life under her roof. But would Edward see things in the same light? Would he respect her privacy if he no longer wanted her for his wife? Somehow she felt he would.

'Edward.' She began again. 'There is something I have to tell you. It concerns my life before coming to Coseley . . .'

About to reply that there was no need to tell him anything, Edward turned to her. Seeing the look on her face, he remained silent. Whatever it was, she had the need to tell it.

'. . . my mother died from childbirth while I was very young. A friend, Mother Polly, took care of me while my father was at work and a woman from the town, Mary Carter, came to the house twice a week, to do the washing and the baking. Then, one day, Mary disappeared and when her body was found floating in Millpool my father was accused of her rape and murder. The official verdict was death by misadventure but that made no difference to the people of Wednesbury – they accused and taunted him for months, until one night he came home drunk. He . . . he mistook me for Mary and said he might as well do what he was accused of doing. He didn't mean to hurt me, he thought I *was* Mary, I know he did, but he . . . he raped me.'

Pausing, Anna gazed out across the heath, into the distance that held her child.

'I have a son, Edward,' she finished softly. 'I have a bastard son.'

He had not taken his eyes from her as she talked. He had seen the emotion in her face, sensed the effort the telling of her rape had taken. She need have told him nothing yet instead had told him all. She could have lied to him but deep within him he knew she had spoken the truth, the whole truth.

'Who has the lad now?' he asked.

'Mother Polly said she would care for him as she had for me,' Anna answered. 'I could not let a child suffer for something he had no part in, and I could not bring him with me with having no place to live and no one who would look after him while I work. But I love him, Edward, I send what money I can to feed and clothe him, and one day, God willing, I intend to have him with me.'

Turning her head, Anna looked him squarely in the eyes. 'I have told you what happened, Edward, and it is the truth. If you no longer wish to call on me then I understand.'

Standing up, he held out a hand and when she took it pulled her gently to her feet.

'Tha's told me lass,' he said gently, 'and I appreciate the telling, though it makes no difference to the feelings I hold for you. What happened was none of your doing, that is what I believe, and will always believe. Marry me, Anna, and we will make a home for the boy, together.'

• • •

The wedding, a year after that day on the moor, was a quiet gathering at the chapel, Maggie Fellen and the Cresswells the only witnesses as Anna joined her life to that of Edward Royce. He'd known that day on the moor that she had not loved him and he had not asked her for anything, even when she had felt the tension holding him like a coiled spring.

Laying a sparkling white cloth across the table, Anna smiled tenderly. She had not loved Edward then, but she did now, with a quiet peaceful love.

I'll not push myself on thee, Anna. On their wedding night they stood in a shaft of moonlight streaming through the open curtains of the small front bedroom in his Slater Street house. 'Tha need have no fear on that score. Ah love thee, lass, an' ah want thee, ah'll not deny, but ah'll lay no hand on thee unless tha wants it. Tha is my wife an' ah thank God every day. An' if that's to be the all of it, then ah can make best of it.'

Her hair had been loose of its pins and he had run his fingers through the dark fiery silk, holding her against him. She had felt the shudder run through him, the quickening of him pressing against the thin cotton of her nightdress, then he had left her, going to lie in the bed they had shared without further closeness for three months. Fear had kept her from loving Edward, fear that the pain her father had caused her would happen all over again, the same terror and revulsion. But that had been a dreadful mistake she knew, her father had been driven mad by lies and taunts. He had tried to drown that madness in drink which had only added to his insanity until he had raped his own daughter without knowing. But like her father Edward was kind and gentle, loving her with an undemanding love, and like her father he would not knowingly hurt her. She was the one hurting Edward, she was causing him pain, pain he did not deserve nor would force her to assuage.

'Edward!' She had called his name in the soft creamy moonlight and heard the quiet, almost sobbing release of breath as she whispered, 'Help me, Edward.'

Now Anna smiled into the fire, her memory sending pictures through her mind. She was to bear his child.

Behind her the latch opened noisily and she twisted towards the sound.

'Tha shouldn't have waited up, lass, tha needs to rest more with little 'un coming.' Leaving his shoes at the scullery door, Edward dropped heavily into a chair beside the glowing range, fatigue scoring lines across his face.

'I get quite enough rest.' Anna tried to keep her own tiredness from showing. There had been too many nights with Edward working into the small hours, but if he could manage, so could she.

'Has anyone stayed up at the new place with you?' Ladling soup into a bowl that had been warming against the fire, she placed it on the table, pushing a plate of bread close beside it.

'A couple of the men, but I sent them home about eleven. Ah can't expect a proper day's work out of a man who's worked half the night afore it!'

'Yet that is what you yourself are doing.' The worry of weeks echoed in Anna's reply. 'You push yourself day and night, Edward, and don't pretend . . . it's wearing you out. Why must it always be you who has to be there? Why can't this partner, whoever it is, take a turn?'

'He's seeing to the sales end, Anna.' More weary than he would ever admit, Edward changed his seat for a chair at the table but the soup remained untouched. Reaching for Anna, he pulled her close, his arms around her thickening waist, head resting on the child in her womb, breathing in the scent of violets.

'King's Choice is mine, the same as this child is mine, and I want the best for both of them, Anna. Don't you see, love, I have to succeed for both of you?'

A rush of tenderness softening her voice, Anna touched a hand to the head lying against her stomach. Edward didn't understand even yet that she loved him whole-heartedly, he had no need to prove himself to her; perhaps it was her fault. She didn't lie in his arms smouldering with passion, but she loved him and he was enough for her.

'You have already succeeded for me, Edward,' she whispered into his mahogany hair. 'And our child will have the finest man in Coseley as a father, it will need no more.'

'I love thee, lass.' Edward did not look up. 'I love thee.' He buried his face closer to the gentle rise that was his unborn child, waiting for a reply he knew would not come.

Anna had married him and kept his house, she answered his physical needs, but not once had she said she loved him.

'Ah'm not wanting to eat.' Stifling the emotion pulling at him, he stood up, one hand grasping Anna's. 'Ah'm away to bed and for once tha can leave the crocks, they'll wash in mornin' . . . and this time, Mrs Royce, tha's not goin' to pretend neither. Ah can see tiredness in tha face.'

'I will bank the fire and come straight up.' Anna smiled into a face weary from more than hard work, and her heart twisted. She was failing him, she knew that, and yet . . .

'No tha won't.' Releasing her, Edward moved towards the scullery where the bucket of coal chippings was always kept. 'Tha's goin' to bed, ah'll see to fire.'

He did not follow at once. Anna had washed her hands and face in the water kept in a jug on the dresser at the foot of the brass bedstead and was already plaiting her hair when she heard his tread on the wooden stair. She wished he wouldn't work so many hours.

'There's water in the jug.' She tied the end of her long plait with a length of white ribbon.

'Ah had a swill in the scullery.' The icy water he had hoped would wash away desire had achieved nothing. His back turned towards her, he slipped off his shirt and trousers.

'Will it take much longer to get the new workshop set up?' Anna glanced at the sinewy back and the surge of warmth she had felt downstairs welled up in her. Suddenly she wanted to take him in her arms, to soothe away the weariness of body and heart.

'A few days, ah reckon. There's one big machine has to be delivered yet. Get that in and we should be all set.'

'Edward.' Turning off the oil lamp, Anna pulled back the curtains, looking down at the sleeping, moon-bathed street. 'It's not too late,' she said quietly. 'You can still withdraw from this partnership and wait until you can launch King's Choice yourself. You have always preferred to be your own boss and don't have to change for me.'

'But ah do, Anna.' He was behind her, his fingers playing with the long plait of her hair. 'Ah want to change the world for you, to give you the best that money can buy . . .'

'You have given me more than any money can buy, Edward.' She turned, seeing the line of his shoulders in the light from the window, catching the dark gleam of his eyes sweeping her face, and the heat from his body burned through her nightgown as she pressed against him, lifting her arms to his neck.

'I have you, and soon I shall have our child. I love you, Edward,' she whispered, shy as a new bride. 'I love you.'

'Anna!' He was hoarse with longing and uncertainty. 'Anna . . . oh, Anna, my love . . . my love.' His arms strong about her, he held her close in the moonlight, afraid that to move would be to lose what God had just given him.

It was Anna who broke away but only long enough to climb into bed and as Edward joined her she slid back into the circle of his arms, happy that tonight he would taste the fullness of her love.

'All things bright and beautiful . . .'

Singing the words of the hymn her mother had taught her so long ago, Anna tidied her already spotless kitchen. Satisfied all was as she liked it, she turned her attention to the gently bubbling saucepan against the fire. It was too early to add potatoes yet, Edward would not be home until late and she did not want them boiled away to nothing in the water.

'All things bright and beautiful, the Lord God made them all . . .'

Lifting the heavy pan, she put it on the hob that gleamed like black silver. Edward said she shouldn't work so hard, scrubbing and polishing, but she loved this tiny house as much as she guessed his mother must have done.

The girls would be here soon. Anna glanced at the clock ticking quietly on the mantelpiece above the fire. She looked forward to the visits of the wenches from the mill, enjoying their gossip and listening to their latest love stories. Anna smiled to herself as she reached down her precious china cups from the dresser. They had been a wedding present from Maggie and she still felt like a little girl playing house every time she took them from their hooks. Laying them ready on their delicate saucers, she took out the fruit cake she had baked that morning; she liked to have something to offer and the girls were always hungry.

'Are yer in, Anna?' Ella Barnes pushed aside the chenille door curtain.

'Of course, come in.' The same happy smile teasing her mouth, Anna welcomed her guests.

Tea made and poured, she handed Ella a small carton, watching her pleased grin.

'Eee, ta ever so, Anna.' Ella took the pill box filled now with a paste of grated horseradish and milk. 'It's workin' just fine. My freckles 'ave almost disappeared.'

They were not so thickly brown, Anna admitted to herself as the girl eagerly opened the box, sniffing at the contents, but that could be the result of her not worrying so much about them rather than the paste.

'Anna,' Rachel Orme's brown eyes gleamed excitedly, 'would yer do my face with cosmetics? You know, like them there rich women in tuppenny novels.'

'It won't be tuppenny novels your mother will be blaming

if I send you home with your face made up,' Anna said, smiling.

'You knows the sort o' women daubs themselves in paint and powder,' Ella mimicked Rachel's mother, 'the sort that's no better than they should be.'

'Oh, go on, Anna,' Rachel pleaded as the giggling died away. 'I've always wanted to see how I might look done up like wenches in Birmingham Music Hall.'

'You might see how they look done up in Birmingham 'ospital if your mother cops you.' Ella Barnes wagged a warning finger.

'But her won't, not if I washes it off afore I goes. Please, Anna, you never knows. I might look like one o' them film stars. Eee, think of it, "The Desert Sheik", starring Miss Rachel Orme.'

'It would tek more than Anna's cosmetics to turn thee into a film star,' Ella Barnes said, laughing. 'That would need a Fairy Godmother!'

'Well, at least I don't need no pastes to get rid of freckles,' Rachel shot, hurt by Ella's remark.

'No, you doesn't, but you could do wi' a load o' concrete to fill in holes where you had the chicken pox.'

'Now that's enough!' Anna had seen exchanges of this sort lead to tears before. 'I think it might be fun to try, Rachel, so long as you scrub it off before you go home.'

Delighted, she settled into a chair in Anna's bright kitchen, tucking the towel Anna handed to her round her neck, protecting the high cotton of her pink blouse.

'When is the babby due, Anna?'

Wiping Rachel's face with a scrap of white cloth dipped in rosewater before spreading a thick layer of ground oatmeal mixed with milk over her cheeks and brow, Anna smiled happily. 'Another month.'

'Is Edward pleased?'

'Of course he is pleased.' Hester came in through the scullery, a feathering of rain sparkling like tiny crystals on her mousy hair. 'Have you had that sort of daft question all night, Anna?'

'I didn't mean to be daft.' Ella's mouth drooped. 'I just asked, that's all.'

'Then tek a poker an' stir your brains a bit! Get rid of all the dust afore you asks the next time.'

Putting a paper-wrapped parcel on the table, Hester took off her shawl, hanging it on the wooden peg behind the door.

'Me mam has sent a matinee coat an' says to tell you there'll be some baby gowns along tomorrow. Her got them from the pawn shop, an unredeemed pledge, but 'er's got them in boiler just to mek sure as they're clean.'

'I'll never be able to thank your mother, Hester, but I am pleased. Every little helps just now with Edward starting his new line.'

Leaving Rachel until the oatmeal dried, Anna turned to Ella.

'Do you want to try?'

'Eee, Mrs Royce, I was 'oping you'd ask.'

'Maggie says to mek sure you're not standing on your feet too long.' Hester cast a stern glance at the girls in Anna's kitchen.

She enjoyed the company of the girls but they had turned it into a weekly visit and she now eight months gone; she should be resting with her feet up instead of running a beauty parlour.

'Maggie worries too much.' Massaging a thin film of cream scented with a hint of wild honeysuckle over Ella's upturned face, Anna glanced at her friend. 'And for that matter, so do you, Hester Cresswell.'

'Well, it needs somebody to. You seem to think you can keep going day and night.'

'I'll come to no harm.' Cutting two slices from a cucumber, Anna placed one over each of Ella's eyes. 'Is Maggie with your mother, Hester?'

'She was when I left. Seems they're havin' some kind of

competition, the way me mam's knitting needles and Maggie Fellen's crochet hooks are flyin'. I tell yer, Anna, that babby of yours will 'ave to wear these woollies till it's twenty-one to get through what that pair are mekin'.'

Behind them Rachel choked back a laugh. 'Don't go on like that, Hester Cresswell. If you meks me laugh it'll crack all of Anna's plaster work.'

'That's about ready to come off.' Pouring water from the hissing kettle into a large pottery bowl, Anna cooled it with a jug filled from the scullery tap.

Watching Rachel cleanse away the dried oatmeal, Hester asked, 'Edward is sure he's doin' the right thing, Anna?'

'He would rather have been on his own,' a tiny frown pulled the arch of Anna's eyebrows, 'but since the palace agreed to the name King's Choice and ordered a complete suite of cutlery, everybody seems to want it. Edward couldn't fill all the orders working alone so this seemed the only answer.'

Removing the cucumber slices from Ella's eyes, Anna wiped the lids with a rosewater-dipped cloth, patting them dry with a fingertip movement.

'A partnership was the sensible solution really,' she defended Edward's action. 'We hadn't the money for machinery and there was no way he could make that amount of cutlery by hand. A sixty-forty split was fair, he reckoned.'

'I don't know about the money side of things,' Hester took the bowl of water, emptying it into the scullery sink, 'but it seems to me your husband is doin' all the work. How many times has he bin home before eleven at night since this thing started?'

Anna stretched her back, feeling the baby kick inside her. Hester was right. Edward was gone all day and well into the night but he wanted to make sure everything was set up the way he wanted it; it was like Edward not to leave things to other people. 'We will have a better life soon,' he had told her last night, holding her in his arms. 'We are on a winner, Anna, and this is just the beginning. Soon you can have a nice house somewhere. P'raps we might even join the toffs in Woodgreen.' He had slept then, worn out from working since first light.

'What time be you expectin' him tonight?' Hester came back, drying her hands, her eyes speckled gold from the softly flaring gas light.

Bending over Ella, touching beneath the lower side of her lashes with a soft black drawing pencil, Anna didn't answer at once. Studying the girl's face, she smudged the lines she had pencilled, smoothing the starkness to a charcoal shadow that emphasised the almond shape of the girl's eyeline.

'I'm not sure. Edward is helping the men get a new machine bedded in. He doesn't know how long it will take.'

'While his partner is getting another trollop bedded in – and we all know how long *that* will take.'

'Eee, Hester Cresswell!' Ella Barnes looked up from the box of cream she had cradled all night. 'You better not let your mam hear you talk like that.'

'Well, it's true.' Hester turned on the girl from Rewcastle's Mill. 'An' everybody knows it. That one is willing to let anybody do the work just so long as it don't tek him from his pleasure.'

'Edward wouldn't be happy if he hadn't seen the job done for himself, Hester,' Anna said, smiling. 'Now make us all a cup of tea.'

'There you are, Ella.' A few moments later she handed the girl a mirror. 'It could be Miss Ella Barnes currently appearing in The Desert Sheik.'

Looking at her reflection, Ella's brown eyes widened with pleasure.

'Eee, Anna, I can't tell meself. Ooh, you be clever in cosmetics! You'll 'ave to teach me 'ow to do this for meself . . . Eee, what would me mam say!'

They were laughing when the beige-bordered chenille door curtain was pushed aside and Eli Curran stepped in from the street.

'It . . . it were a machine, me wench. It slipped.'

Hester's arm about her, Anna watched the men carry a door into her bright warm kitchen, a door on which they had laid the body of her husband.

'It were an accident.'

Eli pulled off his cap and stood twisting it in his hands.

''E were settin' up a press – you, know for stampin' out the metal for them knives an' things – when it slipped an' the lot come tumblin' over on top of 'im.'

Behind her the mill girls clung together holding on to each other, their frightened exclamations punctuating the dreadful hush that had settled, robbing the tiny room of its warmth.

'Where shall we put 'im, missis?'

One of the men helping to carry the door looked at Anna but his question was lost on her. Why was Edward lying down? Why didn't he smile?

'Over here.'

It was Hester who answered. Crossing quickly to the sideboard beneath the room's one window, she scooped up the wooden candlesticks and pottery bowl, dropping them on to the table among the cosmetic creams and lotions.

'We be mortal sorry.' Eli looked more at Hester than at Anna. 'There weren't nothin' we could do, the thing was over an' 'im under it afore you could wink.' He glanced towards the four men standing awkwardly shuffling their feet now their burden was laid down. 'If . . . if we be needed, then you know where to find we.'

'You have grease on your face, Edward.'

Anna crossed to the sideboard, a tiny smile lifting the edges of her mouth, and touched a finger to the smear of greasy dirt crossing his brow and cheek.

'You will have to wash that off before supper.'

'Come away, Anna.' Hester put an arm around her, turning her away as the men left the house. 'Edward won't be wantin' anythin' tonight.'

'Eh, Hester, is . . . is Edward Royce truly dead?'

The girl's words seemed to pierce Anna's mind, chasing away the numbing stillness.

Edward was dead!

Around her the room swirled in a crazy dance and in her womb the unborn child lurched.

Edward Royce was dead!

'You pair!' Hester spoke sharply to the girls as she held on to Anna. 'Stop actin' like bloody mawkins. This ain't the first dead body y'ave seen, an' God knows it ain't likely to be the last! Now go fetch Maggie Fellen an' me mam, tell 'em what's happened. I'll stop with Anna.'

'I did not love him as I should have done.'

Anna sat beside the cold grate that would remain fireless while her husband's body lay in the room.

Sitting beside her, Maggie held back a reply. Anna had said nothing since she and Hester's mother had come running. 'Edward Royce be dead,' was all the two girls had gabbled before racing off. She had said nothing as they had washed the body and dressed it in its Sunday best, just stood silent and unmoving, staring at Edward's face.

'I did not love him enough. He deserved more.'

'You gave 'im all you could, wench,' Maggie said gently. It would be best to talk, to try to draw out the grief locked inside, better if Anna would cry it out.

'Did I, Maggie?'

Anna's eyes turned to the door where her husband's body still lay. It had been placed on chairs brought in by neighbours.

'Did I give him all I could?'

'O' course you did, Anna. You looked to 'im as well as you could an' 'e knowed that.'

'Looking after him was not enough.' Anna's voice was barely audible. 'It was not enough, Maggie, I should have loved him more.'

The weight of the child in her womb making her progress slow and unwieldy, she pushed herself to her feet and crossed to where her husband lay, only the bronze pennies holding his eyes closed saying he was not sleeping.

'It was not enough, Edward.' She looked down at his quiet face. 'You deserved so much more.'

In the hushed stillness she slipped to her knees, taking one hand in hers, holding her cheek against its marble coldness.

'I could not show you for so long,' she whispered, 'I could not tell you what lay in my heart, the *real* love that had grown and filled it. I could not tell you how I felt in those early weeks and now it is too late – too late to tell you it was fear that held me away from you, fear of what had happened before. But I loved you, Edward, I loved you. Oh, Edward, I'm sorry . . . I'm sorry!'

In the shadows Maggie Fellen watched, her own heart moved to breaking, but she made no attempt to bring Anna away. Let her pour it all out. Let the tears of sorrow be her comfort, for it was all the solace life might offer her.

Chapter Six

Anna didn't cry. Nor did the tears fall the day the plain deal box holding his body was lowered into the ground or that same night when pain carried his child into the world.

Hester Margaret was her daughter's given name, but from the moment Maggie had laid the tiny bundle in her arms and she had seen the golden fuzz of hair, soft as a summer morning, Anna had called her Misty.

'You have a half-brother, Misty.' She stroked a finger across the tiny head, feeling the child pull hard on her nipple. 'He has the same colour hair as you but his eyes are blue. I don't know his name and he will never know yours, but you have a half-brother, my little sweetheart, though the two of you will never meet.'

'Be you in, Mrs Royce?'

Anna glanced towards the door, kept on the latch like all the rest in this part of Coscley. Taking the child from her breast, she called, 'Come in.'

She recognised the man who shuffled self-consciously into her neat little kitchen. He was a clerk in Rewcastle's offices.

'Mr Rewcastle sent me, Mrs Royce.'

'It used to be Anna. What happened to change that, Joby?' Putting the baby in a drawer that served for a cot and covering her with a blanket, Anna turned towards the slight frame of Joby Timmins. 'So Mr Rewcastle sent you. What for?'

'He told me to ask you if you would come up to the Mill? I . . . I don't know what for.'

Maybe not, Anna thought, watching his glance fall before her own, but I bet you have a good idea.

'Did he say when, Joby?'

'Aye, Mrs . . . Anna, this afternoon, if you can manage?'

'I'll manage. Tell Mr Rewcastle I will be there at three.' She crossed to the door, holding it open for him. 'Is your family well, Joby? Last I heard your John was cutting his teeth with bronchitis.'

'Aye, but he seems all right now, poor little bugger. There was a time I thought we'd lost him.' Joby Timmins smiled, transforming a face worn by work and worry. 'Thanks for askin', Anna wench. And, Anna . . .' he leaned slightly closer '. . . look out for Rewcastle, he's a sly sod. I don't know what he wants to see yer for . . . well, not all of it any road. Just be careful, eh?'

She had left the baby with Maggie and sharp on three crossed the cobbled yard of the mill. Inside the offices, their walls covered with drab brown paint, Anna looked around with distaste. The workhouse couldn't be much drabber. She was about to sound the small brass bell on a table beside the entrance when Joby Timmins entered from an inner door.

'Mr Rewcastle is waiting for you, Mrs Royce.'

This time Anna did not question his formality. Here he would be expected to address her as any other visitor to the mill. He led her through a long room where several clerks burrowed industriously among mounds of paper though Anna knew their eyes followed her as she passed.

The office Joby showed her into smelled strongly of lavender wax polish and for the first time in her life Anna walked on a rug that had not been pegged from clippings of old clothes.

'Sit down, Anna.'

There was no formality here, she noted, sitting on the edge of the chair Jacob Rewcastle pointed to. Or was it a lack of respect? The great mill owner and an ex-employee? He smiled at her across the huge mahogany desk and Joby Timmins's warning echoed in her mind. 'Look out for Rewcastle, he's a sly sod.'

'I think you know how sorry I am about your husband . . . dreadful accident . . . dreadful.' His smile faded. 'But the business of life must go on. That's the reason I asked you to call and see me, Anna. Business.'

'I don't understand, Mr Rewcastle, what business do you have with me?'

'Not you directly.' He lifted a sheaf of papers, shuffling them together. 'My business was with your late husband. He borrowed a great deal of money from me to buy new machinery and premises, and now,' the heavy shoulders were raised in a shrug, 'now I must call in his loan, Anna.'

'But Edward said he had a sixty-forty arrangement. He was to take forty per cent of the profit from King's Choice in exchange for the money he needed right away to set it up.'

'I'm sorry, Anna. He must have wanted you to believe in him, I suppose.' The papers were shuffled again. 'The truth is your husband borrowed heavily from me, but I'm a fair man and seein' as how things stand with you, I've decided to let you keep the workshop.'

Across the desk small eyes peered at her, from within enveloping fleshy folds. Anna shivered inside. Jacob Rewcastle had no intention of being fair with her.

'After all,' he went on, dropping the papers he was holding on to the desk, 'it'll be little use to me once I get the new line into full swing . . . and you should get a good price for it.'

'The workshop?' Things were moving too quickly for her. Edward in debt to this man? But he wouldn't borrow money, not without telling her, and had spoken only of a partnership.

'Didn't he tell you? The workshop was part of the collateral he put up against the money I lent him.'

'And the house?' Anna's voice was strangled.

'That, too, since you ask.' Pushing himself heavily out of the brown leather chair ringed around with brass studs, Jacob

Rewcastle moved to Anna's side. She was a good-looking wench, with that thick bright hair and clear skin. Put her in a few decent clothes and a man could take her places.

'But you could do better than that hovel.' He brought a podgy hand down firmly on her shoulder.

So that was it, that was the real reason Jacob Rewcastle had asked to see her in the privacy of his own office. He thought he was on to a good thing: a woman who would share his bed and be only too glad to keep her mouth shut. Shoving his hand from her shoulder, Anna was on her feet, her eyes glinting like green ice.

'That hovel, as you put it, was my home. And shared with Edward, infinitely preferable to any you might offer.' She saw the dull flush spread across his heavy jowls but went on scathingly, 'if the house and workshop were pledged by Edward then take them . . . I will produce King's Choice somewhere else.'

'I don't think so.'

The shiver inside Anna turned to a feeling of cold dread. As much as this man had told her, the worst was still to come.

'King's Choice is no longer yours to produce.'

Jacob savoured the telling. This would show this young upstart her bread would be buttered thicker by his hand. He moved behind the desk, leaning back in his chair.

'The design was patented, and the patent is in my name. Edward Royce was no businessman.'

'You bastard!' Anna spat as she realised what he was implying. 'Edward would never do that. He worked too many hours on that design. You've stolen it . . . you're a thief, Jacob Rewcastle, nothing more than a common bloody thief!'

'Take care, Anna,' he warned softly, little eyes travelling over the black cloth coat rubbed bare along the line of buttons, the black gabardine skirt shiny from so many pressings, shoes he guessed had no bottoms to them. 'You're hardly in a financial position to pay off a libel suit. You'd better be sensible. I could see you quite comfortable, you and that daughter of yours.

There was never any contract signed, your husband only put his name to the loan paper, so it would be in your best interest in the long run to do as I suggest. Come on, Anna, you know I'm right.'

'The name is Mrs Royce!' Behind the filmy black widow's veil draped about her cheap hat, Anna's eyes glared. 'And don't bother to go any further. You have everything Edward ever had in his life except his wife, and her you will never possess!'

'Don't be bloody stupid, woman.' Piggy eyes darted to the office window beyond which Joby Timmins was bent over a ledger. 'You're going to find it hard.'

'That's the one thing I can be sure of right now.' Anna walked to the door, twisting the brass knob before she turned to look back. 'But there is also something *you* can be sure of. No matter how hard I find it, Jacob Rewcastle, you will find it doubly hard. I intend to take back all that was Edward's and more besides. My advice to you is: pray. Pray very hard that I stop at that!'

'Is something wrong, Father? I could hear voices all down the passage.'

Pressure from the other side caused Anna to release the door handle and step away. The man who came in gave her a sharp glance; she had seen him several times at the mill, the women pointing him out as Philip Rewcastle.

'I just made this woman an offer only to have it thrown back in my face.' Jacob glanced past them to Joby Timmins. His head was bent over the books but it was a certain bloody bet his ears were cocked. 'I don't like that, Philip, I don't like that at all.'

In his mid-twenties now, Philip Rewcastle knew all about his father's offers, especially those made to women, and despite her widow's weeds this one appeared young and not bad-looking.

'Perhaps the lady didn't like it either, Father.' Philip smiled full at Anna. 'Why don't we see if we can make things more acceptable, Mrs . . .?'

'Royce . . . Anna Royce.'

'What was my father's offer, Mrs Royce?'

Across the desk Jacob Rewcastle lost much of his colour and those small eyes seemed to retract further, almost invisible amidst the puffy flesh.

Anna's fingers tightened about the strap of her shabby bag. This was her first chance of revenge: to tell his son of the offer to become his father's kept woman. Beneath her veil Anna looked at Jacob Rewcastle's only child. He wasn't as tall as Edward had been, in fact he was little taller than herself. A pale grey topcoat emphasised his slender build, a hint of auburn gleamed in hair worn long enough to touch his collar and his side whiskers were worn fashionably level with his ear lobes. There was no moustache framing the attractive, almost feminine fullness of his mouth. Physically at least Philip Rewcastle was the complete opposite of his father.

'Your father offered to let me keep my husband's workshop.' Anna relaxed her fingers, allowing the moment to slide away. This was not the revenge she wanted. 'But it was part of a business arrangement they had made together and as such belongs to your father. It was . . . kind of him to offer its return but I don't want it.'

'This workshop, Father, where is it?'

'Slater Street. You know, runs along bottom of main mill.'

'Oh, yes. And this workshop, Mrs Royce . . .' Philip's eyes returned to Anna. 'Isn't it joined to the house?' At her nod he added, 'Which means that too was part of the arrangement.'

'I've said all I'm going to.' Jacob had recovered his composure but his voice betrayed fury. 'I offered and she said no . . . that's all there is to it. The house and everything beside it was pledged against a loan that cannot be paid. The property will be sold so I can recoup some of my losses. I'm not a bloody Philanthropic Society.'

'All Coseley knows that, Mr Rewcastle. To be frank, all Coseley knows exactly what you are.'

Anna turned to the door, not missing the admiration in Philip's face as he opened it for her. 'Good afternoon,' she murmured.

'Mrs Royce!' Philip Rewcastle dismissed Joby with a shake of his head, walking with her along the drab corridor. 'I'm sorry about all this, I'm sure I can get my father to change his mind.'

'Oh, but I don't want him to!' Anna blinked, finding the daylight harsh after the gloom of the building. 'You see, I wouldn't stay in a house of his even if he paid me.'

'Which constituted his offer exactly or I don't know my father.'

'I must go.' Not by the flicker of an eyelid did Anna confirm the truth of what he said. 'My daughter will need feeding soon.'

'But where will you live? You must let me help you.'

'No!' She jerked her head upward. 'I will arrange for my things to be moved as soon as possible. There is nothing apart from clothing that I want from the house. I trust your father would not deny me that?'

'Mrs Royce.' Anna glanced at the hand touching her sleeve then up at his face.

That was what had been at the back of her mind since he had first stepped into his father's office. Philip Rewcastle had pale smooth skin, she noticed. Smooth and clear as a woman's.

'The house . . . is there a key? We will need to send someone round to make an inventory of the property.'

The word meant nothing to Anna but it didn't matter anymore what happened to it or to Edward's workshop. The only thing that hurt was the knowledge, despite her passionate threat of a few minutes before, that she would never be in a position to take revenge on Jacob Rewcastle.

'You called him right, me wench, Jacob Rewcastle is a bastard and more.' Maggie filled the pot for yet another cup of tea.

It was the only solace she could offer this girl who even

now refused herself the comfort of tears; she had strength, there was no denying that, but strength alone couldn't put food into her child's mouth.

'Well, I can't see Edward handing over King's Choice as easily as that.' Hester cradled her goddaughter. 'It might well be as old Rewcastle said, Edward was no businessman. But he was no fool neither.'

'Aye, wench,' Maggie's spoon rattled noisily against her cup as she stirred her tea, 'there's bin sharp practice somewheres and you can wager your man knew nowt of it.'

Hester placed the sleeping baby in the blanket-lined drawer standing on the floor beside the fireplace and stood looking at the tiny puckered face.

'Edward might have left a paper of some sort. Yer should at least look, Anna. It's not just you that Rewcastle is robbing.'

''Appen Essie could be right. Least ways we might have a little peace if you goes on up there and searches.'

Anna hadn't been back to the house she had shared with Edward since the afternoon of her visit to Jacob Rewcastle's offices, and she didn't want to go now. It had not been an all-consuming love she had had for Edward but they had been happy enough; he always so keen to please her, she secure in the knowledge he would always care for her. But now he was gone and she was back where she had been two years before, living in Maggie Fellen's house, only this time there were two children, two tiny lives who had their beginnings in her and whom she must find a way of keeping.

'There was the box.'

She had barely murmured it but Hester turned sharp hazel eyes on her.

'What box?'

'A wooden one, about that size.' Anna indicated with her hands. 'Different coloured woods made a pattern of flowers on the lid. Edward said his mother had had it as long as he could remember . . . but there are no papers in it, I'm sure.'

'Oh!' Light fading from her eyes Hester Cresswell dropped to a chair, her fingers drumming against the sparkling white cloth Maggie always used. 'But couldn't there have been another . . . say in Edward's workshop?'

'I didn't go in there all that often,' Anna admitted, 'but I wouldn't think so.'

'There's no good in thinking.' Hester stood up, pushing the chair back. 'You've got to look. C'mon, I'll go with you.'

'But you have to go back to work . . . we . . . we'll go tonight.'

'Oh no we won't! You ain't backin' out again, Anna Royce. I owe it to Misty to see you does all you can to get her father's rights. As for going to work, if I thought Jacob Rewcastle would go bankrupt 'cos of me not turning up for shift, I'd never go again.'

'Go on, Anna, leave little 'un. She'll be safe enough wi' me.'

Maggie began to collect the cups. Anna watched her place them on the cheap wooden tray. Maggie liked things nice. Her scrubbed table always wore a fresh clean cloth; her bits and pieces of furniture shone. Suddenly the tears she had denied so long welled into Anna's throat. God, she prayed silently, make it possible, no matter how hard. Let me find the way to pay Maggie Fellen for her kindness to me.

'Eee, Anna, that teks some believing.' Together the two girls walked along Roker Street, turning into the alley that linked it with Slater Street. Hester's clogs rattled loud against the blue-grey cobblestones. 'You sure it was Philip Rewcastle?'

'Of course I am, you've pointed him out to me often enough. Besides, he called Jacob "Father".'

'Aye, and no one would do that lessen they had to!' Hester giggled, wrinkling her nose. 'Poor little bugger. But yer sure he said he'd help?'

'He said I must let him help me,' Anna stated flatly, having already gone over the scene in the office more times than was necessary for Hester to get the picture. 'In fact, he seemed quite kind.'

'I've no doubt, but don't you be fooled by him, Anna. There's summat about that one I can't quite figure.'

'Like what?' She felt a stone bite through the worn sole of her shoe.

Edward had refused to allow her to wear clogs, her feet were too dainty to be subjected to those monstrosities, he'd said, but that was a nicety that would have to go.

'Like the men he goes around with.'

'What's wrong with them?' They turned into Slater Street. The house and workshop were right at the end, separated from the line of terraced houses by a wide area of derelict land.

'It would be more to the point if yer asked what's right wi' 'em.'

Anna, who had only seen Philip Rewcastle briefly at the mill before as he had walked through her own department, found herself wondering where else Hester had seen him.

'He was strange when he were a lad.' Hester linked an arm through Anna's. 'Accordin' to me mam, old Jacob wanted him to learn steel trade from bottom up, on shop floor so to speak, but it wasn't steel trade he wanted to learn. Oh, he was interested all right but only in the men he worked with.'

'Well, wasn't that a good sign, being interested in the men who would one day be his employees?'

'Oh, aye?'

Hester cocked her head sideways, a half-disbelieving look in the glance she directed at Anna. She wasn't that gullible surely? True Anna had none of the coarseness some of the girls at Rewcastle's had, their bawdy jokes usually passing over her head, but Philip Rewcastle . . .

'The business he was interested in had nowt to do wi' steel,' she finished, watching for Anna's reaction.

'Me mam wouldn't say much when us kids were around,' Hester went on when there was none, 'but after a while he went away to some posh school, I believe, and now he's back – and a couple of right queer characters he's brought with 'im.'

'Queer!' Anna's eyes were on the house.

'Aye, bloody queer. One of 'em fancied his chances last week. Came into the packing sheds, they did, Philip Rewcastle and one of his posh friends. Big bloke, and underneath his fancy clobber like to have a few muscles.' Hester caught the corner of her shawl the breeze had freed and held it across her breasts.

'Well, they was strollin' down the shed when this one stops behind me and touches my hair with his fingers. "What about this one, Phil, old chap?" he says, all bay-windowed. "Surely you must have fancied a romp in the hay with this one?"'

'And what did Philip say?' Even now Anna wasn't quite listening.

'"Oh, don't be so bloody stupid, Robert,"' Hester mimicked wickedly. '"You know I have no interest in that sort of thing."' Hester's laughter rang out scornfully.

They had reached the waste land and Anna felt herself shrink inside. She ought not to have come, there was nothing for her here.

'Philip Rewcastle went to walk on then,' Hester was not oblivious to the emotion tearing at Anna and kept fighting it the only way she knew, 'but this friend of his wasn't having any. He puts his fingers under my chin and asks, "What about you, my little pearl? What would you say to an offer like that?"'

'What *did* you say?'

'I told him to stick it up his arse!'

It was just the right thing to say. Anna's laughter joined Hester's, dispersing the ghosts of yesterday.

'Let's go in the back, through the workshop.' Anna pushed open the gate in the surrounding wall, leading the way up the path.

* * *

'I told you there would be nothing here.' They had spent an hour searching the wooden shelves and cupboards, finding nothing but the tools that had been Edward's father's.

'I think we should go.'

'Not yet, Anna, we have the house to search first.'

'But maybe Jacob Rewcastle has had everything taken out?'

Anna thought of the few articles of furniture she had kept so carefully polished. They too had been Edward's parents' and she felt sick that Jacob Rewcastle should have the selling of them.

'And maybe he hasn't.' Pulling her by the hand, Hester walked determinedly across the pocket handkerchief of yard that separated the workshop from the house, then through the scullery into the kitchen.

It was the same as she had left it. Nothing had been moved, nothing taken away.

'There's nothing in here,' Anna whispered in the silence, 'or I would have seen it when I fetched Misty's things.'

'It'll tek no hurt from looking again.' Hester's quick fingers pulled open drawers and, finding nothing, pushed them closed.

'C'mon, Anna, yer no help standing there like a statue.'

As Anna predicted, they found no papers either there or in the tiny front parlour that had been her pride and joy.

'Where's the box you spoke of?' Hester straightened the red chenille table-cloth with an automatic movement.

'Upstairs in our bedroom.' Anna felt the fear return. That was the room she'd shared with Edward. The door they had carried his crushed body home on had been laid on the bed they had slept in together. She couldn't go up there, she couldn't look at it again.

'I know, love,' Hester's eyes were oceans of pity, 'but think of Misty. If you can't do it for yourself, do it for her.'

Steadying herself against the table, Anna drew a long breath. Hester was right, of course, she had to try everywhere, if only for her daughter. She had one foot on the stairs when she heard it, a long pulsing moan.

'Christ! What does you reckon that was?'

'I don't know.' Her own fear matched Hester's. 'Probably nothing, these old houses creak a lot.'

'They might creak but I've never heard one moan afore!'

Overhead there was a bump and the scrape of wood against wood.

'It must be the men from Rewcastle's.' Relief surged through Anna. 'Philip said they would need to make an inventory.'

'I don't know what one of them might be.' Hester's young face hardened. She had heard the same sounds before from her parents' bedroom when they thought she and their Billy were asleep, the same breathy moans. There was somebody up there all right, but whatever they were doing in Anna's bedroom, they were not taking any inventory!

'Stay back of me,' she ordered, stepping out of her clogs.

Anna never could think of it in later years without a feeling of pity. To be found like that, and by two young women!

They made no sound on the stairs and the bedroom door was open. Hester pushed it wider still. Two naked bodies writhed together on the double bed. Smooth creamy arms twined about muscular shoulders, long fingers fastening into dark hair; two smooth legs spread creamy columns each side of those covered with short dark hairs and a bare bottom tautened with each grunting push.

'Oh, please!' It was half a sob as the hard jerking body ground into the one pinioned beneath it. 'Please, more . . . more.'

'I'll give yer more, yer dirty sod.' Hester stepped forward, the clog she held in her right hand slapping against bare buttocks.

The muscled body with its covering of fine dark hairs rolled sideways off the one beneath, and Anna stared. Swathes of sweat-soaked hair lay across smooth cheeks like streaks of dried blood; where the widespread legs joined, a tight-curled mass of the same colour formed a halo around a penis robbed now of strength or vigour. But it was the eyes that held her, amber eyes drowning in agony, the eyes of Philip Rewcastle.

'Well, well!' The muscular man propped himself lazily on one elbow, his throbbing penis jerking with newfound life he made no effort to hide. 'So you changed your mind, little pearl . . . and you have brought a friend. How thoughtful. Don't you think so, Phil?'

'Shut up, Robert!' Philip Rewcastle reached for a shirt lying on top of the tumbled heap of clothing on the floor beside the bed, draping it across himself as he sat up.

'Not shy, are we?' Robert splayed his legs slowly and deliberately. 'Don't hide it. Show the little ladies what they can have if they behave.'

Closing the fingers of his right hand about the throbbing tube he lifted it clear of his stomach holding it up like a baton. 'C'mon girls, which of you wants the first ride?'

'I told you once before what you could do with that.'

Anna listened remotely, as though in another world. A furious Hester wasn't shocked at what she saw; it was as if it was no more than she'd expected.

'Then what about your friend?' He continued to flaunt himself before them. 'I wouldn't mind the odd hour with you, girlie, and from the look of you you could do with a nice little present . . . besides this one, I mean.'

Anna felt sick. They were on her bed, hers and Edward's, defiling it with their unspeakable activities – and now he was asking her to join in.

'That's enough, Robert!' Philip found the courage to look at her. 'I'm sorry, Mrs Royce. To say this is unfortunate would be ludicrous. Instead I will only ask why you are here?'

'The box,' Anna stammered. 'I . . . we came for my box.'

'Where is your box?'

He was very gentle, almost as if he was the one to have

caught her in some dreadful act and was trying to reassure her there would be no punishment.

'In . . . in the drawer of the chest.'

'Then could I ask you to get it and then be good enough to leave? I would get it for you, but for me to move would cause you more embarrassment and you've had enough of that already.'

As if in the grip of some horrible nightmare, Anna walked across the room, pulled open the top drawer of the chest in the alcove below the only window, and took out the small wooden box. Walking back to where Hester still stood in the doorway, she averted her eyes from the men, one still sprawled blatantly across the bed.

'You really don't know what you're missing,' Robert said mockingly.

'Maybe she don't,' Hester bristled, gold specks flashing in her angry glare, 'but I do, mister. A dose of the clap, that's what she's missing!'

'Why, you bloody little snot! I'll break your dirty little neck for that!'

He jumped up but Philip Rewcastle was as quick, nakedness forgotten as he held the other man back, his tawny eyes fixed on Hester.

'You will go now,' he said tonelessly, 'and if you know what's good for you, you will say nothing of what you saw here this afternoon.'

'There weren't a lot to see.' Hester stared hard at her employer's son, scorning his nakedness. 'An' if you be threatenin' me, Philip Rewcastle, you needs bigger assets than that to do it with.'

Outside the sun warmed Anna, freeing her from the icy grip of shock.

Philip Rewcastle and the man he'd called Robert had been making love. She shivered, fingers trembling around the pretty inlaid box. It was unnatural, obscene. How could anybody bring themself to do such a thing?

'Eee, never mind, love.' Hester put an arm through Anna's. 'A lot of strange things 'appen in life, and it's my guess we both have a lot more to see afore we are done. I did try to tell you about Philip Rewcastle. I guessed when you were tellin' me an' Maggie what 'appened t'other day in 'is old man's office that he 'ad more things in mind than 'elpin' you. 'Elpin' hisself more like!

'Can't you see, Anna? He only asked about a key to the 'ouse so he could hold on to it. That way he could 'ave a little love nest for 'im an' that Robert to go to, all locked in safe and sound. Only he forgot the way in through scullery. If that's all the sense them posh schools 'is father sent him to 'ave taught 'im, then I reckon old Rewcastle should get his money back.'

'But even in . . . in there he tried to be kind.' Anna shuddered, seeing again the streaks of sweat-soaked auburn hair across his pale skin; seeing again that smear of blood across her own breast.

'Aye,' Hester pulled her away, guiding her steps towards the alley, 'that's another of his little tricks, I reckon. Get 'imself into folks' good books. That way they either won't see 'is slimy ways or else will turn a blind eye to them. Either way Philip Rewcastle comes out on top.'

Hester grinned suddenly, the cheeky grin of a naughty schoolgirl that lit up her plain little face and deepened her hazel eyes to molten gold.

'But he didn't come out on top of 'is mate Robert, it was the other way round wi' that one. Mind you, Anna, when I told 'im to stick it up his arse, I didn't think he'd take me serious!'

Her tinkling laughter echoed off the sombre line of terraced houses, but Anna did not join in. Whatever Hester thought of Philip Rewcastle, she could feel only pity for him. How strange to feel pity for a man who had everything: money, education, a good background.

But Anna knew with awful certainty that, like herself, Philip Rewcastle had nothing.

Chapter Seven

Anna opened her faded purse, already knowing the paucity of its contents before she did so. It had been three months since Edward was killed and apart from the few pence the girls from the mill gave her for her face creams and hair rinses, there had been no money since.

She tipped the few copper coins into her hand. Scarcely enough to pay Maggie for her board and keep.

'Will you watch Misty for me, Maggie? I'm just going out, I won't be long.'

Reaching behind the door for her black coat, Anna left the house, still pushing her arms into its sleeves. The bell rang over the door of the dark little shop and the dank musty smell of decay swept into her nostrils as Anna stepped inside.

Sam Castleton shuffled forward, puffing from the effort. Suffering from a collapsed lung, the intense heat and sheer physical effort involved in working in the steel mills made his former employment impossible for him so he had opened a pawn shop at the rear of the general grocery stone run by his wife.

'Aye?' Sam asked, the sun behind the figure in the doorway turning it into a silhouette he could not recognise.

'It's me, Mr Castleton.' Closing the door, Anna walked across the dusty floor, pulling her wedding ring free from her finger. 'How much can you let me have against this?'

'Eee, Anna, I didna know it was you.' He picked up the ring, looking inside it for the hallmark. 'Still no work, wench?'

'Not yet, Mr Castleton. Rewcastle's don't want anybody, it seems, and apart from them there's little else in Coseley.'

'Aye, aye.' Sam nodded sympathetically.

This girl had had things hard, and according to talk in Bella's shop, word was old Rewcastle didn't want her given work anywhere, and there were not many in these parts would go against that old swine.

'It's a good ring . . . twenty-two carat. I could let you have three pounds.' It was over generous even for twenty-two carat for the ring wasn't heavy, but what the hell? If she never redeemed the pledge he was out of pocket. 'That do for you, me wench?'

'Yes . . . thank you, Mr Castleton.' Pushing the white ticket and three pound notes into her purse, Anna turned away. 'Say hello to Bella for me.'

'Aye, I will that.' Sam watched the pathetic figure in the black coat and skirt bought from his collection of unredeemed clothing and shook his head.

Coseley could hold only trouble for Anna Royce, old man Rewcastle would see to that.

Back in Maggie Fellen's kitchen, two young girls giggled nervously.

'This wench at work knows some of the wenches in packing sheds at Rewcastle's,' the shorter of them volunteered as Anna took off her coat. 'She said you would sell the two of us some if we came. Eee, Mrs Royce, I 'opes you don't think it a cheek, our comin' to the 'ouse like?'

'No cheek.' Maggie stirred the fire beneath the kettle then reached for the cups on the dresser, her starched petticoats rustling. 'Shy wenches get nowt. If you wants anything, ask for it, I always say.'

'Aye, Mrs Fellen, me mam says that an' all.' The tall and lanky girl smiled, showing good teeth. 'But Chrissy an' me felt a bit awful like, coming to the house.'

'Nobody need feel awful about coming to Maggie Fellen's.'

Cups rattled busily on saucers. 'If I don't want 'em in then I tells 'em to leave.'

'Was it me you came to see?' The three pounds in her purse making her feel a little happier, Anna smiled at the giggling girls, clutching each other's hands in a state of delicious excitement. Had she ever felt as these two did now?

'Aye, Mrs Royce.' The girl called Chrissy spoke up. 'We . . . we'd like to buy some of that there face cream you 'as. Everybody says 'ow lovely it is . . . does wonders for the skin, so they say.'

'I don't think either of you girls needs face cream. You both have lovely complexions.'

'Oh!'

Anna saw disappointment chase laughter from two pairs of eyes. She had told them the truth and ruined their day by doing so.

'However,' she added, salvaging their happiness, 'you need to take care of it if you want to keep it.'

From Maggie's front room she fetched two small white pots, handing one to each girl.

'After you have washed your face, smooth in just a little of this.'

'Eee, it smells just grand.' Chrissy removed the lid, pressing her pert nose to the contents of the pot. 'Ta, Mrs Royce.'

'Yes, ta, Mrs Royce.' Chrissy's friend smiled her delight. ''Ow much do we owe you?'

'Oh, er . . . just leave something for the baby.' Anna hated taking money for anything she made.

'Mrs Royce!' About to cross Maggie's newly whitened front step, the lanky girl looked back at Anna. 'Benjie Freeth 'as just 'ad a big order come in. I heard me dad tellin' our mam last night. 'Appen he might be able to use somebody . . . that's if yer wants a job?'

'I was told you might have a vacancy, Mr Freeth?'

Anna had followed the two girls out of Maggie's kitchen,

hurrying to the little brick workshop standing in the shadow of the huge steel-rolling mills.

Benjamin Freeth, the circular cap that marked his Jewish faith fitting the crown of his head like a saucer, lifted his shoulders.

'So people know already! Time was when a man could have a minute to breathe in Coseley, but now . . .' He shrugged his shoulders again.

'If I was told wrongly, I apologise for disturbing you.' Anna shifted uncomfortably, feeling the rough floor against the soles of her feet. On the way home she would call in Bella Castleton's shop for a cardboard box and cut another couple of insoles for her boots. They were going to have to fight the good fight for a while yet.

'So I'm disturbed already.' A perpetually harassed face creased into a semblance of a smile. 'But to be disturbed by such a pretty face should count among a man's blessings.'

Miraculously finding a chair from beneath a welter of wood shavings, he brushed it clean with a thin hand, indicating Anna to sit down.

'Mine is not a large place, it pleased the good Lord that Benjamin Freeth didn't make it big, but thanks to Him at least I eat every day.'

Tucking his thumbs through the shoulder straps of the coarse carpenter's apron that reached almost to his boots, he watched Anna trying desperately to keep disappointment from showing in her face. He knew from her speech she was not from Coseley and from her clothing that she wasn't finding it easy.

'I couldn't pay a large wage and I could only take you for four days a week.'

Even then he would be stretching his resources, but if the good Lord hadn't stretched out His hand and sent His servant Moses to bring the children of Israel out of bondage there would be no Benjamin Freeth, Cabinet Maker, to give a job to anybody.

'Four days a week would suit me very well, Mr Freeth. Thank you. Thank you very much indeed.'

'I have a job, my darling.' Anna bent over the small truckle bed beside her own where Misty lay sleeping, one arm thrust free from the covers.

He had slept in that same way, Anna remembered, her heart jerking. Almost from birth he had fought to free his arms from the blanket she wrapped him in.

Climbing into bed, she watched the play of moonlight across her bedroom window, seeming to feel again the tug on her nipple, the tiny down-covered head nuzzling her breast. Did her son still refuse to have his arms placed beneath the bed covers? Was his hair still the colour of ripe corn, his eyes as blue as she remembered?

'Oh, my love,' she whispered, turning her face into the pillow, the pain in her heart crushing the breath from her body, 'my little love, I want you so much . . .'

'It doesn't pay as much as Rewcastle's,' Anna explained, cutting the cardboard box Bella Castleton had given her into shape and fitting the new soles inside her boots, 'but then, I will only be working four days. Mr Freeth said he always goes into Birmingham on a Friday. Something about there being no synagogue in Coseley and Saturday being the Jewish Sabbath he's not allowed to work. Seeing there is nobody other than him to supervise the place, I can't work those days either. But it's better than nothing, Maggie, if . . .'

'If what?' Maggie Fellen had listened quietly.

'It . . . it's a lot to ask, Maggie. Are you sure you can manage? Babies can be hard work.'

'Aye,' Maggie's grey stare remained level, 'and are you saying Maggie Fellen is past it?'

'You know I'm not.' Anna flung both arms round the older woman's neck, resting her head against the rich brown hair.

'But I love you, Maggie. You and Misty are my life and I don't want to risk your overdoing things.'

Her arms tightening, Anna pressed her face deeper into Maggie's brown hair. 'I couldn't go on without you,' she whispered. But I have to go on without my son, she added silently.

'*The girl you desired for so long is yet to come . . .*' Kate O'Keefe's prophetic words circled Maggie's mind '. . . *yours will be the caring of it.*' She would have the caring of Anna's child; would to God it had been under different circumstances.

'Thirty shillings a week isn't going to provide any luxuries but it will keep us, Maggie, and we should be thankful.'

'I could manage on less than a pound a week, Anna, I've always told you so.'

'I paid you a pound when there was just me.' Anna moved to the corner by the fireplace looking down at the face of her sleeping daughter. 'I won't pay you less now there's two of us.'

'The child teks no keepin'. You 'as 'er on the breast.'

'And you do just about everything else for her, and will do even more now I've got a job.'

'You could always send a bit less for the other 'un.'

'No, Maggie.' Anna bent to hook a finger into the curling fist of the baby. 'He can never know what I feel for him. I left a part of myself behind when I left my son. He'll never know my touch or my face but I'll not deny him money to keep him fed. Whatever happens, Maggie, I must send that. I . . . can't give him anything else.'

'I understand, love. Don't worry. While Maggie Fellen lives, neither you nor yer little 'uns will go short. Anna . . .' Maggie looked at her closely. 'Do you remember that night Kate O'Keefe read the tea cups in Mary Cresswell's kitchen?'

'Yes.'

'Well, she wasna quite right in what she said. She said I would 'ave the daughter denied my 'eart and mine would be the carin' of it, but she didna say I would 'ave *two* daughters. Misty is the daughter of my heart and I love her as my own, but even that is not the sort of love I bear 'er mother. That one is the daughter of my soul.'

Anna didn't move. Sunk on her haunches, her finger held in the tiny fist of her baby, she at last allowed the tears to flow.

'I don't know what time they will come, Anna.' Benjamin Freeth picked up the beautiful inlaid mahogany box, blowing any last speck of dust from its ivory velvet lining. A lot hung on whether the box met with the approval of the people he was expecting. Anna knew it was to be part of a presentation but to whom and just what it was to hold remained a mystery to her.

'Relax, Mr Freeth, they can only love this. It's the most beautiful one you've made, I'm sure.'

'Yes, Anna, it is the most beautiful. But then, it is to be given to the most important in the land so it is right it should be so.'

'You know,' Anna looked up from the table where she had been polishing the lovely casket, 'Maggie Fellen has a saying: "When a man has done his best, he can look anyone in the eye with pride."'

'Anna,' Benjamin smiled the slow smile that seemed to take an hour to stretch across his fine drawn face, 'that Maggie Fellen, she must be one smart woman.'

'Hello . . . Mr Freeth?'

Benjamin went to greet the new arrival.

'You cut it pretty damn' fine,' he shouted, 'them from London could be here already.'

Anna turned to watch, hoping he would greet his London visitors less irately, then felt a sudden chill touch her. The man handing a large box to Benjamin Freeth worked at Rewcastle's Mill.

'Stop yer fussin'. I couldn't get 'ere afore I was sent, could I?' The man pushed the box hard against Benjamin's chest.

'Seein' they 'aven't arrived yet, yer still 'as time to get that lot tarted up.'

Mumbling under his breath, Benjamin carried the box to the tiny room where Anna worked.

'This is what we've waited for, Anna, it should have been delivered already but . . .' He lifted his shoulders in protest. 'But who is Benjamin Freeth that folks should hurry? Check them, Anna, I don't want the tiniest speck or blemish. Benjamin Freeth, Cabinet Maker, does not supply boxes to hold goods of inferior quality. The best, Anna, that is what this must be. The best.'

'I'll be very careful,' she said, conscious of the old man's pride in his work. 'I'll go over every one.'

He shuffled out, leaving her to untie the string. Inside brown paper several tissue-wrapped articles nestled together. Peeling back the soft white paper, Anna stared at the beautiful hand-made knife . . . she had just unwrapped the first of King's Choice.

Anna laid the rest out before her, the complete range of flatware exactly as Edward had designed them; elegant handles flaring slightly at the bottom housed an intricate crest then flowed in classic lines to the bowls of spoons, the prongs of forks. Each piece was a masterpiece. Some craftsman had turned Edward's dream into golden reality, one he would never see. Edward Royce had poured his very life into the making of King's Choice and now he was dead.

'I took the liberty of bringing Lord Kenmore, Benjamin, seeing as how you might find it inconvenient to leave your workshop.'

Anna pressed the last spoon into place with a vicious movement.

Jacob Rewcastle! She should have known he wouldn't be far away; that was why King's Choice had been brought here instead of the lovely presentation box Benjamin had made being taken to Rewcastle's Mill. Jacob would want no hint that he was involved. It must seem that the project was still in the hands of the small producers it was meant to help. That way royal approval would be retained and King's Choice would be sold all over the world.

'But I never expected . . . you should have warned me, Mr Rewcastle. The place is not fit.' Benjamin's guttural accent thickened with anxiety.

A voice Anna did not recognise intervened brusquely.

'Nonsense. It was His Majesty's wish that we see where all the pieces were made . . . that includes the box.

'Now I would like to see the article to be presented, if I may?'

The cultured voice came nearer and Anna closed the lid of the casket, giving it one last quick wipe.

'Your clothes . . . they will be soiled,' Benjamin protested. 'I will bring it out here, there is more room.'

'Clothes are of no consequence.' In his elegant dark alpaca coat worn knee-length over pin stripe trousers, a silk waistcoat covering his brilliantly white shirt, Lord Kenmore strode into the tiny room at the end of Benjamin Freeth's factory. 'Is this the gift?'

Lifting the silver-topped malacca cane he carried in one gloved hand, he tapped the mahogany inlaid lid Anna had just wiped.

'It is, Your Lordship.' Jacob Rewcastle could not fit into the tiny room.

'Mmm.' Lord Kenmore ignored Anna, squeezed tight into corner. 'His Majesty will be pleased. My dear . . .'

He held out one hand stepping backward into piles of Benjamin's carelessly strewn templates, and handed a woman into the constricted space.

'If you will permit, Lady Strathlyn, I will leave you to make your decision. I wish to speak to Mr Rewcastle and Mr Freeth.'

'Of course, I will join you presently.'

Anna had seen fine dresses displayed in the windows of the shops in Birmingham and covers of magazines showing elegant models, but her mouth opened in admiration of the woman Lord Kenmore handed into the tiny workroom.

She wore a lavender silk twill three-quarter-length coat frogged down the front and with slightly padded sleeves corded in amethyst. The straight skirt worn beneath was of the same colour. On her dark head she wore a small lavender grosgrain hat, amethyst feather trimming shading at the tips to mauve. And even in the Birmingham shops Anna had never seen the like of these shoes! Pointed toes, cut low across the foot, small square heel . . . they were the exact colour of the hat, and covered in lavender lacework patterns picked out with tiny brilliants of amethyst and mauve.

'This is King's Choice?' she asked, touching the box with a lavender-gloved hand.

'Yes . . . yes, it is, ma'am.' Anna bobbed a nervous curtsy. Was that the proper way to address a lady as obviously grand as this one?

'Her Majesty asked if I would try holding them. Some cutlery causes her discomfort.' The woman touched a finger of one hand to the palm of the other. 'Her Majesty has a very small hand.' Then, when Anna did not move, added, 'Would you be kind enough to show it to me?'

Awestruck by the grandeur of the woman, Anna moved awkwardly, bumping against the table. Wisps of wood shavings curled into the air, floating on to the lovely coat, but the woman paid no heed.

'These are exquisite!' she breathed.

The rose blush of Britannia gold glistened against ivory velvet. Edward would have been so proud. Anna lifted a knife from its retaining slot, holding it towards Benjamin's distinguished visitor.

'Perfect.' Lady Strathlyn curled one gloved hand around it, holding it as though about to cut. 'A perfect fit. Her Majesty will find no discomfort in using these, I am sure.'

'Will Your Ladyship try the rest?' Anna took back the knife, laying it among its golden family.

'There is no need. The man who is responsible for the creation of King's Choice is a master of his craft. Their precision and balance, the way they fit into the hand, makes me feel their design was more than just a labour of the brain. Something of the heart is there also.'

'A great deal of his heart.'

'Oh!' Lady Strathlyn heard Anna's murmur. 'You know the designer?'

'He . . . he was my husband.'

'Was?' Cool blue eyes looked straight at Anna.

'Edward died, ma'am.' Anna touched a finger to the box holding the cutlery that was to be a royal gift. 'Before King's Choice was produced.'

'I see. So now you work for Mr Freeth?'

'Yes, Ma'am.'

'Mmm.' Lady Strathlyn glanced at the unpainted walls, the heaps of templates and layers of wood dust covering everything. 'I wonder . . . how do you keep your skin looking so clear and manage to have a real shine in your hair in all this dirt? I find it difficult enough in the palace or my own home. But here . . .' She patted her immaculate coiffure. 'Tell me what magic you use.'

Anna blushed at the compliment.

'I . . . I just use herbal preparations, Your Ladyship. Creams and rinses I make myself.'

They were interrupted by the return of Lord Kenmore and with a slight nod of her dark head Lady Strathlyn left Anna, who did not quite believe what had happened.

'What the devil . . .?' Jacob Rewcastle, coming to collect the box of cutlery, stopped at the sight of Anna. 'What the bloody hell are you doing here?'

'I work here, Mr Rewcastle.' Anna's voice kept an even tone though her heart lurched violently. Any meeting with Coseley's mill owner could only mean trouble for her.

'Do you now!' The piggy eyes became almost invisible. 'And just how long have you been working here?'

'Three weeks.'

'You'll not work another three, that I'll guarantee.' Snatching up the mahogany casket, he stared at her narrowly. 'In fact, Anna Royce, you'll work nowhere the hand of Jacob Rewcastle can reach.'

It was less than three as he had predicted. One week after collecting the presentation box from the workshop of Benjamin Freeth, Jacob Rewcastle bought him out.

'Like my Naomi says, Anna,' Benjamin told her, tears running down his thin cheeks, 'the business . . . we have no child to leave it to and we are both old already. "So sell it, Benjie," she tells me. "Sell it and stay home with your Naomi."' He lifted his shoulders in his predictable shrug. 'And that Jacob Rewcastle . . . sheeesh! A man can do without the trouble he can cause. I'm sorry, Anna, but what else could I do? If I refused to sell he would get a cabinet maker somewhere else and I would still be out of business. But with no money to show for it.'

'Don't worry, Mr Freeth.' Anna fastened her worn black coat and shoved a long hairpin through the black hat, fastening it to her piled up hair. 'I'll find work.'

The trouble was, she thought, walking home with her last thirty shillings, where was she going to find it?

The potatoes peeled and set in a pan against the fire, Anna stirred a spoonful of plain flour into half a cup of cold water. Taking the huckaback cloth from the side of the fireplace, she lifted out the tin tray. Maggie had made faggots this morning. Now Anna poured the flour and water mixture into the pan, stirring it into the juices of herbs and meat. Returning the tray to the oven, she carried the utensils to the scullery for washing.

The meal would be ready when Maggie returned from next door. She liked a chat with Mary Cresswell and Anna had insisted she go this afternoon, just for an hour or so. It would be a change for her not to have to be responsible for Misty. It had not been easy dashing home to breast feed the baby at noon and again at four o'clock, then dashing back to Freeth's, but Benjamin had been very good to her, never complaining if she were a few minutes late. Anna sighed, drying the little pot jug she had mixed the flour and water in. It hadn't been easy, but managing without the meagre wages he'd paid was going to be a sight harder.

A knock sounded through the silent house. Startled, Anna hurried back to the kitchen. Nobody ever knocked in Roker Street. The knock sounded again and Anna held aside the long chenille curtain, pulling the door open at the same time.

'Good afternoon . . . Mrs Royce?'

'Yes?' Anna answered a woman tastefully dressed in brown gabardine edged with a piping of cream braid matching her well-polished brown shoes. This was a woman she hadn't seen before.

'Oh, good!' She seemed relieved. 'My daily woman said you lived here. You . . . you are the lady that makes face creams, aren't you?'

'Please, won't you come in?' Anna remembered her manners.

'Thank you.' The woman stepped into the kitchen, her glance flicking around the neat room.

'It's my daughter's sixteenth birthday in a few days, Mrs Royce, and I would like to give her a little extra present. I know girls of that age like to experiment with cosmetics so I prefer her to have something safe and I have heard such good things of yours. Would you sell me some? A little cleanser perhaps. I . . . I don't know very much about that sort of thing.'

'It's a bit difficult, Mrs . . .'

'Paget. Lorna Paget. We live on the other side of Coseley, Wood Green Road.'

'Will you sit down, Mrs Paget?' Anna offered her a chair. 'As I said, it is difficult for me to sell you creams when I don't know your daughter's skin type. Is it dry or perhaps a little oily?'

'Does it make a difference, Mrs Royce?'

'I'm afraid it does.' Anna looked at the well-scrubbed face of her visitor.

The woman had probably never used more than the odd dab of rosewater in her life but was forward-looking enough to realise the same would not do for her daughter.

Over a cup of tea Anna carefully gleaned the information she needed, and when she offered to deliver the appropriate creams, Lorna Paget smiled gratefully.

'That would be very kind, Mrs Royce. Shall we say Thursday afternoon?'

Wood Green Road was a quiet tree-lined place. Houses here were built in twos but sometimes one house would stand alone in its own well-tended gardens. There were no long rows of terraces, their front doors standing next to the footpath; no perpetual grey blanket of smoke hanging above them; and no sentinel mills standing black and threatening on the skyline.

It must be wonderful to live in a place like this. Anna studied the houses hungrily. Here a child could play while filling its lungs with clean air, instead of the fumes of the steel mills the kids of Roker Street grew up with.

Number twenty-four was a neat, green-painted semi-detached, with white lace curtains closed decorously across the bay window. Turning into the neat flower-bordered drive, Anna felt sharp gravel bite through the thin layers of cardboard she had put in her boots and wondered if she ought to go round the back. That was the usual entrance for tradesmen.

But having already reached the front door she decided against it. The less crunching about on this gravel, the less her feet would suffer. Before she could change her mind she rang the brass bell.

A young lass in ankle-length black skirt, white long-sleeved blouse buttoned high up her throat, a small lace cap on her bright hair matching the starched apron, showed Anna into Mrs Paget's front parlour.

'This is most kind of you, Mrs Royce.'

Anna had wrapped her parcel in a sheet of brown paper Bella Castleton had given her, careful to place the black printed words 'Morton's Finest Quality Sewing Threads' on the inside. Now she waited while Mrs Paget unwrapped it.

'Oh, Mrs Royce, this is so beautiful . . . you must have spent so much time on it.'

She had. Anna smiled ruefully, remembering Maggie's disapproving sniff when she had decided the pretty inlaid box that had been Edward's mother's would hold the creams and rinses she had made for this woman's daughter. But Anna knew Edward would have taken the same pleasure she had in using the box to make a young girl happy.

Mrs Paget lifted the tiny glass jars from their separate compartments, removing the stoppers and sniffing the contents, reading the labels Joby Timmins had written in flowing copperplate script before easing them gently back into the boxes and closing the lids.

'Mrs Royce,' she said, brown eyes tear bright, 'I don't think this is the usual way you package your preparations. It is my belief that this . . .' she rested her hand on the pretty wooden box, '. . . was something that meant a lot to you, and I know the reason behind your giving it away. You wanted to please a young girl you have never even met, to make her birthday more pleasurable by giving her something she can keep and treasure. I won't forget this, Mrs Royce.'

'Five pounds, Maggie! Mrs Paget paid me five pounds!' Anna had run almost the whole way back to Roker Street and now she sat at Maggie's table staring at the white five-pound note. 'That's almost as much as I got in wages for a month at Rewcastle's or at Benjie Freeth's.'

'Aye, wench,'er paid you well. And you can add this to it.'

Maggie reached beneath her white apron, pulling a handful of coins from the pocket of her black skirt.

'While you was away I've 'ad no less than five wenches 'ere, all after buyin' your creams.'

Counting the coins, Anna was amazed to find they totalled almost fifteen shillings. Together with the five pounds Mrs Paget had paid her, she and Maggie would be able to manage for at least four, maybe even five weeks if she were careful, and she could still send money for her son.

'Your mother is very rich, Misty.' Anna dropped a kiss on the head of her sleepy daughter. 'Five pounds fifteen shillings, and it's all ours.'

'Anna . . . I've bin meaning to talk to you for some time now.' Maggie filled the pot from the steaming kettle on the polished hob. 'Sit you down and we'll have a cup of tea.'

'Is anything wrong?' Happiness drained from Anna. 'You're not ill, Maggie?'

'Eee, 'course not! Can't a body 'ave a conversation unless it be from their death bed? I've got summat to say an' I reckon now's as good a time as any to say it.'

She poured the hot brown liquid into china cups. She never could abide those thick pottery mugs big enough to hold half a pint. A woman felt more like a woman drinking her tea from a dainty cup. Anna took hers, adding milk and sugar, stirring too long.

'It's this way, me wench.' Maggie Fellen's grey stare was candid. 'Old man Rewcastle 'as a down on you and intends that nobody in Coseley will give you a job. So the way I look at it is this – it's time you worked for yourself.'

'But how, Maggie . . . doing what?' Perplexed, Anna's brows drew together.

'Wait.' Going across to the fireplace, Maggie lifted down a cocoa tin from the shelf above.

Anna dropped the money the girls paid for her creams into this tin, always a little too embarrassed to count it.

'How long has it been since you looked in there?'

Anna glanced at the chocolate-coloured tin. 'I haven't . . . I mean, I don't . . .'

'Exactly!' Maggie took a triumphant sip of tea, an unreadable expression lurking in the depths of her steady gaze. 'Well, you'd better look now.'

Slightly bemused by the turn her homecoming had taken, Anna eased off the lid, emptying the contents of the tin on to the white cloth. Sorting the coins, she stacked them, silver and copper. Pennies, halfpennies, threepenny bits, sixpences, shillings and florins, sprouted up from the cloth like brown and silver stalks.

'Good God!' Anna leaned back against the chair. 'I had no idea there was so much. It comes to almost eight pounds. I couldn't possibly have made all that.'

'Well, there's no way I could 'ave made it an' it don't grow on trees despite what fairy tales tell you. Anyway that's not the finish of it, y'ave made more than that.'

This time Maggie went upstairs, returning with an oblong cigar box.

'I got this from the carter,' she said, placing it at Anna's elbow. 'He asked if I'd took up smokin'.'

'The carter . . . but why?'

''Cos if I'd asked Bella Castleton for one 'er'd 'a wanted to know the top and bottom of what I wanted it for.'

'And what did you want it for?'

'To keep your brass in. It were gettin' over much for that piddlin' little tin o' your'n.'

Maggie tipped up the box and Anna gasped as gas light gleamed on gold sovereigns, silver crowns, half crowns and florins, all tumbling together in a glittering miser's hoard of coins.

'Maggie,' she croaked at last, 'where in God's name did this come from?'

'It's your'n, girl, all on it. I thought you had no idea 'ow much them creams of your'n was bringing so I took it out of that tin a little at a time and put it under my bed against a rainy day.'

'But all that, Maggie?' Anna whispered, afraid to touch the glistening heap. 'I couldn't have made that much.'

'Look, Anna.' Maggie sat down, facing her across the table that half-filled her tiny kitchen. 'You don't be knowin' what a winner you be on. Whoever taught you 'ow to make lotions and the like gave you a rare gift. Use it wisely, Anna, and you could kiss Roker Street goodbye.'

The gas jet spluttered and the yellow light dimmed then flared steadily, tinting Maggie Fellen's rich brown hair bronze.

'Look, wench, I told you at the start, there's no way you will be given work in Coseley or close by. Old Rewcastle has shit on you but by God 'e'll not wipe his arse on you an' all. Tek the money, wench, and set up for yourself. Keep your head low an' you'll be all right.'

'But, Maggie, this money . . . I know it's quite a sum but is it enough? And will my creams continue to sell? I think the girls at the mill only bought them because they felt sorry for me.'

'Don't be so bloody daft!' Maggie exploded. 'Brass is too bloody 'ard come by an' folk about 'ere gi' nowt away. If they buy owt it's because they want it. And think on this . . . if women 'ereabouts buy a thing it better be good or they tek it back and wrap it round throat of the bugger that sold it. An' I 'aven't heard you choking yet.'

Pushing the heap of coins towards Anna, Maggie smiled. It had hit the girl right between the eyes and she needed a minute to take it all in.

'Try it, wench,' she said minutes later when Anna's eyes showed understanding. 'Tek your money and get the things you need. My front room will serve as a shop if you sets up a few shelves. That way you won't need to splash out on hiring premises. And,' Maggie smiled widely, 'that way, if you falls then your arse won't get bruised so badly.'

'Mrs Fellen!' Reaching across the table, Anna took Maggie's rough hands into her own. 'I have heard more swear words from you tonight than I ever thought you knew.'

'Aye,' Maggie twinkled, 'an' you be like to hear more if you don't heed what I've said.'

'I'll heed you, Maggie.' Anna's face softened into tears. 'And you heed me. I love you, Maggie Fellen . . . I love you very much.'

Chapter Eight

Brushing her wealth of red-gold hair high on her head, Anna skewered it with pins then settled her black hat firmly with a long pearl-topped hat pin.

The deep green suit Edward had purchased for their wedding had been sold in order to buy the black skirt and coat she'd needed for his burying; the skirt and coat that had just received yet another pressing. She must look her best for what she was about to do.

It was six months since Maggie had shown her the money her cosmetics had made. Turning the front room into a shop had cost them nothing. William Cresswell had been coaxed into leaving his beloved pigeons and with his son's help a row of shelves had appeared in no time. Anna had resisted Hester's advice to paint them shocking pink, settling instead for a delicate shade of beige. Plenty of pretty lace, ruched and tied, turned the shelves into inner window displays, holding a select few of the products for sale. Replacing the chenille door curtain with a piece of bright yellow cotton Bella Castleton found for her, Anna had trimmed it with a froth of lace tied with a huge satin bow. Mary and Maggie had insisted they too were going to help and did so by washing the floor free from paint splashes and serving far too many cups of tea.

Anna fastened her coat. Maggie was minding the shop so there was no hurry. Outside the wind whipped about her legs, cutting through the thin coat, and she was glad she had used some of the recent profits to buy a new pair of button boots.

At least her feet would stay dry. The train seemed to take forever to get to Birmingham but once there Anna wasted no time. After posting off the monthly two pounds for her son, she strode along the main street until she came to the little shop, sandwiched between Monsieur Pierre, A-la-Mode Gowns and Beatrice, High Class Milliner. She heaved a sigh of relief. The premises were still to rent. Reading the notice in the window, Anna asked directions, finally reaching the address in Rooth Street.

Abraham Fine listened to her proposal to rent his shop for six months, bright eyes taking in her shabby appearance.

'You say you come from Coseley, Mrs Royce?' he asked when she finished.

Anna's happiness faded. Did Jacob Rewcastle's influence stretch as far as Birmingham?

'Forgive me if I seem impertinent,' he went on in his slightly guttural voice, 'but is it Anna . . . Anna Royce?'

'Yes, Mr Fine, I am Anna Royce.' If he was going to refuse to let her hire his premises then he might as well get it over with. Anna's eyes held his rheumy blue ones. She had survived worse disappointments.

'Then you know my good friend Benjie Freeth?' He smiled. 'A friend of Benjie Freeth's is a friend of Abraham Fine's. The shop is yours, Anna . . . do we sign a paper?'

She hardly heard the babble of voices in the third-class compartment on the way home. She had taken the first step.

In the six months of using Maggie's front room she had made enough profit to put what was left after living expenses into acquiring a second shop. Anna looked at her reflection in the window of the railway carriage. The shabby hat with its veil lifted off her face. The sparkling white cotton blouse fastened high about her neck . . . a blouse that was almost threadbare. But she was Anna Royce, a woman going places. She twisted her wedding ring, redeemed from the pawn shop, remembering her threat to Jacob Rewcastle. Her mouth set in a hard, determined line. Maybe he was not beyond her reach after all.

'But you went to Birmingham last week, you can't want to go again?' Maggie Fellen shook her head. 'An' I certainly won't go gallivantin' off on no train.'

Anna had been to Birmingham only the week before and Abraham Fine had done all he'd promised. Following her little sketch faithfully, the men he'd hired had made the shop ready in two days and she had placed her pots and jars in the lace-trimmed alcoves. Now everything was ready for her big surprise.

'Please, Maggie, just for me. I want to buy myself some new clothes and I'd like you to be there. Please come, Maggie . . . please?'

'I never could refuse you anythin', Anna, an' I'm still as daft. But what about Misty?'

'Mary Cresswell will keep an eye on her, she said as much.'

'You've got things nicely sorted out, ain't you, wench?'

I hope so, Anna breathed silently. I certainly hope so.

'I didn't know you was comin', Essie.' Maggie, feet feeling less than her own in the shoes kept against weddings and funerals, walked between the two younger women, her dark grey gabardine coat and long skirt smelling of mothballs.

'Aye, Mrs Fellen. Anna said I should see the shops in Birmingham and I agreed. Me mam says it's a waste of good brass train ridin' to Birmingham – but eee, I be that excited! It feels like Sunday school outing when we were kids.'

Sunday school outing! Anna glanced away. She and Peter had laughed so much on their last Sunday school trip when he had given her a necklace of pink ribbon with a paper diamond and she had worn it, as proud as the Queen of England. But what good were paper diamonds?

'My feet be killing me. Y'ave traipsed me all over the place and still you ain't bought anything,' Maggie complained.

They had stared in windows and walked in and out of shops most of the afternoon, Anna holding tight to her secret, wanting the moment to last.

'What about a nice cup of tea?' she relented, seeing the crease between Maggie's brows. 'I know a place where they make it just the way you like it.' She pushed a hand beneath the older woman's arm. 'And no one will see if you push those shoes off while you drink it.'

'Eee, Anna!' Hester's head swivelled with each shop they passed. 'I never thought there were places like this. Some of them are big enough to swallow half Roker Street.'

Anna laughed. She had thought the same on her first visit.

'There's one more I want you to see, Hester. It's not a big shop but I think you will like it.'

'Not until I've 'ad my cup of tea and five minutes sit down,' Maggie admonished vehemently. 'Your feet be younger than mine. You two could go on all day but I need a rest or you'll be carryin' me back to that train.'

'You can have your tea, Maggie.' Anna halted, pointing across the street to the elegant lettering painted in gold above a lace-draped window: Anna Royce. 'You can have it in there,' she said.

'Well?' Anna had made the tea in the tiny room at the back of the shop while her companions inspected every corner of it. 'What do you think?'

'Think!' Hester did another round of the prettily flounced shelves then perched on one of the spindly velvet-covered chairs. 'It's lovely, Anna, really lovely. Did you design all this yourself?'

'Yes, I sketched it out the day I hired the place from Mr Fine but it was he who got everything done for me. I just arranged the jars and pots.'

'Eee, Anna, who'd 'a thought it? Anna Royce with 'er own shop.'

'It would never have happened without Maggie.' Anna put an arm around the spare shoulders. 'She showed me the way.'

'You just needed a push, me wench.' Maggie bent over her tea.

'Stand behind the counter, Hester, I want to see what it would be like to be a customer.'

Anna stepped outside and when she re-entered Hester stood smiling behind the gleaming mahogany counter.

'Good afternoon, madam.' She inclined her mousy head just a touch. 'Welcome to Anna Royce.'

'Perfect!' Anna clapped her hands, happiness gleaming in the depths of her green eyes. 'I knew you would be. Hester, I would like you to run this shop for me. I'm asking you to leave Rewcastle's Mill and work for me here in Birmingham. It will mean a train ride night and morning but . . . but this is only the beginning, Hester. I intend to make a go of this cosmetics business. I intend Anna Royce to go a long way and I'd like you to come with me. You will have full control here and answer to none but me in anything you do. Will you do it, Hester?'

'I'll start on Monday . . . an' Rewcastle's can sing for a week's notice!'

Jacob Rewcastle. He must not find out why Hester was leaving the mill. If he did, she could say goodbye to her dream.

'Don't tell them you are coming to work for me, will you, Hester? You know how Mr Rewcastle would enjoy closing me down before I started.'

'I'll think of something, Anna.' Hester came out from behind the counter. 'Eee, fancy! Me, manageress of a real shop. It makes a right fine birthday present.'

'Of course!' Anna said, remembering. 'It's your birthday soon, isn't it?'

'Aye, I'll be twenty next month . . . eee, Anna!' Hester clamped a hand to her mouth. 'Does you remember?'

'I do!' Maggie Fellen regarded them both with steady grey

eyes. 'Kate O'Keefe said that a month afore you saw your twentieth year you would leave mill. You would be mistress in your own place and answerable to one woman only.

'Do you still think Kate's reading of the cups is just a bit of fun, Hester Cresswell?'

Chapter Nine

Anna loosed the button at the throat of her white cotton blouse, feeling the cool air touch her breasts beneath the thin covering. Her worn black skirt was heavy about her ankles and for one mad moment she wanted to tear it off, to fling it away together with her petticoats, and run, feeling the wind on her body.

The moor was a vast ocean of green with tiny wavelets of wild flowers cresting the grass that bent and swayed, first silver, then green, in the ebb and flow of the gentle breeze. How she would love to bring her son to the moor, to see him run with his sister over the soft grass, to watch him pick flowers for Misty as Peter had picked them for her. How she would love . . .

But Anna knew she could not claim the son she had given into the care of his father, she could not hold him in her arms. But she would always hold him in her heart, in her very soul.

As the pain of remembering pulled at her, Anna stared across the wide moor to where Coseley lay, a dark smudge against the landscape. Coseley and Wednesbury, both so alike, both bringing happiness and pain to Anna Royce.

She no longer came often to the moor, the thoughts such visits conjured being harder to bear each time. A herbalist now supplied the oils and essences of the plants she'd once picked, but when she could Anna still liked to gather some for herself; besides the isolation gave her time to be alone, time to think. Her basket was almost full but, reluctant to leave the peace of the moor, Anna walked to the spot where Edward had found her the wild honeysuckle. She smelled the delicate fragrance, touching her face to the scarlet and yellow blooms. It was one of her favourite perfumes, as it seemed to be with the many customers she was getting from the wealthier side of Coseley. Lorna Paget had preached the worth of her cosmetics with the zeal of a disciple and every day brought Anna fresh business.

She still felt dazed at the speed with which it was happening. Opening the shop in Birmingham in October, it had become popular in time for Christmas and she and Hester had both been run off their feet, keeping up with the demand there and in Coseley.

Hester. Anna smiled. The girl was changing. The 'thee' and 'tha' of her speech was fading, but there were no airs and graces. Hester didn't need any. The quiet dignity of her own nature was enough; now her mousy hair gleamed like brown honey and her plain little face had taken on a confidence that gave her a new radiance.

Breaking off a few of the fragrant blossoms and putting them into her basket, Anna turned toward Devil's Finger, the small waterfall that fell a hundred feet into a spray-filled chasm. Misty was at Sunday school with the Cresswell twins; an independent three year old, she loved being with the 'big' children. Anna relaxed. She could afford another hour here in the splendour of the moors before making her way home.

The sound of water falling over stones muffled approaching hoofbeats and Anna swung round, startled to hear a voice suddenly declare: 'Well, well, if it isn't Mrs Royce.' The darkly handsome friend of Philip Rewcastle looked mockingly down from a black horse, its flanks silvered with sweat. 'Aren't you afraid, out here all by yourself?'

'Not in the least.' Summer sun ringed his black head with a circle of blue, the devil's halo. It fitted him to perfection. 'So long as that is the way it is . . . but seeing I can no longer enjoy that luxury, I will say good afternoon.'

'Not afraid of me, are you, Mrs Royce?'

Anna glanced up at the handsome features. Some said the devil was handsome. This man was both, the devil and handsome.

The horse side-stepped nervously at the sound of his crop striking brown leather riding boots. He stared down at Anna, a mixture of disdain and lust in his brilliant eyes.

'Then perhaps you should be, Mrs Royce.'

Blood raced through Anna's veins. This was a man best avoided. He had been dangerous enough with Hester and Philip present, but out here, alone . . . Anna's free hand moved nervously to her throat, fingering the open button, and his hungry look followed, lingering over her breasts.

'Is that the invitation I think it is, Mrs Royce?' He bent forward, using the riding crop to pull at her unbuttoned neckline. 'I thought the last time we met you were more than ready to play.'

Angrily, she swiped away the gleaming cane with its snaking leather strip.

'You disgust me!' she spat. Then she was running as fast as she could through grass that suddenly seemed intent on grabbing her feet, holding her back.

At first only laughter followed her retreat then the drum of hoofbeats told her he was chasing her. Guiding his mount around and in front, he forced her to stop.

'I won't hear of your leaving, Mrs Royce.' An ugly smile twisted his mouth. 'You and I have some unfinished business. Where better to complete it than here?'

'I've got no business with you!' Anna replied, fear mounting inside her. 'You will please let me pass.'

'Will I?'

He was gloating, tormenting, feeding like some evil being on the fear he saw in her eyes. The gleaming cane snaked out, ripping her hair free from its pins, spreading it like a red-gold shawl about her shoulders.

'Lovely!' he breathed. 'Like fire. Do you live up to the

reputation that goes with hair that colour, Mrs Royce? Do you make love with the burning heat and passion of fire?'

There was no room now in that fierce gaze for disdain; it had been overridden, destroyed by the surging tide of lust. It sent a shiver of loathing and fear along Anna's spine. The fact that she was alone and defenceless was nothing to a man like him. In fact, he preferred it that way. If there were none to see him attack, there would be none to answer to.

There was nothing to be gained from talking. Dodging beneath the animal's chest, Anna streaked away, her hair a red banner floating behind her. She had only run a short way and already the breath was painful in her throat when hoofbeats throbbed behind her. Turning her head, she threw a backward glance across her shoulder. Through the hair whipped across her eyes she saw the horse approaching at a gallop, white flecks of foam flying from its mouth like flakes of snow on the breeze. Then her senses reeled, blue and green swirled into a kaleidoscope of colour as earth and sky rotated in turns about her tumbling figure; the horse had been spurred straight at her, its massive black shoulder catching her and sending her sprawling into the grass.

He was dismounted and rolling her beneath him before her senses had steadied. He ripped away the cotton blouse and chemise, his mouth closing over her nipple as his hand threw up the length of her skirts and pushed between her thighs.

'No!' Half-conscious, Anna tore at the head fastened to her breast but his teeth closed cruelly over the tender flesh and she screamed with pain.

Then, as quickly as his weight had rolled on to her, he heaved it away and Anna saw a riding crop strike, finding his face again and again.

Fighting against the brute strength of him, Anna had been unaware of the approach of a second rider. Now as she pushed her skirts down over her legs and pulled the remnants of her torn blouse across her breasts, she looked up into the tortured face of Philip Rewcastle.

'You lying swine, you filthy lying swine!'

The crop rose and fell.

'You told me you wouldn't do this again. You said you were finished with women.'

'Wait!' Flinging up his hands, protecting his face from the cut of the flailing whip, Robert backed away. 'You don't understand, Philip . . . listen to me, please.'

'I understand you, all right, you lying swine.'

But the whip fell still.

Anna had scrambled to her feet and without knowing it moved closer to Philip's chestnut mare, seeking the protection of her rider.

'No . . . you don't understand, Philip.' Robert's voice became soft and pleading, his dark eyes entreating. 'I was passing when I saw Mrs Royce. I stopped to give her the time of day and she asked if I would pull up some plant or other that was too strong for her.'

Scarlet trails of blood trickled across his forehead and through the thick black of his eyebrows, smearing into his dark eyes, but their gaze never flickered from Philip Rewcastle, even when Anna gasped at the outrageous lie.

'What else could I do than assist the lady, Philip? Then, when I was kneeling down, she lifted her skirts, spread her legs and pulled me on top of her.'

'Then shoved her tit in your mouth, I suppose!' Philip laughed, a harsh, haunted sound. 'Really, Robert, what kind of fool do you take me for?'

All the time he spoke Robert had been stealthily moving backwards and Philip let him go, widening the space between them.

'No fool, Philip. I know it must sound ludicrous but it's the truth. The woman wanted me to . . .'

The last was spoken on a note of hysteria as Philip looked down at Anna. For a moment his terrible expression softened, giving way to a gleam of pity.

'There is no need to ask what happened, Anna,' he said

quietly. 'Your eyes speak for you. The blame lies with Robert Daines. But he will never touch another woman, I swear it!'

'Philip.' Anna lifted a hand to the man who smiled a strangely contented smile, then felt it thrown aside as he pressed his spurs to the flanks of his mare.

With a strangled cry, Robert Daines turned and ran.

But Philip followed relentlessly, closing the gap between himself and the lover who had betrayed him. As Anna watched, the dark figure came to the edge of Devil's Finger and turned desperately, seeking another way. But it was already too late. Drawing level, Philip tugged viciously on the reins, snatching the mare's head back over its neck so that she reared.

The whinny of protest was followed by a longer, terrified human one. Front hooves lashing forward as she rose on her hind legs, the mare caught Robert Daines full in the chest, sending him flying, arms spread-eagled, out over the chasm then down, following the Devil's Finger into blackness. There was a momentary pause then the glint of sun on polished wood as Philip's crop whistled down on to the mare's flanks again and she reared once more.

Anna pushed her fist against her mouth, stopping her own screams, watching the animal fight against the slippery shale sliding away beneath her, taking horse and rider on a last journey into death.

They brought the bodies up from the chasm, the men of Coseley, and a specially convened Coroner's Court returned a verdict of 'Accidental death'. A week after the nightmare scene the body of Philip Rewcastle was laid to rest and that of Robert Daines returned for burial on his southern estate, and not once in all that time did Maggie question Anna's return from the moor, her blouse almost torn away, hair cascading loose about her scratched neck.

The whole town seemed unnaturally quiet following the funeral of the only son of Jacob Rewcastle, though his mill continued to belch out its black smoke and men drew molten steel from the fires of its belly.

In the front room she had turned into a shop, Anna moved restlessly, unable to rid herself of the horror of that afternoon. Outside the sound of a vehicle drawn by a trotting horse caught her attention. It was mid-afternoon; tradesmen had already made their rounds, even the 'Auntie Sally' man who could never be tied to any approximate hour to deliver the black syrupy disinfectant from which he drew his nickname.

Moving to the window, Anna caught her breath; a smart carriage drawn by a grey horse had stopped outside Maggie's door and Jacob Rewcastle was stepping out.

'You will come in?' Maggie pulled the door open before his knock sounded on it.

'It's Anna Royce I want to see.'

'I'm here, Mr Rewcastle, what can I do for you?' Anna emerged from the front room, her face blanching at sight of the basket he placed on the table. She had left it behind on the moor. Caught up in the drama being played out before her, she had forgotten it and later been too terrified to go looking for it.

'You *can* do summat for me.' Jacob brushed aside the offer of a chair. 'You can tell me the truth of what happened last Sunday up at Devil's Finger. And don't deny you were there. That . . .' he pointed to the basket though he didn't look at it. '. . . was found close by and I'm told it's yours. That's the truth, isn't it?'

'The basket is mine, Mr Rewcastle.' Anna's knees began to tremble. Why hadn't he been to see her before this? Why hadn't the basket been used to bring her before the Coroner's Court? Why had Jacob Rewcastle waited until now to face her with it?

'Then you were on the moor last Sunday?'

Wincing at the accusation behind the question, Anna nodded.

'And did you see my son?'

Across the table the puffy red face challenged her but beneath the bravado Anna could read the man's fear, a fear that silently answered her questions. She had not been brought to court because he was afraid she had seen what had happened, and afraid she had understood what lay behind it.

Strangely, Anna felt almost sorry for the man who had cheated her of everything she and Edward once had. He would never accept a denial that she had been present when his son had fallen to his death; it would eat away at him like canker in an apple. Fate had given her another chance to strike at him through Philip, but again Anna refused to do so.

'Yes, Mr Rewcastle,' she answered simply, 'I saw your son.'

'Did . . . did you see him fall? What happened?'

Turning away, Anna walked to the black-leaded grate, a fire burning there even though it was June.

To tell the truth about the tortured love that had driven Philip Rewcastle to commit murder would not bring back the dead or wipe away the memory of what Robert Daines had tried to do to her. It would have been easy for Philip to accept the lie the other man offered, to close his eyes to her innocence, but he hadn't. Philip Rewcastle had acted towards her as a gentleman, just as he had when she and Hester had come upon them in the bedroom of Edward's house, and as he had in his father's office. She would not repay that kindness by revealing he was hopelessly in love with a man.

'The dark-haired man . . .'

'Sir Robert Daines?'

'Yes. Your son called him Robert.' Turning to face him, Anna heard her daughter's laughter float in from the tiny back yard shared with the Cresswells and suddenly all concern over what she was about to say faded. Yes, she would lie, to preserve any respect Jacob Rewcastle still felt for his son.

'I was on the moor,' she said levelly, 'near Moses Table, when Robert Daines came up behind me. He rode me down with his horse and while I was on the ground, tried to force himself upon me. It was entirely the actions of your son that prevented him from raping me. Philip dragged him away, telling him what a fool he was, and while he was helping me to my feet, Robert Daines became very angry. He shouted that Philip was a fool, I was nothing but a mill wench and no one would bother if they both took me.

'When Philip pushed him away from me a second time, Robert Daines struck him in the mouth. Philip fell and lay still for a while . . . I think he caught his head on a stone. Robert Daines thought he was dead. Shouting that he would kill me too if I said anything of what had occurred, he began to run in the direction of Devil's Finger.'

Anna kept her glance on Jacob's eyes. 'A few seconds later Philip got to his feet. He shouted something about Robert not knowing the waterfall was there, then jumped on his horse and rode after him. I don't really know what happened next except one moment your son was reaching for his friend, then they both went over the edge.'

'So that's it! I guessed as much.' His face darkening, Jacob Rewcastle bent forward, placing both hands palm down on Maggie's white table-cloth, hatred spewing out with his words. 'My son died for nowt but a whore. Gave his life to save a woman who most likely spreads her legs willingly.'

'Jacob Rewcastle!' Maggie had not moved until this moment. Now she stepped forward, her face sharp with anger. 'This is my house. You 'as what you came for, though God knows yer tormented mind must twist what y'ave 'eard to suit yerself. But there's nowt about Jacob Rewcastle that frightens me so you best leave afore my clog finds your arse.'

Jacob straightened but his livid stare remained locked on Anna's pale face.

'I'll leave, Maggie Fellen,' he hissed, 'I'll leave, but when I have there'll be others to follow. You thought I didn't know about your little enterprise in Birmingham, didn't you? The shop run by Hester Cresswell . . . the one you're renting from Abraham Fine. Well, I do! And I tell you this and all: you've paid your last rent. There'll be no Anna Royce in Birmingham this time next week, and if you have any brains at all you'll see there's no place for you in Coseley or anywhere else I can find you.

'You took my son but by God you'll be sorry. You'll be sorry you ever heard the name Philip Rewcastle!'

'That was only part truth you spoke, wench, but I reckon as the Good Lord won't pay much mind to the rest.' Maggie turned from the window where she had stood watching Jacob Rewcastle drive away.

'Cryin' will get you nowhere. All you gets from that is the 'eadache. Wash your face an' tidy your hair. You can't be goin' out looking like a half-wrung mop.'

Anna sniffed, dabbing a handkerchief to her eyes. 'I . . . I'm not going anywhere.'

'That's all you knows. You be goin' to see Abraham Fine afore Jacob Rewcastle does.'

'But what good will that do? Rewcastle has money and there's little people can do against that.'

'How does you know?' For the first time Anna could remember Maggie snapped at her. 'Not every man in the world worships brass, an' it's my guess Abraham Fine is one of them or why should he 'ave let you 'ave 'is shop for rent he did? Common sense should tell you with a position like that it could fetch twice as much.'

Anna hadn't realised Maggie had quite such a business eye. As she looked at her now, slate-grey eyes cold as the steel that rolled from Jacob's mill, she might have been looking at a stranger.

Anna smiled faintly. 'It might be as well to give Mr Fine a little advance warning of Jacob's intentions.'

She hadn't known what to expect in going to see Abraham Fine but he and his wife Leah listened attentively as Anna told them of the threat to her livelihood.

'Jacob Rewcastle won't be satisfied until I've left this part of the country altogether, Mr Fine and I wouldn't want you to clash with him on my account so I will pay you three months rent to cover any loss while you look for someone else to take over the property.'

'We have heard from our good friend Benjamin the truth of this Jacob Rewcastle, and more of what he has done to you than you have just told.' Leah Fine shook her neat grey head, setting long gold earrings jangling. 'Perhaps now it is time for him to find out the whole world need not dance to his tune, eh, Abraham?'

'What my Leah is saying, Anna, is that we will not sell over your head, not to Jacob Rewcastle nor to anybody else. The shop is yours for as long as you wish.'

'But Jacob Rewcastle would give you a good price, more or less anything you ask, just to get me out . . . and be assured, Mr Fine, he won't give up without a struggle.'

'So who is afraid of a struggle?' Abraham's watery blue eyes strayed to his wife's gentle face. 'For nearly two thousand years our people have struggled . . . it's nothing new.'

'But the Lord has stayed with us, Abraham,' Leah added.

The tinkle of fine china as she poured coffee from a swan-necked pot then stirred in sugar and cream for Abraham sounded loud in the pretty chintz-upholstered sitting room. Anna accepted the cup offered to her, not knowing if she would like the strongly smelling drink. They had only ever had tea at home and Maggie never had anything else except a tin of cocoa in the house.

'Anna.' The skin on his hands almost transparent, the veins showing clearly, Abraham reached forward, putting his flower-sprigged cup and saucer on a mahogany table.

'I said we would not sell the shop over your head . . .' he paused, fixing that pale stare on her '. . . but what if I sold it to you?'

'Me!' Anna swallowed. 'But even if I had enough to buy it,

Jacob Rewcastle could always offer more, and he'd never let you sell to anyone else.'

'A man can sell what is his own to whomever he chooses.'

'Try telling him that!'

'Anna, we have talked of selling the shop for some time now and Leah thinks as I do. Our son Reuben does not want those premises. He already has a fine office for his solicitor's business.' He reached with his thin hand for his wife's, folding it about her fingers. 'It is our wish that you should have the shop.'

Her own hands shaking, Anna put down her cup beside Abraham's. It would be wonderful . . . her own shop . . . she might have the asking price, she was showing a handsome profit both in Birmingham and Coseley.

'Well, what do you say? My Abraham, he wants you to have it. Says you will love it as much as he did.' Leah lifted plump shoulders in the gesture Benjamin Freeth always used. 'Sheesh! Who should love a shop . . .'

I would, thought Anna, I know exactly how Abraham feels; to have given so much of your life to something then have it taken away by someone who wants it only for spite and revenge; to work as Edward had worked only to lose it all; and the losing would be hard for Abraham, even to someone he liked.

'If I can pay the price you ask, nothing would please me more than to take your shop and care for it, Mr Fine, but once Jacob Rewcastle finds out who has offered for it, you will get no peace until you promise to sell to him.'

'By that time it will be too late.' Abraham looked at the elegant long-case clock ticking in the corner of the room, then drawing his pocket watch from his waistcoat, checked it and replaced it in the slit pocket. 'Reuben will be home in a few minutes, Anna. Let's see what he suggests.'

Reuben Fine was tall and dark, almost as dark as Robert Daines though there the similarity ended. His eyes were those of his mother, brown and piercingly observant, but the rest of his features spoke of Abraham. Thick, straight brows topped a slightly hooked nose and his wide mouth smiled easily.

'But nothing could be simpler to remedy, Mrs Royce.' He too listened carefully to her fears. 'It would be sensible for you and my father to sign a legal document of sale . . . I know my father would be happy just to have a verbal agreement but in this instance it would be in the best interests of both of you to go by the book.'

Back at Roker Street Anna went up to the room she shared with Misty. Looking down at the tousle of golden hair and pinkly flushed face of her sleeping daughter, she knew she had been right to take the risk of buying the shop from Abraham Fine.

She had to fight Jacob Rewcastle on his own terms . . . this child, and for all she knew the boy back in Wednesbury, depended on her and she would fight any man for their sake.

Sitting on her bed, she spread out the legal document on the faded blue bedspread.

'We don't rent it anymore,' she whispered towards the old truckle bed Misty slept in. 'It's ours. For better or worse, darling, it's ours and I swear I will make a go of it. Oh, Misty! It feels so marvellous.' Anna held the paper to her breast. 'It . . . it's as if someone had suddenly given me a diamond.'

A diamond! Anna slowly lowered the document, staring unseeingly at the flowing script. '*One day you'll have a whole string of diamonds* . . .' The words danced in her mind, Peter's words. He hadn't meant a tiny scrap of paper glued to a pink string. This was what he had meant. She touched the crisp edge of the document, letting her finger trace the signature: Anna Royce. This was her diamond, her first paper diamond, and one day she *would* have a string of them.

Chapter Ten

Despite his threats, Jacob Rewcastle had not driven her from Coseley or closed her shop in Birmingham. He might be able to influence the men of his circle but the women were beyond his jurisdiction; they liked Anna Royce Beauty Products and they intended to have them. Anna closed her account book and leaned against the hard back of the wooden chair at Maggie's table. Takings were up every week; so much so that in Birmingham Hester was taking on a new girl.

''Ave you thought on what I said yesterday?' Maggie came in from the scullery, her questioning glance directed at the closed book.

'Yes, Maggie, and I can see the sense of it but . . .'

'But what? 'As you not got enough?'

'Money? Oh, yes, it's not that.' Anna rose, carrying the account book over to the dresser and putting it into a drawer. 'It's just that I feel nervous whenever I think of taking on something new.'

'What's new about it? You put the creams an' lotions into a fancy box for Lorna Paget, didn't you? So do it again. I'm sick to my back teeth of 'avin' to tell all those women from yon side that you don't 'ave any. For God's sake, girl, they're beggin' to spend their money an' if you don't be quick, somebody else will up an' tek it off them.'

She was right. Anna watched her black-skirted figure bustle out. Maggie had been right about her starting her own business and she was right in her advice to extend it to suit the more exclusive end of the market.

'Sleepin' money is idle money,' Maggie had said, 'make yours work for you.'

Anna pushed open the door of Wigmore Banking Company, her boots tapping on the tiled floor as she walked to the counter. Reuben Fine had suggested she come here. She was to meet him later at the shop. He always suggested they meet there if she needed his advice any time and Anna had a sneaking suspicion why. Hester Cresswell had turned into an attractive young woman.

'Can I help you?'

From his superior position behind the counter, the teller looked down his thin nose at her. 'Was you wanting something?'

His eyes were darting all over her, from the black hat pinned securely to the piled up red-gold mass of her hair to the shabby coat and shiny skirt.

'Yes, please.' Anna tried to smile but couldn't. There was enough vinegar in the man's face to pickle a barrel of onions. 'I wish to see the manager.'

At the end of the sharp thin nose nostrils widened like sluice gates opening while a thin smile hovered round his lips.

'I'm sure I can see to any business Madam might have.'

It was a definite snub, undisguised emphasis on the word 'Madam'; his open contempt for her clothes said it all. Anna squared her shoulders. Eyes cool as green ice played meaningfully on his own frayed cuffs and paper collar, the dark coat pressed as many times as her own. If she were going to do what she had come here to do, then she would do it properly. And the time to start was now.

'*You* might be sure of that, Mr Burrows.' Her quick gaze had caught the name plaque displayed on the counter. 'I am not. I do not deal with subordinates. I will discuss my business only with your superior.'

She had intended her voice to carry. Now titters of amusement spread among the other men working to either side of the reddening, spluttering Mr T. Burrows.

'I do not have all day.' Trembling inside, Anna maintained a calm front. 'You will tell the manager that Anna Royce is here.'

She had added no 'please', had not said she would be obliged if he would see her. She had issued an order and was surprised at its effect.

John Harris leaned forward, resting his hands on the walnut desk. He had heard of this woman sitting opposite him; one got to hear many things in his line of business and it was his opinion Jacob Rewcastle had robbed her. Business was business, John Harris was the first to admit, but robbery was also robbery and that was what had taken place over King's Choice.

'I will be happy for you to bank with Wigmore's, Mrs Royce.' He rang the small bell on his desk.

'Have this deposited to Mrs Anna Royce and bring her book in here,' he said to the man who answered his ring.

Anna kept her mouth steady, fighting a smile as Mr Burrows kept his glance away from her face. He was taking no more chances with her sharp tongue.

'Er . . . forgive my forwardness, Mrs Royce.' John Harris waited until the door closed behind the departing Burrows. 'But the money you have just placed on deposit, would it not be better to make it work for you . . . investments . . . stock perhaps?'

Anna did smile then, amused that he should choose the same words as Maggie.

'Thank you, but I wish that money to remain untouched. However, I would welcome your advice on another matter, Mr Harris. I . . . I feel I can trust you to guide me in the right direction.'

She lowered her long lashes. There was a time for putting

men in their place and a time for flattery. Lifting her glance, she saw his pleased reaction. Anna Royce was learning fast.

Quickly she outlined her business. 'And now I feel there is an opening for a more lavishly packaged product, one aimed at the more affluent who are looking for an unusual gift.'

John Harris was listening intently. 'So what do you suggest? Will it make another selling line or should I forget it?' Anna asked.

Touching the tips of his fingers to his lips, the bank manager remained silent. His own wife had purchased this woman's products and now bought no other. Handled properly, it could prove a profitable venture and maybe bring additional business the bank's way. There was a discreet tap on the door and Burrows re-entered the office, placing a slim black book on the desk then withdrawing like a shadow.

'It is a laudable idea, Mrs Royce.' John Harris opened the small book, checking what was entered in it before handing it to her across the neat desk. 'But for the bank to back you financially . . .'

'I'm sorry.' Anna watched the movement of hands so different from Edward's. His had never been so white yet there'd been a strength to them, a steadiness and calm which she badly missed.

'I must not have explained myself clearly. I don't want to borrow money from the bank, I do not intend to incur any debt. I want to feel my way slowly, Mr Harris, paying as I go, and this is what I will use to make my start. What I want you to tell me is whether it is enough to begin with?'

For the second time since entering his office, Anna lifted her old carpet bag from where it rested on the floor beside her chair. Placing it across her knees, she opened it, taking out several small thick linen bags. Not all of the words 'fine milled flour' had come off when she had washed them in Maggie's scullery sink but they were clean enough, leaving no trace of their original contents as she placed them on the shining desk.

'There's three hundred pounds there, Mr Harris, but if you think that insufficient, I will wait until I can add more.'

Anna heard his sibilant intake of breath.

'I would say you have ample funds to make a beginning, Mrs Royce. Do you wish to place this in a business account with us?'

Anna nodded, watching the pleased smile spread across his features as he rang the gleaming brass bell once more. An acid-faced Burrows carried her money away.

Anna fastened her carpet bag. She was pleased with the way things had turned out, just as Reuben had predicted she would be. He was a smart man, was Reuben Fine. But then, didn't Hester tell her so almost every evening?

'Mr Burrows,' John Harris showed her out of his office, pausing as they passed the chief teller, 'any time Mrs Royce is in the bank she is to be shown into my office immediately. Please let the rest of the staff know that also.'

Anna walked proudly from the building. What John Harris had just done clearly signalled his support of her, a helpful gesture towards a woman fighting in a man's world. Head thrown back, she strode on determinedly to her meeting with Reuben. Now she had two debts to pay, one to a mill owner and one to a bank manager. She would pay both.

Maggie was right as usual, Anna realised as she slipped on the moss green day suit and studied its effect in the fitting-room mirror. It deepened the emerald of her eyes and complemented the burnished gold of her hair. She had lost weight but that was not surprising, seeing she hardly ever had a moment to sit down, and she wasn't displeased. Her waist was tiny and her breasts high. She didn't need the restrictive whalebone corsets to give her that hour-glass silhouette that was so modish. She ran a hand over the stiff grosgrain. Edward would have loved to see her dressed like this . . .

'But, my dear, of course I took them. I couldn't possibly have disappointed him by refusing, now could I?'

Two shrill voices trilled loudly, their empty falseness jerking Anna from her memories. She would buy the green suit. Taking it off, she draped it across a tiny gilt chair.

'They are lovely – but they're not real, are they?'

'Of course they're real. Rubies are my favourite. I would never settle for less than the best. Fortunately he had drunk himself into a stupor before I had to earn them . . .'

Laughter trilled again, loud and unpleasant. Anna slipped on her brown skirt, fastening the small self-covered buttons. She had no wish to eavesdrop. Reaching for her jacket, she slipped her arms into it, shrugging it on to her shoulders, nimble fingers slotting the buttons through buttonholes.

'Stupid old man!' The woman's voice came clearly through the thin wall separating the dressing cubicles. 'Thinks he can get himself a son and heir and it will be with me. Hah! He doesn't know how wrong he is.'

'Is your friend not married then?'

'Yes, but she won't give him what he wants – probably too old to have any more children anyway.'

Drawing aside the curtain, Anna pushed the green suit into the hands of the assistant waiting discreetly.

'Thank you, I will take this . . . will you please bring it round?'

'Of course, Mrs Royce.' The woman smiled. 'Will you be in the shop or will I leave it with Miss Cresswell?'

'I'll be in the shop.'

'More children!' the thin voice piped as Anna began to cross the carpeted floor of Monsieur Pierre, A-la-Mode Gowns. 'He does already have children then?'

'Should I have the peach or the mauve do you think?'

Anna stepped through the doors and stood outside breathing in fresh air. She wasn't a fool, she knew there were women like that, but suddenly she would have liked nothing more than to shake the breath from the selfish bodies of the two she had just been forced to listen to. Perhaps it was a case of six and two threes. The man, whoever he was, was cheating on his wife and so perhaps deserved to be cheated in his turn. Nevertheless it made her feel a little sick.

'Did you buy anything?' Hester looked over her shoulder from the shelf she was dressing when Anna came into the shop.

'Yes. The assistant will be popping round with it in a few minutes, she has customers at the moment. Do you mind taking it for me? I . . . I have one or two things to see to.'

Hester nodded and Anna slipped quickly into the neat back room before her friend could question the faint flush of anger tingeing her cheeks. The tinkle of the shop doorbell followed but Anna remained where she was. It was probably Reuben, he usually called at this time.

'But I thought I had told you . . .'

Anna's spine tingled. It was the same voice she had heard moments before.

'. . . he only had one son. In his late-twenties he was, I believe, but he was killed. An accident, they said. His horse lost its footing and went over the side of a waterfall or something . . .'

Anna's head reeled and she clutched at the table for support. She was talking about Philip . . . the woman out there in the shop was talking about Philip Rewcastle; and the man who had bought her rubies, the man who hoped for a son, was Jacob Rewcastle.

'*He only had one son.*' The words rang through the dark hours of the night. '*He thinks he can get himself a son.*' They went on ringing in her mind as Anna walked to the station and bought her ticket, and they were still there a little over an hour later when she walked from the small station at Burslem. She felt guilty about leaving Misty and the front-room shop to Maggie yet again.

A freckle-faced boy grinned when she asked if he could give him directions to the pottery. He couldn't be much older than Misty, certainly no more than eight, but already his arms hung well below his sleeves and there was a marked gap between trousers and boots that only will-power held together.

'Aye, I can, missus. Which one does tha want?'

The cheeky grin was infectious and Anna smiled broadly.

'I don't know,' she admitted 'suppose you tell me?'

Wiping the back of his hand under his nostrils then running it down the side of a trouser leg, the lad chuckled.

'Well, tha could tek tha pick of any of 'alf a dozen but nearest one is Seth Gladwin's place. Though whether or not 'e's theer . . .'

Shoulders too wide for the jacket lifted non-committally.

'Why shouldn't he be there?'

''E might be off looking for somebody to buy rest of 'is stock. Seth 'as bin tryin' for weeks now and me dad says it'll be a miracle if 'e finds someone, but if tha wants I'll tek thee theer.'

At Anna's nod the boy turned along the steep cobbled street, his thin legs moving rapidly.

'Ar,' he volunteered, 'Seth is all but finished. Closin' its doors is Gladwin's like a good few others round 'ere.'

A pair of high doors led to Gladwin's Potteries. Anna slipped a threepenny bit into the grubby hand of her chatty companion and walked across the cobbled yard. To her left a huge bottle-shaped brick edifice rose to the sky. The rest of the court was boxed in on three sides by ramshackle buildings, one of which boasted a rickety wooden staircase leading to an upper storey. Anna glanced around, almost wishing she had accepted Reuben's offer to come with her. In her old carpet bag the walnut box Benjamin Freeth had made at his home to her instructions weighed suddenly heavy. The world of Burslem was strange to her.

'Can I help thee?'

Anna turned to the shadowed doorway of one of the side buildings and for one wild sickening moment she wanted to scream. The white potter's apron daubed with red clay reminded her of a smear of blood across her breast, the tawny streaks of hair across Philip Rewcastle's face . . .

'I . . . I wanted to see Mr Gladwin.' Her trembling fingers almost lost their grip on the carpet bag and it took several long breaths to fight away shadows of her yesterdays.

'I'm Seth Gladwin. Tha better come up to the office, tha looks about ready to drop.'

Anna followed him up the shaky staircase and into a tiny office whose organised chaos reminded her of Benjamin's workroom. Offering her the only chair, Seth Gladwin walked over to the high arched window where he stood looking at her.

'What was it you wanted?' he asked when they were both settled. 'As tha can see, there's little left.'

'I . . . I was told you were closing. I didn't know that before I set out.' Anna tried to keep her eyes from the smeared calico apron. 'I might have saved myself a journey.'

'Aye, Gladwin's Pottery is finished.' The whiskered face turned from her, looking down into the deserted yard. 'I'm glad me father isn't alive to see it. This pottery was his pride, his life and mine until . . .'

Anna waited but the man, whom she judged to be in his sixties, said no more, eyes fixed on the emptiness of the yard below as he too walked the corridors of memory.

'There's no more call, tha sees,' he said at last. 'Everybody wants this fancy foreign stuff. Hah! Ah wouldn't gi' tuppence for the best on it.'

Anna glanced at the few pieces in one corner of the room: thick workmanlike jugs and bowls, all in the same uninteresting white glaze. She could understand the change in preference. She too liked even workaday objects to be pretty.

'Is that the only type of pottery that can be made here?' she asked, ignorant of the whole process.

'No.' Seth Gladwin moved to a cupboard covered in a layer of red dust and took a cup from the shelf inside.

'I made this when ah was nobbut a lad and me dad fired it in that very kiln.' He nodded to where the bottle-shaped brick building was visible through the grimy window. 'Aye, ah liked to get a lump of clay and see what my fingers could mek of it.' He gave the cup to Anna. 'But me dad said as 'ow we would mek nowt out of stuff like that. Break too easy, he said, folk wouldn't want pieces as would break easy.'

Anna held the fragile cup in her hands. Delicate as a baby's breath and almost as transparent. She held it up, marvelling at the thinness of it, seeing how the light from the window filtered through. It was beautiful, even without the slim, question mark handle and fine glaze.

'You say you made this?'

'Aye, ah did.' Age had not dimmed his pride in his achievement. 'When ah were a lad ah did a few other bits and bobs . . . they're in cupboard if tha's interested?'

Anna was . . . very interested. Going to the cupboard, she took out pretty fluted jugs and elegant vases, fine as a summer breeze. How Maggie or Mary Cresswell would treasure one of these!

'They are lovely, Mr Gladwin.' She held a fragile teapot. 'I wonder you didn't make more of these instead of heavier ware?'

'No call for 'em. Good strong crocks was what me old dad always said. Gi' folk good strong crocks and tha won't go far wrong . . . only it seems folk no longer want 'em.'

Anna returned the lovely painted teapot to its shelf.

'So now you are closing down, what will you do with the stock you have left?'

'Truth is, ah think ah've sold all ah'm gonna shift. The rest will 'ave to be written off, same as kiln and buildings.'

'But you can get a sale for them, surely?'

'Not round 'ere.' Seth took a whisper-fine cup from the dusty cupboard. 'Reckon this is all ah'll tek from 'ere. Kiln will never be fired again . . . business is finished.'

He placed the cup on the table, turning to stare once more through the arched window.

'There's no selling any of it.'

Anna picked up the carpet bag she had left beside her chair, taking out the walnut box.

'Mr Gladwin,' she said quietly, 'would you be able to make me some small pots to fit this?'

Seth Gladwin turned.

'So that's what tha come 'ere for, Mrs . . .' For the first time since her arrival, he asked her name.

'Anna Royce.'

'Well, Mrs Royce, truth on it is tha's too late. Today will just about see me off. Ah've already finished the last of workers I 'ad.' He fingered the beautifully grained walnut. 'Bloke who made this is a craftsman, ah reckon, knows what 'e's about.'

'The pots I want for inside would have to be fine, like those in the cupboard. Can it be done?'

'It could, but tha needs china clay for that.'

'Can it be got?'

'Oh, aye.' Seth's glance met hers. 'Has to be brought up from Cornwall, though, does china clay.'

There was no breathless heat of excitement inside her nor the damp fear of doubt, just quiet conviction. Going back to the cupboard, Anna picked up a graceful jug.

'Mr Gladwin,' she asked calmly, 'given a buyer for Gladwin's Pottery, how much would you expect to sell it for?'

Fingernails lined with clay pulled at long side whiskers and heavy brows drew together quizzically as Seth Gladwin surveyed the woman who had walked unceremoniously into his works. Still young and with looks that would turn many a head, she was dressed clean and neat without a deal of money spent on it. Her speech was quiet, nowt lah-di-dah, and he had made easy conversation with her. Strange that . . . he wasn't given to talking overmuch to anyone, much less a stranger and that one female.

'I should have counted myself lucky to come out of it with a 'undred pounds,' he answered at last, held by her candid green stare. 'But as it is . . .' He shrugged, holding out the box to Anna.

Taking it, and putting it on the dust-covered bench that served for a table, she held his stare.

'I will pay you one hundred and fifty.'

'A hundred and fifty! Tha must be daft. 'Aven't ah told thee there be no call for pots anymore?' He could have said: 'Put the money down and works is your'n, lock, stock and barrel,' and didn't really understand why he hadn't.

'I would not be producing the sort of pottery you have been making, Mr Gladwin. My line of business calls for something entirely different, that was my reason for bringing the box. I want specialist ware: small jars with lids, hand painted if possible, to fit inside such boxes. Those jars would have to be as fine as this.' She touched the lovely scrolled jug. 'So what do you say . . . will you sell Gladwin's Pottery to me?'

It still took seconds to sink in, to recognise the genuine offer she was making.

'Aye, ah will that,' he spluttered at last. 'If tha wants it, it's thine.'

'I do want it, but there is a condition to the sale.'

'Oh, aye?'

Anna's gaze never flickered. She heard his disappointment, the feeling of 'I knew it was too good to be true', and smiled inwardly. There was a proviso to be met if she were to buy his building but somehow she could not see it causing him much grief.

'Yes, Mr Gladwin, I will pay you one hundred and fifty pounds for Gladwin's Pottery provided you stay on as manager. You will take sole responsibility at a wage of . . . shall we say . . . four pounds ten a week?'

Slowly delight spread over the work-lined face, smoothing away creases and lighting his eyes with an inner fire.

'Ah don't know how tha came to be here, Mrs Royce, but ah thank the good Lord for all 'is blessings.'

'Amen to that!' Anna replied with feeling. 'Now could we settle on how long it will take for you to get production going?'

Seth took the box again, lips pursed under their line of grey whiskers.

'That one is a big kiln, Mrs Royce, and expensive to fire. Tha could fit thousands of the jars the size tha's askin' for into one corner of it.' He glanced up. 'What I'm really sayin' is the cost teken overall will be pretty 'igh if tha only part-fills it.'

'I think, given your help, Mr Gladwin, we can overcome that particular problem,' she returned. 'I want the rest of the space taken up with the type of pottery you have there.' She indicated the delicate pieces she had handled. 'Can you find me the men and women to make them?'

Seth tugged his long grey side whiskers.

'There's bin no bone china med in these part for many a day but the old 'uns still 'ave the skills and the young 'uns the will. Aye, ah reckon we can gi' thee most anythin' tha asks.'

'Does that include painting the designs?'

'Aye, that an' all.'

His tired eyes were suddenly alive again and hope lifted his drooping shoulders. It was little short of a miracle for him and for folk in this part of Burslem. Seth thought of the men and women without work, without money to feed their families; if this woman did take on the pottery there would be many blessing her name.

'You can contact John Harris of Wigmore Banking Co., Birmingham, if you have any queries, Mr Gladwin.' Anna realised he would probably have his doubts about her. 'I will have my solicitor draw up a bill of sale at once.' She turned to go. 'I will leave the box with you, I presume you will need its measurements. As for the rest . . . if I sketch roughly what I have in mind, will you be able to make cups and things from that?' She smiled. 'I'm afraid I'm a total novice when it comes to pottery.'

If she had asked would he fly if she strapped two palings

to his arms, he would have said yes, but all he could do was nod. Tears were too close for him to speak. Walking with her to the gate, Seth fidgeted with the corner of his apron, too shy to offer his hand.

'I'm very glad I came here today.' Anna held out her own hand. 'I think together we will make it work but there is something that would help.' Seth took the tips of Anna's slim white fingers in an effort not to cover them with dried clay but she pushed her hand firmly into his. 'I might not know much about making crockery but I know that a name people have come to depend on can only help us both. Will you agree to my keeping the name Gladwin's Pottery?'

Words still would not come but Anna didn't need them; the answer was in the old man's eyes. If it were within his power, the venture they were about to embark on would succeed.

'Tha's finished then?' The tousled head of the boy who had brought her from the station popped round one tall door, split in a cheeky grin. 'Somebody has to show thee back to station.'

And another threepenny bit wouldn't come amiss, thought Anna, matching his grin.

'If you had told me you intended buying the business, I could have drawn up the contract and come with you . . . I did offer.' Reuben looked at Anna across the table in the back room of the Birmingham shop.

'Don't think I wasn't grateful . . . I just thought it would be taking you away from your work for nothing. Believe me, Reuben, when I went to Burslem yesterday I had no thought of buying anything other than cosmetic jars for my gift boxes.'

'That will be the truth, Reuben.' Hester's neatly dressed hair glinted in the light from the window. 'Anna didn't even know where to find a pottery until we asked the teacher up at the school, so how could she know one was for sale?'

He pushed forward the sheet of paper for Anna to read.

'Well, I think she made a very good deal. You are a clever girl, Anna Royce.'

'Thank you, sir.' Anna dimpled. 'But I would like you to come with me and ask Seth to sign this . . . I want to be perfectly sure it is what he wants too, Reuben.'

'I'll be there, Anna. But right now, may I borrow your assistant for a few minutes?'

What happens if he proposes? Anna thought, seeing the radiance in her friend's eyes as she followed Reuben. His real goal in coming here was Hester. They were in love, deeply in love, but a Jewish-Anglican marriage? What would Abraham Fine have to say about that? Not to mention Mary Cresswell.

She had washed the delicate pieces that Seth had insisted he wanted her to have and now studied one of the delicately moulded jugs. Placed discreetly in a draped niche, or set with one or two pretty jars, it would be displayed to perfection; a ruse secretly intended to catch the eye of her customers. Anna smiled to discover a deviousness that was new to her. She was becoming a true businesswoman with an eye to the main chance.

At the tinkle of the bell Anna turned to the door, her quick glance taking in the customer's blonde hair swept up beneath a classy blue hat, blue panne velvet coat trimmed with tiny blue bows and braid.

'Good afternoon, welcome to Anna Royce.'

She used Hester's words though for some reason she could not imitate her smile. Putting the jug quickly on the shelf she had chosen for it, she placed a small upholstered chair close to one of the tables Hester had suggested might be more acceptable to ladies than hovering at a counter, then waited until the woman was seated. Anna watched the hard face; paint and powder, going some way to disguise the effects of age, did nothing to soften the line of her mouth or the steely light of her blue eyes. Anna repressed a sudden shiver. She had taken a dislike to the woman on sight, but why . . . for what possible reason?

'May I show Madam something?' She had to say something, couldn't stand there staring like an idiot.

'Yes!' It was imperious, a command, and Anna's hackles

rose. 'That jug you were holding just now, I would like to see it.'

Her mouth set hard, Anna handed over the lovely porcelain piece. That voice had told her why she felt so much dislike for the woman in blue. It was the same woman who had come to the shop last week; the one she had overheard in Monsieur Pierre's, speaking so disparagingly of Jacob Rewcastle.

'This is very beautiful.' The woman twisted the jug in gloved hands. 'So very delicate, obviously Italian . . . they are so good at this type of thing. I often think it would be nice if our own country could produce such fine china but . . .' She shrugged, lifting soot-coated lashes. 'We just don't seem to have the skills.'

Anna clenched her teeth, no longer even trying to smile.

'Do you have this in pink?' The woman held out the jug. 'The continentals have such a wonderful eye for colour, you really can't get the like of it here.'

'Not yet, Madam,' Anna heard herself reply graciously while her every urge was to throw the woman out of the door. 'But we do hope to have some very shortly.'

'Ah! Such a distance to transport fragile china, I do understand. Where is it you import from? Milano . . . Roma . . . or Venezia? Oh! That divine Venetian glass . . . do you sell that too?'

'No!' Anna's insides clenched. She had never heard anyone talking of foreign places yet recognised the falseness of this woman.

I'll bet you've never been fifty miles out of Birmingham, she thought acidly.

'Pity. It's such marvellous glass.' Placing the jug on the small round table, the woman admired its graceful lines again. 'Do you have any more pieces like this?'

Grudgingly Anna brought out the rest of the porcelain Seth had given her and listened to the woman's admiration. She might be a gold digger, taking Jacob Rewcastle for all she could get, but she genuinely appreciated the beauty of Seth's work. As she listened Anna knew she had been right; she would be able to sell every piece of fine porcelain the pottery could produce.

Chapter Eleven

Had it really been that long? Anna looked at the two documents she had spread side by side on her bed. Was it really two years since she had bought Seth Gladwin's place, two years since adding the second paper diamond to her string? So much had happened since she came to Coseley: her marriage to Edward, then his death before the birth of her daughter – then had come the loss of King's Choice and the terrible death of Philip Rewcastle.

'*Toil and tears*.' Anna remembered the reading of the tea leaves. 'There's been a lot of that, Kate,' she whispered, 'a lot of toil and too many tears.' But both of the businesses had done extremely well. And now this.

She picked up the cream envelope, looking again at the crest on the flap, knowing the words of the letter by heart. 'Her Grace would be pleased if you would call on the afternoon of 19 May . . .'

'Granma Maggie says are you ready, Mother? Auntie Mary has sent the boys round to say Hester would like you to go next door.'

Anna smiled into the cornflower blue eyes of her daughter. At eight years old, she was chubby and golden-haired as a cherub, and the thought occurred to Anna just as it always did: were those other eyes still that strange transparent blue, was his hair still blond?

'I'm coming, sweetheart,' she said, shoving the papers together and pushing them into their box. Taking Misty's hand, she walked awkwardly behind her down the narrow stairs, her free hand closing around another imaginary hand and her heart aching for the smile and the touch of her son.

Hester was married. Anna thought nothing could ever be so beautiful as that exchange of vows beneath a canopy. Memories of her own wedding flooded her mind. Edward in stiff wing collar and Sunday suit, and herself feeling like a lady in the green outfit he had bought for her and which she had later sold to Sam Castleton to buy her widow's black. But it wouldn't be like that for Hester, she thought, fiercely protective of her friend's happiness. Nothing was going to spoil life for her.

'She's done you proud, Mary.'

'Aye, Maggie.' Mary Cresswell wiped her eyes.

'Her's a grand wench, an' that bloody pretty as well!' William Cresswell put in proudly. 'An' it's your turn next, Anna girl . . . it's time you were wed. It's bloody wicked, lettin' a wench as pretty as you go to waste.'

'You hold your swearin', William Cresswell.' Behind the frown Mary's eyes twinkled. Her William was a quiet man but a sensible one and what he had just said needed saying.

'Well, I'm right, it's not good for a woman to live life alone.'

'But I'm not alone. I have Misty and Maggie and a whole family of Cresswells to keep me company.'

'You knows what I meant and I still says you be wastin' your life,' he defended himself.

'I'll marry you, Anna.' Fourteen-year-old Bobby Cresswell turned a cheerful eye on the gathering. Almost as tall as his father, a shock of hazel hair fell in an unruly mop over his brandy ball eyes, the only thing that distinguished him from his twin brother for George had eyes almost as blue as Misty. 'I quite fancy the older woman.'

'You'll not fancy my toe up your arse, but that's what you'll get if you don't shift!' Mary fetched her son a swift slap on the ear. Wedding reception or no wedding reception, she was having no lip.

''Is bloody ears are far too big. I keep saying it's time William clouted 'em for 'im but I might as well talk to meself for all the notice that one teks. It's a good job 'e's startin' work tomorrer, that'll tek some of the lard out of 'im.'

Anna smiled at Bobby's infectious grin.

'Make a good job of working with Benjamin Freeth, and who knows? I might take you up on your offer, Bobby Cresswell.'

She had set Benjamin up in a small workshop where he made the wooden presentation caskets that held Anna's small jars of cosmetics. These had been a winner right from the moment they were introduced and now he needed assistance. Bobby was quick to learn and the old man had taken him on as an apprentice, along with his brother. Anna sighed inwardly. Two more lives tied up with her own.

A week after Hester's wedding Anna caught the London train. Reuben had agreed Hester should remain in charge of the shop. They were a modern young couple, he said, he didn't expect her to stay home all day just because she was now a married woman. Mary had said nothing to this. After all, women in her walk of life only stopped going to the mill long enough to give birth. A week later they were standing at the benches again. It was enough for her that her daughter was happy. Misty and the front-room shop were left to the care of Maggie.

Anna again felt guilty at leaving her daughter, even though it was only for a couple of days. Soon now she would take a few days off from the business and spend them just with Misty.

Leaning her fiery head against the seat, Anna closed her eyes, the words of the letter in her bag matching the rhythm of the train's wheels passing over the points. 'Her Ladyship would be pleased . . . Her Ladyship would be pleased . . . The letter had said 19 May. That was tomorrow. First she must find a hotel.

Stepping from the train at Euston Station, the noise and bustle of the crowds was overpowering and Anna hesitated.

'Do you 'ave to stand there right in other folks' way?'

An old woman with a covered straw basket on her arm bumped past, muttering angrily. Steam belched loudly from a massive green and gold engine and Anna started nervously at the shrill whistle of the guard; a cloud of black particles, floating in the grey breath of a departing iron monster, wreathed about her face, closing off the breath from her lungs and making her cough. Tears stinging behind smarting eyelids, she hitched the new valise she had bought for the journey more firmly in her hand, missing the comforting worn handle of her old carpet bag.

Outside, the street held a dark promise of rain. A breeze intent on mischief tugged at a strand of her red-gold hair, freeing it from the restriction of hat and pins then chasing it across her face. Yet even here there was little relief from people pressing and pushing from every side. It seemed to Anna that the whole world lived in this one street in London, and that the whole world was intent on pushing her out of the way. Buildings so tall and grand they terrified her rose all around, grey and suffocating as the walls of a tomb; nifty hand carts filled with fruit and vegetables were darting like coloured butterflies almost beneath the iron-bound wheels of carriages and cabs, and all the time the cries of street traders added to the din.

'Watch yer back!'

A barrow loaded with oranges was pushed close to her and Anna moved a step forward then retreated with a startled cry. A black lacquered carriage, its driver resplendent in black top hat and coat trimmed with red braid, whisked past just inches from her toes, throwing mud on to the skirt of the green suit she had bought at Monsieur Pierre's.

'Will you be wantin' a 'ansom, miss?'

A dirty-faced character, the front of his coat adorned with greasy marks, sidled from the crowd to stand too close to her.

'A . . . a what?' The strident yell of a costermonger exploded, confusing Anna with its suddenness.

'A 'ansom. You knows . . . a 'orse and carriage.'

'Oh . . . yes. I suppose so.'

Two dirty fingers were inserted in the character's mouth and he gave a loud whistle. Down the street a driver laid his whip to the flanks of a tired horse.

'Where you wanting to get to?'

Fumes of gin gusting from him, the sleazy man questioned Anna as the carriage halted beside them.

'I . . . I don't really know.' Confusion still dulled her mind, making it difficult to think. 'I was hoping to find a quiet hotel.'

'You ain't bin to London afore then?'

'No.' Anna hitched her valise closer in aching fingers.

'That explains why you was lookin' a bit lorst like.' His calculating gaze moved to the black valise as his grimy hand reached for the cab door.

Involuntarily Anna shrank away. The man's hand was filthy, dirt ingrained in the skin. Even the men at the mill never seemed this dirty, not after ten hours of forging and rolling molten steel, and they certainly didn't smell like he did. The gin was bad enough but each time he moved, the sour smell of ancient sweat rolled from his body in sickening waves.

'You leave it to me, miss.' He smiled, showing blackened teeth. 'I knows a quiet place . . .'

'I'm sure you do!' A black malacca cane dropped on to the hand that touched Anna's sleeve. 'Too quiet . . . Muswell Hill graveyard being the prime favourite, I have no doubt.' The cane tapped lightly several times on the grimy hand before the man who had joined them spoke again. 'On your way, you rogue, before I send for a constable. The lady can do without your kind of help.'

The black tip of the slender cane remained resting for a few seconds on the knuckles of the other man's hand, then it was lifted. Muttering about 'bloody interfering sops', the fellow sloped away into the station.

'Forgive my intrusion,' the voice at her elbow began

again, 'but I could not allow a lady to be accosted by such a rogue.'

'He was trying to help.' Anna brushed a hand over the mud on her skirt, succeeding in transferring most of it to her pale grey glove. She knew the stranger was watching and suddenly felt like an awkward girl.

'That was obvious, but it was himself he was intent on helping – to your purse, the moment he got the chance.' Opening the carriage door, he took the valise and put it inside. 'Will you allow me to give the driver the address to which you wish to be driven?'

Again Anna felt foolish. She had no place to go, having thought to ask after a suitable hotel once she arrived in London. She had not dreamed it would be like this, so crowded and impersonal, and after the last few moments felt even more inadequate.

'Perhaps I might suggest The Conway? It is a small genteel residence most suited to a lady travelling alone. It stands in Leicester Road, not far from here.' He smiled for the first time. 'Handy for any business you might have in this, our fair city.'

Taking her silence for acceptance, he handed her into the musty-smelling cab.

'I would take you there myself but I have the misfortune to be meeting someone . . . an old friend. In the circumstances I will take the liberty of offering my card now instead of calling at your address and leaving it there.' The smile flashed again. 'My poor dear mama would have a touch of *mal-de-mer* were she to hear of it.'

Reaching into an elegant silver case he withdrew a card, handing it to her before closing the door. Stepping one pace back, he gave a half bow. 'If I can be of any assistance during your stay, a sixpenny runner will find me at that address.'

He called to the cabby then, giving the name of the hotel, and Anna heard the whip crack and felt herself jolt forward as the horse heaved against the traces.

He had been tall, the sand-coloured velour of his coat complementing, almost caressing, the upright line of his body. His voice and manner were authoritative; hair free from pomade curled almost boyishly over his forehead; side whiskers traced his cheeks down to the line of his jaw. But it was his eyes Anna remembered most. Changing from grey to twinkling blue as he had spoken of his dear mama, then back to grey as he became serious once more. He had been charming, her knight in sandy armour, but who had he been and why bother to help her?

Anna looked at the card she still held between her fingers. 'Charles Lazenby', it read simply in bold black print, and Anna was too stunned to read the address.

'Her Ladyship will see you now.'

Smiling nervously, Anna followed the portly figure along acres of carpeted corridor.

Dressed in a black cutaway suit over a brilliant white shirt, he not only resembled a penguin in appearance but waddled like one too. Knowing she would fall flat on her face if she didn't stop gawking at her splendid surroundings, she forced her eyes to remain on the butler before her.

'Mrs Royce, Your Grace.'

His announcement over, the penguin closed the gilt-embellished door, leaving Anna alone on a blue carpet so vast it reminded her of the sea the day she had taken Misty to Rhyl.

'Do come in, Mrs Royce.' A woman rose from a small writing table beneath a sun-filled window, its light reflecting on the lavender silk of her dress, touching the immaculate coiffure of slightly greying hair. 'It was good of you to come . . .' Stopping mid-sentence, she lifted a pair of gold-rimmed lorgnettes, studying her visitor more closely. 'But I've seen you somewhere before. Yes . . . yes, of course, King's Choice!' She dropped the eyeglasses, letting them hang by a slim gold chain. 'You were the girl who worked at . . . at wherever it was.'

'Benjamin Freeth's, Your Ladyship,' Anna supplied with the suggestion of a curtsy.

'Ah, yes!' Lady Victoria Strathlyn waved a thin white hand. 'But you were such a frightened-looking little thing. My dear, how you have changed.'

Anna blushed, fighting the urge to look down at her skirt. She had rinsed off the mud as soon as she had got to her hotel room but a faint stain remained on the material.

'Sit down, Mrs Royce.' Giving a sharp tug to an embroidered pull hanging beside the stone fireplace, Lady Strathlyn settled into a high-backed chair. 'You must be wondering why I took the liberty of asking you to come all this way?'

Anna had been wondering. In fact the question had not left her mind since the letter had arrived, but she could wait. She was used to it by now.

A maid in a white lace-trimmed cap and apron entered with a tray, and as she laid it on a table beside her mistress, Anna gave a surprised gasp.

'Is something wrong, Mrs Royce?' Lady Strathlyn was watching her closely.

'No . . . no, it was just the surprise of seeing my china.'

'*Your* china?'

A tiny smile curving her mouth, Anna lifted her eyes confidently to the woman serving her tea. She had known the lovely porcelain produced in her pottery was worthy of the finest houses in England and now the proof was here in front of her.

'I always tend to think of it in those terms, Your Ladyship. I suppose because it is an Anna Royce design.'

'You mean, you are responsible for this?' Victoria Strathlyn looked from the tray to Anna. 'But I thought you worked for Mr . . . for that cabinet maker?'

Easing off her gloves, Anna accepted her tea, loving the touch of the paper thin porcelain cup and saucer.

'I did, but that was a long time ago. Now I manufacture my

own beauty preparations and am responsible for Gladwin's Pottery.'

'I must congratulate you on both, Mrs Royce. Each is exceptional in its way, and that brings me to why I asked you to call at Beldon House.'

Returning her own cup to the tray, Lady Strathlyn looked up. The woman sitting opposite her was no longer a half-starved, harried young girl. She handled herself well; she was polite in her speech and manner, but not unduly deferential. Whatever had happened to Anna Royce had changed not only her circumstances, it had changed the woman herself.

'Some weeks ago my son bought one of your beauty boxes for his sister. She showed it to the Princess . . . they have been friends from childhood . . . and in turn the Princess asked that one be made for her. As you will appreciate, Mrs Royce, Her Majesty could not journey to Birmingham where I believe my son purchased his sister's gift, nor would propriety allow that the Palace contact you directly. But like all mothers, Her Majesty desires to give her daughter the present she has asked for. Therefore it fell to me, as Lady-in-Waiting to Her Majesty, to write to you.'

Anna's mind began to spin. The Queen! The Queen had asked for her cosmetics. The Queen wanted to give her daughter an Anna Royce beauty box.

'Would you be prepared to supply one?'

'What? I . . . I'm sorry.' Anna pulled her thoughts together. 'Forgive me, Lady Strathlyn, but . . .'

'I know, my dear, it is not every day the Queen asks for one's products. You do realise, I presume, that my letter could not enlarge upon the true reason for your coming to London. Her Majesty does not approve of her . . . shall we say . . . private matters, being widely known.'

'I understand perfectly, Lady Strathlyn.' Anna put down her cup with fingers that shook.

* * *

'Excuse me, madam.' One of the hotel maids entered Anna's room when she called: 'Come in.' 'A gentleman asked me to deliver this, he's waiting downstairs.'

Anna took the familiar card and smiled at the request scrawled across the back of it: 'Have dinner with me and make my miserable life happy.'

'Would you ask the gentleman to wait? Please tell him I will be down in a few minutes.'

She had no intention of making his miserable life happy by dining with him, but she did want to thank him for his kindness yesterday. The maid curtsied and withdrew, leaving Anna to tidy her hair. She had taken a bath since returning to the hotel, hoping the warm water would help soothe her mind, but try as she would the wonder of the afternoon would not be dismissed and she still felt half-dazed. Pushing a last pin into the heavy swathes of her hair, Anna looked at herself in the cheval mirror.

'You have met a Lady-in-Waiting to the Queen,' she whispered. 'What will Maggie have to say about that?'

Charles Lazenby smiled as Anna joined him, his teeth white against his tanned skin. Why hadn't she noticed he was tanned when he spoke to her yesterday?

'Good evening, thank you for agreeing to come downstairs.' The voice was the same: musical, soft, yet not without strength, and the grey-blue eyes held open appreciation as they settled on her.

A faint blush painting her cheeks, Anna answered.

'I must thank you, Mr Lazenby, for helping me yesterday.'

'You find the hotel to your liking?'

'I do,' Anna nodded, her gaze shifting around the foyer. 'I could not have chosen better, Mr Lazenby.'

'Then if you are pleased, perhaps you will reward my efforts.'

'Perhaps!' Anna was amazed at her own answer, amazed how at ease she felt with this tall elegant man, amazed at the way she allowed herself to be drawn towards a sofa in a secluded alcove.

'My reward, should you grant it, Mrs . . .?'

'Royce . . . Anna Royce.'

'My reward, should you grant it, Anna, is that you call me Charles.'

'I don't think that is too much to ask after the help you gave me yesterday.'

His smile widened. 'Kind as well as beautiful, Anna, your bounty is double.'

Why did she not object to an almost total stranger addressing her by her Christian name? Anna thought as Charles Lazenby smiled again, his eyes changing from grey to twinkling blue. Surely it was not the most acceptable procedure but suddenly social etiquette no longer seemed so very important.

'And the answer to my question?'

'What question?' She frowned.

'My dear Anna, have you forgotten already? I asked if you would dine with me this evening?'

She had forgotten and his reminder brought her up sharp. He was little more than a stranger. She had spoken to him yesterday for the first time in her life, and that had come out of the blue. There had been no formal introduction, no one to vouch for him; it would be sheer madness to trust herself to him; better by far to thank him again and return to her room.

'No, no thank you.' She was terrified enough of the Conway: she had never stayed in a hotel in her life and worried that each move she made would be a wrong one. The thought of eating in a public dining room scared her even more.

'Please, don't say no, Anna.'

Perhaps she did owe him something in return for his assistance yesterday, and maybe, in the future, her business might require she dine in a public dining room. A start would have to be made sometime, it might just as well be now.

Putting on a brave face, Anna smiled.

'Very well Mr Lazenby, I won't say no.'

Seated at a secluded table, Anna stared at the array of cutlery and glasses set before her. What on earth were they all for? Nothing but a knife and fork was used in Roker Street, and only a spoon if the meal were broth; it had been the same in Wednesbury.

In deferential silence a waiter placed a small dish before her.

Did she use a fork or a spoon? Anna's hand hovered in her lap. Edward had shown her a setting of King's Choice but she had only appreciated its beauty, without asking what each implement was used for.

'How was your day, Anna?'

Charles picked up the fork furthest from his plate. Breathing an inward sigh of relief, Anna followed suit.

At last the meal was finished and she relaxed with her favourite cup of tea though Charles had expressed a preference for brandy. Around them other diners stole surreptitious glances at the tanned features of her handsome escort.

'I still can't believe what happened. It's too much like Bella Castleton's tuppenny novels.'

'Whose tuppenny novels?'

'Oh, they're not Bella's, not really,' Anna laughed. 'She doesn't write them, just sells them in her shop in Coseley . . . that's where I live. The girls at the mill love to read them. Filled with such soft notions as the rich young lord marrying the poor working girl, they are. Totally removed from reality. Perhaps that is their chief attraction.'

'And that idea holds no attraction for you, Anna?' There was an undercurrent in his question, a strange intensity that held them silent for a moment.

'I believe in facing reality,' she said, meeting his penetrating stare. 'It doesn't happen that way in real life. Girls like those in Coseley don't marry lords, rich or poor. Work is all they know or will likely ever know.'

'But you, Anna, given the opportunity, would you marry a rich lord?'

'Rich or poor, lord or mill worker, it would make no difference if I loved him.' Anna lifted her head, the movement stealing light from the chandelier then returning it in a thousand tiny red-gold sparks. 'But I don't believe in fairy tales . . . at least not that sort.'

She had thought her straightforward answer would dissuade him from his close scrutiny but it remained just as intense and his eyes had the look Edward's had often held when they had walked together on the moors above the village.

'What happened today was like a fairy tale. I still can hardly believe it.'

'Tell me about it and perhaps my cavalier actions can be practised once more.' Lifting his brandy glass, he eyed her closely. 'Though I shan't be able to say I don't believe in fairies, for you, Anna, have the golden beauty of Titania herself.'

'Who?' she asked quizzically.

'Titania . . . Queen of the Fairies.'

'Oh! Well, it wasn't the Queen of the Fairies I went to see this afternoon,' Anna replied. It poured from her then, the whole business of going to Beldon House, and Charles avidly watched the movement of her lovely face and the emerald fire in her eyes. She was every bit as beautiful as on the day he had seen her cross a street in Birmingham where he had followed her into a shop, only to find as he walked in that she was no longer visible.

'Oh, heavens!' Anna pressed a hand against her lips.

'Heaven is not my domain, Anna, but I will move it and earth too to take that crestfallen look from your face. Whatever it is that is worrying you can be overcome, you know . . . you have only to tell me what it is?'

'Me and my big mouth. Maggie says it's as big as a Parish oven and one day it will get me into trouble, and she's right.'

'You have a delectable mouth, Anna.' Charles replaced

the brandy glass on the table, topping up its contents from a cut-glass decanter. 'I'm sure it could give offence to no one.'

'You don't understand,' she said through her fingers, 'I promised Lady Strathlyn I wouldn't tell anyone that the Queen has asked for my beauty box – and in less than four hours I've revealed it all.'

'Have you told anyone other than myself?'

'No . . . just you, but it is still unforgivable, I made a promise and I've broken it. If the Palace or Lady Strathlyn were to find out . . .'

'They will never hear it from me, Anna.'

There was no reproach in his voice, just sadness. He had shown her kindness and she was repaying it with mistrust.

'Oh, I didn't mean it to sound that way!' Impulsively she put a hand on his.' Of course I don't think you would repeat what I've said. It's myself I can't trust . . . me and my big mouth . . . how long before I blurt the whole thing out again? And next time it might be to someone not so understanding as you.'

Closing strong fingers over the hand on his own, Charles Lazenby looked at the woman seated opposite, knowing he wanted her. Taking a moment to quell the strong desire her touch had stirred in him, he smiled reassuringly.

'It was the excitement that loosened your tongue, Anna. Given a few days it will fade. You will not feel the same need to share it with anyone. Believe me, you will not betray the confidence of Her Majesty.'

'I do hope you're right.' Anna was still not convinced. 'Maggie will give me a right tongue lathering when I get home, and it will be no more than I deserve.'

'You are returning home tomorrow?' he forced himself to answer naturally.

'Yes, the eleven o' clock train.'

'But you have seen nothing of London. That is a pity, Anna, for though you might have difficulty in accepting it after that fracas at the station yesterday, it does have some beautiful sights.'

Withdrawing her hand from his, Anna played absently with her white damask knapkin. She had never used one before, and as with the cutlery only knew what to do with it from watching Charles. He was from an entirely different background to herself; everything about him, clothes, speech, manner, made that glaringly obvious. He was part of the world Jacob Rewcastle had tried to buy Philip into by sending him away to college. He might even be of the aristocracy, the wealthy titled gentry that had bred Sir Robert Daines, but there the similarity ended. There was no spiteful cruelty in this man, of that she felt certain, no unnatural trait that wanted only to see others cower before him.

'I would like to show you some of the city, Anna,' Charles began earnestly. 'Its theatres and art galleries, buildings and parks. The Albert Hall, Saint Paul's Cathedral . . . there are so many things I know you would enjoy.'

'I would enjoy seeing them, Charles.' She twisted the napkin, it helped keep her eyes from that handsome face. 'And Misty would love hearing about them, but there just isn't time.'

'Misty?'

'My daughter.' Anna did look up then, a tender smile playing about her lips. 'She's almost nine and interested in everything. In fact, Maggie says she's such a fidget, wanting to know the top and bottom of everything there's no keeping up with her.'

'Then why doesn't she give her some of those books to read?'

'Books!' Anna looked perplexed. 'What books?'

'Bella Castleton's tuppenny novels.'

Anna laughed aloud, drawing several enquiring faces her way.

'Maggie would never have that. Maggie Fellen took me in when I moved to Coseley. We live in the same house and she looks after Misty most of the time. Too much of the time, if truth be told.' The smile left Anna's eyes. 'I leave too much to Maggie, I know I do, nearly all my time is given to the business. It's not fair on her, and I've tried telling her so and getting her to agree to some help but she won't hear of it. Keep yourself busy and there will be no time for the devil to put his oar in, is Maggie's philosophy.'

'She sounds a sensible woman.'

'She is.'

'Then why not do as she says? Why sit here all evening when you could be busy seeing some of London? And think how fascinated Misty will be when you tell her all you have seen.'

It was a temptation. Misty and Maggie both would be enthralled to hear of what she had seen, but Anna hesitated. It wasn't right to go gallivanting about the place with a man who was almost a stranger . . . and especially not at night.

'I could hire a chaperone.' Charles smiled, understanding her dilemma. Edwardian England had not changed so much. It still imposed tight conventions upon women; its fierce public morality always ready to shred a tarnished reputation.

'But today has been a strain, it has tired you. Maybe a carriage ride through Regent's Park in the morning before you take your train?' He rose to his feet, tall and elegant in a deep blue evening coat reaching almost to his knees. He raised her hand gallantly to his lips. 'You will ride with me tomorrow, Anna?'

His mouth whispered the question but his eyes asked more. Deep dark tunnels, they drew her inexorably where she had no wish to go. There was no sense in prolonging things, nothing to be gained from agreeing to ride with him tomorrow. But on the other hand, Anna told herself flatly, there wasn't much to be lost either. When she got on that train tomorrow Charles Lazenby would melt from her life like mist in a summer sun.

At her nod of agreement he touched his mouth to the back of her hand and walked from the hotel, the elusive violet scent of her perfume filling his nostrils, his mind already wrestling with the problem of how to keep Anna Royce in his life.

Chapter Twelve

Anna had been back from London a week when Charles came to Birmingham.

'He left this, Anna.' Hester, wide-eyed with curiosity, handed Anna a familiar card. 'And he said he would call every day until he saw you. He's already been here twice but I thought I'd better not say where you lived.'

Anna took the card.

'You did right, Hester. Maggie's making enough fuss over moving house, she's no desire to live over against Woodgreen. "Yon side's too lah-di-dah," she says, so heaven knows what she would do if Charles Lazenby landed on her doorstep!'

'He was quite a looker.'

Anna laughed outright.

'You don't have to ask, Hester Fine, I've known you too long. What you mean is, who is he and how did we meet?'

Hester's hazel eyes twinkled.

'Kettle's on, come and tell me the whole story.'

'And now he's in Birmingham and intent on finding you, Anna?' Hester had listened wide-eyed. 'Eee . . . it really is like Bella Castleton's tuppenny romances. Just think . . . Lady Lazenby.'

'Now don't go getting ideas, Hester.' Anna tried to sound calm but as the bell tinkled and her friend disappeared into the shop, Anna's heart was racing.

Eight o' clock, Charles had said, earlier that morning when

leaving his card with Hester and even that was too long to wait before seeing her again. In the back room of the shop Anna slipped into the turquoise taffeta gown she had bought that afternoon from Monsieur Pierre's. It had been wildly expensive but for this one occasion she forgot the cost. She looked at herself in the mirror. Her stomach was flat and her breasts high, even after carrying two children . . . two. The eyes looking back from the mirror changed from green to transparent blue; her son would be almost thirteen now. Was he strong . . . would he be tall . . . did he know about her?

'I'll leave the door on the latch. Eee, Anna, you look gorgeous!'

Hester stood admiring her in the doorway.

'You're going to make the loveliest Lady Lazenby they've ever had.' She darted across the room, taking Anna in a close hug. 'Have a lovely evening,' she said, 'you deserve it.'

There was little time before Charles arrived and Anna, unable to keep still, began to rearrange a lace-draped alcove, placing a tall-necked, cloud-pink porcelain vase at its centre. 'The Italians have such an eye for colour.' She laughed at her own mimicry.

'I agree, but even the most gifted of them could not capture the beauty standing before me.'

Startled, Anna whirled round, colour tingeing her cheeks.

'Charles! I . . . I didn't hear you come in.'

'I had not meant to startle you but will not apologise for having done so.' He moved forward, smiling down at her. 'No man should apologise for being the cause of such wide eyes . . . such beautiful eyes.'

'I was day-dreaming,' Anna replied, a flurry of nerves filling her stomach.

'I think I too am day-dreaming.' His low, seductive voice wreathed about her like black smoke. 'That can be the only explanation for what I am seeing, a dream too beautiful to be true.' He watched the colour deepen in her cheeks, the brilliance of her eyes against the translucence of her skin.

What he had thought in London was true: Anna Royce was the most beautiful woman he had ever seen.

'I thought The Royal Hotel for dinner, if you have no objection?'

He stepped aside at the negative shake of her head, making no attempt to touch her as they went outside to the waiting hansom. He could wait.

'The key.' Anna turned back to the door. 'I mustn't forget to lock up. Hester would have a fit.'

Handing her into the hansom, he caught the elusive fragrance of violets, a fragrance that had haunted him ever since meeting this woman, as she had haunted his mind.

Anna's nerves were stretched taut. She trusted Charles Lazenby, it was her own disturbed emotions that made her nervous.

Their table was in a secluded alcove, some distance from the four-piece orchestra, and Anna, conscious of eyes following them as they crossed the beautifully appointed room, was glad of the privacy it afforded.

All around waiters moved on silent feet, black tailcoats worn over white shirts, and not one of them resembled a penguin.

'What are you hiding behind that Mona Lisa smile?' In the soft light her hair was a vivid crown, all the more alluring for not being adorned with a silly assortment of the feathers so beloved of society women.

'A what smile?' Anna asked, blushing again at what she saw in his look.

'Mona Lisa. It is a painting by Da Vinci, famous for the smile on the face of its subject. It has haunted men for centuries, driven them mad wondering what lies behind it. The same way that your smile is driving me mad now, Anna.'

'Well, I won't let you go mad wondering.' She met his eyes as she told him what had amused her. Listening, he smiled inwardly. He had always thought of Groves as a penguin waddling importantly through Beldon. Strange Anna should see him in just that way.

'What did you think of Beldon House?' Charles asked as their glasses were replenished.

'Whew!' Anna raised her eyes towards the ceiling. 'It defies description. I can only say it was absolutely breathtaking – all those pictures of people in strange clothes, and the furniture . . . I never thought such things existed.'

'And the people?' He watched the animated play of her delicate oval face, the fluttering descriptive movements of her slender hands.

'I only saw Lady Strathlyn.' Tentatively she sipped the wine he'd poured into her glass. 'I suppose there might be a husband somewhere but I know there's a daughter and a son because her Ladyship mentioned them. She was very nice. I expected . . . I don't really know what I expected.'

Creamy shoulders lifted in a shrug, closing the enticing valley between her breasts which peeped tantalisingly over the décolletage of her turquoise gown.

'Will you allow me to escort you home?' he asked, forcing his eyes away from the tormenting sight.

Surprised by the suddenness of his question, Anna glanced at his unfinished brandy. Had she said something to displease him? Had he for some reason become embarrassed at being seen with her? Not wanting to add to any possible unease, she rose.

Taking the short silk-lined cape from the back of her chair, Charles placed it around her shoulders, one finger touching the long curve of her neck beneath the sweep of her hair. Outside the night was a mixture of warm moonlight and darkest velvet sky. Anna couldn't resist staring up at it. It was a sky made for more than just a journey home. This was a night for walking on the heath, for making love in the shadows of Moses Table.

'Allow me, Anna.'

Charles touched a hand to her elbow and she was glad the darkness of the hansom hid the blushes painted by her thoughts. At her side in the shadowed closeness his arm touched against her, then as she would have moved, went about her, drawing her against the hardness of him, his other arm sliding around her back, the palm of his hand between her shoulder blades, its strength preventing her from pulling away – always supposing she had wanted to.

'Anna,' he breathed against her ear, 'my beautiful Anna.' His lips trailed her cheek, pressing a feathering of kisses to her parted mouth. 'My beautiful, beautiful Anna.'

Her eyes closed, everything spinning together in the dark as his mouth closed over hers.

'You're so lovely, Anna.' He broke away. 'I can't tell you how lovely. You are like an exquisite flower, so soft and fragrant.' His voice sounded faraway, drifting in her mind like an echo; a voice within a voice, carrying her on a spiral away from her own common sense.

'Anna.' He still held her close, his mouth against the perfumed silk of her hair. 'I want you to come to London with me. I want you to be with me always. I've wanted you since I first saw you cross a street here in Birmingham. I followed you into a shop, only to feel like a child that had lost some precious toy when I found you were not there.'

'You saw me in Birmingham?' A pulse beat in her brow, resting against his temple. From the recesses of Anna's mind came Lady Strathlyn's words: 'My son purchased it for his sister . . . Birmingham, or so I believe.'

'Lady Strathlyn's son bought an Anna Royce beauty box.' She drew away from him. 'He bought it for his sister.'

'I must confess . . . it was I.'

'But, but your name . . .'

'Is different to my mother's? She took her name and title from a second marriage.'

Pulling free, Anna sought his eyes in the gloom.

'Why didn't you tell me that night in London when we had dinner together? You let me go on about Beldon House and never said a word . . . why?'

He tried to take her back in his arms but Anna resisted, a little of her pleasure gone.

'You were like an excited child, Anna.' He took her hand in his, pressing the palm against his mouth. 'To tell you I knew the house would have robbed you of that excitement, and robbed me of seeing the pleasure in your lovely face as you talked. Why should I do that when the fact of where I live is unimportant?'

'Then why didn't I see you there?'

He released her hand. Light from a street lamp caught her eyes, endowing them with sudden brilliance. How could he tell her he had deliberately stayed away? That his mother was too shrewd a woman not to guess at the feelings he harboured for her visitor?

'Didn't I tell you I was meeting someone? The day you visited Beldon, I was with a very old friend who was returning from Europe.'

The carriage rolled smoothly on, the clatter of the horses' hooves loud on the cobbled road, the encouraging commands of the driver urging them on. Everything seemed the same as it had a few minutes before but somewhere there had been a change.

'Does that answer your question, my sweet interrogator?'

His hand still cupped her chin. Anna pulled away. She didn't know whether it answered her or not. Charles had no need to lie to her yet something inside warned her that he had.

'So, will you come with me to London, Anna . . . please?'

'And what would Lady Strathlyn say to that?'

'She wouldn't have to know,' he returned quickly.

Anna felt the last of her enjoyment drain from the night and her body tensed, waiting for what had yet to come.

'We would gradually introduce the idea of our being together.'

If he had any sense of the impropriety of his proposal, he didn't show it.

'I see!' Anna gathered the silk folds of her cape, holding

them almost protectively across her breasts. 'And will you be living at Beldon House too while this . . . acclimatisation . . . is going on?'

'Beldon House?'

She felt him turn, felt those cool eyes regarding her in the dimness, but made no effort to meet them.

'Of course! That is where I would be living if I came to London with you, isn't it?'

'No, Anna!' He was so casual. 'I had thought of something a little more private, somewhere we could more easily be alone. I could find you a nice little house in the suburbs, away from the bustle of London.'

And from Beldon House. Anna swallowed, tasting bitterness. That was what had really brought him to Birmingham. He wanted a new toy, one that would warm his bed. Well, he certainly fooled you, my girl, she thought with a grim smile. You thought he was helping you up there in London when all he was doing was softening you up, and now he's moved in for the kill. Suddenly she wanted to laugh, loudly and hysterically. Charles Lazenby was no different from Jacob Rewcastle except that when it came to the business of wanting a mistress, the older man didn't beat about the bush.

The carriage stopped in the quiet street in front of Hester and Reuben's house and Anna jumped down without waiting for help, not wanting him to touch her. On the footpath she turned to look back at the man leaning out of the window, his handsome face clearly visible in the moonlight.

'Anna . . .'

'That's a high wall you are sitting on,' she interrupted, 'it separates your world from mine. You should make up your mind which side you want to be on . . . it could be a long painful fall.' Forcing a smile to her lips, she went on, 'It was a pleasurable evening but as for your invitation, thank you, no. I will not be accompanying you to London.'

Climbing the stairs to Hester's spare room, Anna willed her jolted nerves to settle.

'Mark it down to experience,' she whispered, stepping out of the turquoise gown. 'You won't make the same mistake twice.'

'We just can't manage, Anna. Orders is floodin' in wi' each day, an' though I've taken on new 'ands, we can't keep up.'

'So what do you suggest, Seth?'

'I 'adn't wanted to bother thee, I knows tha's busy, but it seemed to me as tha should be told. It's a regular avilanche we bin gettin'. Orders for everything from a vase to a full bankitin' suite.'

Anna smiled at the old man's pronunciation but his meaning was clear enough. John Harris at Wigmore Bank had already told her of the rapid upward surge in her profits and advised her to invest them. She would do that, of course, but after her own fashion.

'So what do we do?' she asked again.

Seth pulled his side whiskers and pushed his lower lip before answering.

'If tha wants to fill these orders . . . and tha'd be a fool not to . . . then only way ah sees it is to get another place. This'n just ain't big enough.'

'Any suggestions?' Anna watched another tug of his whiskers, another pensive twist of the mouth.

'There's several seein' as nobbut us seems to be working. Theer's Boucher's down the road aways. Jeremiah 'ad two kilns a firing theer at one time. An' then theer's Myton's, they 'ad two an' all, mostly piss pots they med.'

Anna glanced away, a smile threatening.

Seth's choice of language was just his way; he meant no offence and she would take none.

She asked instead, 'Which would be best for our use, Seth?'

'Six an' two threes, Anna. They would both do. Both back on to cut, as this place does. Tha could still get pots away by barge.'

'Pots' was hardly an adequate description of the beautiful fragile porcelain but the old man would not thank her for another; they had been 'pots' whatever he or his father had produced, and 'pots' they would always be to him.

Anna went to the window overlooking the cobbled yard. It was no longer desolate and empty as it had been that first day. Now men and women hurried busily between drying sheds and packing houses, and the faces that glanced up smiled as they caught sight of her.

'Two kilns, Seth,' she said quietly. 'That would make them expensive.'

'Ah reckon not.' Behind her, he could see the set of her head, the determined grasp of her small hand on a window bar. 'They 'as two kilns right enough, whereas this place as just the one, but they've stood empty a lot longer'n Gladwin's an' all. Way ah sees it is this.' He pulled his whiskers, particles of dried clay flaking from his hands. 'Thee mek tha offer for whichever one tha chooses an' leave it at that. Neither Jeremiah Boucher nor Joseph Myton is like to refuse. They'n 'ad them dead potteries on their 'ands too long.'

Anna tapped a finger against the dusty glass. Could she work both places? Would the craze for her dainty tea services and elegant dinner suites last, or was she riding the crest of a wave that would ebb, leaving them empty again? Her finger ceased its movement. What she had done once could be done again. If and when fragile porcelain lost its hold on the market then it would be up to her to find something to take its place.

'What about the running of another place, Seth. You can't be in both. Can you find a man you can trust?'

'I reckon so, I knows all folk hereabouts and they'd give their hearts for a chance of a job. They'll serve thee well, Anna, as do the ones 'ere at Gladwin's.'

'But without you to teach them, Seth, will they be able to produce the type of ware I've come to expect?'

Seth tucked his thumbs beneath the string that held the clay-covered apron to his waist.

'There are some older ones who can teach the young 'uns, same as we did here. And besides,' his head thrust forward authoritatively, 'they'll have Seth Gladwin to answer to should they not come up to scratch.'

'Get them then, Seth, as many as you think we will need to run both Boucher and Myton, and leave the rest to me . . .'

'Tha's thinkin' o' gettin' both? That be four kilns extra to this 'un. I know tha has some kind o' magic in thee, lass, but . . . but does think tha can fill 'em all?'

'It's no magic on my part, Seth. Your skill has brought all this about, and I think it will keep us going for a long time yet.'

Turning from the window, Anna picked up the bag she had left on the dust-covered table, making a mental note to get the office cleared and into working efficiency.

'Can you find a sign writer?'

'A sign writer?' Seth repeated, his bushy brows drawing together in concentration. 'Theer's bin no call for such in these parts for long enough but I reckon I knows one. But what does want sign writer for?'

'Read this, Seth.' Handing him the letter, Anna watched him read and then read again, his old hands shaking. At last he looked up, tears channelling the lines of his face.

'If only my old dad could 'ave seen this.'

'The whole of Burslem is going to see it, Seth,' Anna said proudly. 'We are going to have a sign painted the width of those doors out there: "Gladwin's Pottery. By Appointment to His Majesty the King. Suppliers of Fine Porcelain."'

'But 'ow did tha manage this, lass?' He still held the letter in trembling fingers, looking first at it and then at the young woman who was breathing new life into his own.

'Remember the blue and gold banqueting suite you made nigh on a year ago? It was accepted by the Palace, and that,' she nodded towards the letter, 'is the outcome. We've only just started, Seth. Whatever the King has, all the big nobs want the same. You think we are flooded with orders now but just you wait . . . before very long Anna Royce china will be in every fine house in the country.'

She slipped the letter back inside her bag. This was the third of her paper diamonds, but precious as it was, it was not the one she desired most. That was King's Choice. And sooner or later, Edward, she vowed inwardly, I'm going to get it.

'Mary Cresswell is a well-meanin' soul and 'as bin as good a neighbour as a woman could hanker for, but I don't think as how 'er's right for shop.'

'I thought the same, I must admit, Maggie.' Anna looked up from checking her accounts. 'I will have to get a younger woman . . . question is, who?'

The front room that was part of Maggie's old house had been left mostly to Mary's care since they had moved to Woodgreen. Busier than ever, Anna found less and less time to go there.

'An' 'ave you thought of one in Birmingham? Young married wenches 'ave a way of gettin' pregnant.' Maggie watched Anna's pale face, her eyes enormous inside dark circles. Anna worked too hard, driving herself all the time, and for what? A revenge that would kill her in the getting.

'What if Hester starts a child? I can't see Reuben bein' so happy with her workin' when that happens, an' don't tell me you can manage yourself, y'ave enough on your 'ands.'

The same thought had plagued Anna for months now. How would she manage without Hester? True Ellen Passmore, the girl Hester had taken on, was confident and efficient, but had she got Hester's touch . . . could she make every woman who came into the shop feel cosseted, that Anna Royce existed solely to please her? These were all questions that needed answering.

'I will talk to Hester and sort things out but right now I must finish looking over these accounts. I'm seeing John Harris at the bank tomorrow and I want all the facts at my fingertips.' Keeping the accounts herself was time-consuming but there was only one other she would trust to do them in her place. Tomorrow she would go to see Joby Timmins.

'Something is pushin' you, Anna wench.' Maggie refused to be dismissed. 'I don't know what. All I do know is it wasn't pushin' you a few months since an' it's nowt to do wi' Jacob Rewcastle neither. You tek it steady, lass. The devil still rides though the back be sore, Anna. There's no chuckin' 'im off when y'ave 'ad enough.'

Maggie was right, of course. Anna, her head still bent, closed her eyes wearily then opened them again as the handsome face of Charles Lazenby imprinted itself upon the lids. Something *was* pushing her, burning as strong as the desire to regain King's Choice, and tomorrow she would take the first step towards dousing the flames.

Unlike a tuppenny novel heroine she wouldn't have a title but, by God, she would have everything else. She was only a mill girl, only good enough to be a rich man's mistress, was she? Well, watch me, Charles, she vowed silently. Just watch what a Black Country girl can do.

John Harris ushered her into his office with a glance at the long-faced Burrows. He had been hoping Anna would call at the bank; her profits were on a meteoric rise. It would be to her benefit to consider using some of the money for further investment.

'That's sound advice, Mr Harris.' Anna listened to his recommendation that she should buy stocks. 'But I have an idea of my own.'

John Harris smiled.

'You usually have, Mrs Royce, and so far they have all been sound. However, the way you are piling up capital, I felt I ought to offer my advice.'

'That is always welcome, Mr Harris,' Anna flashed him a smile, 'but I have decided on what I want to do . . . only to be frank I don't quite know how to go about it.'

John Harris pressed his hands together, tapping his fingers

against his lips and watching Anna with shrewd, assessing eyes. The shiny black skirt and worn coat were gone, replaced by a grey gabardine suit. Button boots he guessed had seen more cardboard insoles than she would ever admit had given way to smart leather shoes. Mrs Anna Royce had changed and not just in appearance. As she talked he sensed a deepening determination, a will not only to succeed but to excel.

'I wish to expand my business.' Anna watched for a reaction but saw none. 'I want bigger premises and they must give me access to the larger towns.'

'Have you thought of building your own? That way they would be tailor made to your requirements.'

Anna waited only long enough to exhale.

'The shops I want are already built. Tell me . . . have you heard of Ellis Hardware?'

A puzzled frown drew his brows together slightly and his hands were lowered to the desk.

'Yes, but . . .'

'I want them!' Anna intervened.

'Have you any idea of the business they are doing?'

Anna was prepared, she had guessed he would ask this.

'I am quite aware it could be better,' she answered levelly.

'But hardware!' John Harris sounded concerned. 'Forgive me, Mrs Royce, but is that really your line?'

Anna stared determinedly at the man on the other side of the shining desk.

'That is exactly what I want,' she stated flatly. 'Will the bank back me with a loan should my funds prove insufficient to cover the purchase?'

'You are very much in the black, Mrs Royce, a strong healthy balance, but . . .'

'I have no time for buts, Mr Harris.' Anna's eyes flashed like emeralds embedded in ice. 'Only answers. If you can't meet my requirements then I must place my business in other hands.'

Three months later she became sole owner of Ellis Hardware and the same day cancelled all orders to Rewcastle Mill. She had one more paper diamond and the biggest, most brilliant of all, had come one step nearer.

Buying the chain of hardware stores had taken up all her attention, or was that her excuse for not talking to Hester about more staff? Anna knew she had been putting off the moment but now she must face it. All the way to Birmingham the question gnawed at her. What will you do if Hester leaves? And when she finally walked into the shop, she had still found no answer.

'Well, I'm not pregnant!' Hester's pretty face was flushed. 'And I'm not leaving or likely to be yet, despite what Maggie Fellen thinks. Because they had a kid the minute the wedding ring went on their finger, they think everybody else is the same.'

'Maggie didn't mean it that way,' Anna soothed her friend's ruffled feelings. 'She only meant to point out that I should be prepared for any likelihood, such as your being away from the shop for a while.'

Spooning sugar into the tea she had poured, she gave the cup to Hester.

'You know . . . if you only went down with a cold for a few days I would be in a right mess. I already seem to have to be in a dozen different places at the same time.' She took her own tea, stirring it absently. 'Honestly, Hester! We are going to have to do something. Ellen is good, I know, but we couldn't expect her to have to manage alone.'

'I've been giving the same matter some thought, I must admit, Anna.' Hester sighed. 'I feel as you do about Ellen. She's quick and works well but . . .' Putting her cup on the table that separated them, Hester leaned forward.

'Look, Anna, I don't know how you will feel about this but what about taking on some young girls and giving them one evening a week staff training? I thought in addition you might offer them a small commission. That way they will learn the gentle art of selling more quickly, don't you agree?'

'Sounds a good idea.' Anna nodded.

'I've also been thinking about your porcelain. You can't show much of it here.'

'True!' she interrupted. 'But with buying Ellis Hardware, I don't want to take on another shop just yet. But there is another way of showing customers a wider range of what Gladwin's Pottery produces.'

'How?'

Anna pushed her cup aside.

'Why not a catalogue?' she asked. 'We could have very posh ones printed and place them discreetly on the tables. That way customers would be able to see the whole range: designs, colours, the lot. Then if they wanted anything we could take their orders here in the shop!' She sat back. 'What do you think?'

For a long moment Hester remained straight-faced then her mouth widened into a beaming smile.

'What do I think?' she said delightedly. 'I think you're a blooming genius, Mrs Royce!'

The catalogue proved an immediate success: it had a cover of silver card, with scarlet and gold royal arms topping those marvellously influential words 'By Appointment', and inside the first page showed a spray of pink and burgundy fuschias trailing tastefully from the top left-hand corner to the bottom right, enclosing an elegantly scripted 'Exclusive to Anna Royce'.

Every day brought a flood of orders as more and more people discovered her pretty china, and more of the newly rich steel magnates wanted what was in the homes of the gentry. All three of her potteries were working and still demand exceeded output, but Anna would not exchange quality for quantity. She must keep all her products absolutely perfect.

On that she was building her reputation. On that she would string her paper diamonds. On that rested the future of her daughter and of the son for whom she longed, the son who would never know her.

Chapter Thirteen

From the curtained alcove of her bedroom window Anna watched her daughter in the garden below. At eleven years old she was gangly as a young colt, all arms and legs, and growing at a frightening rate.

It seemed only yesterday that Misty had been born, only yesterday Edward had been taken from her, and only a little more than yesterday since she had left her son.

Her son! Anna leaned her head against the cool glass. Would this longing for him ever leave her? Would she ever have the courage to claim him?

She closed her eyes, seeing again the tiny crumpled face, head covered in golden down.

It would not take courage to claim him; the courage had come in leaving him in Wednesbury. They had been so close to sending for him, Edward and herself, but he had died before they could and now . . .

Anna opened her eyes, letting them fix on the tall chimney stacks of the steel mill, a skyline so like the one of her childhood.

Now she could not face up to what might happen if she disrupted his life; could not take the risk of seeing nothing but hatred in those pale blue eyes, of being condemned for leaving him.

'I did leave you, my little love,' she murmured, her very soul twisting with pain. 'I did leave you but I did it for you, so you could live in peace. I love you, my son, my child . . . I love you so much and I always will.'

Lowering her glance to the garden she saw in her imagination a tall young lad with hair like corn silk, the picture only deepening the longing that was always within her.

He would be working by this time, always presuming there was work to be had in Wednesbury. Would he come bouncing in at night when his day's work was done, like the Cresswell twins did? Was he as happy as they and as healthy? And her father, what of him . . . was he still alive even? Anna's heart twisted, knowing she would never go back; she could not take the risk.

Yes, she had done what she could for her nameless son, but what about Misty? She deserved more than Coseley could provide. Stepping away from the window, Anna sighed. This was not going to be easy.

'But I don't want to go to school! I want to stay with you and Grammie.'

'I know you do, darling, but Grammie needs a life of her own too. She has looked after both of us for so long and running this house is not easy. We can't expect her to go on forever taking responsibility for us.'

What I really mean is, she can't go on taking responsibility for you, Anna thought guiltily, and it was happening more and more often. As business boomed she was called on more regularly to give directions or decisions, often leaving Misty with Maggie or the Cresswells.

'Try to understand, sweetheart, it's for your own good.'

It wasn't the whole truth and Anna looked to Maggie for support but the look on those well-loved features told her she was on her own.

'I do understand.' The golden hair, still like so much summer-morning mist, swirled about Misty's face. 'You want to get rid of me. I . . . I'm in the way here . . . a nuisance under your feet.'

'Oh, Misty, that's not so and you know it!' Anna tried to take her daughter in her arms but the child twisted away, her mouth tight. 'You could never be in the way, either of me or Grammie.'

'Then let me stay. You say the business is taking too much of your time so why not let me help? That's all I want, to help.'

From her chair against the fire Maggie Fellen watched the child she had nursed from birth, reading the pain of rejection in that small face as clearly as though it were a book in her hands; and watching too that older child who had come to her out of a dark, rain-torn night. It wasn't an easy decision Anna was making but it was one that had to be hers alone.

'And I want you to,' she was saying softly, 'that is part of the reason I want you to go to boarding school. I've seen your sketches, darling, they are good . . . very good. I want you to develop that talent, to learn presentation and design, experiment with colour and materials. None of which you can do here.'

That much at least was true. Misty had inherited Edward's eye for drawing and was already showing signs of Anna's own flair for design, and there was no school in Coseley that could take that talent and mould it. Anna took a breath and plunged on.

'Think of it, Misty. If you can learn those things, you can join the business. We could use a good packaging designer.'

'You really mean that? You . . . you're not pretending, are you, just to get me to agree to go away to school without a lot of fuss?'

Her cornflower blue eyes were no longer tearful and Anna breathed a silent prayer of thankfulness. Who could blame Misty if she did kick up a fuss? Certainly not a mother who knew the heartbreak of losing a parent.

'No, darling, I'm not pretending.' She smiled at her half-grown daughter. 'You do well at school, learn as much as you can, and when you leave there will be a place for you in the business.'

'I suppose you knows what you be doing.'

Misty had gone to bed and now Maggie voiced her critical concern. 'Misty is your daughter after all.'

'You must agree it's for the best, Maggie?' Anna settled on the floor, her head resting against the knee of her old friend. 'She really hasn't anyone here she cares to be with other than the Cresswell twins, and they are getting a bit too grown up to drag a schoolgirl with them everywhere they go.'

'Mmm, I sees your point, Anna, and I goes along with what you said about girl needin' the kind of schoolin' that ain't to be got in Coseley. But what did you mean about me needin' more rest? I be as good as ever I was an' don't you go sayin' any different, Anna Royce.'

'You know I only said that so Misty wouldn't argue.' Anna pressed lovingly against Maggie's knee. 'You are as strong as ever you were, we both know that. I said it because I simply didn't know how else to persuade Misty.'

'Well, that didn't do it.' Maggie stroked a hand over the shining red-gold hair. 'It was your promising her a place wi' you did that. My question is, did you mean it? Do you intend doin' as you said? I love that child as I would one of my own an' I couldn't stomach seein' 'er disappointed.'

'Of course I meant it.' Anna looked up, surprised Maggie should harbour any doubts as to her sincerity. 'Misty's sketches are good. Given the right training she could well become a very competent designer, and if things continue as they are now we will need someone like that.'

Returning from the long journey to Kent where Misty had been entered into the Haworth School for Young Ladies, Anna climbed into the trap brought to pick her up from the station.

'Did little 'un settle all right?'

Anna tried to smile. Whatever was said to the carter one day was all over Coseley the next.

'Yes, she was already making new friends when I left.' It was a valiant lie but she needed to hear those words, to reassure herself that the tears flooding her daughter's eyes would be gone by now.

'I be glad to 'ear that, Mrs Royce.'

He hadn't believed her, the flat tone of his voice said so, and Anna was glad when he lapsed into silence. She had tried telling herself that boarding school would be best for Misty, but was it, or was she risking her daughter's happiness in order to lighten her own load?

It was late when the trap turned around and the carter called goodnight but Maggie was waiting, the letter in her hand.

'But why, Maggie?'

'Didn't John Harris tell you?'

'No!' Anna slumped into one of the upholstered wing armchairs that graced the tasteful sitting room, a bewildered look in her fine eyes. 'And his letter never mentioned it.'

'Can't say I blame 'im for not writing thing like that down. Letters 'ave ways of fallin' into wrong hands.'

'But selling the mill!'

She still could not take in what the manager of Wigmore Bank had told her. Jacob Rewcastle was selling up . . . completely. She might once have danced around the room with glee at hearing it, but now . . .

'I've bin expecting something like this,' Maggie said, her own expression as troubled as Anna's.

'But he's closing down completely . . . the whole lot . . . rolling mills, everything. Why, Maggie?'

'Money!' the older woman answered dourly. 'What else? Jacob Rewcastle 'as spent 'ard and fast since his son's death, spendin' on them fancy bits of is'n, spendin' too much trying to rebuild what's dead and gone. It 'ad to come,' she shook her grey-streaked head, 'an' now it's here.'

Anna closed her eyes, leaning back against the softness of the chair. Yes, it was here, and it was her fault. God! She hadn't meant for this to happen. Cancelling all Ellis Hardware contracts had been her way of hitting out at Jacob Rewcastle, but they were Rewcastle's major buyer. Without them he had found it hard to survive and now it seemed he wanted cash more than he wanted his mill.

'It'll butter no parsnips, you blamin' yourself.' With her usual insight Maggie went to the heart of Anna's worry. 'Jacob Rewcastle can put this on nobbut himself. A man like him,' she went on scathingly. ''Avin' a bit on the side 'as long been the prerogative of his sort, and I suppose as it'll go on that way, but to fall for the tongues of lying trollops! Still, you knows what folk say . . . there's no fool like an old fool.'

Wasn't there? Anna's thoughts leaped to Charles Lazenby. She wasn't so old but she had certainly been fooled. He had never tried to contact her since that night more than a year ago.

'It's his wife as I'm sorry for.' Maggie's voice cut through her thoughts. 'To lose an only child the way she did, then 'avin' the shame of a man who meks a fool of 'imself with every loose woman he can find. Tcchh! Jacob Rewcastle needs a boot up 'is arse an' even then I doubt it would knock sense to his head. Closin' mill—! Eee, who would 'ave thought?'

'What about Coseley? Rewcastle's Mill is the only employment here . . . what of the men and their families, how will they keep them?'

Maggie expelled a long, troubled breath, head moving slowly from side to side.

'It's going to be 'ard, Anna, 'ard on everybody, I'm thinkin'. There'll be tears in a good few houses down yon side when they learns of this.'

In bed Anna stared into the darkness. She hadn't wanted this. Her sole aim in buying Ellis Hardware and closing its doors against Jacob Rewcastle had been to pay him back for what he had done to her, to pay him back for taking

King's Choice; but she didn't want revenge at the expense of people who had shown her only kindness, had accepted her as one of their own. At last pearl-grey fingers of dawn played across her face, turning pink then yellow. She knew what she was going to do now but the knowledge took away none of her worry.

She would be in London for a week, all the time she could spare, and it had taken one of those precious days to find the shop. She was taking a hell of a risk, opening another shop at this time, but she needed a wider market and this could prove the most lucrative of all. The shop she had found was small but the location opposite St James's Park was excellent. Quite a bit of carriage trade passed along Birdcage Walk, either to the park or into Buckingham Palace Road. This meant her 'By Appointment' sign would be seen by the wealthy or those who served them.

Paying three guineas a week rent for three months in advance made Anna grimace. It was scandalously high, but that she supposed was London, a fact her own prices would reflect.

She had chosen well. The building could have been custom-built with its deep-set alcoves and graceful niches, and Anna used them to full advantage, displaying her porcelain there and on pretty, lace-draped tables that looked as if just laid for an intimate luncheon or afternoon tea.

'Phew!' Anna pushed a straying strand of hair upward, securing it beneath a tortoiseshell comb. 'I never thought we would be ready in time. You've been marvellous, Emma . . . thank you for all your hard work.'

Emma Sanders, born of money-conscious, middle-class parents then rejected by them for daring to fall in love with and marry a working man, was one of the girls Hester had taken on for staff training, and although that was just weeks ago, both Anna and Hester felt confident she could now handle the London shop alone.

'We are both very grateful to you, Mrs Royce.' Emma's face was beginning to lose the haunted look it had held and not all the colour in her cheeks was due to the hard work of setting up the last of the displays.

'William and I still cannot quite believe it . . . a place of our own. You needn't worry.' She smiled, suddenly transformed by the happiness that lit her violet eyes. 'William and I will make the shop work, I promise.'

'I know you will, Emma, but the rooms over the top are not big . . . are you sure you can manage?'

'We will be together, Mrs Royce.'

Anna didn't need to hear any more. Understanding completely what the girl meant, she turned away, checking yet again the elegant displays, nervously rearranging a beauty box here or a jug there.

She had chosen her site well. With two days to go before she must return to Coseley, her books were already filled with orders that would keep Gladwin's Pottery working for weeks ahead and the catalogues had been an enormous success. Her beauty boxes, too, craftily placed in the tiny boudoir alcove, had not gone unnoticed. Benjamin Freeth and the Cresswell boys would be delighted with the several dozen orders already placed.

Behind her the tiny bell William had fastened above the door tinkled. Anna collected her thoughts, with Emma already busy with a customer, she must attend to the one who had just entered the shop. Taking a last nervous breath she turned, the smile that had come automatically to her lips fading.

'You came to London after all!' he said quietly, giving a slight bow to an overdressed dowager dragging a vinegar-faced companion in her ample rear. 'I am so glad, Anna.'

'Are you, Mr Lazenby?'

'You know I am.' He smiled into her eyes. 'You must have

dinner with me tonight so that I may tell you how much I have missed you.'

The smile was the same, slow and disarming, lifting the corners of his mouth in a dangerous, deceptive curve. His eyes, slumbrous, hypnotic, would drown the unwary.

'Thank you, but I am too occupied with the shop.' Pin pricks of sweat touched her brow like warm mist; her palms felt moist. He had taken her by surprise. Somehow she had never thought he might come to the shop. In the rush of her decision to open up here, she had forgotten he too lived in London.

'Nonsense.' He stepped in front of her, trapping her against one wall. 'You have someone here with you. She can see to whatever needs seeing to.'

'I prefer to do that for myself.' She had been surprised, taken off guard, but now she was herself again. His eyes no longer seemed hypnotic as she stared coldly into them. 'If you will excuse me, I have customers waiting.'

'Anna, listen to me.' He moved as she did, blocking her way. 'I can do so much for you . . . this shop, your porcelain. I can help open doors you never even knew existed.'

Sunlight reaching through the bow-shaped windows touched his fair hair, turning it to bronze where it curled softly above his collar. It would be so easy to accept his offer. Beneath the starched high collar, her throat felt hot and dry and she had to draw a long breath.

'Your price is too high, Mr Lazenby,' she said unsteadily. 'My tableware must succeed on its own merits, I won't sell myself in order to promote it.'

'Charles!'

The petulant cry ringing across the salon was her means of escape and as he turned Anna took it.

'Come here, Charles . . . I want your opinion on this.'

Hands trembling, Anna tried to concentrate on the plump dowager and her dilemma over which dinner service she should choose but she could not close off the strident voice.

'The colours are well toned, Charles, don't you think, but is it right for Abbotts Ford?'

'I'm sure whatever you choose will be perfect.'

Anna heard the rustle of satin as the dowager moved to another alcove, Charles Lazenby could charm ducks from the water when he spoke like that. Desperately wanting to get away to the privacy of Emma's upstairs rooms, she could only nod and try to smile as her portly customer continually changed her mind.

'But it must be perfect for both of us, Charles, it must please us both for we will be using it . . . once we are married.'

The dowager lifted her feather-adorned head, smiling fatuously in the direction of the over-sweet sentence, but Anna refused to look up. If Charles hoped the news would shock her, he could hope again.

It was two years since he had followed her to Birmingham and she had refused to become his mistress. That was more than enough time to get himself engaged. That was not what galled her. It was the fact that in the face of his coming marriage he still wanted her to be his mistress. That was the pill that was too bitter to swallow.

Putting down a flower-sprigged sauce boat, Anna walked into the back room which served as a store room. If the dowager didn't buy her china because of being abandoned, then hard luck.

'It isn't what you think, Anna.'

His gentleness had the effect of petrol on a low flame. Every nerve ending flared with sudden all-consuming rage, destroying any last vestige of respect she might otherwise have held for him. Skirts rustling against the rough stone floor, Anna whirled round to face Charles Lazenby who had followed her into the store room.

'Anna, it isn't . . .'

'I don't think anything!' Her voice was cutting. 'I'm not interested in you, in what you do or who you do it with! In short, Mr Lazenby, I prefer not to be burdened with the wearisome task of having to make polite conversation with you.'

Breasts heaving with every breath, Anna studied the handsome features already indelibly printed on her mind, then so quietly she was only just audible added: 'If you are the gentleman you imply then you will not impose yourself upon me again.'

Less than four paces away Charles Lazenby's mouth tightened, his fine nostrils flaring with the effort of holding his temper in check. His eyes became cold. Anger clearly visible in their depths, he stared at her for a long moment. Then, with one tap of his silver-topped malacca cane against a gloved palm, said tersely, 'Your servant, Mrs Royce.'

'I don't believe this at all.' Anna read the neatly penned note again before handing it across the breakfast table to Emma. 'I think this is a ruse. Charles Lazenby is using his mother's name to get me to go to Beldon House. I don't think Lady Strathlyn wants to see me or my catalogue.'

Emma read the letter and handed it back to her.

'But why . . . for what reason . . . I mean, why use his mother's name?'

'Because he knows there is no way on God's earth he would get me to go anywhere to see him.' Yesterday had left Anna badly shaken. She could not take another encounter with Charles . . . not yet.

'But if the note really is from Lady Strathlyn,' Emma said in concern, 'it would place the shop in jeopardy if you snubbed her. She is bound to have influential friends.'

You don't know how influential, Anna thought, folding the note back into its crested vellum envelope.

'Can't you excuse yourself? Say how busy you are with the shop being so newly opened.'

'Not if we wish to extend our clientele, Emma.'

'What if you were not here?' William folded his newspaper.

'But I am here, William!'

The strain of the last week, the threatened closure of Rewcastle's Mill and all that it entailed, rang in Anna's sharp reply. Lady Strathlyn had been very kind to her. How could she repay that with a deliberate lie?

'But if you were not in London, surely she could not hold it against you if someone else acted for you?' He answered with plain good sense.

'But as Anna said . . . she is here, William. It would be gross bad manners to pretend otherwise.' Emma placed a hand over that of her husband.

'She wouldn't be if she took the afternoon train home.' William looked from one quizzical face to the other. 'Simply send a catalogue and more samples . . . I could take those and a note from Emma. If she said you had returned to Coseley, leaving her with permission to open any letters not marked 'Private' and deal with matters arising from them, surely that would remove any suspicion of deliberate rudeness?'

'And get me off the hook,' Anna admitted. 'But can you two manage here?'

Smiling at William, Emma's eyes darkened to that lovely shade of violet. 'We can manage, Anna,' she said softly, 'we have each other.'

'Excuse me, ma'am.'

Anna turned from the window where her eyes had barely noted the passing countryside. A man, dark-haired and dark-eyed, smiled openly at her and for a fleeting second Anna felt she knew him.

'I . . . I know it's not polite to address a lady y'ain't been introduced to but there being nobody here to do that, I thought I'd just up and take the risk.'

Anna noted the clear complexion, the hair cut higher than the collar, shorter than the way Charles wore his, and the clothes. The dark worsted suit was more workmanlike than fashionable but the wide honest smile more than made up for that.

'Fact is, ma'am, I was wondering if you was taking this train all the way to Birmingham?'

'Yes.' Anna was surprised at the question but answered anyway. 'But I go on to Coseley.'

'Say now, if that ain't pure coincidence. I'm going to Coseley too. My mam lives there . . . say, you might know her. Name of Maggie . . . Maggie Fellen?'

Andrew! It was all she could do not to gasp . . . this man was Andrew, Maggie's son. She looked into his grey eyes, so much darker than his mother's, and some tiny imp of mischief made her hold her tongue.

'Lived in Coseley all her life, has me mam,' he went on when she did not speak. 'I went to America a few years ago and she wasn't too pleased about that but I've done all right and now I'm here to fetch her back to the States. She's gonna live in comfort from now on. I've got this ranch in the Mid-West and I've had a place built on it in case Mam wants a house to herself. Independent is me mam, always was.'

'Does your mother know you want her to go and live with you in America?' Anna was giving nothing away.

'Shucks no, ma'am.' The smile broke out again, like a lad who had been given a threepenny bit. 'I have to break news like that gently. She won't want to come first off, but she'll change her mind. After all, there's nothing here for her.'

'Perhaps not,' Anna replied, resisting the temptation to smile, 'but the habits of a lifetime can be hard to break.'

'Ya only have to do it once, ma'am.' He grinned boyishly. 'Like most things, ah reckon, rest comes easy after that, and I want me mam with me for what's left of her time.'

He was right. Anna felt her heart lurch. Habits could be broken and family was family after all. Perhaps Maggie would go with her son. It was too painful to think about on top of everything else so with an effort she pushed the prospect away.

'I wonder how she looks?' Andrew Fellen rambled on, unaware of the heartache he was causing in the smartly dressed woman sitting across the compartment from him. 'She always tried her best to look smart, did me mam, even though it could never have been easy for her after . . .'

He broke off in mid-sentence; Anna could have told him she knew his father had left when he was still young, but from the look that suddenly closed his face, felt it would be tantamount to interfering so said nothing.

For several minutes the rhythm of the train and the huff of the steam engine were the only sounds in their closed world, and then, as if he had come to some decision, Andrew began again.

'I didn't think life was too bad when I were a lad and me father worked at Rewcastle's Mill. On Sunday afternoons he would take me with him up on to the heath. Me mam would create at that, said we should both be in Chapel, but Father would have none of it. He said there was more to be learned by watching birds and looking at plants and creatures God had made, and he was right. I reckon I learned more from him than I could from any Bible-punching Baptist Minister.'

His face had softened as he talked of his father and the stony look had left his dark eyes, but the heartache he had talked away had settled in Anna, arousing memories of her own carefree childhood and the parents who had been her life, bringing back all the agony of their loss.

'Winter was good too in its own way.' Maggie's son did not see the pain, could not read the distress in those wide green eyes fixed on his.

'The fire was always way up the chimney and the kettle on the hob. Mam would make toast thick with dripping and a mug of tea with three spoons of sugar. When me dad came home from mill he would take hot plate from the oven, wrap it in cloth and put it in my bed. Then we would sit downstairs by the fire together and look through his book while me mam did her crochet.

It were all pictures of ships. Mad about ships were me dad.'

I know, Anna thought watching him, and I know the misery that madness brought your mother. But even so she smiled inwardly as the brogue of childhood slipped back into speech.

'Talk about ships from morning till night, would me dad, supposin' he could get anybody to listen. Mam said he were just plain daft. He'd far better find summat useful to occupy his spare time.' His lids half-closed, narrowing the dark eyes as he stared into the past. 'It seemed me mam never could understand that was his way of relaxing, that an hour with that book brought him a pleasure nothing else could give; and after sloggin' his guts out in that mill for twelve hours every day any man deserved all the pleasure he could get.'

Beyond the windows sheep and cattle browsed peacefully in soft meadows; in the distance a church spire reached a bony finger to the sky, reminding Anna sharply of the smoke-blackened Parish Church that dominated Wednesbury from its own green sloping hill.

'I suppose he stuck it as long as he could.' His voice was softer, the hindsight of maturity not quite masking the raw pain. 'Then one day he just walked out. I thought my world had ended but me mam never said one word and if I tried asking she shut me up sharpish.'

'Did your father ask her to go with him?'

'Never knew. Like I told you, me mam would have nowt said after me dad had gone.'

Shadows lengthening in the compartment touched his face, softening the line of features sharp cut as his mother's, concealing the sorrow in his eyes.

'I left school then. I were twelve and got a job in the mill . . .'

The door slid open and Andrew stopped speaking, turning his head towards the gathering night. Anna watched the uniformed conductor turn up the wick of the polished brass oil lamps fastened to the sides of the compartment, watched yellow flame spurt along the tall glass funnel as the wick caught the flaring life of the match he held to them, then smiled good evening as the attendant touched his cap to her. To Andrew Fellen she said nothing; respecting the silence of a man mourning lost years, lost love; feeling the twist of sympathy. She knew that pain, she had travelled the same path.

'I had to get a job.' He began to speak suddenly, the words rushing out of him like some long withheld torrent. 'I didn't want me mam breaking her back, killing herself in that lousy sweat shop of a mill for a few paltry shillings, like all the others in Roker Street. There were only two of us, we had no family of kids, so I reckoned we could manage on the bit old man Rewcastle paid young lads. And we did manage until . . .' He halted again, hands twisting viciously against each other and his mouth thinning, the strength of his emotions draining it white.

'Forgive me, ma'am.' He leaned his head against the white antimacassar of the seat. 'I've rattled on like a child, I beg your pardon.'

Anna smiled then turned her head to the darkened vista, knowing the value of silence.

Conversation had kept Charles from her mind but as Andrew took her hand, helping her down to the platform, the spectre of him rose vividly. He had taken her hand that way. Like Andrew he was so tall she had to tip back her head to look into his face. Waiting while Andrew brought her bag from the train, Anna looked past him, catching the dark silhouette etched black on the deep grey evening, a shadow that darted towards the engine, beginning to pull away.

'No!' Pushing Andrew aside, Anna flew along the platform, grabbing the shadow intent on throwing itself beneath the massive wheels.

'Leave off!' it screamed, struggling so violently Anna almost lost her hold.

'What the hell . . .' Andrew Fellen twisted the struggling figure into his firmer grip.

'Leave off . . . let me go, you bloody interferin' . . .'

Anna heard the thud of clog against bone as the shadow kicked out viciously, the grunt of anger and pain followed by a rattle of breath as Andrew's strong hands whipped it back and forth.

'Do you be knowin' you can get yourself killed arsin' about in front of a railroad train?' he shouted, anger restoring his native dialect in full.

''Course I bloody well knows.' The struggling stopped and the figure fell against his chest. 'Why else does think I be 'ere?'

Anna's hand flew to her throat as she tried to catch the night-veiled face. Who was it . . . who in Coseley was desperate enough to want to commit suicide?

'I'll take her.' She reached for the sobbing girl, feeling the bones beneath a pathetic covering of flesh.

'It's all right,' she soothed, guiding her towards the arched entrance that led on to the cobbled road. 'It's all right now.'

'Say, ma'am . . . where do we get a cab around here?'

Only then was Anna aware of the tall figure following behind.

'We don't,' she said.

'Then how in the hell is a guy supposed to get where he's goin'?'

The accent Anna presumed to be the gift of America returned but where once she had found it pleasant, it now grated.

'He walks!' she snapped irritably. 'The same as a woman.'

'What possessed you to do a daft thing like that?' Maggie handed a cup of cocoa to the girl, now bathed and dressed in one of Misty's nightgowns.

'I thought it best an' I still do.' Red-eyed defiance met Maggie's stony glare.

'Best!' Maggie shoved the cup into the girl's hand, noting the skin yellow against the white pillows of Misty's bed. 'Best . . . to throw yourself under railroad engine?'

'At least that way I get to kill meself, and it's only what me mam'll do any road when 'er finds out.'

'Finds out what?' Anna asked. Looking into those drowned eyes was like looking into those of her own daughter, so blue, and the child would be pretty had her face not been so thin, and puffy from crying.

'Finds out I be pregnant.' She began to wail all over again. 'Oh, me mam'll kill me, I knows 'er will!'

'What about lad as put you up the spout?' Maggie asked without preamble. 'Is 'e going to marry you?'

''E can't.' The wail sharpened and Anna removed the cup before the girl's trembling hands slopped cocoa on to the white sheet. ''E's no lad, an' besides 'e's married already. Oh, God!' Dropping her face into her hands, the girl sobbed. 'Oh, God, me mam . . . an' the neighbours, won't they just love this?'

Turning away Anna set the cup on the marble-topped dresser, hiding the agony that had leaped to her eyes. She knew what this child was going through and the ordeals yet to come.

'Who be your mam?' Maggie pushed a large cotton handkerchief into the girl's thin hands.

'Connie Stevens . . . me mam's Connie Stevens. We live down by cut side. 'Er'll not tek me back once 'er knows.'

Maggie's brow wrinkled into a frown. She knew the cutsiders, living in shacks thrown together from anything, overrun with kids and rats, dirt and filth everywhere. And she knew Connie Stevens; large, loud-mouthed and aggressive, more interested in the gin bottle than her large brood that swarmed the banks of the canal up against the mill, living on anything they could lay their thieving hands on. Why this one should want to return was beyond understanding until you remembered the alternative was the workhouse.

'Wipe your snotty nose an' get yourself off to sleep,' she said, gently covering the puny shoulders with the bedcovers. 'Mornin's soon enough to sort that out.'

'Wench was right.' Downstairs she told Anna what she knew of the folk who lived alongside the canal. 'Connie Stevens will kill 'er an' all but not on account of any neighbours. It'll be 'cos the kid will no longer be fetchin' in money for gin. Poor little thing, life's 'ard enough down there without this. But she's bin a bloody fool when all's said and done an' none to blame but 'erself.'

'It doesn't always happen that way,' Anna answered quietly, her own rape vivid in her mind. 'We musn't judge until we know.'

A loud bang at the door brought their glances together before Anna went to open it.

'I'm sorry.' She blushed as the man standing on the whitewashed step finished speaking. 'I meant to tell you but when I saw that girl try to throw herself under the train, it completely slipped my mind.'

'Then it's as well Mrs Cresswell still lives down there, isn't it?'

'Who is it, Anna?' Maggie emerged from the sitting room.

'A visitor, Maggie.' Anna smiled. 'For you.'

She was silent for a second, mouth opening and closing, the blood draining from her lined face. Andrew too stood silent and immobile.

'Mam . . . oh, Mam!' Then he was across the hall, gathering his mother into his arms, his face pressed against her grey-streaked hair.

'Oh, Mam!'

Closing the door, Anna walked upstairs.

Anna smoothed the bodice of her grey corded day suit and pushed a stray hair under the lime green hat. The curling feather gave it a jaunty air but didn't reflect her feelings. She had visited Wigmore's Bank often enough but today she was nervous. Pushing open the door, her footsteps seemed to echo on the tiled floor as they had seemed to do that first day almost ten years ago, and catching sight of the watchful Mr Burrows, her spine tingled. Entering the hushed confines of the manager's office, her mouth was dry but the palms of her hands felt moist with sweat.

'That's it in a nutshell. By taking over Ellis Hardware I have been the cause of Rewcastle Mill's closing and I had not reckoned on that.'

Anna twisted her fingers together awkwardly. This was worse than being in the dock but she couldn't back down; she would go through with it no matter how awful it felt.

John Harris watched her closely.

'Then what did you reckon on?' he asked quizzically.

'I thought he would just sell King's Choice.'

That he could believe. She wanted only what Jacob had taken from her.

'It never occurred to me he would just throw the whole lot up,' she rushed on. 'I feel responsible, it will be my fault if the people of Coseley lose their work.'

'So what is it you want to do?'

'I want the bank to extend my credit, I want to take over the mill.'

'You!' John Harris was clearly astonished. 'But you have cancelled the main outlet for their products.'

'What I have closed I can reopen.' Confidence returned, bringing Anna's chin up firmly. 'I can resume the sale of hardware through Ellis Hardware and that way no one will lose.'

'But hadn't you intended those shops to be new outlets for your porcelain?'

'Yes, but in the face of what has happened I have changed my mind. The money allocated to re-designing the interior of those shops will help buy the mill. For the present it will be more sensible to lease smaller premises to launch my tableware.'

'Then you still intend to carry on with your plans for widening your market?'

'Most definitely, Mr Harris. The purchase of Rewcastle Mill will not affect my decision on that. As you yourself said when I approached the bank concerning Ellis Hardware, my profit margins are very healthy, I can repay a loan with no problem. In fact, my only problem at the moment is, do I borrow money here or from some other bank?'

The following evening John Harris called on Anna at home.

'Mrs Royce,' he said formally. He had waited until she had written her name across the foot of a close-written document, agreeing to a loan of three thousand pounds. 'I think you should know the directors of the bank are friends of Jacob Rewcastle. Take my advice, tread carefully.'

'I don't want my name put forward as a prospective buyer, Reuben.' Anna sat in Reuben Fine's office in the centre of Birmingham. 'If Jacob Rewcastle got wind of it he would see every man in Coseley starve before he would sell. Can I put in an offer to buy using a different name, one which Jacob might not so easily recognise?'

Reuben thought for a moment. 'You kept the name Gladwin for your pottery, and Stoke-on-Trent is a fair distance from Coseley. It could be an even bet that Jacob will not know much of the town, or recognise the buyer, and given that should he want to sell badly enough he might not pay too much attention to the name. It is a risk, Anna, but if that is the way you want it then we can try.'

'It is the way I want it, Reuben.'

Pushing his spectacles back onto the bridge of his nose, Reuben looked at Anna. Her face was pale and there were dark shadows beneath her eyes. He guessed what was driving her, but the need was not only to recover King's Choice. He knew there was a need in her that went deeper than that; he had known since that night she had talked with Hester and himself about the possibility of acquiring another shop. The talk had drifted to the past and it was then she had told them of her rape and of the son she had in Wednesbury. That was the driving force behind all that Anna Royce did, the need to have both of her children with her.

'We can sort the business of the mill, Anna,' he said, looking at her through the thick lenses of his spectacles, 'but what about you? You are pushing yourself too hard, taking on too many commitments. You can't burn both ends of a candle and not expect it to go out.'

'I am all right, Reuben.' Anna's smile was deceptively bright. 'So long as I can keep the men in work. Get that mill for me.'

Chapter Fourteen

Jacob Rewcastle entered The Fighting Cocks public house, making his way to the back room where he regularly met his business associates.

Business! He clamped his teeth together hard, face thunderous. His business had gone downhill since the sale of Ellis Hardware; a great deal of his trade had been with them, and now he was about to lose the steel mill.

To whom? The question had puzzled him for days. Who in Coseley had the money to buy out Jacob Rewcastle?

'Evenin', Mr Rewcastle, sir.'

The landlord greeted him as he strode through the smoke-filled bar, packed with men in tattered jackets, their moleskin trousers held up with wide, heavy-buckled belts.

Nobody, that was who, Jacob answered his own question, ignoring the landlord. There was nobody hereabouts could find that kind of money. Like as not the mill would go to some bloke from Brummagem.

Yes, it would be bought by somebody in Birmingham. He didn't really mind being out of business. The eternal rat race of undercutting the next man, always having to watch the market for signs of a slump – no, he would not mind being out of that now he had no son to leave it to.

No son!

The thought struck him like a physical blow as it always did.

Philip was dead and all because of that bitch.

Opening the door, he was greeted by several men already seated in leather armchairs, brandy glasses at their elbows.

Letting the door swing to behind him, Jacob returned their greeting. These were the men who would help him take revenge on that Royce woman. With their help he would see the bitch in the workhouse where she belonged, her and her brat!

Removing his overcoat and tall black hat, Jacob accepted a glass of brandy, carrying it to his accustomed place beside the glowing coal fire.

He had been too soft on Edward Royce's wife, had only threatened to put her out of business up to this point, but now he would make that threat a reality. If Jacob Rewcastle had no business then Anna Royce would have none, and if he had no child to come after him then she would have none either.

That kid attended some boarding school. It wouldn't be too hard to get somebody to see to it that one afternoon she had an accident!

'Now then, Jacob,' a voice hailed him from a deep armchair. 'Be you still set on giving up the steel?'

'I am.' Jacob took a pull at his brandy, pressing his tongue against the roof of his mouth as the liquid burned his throat.

'Can't say I blame you,' the voice replied. 'I would do the same if I hadn't a son to leave it to.'

You bastard! Jacob's thoughts burned like the brandy. You never fail to rub it in, never fail to make some remark, but you ain't got the courage to come right out with it, say what you mean. Jacob Rewcastle hasn't got it in him to make another son.

But he must keep his thoughts to himself. At least until he had what he was looking for, and that was the help of these men in destroying Anna Royce.

But he had to tread warily, take care what reasons he gave for enlisting their aid. They were men of the world as he was, men who wouldn't think twice about tumbling a woman, but at the same time they would have no sympathy with a homosexual nor with the father of one; it must not come out that Philip had been of that tendency.

'But why put the woman out of business?'

The man who put the question fingered bushy side whiskers, his eyes watching Jacob through the a haze of cigar smoke.

'Ar, why bother?' another put it. 'She won't survive long anyway. Business be for a man. Ain't no woman capable of runnin' more'n a kitchen.'

'This one is,' Jacob said over the murmurs of assent. 'This one has a head on her shoulders, and if she ain't stopped she's likely to have all of Coseley in her pocket in a few years' time – and that won't sit easy with a few in this room.'

'But what does she do? I mean, to be a threat the woman has to have money, so where does it come from? After all, she cannot manufacture the loot out of thin air, can she?'

Jacob turned a cold eye on the snappily dressed son of a late colleague. She could make mincemeat out of you. For all your public school way of talking, you ain't got a decent brain cell in your head, he thought. Swallowing a little more brandy, he drowned the desire to speak the thought aloud.

'She can do the next best thing,' he answered, swirling the contents of his glass. 'How many in this room can pick plants off the heath and turn 'em into face creams and sweet-smelling lotions?'

'Is that what 'er business be, Jacob?'

'Some of it.' Jacob turned his glance to the older man. 'I'm told as she also has considerable interests in some fancy china place up along Stoke way. I tell you, that woman has her head on right way round. Face paints and fancy china – the things every woman wants, and every woman with money, and even some without it, will have.'

Going to the table to replenish his glass from the several bottles laid on it, he looked at each man in turn.

'You all of you have wives *and* them you passes off as wives on the side. Tell me, which of those women has no liking for fancy cups and saucers and pretty china doo-dads? Which of them don't put powder and paint on their faces, even if they don't own to it, eh? Which one of your wives would be content knowing the one next door had summat she hadn't got? None of 'em, and you know it. That woman has chosen her business well and it'll grow, my friends, it'll spread like ripples in a pool. And then her money will grow with it, and with that money she will *buy*. She will buy any business she can lay hands on, and like as not that business will be *yours*.'

'Be you certain that your warning don't 'ave no foundation in what 'appened to that lad o' your'n?'

The man who had first addressed him now spoke up again, his face partly hidden by the wing of his armchair.

Jacob's nerves tightened. That one was always on the bloody ball, there was no pulling the wool over his eyes.

'It does have a part in it,' he answered after another pull from his glass had settled his nerves. 'My lad lost his life protecting a whore, because that's what she be. Who else but a whore would be up on the heath alone? She was expecting the man who tumbled her, and spread her legs willing enough till my lad come across them. Then she starts to scream rape. Think on it, the lot of you. It was my son that time. Whose will it be next? Which of you will be like Jacob Rewcastle? Which of you will have no son to follow after you? Don't think it can't happen again 'cos it can, and it will – unless we drive that bitch out of Coseley!'

Outside The Fighting Cocks Jacob climbed into a hansom. It was late, but not too late for the establishment he was headed for.

'Railway Station.'

'Station it be, sir.'

The cabbie whipped up the tired-looking horse and Jacob leaned against the shadowed upholstery.

They had taken his warning, albeit only when he had wondered aloud how their wives would react to learning of some of the bawdy houses their husbands frequented. Soon Anna Royce would find herself back where she started. But that won't be the end, he vowed silently, it won't end till you're in the workhouse.

She had taken his son, killed him as surely as if she had put a gun to his head. Had she not been on the heath that day, Philip would not have died. He gave his life to save hers, Jacob told himself.

But in the darkness of the hansom cab he closed his eyes, trying to shut out the truth that could never be escaped for long. Philip had not given his life to protect Anna Royce, he had died as a result of his own jealousy; jealousy that Robert Daines, the man he was in love with, could want a woman.

No one had told Jacob so, not even the Royce woman. But she had not needed to. He had seen the way his son's feelings were directed, seen it from the earliest days of his boyhood. But that knowledge must remain his alone and while Anna Royce remained in Coseley, he could never be certain that it would.

'You are telling me the truth, Amy?'

Anna watched the girl struggling to fasten the threadbare dirty blue coat across her thin chest. Several times too small, it had already known many owners.

'Yes, Mrs Royce.'

Maggie shook her head at the whisper.

'I be going with you. That one is as sly as a cartload o' monkeys.'

'No, you stay here with Andrew, I can manage.' Anna knew the temper of the older woman. Fastening the last of the row of shiny bronze buttons that adorned her dove grey corded suit, she pushed a bronze-knobbed hatpin through the hat perched on top of her heavy folds of hair. She no longer looked like the drab widow who had visited Wigmore Bank years before.

'He'll deny everything, you knows that.'

'Yes, Maggie, but it won't stop me. I'm going to face him with this, he's not getting away with it.'

'You might try!' Maggie was abrupt with her. 'But you'll get nowt. It's 'er word against 'is'n an' there's no justice where there's money. That one could buy his way out even if wench 'ad means of bringin' 'im into court, which he knows nicely she 'asn't. Still . . . go if you must, but don't say you went without a tellin'.'

Amy Stevens close by her side, Anna walked from Woodgreen through the streets of Coseley, the sound of clogs loud on the cobbles as whole families went to Chapel. She hadn't been since Edward had died. Where was the love and mercy that allowed a child to be raped, and that could have saved her husband from death? No, she hadn't been to Chapel since that day and wouldn't be going today.

'Don't start snivelling again,' she said tartly to Amy as they followed a winding drive lined with glorious copper beech trees.

'Mrs Anna Royce to see Mr Rewcastle.' Her tone was still sharp as the footman opened the heavy oak door of Highfield House.

'The tradesman's entrance is at the rear, through the arch and to the left!' His features wrinkled disdainfully showing positive disgust when they reached Amy, trembling by Anna's side.

Stepping back, he began to swing the heavy door to but Anna was inside, dragging the girl in after her.

'You get smart with me and your rear will feel my foot – and not only through the arch and to the left but all round every inch of this stinking pile! Now move or I'll find Jacob Rewcastle for myself.'

'What is it, Newton . . . what is all that noise?' Halfway down the carpeted stairway stood Beatrice Rewcastle, her watery blue eyes taking in the scene below.

'Amy?' She took two steps down, skirts rustling with each movement. 'Where have you been?'

'I . . . I . . .' Visibly terrified, Amy tried to hide behind Anna.

'Well, wherever it was you are no longer needed in this house, and do not bother asking Cook for a reference – there will be none forthcoming. Don't think you can leave without any sort of explanation then creep back here a week later and expect me to keep you on. Newton!' She switched her watery glance to the smirking servant. 'Get these . . . people . . . out of here and see them off the grounds.'

A silken swish of her skirts and she had turned about, one foot already on the step above.

Anger at Jacob's treatment of the girl swept through Anna. Anger so strong it burned away her usual good manners.

'If Newton needs his legs to carry out his duties in this house then I suggest he keep his distance. One step nearer and I'll kick them from under him.' Anna's eyes sparked like lightning in her furious face. 'And as for Amy's job, that's not why she's returned to this mausoleum.'

'Just who *are* you?' Jacob's wife was unused to the lower classes speaking back to her or at least not with the cool authority with which Anna spoke.

'It's not who *I* am should worry you, Mrs Rewcastle, if that is who you are . . . and unless you want this maukin to hear what we've come about, and I think he would rather enjoy what I have to say, then you will send for your husband now.'

Beatrice Rewcastle blanched visibly, long thin fingers gripping the gleaming mahogany balustrade. For a moment she wrestled with Anna's revelation.

'What the bloody hell is all this?' A door was thrown back and Jacob Rewcastle strode into the hall. 'Newton, what the bloody . . .?' He coloured fiercely as he saw the visitors.

'What are you doing here?' he demanded.

'I think you know that already but I can tell you just the same.'

Anna met his furious glare, unflinching. There was a time she might have been as afraid of Jacob Rewcastle and his wife as Amy was now but hard knocks had long driven that sort of fear away.

'Amy tells me that you . . .'

'You bugger off!' Jacob barked at the black-coated Newton. 'And you, Beatrice, get yourself back upstairs.'

'But, Jacob, I . . .'

'Don't bloody Jacob me!' His voice ricocheted from the panelled walls like bullets. 'I told you to get back upstairs. This has nowt to do with you.'

His eye caught the movement of a black coat.

'I thought I told you to bugger off . . . stand there with your bloody earholes flapping and you're likely to get the buggers knocked off!'

Beatrice Rewcastle's face flushed a deep carmine red but she turned and walked back up the stairs as Newton vanished.

'Now then!' Jacob's piggy eyes returned to Anna. 'I don't entertain the likes of you in my house. If you have business with me then you can call at the mill . . . maybe I'll see you there. As for you,' the glance narrowed to slits as he turned to the pathetic figure of Amy, 'there's no work for you here or at the mill so get out, and if I see you here again I'll have you up at quarter sessions.'

'That would suit Amy admirably. I'm not certain the magistrate would be interested in what she had to tell him,' Anna was superbly cool, 'but even if he were not, there are those in these parts who no longer take the view that a man seducing a young girl on the grounds of being her employer and having a great deal of money is right or in any way acceptable. The magistrate may not take a serious view of what you have done to this girl but there are opinions other than his in Coseley, opinions which can be brought to bear where a magistrate cannot reach.'

Jacob felt the warning even through his rage. The bitch was right. There were those in Coseley and outside of it had a dose of religion, especially the women. Offend their finer feelings and he could kiss goodbye to any support from their husbands.

'As for myself, I'd prefer to conduct this business at the mill.

There are so many more listening ears and willing tongues up there. They will carry word of what you have done to this child to a far wider audience than we have here and will feast on this titbit for a long time to come.'

'What's that bloody lyin' slut been telling you?' Veins stood out like thick cords in his short neck and his voice dropped to a menacing hiss.

Anna read the danger in that bloodshot glare, the hostility curving the flaccid mouth, but at the same time recognised the fear behind both. Jacob Rewcastle was in no doubt of what had brought them here.

'There is always the possibility that Amy is lying, Jacob Rewcastle,' she said quietly, 'but we both know there are far greater liars. As for her being a slut, I don't think a man with the morals of a rutting dog is qualified to judge on that point.'

From the curve at the top of the stairs Beatrice heard a low curse, the door of her husband's study opening and closing, then remained straining to listen.

'I'll give you two minutes.' Inside the tobacco-stained room Jacob removed the heavy gold hunter from his waistcoat pocket. 'Afterwards you have a choice. Walk out or I'll throw you out, and enjoy doing it.'

'I'm sure you would.' Unperturbed, Anna faced him in the masculine, book-lined room. 'But then you enjoy mauling a woman, don't you, Jacob? With or without a reason.'

'You bloody bitch!'

'Amy is pregnant. She claims that you are the father of the child she is carrying!' Anna matched his snarl.

'What's that you say?' His lips remained still, words emerging through clenched teeth.

'You are the father of Amy's child . . . what do you intend to do?'

Amy had stayed close to Anna during the rapid exchange. Now, as Jacob Rewcastle's anger flared a new, she turned her face into the other woman's shoulder, sobbing hysterically.

'Do!'

Beyond the closed door Beatrice had heard the accusation and waited for his reply.

'I'll tell you what I'm going to do. I'm going to wring her bloody neck. I know her sort, splaying her legs for any that fancies a ride then looking round for the best bet to hang the consequences on. She must have the clap up to her eyes, the bloody trollop. And you think I'd fancy that?'

'You would fancy anything in a skirt.' Anna wrapped one arm around the sobbing girl, her face a cold mask. 'The only difference being, you pay some trollops for their services . . . like a ruby necklace for a certain blonde.'

His angry exclamation carried to Beatrice whose fingers clawed into her brown bombazine skirts. She had guessed at the activities keeping him from the house until the early hours but while he was keeping his filth from her door she could accept it. Now . . . with a common servant, and her no more than a child . . . Her fingers curling closer into her rustling skirts, she turned away.

'How do you know about that?' Inside the room Jacob's face contorted with fresh fury.

'Let's just say I know.' Strangely, in the face of his anger Anna felt herself grow calmer. What few reservations she had harboured at the thought of confronting Coseley's wealthiest man had disappeared altogether. She no longer cared what he or his money could do.

'You took advantage of your position as Amy's employer,' she went on, watching the hatred play across the bloated features. 'You gave this child an ultimatum: either she consented to play your dirty little games or she was out of a job. You knew the terror such a prospect would hold, especially for a cutsider; they have little or no choice as it is with you refusing them work at the mill and God all else to do in Coseley.

'You knew if she went home and told her mother that the paltry few shillings she got for working her heart and soul out here would no longer be forthcoming, then her life would be hell. And like the vulture you are, you preyed on that.'

'And that dirty little whore told you that, I suppose.'

Moving to the fireplace, he turned to face them, legs spread, hands behind his back, arrogant, conceited and totally contemptuous.

'If she is a whore then it's you who made her one,' Anna retorted.

'I ain't a whore, Mrs Royce, truly I ain't. I ain't never bin wi' a lad . . . me mam would kill me.' Amy lifted her head, leaving a damp tear stain on the front of Anna's coat. 'I ain't never bin wi' anyone 'cept 'im an' . . . an' then it was only because 'e said as 'ow I couldn't work 'ere no more lessen I did!' Tears washed down her face. 'Oh, I daren't go 'ome, Mrs Royce. I daren't tell me mam.'

'Don't be frightened, Amy.' Anna still held one arm protectively about the girl. 'We will see your mam after we leave here.'

'Which is right now!' Jacob pulled the watch from his waistcoat pocket. 'Two minutes was what I told you and that time is up.' He flicked the gold hunter, sending it spinning into the slitted pocket. 'But I'll spare the time to tell you this. You'd do better to find yourself a man and spread your legs for him. It'll get you more in the long run than tryin' to hang that trollop's bastard on me.'

'That's all you think a woman capable of, isn't it?' Anna's glare was lacerating. 'Find yourself a husband and home then stay there. And if you can't, then let someone else's husband set you up in a cosy little place where you can spread your legs for *him*. That's what you wanted me to do, isn't it? And you deny you seduced this child! I told you once before, Jacob Rewcastle, and now I tell you again, you are nothing but a bastard.'

Maggie had said she would get nothing but she had needed to try, if only to let him know that others besides Amy knew what he had done. Walking home to the sound of church bells, Anna found herself wondering once again if there really was a God.

'She will be all right there. It has given her a job that will keep her and the baby, and Mary Cresswell will love having someone to fuss over, though I was surprised when your mother suggested Amy take on the front-room shop.'

'My mother was always a pushover for a hard luck story.' Andrew looked down at the woman walking beside him and couldn't help wondering what had brought her to Coseley and his mother's door.

'There are a good many have cause to be grateful to her, Andrew, myself among them.'

'Gee, Anna, I didn't mean . . .'

'I know you didn't, Andrew.'

'Me mam always said as 'ow I had a big mouth.' He grinned, adopting the speech of his youth again.

'Mmm, but a nice one.'

They walked in friendly silence on the heath, above the smoke of the mills, and Anna lifted her face to the sharp kiss of the wind. She hadn't walked on the heath since Philip Rewcastle had ended his life there.

'I used to play up here as a lad.' Andrew pushed his hands into his pockets. 'Over there against the Devil's Finger. My mother used to say it pointed the way to hell and that's where I would finish up if I fell over the edge. Want to take a look?'

'No!' Anna sat down, tucking the russet folds of her skirts beneath her. She did not want to peer into the blackness of that hole, to look into the place where two men had met their death.

'I've had enough walking for now, let's just sit and look at the view.'

'That's no view for you, Anna.' Andrew settled at her side. 'There are places on this earth would take your breath away and I want to show them to you.' He turned towards her, taking her hand in his, dark eyes aflame. 'I want you to come to America with me, Anna . . . I want you to be my wife.'

'Your wife!' She gasped. 'But you've only known me for two weeks.'

'Two weeks, two lifetimes . . . what the hell difference does it make? Anna, I love you. I've loved you since you spat like a scalded cat on that railway platform down there . . . I love you and I want you to marry me.'

Anna's eyes gazed across to the horizon. 'I love you and I want to marry you.' Andrew had said both . . . Charles had said neither.

'Please, Anna . . . say you will?'

At her side Andrew waited.

'You don't know about me, Andrew,' she said after a long interval. 'About my background.'

'And I don't want to know because it doesn't matter, it's you I love . . . you I care about, not your background.' He took her face in his hands, his eyes drowning in hers.

'Understand me, Anna, I love you. Nothing in the universe will alter that.' Holding her face, he lowered his mouth to hers in a fiery lingering kiss.

It was sweet as Edward's had been but there was no music in her head, no brilliant starburst against her closed lids. But Andrew wanted her for a wife, not a mistress, perhaps that was why she lifted her arms to his neck and returned his kiss.

'Why did you go to America?' she asked later when, taking her kisses to mean she would marry him, Andrew lay happily on his back, a long blade of grass between his teeth.

''Cos old man Rewcastle gave me the sack!' He squinted up into the sky. 'That son of his tried the old come on with me but I wasn't taking it as some had just because his father owned the mill and our lives with it. I told him I would break his hands off and stuff them up his arse if he tried anything again. His answer was: "There is only one letter's difference between hiring and firing, Andrew Fellen." I said the letter was "F" and that his old man could stick his fucking job, then I punched the living daylights out of him.'

Spitting the blade of grass away as if clearing a nasty taste from his mouth, Andrew sat up, his gaze ranging over the tall black chimneys and high imprisoning walls of the steel mill with its sentinel rows of terraced houses.

'That bloody family,' he muttered. 'They've a lot to answer for but I think the old man was more to blame, buying Philip his nancy boys . . .'

'Philip is dead, Andrew.' Anna glanced towards that awful place. 'He . . . he fell over Devil's Finger.'

'So Mam said.' His head turned, following her glance to where the ground cut steeply away. 'He didn't have much of a life, for all his father's money, and underneath his pansy ways I believe there was the makings of a man. After I'd knocked him half-daft, I told him if his old man took one step against my mam, I would kill him. Then, I remember, he stood up and glared at me. He had tiger-coloured eyes that seemed to glow, and he said, "Whatever else I might be, I am still a gentleman. I do not take revenge on women."'

'And that was when you left home?'

'What else could I do, Anna? There was nobody in Coseley or for miles around who would risk incurring Jacob Rewcastle's wrath by giving me a job, and I wasn't going to let me mam keep me.' Andrew jumped to his feet, his smile wide and stubborn. 'But I'm back now and I've got you. Let's go tell Mam the news.'

Why couldn't she smile? Why was there only emptiness where there should have been something, even if that something was not happiness? Walking beside him, Anna could not help remembering that other tall figure, the figure of Jacob Rewcastle's son.

'Beggin' yer pardon, Mr Rewcastle, sir, but I 'ardly thinks as 'ow the lady should be in foundry.'

'Who the bloody hell asked you?' Jacob Rewcastle turned

florid heavy jowls towards the man who spoke. 'You're bloody paid to puddle iron, not to think.'

'Jos is right, Mr Rewcastle.' Eli Curran, smart in a stiffly starched collar, came to Jos Ingles's side. ''Tis dangerous, men are just about to tip the basin.'

'That's you, ain't it, Curran?' Jacob peered through bloodshot eyes, swaying unsteadily. 'Why're you all dressed up in a monkey suit . . . have you been to a funeral or summat?' Laughing at his own unsavoury joke, he placed a hand beneath the arm of his woman friend. 'You'll like seeing this, my dear, it's like fireworks on Guy Fawkes Night.'

Eli felt the weight of being appointed foundry manager weigh heavily. He had never argued with Jacob Rewcastle before. Nobody had argued with Jacob Rewcastle before.

'I be sorry, Mr Rewcastle, but I must ask you to take the lady out of the foundry. We can't tip basin wi' 'er so close an' all.'

The cords in Jacob's neck bulged; rage deepened the colour already high in his face.

'Take the lady away, you say?' His bellow rang above the clang of rolling beds where ingots of red hot metal were rolled into long strips. 'It's not a lady who'll be leaving, Eli Curran, *you* will. You can pick your bloody tin up right now. You're finished at this mill, do you hear me? Finished.' He glared round wildly. 'And that goes for all the rest of you who want to say their piece. Now tip that bloody basin!'

Jos Ingles shrugged at the man standing on the other side of the crucible filled with molten metal. Jacob Rewcastle carried a lot of clout. It would be asking for trouble to cross him.

Raising the wooden poles that supported the crucible, the two men operating the tip began to pour, the molten metal giving off a shower of sparks as it ran into the moulds placed on the ground.

Jacob grabbed his companion out of the way of the showering sparks and stepped backward. Catching his heel in one of the narrow channels dug in the earth floor for draining any spilt metal, he lurched sideways. As he threw out his free arm in an attempt to arrest his fall, he fell against Jos Ingles sending him sprawling beneath a glowing stream of molten metal.

'What happened?' Crossing the mill yard Anna was in time to see the blackened, burned figure being carried into the shed beside the offices.

'Jacob Rewcastle, Mrs Royce, he brought a woman . . .'

'Tell me later!' she ordered. 'Get the doctor, Eli, and send a couple of the women to Molly Ingles. Tell them to stay with her till she's calm then one of them come to me here.'

Two minutes later, her whole body stiff with anger, Anna faced Jacob Rewcastle.

'What are you doing here?'

On his feet again he leered at her, the fumes of his breath blinding. 'Well, well! If it isn't Mrs Royce! You're like horse shit, woman, you're everywhere.'

Around her, faces pale beneath sweat-streaked dust, the men waited. Anna breathed deeply, her glance taking in the weeping girl before returning to Jacob.

'Horse shit, Mr Rewcastle, has at least one use,' she replied icily. 'And that makes it at least one hundred per cent up on you.'

With all the swiftness of a summer storm his drunken humour faded. Piggy eyes receding to nothingness, Jacob Rewcastle stared at the only woman who had ever defied him.

'I told you once before,' he grated, 'if you set foot on my property again, I'd have you whipped off.'

'So you did.' Anna held her ground. 'But this is no longer your property, you sold it some months ago.'

'What if I did!' Jacob's face turned a dark red.

'Then having sold it, you have no right to be here.'

'Rights!' Jacob laughed harshly. 'I have all the bloody rights I need, seeing the man who bought this mill be a good friend of mine.'

'That is not true.' Anna said as he glanced triumphantly at the girl he had brought with him. 'You have never been a friend of the owner of this mill.'

'Eh!' Jacob shipped back to her, anger turning his face to purple. 'How would you know?'

Anna felt the flick of her nerves. She had taken every precaution against his finding out just who it was had bought his mill, but now she no longer cared: she wanted him to know.

'Because you have never been a friend of mine.'

'Nor never bloody likely to be!' he spat. 'But I don't see how that has anything to do with it.'

'Then I will tell you,' Anna said calmly. 'I am the one who bought this mill. It belongs to me.'

'That's a lie!' Releasing the girl's arm he took a step forward. 'This mill was bought by Gladwin Pottery of Stoke-on-Trent.'

'Which also belongs to me.' Anna's voice was quiet. 'You should instruct whoever acts for you to look more carefully at any purchasers you may deal with in future. But now I am telling you what you told me, stay off my property.

'Eli,' she glanced quickly at her foundry manager, 'should Mr Rewcastle show his face here again you have my permission to throw him out. I will take the consequences should anyone bother to complain.'

The listening men didn't muffle the comments that brought an apoplectic gasp from their former employer.

'I should have trodden on you from the first, broken you together with your bits of bloody crockery!'

'But now it's too late, Jacob.' The sight of Jos Ingles's burned body stamped on to her mind, Anna no longer cared who heard. Her voice, cold and clear as a mountain stream, vibrated from the roof beams.

'It was my bits of crockery bought your mill and it's my bits of crockery paying these men their wages. You're finished, Jacob Rewcastle. Not only are you a nobody, you're a nothing.'

'You told me you would take more than my son,' he hissed, purple with rage.

'Philip was the one good thing that ever came out of you.' Anna was impervious to the hatred he spat at her. 'And though you spend money on a hundred like the woman standing at your side, you will never replace him. You would be better advised to look to the son you have.'

'Son!' Hatred and anger, a powerful admixture, brought Jacob a new clarity of mind. 'I've got no son, you've seen to that.'

Anna looked steadily at the man she despised.

'Amy Stevens was delivered of a child two nights ago,' she said quietly. 'The child was a son . . . your son.'

'I'll be back in two or three months, Anna, and then we'll be married.' Andrew gathered her into his arms. 'God, I wish I didn't have to leave but I have to return to the States to settle my affairs and sell the ranch.' He touched his lips to her hair, hand cradling her head. 'I love you, Anna,' he whispered. 'I love you . . . the days are going to be hellish dark until I see you again.'

Still his arms held her and Anna made no attempt to move, ignoring the stare of the station master-cum-porter-cum-ticket office attendant-cum-caretaker. The man who watched was all of those, in fact he was the only employee at Coseley Station as he had been on the night Anna had arrived. She had come on since that rainy night, that much he knew, but it hadn't changed her none. She was still the quiet wench she had been when Maggie Fellen had taken her in. Leastways with all except Jacob Rewcastle, and there was none in Coseley held that against her. No, this place was the better for her coming and if Maggie Fellen's lad could bring her happiness then there was none in Coseley would mind that. Picking up a broom, he shuffled away to the other end of the platform.

'Oh, Anna.' Andrew's arms tightened round her. 'The days are going to be so dark, so hellish dark.'

They would be dark for her too. Anna lifted her mouth to his goodbye kiss. But for a different reason. Andrew Fellen was a man who deserved the whole of a woman's love, the love a woman should hold for her husband, a love that held her heart and soul – and this was a love she couldn't give him. She closed her eyes, shutting out the cowardice that held her to an unspoken promise. Yes, the days ahead would be dark for her too, dark under the shadow of her own guilt.

Watching the train steam out of the station, and the figure waving until a curve in the track carried him from her sight, Anna felt that guilt settle heavier on her shoulders.

'You 'ave a visitor.'

Anna had walked slowly from the station, unwilling to go home, unwilling to face Maggie, convinced she must know the truth of her feelings for Andrew; she had that uncanny knack of knowing Anna's feelings almost as well as she knew them herself, and looking at those penetrating grey eyes now, Anna was convinced she knew it all.

'Visitor?' She slipped off her coat, letting Maggie take it from her. The last thing she wanted was a visitor. She wanted to be alone with Maggie, to sit with her and reason out the happenings of these last weeks, let Maggie's down-to-earth common sense sort out the tangle matters had taken.

'Ar, that's what I said.' Maggie folded the coat, nodding towards the sitting room. 'I've put 'im in there. I said as 'ow you'd gone to railway station but 'e said as 'e would wait.'

Removing her hat, Anna touched a nervous hand to her hair, her look questioning, but Maggie had already turned away. Smoothing her hand over the pale cream of her blouse and her green skirt, she breathed deeply, a feeling of sickness rising in her stomach.

Opening the door of the sitting room, her eyes flew to the man who stood at the fireplace and the sickness faded. Her visitor was not Jacob Rewcastle.

'Mr Harris.' Anna glanced behind her, not wanting to close

the door on Maggie, but seeing the hall empty she stepped forward, closing the door.

John Harris accepted the chair she indicated.

'I didn't wish to intrude, Mrs Royce, but I thought I ought to bring this in person.' Taking an envelope from the pocket of his black three-quarter-length coat, he held it out for Anna to take.

'There was no need for you to put yourself out, Mr Harris.' Anna felt she should smile but couldn't. 'I would have come to see you at the bank tomorrow.'

John Harris looked at her, unsmiling.

'I think when you read that you will understand why I had no wish to wait until tomorrow, Mrs Royce.'

Taking the envelope and tearing it open, Anna scanned the contents.

'I'm sorry.' John Harris stood up. 'If there is anything at all I can do . . .'

'Thank you.' She mouthed the words unconsciously, her mind stunned. She sat unmoving as the manager of Wigmore Bank let himself out, her eyes resting unseeing on the words of the letter he had just given her.

The bank had foreclosed.

They were calling in her loan.

Jacob Rewcastle had not called to see her but somehow she felt he was here in this room, and he was laughing.

Chapter Fifteen

Anna walked from the station into a street that had changed little in the years since she had seen it last.

One or two heads turned to look at the smartly dressed woman, a dark veil shrouding her hair and face, but as quickly turned away. Folk in Wednesbury were too busy earning a living to spend time gawking after a stranger.

Booking into The White Horse Hotel, she asked for a sixpenny runner to take a sealed letter to Polly Shipton.

'How . . . how did it happen, Polly?' she asked later greeting the woman who had delivered her son.

'It was suicide. 'E 'ung isself, Anna.'

'Oh my God!' Anna paced impotently about the room. 'But why, Polly, why?'

'Who knows the answer to that 'xceptin' the Almighty, me wench? P'raps 'e'd 'ad as much as he could tek.'

Like a wounded animal Anna didn't know whether to run or stay. It should not cause her this much pain . . . not after so long.

Turning to the window, she asked, 'Did he say anything . . . leave a note?'

''E said nothin' to anybody . . . the lad is as surprised as the rest on we. Knocked 'im sideways this 'as.'

The lad! Anna twisted her hands together. It must be her son Polly was talking about. Who else was there to be so upset at her father's suicide?

'How is he, Polly?' she asked quietly.

'A fine lad, Anna.' Behind her the old woman's voice carried obvious pride. 'Tall as 'is . . .'

'His father.' Anna finished the sentence. 'Did he know, Polly . . . about me?'

'No, me wench, Jos never 'ad the courage to tell 'im an' I thought as it was none of my business.'

'I see.' Anna's voice dropped to a whisper. 'And his name? What did my father name him?'

'Aaron . . . 'e were christened Aaron.' The old woman smiled. 'Learned 'is letters well 'e did at St Bart's until 'e were thirteen, then 'e left to set on for Joby 'Ampton. Jos didn't give much to that but said as 'ow lad 'ad a choice of 'is own.'

Anna's nails bit into her palms and her lips were white with tension but she knew she had to ask the question.

'And me, Polly?'

''E never spoke your name but 'e thought on you often, but what with the pain of what 'e did to you . . . I just 'ope as now 'e 'as found peace.'

'I . . . I can't see him, Polly.' Anna's hand trembled violently.

'I know, me wench.' Polly Shipton pulled the checked shawl closer round her thin shoulders. 'Anyway, Aaron 'ad 'im screwed down last night. Reckoned as there'd be none save 'imself an' me would be payin' respects.'

'When . . . when is it to . . .' Anna broke off, the words choking in her throat.

Crossing to the door, her crippled leg dragging heavily behind her, Polly looked back.

'Tomorrow mornin', eleven o'clock, at the Parish.'

It was time.

Anna sat on the edge of the bed in her small room in the hotel, as she had most of the night, reading over and over again the special delivery letter Polly Shipton had sent her.

'I thought as 'ow yer should know yer father died last night.' The words seared into her brain. Her father was dead, he had died without hearing her say she had forgiven him. But had she forgiven him? Could she forgive him? In her most secret heart Anna heard the words: Not yet . . . not yet. And now her father was dead, today would see the burying of him and she must be there. At least she could give him that.

'Will you be wantin' a carriage, Mrs Royce?'

Fat balding Harry Fletcher, who had been landlord of The White Horse when she was a child, danced attention on her as Anna walked down the polished wooden stairs to the lobby.

Inside she smiled acidly. Would he dance the same attention if he recognised the woman who had checked into his hotel last night as Jos Bradly's daughter? It was a safe bet Polly's tongue would tell him to mind his own business should he ask who it was had sent for her last night.

'I can send to Joby 'Ampton's for one, won't tek but ten minutes.'

Joby Hampton. Anna remembered the tall friendly man who owned the steel works that had employed many of the men of Wednesbury when the coal seams began to run out. His pride and passion had been his horses, trotters that drew his two-wheeled racing traps. Her father had driven many a race for Joby and sometimes in the evening he had gone to help exercise the horses. He had taken her with him then, swinging her squealing with delight into the trap when Joby had said she could ride with him.

'No, thank you.' Anna stood waiting as Harry Fletcher opened the door that gave on to Holyhead Road. 'I'll walk.'

A slight drizzle began to fall as she walked up along Lower High Street towards The Shambles. The last time she had walked these streets her heart was breaking. It was breaking still. People glanced as she passed but paid no more heed and Anna spoke to no one. There was no need. Every street in the tiny town was engraved on her heart. Passing The Pretty Bricks public house, nicknamed for the maroon-glazed tiles beneath its bottle-glass bay window, she walked halfway up steep Ethelfleda Terrace, stopping short of the house that had been her home. Below her the houses she had passed, all with closed curtains, pretended grief at the passing of Jos Bradly.

Hypocrites! Resentment flared in Anna. You tortured him with your lies about Mary Carter, accusing and backbiting, until you drove him mad.

It was you who raped me, every single one of you.

Standing half-hidden behind a tree, she drew little notice from the women grouped about the gate of the house: they were too engrossed in their morbid occupation to pay her much heed. From where she stood on the gentle swell of the hill Anna watched the wooden ladder placed against the bedroom window; watched as with the aid of ropes the rough coffin was lowered down then carried, not along the garden path and through the gate, but across the tiny garden where it was passed like some nameless parcel over the low wall.

It was a matter of yards to the lych gate but the men carrying her father's coffin did not carry it beneath its shelter but set it on the ground, leaving it there while Polly Shipton and the tall lad with hair the colour of Misty's followed the vicar into the church. He had been right, her son, there were only two to pay their respects.

Anna glanced over to where the group of women was dispersing. The show was over. Now they would gather like scavenging crows to pick over bits of her father's life. Alone in the rain, Anna kept her silent vigil, unable to walk the few yards to that lonely coffin; equally unable to turn and leave it.

They came at last from the church, her son and cripple Polly, followed by the vicar and four men who had doubtless been well paid to carry this particular coffin. Anna brushed the rain that clung like tears to her cheeks. Now finally her father would be taken to his rest in the churchyard. Trembling from head to foot, she watched the four men lift the coffin to their shoulders and carry it outside the wall of the churchyard to where a large hole gaped black beneath a huge oak tree. Of course. Anna bit her lip to stifle the cry in her throat. Her father would not lie in the sanctified ground of St Bartholomew's Parish Church. He was a suicide, he had suffered a suicide's funeral, yet still his punishment was not finished. His body had received no blessing, his grave would know no tombstone.

'Was I wrong, Polly?' Back at The White Horse Anna looked at the woman who had cared for her son. 'Should I have stayed?'

'Nay, wench.' Polly Shipton saw the anguish tearing at the woman who paced the room. The wench had always been pretty; now she was beautiful, with the creamy colouring and classic bone structure that had been her mother's and the proud bearing that was a legacy from her father. Oh, yes, he would have been proud of her, would Jos Bradly.

'You would never 'ave survived, not against the bitches as 'aunts this town.'

'But my son, Polly, I left him, I turned my back on him.'

'You left 'im, 'tis true.' Polly made no attempt at denial. 'But turned your back on 'im you never did. You sent money regular though it must 'ave been mortal 'ard on you . . . aye, wench, afore you asks Jos knew where it came from though 'e never commented . . . like I says, you 'ave nowt you should 'old against yourself. Go. Get you away back to where you 'ave made yourself a good 'ome. You 'ave a daughter you must think on an' it seems you 'ave a good friend in that Maggie Fellen.'

'As I have in you, Polly.' A thin smile touched Anna's mouth. 'I have a son too and I love him.' The smile faded. 'I loved him when I left him with you.'

'You went to the 'ouse?'

'Yes.' Anna stood at the window, looking out over the one decent street the town could boast. 'While you were at the graveside. I . . . I hadn't the courage to see . . .'

'Ar, wench,' Polly nodded, 'did 'e see you there?'

Anna could only nod.

'An' did you tell 'im?'

Anna turned from the window, tears coursing from her eyes.

'I couldn't, Polly. I hadn't the courage. I love him but I . . . I can't risk his hatred. Better he never knows me.'

'Ar, you 'ave your life an' lad 'as 'is. Best leave it that way.'

'But it sounds so heartless put that way.'

Polly Shipton pulled her checked shawl higher on to her shoulders.

'An' is it less 'eartless to tell 'im now? I tell you, Anna, lad's 'ad as much as 'e can 'old. Tell 'im if you will but not yet. 'E can't tek another blow like the one 'e 'as just been dealt.'

She was right. Anna watched her crippled friend limp to the door. Her son was tall and strong but it was the strength of youth. Tax it too hard and it would break.

'He will always be cared for, Polly,' she whispered, 'as long as I have a penny, it will be his.'

'You 'ave no need to tell me that, me wench.' Polly's lined face broke into a smile. 'Hasn't it always? But from now on you must see to some other road of gettin' it to 'im. I can no longer pass it off as comin' from 'is grandfather.'

'His grandfather?'

For a moment the question hung in the air then Polly answered.

'Ar, that's what Jos told 'im an' I saw no reason to change it.'

'Did . . . did he ever ask about me?' Anna asked tremulously. 'Did he ever ask about his mother?'

'Ar.' Polly Shipton gazed levelly at the daughter of the man they had buried less than an hour since. 'Ar, 'e asked about you all right. I told 'im you was dead.'

'But why didn't you discuss it with me first?'

Sitting in Hester's pretty sitting room, Anna looked at her solicitor.

'It all happened so quickly, Reuben. John Harris brought the bank's letter in the evening and next morning I got one telling me my father was dead. That drove all else from my mind.'

'Is there anything you can do, Reuben?' Hester was close to tears.

'Under the terms written here the loan can be called in any time.' Reuben tapped the document he was holding.

'It was a stupid risk to take in the first place, Anna, buying Rewcastle's Mill. You must have known that you were putting most of your eggs in one basket.'

'My only thought was of all those men losing their jobs.'

'But why, for what reason, should the bank act this way?'

Reuben Fine shook his head, peering at his wife over the spectacles he had taken to wearing. 'From what Anna says it sounds like collusion.' Someone, somewhere, had called in some favours and Anna was paying the price.

'But I still don't understand.'

'There's nothing to understand, Hester.' Anna had gone through the whys and wherefores a thousand times since opening that letter. 'It's my bet Jacob Rewcastle is at the back of this. It's my own fault, John Harris warned me the directors of Wigmore's Bank were friends of his.'

'But what does he get out of it?'

'Satisfaction!' Reuben glanced at his wife. 'Jealousy . . . revenge . . . spite. Each is a powerful motivator, but reasons we can discuss later. Right now we need to find a solution.'

'I've counted every last penny of cash.' Anna produced a list from her bag, handing it to Reuben. 'There are accounts yet to be paid but I can't guarantee the money will come in time and as things stand I'm short some three hundred pounds.'

'Seven days!' He blew down his nose. 'Whoever dreamed this up didn't give you much time.'

'That old swine would make sure they didn't,' Hester said, 'but we've got a bit put by, Anna, you can use that if it will help.'

'Thanks.' She patted her friend's hand. 'But I couldn't take what you and Reuben have worked hard for, I couldn't live with myself if I lost it. Besides,' she saw Hester's rueful look, 'it's not the end of the world. I've lost the mill but I still have the shops.'

I have failed you, Edward, Anna thought as the train carried her home from Birmingham. I tried to get King's Choice for you but I failed.

'It'll be none but 'im.' Maggie listened to the reason for Anna's new worry. 'I told you that Jacob Rewcastle was as sly as a cartload of monkeys. If 'e couldn't put one over on you one way, then 'e would find another.'

'Well, he has found one I can't fight, Maggie. Joby Timmins has gone through these figures with a fine-toothed comb and I have done the same, but I am still three hundred pounds short. Another month, Maggie, another month and I could have paid the lot.'

For several minutes more Anna gazed at the neatly entered columns of numbers, their totals emblazoned in red ink, then slammed the black bound ledger shut.

'He has won after all, Maggie,' she said resignedly, 'Jacob Rewcastle has won. In a week there will be no Bradly Engineering and King's Choice will be gone.'

'You tried your best, wench,' Maggie said softly. 'Nobody could have done more.'

'It was not enough though, was it?' Anna stared at the ledger.

'I knows this be more easy said than it be to do, Anna, but try to put it out of your mind. The mill has to go, and that be all there is to it, you have other ways of keeping a roof over your head, Rewcastle hasn't took the lot.'

'I don't mind losing the mill, but to lose it to him! What would Edward say?'

'He would tell you what I've told you already. It ain't through no fault of yours that the mill be going, he would see Jacob's hand in this as I see it. He's got his friends to put their heads together and they have come up with that letter. Foreclosing! That be a bit of conniving if ever I seen it.'

'Connivance or not,' Anna sighed, 'it has taken the mill out of my hands. I only hope it will not affect the workers.'

'We can only wait and see, wench. Won't do no good worryin'. What the Lord has set to happen will happen whether you worry or you don't. But the way I thinks is this: He has let you work too hard and too long only to take it from you now. My mother had a saying, "God is good, if He don't come, He sends." Something will turn up, wench. I be sure of it.'

'I wish I had your belief, Maggie.' Leaving the ledger on the table, Anna crossed to where the older woman sat and sank to her knees, resting her head in the wide lap. 'But not having that doesn't matter, as long as I have you.'

Maggie touched a hand to the red gold hair of the girl she loved as her own, remembering what Kate O'Keefe had said. But Anna was more than the daughter of her heart, she was the blood in her veins, and even when she was wed to Andrew she would not mean more.

Undressing for bed, Anna turned over events in her mind. She was in no doubt that Jacob Rewcastle's hand was behind the calling in of her loan. He would have called on his cronies, most probably holding some threat over their heads. Either that or it was the old pal's act, men closing ranks against a woman who dared to enter their world; a woman who had the audacity to presume she could hold her own in the field of heavy industry.

Pulling a brush through her hair, she stared at her reflection in the mirror of her dressing table. She was no longer the girl who had been driven from her home, a girl who had given up her son in the face of other people's spite.

He thinks I am dead.

The hand holding the brush fell to her lap and the gaze resting on the mirror no longer saw her own reflection but instead the tall figure that had followed her father's coffin, the over-large suit in no way diminishing her pride in the way he carried himself.

He was her son. The child she longed for in every waking moment, the child whose tiny body she seemed to feel against her own every time she lay down to sleep; the son she would never hold in her arms again yet whom she would hold in her heart forever.

'Aaron,' she whispered, 'don't hate me too much, my son. I left for your sake, not for my own, what I did, I did for you, for the sake of my child.'

'Maggie Fellen is a strong woman.' Doctor Merrow pulled on the chamois gloves that had long since passed their best and took up his black Gladstone bag from the hall table. 'But I've known the strongest horses to fall, Anna, and this last blow . . .'

The doctor who had brought Misty into the world shook his head slowly before going to the door.

'We all need courage to go on living sometimes but that woman is going to need more than most. Take care of her. We don't have too many of her kind.'

Anna held the door ajar, her own face pale and drawn. 'I've asked her so many times to have help, this house isn't Roker Street, but she would hear none of it, do you think that now I should insist?'

'No, Anna.' The doctor touched a hand to her arm, his smile gentle on a face lined before its time. 'This is the wrong time to impose any kind of change. She needs to do the things she's always done, she needs things to be as normal as possible. It's a bad business, Anna, but with the Lord's help and yours she'll pull through.'

She watched the doctor, his shabby collar turned up against the cold, climb into the small trap, take up the reins and urge the bay mare into a gentle trot, before she closed the door and returned to Maggie's bedroom. The woman she loved with all her heart was sleeping, the laudanum draught the doctor had given her doing its work. Anna gazed at the sleeping figure, so small and lost in the bed she had once shared with a man who had walked out on her. The passing of the many years since showed on her tired face. *WHY*? screamed Anna's heart. *WHY*? The old clock on the mantel chimed softly as she left the room. Going to the small room off the hall that she had turned into an office, she lifted the telephone, cranking the handle at the side.

'Good afternoon, Miss Grant, this is Anna Royce,' she told the headmistress of Haworth School for Young Ladies. 'My daughter has asked permission to spend the holiday with the Rothmans in Switzerland. Would you tell her, please, that if the invitation still stands, she may go?'

Replacing the ear piece on the hook, cutting off any questions, Anna walked into the sitting room. For a moment she stared around the room, so empty without Maggie, then crossing to the huge Christmas tree in the corner, began to strip it of its tinsel and delicate glass balls. Gathering the brightly wrapped presents, she pushed them into a cupboard under the stairs. There would be no celebration in this house. Picking up the yellow envelope from where Maggie had dropped it on the mahogany table beside the sofa, Anna held it for a minute: such a small envelope to carry so terrible a message. Screwing the envelope into a ball, she flung it into the fire. Maggie would have no need of it to remember what was written inside.

'Appendicitis' the shipping line had telegraphed. Andrew had developed appendicitis a week off the Azores. They had made all speed but had been too late. He had died on board.

'I should have known,' was all Maggie had said. 'I thought that this time Kate O'Keefe was wrong, but I should have known.'

'*One ye will see again in this life but once only*.' Again the Irish woman's prediction had proved true. And what of the words spoken to Anna Bradly? '*The man who will encircle yer heart is not in this land*.' Anna's mouth tightened. This was the end of the prediction. She had married Edward and he had died; she was to have married Andrew and he had died; Philip Rewcastle had taken his own life and that of Sir Robert Daines after becoming involved with her; her father had committed suicide because of her. But there would be no other. No other man would lose his life because of the jinx that was Anna Royce.

'Oh, how beautiful, you spoil me dreadfully!'

'They be nowhere near as beautiful as your eyes, my dear!' In a private room of the Birmingham Royal Hotel, Jacob Rewcastle fastened a necklace of sapphires about the neck of his latest paramour. His hot eyes lingered over the magnolia of her jutting breasts and his body quickened at the thought of what was to come. Young and pretty, she welcomed his embraces. She would give him what the girl Amy had claimed yet he did not believe. She would give him a son.

She would give him a son to replace the one that bitch had taken from him. He had thought to harm that daughter of hers. Pity the brat had been whisked off to some school or other before he could, but there would be other chances. Stroking a podgy hand over the taut young breast, Jacob smiled. He was not through with Anna Royce though his associates would see her finished in business. Tonight would see the start of a new beginning, a new son for Jacob Rewcastle.

'You must let me thank you properly, Jacob.'

She turned to him, her eyes meltingly soft. Slowly she removed the cravat from his throat then dropped her hands to the buttons of his waistcoat, expertly slipping them loose. Blood beat a throbbing rhythm against Jacob's temple, deepening his florid complexion. The girl was a fever in his blood. Pushing his hands away, she continued to touch and stroke, building the fires of passion as she stripped him.

The sheets of the bed were cool but the heat within him soared as Jacob watched the girl lift her arms, carrying her shift above her head; saw her free long slender legs from a pool of silken petticoats. He felt the breath snag in his throat as she shook her black hair loose, letting it fall in a cloud about her shoulders. Climbing into bed beside him, naked except for the sapphires about her neck, she pressed the cool column of her body against his.

'Put out the gas, my dear,' Jacob whispered hoarsely.

'Why?' The girl pushed herself to her knees, a pout on her red mouth. 'Does the sight of me not please you, Jacob?'

The beating in his temples intensifying, his eyes slid from the pretty childish features to the dark triangle at the base of her soft belly. He was so bloody lucky, finding a girl like this. Every minute with her was a pleasure, especially when those minutes were spent in bed. He closed his eyes, brain throbbing like a steam engine as she bent over him, brushing her nipples against his lips.

To hell with what society might think. Fingers clumsy with passion, Jacob grabbed a soft breast, sucking at it like a hungry infant. To hell with what anybody thought, he was going to make this girl his wife.

His mouth still clamped around his soft prize, he rolled her beneath him. She gave a cry as he penetrated her, as though receiving him for the first time, and the pleasure of it increased the pounding in his head. The pressure behind his eyes threatened to force them from their sockets with every thrust into that warm moistness. He had fixed that bitch Anna Royce and tonight he would fix the only other thing he wanted. Tonight he would fill this girl with his child.

'This is for my necklace, Jacob.'

Beneath him the velvet eyes smouldered, but his own closing against the pain of passion, Jacob missed their expression of loathing.

'You like this, don't you?' she whispered, contracting then releasing the muscles of her vagina, sucking at his bloated penis. 'Tell me you like it, Jacob.'

Jacob Rewcastle didn't answer. His lower jaw falling slackly, he choked in the back of his throat, dropping full on to the girl beneath him.

For a minute she lay listening to the sounds of Jacob fighting for breath then, heaving him away, rolled from the bed.

Replacing her clothes, tidying her hair carefully beneath a trim red bonnet, she looked again at Jacob, her mouth parting in a cold smile as his eyes begged for help.

'Not from me, you slimy bastard.' She laughed quietly. 'You'll get no help from me.'

Picking up first his jacket then his trousers, she removed every penny then closed the door behind her and walked from the hotel, nodding to the night porter as she went.

Chapter Sixteen

The long days of Christmas were over and though Anna was reluctant to leave Maggie she was glad to be free of the house. It had been hard letting Misty go to Switzerland – the time she had with her daughter was precious – but home had been no place for her this year.

Misty was growing up fast. Anna closed her eyes and saw in her mind the pretty smiling face, eyes blue as a cornflower and the pale blonde hair. Her daughter would be a beautiful woman. Opening her eyes, Anna stared out of the window of the train carrying her to London. The house had been so quiet, it would have been unfair on a young girl, so full of all the gaiety of life, to insist she come home for the holiday, a home heavy with sadness and fear, fear that Maggie might not recover from the death of her son. It might have been easier on them all if Maggie had cried, instead of this awful dry eyed quiet . . .

Across the compartment a man cleared his throat then noisily refolded his newspaper. Anna glanced across at him, then returned her gaze to the passing fields as he settled back to his reading.

Maggie had said almost nothing since receiving the telegram that had told her, so coldly and abruptly, of Andrew's death at sea, but Anna had heard her murmuring, 'One ye'll see once more.' The words of Kate's prophecy.

But Maggie was keeping her tears inside, Anna thought. Keeping them to shed in the long lonely hours of the night, as Anna kept hers. Allowing only the shadows to see her pain, to know the extent of her suffering.

Maggie had lost her son as Anna had lost hers. True, Aaron was not dead in the sense that Andrew Fellen was dead, but he was just as lost to her.

Don't tell the lad just yet, Mother Polly had warned. And she had not told him. She had left Wednesbury without telling her son who she was. That had been as painful as leaving him that first time.

In her lap her fingers clenched with the memory that had never truly left her. Could telling him have been worse than this, worse than the hurt that ripped through her every time she thought of him, every time she saw a mother with her son, every time she spoke of him in her prayers? And if he had turned his back on her, what then? Could she have stood the pain of that?

One day she might have to.

Watching the passing scenery her fingers curled even tighter, but the bite of her nails into her palm was nothing compared to the bite of the thoughts in her mind.

One day she would have to face that threat, for Aaron had the right to know his parentage.

Beatrice Rewcastle looked at the still figure of the man they had carried from that room in the Birmingham Royal. Doubtless he had gone there with some woman, one who had robbed him then left him to choke his life away.

'You should have died,' she murmured, 'why should you live when my son is dead?'

Jacob's right eyelid twitched then opened, leaving the left one closed, paralysed by the stroke that had taken all power of movement from the left side of his body.

He swallowed, but distaste returned as quickly as he tried to rid himself of it. His body might be half dead, but not his mind. Whatever had struck at him in that hotel room had not affected his brain, or his sight, he thought, gazing at the woman who stood at the bottom of the bed. He knew what he must do, and it was almost as galling as having to look at her!

'I want Brown,' he muttered. 'I want to see 'im. Tell 'im to come in the mornin'.'

'What for?' Beatrice asked.

'Mind your own bloody business!' His uncertain temper remained unaltered. Try to keep him as quiet as possible, the doctor had warned. He could suffer a second stroke at any time and that would certainly kill him; don't let him excite himself and he might pull through.

'Couldn't you see him next week?' Beatrice watched the purple patches on her husband's face. 'The doctor said you were to have complete rest and quiet.'

'Doctor! 'E's as bloody daft as you!' Jacob exploded. 'Send word to Brown to get 'is arse over 'ere in the mornin', and bloody well do it now!'

Lips tight, against the smile that so wanted to curve her thin mouth, Beatrice pulled the bell cord hanging beside the huge bed.

'Daisy,' she said as a maid answered her summons, 'tell Newton to send over to Lawyer Brown, he is to say that Mr Rewcastle would be obliged if he would call tomorrow.'

'Obliged!' The thunder was muted by twisted, half-closed lips but Jacob's one eye flashed brilliant with anger. 'Who said owt about bein' bloody obliged!' His heavy head lolled towards the maid standing nervously near the door. 'You tell Newton 'e is to say as Jacob Rewcastle 'as business with 'im an' 'e is to 'ave 'is arse over 'ere in the mornin' afore nine o'clock.'

'Yes, sir.' Not daring to look at her mistress, the girl scuttled from the room.

Beatrice folded her hands over her brown bombazine skirts. Her grey hair was parted along the centre and pulled severely over her ears into a tight bun on the nape of her thin neck, it only accentuated her rapier-honed features.

Jacob squinted at her, distaste thick in his mouth. She looked like a freshly sharpened pencil.

'You can bugger off,' he slurred. 'I can do wi'out your parsimonious face.'

'I agree I was never pretty, Jacob.' Beatrice didn't move. 'Never pretty enough to work you into the kind of filthy frenzy that has left you less than half a man.'

Struggling to lift himself, he dropped back in breathless defeat.

'Wha . . . what do you be knowin' of passion, you bloody vinegar-faced bitch? You who 'as always been too miserable to open your mouth, let alone your legs.'

'That didn't really bother you, Jacob,' she said acidly. 'You had my money. Enough to buy all the women you wanted.'

'An' enjoyed 'em all.' Jacob's twisted mouth screwed into a smile. Beatrice continued to smile also, a smile of satisfaction.

'But that is all over now, Jacob. You are crippled. Oh, not in your mind and that is good. You still have full control of that, and with it you can think of all these long hours you have left . . . to spend alone in that bed.'

'The devil take you, you bloody bitch!' He seethed, his right hand grasping fruitlessly at the bed cover. 'The devil take you!'

'Devil or God,' Beatrice returned calmly, 'I would willingly go with whichever put you there.'

Two hours later she held the letter Lawyer Brown had sent in return to her husband's message. She could guess why Jacob wanted to see him. She had heard of the birth of Amy Stevens' son.

Putting the letter on the tray which held a cup of mulled wine, she nodded to Newton to carry it upstairs. A smile on her narrow face, she turned into the sitting room. With that nod Beatrice Rewcastle had sentenced her husband to death. Who would know it was poison and not a second stroke had taken him to his grave?

• • •

Anna tried to relax in the hansom carrying her across the city to the shop she had set up in London. Everywhere was noise. The shouts of men loading wagons, the clang of trams and the clatter of horses' hooves. She should be used to the noise, after all she visited Birmingham regularly enough, but this . . . Anna leaned back in the carriage, even Birmingham was no match for this madness.

What would Maggie make of it? She smiled at the thought. She would probably use one of her favourite phrases, 'everybody rushing around like a man with his arse on fire looking for a bucket of water to put it out'.

Maggie. Anna's thoughts turned to the woman she had left behind in Coseley. She had always been so strong, always ready to push on when Anna herself had wanted to give in. It had been Maggie who had helped her when she had arrived penniless on her doorstep, Maggie who had been so understanding when she had told her of her son, and it was Maggie who had been there for her when Edward was killed.

Please God, take care of Maggie, Anna prayed silently as the hansom dropped her at the shop.

'I hope you approve, Anna.' Emma showed her the small tea room she and William had created from an almost derelict side building. 'We thought that if we served tea and cakes after the clients had browsed through the shop, they would probably look through the catalogue and order their purchases before leaving the premises. It seems to have worked rather well,' she added nervously.

'I think it's a marvellous idea. Thank you, Emma. No wonder the shop is so popular. Your William makes a lovely cup of tea.'

'He is wonderful, Anna.' Emma's nervousness faded and her violet eyes glowed with a soft secretive warmth that tugged at Anna's heart. 'He works all day unpacking deliveries, making up orders, brewing pots of tea – he has even learned to make cakes and scones. Then in the evening he takes out deliveries.

That was why we bought the hand cart, Anna. We tried to do without it because of the expense but . . .'

'It was the sensible thing to do, Emma,' she interrupted, 'as was this tea room. You and William have proved your worth and that is why I am putting you on a share basis. From now on, Emma, you take the same as Hester. Two per cent of what this shop makes is yours, over and above your salary.'

When Emma's tears of happiness had subsided, Anna continued, 'Did William take my apologies to Lady Strathlyn?'

'Yes, Anna, and Her Ladyship *had* asked you to call. She questioned William very closely.'

Then it had not been a ruse. Charles had not wanted to see her. Wrong again, Anna, she thought grimly. But then, you were wrong about Charles from the start.

'Whew!' Anna wiped the perspiration from her face. 'We are all going to have a cup of tea, and this time, William, *I* will make it.'

'It's beautiful, Anna, quite the loveliest yet.'

The three friends sat together in the salon which had taken the whole day to set out.

'Credit where it is due, Emma.' Anna sipped gratefully at the hot tea. 'I only design the china. It's Seth Gladwin who does the rest.'

She looked at the setting the three of them had created; unable to afford a huge dining table they had laid floor boards across piles of house bricks, covering the whole down to the floor with a flowing damask cloth William had found on the rag market and which Emma had boiled until it was white as new snow.

She had proved invaluable in so many ways: taking Anna to the Saturday night market in Petticoat Lane to find elegant wine glasses; refusing to pay more than tuppence each for the chairs the junk man wanted sixpence for, then rolling up her sleeves and helping scrub and polish them until they shone. She had folded napkins into white pleated fans and laid the King's Choice cutlery.

Edward would have been so proud. Tears trembled along Anna's lashes as Emma lit two four-branched candelabra that only that afternoon had been black with the dirt of ages. Pale translucent candlelight spilled in soft lemony pools, tinting the glasses and playing gently over the exquisite claret and gold china. Royal Edward, Anna's own design and choice of colour, brought into vivid, beautiful reality by Seth Gladwin's skilful hands. Emma was right: this was her most beautiful range of china yet.

'A gentleman to see me?' Anna wrapped the glistening folds of her wet hair into a towel. Something had happened at the shop. It must be William come to tell her for only he and Emma knew where she was staying. Reaching for a peignoir, she fastened it hurriedly. She had only left the shop an hour ago.

'Ask him to come up,' she said, tightening the towel about her head. William would understand her informality . . . nothing must go wrong with tomorrow's launch of Royal Edward.

'Yes, ma'am.' The blank-faced hotel maid bobbed a curtsy and two minutes later a knock sounded on the door.

'Come in, William,' Anna called from the bathroom, then stared in disbelief as she emerged.

'Hello, Anna!' said Charles softly, his eyes drinking in the flushed loveliness of her face.

'How . . . how did you know I was here?' The first stunning blow of surprise fading, Anna found her tongue. 'Did Emma tell you?'

'No.' The well-formed mouth curled to a smile. 'And I very much doubt if that worthy lady would tell me anything I asked her.'

'Then how?'

'I saw you walking along Queen Anne's Gate. It was an easy guess you would be staying at The Conway.'

'How very shrewd of you,' Anna returned acidly, 'and how thoughtless of me. I shall know better than use this hotel in future.'

'If I knew you were in London, Anna, I would visit every hotel until I found you.'

If he thought to flatter her, he had made a mistake. All the latent anger and misery of the months since Andrew's death, and the travesty of a funeral that had been accorded her father, suddenly broke through.

'And tell your wife what?' she blazed. 'Or have you got your seedy little life so well ordered you don't have to tell her anything? Perhaps she is so pleased to be Mrs Lazenby that she turns a blind eye to your excursions. Or could it be that, like myself, she is not interested in what you do?'

'My wife . . .'

'Don't bother to tell me she doesn't understand you, Charles.'

'Anna, I must talk to you.'

He stepped nearer and her chin came up defiantly.

'Why? Isn't she interested in listening to your lies either? And if all you have to talk about is some nice little house in the suburbs, you can save your breath, Charles. Now, please go. As you can see, I am not prepared for visitors, especially unwelcome ones.'

'What gives you the idea that I am married, Anna?' He asked it softly, no trace of rancour in his tone.

'Are you telling me you're not?' Eyes filled with scorn were fixed on him disbelievingly.

'I mean just that.'

He was cool, she had to give him that.

'Then the girl who was selecting china was your mistress! A bit young, I would have thought, even for you.'

He remained perfectly still, only his eyes hardening beneath the fall of fair hair still worn without pomade.

'The young lady I was escorting the last time you and I met was not my mistress, Anna, she was my sister.'

She felt the room revolve about her. His sister . . . and she had accused her of being little more than a high-class trollop!

'I . . . I'm sorry.' It was all she could say.

His smile returned, softening his eyes. He was so devastatingly good-looking, no woman could be blamed for becoming his mistress.

'I will accept your apology only if you accompany me to the theatre and then dine with me afterwards?'

Anna walked to the window, looking out over the darkened street.

'I can't,' she said. 'As you can see, I am not dressed for the theatre.'

'Then we will dine here, in this room!'

'No.' Anna turned sharply. 'That would not be proper.'

Charles Lazenby was naturally charming, and knew now to use that charm, but he was a fool if he really believed he could hoodwink Anna Royce.

'Wait for me downstairs.' She saw the smile curve his mouth again and her own lips tightened. Charles would get his apology . . . but that was all he would get.

Fastening the tiny pearl buttons of her cotton gloves, Anna gave herself a long look in the mirror. The cream grosgrain dress with its wide belt and fashionable hobble skirt, stopping short of her ankles, emphasised her slim body and accentuated the shining red-gold of her hair. Her skin was as soft and creamy as it had always been, and for all that she had suffered, not a line marred her face.

'You make a presentable picture, Anna Royce,' she whispered. 'Presentable enough for any man's mistress, but not acceptable enough for a wife.'

Turning, she picked up the cream silk chiffon scarf lying on the table and tucked it into her belt. At thirty-four years old she should have been at home with a husband and family instead of going for a picnic with a man who had no intention of ever offering her a legitimate position as his wife. Why did you say you would go? she asked herself for the umpteenth time. Why didn't you stick to your plans and say you were returning to Coseley this morning? But she hadn't, she had accepted Charles's invitation before he had left the hotel last night, and now she must go through with it.

She had reached the lobby when Charles came in. Dressed in a thigh-length belted slate grey coat, teamed with breeches and knee-length leather boots, he drew every eye as he slipped off his gauntlet gloves and raised her hand to his lips.

'You look very beautiful, Anna,' he said, eyes filled with admiration. 'Like some pale goddess who will suddenly melt away in a pearly mist – only I'm not going to let you melt away, now or ever. I thought we'd go somewhere along the river. The parks are always filled with people you simply have to stop and speak to, and I'm not ready to share you with anybody.'

He didn't smile as he looked down into her face and Anna did not blush as she once would have done. She had the measure of Charles Lazenby, she was under no illusions about him.

'Your coach, ma'am.' The seductive smile giving way to a delighted boyish grin, he stopped beside a green horseless carriage, its lacquered coachwork and huge brass headlamps gleaming in the morning light.

'I'm not riding in that!' Anna stepped emphatically backward.

'Why not?' His grin widening, Charles took her arm. 'It won't bite you. It is only a motor carriage.'

'Is that what you call it?' She cast a disparaging glance along the shining length of the vehicle. 'I saw one of these in Queen Anne's Gate. Noisy smelly things! I don't like them.'

'You haven't given them a chance. Come on, Anna, be fair. If you don't like it after you have given it a go, I will never ask you to ride in one again.'

Against her better judgement she climbed into the high leather seat, her hands gripping tight to the side.

'Relax,' Charles laughed, 'and I should fasten that pretty hat on with something. It can be breezy riding in this.'

'I prefer a hansom,' she grumbled, tying the chiffon scarf about her head. 'They are much more civilised.'

'But not half the fun.' Charles cranked the starting handle and the huge machine jerked into life.

'You'll see, Anna,' he called over the noise of the engine. 'By the time we get home you will love this asthmatic monster as much as I do.'

Don't count on it, she thought, every bone in her body jolting as they drove away. Give me an old cart any time.

The sound of a stone hitting water caused Anna to open her eyes. She watched concentric circles widen in the sun-sequinned river. Along the banks, huge trees dipped their branches in worship, and somewhere among their foliage birds sang a hymn to their creator.

'Sorry . . . did I wake you?'

'I wasn't asleep.' She sat up. 'I was thinking about the last time I went on a picnic . . . it seems so long ago.' Perhaps it was the magic of the moment, Anna could never decide why later, but easing her back against a tree trunk she told Charles of that Sunday school outing, of Peter and her paper diamond.

'Peter was right.' He turned to her as she finished speaking. 'You should have diamonds, Anna, but not paper ones.' He caught her hands, his eyes fathomless and serious. 'I want to give you those diamonds, Anna, I want to drown you in them.'

He had taken the moment, her lovely peaceful moment, and shattered it. Feeling she had lost something irreplaceable, Anna was overcome with rage. She had tried for so long to keep calm but now her angry reply sent the birds wheeling from the trees.

'How many more times do I have to say it? How many more times must you hear it before you will accept it? I will not be your mistress!'

Anger draining her, leaving her empty of any feeling at all, she walked to the edge of the river, staring into its depths.

'Why?' Charles asked, stamping a boot against the riverbank. 'Because of your business? How many paper diamonds does it take to make a string, for Christ's sake?'

'No, it is not because of my business.' Anna felt strangely calm, the anger of a moment before dissipated. He had made her a totally unacceptable offer, one that should preclude her ever speaking to him again, but deep down she had a feeling that beneath the arrogant self-assurance, Charles was a kind and caring man.

'Not my business,' she repeated, 'but my morals. I am not a whore and I will be no man's mistress.'

Charles Lazenby looked at the woman, her head held high, and admitted he had lost. He had thought to make Anna Royce his mistress but once again his gamble had not paid off.

'I beg your pardon, Anna.' He smiled sheepishly. 'My behaviour has been reprehensible, and I apologise. But with your beauty, you cannot condemn me for trying. Will you forgive me?'

'If I have your word you will never refer to it again?'

'You have it.' He gave a slight bow. 'But might I ask that we be friends, Anna?'

She smiled.

'No one can ever have too many of those,' she said, 'especially me.'

'Then as one friend to another, Anna, may I ask you once again to call me Charles?'

How many paper diamonds does it take to make a string? Charles's question echoed in her mind as he drove her to the railway station, but it was a question to which she found no answer. She had thought only to take back King's Choice but now she could not stop, the livelihood of too many others was tied in with her own. '*The lives of many will be bound to yer own* . . .' How true Kate O'Keefe's word were proving, but how much more must she do? Charles had been right to ask – how many more paper diamonds *would* it take? With sickening certainty Anna knew she had become caught in a web of her own making, chained by manacles strong as her lust for revenge.

'Would you prefer it if we came to the house?'

'I would appreciate it,' Anna answered Reuben's question.

'We could call around seven this evening, is that too late?'

'No, seven will be fine.'

'Seven it is then, Anna.'

I could have done without having to see anyone tonight, Anna thought, feeling the weariness that seemed at times to eat into her bones. But she had not wished to refuse Reuben's request she see this friend of his father's.

Hearing the quiet click that told her Reuben had hung up she replaced the telephone on the hook. He had said it was a matter of business.

More business. Anna leaned back in her chair. Why discuss more business when she was losing half of what she had? Why not give it all up? Paper diamonds. That was what Peter had said. But she would give them all and more besides, everything she had fought tooth and nail for, if only her son were with her. If she could only have both of the children she loved so much. That would be the brightest diamond of them all.

She had kept the promise to take back King's Choice, in doing so had acquired a few more paper diamonds, but she would trade them all for one smile from her son's proud young face.

'I love you Aaron,' she whispered, pushing up from her chair. 'You may never know it but I love you, my son.'

Reuben Fine arrived at seven on the dot, bringing with him an elderly man he introduced as Emanuel Goldberg.

'Such a name, sheesh!' The man shrugged his shoulders, blue eyes twinkling behind heavy framed spectacles. 'But my friends are good to me, they call me Manny. Maybe you will call me Manny, Mrs Royce?'

Feeling an instinctive liking for the short grey-haired man, Anna took the hand he held out to her.

'We might do a deal.' She smiled. 'I will trade Manny for Anna.'

'Sheesh, Reuben my boy!' The eyes holding Anna's twinkled like blue sequins. 'You say the woman is not Jewish . . . so where did she get such a head for business?'

Taking both of their coats, Anna hung them in the coat closet standing against one wall of the hall, then led the way into the sitting room.

'Will you take some tea?'

'No, my dear.' The old man replied smilingly. 'It was good of you to agree to see me, I should not take even more of your time.'

'It will take very little of my time to make tea.' Anna appreciated the thought behind his refusal and her smile was warm.

'Then I shall say yes, a little tea always helps the business of business.'

In the kitchen she collected china on a tray and brewed tea in a china pot, and all the while she could hear the voice of Jacob Rewcastle in her head. 'You've lost it after all, Anna Royce. You've lost the mill that was mine, and you'll lose that son of yours, the same as you took mine from me. You'll lose it all . . . you'll lose it all.'

'I hope Maggie is well.' Reuben got to his feet, taking the tray from Anna as she came back to the sitting room, then settled himself once more in a comfortable armchair, his small Gladstone bag at his feet.

'Yes,' Anna answered, glad that Maggie seemed, at last, able to come to terms with Andrew's death. 'She is over at the Cresswells'. She goes there once a week, she says it is the only real natter she gets to have any more.'

'She will get that all right.' Reuben smiled, taking off his spectacles and rubbing the lenses with his handkerchief. 'My mother-in-law can talk the wheels off a wagon.'

'Don't let her hear you saying that, Reuben.' Anna smiled across at him. 'Mary can have a sharp tongue as well as a busy one.'

'Don't worry, Anna, that is something I know well already, being her son-in-law entitles me to no exceptions.'

'She and Maggie are two of a kind,' Anna replied. 'They say what they mean, regardless of who is on the receiving end. But they are without price, both of them.'

Manny Goldberg kept his eyes on Anna while she and Reuben were talking. This was a strong woman, despite the marks of tiredness on her face. A woman of character and principles, one who, he felt, would not easily break a bargain once it was made.

Manny took the tea she poured for him. 'Anna,' he said. 'I asked Reuben to bring me here this evening. His father is my dearest friend, a man whose word I can depend on – and that word was that there was none better than Anna Royce with whom I could do business.'

'Business?'

'Let me explain.' Manny stirred sugar into his tea. 'I have shops in the Hague, Amsterdam, Rome and Zurich. Shops that sell only the finest.'

He looked up at her, eyes a little enlarged by the thick lenses of his spectacles.

'I wish to introduce a range of fine china into those shops, china of the highest quality, and my friend tells me you have such a product.'

'I think my china will match any you can find elsewhere.'

'It must not match.' He raised the delicate cup. 'It must surpass. The name Goldberg has a reputation in Europe for supplying only the best.'

Anna waited, watching the way in which he balanced the fragile cup in his hand, the way he held it to the light.

'This is one of yours?'

He smiled as she nodded. 'It is exquisite, truly exquisite. My friend the father of Reuben was correct in his advice – yours is the best I will find.'

Placing the cup and saucer on a table beside him, he looked at Anna.

'Can you supply these to Manny Goldberg?'

'I . . . I am sure we could,' Anna answered, surprised. 'Perhaps you would like a catalogue of our designs?'

'Oh, he's got one of those, Anna, Hester saw to that.' Reuben grinned.

'Yes, I have your catalogue, but I will need more for my shops. Customers like to be given a choice. And when they cannot say, "I like this better than I like that", they buy both. Sheesh!' He smiled, lifting his shoulders in a shrug. 'It's business.'

'Hester also showed him one of your beauty boxes.'

'She did, she did!' Manny Goldberg laughed, the spectacles sliding along his nose so that he was looking at her over them.

'She is a smart girl, that Hester, you have the best for a wife, Reuben my boy.' Pushing the spectacles back into place, he returned his gaze to Anna. 'The beauty boxes are made by Benjie Freeth, I understand? That is good. Every one will have the highest workmanship, be a thing of beauty in itself. Can you also supply these to me?'

Anna nodded again, hoping she was not taking on too much.

'Then I have a proposition to make and it is one I wish to put to you in the presence of your solicitor. It is this.' He pushed again at his spectacles. 'You agree to make Goldberg's the sole agent in Europe for Anna Royce products. In return I will pay ten thousand pounds for the franchise. After that we agree a separate price for your china, and another for beauty products.'

'You . . . you mean you are willing to pay ten thousand pounds to become the sole outlet for my products?' Anna choked with surprise at what he had just suggested. 'But I can't . . . I mean . . .'

'It is a good offer, Anna,' Reuben said.

'Is my proposal not acceptable? Does Manny Goldberg not offer enough money?'

'No, please, it isn't that!' Anna blushed at the thought of appearing greedy when it was the sheer magnitude of the offer that had caused her to protest. 'I am flattered you wish to sell my china through your shops, but . . . but I can't take all that money over and above what is paid for each product. It . . . it seems like . . . well, like robbery!'

Throwing back his head, the Jew laughed, setting his spectacles once more on his nose.

'Robbery?' he chuckled. 'Manny Goldberg doesn't get robbed. Being the only man in Europe to sell Anna Royce will make me money, make *both* of us money. When your products can be bought nowhere else then people will come to Manny Goldberg. So, Anna, what do you say? Do we have a deal?'

'It's nothing unusual, Anna,' Reuben said as she looked at him, a question in her eyes. 'A great deal of business is done on the same lines. A man wants something, then he has to pay for it.'

'It still seems a great deal of money to pay . . .'

'Money, sheesh!' The shoulders rose in the shrug that seemed second nature to the man. 'Manny Goldberg respects it as a man should respect his mother. Be assured, I do not throw it away. I expect to recoup it many times over. So, Anna Royce . . . are we agreed?'

At her smile the man rose to his feet, taking a package from the pocket of his coat and handing it to her.

'Reuben will make out an agreement. That is the ten

thousand.' Behind the thick lenses his eyes smiled at the look of astonishment that crossed her face. 'Manny Goldberg keeps his word.'

Anna shook the hand he offered. 'And I will keep mine,' she said, her throat thickening, 'I will keep mine.'

'*One way or another the Almighty will send what you be lookin' for.*'

Maggie's words of a few nights before stirred in her memory as she closed the door behind the departing men. The money Manny had given her would mean she could keep the mill and King's Choice, but more important, it would keep her son in her life.

'. . . the Almighty will send what you be lookin' for.'

It felt like a miracle but the whisper that slipped from her was not addressed to God.

'Thank you, Edward,' she murmured, 'thank you.'

Chapter Seventeen

'You knows your own business best, Anna, but I would 'ave thought it daft to keep running that place at such a loss.' Joby Timmins looked from the ledgers to her.

Reuben and John Harris had both virtually called her a fool for buying Joby Hampton's Wednesbury foundry. Now it seemed they'd been right.

'So what do I do, Joby?' she asked in a tired voice.

'Seems to me nobody knows steel trade like Eli Curran. Why don't you send 'im to this Wednesbury place? 'Appen he might find out why place is a millstone about your neck.'

She hadn't thought of that and thanked the clerk for a suggestion that might just bring a solution.

'Can I go too?' Misty asked when Anna told her and Maggie what she planned.

'What on earth for?' Anna looked at her daughter. At seventeen she was chic and sophisticated, the perfect product of a boarding school for young ladies; so very different from what Anna herself had been at that age. 'There is nothing you can do there, it's just a small steel foundry.'

'I know.' Misty perched on the arm of her mother's chair, one finger toying with her hair, 'but I want to know more about the business than designing packages for cosmetics.'

'Your designs are very good, darling. They are responsible for the popularity of Mistique.'

'I enjoyed that, Mother, the sketches and talking to the

printers and everything, but that doesn't mean I wouldn't enjoy seeing the inside of a foundry too.'

Anna smiled, trying to imagine her elegantly dressed daughter among sweating workmen stripped to the waist against the heat of the coal furnaces.

'You would have to wear something more durable than those.' She nodded towards Misty's pale blue calf shoes.

'That means I can go . . . yippee!' The girl danced excitedly round the sitting room until Maggie called for her to stop.

'You mind you do as Eli Curran tells you,' Maggie warned. 'It's no cake walk inside a rolling mill.'

'I will, Grammie.' Misty rested her golden head against one that had turned pure white soon after hearing of her son's death.

'Grammie is right,' Anna said in a tight tone, 'you do exactly as Eli says.'

Misty glanced at the clock on the wall of The White Horse dining room. She and Eli had eaten together this evening as they had every evening since they had been in Wednesbury, and she knew Eli would want to follow his usual pattern of going to his room, writing up a few notes for her mother then going on for a pint of beer. But this evening Misty had no intention of following her own usual pattern. Tonight she was not going to lie on her bed and read, going slowly out of her mind with boredom.

'I thought I would walk into the town, Eli.' She folded a heavy white napkin, paying it more attention than was warranted.

'Eh? You can't do that, wench! This 'ere is a strange town. You can't go gallivantin' about like you do in Coseley.'

'Why not?' She smiled, hiding iron determination behind a soft expression.

''Cos you never knows who might be about.'

Misty laughed, showing pretty white teeth. She had to play this one very smart.

'Oh, come on, Eli, there are no monsters lurking in the

bushes. In fact, I've seen precious few bushes around here at all.'

'You knows what I means, miss.' Eli was testy. He was responsible for Anna's girl. ''Sides, there's nowt to this town 'ceptin' little 'ouses and factories so what does you want to go looking for?'

'The landlady here says there is a market on tonight. It goes on until after midnight. I must see it, Eli, the girls at school would never believe it.'

'If you must.' Displeasure adding to the lines already cutting across his brow, Eli pushed his empty plate away. 'Wait on five minutes till I write up fer your mam an' then I'll come wi' ye.'

'No, Eli.' His sharp glance told her she had been too quick. Leaning forward, she squeezed his hand in hers, voice pleading. 'I can't look at any womanish things I might find if you are there.' Eyelids lowered, she even managed a blush. 'I . . . I would be far too shy.'

She had a point, and Eli was itching to be away to The Turks Head pub, just a few yards along the street. He had struck up a friendship with some of the local men; one that was telling him far more than that manager up at the foundry.

'But I can't leave you to walk about place on your own.'

Misty's smile was inward, secretive. Eli was already halfway to where she wanted him.

'I know you want to take care of me, Eli, but the people here seem friendly enough and I won't stay out late, honestly.' She increased the pressure on his leathery hand, her blue glance wide and candid. 'Please, Eli . . . I want to see the market. We never have anything like it in Coseley and the staff of the Haworth School for Young Ladies would drop dead at the mention of the word!'

Eli grinned. He'd always liked this wench of Anna Royce's and having grown up with the Cresswell twins she could take her own part with the best of them, he reckoned.

'You mind what y'ave said then, young miss, an' mind you gets yourself back 'ere reasonable like.'

The smile she gave him was pretty, masking the thrill of triumph. She was learning more at that posh school than was on the curriculum.

The grey sky of evening assumed a scarlet cast as the iron foundry opened its blast furnace. Below the hill that held a grim stone church, market stalls nestled among the cluster of tiny terraced houses. But Misty wasn't interested in them.

Aaron lived on the hill close to the Parish Church he had told her when she had stopped to speak to him on the tour of the foundry with her mother, and she had learned enough from Eli to know this was the last opening of the furnaces for the day shift. Soon he must pass this spot to get home.

Touching the pale gold hair she had piled on to her head, she smoothed her sapphire velvet suit, glad she had brought it with her and confident the well-cut line enhanced her slender figure. She wanted to appear older, more mature. That way Aaron would take notice.

A slight breeze caught a blonde tendril, weaving it among her thick lashes, and she turned her head, letting the same breeze blow it off her face. It was then that she saw him, tall and broad, his long stride making easy work of walking up the steep hill.

'Good evening, Mr Bradly!' Misty smiled as he drew level.

'Good evening, Miss Royce.' Aaron hesitated, unsure whether or not to walk on. 'You shouldn't be up here all by yourself. It will be dark soon.'

'Oh, not for a while yet, Mr Bradly, and it is such a pleasant evening I thought I would try to see a little of Wednesbury before I have to return home.'

'Was there no one could see it with you? Do you have to be alone?'

'There is only Eli.' She liked the way he looked into her face, an open confident glance with none of the shiftiness she had seen in some of her mother's employees. 'And he was very busy. Besides,' she lied competently, 'I wouldn't have wanted to tire him further by asking him to walk with me, not after a long day's work.'

'Well, you can see all of Wednesbury from here.' Aaron pushed a hand into his hair, holding it against the breeze. 'What there is to see. I recommend you take a look and then return to The White Horse.'

He was walking away, leaving her standing.

'But there must be more than houses and factories?' Misty started after him, her attempts at worldly sophistication abandoned. 'There must be some pretty places to see, and I wouldn't be alone if *you* showed them to me.'

He stopped and turned, showing no surprise at her forwardness.

'You won't go until somebody does . . . that somebody had better be me, I suppose. Wait there.'

This time he did stride away and Misty felt a glow of triumph as she watched his broad upright figure.

'There is Hob's Hole.' Foundry grime washed away, burn-sprinkled trousers changed for neat dark worsted, a white open-throated shirt showing a little of his wide chest, Aaron walked her slowly down the hill. 'Folk go there sometimes to get away from all this. That's when they're not too bushed.'

'Bushed?'

'Yes,' he answered without looking at her. 'Tired. Worn out from grafting for a living.'

'And you go there?'

'I like it despite its name. It's a wide pool rather like a lake, I suppose. When the weather is hot the lads swim there after they've finished work.'

'And the girls?' Misty could not resist a mischievous smile as he threw her a quick glance.

'They don't swim, but quite a few of them go along for the view.'

'Is it such a pretty place?'

He roared with laughter then, blond head thrown back.

'I was teasing,' he said at last. 'They go to see the lads – they swim naked.'

Misty held his glance with sparkling eyes.

'I would still like to see Hob's Hole, with or without the vagaries of its view, Mr Bradly.'

'Then see it you will, and on your head be it if one of the men has decided on a dip.'

Taking her hand to help her over a low stile, Aaron kept it in his own as they crossed a broad meadow, the small tree-fringed lake that was Hob's Hole reflecting the crimson of the lowering sun. She would be gone soon, leaving his drab life drabber, but for the moment they were together.

Picking up a pebble, he sent it bouncing flat across the dark water, spreading circles in its wake. Hesitating only a moment, Misty selected a stone and skimmed it expertly after Aaron's.

'I learned to do that before I went to school,' she said, grinning.

Across the pool a man's low voice mingled with a woman's laughter and Aaron turned, taking Misty's hand.

'I'm on the first shift tomorrow,' he said, a hint of shyness in his voice. 'That means I shall be finished at two o'clock if you've a fancy for a walk?'

Her fingers twining in his, Misty smiled. 'I've a fancy.'

'I don't care for the way things are being run, Anna.' Eli Curran sat a little uncomfortably in Anna's finely furnished sitting room. He hadn't needed the two weeks they had stayed in Wednesbury to sort out the steel mill's problem or to realise that missis's daughter seemed reluctant to leave.

'What exactly do you think is wrong, Eli?'

'Steel,' he answered bluntly. 'It's nowt short o' rubbish, what's bein' turned out down theer. You can't be blamin' folk for not wantin' to buy the stuff. It's a wonder place 'as gone on as long as it 'as.'

'Why is that, Eli? It seemed to do all right when I was a . . . down there.'

Eli Curran caught the swift correction but his lined face gave no indication. Anna Royce had done all right by him and by Coseley and was entitled to her privacy.

'Seems since old gaffer went and works was sold to Bradly Engineering, that manager – what's 'is name? – seems to think it meks no matter 'ow much shit is in the pig iron he uses. Some young lad tried tellin' 'im it were no good but he were told to shut up or get out.'

'I see.' Anna rose. 'Thank you for going, Eli, I'm very grateful.'

Seeing him to the door, she closed it, leaning against the hard wood. Why was fate drawing her back to the one place she didn't want to be?

'I don't want to go,' she whispered into her hands. 'Please God, I don't want to go.'

'There just ain't the call there was a year or two ago.' The manager of the Wednesbury steel mill eyed the red-haired woman and the slip of a girl at her side. He remembered that one from a month or so gone, come here with that snipe-nosed bugger Curran who thought he knew everything.

'Isn't twelve months rather quick for the steel business to fall off as drastically as you say, Mr Dean?'

'It was fallin' off afore place was sold.' Samuel Dean didn't like being questioned, much less by some toffee-nosed bitch of a woman. What did she know about puddling iron?

''Course,' he went on, 'there was ways of cuttin' costs but Joby Hampton wouldn't 'ear of it.'

'Like what?' Across the dirt-packed floor two men heaved on the heavy link chain that lifted the iron door of the furnace. From where she stood Anna could feel some of the heat that ran hell a close second, but she didn't move back.

'Well, he 'ad no need of puttin' best quality pig iron into smeltin', he could 'ave used a lower grade.'

'Like you have been doing.' She said it quietly, her eyes on the sweating men shovelling coal into the red hot maw of the furnace.

'Is that what you would have done?'

Anna stopped, addressing her question to Aaron, the muscles of his arms and shirtless back rippling with the effort of pulling bars of glowing steel across the rolling beds, teasing them into ever more slender rods, feeling the same pride in him as she had felt watching him follow after her father's coffin.

'There can be no excuse for shoddy work.'

Transparent blue eyes lifted momentarily to her own and again she experienced a glow of pride. Her son was not afraid to speak his mind, neither did he make an effort to hide the fact he had overheard their conversation.

Directing his stare to the foundry manager, he added. 'It is a poor workman blames his tools.'

'My sentiments exactly.' Anna nodded. 'I hope you will continue to think that way once you replace Mr Dean, as manager of this foundry.'

Anna watched her son straighten in front of her, watched the surprise flare in his blue eyes.

'Eh!' Beside her, Samuel Dean's heavy face darkened. 'What's that yer say? What the bloody hell does yer think you're playing at?'

'I assure you I am not playing.'

Anna's voice was suddenly cold and hard as the bars of steel stored in the yard.

'And hell has nothing to do with it. *I* am giving you your tin, Mr Dean. I will not have men with your sly underhanded ways in my employ, and I will most certainly not have them in charge of my foundry. I will have the clerk make up your wages . . . you are finished at this foundry, as of now.'

Turning to leave she caught Misty's amazed expression and gave her a quick wink. If her daughter was going to learn then she must learn it all, especially how to kick a man's backside.

* * *

'You still look after him, Polly?' Anna sat in the tiny kitchen that was filled with so many memories.

'Ar, me wench, I do, much as 'e'll let me. Says it's too much for a woman my age to cook and clean. Huh!' She picked up a bucket, throwing a heap of coal onto the glowing fire. 'I told 'im I could do a day's work as good as 'im any day, cheeky young bugger! Mind you, Anna, I was glad enough when 'e said it would be easier for me if I moved in 'ere. That hill were gettin' to be a bit much.'

'He hasn't got himself a girl then?'

'Not courtin' strong if that's what you'm askin'.'

Polly picked up a small hand brush, sweeping the dust of the fire from the hearth. 'But I reckon 'e be sweet on some wench, he's bin maudlin' this last month or more.'

'Polly!' Taking the brush from the old woman's hand, Anna pressed her into the one chair the kitchen boasted.

'I've made some financial arrangements for . . . for Aaron.' She hesitated, still feeling the strangeness of speaking her son's name. 'When he is twenty-one he will come into quite a bit of money. Try to see for me that he spends it sensibly, doesn't squander it.'

'You need 'ave no fear on 'im doin' that, Anna. One thing Jos always told 'im was you look after the pennies, the pound will look after itself.'

He would say that, Anna thought, turning towards the door. Her father had not stinted her or her mother but had always tried to take care of his money.

'I don't know whether I will come to Wednesbury again, Polly,' she said, staring out towards the blackened walls of the Parish Church, 'but if I don't, you will always have my love and thanks for what you have done.'

Polly eased her body slightly, lifting the weight from her crippled leg, as she stood in the open doorway watching the woman in a smart green suit walk slowly past the wall of the churchyard to stand beneath the oak tree, looking at the bright flowers growing among the grass that covered a lonely grave.

'You've had a hard life, Anna Bradly,' she whispered into the soft air of the afternoon, 'an' I'm thinkin' there's more of the same yet to come.'

Chapter Eighteen

Spooning extra sugar into the pretty china cup, Anna stirred it vacantly, her mind miles away in Wednesbury.

She could not help. There was nothing she could do. All day the thought had plagued her, all day the worry of it had weighed on her like an iron bar, and all through the day she had found no solution.

The heat of the drink she was stirring travelled up the metal spoon, its sting bringing Anna back to the present. Taking up the cup and saucer, she carried it to Maggie's bedroom. Ordinarily she looked forward to this small ritual that had grown up since Maggie's illness; she valued the quiet minutes with the woman who meant so much to her.

'You looks done in, wench.'

Propped up on vast pillows, their frilled white slips starched stiff, Maggie took the cup of cocoa.

'You shouldn't 'ave bothered makin' this. You 'ave enough to do wi'out waiting on me.'

Anna smiled but the smile was tired.

'I like to do it, it's the only real time we seem to get to talk anymore.'

'That be the truth an' all.' Maggie patted the side of the bed. 'Sit you down for five minutes. I knows y'ave 'ad a long day but there be summat as needs to be said an' it won't improve wi' the keepin'.'

Anna shook her head.

'It will keep at least until tomorrow. You have had a long day too. You don't rest nearly enough.'

Maggie was right as always, it had been a long day and one that had added another worry to the list that seemed ever ready to plague her.

Maggie's eyes were faded but they had lost none of their keenness. Now they seemed to reach inside Anna's mind, to read the worry there.

'It might 'ave been a long day, wench,' she patted the bed again, 'but it'll be a damn' sight longer night if you don't tell me what it is be ailing you. There's a worry in you an' don't go denyin' it. We have shared the same house too long for you to go trying to pull the wool over my eyes. It ain't bad news about Misty, is it?'

'No.' Anna sat down on the bed, reaching a reassuring hand to her friend. 'Misty is fine. She is doing well at school, and every letter is filled with the new friends each year's intake brings and the madcap things they get up to. My only worry about her is that she may never want to leave school, never want to come home.'

'There be no real fear of that.' Maggie put her cup aside on the small night table beside her bed then put her hand over Anna's, holding it between both of her own. 'That one has her heart with her mother.'

For a few seconds neither said a word, only the ticking of Maggie's old clock audible. Then, with the foresight that always seemed to lead her to the heart of any trouble, Maggie spoke.

'If it ain't Misty that be worryin' you, an' I knows it ain't the business, not since you paid off them vultures at the bank, then it 'as to be the other one. It be your son, your lad. That be what's gnawin' at you. Tell me if I be wrong?'

But Anna could not tell Maggie she was wrong, though again she could not tell her she was right; she could not place her own worry on those frail shoulders which had been bent often enough on her account. Yet to tell her nothing at all would do as much harm. Maggie would, she knew, lie awake most of the night wondering.

'I think I am just overtired,' Anna said, knowing this would not satisfy Maggie.

'You be that all right, but there be more to it than tiredness. You 'ave a sadness about you that ain't no fault of workin' too hard. Won't you tell me what it be, Anna? Might be as together we can put things right.'

Anna looked at the lined hands that held her own. Maggie had helped so many times and in so many ways but this time there was nothing she could do. There was nothing either of them could do.

'Seems like lad will be leaving . . . he don't seem to have the heart he once had for his work.'

The words of Polly Shipton's letter ran through her mind as they had since it had arrived that morning.

'. . . and unless he should write, I won't be able to tell you for where.'

Her son would be gone from Wednesbury and she would lose the one tiny thread that held him to her. The thought sent a shudder through her and Maggie's hand tightened on hers.

'Tell me, wench,' she said softly. 'Don't shut me out now.'

'Oh, Maggie . . .' Anna drew a long sobbing breath. 'I don't want to lose him. I love him . . . I love him.'

It was too much. She had not meant to place her burdens on the other woman's shoulders but the sheer love in Maggie's voice had broken that resolve and slowly, between sobs, the story of Polly's letter came out.

'So you see,' she finished, 'I can't do anything to hold him there in Wednesbury, and I feel . . . I know . . . he would not come here to me. He is proud, Maggie, every line of his body tells you that. Too proud to accept a woman's charity.'

'Ar.' Maggie nodded. 'That I can believe. The folk of the Black Country 'ave little 'ceptin' pride, but that they 'ave in great measure. Your lad wouldn't take kindly to your sending for him now, but this I feel certain of – you won't lose 'im,

Anna. The love you 'ave always held for that lad of yours is too strong. A way *will* open, wench. God is good, 'e won't take away what you 'ave cherished all these years. One way or another the Almighty will send what you be lookin' for.'

God is good.

In her own room Anna felt the bitterness in her throat. Where was His goodness when she was being raped? And where His goodness when Edward was crushed to death beneath a machine? And where would it be when she lost her son?

'. . . he don't seem to have the heart he once had . . .'

The words Polly had written refused to leave her mind.

She knew the pain and loss he must still feel at losing Jos, but would leaving Wednesbury heal her son's pain?

Anna knew the answer. It was one she had learned so long before. Pain and longing, the sort of longing she had for Aaron, was not so easily left behind.

She had wanted to tell him. Wanted him to know she was his mother. But she had held back, telling herself it was for his sake she said nothing. But was it? Anna buried her face in her hands. Was it for Aaron she had said nothing, or was it because she could not face what she might see in his eyes?

'I can send money,' she whispered into the stillness as if answering some accusation, 'enough for him and for Mother Polly.'

But what of the foundry? Anna dropped her hands and stared into the shadows of her bedroom. She had made Aaron manager. But if he were no longer there did she still want it? Did she want the worry of another foundry? Did she want to be responsible for so many other lives?

What would happen if she closed it?

Anna let the thought hover in her mind.

What of the other men who worked there? Men she knew had nothing but the money they earned each week.

'Why should I care about them?' Anna flared, throwing back

the accusation. 'Did they care what happened to me? Did they care about what they did to my father? Did they care that their lies and torments drove him to take his own life?'

For all the truth of her protestations, Anna knew she *did* care about the people of Wednesbury. She did care about the hardship and suffering her closing the foundry would bring.

Across the years Maggie's words came back to her: '*Some will cry an' others will starve, it's nothing as 'asn't 'appened afore.*'

Some will starve.

In her lap, Anna's hands tightened into a ball. Where was the goodness of the Almighty in that?

'*It's yer back their fortunes will ride on* . . .'

She had seen the owning of Wednesbury foundry as a way of meeting with Aaron, of speaking with him, but to close it because he left . . .?

That was her only real reason and Anna knew it was not reason enough. Bringing hardship to others would not heal her pain, it would not soothe the hurt that came in the night. She might never see her son again if he left that town, but if he had decided his work was no longer what he wanted she could not force him to stay.

'What do I do, Edward?' she whispered. 'What do I do?'

'Where are you going?'

Anna looked up from the newspaper she was reading, seeing her daughter, already half way out of the door of their room at The White Horse.

'There's someone I want you to meet, mother.' Misty's eyes sparkled and her cheeks blushed to a soft pink. 'He . . .'

'He?' Anna's eyebrows rose. Her daughter's interest in the steel foundry had waned rather quickly she had noticed, and her excuses for going out alone in the evening had increased, but she had not thought there to be a 'he' at the root of it. A boy, here in Wednesbury? Surely not. Misty had not had time to make an acquaintance, much less find herself a boyfriend, even in the two weeks she was here with Eli.

'Yes, mother . . . he.' The colour in Misty's face deepened. 'There is a man I want you to meet. He . . . he will be waiting for me downstairs.'

Anna opened her mouth to speak but Misty was already gone, the door banging behind her. She had not referred to him as a boy but a man. And she *was* interested; a girl's eyes did not sparkle and her cheeks turn pink if she had no interest in the man she spoke of.

Anna tried to return to her newspaper, telling herself that, knowing her daughter, this could just be a flash in the pan.

'Mother!' Half an hour later Misty bounced back into the room. 'Mother, this is the man I told you about, he wants to ask your permission for us to become engaged.'

Told her about! The only thing she had heard about this man had been that he was waiting downstairs. Half smiling at her daughter's thoughtless impetuosity, Anna looked up.

He was holding Misty's hand. Their fingers were closely entwined. Anna's own fingers tightened on the newspaper, then slowly, as if held in some terrible nightmare, she lowered it, staring almost hypnotised at the pair standing proudly before her.

It wasn't true! This couldn't be happening! This could not be the man Misty had meant was waiting for her.

'. . . *I reckon 'e be sweet on some wench. He's been maudlin this last month or more* . . .'

Polly Shipton's word returned to her mind, sending her senses reeling.

But it couldn't be! She had got it wrong. Misty would have told her before now if the two of them had met when she was in Wednesbury with Eli Curran. But would she? She had not mentioned him during the whole of the past week.

But she must see! Anna stared at the couple laughing into each other's eyes; eyes so very blue, so very alike. Misty must see . . . the same eyes, the same hair . . . she must see the likeness.

'Mother.' Misty stepped towards her, pulling the man along with her. 'Mother, this is Aaron.'

'. . . *he wants to ask your permission for us to become engaged.*'

Misty's words ran wild in Anna's mind, tumbling over and over, banishing all rational thought, leaving only panic.

'Mother!' Misty bent towards her, anxiety replacing the happiness on her face. 'Mother, are you all right?'

'Yes . . . yes . . . I'm all right.'

Anna swallowed hard. She was not feeling all right, she felt as if she were drowning, but then how should she feel faced with this: her daughter and her son wanting to marry?

Not this! Oh, dear God, not this!

Somewhere in the vacuum that had once been her mind, Anna prayed.

At her side Misty reached again for the hand of the man she loved.

'Mother, Aaron and I want to become engaged.'

With a supreme effort Anna dragged herself from the hell that threatened to engulf her totally.

'Engaged? Is a week of knowing one another enough for a decision like this?'

'Oh, I have known Aaron for longer than a week,' Misty bubbled on, not giving him a chance to answer. 'We met the last time I came to Wednesbury and have written to each other several times since then.'

Written to each other? Anna wanted to scream at the ludicrousness of the statement. A couple of weeks of knowing someone, a few letters . . . and on the basis of that she planned to ruin three lives?

'Two weeks when you were here with Eli and a week here with me – I hardly think that a proper basis for an engagement.'

'But Aaron and I think it is. We know our own minds.' Misty's tone held a childish, petulant note.

Anna looked at her daughter, then for the first time since he had entered the room, her eyes met those of her son: those pale yet intensely blue eyes, the eyes of Jos Bradly.

'No, you do not.' She spoke quietly. 'You only think you do. You know nothing about each other.'

'We do!' Misty flashed. 'We know all we need to know.'

Do you? Anna felt her heart twist. Do you know all you need to? Do you know that Aaron is your half-brother?

Aloud she asked: 'And you, Aaron? Do you think three weeks and a few letters a sound basis for marriage?'

'It is a short time, Mrs Royce, I agree . . .'

He holds himself like my father, Anna thought as he answered. He even sounds as my father used to before . . .

'. . . but we do not wish to be married just yet, we simply wish to become engaged. That is all we ask.'

But you can't! Anna's brain screamed. Don't you see, you can't become engaged? Can't you see who you are?

'You may see that as asking very little,' she returned, her calm voice totally belying her feelings. 'But *I* see becoming engaged as a serious undertaking, one that requires a firmer foundation than a few meetings and a few letters. I'm sorry but I will not give my permission.'

'If your objection is because we have only known each other for a short time, Mrs Royce, then Misty and I will wait for a while.'

He held her eyes, though at his side the hand that was free clenched with tension.

'No, I don't want to wait!' Misty sounded like a child denied her own way. 'Why should we? We are both old enough to know our own minds so why shouldn't we become engaged now?'

'You might feel you know your own mind.' Anna switched her glance to her daughter, seeing the disappointment that pulled her mouth down at the sides. She tried to sound as gentle as her own terror and shame would permit. 'But in a month or so you may feel differently, you are still so very young.'

'Waiting will make *no* difference to the way we feel, will it, Aaron?'

'Waiting will not make a difference to the feelings I have for Misty, Mrs Royce, but if it will make a difference to the way you feel about our being together, then we will wait.'

'No!' Misty clung to his hand, tears running down her cheeks. 'No, Aaron, I don't want to wait!'

Releasing his fingers, he looked again at Anna.

'How long would you like us to wait?'

It wasn't a question of that. No matter how long they waited they could never be man and wife. So why not tell them so, why not tell them the truth of their birth? Anna knew she should, but also knew she could not.

'Make no attempt to see each other or to communicate for six months and then . . .'

'No! I won't . . . I won't . . . it's unfair! You're cruel, Mother, you have no feelings . . . you have no feelings!'

Running out of the room, Misty slammed into her own bedroom and Anna heard the key turn in the lock.

'Six months, Mrs Royce!'

Turning abruptly, Aaron walked out.

Anna looked down at the newspaper still held in her lap and realised only now the strength with which she had been gripping it. It had sent her fingers right through the pages.

'It's unfair' her daughter had said, and there was some truth in the words. The whole of life had been unfair to Anna Royce, but her daughter had been wrong to say she had no feelings.

With her heart splintered inside her, Anna knew just how wrong it was to say she had no feelings.

Chapter Nineteen

Anna let fall the designs for her new range of china. It was almost two months since she had refused Misty and Aaron permission to become engaged; two months in which her daughter had hardly spoken to her. She had thought that sheer youth would cause Misty's feelings for Aaron to change. She had never known the girl want anything for more than a few weeks. In Maggie's words, she changed her mind as often as a collier changed his shirt.

Not this time!

Anna leaned tiredly back in her chair.

She had tried so many ways to deflect Misty in these last few weeks: asking her to accompany a consignment of goods to the Goldberg shop in Rome; suggesting the cosmetics design department would welcome some help. But no matter what she said or asked, it met with the same polite but frosty refusal.

Determined to keep on trying, Anna looked across the room at the girl who sat idly thumbing a women's journal.

'Darling, would you take a look at these?' She held up the sketches. 'The shapes are so beautiful, I can't decide if they would benefit from being painted or if they should be left as they are.'

Rising from her chair, Misty dropped the journal on to a table.

'I am sure you *will* decide, Mother. You decide on everything else.'

Maggie looked up as the girl strode towards the door of the sitting room feeling her patience to be at an end. Maybe Anna hadn't done the right thing by both of her children in not telling them outright why they couldn't marry, but this kind of treatment of her mother had gone on long enough.

'Misty!' she called after the girl. 'Wait on a minute, I be wantin' to say summat.'

'Yes, Grammie?'

'Sit you down.' Maggie felt the familiar stir of her heart at the term Anna's daughter had addressed her by ever since she first learned to talk, but she would not let the love it roused deter her. It was high time the girl was made to recognise a few home truths.

'Now then . . .'

She stared at Misty, perched in front of her, and her grey eyes were hard.

'. . . don't you be thinkin' I be so old as not to remember what first love was like, or to think I don't know what I be talkin' of when I say denial comes 'ard.'

Opposite her, Misty's blue eyes clouded but Maggie resisted the urge to take her in her arms and tell her Grammie would make it all right, as she had so many times in the past. The child had felt her feet, had a taste, however brief, of the sweetness of life, and it could not be long before she had a taste of the sour, but in the meantime she must not be allowed to think she could go on hurting her mother.

'We none of us takes kindly to being told we can't 'ave what we believe to be our 'eart's desire, but that don't give we the right to snipe at them as has the saying of it.'

'Maggie . . .'

'Don't Maggie me, Anna!' The older woman's voice was sharp. 'I know what be goin' on an' I know what I be goin' to say, an' it be no use you tryin' to stop me.'

She turned a harsher look on Misty than the girl could ever remember seeing from her.

'You just remember, your mother has worked 'ard to keep

you ever since you was born, worked almost every hour God sent to give you as much as 'er could. You might not realise it but the love 'er 'olds for you be one no bond will break, an' it be that love that made 'er say no to you. No matter 'ow you might see it now that refusal was made for your own good, but whether you ever comes to see it that way or you don't, you won't carry on speakin' to your mother as y'ave been doin' this last couple of months.

'You try it again and it'll be Maggie Fellen you'll answer to, an' your smart arsin' will get you naught but a smack across the mouth. You want to be married, to take on the responsibilities of a woman? Then try actin' like one instead of comin' the spoilt child!'

Lying in bed, Anna watched moonlight creep through the clouds and play across the walls of her room.

Maggie had been sharp with Misty but even when the girl had run sobbing from the sitting room, she had been unrepentant.

'It needed sayin', Anna. You can't go on coddlin' the wench all 'er days. 'Er be growin' up Anna, 'er be growin' fast.'

Yes, Misty was growing fast, soon they would lose her to a husband – but not to Aaron. No matter how much Misty begged or pouted, she could never have Aaron.

But Maggie's chiding had not ended with Misty.

'You be wrong, Anna,' she had gone on. 'You be wrong in not tellin' them two children of your'n the truth of who they be.'

'I can't, Maggie . . . I can't! If I tell them, I will lose them both. They will turn their backs on me.'

The chill warning of the answer she received circled Anna's heart with a ribbon of fear.

'You be like to lose 'em to a worse fate than that of turning their back on their mother. They be like to 'ave the world turn its back on them. They be little more than children for all the fancy education y'ave given to the wench, an' the education a 'ard life 'as given to the lad. Young blood runs hot, Anna, hot an' fast. They two 'ave abided by what you asked up to now, but for how long will at last? You 'ave to tell 'em, wench, tell 'em afore they does summat you'll all 'ave cause to regret.'

How long would they go on? Anna watched the pale light play among the shadows. Misty was stubborn. It could just be she would go to Aaron, despite what he had said, go to Aaron and . . .

No! Above the sheets, Anna's fingers curled into her palms, pressing the nails into her flesh.

'You be like to lose 'em to a worse fate than that of turning their back on their mother.' The words echoed in her mind, heightening the fear of what Maggie had said. It was too dangerous to let things go on as they were. Misty had not lost interest as Anna had hoped, had prayed; her determination to marry Aaron seemed as strong as before.

'Now *you* as well as Misty must accept things can't be as you want them,' Anna whispered to the shadows. 'You must face the reality. You have to face them, protect them instead of yourself.'

Protecting herself! Anna closed her eyes, pressing the lids hard together as at last her mind allowed her to see the full truth of why she had not told her children of their relationship.

She had been protecting them but she had been protecting herself more; shielding herself from the horror she knew she would see in their eyes when she told them: shielding herself from their condemnation.

But in shielding herself she had left them open to much greater heartache. She had known the misery of rape. She must not allow them to know the misery of incest.

Waiting in her room at The White Horse, Anna tried to still her dancing nerves.

She had brought Misty with her to Wednesbury. She and Aaron deserved an explanation and she would give them it, born at the same time. That way they would at least have each other's support.

'You sent for me, Mrs Royce?'

Anna looked at the tall figure of her son, his white shirt open at the neck. Will his sleeves be rolled above the wrists beneath his jacket, as my father's always were? she thought.

'I asked you to come so that what I have to say can be heard by both of you.'

'We haven't changed our minds, Mother.' Misty stood at Aaron's side, her whole attitude defensive. 'We still want . . .'

'I know what you and Aaron want!' Anna interrupted, her tone sharp though it was not anger that coloured it. 'You and Aaron want to become engaged, but I am afraid that is impossible.'

'But why?'

She had thought a few weeks ago she would have no need to explain why, that the chameleon nature of youth would carry them both along to new desires.

'The time you stipulated is not up yet, Mrs Royce. You do not have to give us your decision yet.'

But I do . . . I do! Anna's heart screamed.

'I think she does.'

'No, Misty.' Aaron looked at the girl whose head was just level with his shoulder. 'Your mother stipulated six months and we will hold to that.'

'It would make no difference.' Anna met the eyes of her son, so like the eyes of the man who had fathered them both. He deserved that at least. Deserved to have her look him in the eyes when she told him the truth.

'Why?' The demand was Misty's. 'Because Aaron has nothing, is that it?'

Why was this happening to her? Anna felt the bitterness of years gone by rise like bile in her throat. Hadn't she been through enough?

'*There be tears in yer cup an' it's refusin' to be dried so they are . . . ye are not to be havin' an easy life . . . toil and tears are the price ye'll pay.*' Kate O'Keefe's words rang across the years, and still they were proving true.

'Why?' Misty demanded again. 'Is it because he hasn't the money Anna Royce has got?'

'I am not afraid of work, Mrs Royce.' The almost transparent blueness of his eyes met hers. 'I can make enough to keep us both. Maybe Misty won't have so many of the fine things she has now, but she will have enough.'

'Money does not enter into it.'

Even as she answered Anna felt detached, isolated, apart from the scene being played around her, only the sickening lurch of her heart telling her it was real.

'Then what does?' Misty snapped. 'If money is not the reason why Aaron and I can't become engaged, then what is?' Her cheeks taking on the red flush of anger, she glared at her mother. 'Or isn't there one? Tell us, Mother, *if you can.*'

Anna was silent for a few seconds, a silence in which she fought for the strength to say the words that would blight their lives and completely destroy her own.

She spoke at last, her voice dull and flat.

'I refused my permission for you to become engaged because nothing could ever come of it. You two can never marry . . . you are half-brother and sister.'

'That's a lie!' Misty gasped. 'A cruel, wicked lie!'

'I only wish it were,' Anna answered, agony in every word. 'But I am Aaron's mother, as I am yours.'

'It *is* a lie.' His face darkened. 'You are not my mother. She died soon after I was born.'

Anna was weary. It seemed all of a sudden that nothing mattered any more. The will that had kept her going through the years of unhappiness was suddenly sapped, drained by the bewilderment and shock on the faces of both her children.

She had done this to them, she was the one bringing that shock and unhappiness, she was the one breaking their hearts.

'Who was it who told you your mother died soon after you were born?' She forced herself to meet his eye. 'Was it crippled Polly Shipton or was it Jos Bradly?'

A new expression in his face, Aaron stepped towards her, the tense lines of his body holding a threat.

'What do you know of Jos Bradly?'

Anna swallowed, every part of her crying out to be free of this, free of the hurt in her son's eyes, of the horror on the face of her daughter.

'I know that he was your father . . . and mine.'

'No! No, that's not true, that's a filthy thing to say.' The strain of the last weeks broke in Misty and she rounded on Anna, her claws unsheathed. 'But you *would* say it, wouldn't you? You would say anything to prevent my marrying Aaron, stop the daughter of the wealthy Anna Royce, the expensively educated daughter of the self-made Anna Royce, throwing herself away on the son of a foundry worker! Well, you can keep your money, Mother, I want no more of it. And I want no more of *you*, either.'

'Misty, let me tell you . . .'

'No!' Misty's breasts rose and fell with the effort of breathing and her young face became a mask of scorn.

'Let *me* tell *you*. Let me tell you the real reason you refuse to allow me and Aaron to be together, why you really refuse to let us marry. You, my beautiful mother, my so clever and efficient mother, my so very hardworking and devoted mother. Oh, I remember all that Maggie said. You had your reasons for keeping Aaron and me apart, but did Maggie know it all? Did she know all of the truth or merely the bits you chose to tell her? Did she know about Charles Lazenby? Did she know that for all your looks, you could not inveigle him into marriage? Did you tell her he did not find you good enough to be his wife, and that what you can't have, your daughter won't either?'

Anna looked at her daughter, at her anger and her hurt.

'Misty, you don't know what you're saying.'

'Oh yes I do!' she replied scathingly. 'I know all about your furtive little trips to London, running off to the bed of your fancy man. You're no different from Amy Stevens, except she got pregnant and you didn't.'

Deep within Anna the fires began to stir, melting away the numbness. This was the child she had struggled for, worked day and night for so she would never know the bitterness of poverty. Her hands closing over the arms of the chair, she struggled to control a rising tide of resentment.

'That expensive education you spoke of does not seem to have done you much good,' she said quietly. 'You are still a little girl, Misty, a child with more mouth than sense.'

Aaron had not moved during the exchange between Anna and Misty and remained unmoving when the girl slammed out of the room.

'I don't believe you, Mrs Royce.' His eyes, intense and unblinking, were fixed on her own; his voice throbbed with anger.

'This is your way of keeping Misty and me apart. Keeping her from marrying a man who, to your way of thinking, has nothing. And it's a bloody dirty way, sullying the name of a man who can't answer for himself!'

At his sides Aaron's fingers curled and uncurled and his square jaw, so like that of the father he was defending, set in a grim line, so that his next words were squeezed out.

'My grandad would never have done what you accuse him of. If you say it once more, I'll make you sorry for it, woman or no woman.'

Only her fingers moving, clenching and unclenching on the arms of the chair, Anna knew she had to finish what she had started. She had to show him once and for all that he *was* her son and that Jos Bradly had indeed been his father.

'Did your father hang himself?' she asked.

It had taken him by surprise, her quiet question. She saw him recoil, surprise and something else, something close to despair, passing across his face.

'Did he tear some cloth into strips? And did he plait those strips together?'

She went on inexorably though her pain matched his own.

It would do no good to leave even the tiniest margin of doubt. He had to know it all.

'That cloth, Aaron,' she asked, her voice a little above a whisper, 'was it pale blue cotton with darker blue cornflower sprays all over?'

The fierceness of his anger giving way to uncertainty, Aaron's face paled.

'How . . . how did you know that? I burned that cloth . . . I burned it before anyone else saw him.'

Tears thickening her throat, Anna told him.

'I was wearing that dress the night he came home the worse for drink, the night he raped me, thinking I was Mary Carter.'

The last trace of colour drained from his face and his hands doubled into fists. Anna could see he was fighting to control the rage and misery burning in him. But she had been forced to tell him, to save both Misty and him from creating their own tragedy.

'That is a lie.' He spat out the words. 'A dirty, stinking, rotten lie, and I'm . . .'

'I think you should ask Polly Shipton about that.'

'I don't need to ask anybody!' he shouted down her interruption. 'I know my grandad. If he did rape you, which I won't ever believe, it would be because you teased and tormented him until he didn't know what he was doing . . . you are a whore, Anna Royce, *that* is what I believe. A dirty, disgusting whore . . .'

'Aaron!'

Anna's cry was of pure anguish but it did not halt the flow of words streaming from his mouth or dim the hatred in his eyes.

'. . . yes, Mrs Anna Royce, you are a whore, and one of the kind who enjoys seeing others suffer. You are one of the lowest kind of people, the sort not worth the talking to . . . and as for your job, try sticking it up your arse! I wouldn't work for you if hell fetched me!'

He had reached the door and was opening it before Anna spoke. Then, though her legs shook, she stood up and her voice was calm beyond her belief.

'Maybe hell will not fetch you yet, Aaron, but it will certainly come for many of the men you work with, to say nothing of their wives and children.'

Aaron swung to her, his blue eyes still molten with rage.

'What do you mean?'

Anna held the gaze. Inside she was crying to take him in her arms, to take both of her children and hold them, tell them it wasn't what they thought, she was as much a victim of fate as they were. But even to try to touch her son at this moment would send him over the edge of reason.

'What I mean is this,' she went on quietly, 'if you do not work for me then that is your choice, but go and you take every man in that steel mill with you. And think on this also, Aaron. The money that bought Joby Hampton's place was nothing. There is enough to buy most of Wednesbury, and mark me well – I *will* buy it, every stick and stone of the places that provide men with work, and I will close them, *all* of them. You leave Bradly Engineering and you take almost every man in this town with you, and that is *your* choice.'

Chapter Twenty

Locked in her room in The White Horse Misty watched the door handle turn and heard her mother's voice asking her to open the door, to let her just explain.

But there could be no explanation; there was nothing her mother could say to explain what she had done. Aaron was right. She had heard him shout that Anna Royce was a whore, and she was . . . she must be, and of what sort to lie with her own *father*?

Staring at the twisting handle Misty wrapped her arms about her chest, trying to still the trembling of her body. Her mother . . . with her own father!

'I don't want it to be true,' she sobbed quietly, 'I don't want it to be true . . . please, please, I don't want it to be true.'

But beneath the pain and horror she knew it *was* true. Why else would her mother have said so terrible a thing? Why sow the seeds of so dreadful a doubt? Certainly not because she could find no other way to prevent a daughter's marriage to a penniless steel worker, Anna Royce was too powerful for that.

'I hate you,' she whispered, her body shaking from head to foot. 'I hate you . . . I hate you.'

In her own bedroom Anna sank to the bed, staring unseeingly at the wall. Aaron had left with anger on his tongue and hatred in his eyes and Misty would not let her come near, would not answer when she called. Both of them . . . both of her children spurned her. Neither of them had asked how or why, seeing only their own pain, seeming to think she felt none.

But she could place no blame on them for that. What she had told them had snatched away more than a marriage, broken more than their dreams – it had broken their hearts.

'I didn't know,' she whispered. 'I never thought that when Misty came to Wednesbury that first time she would become involved with Aaron. I didn't think . . . Oh God!' She dropped her head into her hands, sobs wracking her. 'When will it end . . . when will it end?'

The note was under her door when Anna woke. She had lain sleepless until long after the first spears of dawn drove back the night.

Opening the slip of paper she looked at her daughter's extravagant hand. There was no heading. Anna felt a new twist of pain add to the pounding of the headache that was almost blinding her.

> I will make my own way from here. I want nothing more from you and no more to do *with* you. You are no longer my mother. You are a despicable woman, one who cares for nothing and nobody save herself, and you deserve to suffer. I hope that the very worst life can throw at you hits you full in the face!

The unsigned note slid from Anna's fingers. She deserved to suffer? Despite the pain she suddenly wanted to laugh. She deserved to suffer! Didn't Anna Royce know what suffering was? Hadn't she known it since she was seventeen years old? And what had life left that had not already hit her full in the face?

'I don't know where 'er went.' Maggie ran a worried hand over her white hair. ''Er come back sayin' you was stoppin' a while longer to sort things out an' 'er was goin' back to school.'

'She didn't arrive, Maggie, I telephoned.'

'Eee, what would you do wi' 'em?' Maggie poured the all-healing tea, handing Anna a cup. 'Try not to worry, Anna. That wench of your'n might be young but 'er's got all 'er marbles. Take care of 'erself, will Misty. Give 'er a week or two an' 'er'll come 'ome. It was the shock of 'earin' you say you was the lad's mother. Give 'er time, an' like I says, she'll be 'ome.'

'I don't know, Maggie.' Anna touched a trembling hand to her mouth. 'I keep seeing the look on her face – so angry, so unhappy.'

''Course 'er was.' Maggie held on to her practical manner. Anna couldn't stand up to seeing how worried she really was. Misty was headstrong as she was pretty and there was no telling what she might do, but panicking would do none of them any good. 'It be about the only time as 'ow 'er ain't 'ad exactly what 'er wanted and it knocked 'er sideways. No child likes bein' told no, Anna, but this time it 'ad to be. 'Er knows deep down that you would deny 'er naught wi'out good reason an' when 'er temper 'as cooled down 'er will be 'ome, you can depend on it. But the other one! There's a different kettle of fish altogether. Strikes me 'e'll not come to terms wi' you as easy.'

In her mind Anna saw again the doubled fists and the hatred that darkened those pale eyes.

'He will never accept me, Maggie, even should he accept the truth of his birth.'

'You be wrong there, wench, of that I be convinced. From what you 'ave told me the lad 'as pride and 'e 'as 'ad a knock to that pride, a shock that will take some getting over, but 'e 'as a strength of character and a knowin' of what's right an' wrong that 'e gets from you, an' what you in your turn got from 'im as fathered you. That lad stood by them as 'e worked alongside of, same as you when you took on Rewcastle's Mill. Though you gave 'im a hard time, Anna. What you said was naught short of blackmail an' that ain't like you. Why did you say what you did? Why did you tell the lad you would put 'alf the men of that town out of work?'

Anna stared into the fire.

'Because I love him, Maggie, and I could think of no other way of keeping him. If he leaves Wednesbury I will have lost him for good and I couldn't bear the thought of that. I want him so much and that seemed the only way.'

'Even if he despises you for it?'

'Even so,' Anna answered softly. 'He is my son, the child I have never stopped aching for. I would rather have him with me, hating me, than lose him altogether.'

In the quietness of the sitting room, Maggie watched the shadows of despair play over the face of the woman she had laughed and cried with, the woman she loved as a daughter. What had she gone through in Wednesbury? What hell had opened up for her there?

'But whatever Aaron decides, I know he can take care of himself, he has grown up with the world howling at his back, but Misty . . .'

Anna hesitated, feeling the dread she had carried back to Coseley well up afresh.

'. . . She knows nothing of the world, she has always been so protected.'

'I've told you, Anna, that girl o' yours will take care of 'erself. 'er ain't the helpless little wench you seem to think 'er is. Give 'er time and 'er will be back, safe and sound and cheeky as ever.'

Anna looked up, the fear that haunted her showing dark in her eyes.

'Do you think she will have returned to Wednesbury? Do you think she might go back to Aaron, despite what I told them? Oh God, Maggie, what will I do if . . . if . . .?'

Maggie's hand stroked the red-gold head that bowed itself against her skirts, feeling her own heart breaking as Anna's was.

''Er won't go back there, me wench,' she soothed. 'Don't you go worryin' yourself wi' that thought.'

'But . . . but what if she didn't believe me?' Anna sobbed. 'What if she still believes the whole story was a lie?'

''Er'll 'ave believed it.' Maggie knew the comfort she was trying to give was grounded in sand, holding no foundation, but Anna needed something to hold on to. 'Anybody seein' the pain on your face would know you were tellin' no lie. And even if 'er didn't believe, I reckon that lad would, and should 'e not, 'e seems to 'ave enough backbone to pack 'er off back to 'er mother till things were sorted. Draw your strength from that, Anna. That son of yours won't touch Misty, not in the way you be feared of.'

Watching the dawn break over houses huddled like grey sparrows around the tall steel mill, Anna's mind still rocked with doubt and questions despite Maggie's assurance.

Had Misty returned to Wednesbury?

Had she and Aaron gone off together?

No, had that happened Polly Shipton would have told her. So where was her daughter? Tomorrow she must contact the police. For all Maggie's confidence, the thought of Misty alone terrified her.

And what of Aaron, what of her son? Would he place any value on her threat to put men out of work or would he see it as just that, a threat to be ignored? Would he stay on as manager of the steel mill or would he go?

Anna leaned her head against the cold glass of the window pane. Whichever way he chose, he had turned his back on her, as had Misty. She had lost both her children.

The letter had arrived the next morning. A cold informal missive in which Misty informed her that she had money she had not used from her allowance, that she was safe, and would Anna not attempt to have her brought back to Coseley?

That had been six months ago.

There had been other letters since. Letters as cold and distant as the first, but at least they had proved Misty was well and coping on her own as Maggie had predicted she would. But knowing that did not ease the heartbreak her leaving had caused. Yet knowing the terrible hurt her daughter had suffered, and the girl's own heartbreak, Anna had complied with her wish not to be brought home.

Perhaps Maggie would yet prove right. Anna stared into the heart of the living-room fire but none of its brightness penetrated the dark shadows of her despair, nor any of its heat warm the coldness that gripped her heart. Perhaps Misty's temper would cool, perhaps she would soon be home.

And what of Aaron? There had been no word in those six months, either from Polly Shipton or from the foundry, so he must still be there. She could so easily have found out but had made no move to enquire, done nothing that might possibly embarrass her son further, though she doubted he could ever now be brought to see her house as his home.

A knock at the door sent shudders of fear through Anna.

'Sit you still, I'll see who that be.'

But Anna was at the door before Maggie had finished speaking. Was it Misty come home or a message to say her son had left Wednesbury? Her hand shaking, she opened the door.

'Charles!'

Surprise mixed with an inexplicable feeling of relief as Anna stared at the tall figure of Charles Lazenby.

'You did write to me, didn't you?'

Charles looked at the woman whose blunt refusal of his advances had roused in him a respect he had rarely felt for one of her sex. Was it work that had circled those eyes with dark rings, taken all colour from her face and so much flesh from her bones, or was there something other than business troubling Anna Royce?

'Yes . . . yes, I did write.' Flustered by the sudden appearance of the man who had wanted her to be his mistress, she stumbled over the words. She had forgotten the letter she had written him months ago. 'But I . . . I only wanted your advice.'

'That is all I am bringing!' He smiled down at her.

'Don't you think you should be lettin' man in, whoever 'e be?'

Behind her Maggie's voice was reassuring. The sight of Charles on her doorstep had thrown her. Stepping aside, she closed the door as Maggie appeared.

'Maggie,' she said, 'this is Charles Lazenby. Charles, meet my best and oldest friend, Maggie Fellen.'

Anna knew her friend stood on ceremony for no one, regardless of who they might be, so was not surprised by the blunt, 'Y'ad best come in, sittin' room be through 'ere.'

A smile touching his lips, Charles laid his gloves and cane on the hall table then followed Maggie.

'Your daughter is well, Anna?' Seeing the shadow flit across her pale face, he tactfully left further enquiries unspoken.

''Ow about a nice cup of tea?' Maggie asked the inevitable question. 'Or p'raps you prefer summat stronger?'

'A nice cup of tea would be most acceptable, thank you, Mrs Fellen.'

Waiting until she had left the room, he said quietly, 'Anna, I am asking no questions but I want you to know that should you feel you need my help, you have only to ask.'

Her smile was weak and left her mouth almost instantly but she said nothing. She knew he was referring to Misty but that problem was hers and hers alone.

'Your letter referred to the horseless carriage,' Charles continued, covering her silence. 'Are you thinking of going into that business?'

'I had thought of it.'

'But I seem to recall your telling me they were noisy, smelly things?'

Anna nodded.

'And you said they were the future, if I remember rightly.'

Waiting while the returning Maggie set the tea tray on a table beside one of the wing-backed armchairs, Charles accepted the cup she offered.

'Thank you, Mrs Fellen,' he said again, smiling at the older woman. 'Would you allow me to call you Maggie? I should like us to be friends.'

'Ar, lad, you do that.' Maggie returned his smile, a thing that had rarely happened since her son's death. 'If you be good enough for Anna, you be good enough for me.'

'I could ask no more, Maggie.' It was said with a warmth she knew was genuine.

His tea drunk, Charles returned his cup to the tray.

'So, Anna, you have thought of going into the horseless carriage trade? At least, your letter intimated as much.'

She had not thought much about it in these recent weeks but now her mind returned to the possibility.

'If you are still so sure that they are the future, then yes, I am interested.'

'They are, Anna, I am convinced of it. I have just returned from the Continent, which explains my delay in coming to see you and your receiving no reply to your letter. The motor carriage is creating quite a stir over there. At the moment they are merely a rich man's toy but soon they will be more than that. In twenty years or less they will have replaced many of the forms of transport we have today. The future is in engines, Anna, and the man who produces the best could hold tomorrow in his hand.'

'You seem very sure of that.'

'I am.' Charles leaned forward eagerly, his hair bright against the brocaded velvet of the chair. 'I am as sure of that as I am that day follows night.'

Maggie had sat silent through their talk. Now she stood up, taking the tea tray with her.

'Don't go, Maggie.' Anna put out a hand to her friend.

'Nay, wench,' she shook her head, 'I 'ave little understandin' of 'orseless carriage an' less interest. Be it all same wi' you, I would rather be doin' summat useful.'

After Maggie had left the room Anna stood up, her hair fiery in the light of the lamps.

'Anna.' Charles came to stand beside her. 'Anna, asking you to become my mistress was a mistake, one of the biggest and most foolish of my life. It was an insult to you, and I apologise most profoundly.'

'Charles, it . . .'

'No, Anna. Hear me out please.' Reaching for her hand, he held it in both of his. 'There is something I have to say. I have wanted to say it for some time, but at the last moment my courage always failed me, I could not risk facing the anger I saw in your eyes when I asked you . . .'

'Charles, that is in the past,' Anna said gently.

'Yes.' He smiled ruefully. 'And it always will be there, a shadow between us. God, why did I ever say such a stupid thing?'

'Charles, that day, by the river, you promised you would not refer to that, ever again.'

'That is one more apology I must make, Anna.' His smile faded but he kept hold of her hand. He had been fool enough to offer to make this woman his mistress, an offer that had troubled him for many months before realising its cause. 'But I must tell you, my dear, I was wrong, terribly wrong, I did not recognise my feelings for what they were, but I know them now, Anna. I know that I love you and that I want you to be my wife.'

Charles loved her. He wanted her for his wife. A year ago she might have shouted for the sheer joy of it, but now? Now she felt a little sorry. Not for herself, but for Charles, knowing what her answer must do to him. She could not become his wife and carry on with her business, that she knew.

'You don't know what you are asking, Charles,' she said looking up at him.

'I know I love you, Anna, and that is all that matters.'

'No, no it is not, there is much more to it than that.'

'What more could there be, Anna?'

Pulling her hand free she turned away from him. 'The responsibility, Charles. A wife must be able to put her husband first in all things. To do that I would have to give up my business.'

'Damn your business!' Catching her by the shoulders he swung her back to face him. 'I can give you all the money you will ever need!'

'And that would be enough, would it?' She lifted her glance to his, her eyes moist. 'No, Charles, it would not. That is what I mean by responsibility. I could not abandon all those people who work for me, I am a part of them, a part that can never be Mrs Charles Lazenby.'

'Anna!' With one swift move he pulled her into his arms. 'You wanted me once, you can't deny it.'

'Yes, I wanted you, once,' she whispered against his shoulder, 'I would not be hypocritical enough to deny that. But wanting is not loving.'

Holding her there, against him, he was silent for a moment, then. 'Are you telling me you do not love me, Anna?'

Pushing free of his arms she looked at him. 'I am telling you I will not marry you.'

'But you could continue to run your business, and still be my wife.'

'No, Charles.' Anna shook her head. 'That would not work, you know it and I know it.'

'I love you, Anna.' He smiled, a soft, half apologetic smile. 'I am sorry I left things too late.'

'But never too late for friendship?'

'No, my dear. Never too late for that.'

'Then can I ask, will you come with me to Wednesbury?'

'To where?' He knew it was useless to press her further to marry him, he had had his chance months ago and had missed it.

'Wednesbury,' Anna replied. 'If I am to go into motor

carriage production, as no doubt you would advise, then I would value your opinion of the place I have in mind as a factory, and of the man I have a mind to put in charge.'

Leading the way back to the hall, Charles picked up his gloves and cane then turned to Anna, the smile he gave her hiding the hurt of her refusal.

'Wednesbury it is then, and thank you, Anna, for asking me.'

Watching him leave, Anna felt weary. She would go to Wednesbury even though she would rather stay here in Coseley until some word came of her daughter's return, but she knew she could not afford the luxury of isolation. People depended on her.

The string of paper diamonds hung heavy about her neck.

'Anna, allow me to present my very good friend, André Levassor.' Charles half turned to the man he had brought with him to Wednesbury. 'André . . .'

'No need for you to tell me, Charles.' Black eyes smiled into Anna's. 'Who but Anna Royce could have the beauty of Aphrodite and the hair of a Titian nymph? Who but the woman Charles talks of so often, yet described so ineptly; but then, I am being unfair to Charles, yours is the beauty only a poet could describe.'

'Give her a chance, you rogue.' Charles smiled. 'At least tell a lady your name before you try to charm her off her feet.'

'Forgive me.' The smile deepened turning his eyes to velvet darkness. 'I am André Levassor. *Enchanté*, Anna.' Taking her hand he raised it to his lips.

'You are interested in motor carriages?' It was not the most intelligent of questions, why else would he be here? Embarrassed, she drew her hand away.

'André comes to England whenever he can.' Charles guided her toward the door that led onto the street. 'That being when he can tear himself from the racing circuit.'

'You race horses?'

Holding the door for her to pass through, Charles laughed. 'Not horses, Anna, our M'sieur Levassor races motor carriages.'

'What!' Anna halted in midstride. 'But isn't that awfully dangerous?'

'It is fun.'

Climbing into the hansom, Anna kept her thoughts to herself. She would not call haring around in a motor carriage fun.

'This is the way Anna prefers to travel,' Charles said as they climbed in beside her. 'She reckons motors are "nasty, smelly things".'

'Then I shall agree with her.' André Levassor smiled. 'At least until I can change her mind.'

'That is my plan, Mr Bradly.'

The two men she had brought with her at her side, Anna walked the length of the steel foundry.

'Motor carriages!' The son who detested her glanced not at Anna, but from one to the other of the tall elegant men she had introduced, Charles Lazenby and André Levassor. 'The men here know nothing of building motor carriages.'

'Do you?' Anna steadfastly ignored his refusal to pay her any attention.

'Not the body work, no.' Still he did not look at her. 'But I think I know a fair bit about engines.'

'I see. And where did you learn about them?'

His look still not for her, Aaron returned, 'The man who owns the coal mine along Lea Brook has a car, and he often lets me work on the engine.'

'Car?' Anna raised a quizzical eyebrow.

Aaron turned a cold glance on her. Not once had he smiled at her, not once had he mentioned that awful night at The White Horse, and not once had he mentioned Misty.

'It is a Mistral.' He glanced at André. 'One of yours, I believe, sir.'

'*Oui.*' The Frenchman nodded. 'My grandfather is also crazy for the motor carriage. It was he who began the production of the Levassor engine.'

'It's one of the best, sir, the Mistral is a very good car.' He turned to Anna, the warmth vanishing from his eyes. 'It was brought over from the Continent, and though strictly the term for such a conveyance is "motor carriage", it tends to become shortened to car.'

That's me with my wrists slapped. Inwardly Anna smiled. Well, my lad, she thought, car or motor carriage, you are going to build them.

'And which Levassor engine does your friend's car have?' Charles broke in.

This time Aaron did smile as he answered and the light that leapt to those amazingly blue eyes tugged at Anna's soul. If only he looked at her with the same enthusiasm.

'Two cylinder, sir.'

'And its capacity?'

'Two and a half horse power. I believe it is their newest design.'

'Is he right, André?'

'He is indeed, Charles.' He switched to Aaron. 'You are very well acquainted with motor engines. Perhaps we can talk together, you might like to hear about my latest, the one I am putting in my racing machine.'

'You race motor cars, sir?' Aaron's eyes gleamed. 'That must be the most exciting thing in the world. Lord, what wouldn't I give to have a look at one of those engines. How many horse power do they have?'

Anna listened to her son, pride in him warming her. Polly Shipton had said he had learned well and it was obvious she had not tolerated any of the local slackness of speech, just as she had tolerated none with his mother. Mother . . . that was a title he would never afford Anna.

'Do you feel you could manage the engine side of the manufacture of motor carriages if someone else were brought in to organise the building of the coachwork?'

The question, put so abruptly, stopped her son in his tracks, so that for a moment he made no answer.

'I could have a real good try.' His shoulders straightened visibly, and this time he did face her, looking squarely into her eyes with none of the deference that was usual between workman and employer. 'And if I am no good, *you* may have the pleasure of telling me so.'

'He is a good man and an intelligent one.'

They were having dinner at The White Horse and Charles was speaking of Aaron. He had been impressed with the knowledge and the efficient way of dealing with the men under him that a man so young had shown.

'A bit young, I grant you, but he has a brain and a mind he is not afraid to use. I think you could do worse than put him in charge of your new motor carriage works, Anna.'

'Then you think this town is a good site for it?'

'As good as any other, I should think, given the work force.'

'There will be no shortage of that here,' she answered. 'But how do you think the foundry will convert into a motor carriage works?'

'Quite easily,' Charles sipped his brandy, 'though I think such a move would be inadvisable.'

'In what way?' she asked.

'Well, were I beginning such a venture, I would look to the future. Motor carriages are going to be a major part of that future, Anna. We are seeing the birth but the industry will grow, and that growth will need steel, lots of it. Yours won't be the only motor carriage works, and each one will be needing steel. That being so, you could find yourself facing delay if that need is not met. Maybe even forced out of production should you meet another Jacob Rewcastle.'

'But I have the steel mill in Coseley, I can always use that.'

'You can, of course.' Charles took a further sip at his brandy, savouring the warmth in his throat. 'But what of the industry that mill is already feeding? Will you discontinue that side of your business? Closing one in order to open another is not always good practice, Anna, to say nothing of the people it would put out of work.'

She nodded.

'You're right of course, Charles. I hadn't thought things through properly. I'm jumping in with both feet again and I haven't noticed the puddle of mud.'

'There need be no puddle, Anna. Leave Coseley mill as it is and let *this one* here in Wednesbury go on producing steel. It seems that young fellow in charge has the place very much back on its feet. If finances permit, I would go for building an entirely new place to house your motor carriage construction, somewhere in the vicinity. That way you will have your own guaranteed supply of steel.'

Anna pursed her lips, her thoughts moving rapidly.

'That makes sense, Charles. I could build here or in Darlaston. That is not too far, three miles at most, and from what I remember that town needs work as much as Wednesbury.'

'Whichever you choose, Anna, be sure there is room for component works.' This time it was André who spoke. 'Motor carriages have more bits and pieces to them than is obvious from looking at them.'

'I'm going to need help, M'sieur.' Anna smiled, hoping the form of address she had heard Charles use sounded the same coming from her. 'I have never done this sort of thing before, it has always been the straightforward buying of an established business.' She turned her glance to Charles. 'I don't know if I'll cope.'

'You'll cope, Anna, you always have, but if it would help, I could always look the area over with you?'

'And I am always willing to give advice on the building of your engines.'

'Whenever you are in England, that is.' Charles smiled at his friend.

'You know, Charles.' André picked up his glass, swirling the brandy around its sides. 'I think that might be more often than you think.'

'Thank you, both of you,' Anna said gratefully. 'But where do I find a coach builder to set the other side going? I need someone to train men to the work. Most of the men of this town have only ever known steel making.'

'I can arrange that, Anna, if you will allow.' Taking up his own glass, Charles leaned across the table, the light of the flickering gas lamps enhancing the blue of his eyes. 'To the success of your venture. And to you, Anna, may you be successful in all you do.'

'*Oui*, Anna.' André held his glass beside that of Charles. 'May you be as successful as you are beautiful.'

As she reached her own glass toward theirs, Charles caught the scent of violets, and again he felt a stab of regret. He had thought to seduce this woman, to use her for his own pleasure. But he was the one who had been seduced, ensnared by his own stupidity.

Touching her glass to each of theirs, Anna spoke softly.

'Charles. When you came to Coseley you said we could be friends, but after hearing what I am about to say you may wish to withdraw from that.'

Seeing the play of emotions on Anna's face, André Levassor rose to his feet. Whatever she was about to say to Charles was obviously going to need courage. 'I will leave you together, you will want privacy.'

'No, M'sieur Levassor!' Anna looked at him. The time for secrets was over. From now on she would hide nothing. 'You too were kind enough to offer your help, and you also must be given the chance to rescind that offer.' She glanced down at the glass still held in her hands. They had both offered their assistance. Inevitably that would mean them talking with Aaron, and in so doing they might accidentally learn of her relationship to him. She did not want that. She preferred to tell them herself.

'Charles, M'sieur Levassor.' Lifting her head she spoke clearly and without embarrassment. 'The young man you spoke with earlier today, Aaron Bradly. He is my son . . . my bastard son.'

'New places be doin' well, Anna.'

Spectacles perched on the end of his nose, Joby Timmins ran a practised eye over the monthly returns.

'Sovereign Motors was a right good move on your part. Growin' at a faster rate than anythin' I've ever known. But then, you always 'ad a good eye for business, wench.'

'It's what is known as the Midas touch.' Anna closed the heavy ledger and stood up, pressing her palms into her back, stretching her aching body. Charles had kept his word; he had helped her choose a site for her motor carriage works, and André Levassor had helped tremendously with the engine side of things. Anna had liked him. Liked his quick smile and easy personality.

'A what touch?' Joby went into the hall, picking up his flat cap from the table Maggie kept polished to a glassy shine.

'Never mind.' Anna's smile flashed as she opened the front door. 'It was good of you to come to the house, Joby, I couldn't get to the office.'

'Think no more on it, Anna. You pays me well for what I do.'

'Well, can I send you home in a Sovereign?' she teased, knowing the old man's feelings about motor carriages.

'Nay, wench, I'll walk. No disrespect to you but you can give me a good 'oss afore one o' them contraptions any day.'

'Good night then, Joby, and remember me to your son when next you write to him. You and your wife must be very proud of him, getting a place at grammar school. And King Edward's, no less. Tell him there's a place for him with me if he fancies it once he is finished there.'

'I will, Anna, and thanks, me wench.'

Watching until he turned out of sight around the end of the drive, Anna closed the door. Joby had spoken true about Sovereign Motors. In the two years since starting out at Wednesbury she had bought more factories, and each was now producing motor bodies and components. More paper diamonds adding to the weight about her neck. She did have that legendary Midas touch, everything she took on made money, so why did none of it make her happy?

She was halfway up the stairs when the front door swung back on its hinges and Misty threw herself into the house.

'Mother!' As if she had merely been away for a school term, she came tearing across the hall and up the stairs. 'Mother, it's so lovely to be home.'

Flinging both arms about Anna's neck, she hugged her rapturously. Then: 'Grammie! Where's Grammie? I simply have to see her.'

'In . . . in her room.' Flabbergasted, Anna watched the flying figure of her daughter disappear around the head of the stairs.

'Mrs Royce?'

Turning sharply, Anna almost missed her footing, having to grasp the mahogany banister to prevent herself from falling.

'I apologise if I startled you.'

From the well of the hall a man stood watching her. Dark hair parted down the centre was slicked to either side, carrying on to side whiskers that touched his jaw; on his top lip a moustache blossomed in a small curve. His eyes, bright and darting as a ferret's, ran over her with swift appreciation.

'Misty insisted I come with her. I hope I'm not intruding?'

He stepped forward and Anna knew a sudden insane desire to turn and run.

'Of course not.' She forced herself to move. 'Do come in, Mr . . .?'

'Saverry,' he answered. 'Edwin Saverry.'

It came back nimbly, as practised as the smile that

didn't reach his eyes, a smile that sent a shiver along her spine.

'You two have introduced yourselves . . . good.' Misty sprinted down the stairs, grabbing Anna by the hand. 'Now come and let me get a good look at you.'

In the sitting room that Anna had vacated just minutes before Misty held both her hands, spreading her arms wide and looking her mother up and down.

'Doesn't she look just marvellous, Edwin . . . didn't I tell you my mother was beautiful?'

'You did.' The quick ferret's glance swept over Anna, resting fractionally too long on her firm breasts before returning to her face. 'But your description did not do her justice, Misty.' The thin mouth curved into that same sickly smile. 'Your mother is not just beautiful . . . she is very beautiful.'

'Isn't he charming, Mother?' Misty broke loose, crossing to Edwin Saverry and passing her arm through his.

Too charming! Anna pulled the bell rope beside the fireplace.

'She's new,' Misty said as the maid left to fetch the tea Anna requested.

'Yes.' Anna sat in one of the green wingback chairs, feeling those too bright eyes trace her every movement. 'Maggie isn't getting any younger and I don't like leaving her alone in the house when I'm away.'

Curling down on to the carpet, one arm resting on Edwin's knee where he sat opposite Anna, Misty lost some of the vivacity that had burst from her since she had run into the house.

'I didn't think Grammie looked well, Mother. Her hair is so white and I never saw her cry before, not ever.'

'She has had a great deal to contend with,' Anna said, still slightly amazed at how calmly she had taken Misty's sudden return. 'The news of Andrew's death almost killed her, and the last two years have proved a dreadful strain. You could at least have visited even had you not wanted to come home to stay.'

'I did intend to, Mother, honestly I did, but Paris was so very exciting. Something new to do every day, a new interest every minute, takes your mind away from mundane things. And I *did* write.' Misty dismissed her actions and her mother's mild reproof with the inconsequence of youth.

'So coming home to your family was mundane, and the worry you gave them of little importance!'

Anna could not hide the recrimination in her voice, and across her daughter's pale gold head Edwin Saverry looked swiftly at her.

'Misty got caught up with a young crowd on the Left Bank, Mrs Royce. I am afraid they give little thought to parents.'

'And you do?'

'Yes, Mother,' Misty answered for him. She turned an adoring look up to his face. 'It was Edwin who told me how selfishly I was behaving. It was he said we should come home.'

The maid carried a tray into the room and, placing it in front of Anna, asked if she should prepare something for them to eat. She left as Misty shook her head.

'We should come home?' Emphasis heavy on the first word, Anna resumed their conversation.

Misty gave Edwin the same infatuated glance.

'Yes, Edwin said we should both come. We are going to get engaged but he insisted we come and ask you first.'

Anna felt as though a heavy weight had descended on her. Two years ago it had been the same, only then her worry had been that her daughter's choice of a future husband had been her own half-brother. Now she had chosen instead a man who made Anna's flesh creep.

She looked at the girl whom she had last seen running in tears from that room in The White Horse Hotel. She wasn't weeping now; her face held a soft radiance, a glow of happiness that radiated from it like a beacon. Anna had seen that same look before, seen it when Misty had introduced her to Aaron. And she had seen it die when she'd said they could not marry.

She couldn't do that again, she could not destroy her daughter's happiness a second time.

'That was very thoughtful of you, Mr Saverry.'

Anna poured tea into paper thin cups, sparing herself from looking into his eyes, feeling her unwarranted dislike of the man harden with each moment. It was unfair, she told herself, unfair to harbour such feelings on so short an acquaintance, but telling herself so did not erase the dislike, or the feeling that Edwin Saverry was not a man to be trusted.

Picking up a cup, Anna held it out to him, and in doing so was forced to meet his pallid eyes.

'I would prefer a whisky, Mrs Royce.'

Anna withdrew the cup, grateful he had not taken it; grateful his fingers had not, even accidentally, touched her. Strange how the very sound of his voice turned her cold.

Jumping to her feet, Misty poured a straight whisky and handed it to him, pressing an adoring kiss to his almost languid hand.

Quailing inside Anna asked: 'How long have you known Misty, Mr Saverry?'

'Simply ages, Mother.' Misty danced round to the back of his chair, reaching her hands over the back of it and resting one on each of the man's shoulders. Her eyes, when she looked across at Anna, sparkled like blue diamonds. 'Long enough to know what we both want.'

I've heard those words before, Anna thought, looking at her daughter. The last two years might never have been. The joy in the young face was the same as it had been then, the eagerness matched that which she had shown in the Wednesbury hotel. Only the man was different.

Anna had so wanted this to happen. She had been convinced that with time Misty's feelings for Aaron would change. But this change was giving her no pleasure. She could feel no relief, no happiness for her child. Misty's first love had been doomed from the start. Why did she feel that this one was destined to follow the same path?

'Perhaps we have not known each other so long as your mother would wish?'

One limp hand lifted, fastening over the one that rested on his shoulder. The eyes that met Anna's were challenging. He was daring her to refuse permission.

'. . . in which case we must wait. A little while more will do no harm, my sweet.'

'Mother, please don't say that!'

Misty's look was one of pure pleading and Anna felt the weight at the pit of her stomach grow heavier still.

'Edwin and I love each other . . . I don't want to wait, I want to get married now.'

It was all the same: the impetuosity, the warmth of her feelings, even the words. It all seemed like a dream, some awful recurring nightmare. Except Anna knew this particular nightmare was real.

There was no point in prolonging this. She would not deny her daughter a second time, could not destroy the girl's happiness because of her own feeling of dislike for the man Misty had chosen.

Opposite her the pallid eyes of Edwin Saverry smiled at her. A cold sly smile, a smile of triumph.

Why? Anna asked herself as she held out her arms to her daughter. Why is this happening again?

'*Toil and tears*' . . . the words of so long ago drifted back. '*Toil and tears.*' Was fate about to deal her another blow?

Chapter Twenty-one

'Buy all the lovely things you want to, darling. I just wish I could come with you but I'm really tied up at the moment.'

'Don't worry.' Misty kissed her mother's cheek. 'Edwin is coming to Paris with me. He will keep an eye on me, though I shan't let him stop me buying the most fabulous trousseau a girl ever had.'

'I couldn't deny you anything, my sweet.'

Edwin Saverry's words were for Misty but his eyes bored into Anna's. He had been a guest in her house for a month and even though it meant losing Misty for a week or so, Anna couldn't help but feel glad he was leaving. There was something about her daughter's fiancé she disliked intensely.

Maggie had summed up the fears of both of them a few days after his arrival.

''E's no good, Anna. 'E'll bring naught to 'er heart but sorrow.' And in those words Anna heard the ring of truth.

'You'll be here when we get home?'

'Of course.' Anna touched a finger to her daughter's brow, smoothing away a frown. 'I'm going to London on Thursday but I will be home the following Tuesday, I told you that. Now stop worrying and go or you will miss the train, and that means a long wait for the next. We don't get so many through Coseley.'

It had been a long day. Business meetings with Reuben and John Harris had left her feeling tired. Charles had been right when he said motor carriages were the future, and the way her ventures were expanding she was holding a lot of tomorrow in her hand.

Stirring an extra spoon of sugar into Maggie's cocoa, she carried it up to her bedroom.

'They be gone then?' The frail figure in the wide bed smiled thinly. 'I could 'ave hoped for better but the days of choosin' for the young 'ave gone. They'll 'ave their own way, though the 'aving of it chokes 'em.'

'We could be wrong, Maggie. He might be good for her.' Anna heard the hopelessness in her own voice.

'Ar, an' pigs might fly!' Maggie retorted. 'But there be naught to be gained by moping so get you to your bed and leave matters to take their course. And think on this, Anna. At least mother and daughter be together again, so if things should go wrong, 'er will come 'ome to you.'

'But ought I to have told Misty how I feel about Edwin?'

'What, and 'ave 'er run away a second time, an' this time do summat rash? If you 'ad done that you might 'ave turned the girl's heart against you for good. No, you could do naught but what you be doin'. Let 'er make 'er own choice an' pray 'er won't be hurt by it.'

She would pray. In her own bedroom Anna slipped her nightdress over her head. She would pray but would the Almighty listen?

'. . . if things should go wrong, 'er will come 'ome to you.' Maggie's words in her mind, Anna slipped into bed.

But what of Aaron? He barely acknowledged her as an employer; he would never acknowledge her as a mother. No, her son would never turn to her.

Hovering between sleep and waking, Anna wasn't sure just when she became aware of the figure standing beside her bed.

'You're not asleep, Anna. But then, if you were it would be a pleasure to wake you . . . like this.'

The dark shape bent swiftly, clamping a moist mouth over hers. Caught in a vice of terror, her brain numbed, Anna lay still.

'I knew you wanted that.'

Edwin Saverry! Anna's heart lurched. Edwin here in her room? But he should be with Misty on their way to Paris. So where was Misty? Had she come back too? No, in the numbness of her mind Anna knew that had her daughter returned to the house, she would have come straight to her . . .

'I knew you wanted me,' Edwin whispered against her mouth, and just the knowledge of who had entered her room dissolved most of Anna's fear and her brain began to function.

She must not scream. That would wake Maggie. Maggie! Anna's fears took on a new twist. Edwin Saverry knew she was in the house and Anna felt he would not hesitate in harming even an old woman.

'Can't we have the light on?' She forced herself to stay calm, hoping the loathing coursing through her didn't show.

'Another kiss and then the lights.'

He caught her mouth in a hard kiss. One hand slipped under the sheet, finding the vee of her nightdress then beneath it the firm mound of her breast.

Revulsion rising in her like physical sickness, Anna twisted her mouth away.

'I . . . I always prefer to make love with the light on, Edwin.'

It was a risk but she had to take it. Edwin Saverry was slight in build but that gave no positive indication as to his strength. If he decided to try and take her now she might not be able to fight him off. Above her she heard the harsh intake of breath and as he moved to switch on the new electric light, Anna rolled from the bed.

'What the hell do you think you are doing?' she demanded as the room flooded with light. 'And where is Misty?'

'She's on the boat train for Paris.' He smiled, the same sly repulsive expression she had seen so often during his stay in this house. 'I told her there was something I had to take care of.'

'Then why are you back here?' It was a silly question in view of what had happened but it gave her time to think. The maid was not in the house, but then he would know that having lived here for a month; there was only Maggie, and Anna couldn't risk her being harmed.

'You know why I'm here. Because it's *you* I want.'

She hadn't reckoned on the speed with which he moved. Before the sentence was said he had closed the gap between them, his hands fixed on her like grappling hooks, his wet lips seeking hers.

'But Misty?' Anna twisted again, managing to avoid the onslaught.

'Misty!' One hand fastened in the silk of her nightdress, dragging it off her shoulder, then slid it down to her breast, squeezing and moulding.

'I don't want Misty,' he breathed thickly, 'I want you.'

The strength of him pressing against her forced her back on to the bed and in doing so brushed her against the rosewood cabinet that stood close beside it. In desperation Anna reached towards it, clutching the heavy cut-glass three-branched candlestick that stood on it. She brought it with all her force against the side of Edwin Saverry's head.

Was he dead?

Had she killed him?

'I don't care.' Anna's whole body trembled and her fingers convulsively gripped the candlestick. 'I don't care . . . I don't care.'

It seemed she travelled through eternity as she stood watching the still figure sprawled on her bedroom floor but at last he moved, moaning as he opened his eyes.

'Get out!' Anna hissed as he touched the cut oozing a trickle of blood from beneath his brilliantined hair. 'Get out now before I hit you again! I don't know what the hell you thought you would get by coming back to this house, but whatever it was, you are mistaken.'

Pushing himself to a sitting position, he pulled a handkerchief from the top pocket of his snuff-coloured jacket, wincing as he held it to his head.

Stepping back, a little afraid he might renew his attack despite the blow she had struck him and the candlestick she still held, Anna watched the bright crimson stain seep slowly into the perfectly laundered square.

'Maggie was right about you.' Her lips felt tight, unwilling to move. 'You're no good . . .'

'Maggie!' He spat the name viciously. 'That bloody old bitch!'

'A bloody old bitch she might be but she got your measure.' Anna glared. 'Now you had best leave before I call the police.'

He looked at her, a line of blood snaking down his cheek, undulating into his moustache.

That is what you are, Anna thought as he watched her, a slimy, no good snake.

'Why don't you do that?'

His pallid eyes gleamed in the light of the room, sending new tremors of fear through Anna. She had disliked this man from the moment of their first meeting. Now she despised him.

'Why don't you send for the police? By the time they get here I could be undressed and in your bed. Now wouldn't *that* make a nice little headline? Anna Royce of Sovereign Motors steals daughter's fiancé.'

'You could be in my bed or you could be dead!'

'I could be dead . . . but I won't be.'

He smiled again and Anna knew the true depth of her feelings for the man her daughter was about to marry; the real measure of her hatred.

'Don't be too sure of that.'

'Oh, but I am. You can't hurt that daughter of yours, can you? Not after what has gone on between you. Aren't I right, Anna?'

'You swine!' She raised the candlestick a little higher, every cell in her brain screaming at her to bring it down again, to strike him until that sly smile dropped from his face, until those pallid gleaming eyes were closed for good. 'You swine, I'd like to kill you!'

'But you won't.' Taking the handkerchief from the cut, he looked at the vivid stain then folded the cloth, reapplying it to the still bleeding wound.

'It is as well you don't want Misty because I would never give my consent now. I would never let her marry a swine like you.'

Edwin Saverry dabbed at his head, his bright ferret's eyes on Anna's pale face.

'I don't want her, that's true, but it doesn't mean I am not going to marry her. And you, my dear mother-in-law to be, can do nothing to prevent it. You see . . .' he screwed up the handkerchief savagely between his hands before stuffing it back into his pocket '. . . I would tell your daughter you planned this, that I came back here because you had begged me to, that you wanted me so badly it didn't matter I was engaged to her.'

'Misty would never believe that!' Anna gasped.

Climbing to his feet he swayed unsteadily, thrusting out an arm to steady himself. Still wary of what he might try, Anna lifted the heavy candlestick again.

'You think she wouldn't believe that of you?' At her movement his eyes darkened, narrowing to vicious slits. 'She wouldn't believe that of her darling mother? But I think she would. After all, she is only too familiar with your background . . . a bitch of a mother so in heat she gave herself to her own father . . . the half-brother she has in Wednesbury. Think about it, Anna, who do you really think she would believe?'

'Where did you hear that?' Anna could not believe Misty would tell him about Aaron. 'Misty would not . . .'

Straightening his jacket, running a hand over his slicked

down hair, Edwin Saverry looked at the woman he had tried to rape.

'Wouldn't she?' He smirked. 'Not tell the man she loves of the silly flirtation with a young man who turned out to be her half-brother? Not tell the man she is to marry of her mother's bastard son? You see, Anna, your daughter hasn't enough sense to know when to keep her mouth shut. She wanted to start our marriage off on the right foot, no secrets; so very right for a stable relationship between a man and his beloved wife, don't you think?'

Anna's arm fell to her side though her hand still gripped the candlestick.

'How much do you want?'

Loathing, disgust and fury fought within her as he smiled.

'Oh, you can't buy me off! I might not have got the particular cherry I wanted but I still have the tree.'

'What do you mean?'

The smirk on his face widened, showing teeth that were almost too white, and the small feral eyes gleamed with the warmth of ice.

'What do I mean? I mean your daughter. She's got nothing in her head, and nothing between her legs I can't get anywhere else – and much more enjoyably. In fact, all the stuck up little cow *has* got going for her is your money, and sooner or later the lot of it will be hers . . . and mine!'

'No . . . no, it won't! Neither my money nor my daughter will ever be yours. As soon as Misty returns from Paris I will tell her what you are and what you tried to do tonight, and when I do there will be no marriage.'

'And should you try that, you will find yourself once more without a daughter.'

His smile was gloating and revulsion spread through her, burning like a forest fire.

'If it means I have no daughter then so be it. I would rather that than have her married to you.'

• • •

'I still don't know if it's the right thing.' Anna sat in Hester's sitting room. 'The business is doing fine as it is, I really see no need to expand.'

'Why stand still, Anna, when you could bring employment to so many more people?' Reuben asked over his spectacles.

Bring employment to others. Anna sighed inwardly. She had done that on so many occasions, but what had it brought her other than a great deal of worry? Why enlarge on that? Why add to the burden?

'There's a lot to think of, Reuben.' She was still doubtful. 'The risk . . .'

'Where's the risk?' Hester intervened quickly. 'You heard what that woman said.'

Yes, she had heard. It was her visit to the shop in Queen Anne's Gate two months ago that had triggered the idea she had since discussed several times with Hester and Reuben. Two women had been buying her china.

'If we had this in the States –' one of them had been holding a Royal Edward plate, tracing the exquisite design with a finger '– there surely wouldn't be a house without it. Why, I tell you, when we get this home we are going to be the envy of Washington. There won't be one single woman wouldn't pay a fortune to have the same.'

Maybe Reuben was right, maybe new markets were to be had in America, but did she want to be the one to take them?

'Truth is, Anna,' Hester's toffee drop eyes looked concerned, 'you need a break after the business of Misty breaking off her engagement.'

It was true. Misty's marriage to Edwin Saverry would no longer take place. Anna could still feel the relief that had swept over her when Misty had returned only days after leaving. They had met up with friends when they got to Paris, she had said, and Edwin had drunk too much. She had been in the bedroom of the friend's house showing her the silk lingerie she had bought. Edwin was talking to the husband, his voice drifting in from the living room getting louder with every glass of wine. He boasted he had been back to see her bitch of a mother, told her that all her daughter had was money and that he would take that while taking his pleasures where he fancied. Misty had come home the following day.

Anna remembered expecting the girl to dissolve into floods of tears, but there had been none. It was better she found out now rather than after marrying Edwin Saverry, Misty had said. In her heart, Anna thanked God. Her daughter had grown up.

'Why not go to America, Anna?' Hester cut into her thoughts. 'Give yourself a holiday.'

'But I can't go toddling off to America.' She gave a thin laugh. 'The business won't run itself. I really ought not to have asked you to go, I don't know how I can manage without you, and Reuben has his practice.'

'We talked about that when you first mentioned a trip to America, Anna.' Reuben looked at her over heavy-rimmed spectacles. 'We both agreed a holiday was due to us and this is an opportunity that may never come again.'

'I wouldn't call it a holiday, Reuben,' she said. 'Going to sound out the prospects for a new market, especially in a foreign country, can't be any joy ride. In fact, I'm sure it would terrify me.'

'It might be a bit scary,' Hester agreed. 'But you would have Reuben and me with you. You really should come. If anyone deserves a few weeks off, you do.'

'Say you will come, Anna.' Reuben added his voice.

Her thoughts chaotic, Anna shook her head. Since Andrew died Maggie seemed so frail, hardly strong enough to stand up to life anymore. And Misty. How could she leave her daughter so soon after that awful business with Saverry? She had shown no real regret, no depth of emotion of any sort other than anger. But that did not mean she held none, and if they surfaced, Anna wanted to be close, not half way across the world.

'I will come next time.'

Hester guessed that the reason for Anna's refusal was to be with Misty.

'We understand.' Her quick glance silenced the suggestion Reuben had been about to make. 'You're right, Anna, there is always next time. And if America is as wonderful, or as shocking, as I hope, then we will take me mam and Maggie with us.'

A smile on her lips, Anna rose to leave.

'Now *that* would take some arranging. Maggie has not stopped complaining about Birmingham yet.'

Slipping her arms into the coat Reuben held for her, she did up the row of buttons that reached from waist to throat.

'Was Maggie not impressed?'

Anna slanted a glance at Reuben, knowing his question was tongue in cheek. 'Oh, Maggie was impressed. Said everyone was "haring about as though the devil were after them . . . forgot 'ow to walk, they 'ave."'

Reuben smiled at Anna's mimicry. 'We will compromise. We will take the ladies to London and if they enjoy that, then who knows? It could be: Stand back New York!'

Smoothing on her gloves Anna picked up her bag.

'You know what Maggie would say to that, don't you, Reuben? "Ar, an' pigs might fly!"'

Anna looked across at her daughter. She had sat for over an hour, her pencil resting on a paper in her lap. Anna had watched her closely since her return from Paris, dreading any signs of unhappiness, which, strangely, had not shown yet. Today's faraway mood was the first time Misty had been other than her old bubbly self.

'How are the new designs coming?'

'Mmm? Oh, all right. They are coming along.'

'Misty.' Anna decided to ask the question that plagued her. If it brought on a storm then perhaps it would be for the best, at least storms usually cleared away clouds. 'Do you have any regrets, at breaking your engagement?'

'Regrets!' Misty's head jerked upward, her eyes wide. 'That's the very last thing I feel. Believe me, Mother, I thank heaven every day that I found out about Edwin Saverry when I did. How on earth could I have let myself be taken in like that?'

'It happens,' Anna replied.

'But it wasn't as if I was not warned about him.' Misty let the pencil fall from her fingers. 'My friends tried to tell me what sort of man he was, but I wouldn't listen. I had to have my own way, just like before.'

Anna held out her arms, and as Misty came to her she folded them about the slight figure. 'Don't blame yourself for that.' She murmured against her daughter's hair. 'It was my fault, I should have told you about Aaron before.'

'I wish Aaron were with us.'

'So do I, dear, but he refuses to have anything to do with me.' Anna felt her heart tighten. Aaron would never own her.

'He will learn, one day,' Misty said, her head resting in Anna's lap. 'The same as I did, but I hope he doesn't learn with someone like Saverry. It was awful, Mother, listening to him bragging about what he had done.'

Anna sat quiet. Misty had given her a bare explanation of what had gone on in her friend's house, maybe now she was ready to tell more.

'He said he had told me he wanted to see an old friend before joining me in Paris.' Misty talked softly, but with no trace of sorrow in her voice. 'But that he had come back here, to this house. He said he had asked you for money, and I could guess *how* he asked. But it was clear, for all of his boasting, that his devious little plan came to nothing, he was too angry to have been successful. The next morning he came to my hotel. He tried to pretend his whole outburst had been intended as a joke. Huh!' Misty's shoulders shook. 'Some joke. The man must have a sick mind. When I told him our marriage was off he tried to threaten me with Aaron. He said he would tell the world of Anna Royce's bastard son, a son born of her own father, unless he were well paid to keep his mouth shut.'

Anna sat perfectly still. Edwin Saverry would do what he threatened. She did not care for herself, but what of Aaron? What would it do to him?

'I told him to go ahead,' Misty went on. 'But I advised him to spend whatever he got quickly. I reminded him I had lived on the Left Bank months before he came to Paris. I had friends there who knew the right people, people willing to do anything for the right amount of money. I told him that given your money and my connections he could very well be found one morning, floating face down in the Seine.'

'Misty!' Anna lifted her daughter's head to look into her face. 'Misty, you didn't.'

'I most certainly did.' Misty grinned. 'And given the look on his face, Edwin Saverry believed it.'

'A visitor for you, mum.'

Anna glanced to where the maid stood in the doorway.

'I've asked him to wait in the sitting room.'

'Tell him I will be there in a moment.' She would have liked more time alone with Misty but the girl was already on her feet.

'I will come with you.' Misty held out a hand. 'Whoever it is we will see him off together.'

'André!' Misty bounded across the sitting room. 'We were not told it was you. We came to see you off!'

'But you would not be so cruel to an old man.'

Anna watched the greeting between the two. André Levassor had called several times since that first meeting in Wednesbury, and each time Misty was happy to see him. And she, Anna, how did she feel?

'You do not mind, Anna? That I come uninvited?'

Glad her thoughts had been halted, Anna held out a hand.

'Since when do such good friends need an invitation? But

when you were here last you said you would be in Europe for several months.'

'*Oui*, that is true.' He took the chair Anna indicated. 'But I found myself with a few days to spare, so,' he shrugged his shoulders, 'I came to look at the designs Aaron has for a new motor engine.'

'You have seen Aaron?'

'*Oui*.' He answered Anna's question.

'And how is my obstinate brother?'

Anna caught her daughter's smile and felt a surge of warmth at her complete acceptance of their relationship.

'He is well.' André smiled, then looked at Anna. 'He is a very good designer of engines. I would suggest you go see for yourself, but not today, Anna. Today, I ask you spend with me.'

Anna felt the colour rise in her cheeks. 'I . . . I'm sorry, André, I have . . .'

'You have nothing to do that won't keep.' Misty cut short Anna's refusal. 'And if you are going to mention Grammie, then don't. She has promised to tell me all of the tricks I got up to with the Cresswell twins, and that is likely to take a week at least.'

'There, you see, Anna, you have no excuse. So, you will come?'

'I really should not have given in so easily,' Anna said as André drove the carriage he had hired for the day before coming to the house.

'Did you not want to come?'

'Yes.' Anna replied truthfully. 'Yes, André, I wanted to come.'

They had driven to a small inn where they had been served lunch by a red cheeked woman who smiled constantly, and now Anna knew she was happy not to have missed their day together.

Calling the horse to a halt, he jumped down from the carriage. 'I have something I must say to you, Anna.' He held up his arms, wanting to help her down. 'Tomorrow I must leave, but before I go . . .'

Circled by his arms as he helped her down, Anna felt suddenly nervous.

'Have you enjoyed our day together?' he asked, and when she nodded, 'That is all I ask, that you be happy with me.'

Gently, he turned her toward him and Anna felt herself being drawn into the depths of his dark eyes. 'You will always be happy with me, *chérie*, through all the long days and nights that are left to us. Come with me to South America and when the racing is over I shall take you to Bordeaux. You will love it there, Anna, the vineyards and the streams. But most of all, I want that you will love being my wife.'

'Your wife!' Anna gasped. 'It seems no more than yesterday we met.'

'Who knows when yesterday began?' he asked softly, taking her face between his hands. 'We have known each other for eternity Anna, you feel that, as I do.'

He kissed her then, his mouth tender yet firm and Anna realised with a sudden blinding clarity that she wanted him to kiss her. She wanted him to hold her, wanted to go with him to South America. She wanted to be his wife.

'We will marry in Bordeaux,' he said, when at last he released her mouth.

'No!' Anna pushed free of his arms. 'I can't marry you, André, I can't marry anyone.'

'Why? Because of your paper diamonds?' He laughed softly, pulling her back into the circle of his arms. 'That was an excuse, *chérie*. You refused to marry Charles not because of your business, but because, deep in your soul, you were waiting for me.'

Anna held her face against his shoulder. Maybe he knew already, maybe he had heard it from Aaron, but she must tell him herself.

'My business was not the real reason,' she said quietly. 'There is something more.'

One arm about her trembling body, one hand gently caressing the head buried in his shoulder, André Levassor listened, letting the hurt pour from her; listened as Anna whispered out her past; her father's raping her, her illegitimate son, and lastly her fear that any man who became involved with Anna Royce would die as a result.

'We do not need to fear the past, *ma chérie*,' he murmured as she stopped speaking. 'What we will have in our future together is all that is important . . . nothing else matters.'

Charles had said that and she had refuted it, but with André the words brought a sense of peace, a kind of rightness as though fate had at last given her life a benediction.

'There can be no more excuses, Anna.' His fingers brushed the silken folds of her hair. 'No running away from the truth. You belong to me, you always have done. I will not let you go. What happened long ago was not of your doing, it is over, *chérie*, and we need never speak of it again.'

Lifting her face, he kissed her gently and as Anna opened her eyes she saw behind his dark head a shooting star curve across the evening sky, a glittering moment of beauty, a scanty reflection racing over a dark earth before ebbing away into nothingness, leaving the sky darker for its passing. Was this an omen of what was to be for her? Was meeting André to be a brief moment, a brilliant starburst of happiness that would pass, leaving her life darker and emptier for his leaving?

His mouth closed again over her own and Anna pushed away the inner warning.

'This has to be, Anna.' His mouth touched her closed eyelids. 'We both know it. We have carried this love within us, waiting, searching for the one to whom it truly belonged. But now that search is ended. I love you, Anna, I love you and I want you to be my wife. Shhh.' He touched a finger against her lips as she made to speak. 'The past is gone, *chérie*. It is finished. It does not matter anymore. We have each other, Anna, and we have the future, that is enough.'

Standing there, the sweet smell of meadow grass in her

nostrils, the feel of André's arms about her, Anna knew she loved this man, loved him not with fierceness but with a gentle, calm love that filled her with a contentment she had not known before. On the breeze that touched her hair she seemed to hear the words of Kate O'Keefe.

'*Toil and tears . . . The lives of many will be bound with yer own. Ye will have the carryin' of them, for 'tis yer back their fortunes will ride upon. Ye will work all the days of yer life, but that life will prove to be a great one . . .*'

Toil she had had, building her life, and tears she had shed for a father she loved and a son who would not own her as his mother. And there were many whose lives and fortunes were tied to her own. She had come a long way from Ethelfleda Terrace, and from Roker Street. She had her paper diamonds. For all she knew, the toil, and maybe the tears, were not over yet, but Kate O'Keefe's prediction had proved true. Down to the very last words.

'*The man who will place a ring about yer heart is not of this land.*'

André Levassor was that man.

'No . . . no more!'

Her face drained of colour, Anna stared at the small buff-coloured envelope that held the wireless telegram.

'I won't . . . I won't let it happen again . . . oh, please God, not again!'

'Steady, me wench!' Seeing Anna tremble, Maggie dismissed the delivery boy then closed the door. 'Don't go gettin' yourself all riled up, Anna, you don't know what be in that envelope yet.'

It must not be them. Mouth clenched against the fear that was swallowing her, Anna allowed herself to be pushed into a chair.

It must not be Hester and Reuben. They were on their way to America, they were safe aboard that ship . . . they had to be safe. Oh, why had she agreed to their going? Why had she allowed herself to be talked into looking for new markets?

'You 'ave to open it, wench.'

At her elbow, Maggie held out the dull yellow envelope. Anna stared at it, her teeth clenched. If she did not open it then nothing would happen to Hester and Reuben, if she did not touch it then everything would be all right.

Maggie looked at the stricken face, seeing again that of a girl, no more than a child, who had come to her out of the rain; a girl she loved but could not protect from the blows it seemed life was determined to deal her.

'See 'ere, Anna,' she said gently, 'I knows what you be feelin', the fear that haunts your heart. But it be a fear that be groundless. No matter what you 'ave told yourself, you 'ad naught to do with Edward's death nor that of Philip Rewcastle an' his fancy friend. Same as the death of your father was none of your makin'. You can't be holding these things against yourself, just as you can't go through life thinking you be a jinx on any man who looks on you!'

'I let them go.' Anna seemed not to hear. 'I let Hester and Reuben go, I thought they would be safe . . .'

'Anna, stop mewlin' like a babby!'

Maggie's voice cut through her fear, sharp with anger, anger for the years of anguish and heartbreak she had watched her friend live through, anger that it was still not finished.

'You don't even know if that there telegram be about Hester and Reuben at all. You be buildin' walls wi'out bricks.'

'I thought they would be safe.' Anna's mouth trembled.

'Ar, I know you did, wench. And safe they will be.' Maggie's anger had not faded but was muted now by a softer tone. 'Like as not this 'ere telegram be to tell you they have arrived in America and be 'aving a rare old time, but you won't know 'less you opens it.'

Her hand shaking, Anna took the small envelope, drawing out the slip of paper it held. Slowly, having to force herself to look at the bold black print, she read the words then re-read them, unsure if the fresh flood of pain that surged through her was that of relief or of guilt.

The telegram was not from Hester and Reuben.

Anna sat in the train carrying her to Wednesbury. She had been so terrified for her friends that no other thought had surfaced in her mind. Turning to the window, she watched the spume of smoke from the engine drift like black foam over the passing fields.

The telegram had not been from Hester and Reuben, that had been the relief, but it had been from her son, and that was a cause of the pain.

Worry had pushed many things to the back of her mind, so far as to be almost forgotten.

The carriage wheels screamed against the brakes as the train pulled into a drab little station, the painted sign on the wall of a waiting room proclaiming it as Bilston. Anna pulled in her feet, tucking them beneath the slatted wooden seat as a large woman with several baskets struggled to manoeuvre herself from the carriage to the platform.

She could have travelled first-class with a lot more comfort. Anna watched a thin man in shabby jacket and trousers take the place the large woman had vacated. But for all her success in business, she still felt a trifle uneasy at what she saw as unnecessary spending on herself.

Hissing and spurting like some childhood monster, the train moved and Anna found herself listening to the clicking of its wheels. She had loved watching the trains pass along the track that ran through Wednesbury. As a child it had been a regular summer evening walk with her father when he had taken her to sit on the bank above the sidings of the Great Western Railway and sung little rhymes to match the rhythm of the trains going by. Then he had lifted her to his shoulders and carried her home along Dudley Street, stopping on the way to buy two ounces of Tigs Herbal from the sweet shop on the High Bullen.

So many things had been pushed to the back of her mind, hidden but not forgotten. She would never forget.

The train groaned again, juddering as it came to a stop once more.

'Be you wantin' Wednesbury, missus?'

Anna had not realised she was standing in the compartment doorway and murmured an apology to the thin man standing behind her, waiting to leave the train.

Glancing along the platform and beyond, Anna saw the grassy bank above the sidings. No, she would not forget.

'I had no intention of letting you know Polly was dead, but then I realised she would have wanted you to be told.'

Anna sat in the tiny back room of the house that had been her home for sixteen years. Everything was the same: the grate black-leaded to a silvery shine, the smoke-blackened kettle on the hob, a mat of clippings on the floor, the scrubbed table top white beneath the cloth of deep red chenille that had been her mother's treasure.

'I got your telegram yesterday evening.' Anna brought her thoughts away from the past. 'Was Polly ill, Aaron? Did she suffer at all?'

She caught the shudder her unconscious use of his name caused.

'Heart attack,' he returned coldly. 'But Doctor Shaw said she would have felt no pain. More like a door closing in her face, he reckoned.'

'Thank God!' Anna whispered. Then: 'Is there anything I can do?'

'Nothing!' He almost spat the word. 'I don't need your help. In fact, I don't need you for anything.'

'Aaron, please.' Anna's heart was in the cry. 'Can't we at least try to be friends?'

'Friends?' His laughter was harsh. 'We could have been so much more than that. Oh, I know the truth of what happened in this house, Polly told me. I know the getting of me was not your fault, but you turned your back on me. At least he stayed.' He flung an arm towards the tiny window beyond which the oak tree stood outside the wall of the church. 'He had the courage to own me, didn't turn his back and bugger off without a thought.'

'Yes, he had the courage to stay,' Anna answered quietly. 'He had the courage to face the tongue wagging and the back biting of people we had always thought of as friends, and I did not. All of that is true but I never forgot . . .'

'Oh, yes.' Bitterness twisted the face that swung back to her, the translucent blue eyes darkening with pain. 'Polly told me about that as well. Conscience money. You thought that would cover everything, didn't you? Well, hear this. All the money in the world couldn't dry the tears of a child longing for its mother . . . money might be your universal salve, Mrs Anna Royce, but it doesn't cure all ills and it doesn't buy me. I'll take no more of it from you. I've told you before, I'll pay back every penny you ever sent to Polly Shipton. I don't want your money and I don't want you!'

Anna stood up. The unhappiness that had driven her from this house all those years ago was driving her still.

'The funeral,' she said quietly, 'I would like to be there if you have no objection?'

'Church and cemetery are open to everybody.' He turned his back dismissively.

That was a way of telling her there was no welcome for her in this house, not even to say a last goodbye to a valued friend. Swallowing the deliberate insult, together with what was left of her pride, Anna asked again. 'Would you mind telling me what time the service will be held?'

When he didn't answer she took the few steps that carried her from the little whitewashed room.

'Ten o'clock.' His words followed her through the closing door.

• • •

In the room she had taken at The White Horse Anna removed the jade velvet travelling suit and silk-trimmed hat that had drawn many questioning looks in that third-class railway compartment, then stood staring at the splash of colour against the plain buff bedspread. They were a far cry from a cornflower-strewn cotton frock. She had come a long way from Ethelfleda Terrace. She had her paper diamonds and knew the string that at times lay like a yoke about her neck would grow heavier yet.

'The lives of many will be bound to yer own. Ye will have the carrying of them.'

It was true. Anna continued to stare at the suit, green as that grassy bank of long ago. The lives tied to her own increased as her business prospered, but where was the happiness that should bring?

'Toil and tears, Kate,' she murmured into the silence of the room. 'You promised me toil and tears and I have had both. Your words were true, down to the very last one.'

She had consented to become André's wife. When he returned from racing in South America they would be married. She had once thought herself in love with Charles Lazenby.

After hanging her suit in the wardrobe, she crossed to the wash stand where she poured water from a plain heavy jug into a matching bowl.

But like her daughter's love for Edwin Saverry, her own had proved to be an infatuation, a mere illusion of love that had faded long before her meeting André.

Yes. Anna dried her face. She had come a long way since sitting on a bank watching trains pass by, and tears had followed her, almost every step of the way.

For a second time Anna stood waiting for a coffin to be carried from the house in which she had spent her childhood. This time there was no group of women, shawls drawn tightly about their heads, waiting at the gate for the coffin to pass by. This time there was no spectacle for them to gawp at, no suicide's coffin to be lowered from a bedroom window and passed over the garden wall. This was just the funeral of an old woman who had stood by Jos Bradly and reared his daughter's bastard child. But Anna knew that though she stood alone in the street, more than one pair of eyes watched her from behind piously closed curtains.

They would have guessed by now the identity of the woman dressed in a grey suit edged with black frogging, her auburn hair caught beneath a black veiled hat. She had stayed out of sight when her father was buried, but no more. From this day on they would all learn who it was held their town in her hands.

The door of the house opened and the plain coffin was carried out, its one simple wreath of white lilies telling Anna that even the house-to-house collection of pennies and tuppences, those contributions of friends and neighbours that customarily helped to bury one of their own, had been denied Polly Shipton; she had lived with the stigma of helping Jos Bradly and it was one she was to die with too. Aaron's tribute alone graced the wooden box that held her body.

His solitary figure, dressed in dark trousers and a coat that was too big, which Anna guessed had been bought as an unredeemed pledge from Thomas Bennet's pawn shop, followed it from the house, falling in behind the pall bearers who would carry it the few yards to the church.

Anna's hands tightened around the flowers she was carrying. Head held high, Aaron had not acknowledged her presence in any way. But she would not let his hostility deter her. Polly Shipton deserved her respect and no one would prevent her from paying it.

Following beneath the lych gate to the graveyard where the body of her father had not been allowed to rest, Anna paused, wanting to place her own posy of pink and white carnations beside the white lilies, yet not wanting to offend.

'I'll tek 'em, mum.' One of the bearers held out a work-grimed hand, and when Anna gratefully passed him the flowers, placed them on the coffin.

Walking slowly behind the son who ignored her still, Anna stepped into the church she had not entered since the day she had been churched, the day she had been made to pray for forgiveness for a sin that was none of her making. On one side of the altar steps a plaster virgin held her son whilst from the other a forgiving Christ held out his hand towards the box that held the body of the last friend Anna had in Wednesbury. Her eyes passed the painted figures, going to the high altar with its gleaming cross and chalice.

Where was her forgiveness? When would her dues be paid?

'. . . we are come together to give the soul of our friend Polly Shipton into the keeping of God . . .'

Polly Shipton had no friend in Wednesbury, Anna wanted to scream. Because she stuck by a man and raised his bastard child, the people of this town turned their back on her. She was a social outcast, as was the man their accusations and malicious talk drove to take his own life. Polly Shipton had no one but my son.

No one but her son. The voice of the priest droned on but Anna heard nothing save the sound of her own pain. Polly had cradled the child she had left, held him to her body in the night, soothed him when he cried, taken the flowers his tiny hands had picked, watched him grow and learn. Polly had known his love, and she his mother knew only his hatred.

'We thank God for the life of Polly Shipton . . .'

The change of voice recalled Anna to the service and she looked to where Aaron now stood at the lectern, the great Bible supported not on the outstretched wings of a brazen eagle as was customary but on the back of a fighting cock, the special gift to this church of a grateful King Charles II.

'. . . she lived not for herself but for others . . .'

Anna caught the break in his voice and fought to hold back her own tears. He was so tall, her son, his body showing muscular and strong even in the suit that hung from him. From the great east window a single shaft of sunlight touched his blond head, as if Polly herself were touching it for the last time.

'We have so much to thank her for ... we will not forget ...'

No, Anna watched Aaron's proud face, he would not forget how Mother Polly had loved and cared for him ... nor how his own mother had left him!

It was over. Polly's body had been lowered into her grave, set against the enclosing wall at the rear of the ancient, smoke-blackened church. Priest and bearers were gone and Anna stood alone, staring at the dark hole still waiting to be filled with earth. Polly Shipton had given up a lot for Anna Bradly; forgone the friendship of neighbours she had known for years, making herself as much an outcast as the man and boy she kept house for. Even the finding of a tinker trapped in a mine shaft up along Dangerfield Lane, and his deathbed confession to the murder of Mary Carter, had not eased Jos Bradly's burden. He had raped his own daughter and they would not forgive. Now Polly too was gone and with her the last vestige of loyalty Anna might still feel towards Wednesbury.

Anna walked slowly along the bank of the Tame, the gentle song of its water soothing her frayed nerves. There would be no train for Coseley until morning and she had no wish to sit in The White Horse nor yet to visit any part of the town. After today Wednesbury would hold nothing for Anna Royce.

Above her head birds called loudly, disturbed by her presence, while a lone butterfly fluttered from blossom to blossom in search of its kind.

But the butterfly wasn't orange. Anna sat down on the soft earth, drawing her knees up to her chin. No, there were no orange butterflies, no children laughing and calling, no Peter, just her and her memories.

'I've got them, Peter,' she murmured, 'my string of diamonds ... but the cost was too high.'

A leaf floating on the dark water carried Anna's gaze downstream. She and Peter had so often raced leaf boats during those Sunday school outings . . . had Aaron been a part of such outings, had he climbed trees or fished for tiddlers, had her son fallen into the stream? She would never know. She felt the pressure of dry sobs in her throat. There were so many things she would never know.

Cramped from sitting, Anna got to her feet, brushing grass from her skirts. There was one more thing she had to do before turning her back on Wednesbury for the last time.

Heads turned as she walked the familiar streets leading to Ethelfleda Terrace and the house close to the church, but this time it was no frightened girl they watched, her head bent and hidden by a shawl. This time it was Anna Royce, head held high and confident. A woman no other in this town would dare throw dirty insinuations at; a woman who could crush their lives as easily as they had crushed Jos Bradly's.

Pushing open a door she knew would not be locked, Anna stepped into the tiny whitewashed room, every inch of which was engraved on her heart. Aaron sat beside the fireplace, his head slumped in his hands. Anna's heart jolted, every instinct telling her to take him in her arms, to drive away his unhappiness with the force of the love she held for him, but she did not move.

'I know I am not welcome here.' He swung to face her, the full extent of his misery exposed for only a moment, then he was on his feet, the guard of anger dropping over his pale blue eyes, and Anna rushed on before he could say anything.

'My presence in this house is unwanted, but please remember this was my home before it was yours and what I have to say to you will be said inside these four walls.'

At his sides Aaron's fingers clenched into tight fists; his teeth clamped together as he fought the tide rising within him. She had no right here, this woman who claimed to be his mother, the woman who had turned her back on him.

'What my father did caused pain to both of us,' Anna went

on, aware of the emotions ripping him apart, aware her words could only heighten his pain, aware also that they must be said. 'But he wasn't responsible for his actions. My father was incapable of deliberately harming me and I am sure he never once harmed you. Joseph Bradly was a decent man driven to insanity by mindless fools and others who kept the lie alive, even after Mary Carter's killer was found. Men and women who fed the gossip and kindled the scandal to draw attention from their own dirty work.'

'But he stayed!' Aaron's answer was filled with quiet rage.

'Yes, he stayed.' Anna saw his fury but didn't flinch. If she backed down now the rest of her words would never be said. 'He stayed and I went. You think that was the coward's way out. Well, maybe it was, maybe I was wrong to do what I did, but if so, I did wrong for the right reasons.'

Beyond the tiny window evening shadows began to gather a purple veil about the black-spired church.

'Had I stayed then people would have said I was his whore – as some already had – and we would both have finished up being whipped from the town. How would my father have felt then? A daughter and a newborn child and nowhere to go. Well, perhaps you think I should have faced that, or at least have taken you with me. So think of this too. I had no idea where I would go or how I would live. I had no money, not even enough to buy you milk . . . when I left Wednesbury I had money for a railway ticket and nothing else besides.'

Anna saw his mouth soften but it was the softening of contempt.

'Yes, I know, Aaron.' She read his thoughts. 'Why didn't I come for you when I was earning? Don't think I didn't want to, but Coseley is no different from Wednesbury. They don't take kindly to women who have children out of wedlock, won't entertain it in their own, so what chance for me, a stranger?

'And later, once I *was* married?' Anna parried his next

question. 'Edward wanted to bring you to Coseley and was planning to do so, then he was killed and I was back where I started. Call what I have said explanation or excuse, whichever you choose, but it is the truth. And it is the truth when I say that never, for one moment, did I stop loving you, and never, for one moment, did I stop missing you. You are my child, Aaron. I love you and I miss you as I always will. You despise me for what I did to you, that is understandable, and when I leave this house you will never want to see me again. That too I understand. But it will not change the way I feel, it won't change the love I have for you. You are my son, Aaron, and I will thank God for that every day of my life.'

Anna followed the path that led from the lych gate to St Bartholomew's, turning aside before reaching the heavy door to step across the turf to a headstone set against the curtain wall.

Beyond the gate, partly hidden by the same tree that had sheltered Anna as she had watched her father's coffin lowered into an unmarked grave, Aaron watched the woman who was his mother. Why had he been stupid enough to send her word of Polly's death? Why hadn't he told her flatly to go back to where she came from? Why hadn't he told her he would never feel anything for her but hatred and contempt?

Across the churchyard Anna stooped, laying one red rose on the grave he knew held his grandmother. Aaron stepped further behind the tree, watching the graceful figure start down the path.

Why was he standing here? What was he waiting for? Hadn't this woman caused him enough pain already? He had guessed she would make one last call on her mother's grave before leaving, and despite himself had waited at the window of the house until he had seen her walk past. Then an urge stronger than his will had drawn him to the church, drawn him to the woman coming out through the lych gate, the woman he would not meet again after today. His eyes followed the grey-clad figure as she moved across the grassy hill towards a huge oak, its branches spreading a wide canopy over the unmarked grave of the man who had been his father and hers.

She could not know he lay there. Aaron remained still but his mind ran in circles. Polly might have written, telling her of her father's death. Yes, Polly might have written but she would not have told her of the place of his lying and Anna Royce had not followed his coffin. There was no way for her to know where that grave had been dug, yet she had gone straight to it and now, as he watched, sank to her knees.

Beneath the great spreading branches Anna touched the green earth with one hand.

'You did not mean to hurt me, Father,' she whispered. 'I have always known that. I could not come back, I was not as strong as you. But I never stopped loving you.'

Lifting the tiny bunch of cornflowers and buttercups she had picked from the open heath that lay to one side of the church steps, flowers she had so often picked with her father, Anna put them to her lips then placed them on the soft turf.

'You took good care of him, Father,' she said softly. 'You loved him as I love him.'

Tears too strong for her to hold spilled down her cheeks. Anna stood up. Spread out below the hill, Wednesbury sprawled beneath the pall of smoke from its foundries and tiny back room workshops, while beyond it stretched the heath where Mother Polly had taught her the art of using plants and flowers. She let her eyes rove, seeing one more time the playground of her childhood and the arena where her misery had begun, then glanced at the house that held so much of her heart and so many of her memories.

'Mrs Royce.' Aaron stepped from the shelter of the tree as she drew level. 'I . . . I was waiting for you.'

'Oh!' Anna halted, her head tilted back, forced to look up to reach those intense blue eyes. 'You have something you wish to say to me?'

The dark, over-large jacket hung loosely across his shoulders but to Anna that in no way detracted from the dignity of the young man who faced her; a dignity that was inborn, a dignity that was so much a part of him.

'Yes . . .' He hesitated only fractionally. 'I wanted to say thank you.'

'*You* wish to thank me? I see nothing you need thank me for.'

'Maybe you don't, but I do.'

Behind the wisp of grey veil that covered her face, Anna's eyes held surprise and admiration. Whatever her son had to say, it had taken a man's courage to bring him after her.

'Then perhaps you will tell me what I have done that warrants your thanks?'

She kept her voice cold, almost impersonal, fighting the urge to cry out for him to love her.

'For coming here,' he replied. 'For coming to Polly's funeral.'

All around them the afternoon sky leapt to brilliant crimson flame, silhouetting the church and the cluster of surrounding houses as the steel foundries opened their furnaces.

Anna gazed at the scene she had known from childhood.

'I did not have to come.' She spoke without looking at him. 'I came because I wanted to. Polly Shipton stood by me when nobody else in Wednesbury would. I was proud to follow at her funeral and I will always be proud to have been her friend.'

'You are the only one she had apart from me and him.' Aaron nodded towards the oak tree. 'You saw the turnout for yourself.'

'Yes, I saw. My only comfort is that she must have found it worthwhile. Rearing you, I mean.' She looked at him now. 'She must have loved you very much.'

Seeing his mouth tighten, herself feeling the emotion she knew he was fighting to hold in check, Anna resumed the walk down Church Hill, the walk that would take her away from her son.

'I don't care what your reason was for coming, I still thank you for it.'

Anna turned. A slight breeze caught her veil, and lifted it clear of her eyes.

'I believe André Levassor has been to see you recently?'

'Yes.' Aaron did not close the gap her few steps had placed between them. 'Yes, he has been several times since you were last here.'

Anna caught the fluttering tulle, folding it back across her hat.

'So I understand. Might I ask what you thought of him?'

'He didn't stay all that long either time he came, he always had something else on hand.'

Why was she standing here prolonging the agony? Why didn't she go, why add to the pain his walking away would bring? But she didn't go. Instead she asked, 'But even so, you must have formed some opinion of the man?'

There was still a space separating them but Anna realised the few feet of earth was not the only space between her and this man who was her son; a gulf too wide for him to bridge stretched between them.

'Yes,' Aaron answered. 'He seems a nice enough chap, no airs and graces, and he certainly knows a hell of a lot about motor carriage engines. A man could learn a lot from him. He says what he thinks, you know where you are with him.'

'Has Mr Levassor given any opinion on your handling of motor carriage engines?'

'Yes, he has,' Aaron answered bluntly.

'And?'

'He said I had a good working knowledge of engines and of the motor car as a whole.'

He still called it a motor car, Anna thought remembering the first time.

'Did he ask you to go and work for him?'

'He did not ask that, but he said if ever I wanted to leave off working for you, then I could go to him.'

André had asked her son to go to him and suddenly she knew why. He knew her dread of losing all contact with Aaron and if he worked for André she would at least receive the odd word of him.

'Aaron . . . Mr Bradly . . .'

Anna's glance passed to the tiny patch of blue and gold lying at the foot of the oak tree, and curled her fingers into her palms to stop their trembling as she looked back at her son.

'There is something I wish to tell you, but before I do I want you to know that André Levassor has asked me to become his wife!'

Aaron stared at the woman he had spent so many hours of his childhood dreaming about, so many hours listening to Mother Polly telling him of the courage it had taken for her to leave her child. And the woman had courage. That he had been forced to admit: she need never have returned, never have owned him as her son. But she had returned, bringing with her the power to destroy this town as it had destroyed her father. With a single stroke of a pen she could have taken away the livelihood of almost every man in Wednesbury, instead of which she had developed new industries, giving life to a town that had once driven her away.

'What's that to me?' he asked, stubbornly pushing his thoughts away.

Anna's head tilted backward as she looked up into his face, drawn with tight lines.

'You are my son.'

The simple statement hit him more forcefully than a blow and for one fleeting moment the longing showed in his eyes. 'And what answer did you give?' he asked, once more guarded and hostile.

Anna dug her nails into her palms. 'I accepted, Aaron,' she said as he turned away. 'I told you some time ago that should you leave my employ I would close not only my own business in this town but many more beside. I want you to know that what I threatened no longer applies. You have my word no one will lose his job as a result of your leaving. If you wish to work for André Levassor or for anyone else then you are free to do so. But though you might remove yourself from my life you will never remove yourself from my heart. You are my son, Aaron, and I will never stop loving you. André and Misty want you as I want you, to be part of the family, but we understand you have to do what your heart tells you.'

Turning again to face her, Aaron met the eyes of the woman he had hated for so long. Now he knew why he was here, now he knew how to put into words the thoughts that had plagued him through a long, sleepless night. He stepped toward her, the rage and hate that had held him icebound for so long melting away. 'I much prefer to work with my family,' he said softly, 'and with my mother . . . if she still wants me.'

In the branches of the oak tree birds called softly to each other and the tiny splash of cornflowers and buttercups that lay beneath it seemed to gleam with a new radiance, 'She still wants you, Aaron . . .' Anna whispered softly, 'she still wants you.'

If you enjoyed FOR THE SAKE OF HER CHILD,
here's a foretaste of Meg Hutchinson's new novel,
A HANDFUL OF SILVER:

A Handful of Silver

'She is a what!' Morgan Cosmore's hands tightened about the arms of his chair, his long fingers whitening under the pressure. 'You would hand me a cripple for a wife! What am I supposed to do with that?'

Between cushions of fat his father's eyes were vicious. 'I'm handing you a bloody engineering works. What you do wi' the wrappin' be yer concern.'

'I will tell you what I will do with the wrapping, Father, I will leave it where it is and you can look for your salvation elsewhere. I will not tie myself to a cripple! I can't and I won't.'

'Won't?' Ezra Cosmore's eyes receded further into the puffy flesh surrounding them. 'Don't you bloody tell me you won't!'

'Father, please . . .'

'Don't bloody "Father, please" me. You'll do as I say!'

'No, Father, I can't, not this.'

'Oh, you can't, eh? Well, let me tell you summat. You marry that girl or you be finished in this 'ouse, do you 'ear me? Finished. An' then where do you go? An' where do you get the money to indulge yer fancy habits? You tell me no an' you be on yer own, an' then how would you earn a livin', eh? That would be interestin' to see, you as 'ave never struck a blow in yer life – how would you do it, eh? Tell me that, Mr bloody Smart Arse!'

'Well?' he demanded again when his question was met with silence.

Morgan's hands gripped the arms of the chair harder. He would have liked it to have been the throat of the stocky man standing facing him, legs straddling the hearth, his habitually florid face almost scarlet with temper. 'I . . . I don't know, Father.'

'"I don't know, Father. I don't know, Father,"' Ezra mimicked his son. 'Too bloody true you don't know! But know this – you marry Kerral's daughter or you'll find out, an' it'll be the quickest bloody thing you 'ave ever learned!'

'The girl, Father, what has she to say to this?'

'The girl! Who the bloody hell cares what the girl has to say? 'Er'll do as 'er's bid, same as you.'

'So she has been given the same choice as I have?'

'Arrh, Hobson's. God knows you be no catch, but you be the best 'er'll get.'

'Tell me, Father, how come I am the best Josiah Kerral's daughter can hope for?'

From his chair beneath the high window Morgan Cosmore watched the vindictive smile spread over his father's loose-lipped mouth. There was no love lost between them; his father had disliked him from the earliest times he could remember, always accusing his mother of namby-pambying him, blaming him for the fact she could bear no more children and on her death, ten years ago, marrying again and threatening to disinherit Morgan for the son his new young wife would bear. But there had been no son, only a daughter who had carried her mother with her to the grave.

'I 'ave already answered you on that one.' Ezra ran his tongue over his flabby lips. 'Who else would tek on a cripple?'

'Who indeed?' Morgan rose from his chair with a fluid grace that spoke of the strength in his well-muscled body. 'So I am to be the sacrificial lamb, eh, Father? Ezra Cosmore's lad will take the cripple.'

'You'll be tekin' 'er money an' that's all as need concern you. You won't be called on to do anythin' else.'

'Oh!' Morgan looked at the man who had fathered him,

feeling a potent mixture of dislike and contempt. 'Like what, Father?'

'Like . . . like . . . you know bloody well like what!' Ezra's scarlet face took on a deeper purplish shade. Morgan knew very well what was meant, he just wanted to be awkward the same as always, but he could be as awkward as he liked – he would still marry the Kerral wench. Everything depended on the money that would bring.

'Do I?' Morgan's mouth relaxed into a taunting smile. 'How can you be sure, Father, when you haven't told me? You have always said that if I am to get anything right, you must tell me how and when. So you had better tell me now. What is it I will not be called upon to do?'

'Go to hell, blast you!'

'I am very glad to do that, Father. I had a real fancy for going to hell.'

'Listen to me.' Ezra's head jutted forward on his thick neck and his piggy eyes gleamed. 'You may think yerself very clever wi' yer smart answers but they'll all end up the same. You'll say yes.'

'And if I do?'

'There's no ifs,' Ezra cut in sharply. 'You refuse an' we be done for. The business be up to its eyes in debt an' even this 'ouse be mortgaged for more'n it's worth, so you see, my lad, you give me any ifs an' buts an' we might well finish up wi' nothin'.'

'That's hardly likely, Father.' Morgan studied a perfectly manicured fingernail. 'After all, as you say, who else will take on the cripple? But what if the cripple should refuse? What if she refuses to exchange her fortune for me?'

'The girl will 'ave no say in the matter.' Ezra turned to a side table, selecting a cigar from a box, biting off the end and spitting the stub into the fire. ''Er will do as 'er father tells 'er.'

'Like all good little boys and girls should.' Morgan laughed drily. 'They should not object to being sold off and mated like cattle to satisfy their parents.'

'I never 'eard you object to spendin' my money.' Ezra stooped, pushing a wax taper into the fire. 'An' I doubt you'll object to spendin' that which the wench will bring with 'er.'

'I shall have no objections whatsoever to spending her money.' Morgan watched the older man light his cigar then replace the taper in a delft pot on the mantel. 'But what is in this marriage for you? What do you hope to get out of it?'

Blowing a cloud of smoke into the air, Ezra watched his son through the lavender haze. He was going to take some getting to the altar but get him there Ezra would – or break his bloody stuck-up neck in the trying! 'What do you think I 'ope to get?'

'I think you hope to get your so-called business back on an even keel,' Morgan answered evenly, his eyes watching every nuance of expression flicker across his father's face. 'But you will not do that through me. I will not be saddled with a cripple to save a business that hit the rocks years ago!'

'Then what will you do if you won't marry the Kerral girl? There be no more money left, it's just a matter of time before they foreclose on this 'ouse an' then you'll be out on the street. An' will yer fancy London friends tek you in, then? Will any one of 'em find you a home or finance yer trips abroad every fart's end? Oh, yes, they'll do all of that all right . . . like bloody 'ell they will!'

Morgan continued examining his fingernails as his father's temper suffused his face with a deeper shade of carmine. With luck he would have a heart attack here and now and then Kerral could keep both his money and his gimpy offspring. 'I was unaware Kerral had a daughter,' said Morgan quietly.

'That don't surprise me.' Ezra blew out another stream of smoke. 'You ain't bin aware of anythin' goin' on in Darlaston since you 'ave bin eight years old.'

'You can't blame me for that, Father.' Morgan smiled, showing teeth scrupulously cleaned with bicarbonate of soda. 'You had me sent away to school when I was eight years old.'

'A good job I did an' all,' his father shot back. 'Get you away from yer mother's namby-pambying. Christ! A few more years of that an' 'er'd 'ave 'ad you actin' like a big soft wench – not that that school made much of a job of turnin' you into a man. All you think of is fancy clothes an' fancy women.'

'Poor Mother,' Morgan sighed affectedly, knowing it would send the older man's temperature soaring. 'She always was your whipping boy, wasn't she, Father? She always bore the brunt of your mistakes.'

'Mistakes!' Ezra sucked in a mouthful of cigar smoke. 'What bloody mistakes?'

'Oh, you have made them, you know.' Morgan dropped back to the chair again, hand resting on his knees, eyes lifting to the man straddling the hearth. 'Not that you would admit to any, of course, but you have made mistakes – and perhaps sending me to boarding school was one of them. Maybe if you had kept me here with you, you would have done a better job of turning me into a man.'

'I couldn't 'ave done a worse one!' The words shot out on a stream of strong-smelling smoke.

'Of course you couldn't, Father,' Morgan continued his quiet needle-prick offensive, 'we both knew you were the best man for the job, whatever the job. Mother, I presume, learned so from the first day of her marriage. And I learned very early, Father. I learned that the best way to avoid your belt was to avoid *you*.'

'You needed the belt.' Ezra spat into the fire then turned back to his son, surveying him in the depths of the velvet-covered wing-back chair. 'To knock summat into yer 'ead beside drawin' bloody pictures. Yer mother was too soft wi' you. "Artistic" 'er said you was, when all the time you was too bloody idle to do anythin' else.'

'Yes, well, you soon put a stop to that, didn't you, Father?' Stretching out his legs in front of him, Morgan crossed one foot over the other. 'That school you sent me to gave me no lessons in art. Those periods were replaced for me with extra physical activity. That was on your instruction, wasn't it?'

'Yes, it was on my instruction.' Ezra flung the half-smoked cigar into the fire. 'What bloody good is paintin' an' drawin' in an engineerin' works, eh? Answer me that. An' if you can't, I'll tell you what good it is – none, no bloody good at all.'

'I am sure it isn't, Father.' Morgan smiled, watching the blood rise again in his father's face. 'If you say so.'

'I do say so! An' I say this an' all. It be time you stopped all this gallivantin' off to London an' Christ knows where else an' started to 'elp out in the business.'

'Oh, no, Father. I would not presume upon your territory.'

'Territory!' Ezra sat down heavily in a chair set beside the stone fireplace. 'What you on about? What territory?'

'The business, Father,' Morgan answered blandly. 'I would not presume to interfere with anything you do. What need is there when you do everything better than anyone else can? Besides you have made a perfectly good job of bankrupting us up to now. It would be foolish of me to try and prevent your finishing it. But I would ask this – merely from interest, you understand. How long has it been this time since the men were paid?'

'And let me ask this.' Ezra's eyes were almost obliterated now by the folds of flesh surrounding them. ''Ow long 'as it bin since you last bought one of them fancy suits? The price of one of them would pay every one of the 'ands for a month or more. You leave off yer fancy livin' an' mebbe we wouldn't be nigh on bankrupt.'

'Since we seem to be discussing my expenses and their effect upon the business, I think it only fair to cast an eye over yours, Father.'

'Mine?' The eyes widened pushing back the barricade of fat.

'Yours, Father.' Morgan flicked a finger along the seam of his expensive cashmere trousers. 'Your clothes . . .' He mimed a shudder designed to raise his father's blood pressure. 'I don't know the cost of them but I would advise your tailor to make more of an effort, so they look less like pawnshop rejects. Then of course there is the running of this house. Your table is not exactly that of a man close to bankruptcy though the costs of your wine cellar would bankrupt the old lady of Threadneedle Street. And, of course, we must not forget those regular visits to Birmingham. They do not come cheaply, I'll warrant.'

'Visits to Birmingham!' Ezra almost choked. 'What do you know of my visits to Brummagem?'

Morgan suppressed a yawn with a languid theatrical movement of his hand. 'I know a good deal about them, I have done for some years now. For instance, there is a certain dark-haired beauty name of Maria at the house of Mrs Morrison – though the nearest that woman came to being "Mrs" was lying on a bed with another woman's husband. Then we have the Conroy Club, private, for members only. A little more respectable with its air of gentility but offering the same amenities. You appear to have a favourite there too, Father, or should I say two favourites? Amelia of the baby blonde ringlets, and Consuela, the doubtful red head of equally doubtful South American origin. You prefer to have them together, do you not? And then . . . but need I go on?'

'I earn my money,' the older man parried, 'and I 'ave the right to spend it any way I want.'

Morgan fingered the seam of his trouser leg, smoothing its already perfect symmetry. 'Whereas I do not earn mine. My allowance is a symbol of your charity – a charity never graciously given but always gratefully accepted, and the spending of it always greatly enjoyed.'

'Arrh, well, the enjoyin' be about to stop for the pair o' we unless you bring 'ome Jos Kerral's money.'

'Not to mention his daughter.'

'Yes, well,' Ezra leaned back in his chair, eyes once more guarded, 'we can't 'ave one lessen we tek the other.'

'We being *me*, Father.' Morgan looked up suddenly, his gaze cold. 'You take the money while I take the cripple.'

'You won't 'ave to 'ave no truck wi' 'er once the weddin' be over.' Ezra's voice took on a placatory tone. 'You can carry on much as you 'ave bin doin' then.'

'So I can leave my crippled wife with you, can I, Father? You will spend your nights entertaining her whilst I am in London or abroad? A very different sort of entertainment to that you are used to. Are you sure you want to go through with it after all?'

Ezra understood his son's tactics. Threaten to leave the woman here in Darlaston, give his father the caring of her, and it would change his mind. If a soul could smile Ezra knew his was smiling now. 'There'll be little need for either of us to entertain 'er,' he said. 'A woman to see to 'er will be all 'er'll be wantin'.'

'And all she will be getting if it is left to me, Father.' Morgan's gaze lost none of its coldness. 'Tell me, how old is this prize I am to be presented with?'

'Just on twenty, so Jos tells me.'

'And did he tell you what she looks like? Or maybe you have seen her for yourself? Is she pretty, Father, as pretty as Maria?'

'I . . . I 'aven't seen 'er.' Ezra looked towards the fireplace, avoiding the accusation in his son's eyes. 'But what does it matter if 'er be pretty or plain, as long as the money be there?'

'No matter.' Morgan resumed his study of the seam. 'Seeing as I will not be called upon to look at her, at least not often, and maybe not at all if her face is marked by her disability.' He leaned forward, the seam forgotten as a new thought struck. 'Her face is not disfigured, is it? Because if it is you can kiss goodbye to all of your well-laid plans.'

''Er face be all right,' Ezra answered, hoping the gods would make it so. ''Er father assured me on that point.'

'If only he had assured *me*.' Morgan leaned back in his chair but his eyes displayed an inner wariness. His fox of a father would stop at nothing to get his hands on Jos Kerral's money. A little thing like planting a disfigured wife on his son would cause him no worry at all. 'So just what form does the girl's disability take? Exactly how is she crippled?'

'It's 'er legs.' Ezra faced his son. Cripple or no cripple, he was going to take the girl for his wife, and the sooner he accepted that fact the better. ''Er father says 'er be crippled in the legs. 'Er can't walk but apart from that 'er be all right.'

'And I am to be thankful for that, am I?' Morgan laughed. 'And what of the family line? What of the dynasty you dreamed of founding? Is she capable of bearing a child?'

'How the bloody 'ell should I know!' Ezra's temper reached breaking point. 'What do you want, a bloody doctor's report?'

'No, Father.' Morgan became colder, his own temper more controlled as that of his father ran wild. 'Neither do I want a cripple for a wife, pretty or otherwise. You want Kerral's money, you marry Kerral's daughter.'

'You think I 'adn't thought o' that?' Ezra shouted, his face contorted with a rage he could no longer confine. 'Well, you be wrong, but Kerral won't tek an older man. He wants a young buck for his daughter, though for what I don't know. Bloke as gets 'er will 'ave to spread 'er legs 'isself afore 'e can mount 'er.'

'That would not have bothered you, would it, Father? Though the fact she could not writhe and heave beneath you, or straddle you as you would a mare, might have detracted from your pleasure . . . But then, you will not be having the pleasure, will you? Seeing as her father deems you too old for the servicing of his daughter.'

'Watch yer mouth or I'll . . .'

'Or you will what, Father? Take your belt to me as you did every night for so many years? I don't think so, not any more. Those days are gone, finished, as this conversation is finished. I shall return to London in the morning.'

'And when the money stops,' Ezra glared at the man rising so easily from the chair, all the swagger of youth and good health in the movement, 'what will you do then?'

'I will just have to do what I have always done.' Morgan strode to the door of the oval-shaped room. 'I will have to wait for you to tell me!'

Yes, that's what you have done all yer life, Ezra thought as the door slammed behind his departing son. Waited while someone else did the grafting. Waited and let some other bugger do the thinking for you. Well, I have thought this out for you, my bloody smart arse son. You marry that wench and bring her money into this house, and after that you can go to the devil as quick as you like!

'Miri, how long have we lived in this house?' Esther Kerral turned to look at the middle-aged woman busying herself with clearing the table at which both of them had just taken their midday meal.

'That's a strange question.' Miriam Butler hesitated in her task, her quick glance taking in the girl seated now at the window of the small house set in the grounds of the larger, grander Rowena House. 'You know how long we've lived 'ere. Some sixteen years.'

'I was almost four.' The answer was quiet, musing.

'Arrh, nigh on.' Miriam resumed her bustling, loading dishes on to a serving trolley then removing the white cloth and folding it into a drawer of a long oak sideboard.

'Why?'

The loud agonised query took the older woman by surprise, causing her to stand a moment looking at the face of the girl she had reared – a face as beautiful as any she had ever seen but twisted now with hurt and pain. Dropping the table napkins into the drawer she quickly crossed the sunlit room, sinking on to her haunches beside the girl. 'Essie love, don't. Don't dwell on that, it does no good. What's done be done. Best to let it lie.'

'Best to let it lie?' Her soft brown eyes widened with fresh pain as she turned her glance to a line of tall conifers edging the bottom of the garden, masking the flat green of the lawns surrounding Rowena House. 'That is what he has done for sixteen years – let me lie here where I cannot be seen. Lie here, unwanted and forgotten . . .'

'Shhh, Essie.' Taking the girl in her arms, Miriam crooned softly, trying to ease the hurt, knowing she couldn't, that nothing could take away the pain of what Jos Kerral had done to his own daughter. 'Shh, my wench, try not to tek on, that man ain't worth yer tears.'

'No.' Esther pushed away from her arms, decision straightening her shoulders. 'That man is not worth any woman's tears.' She passed a finger over her cheek below her eyes and looked at the film of moisture that clung to it. 'And I vow before God these are the last I will ever shed on his account.'

'We could go for a turn in the gardens? It's a lovely day.' Miriam rose to her feet, a cold worm of fear nibbling at her insides as it did more and more often these days while watching Esther's disappointment turn to resentment, and resentment to cold, challenging anger.

'Yes.' Esther dried her finger on her handkerchief. 'A stroll in the garden would be nice, Miri.'

'I'll just wash these few crocks first.' She turned thankfully back to her task of clearing away the remains of their meal, yet even as she wheeled everything into the kitchen instinct told her there was trouble in the air. Esther had appeared calm at her suggestion of a stroll but Miri knew better. Rejected and despised for all these years, the girl was close to breaking point.

Left alone in the dining room, Esther stared at the row of conifers standing like a line of green-uniformed dragons, guarding the house she was not allowed to enter, the house where she was born, the house her father had lived in for sixteen years without once seeing his daughter. The last time she had seen him she had been four years old. It took no effort for her to look back over the years to the day her mother had died.

Despite the sunlight tumbling in through tall windows, the house had seemed dark for days. She remembered asking so many times to see her mother but each time she had been shushed by her nurse and told her mama was sleeping. Then had come that afternoon. She had woken from her nap to find the nursery empty, her nurse nowhere to be seen. At first she had played with . . . yes, with large gaily painted wooden blocks, placing one on another until the line had fallen, sending one tumbling across the floor towards the open door. Her mama was through that door, her child's mind had told her as she went to retrieve the block, she would go to see her. The fact that she met no maid as she made her way along the curved corridor that led to her mother's bedroom held no significance for her four-year-old mind. She had been a few feet away from the door when it had opened and her father had stumbled out, a hand held across his eyes.

'Papa.'

She had laughed up at him, her high piping voice echoing through the stillness of the house, and he had dropped his hand and turned towards her.

'That *thing*!' His voice had been evil in its low intensity, his face twisted with disgust as he watched her drag herself along on her bottom, her useless left leg trailing behind her. 'That thing killed my wife!' Suddenly he lunged forward, his booted foot kicking viciously at her legs and back. 'That thing killed my wife . . . that thing killed my wife . . .'

'Mr Kerral, stop!' A woman in a white apron over a blue dress, a white cap standing high on her head, had run out of Mama's bedroom, catching at Papa's arm, trying to pull him away. But the foot had gone on kicking her until Miri had come flying along the corridor and scooped her into her arms, running with her back to the nursery, locking the door behind them. And all the time his frenzied shouts had followed: 'That thing killed my wife . . . that thing killed my wife!'

That had been the last time Esther had set eyes on her father or he on her. She had been brought here to this house with only Miri to care for her, and here they had both stayed. It was only recently that she had learned the reason for her mother's death. The doctors, it seemed, had diagnosed a malaise caused by her child's crippled condition but Miri had declared that Mama had died from the consumption she was already suffering from on her marriage. Those doctors had been wrong, Miri said. The same doctors who had said Esther would never walk.

He had made sufficient allowance for the running of the house he had banished her to, that father of hers. Esther smiled coldly. Henry VIII had made allowances for the household of his daughters, Mary and the young Elizabeth, but that had not made them feel any more secure. They had suffered their father's rejection as she had suffered hers; they had waited for the knock on the door as she waited; they had longed to be sent for, to be told of the love their father held for them, as she had, and they, like her, had wept long hours when that call did not come. But she would weep no more, she had cried her last for Josiah Kerral.

There had been no questions about her well-being, as there had been none regarding Miri's household expenditure. Any extra items, such as the adult-sized bath chair Miri had requested when the one Esther had used for years finally became too small, were met immediately and Miri had managed to talk him into setting aside a tidy sum for Esther; she had dreaded the possibility of his remarrying and having other children and his first child being abandoned completely. The money had accumulated under the guidance of the owner of Long's Bank, until now she was fairly wealthy in her own right. No, her father had not denied Esther money, only his love.

She had been given to Miri lock, stock and barrel, and Miri had loved her as her own child. That love had been doubled when Miri had married a school master who taught the children of the town in St Peter's Church of England school on the green, whenever the local families could pay the threepence a week it cost to send them there, or when the 'whipper in' could catch them playing truant – which it seemed was not often. Playing away was a skill nurtured by every worker's child in Darlaston and one that regularly defeated the school board man.

John Butler had taught Esther too, sitting at the table in the evening after supper, gently explaining when things seemed beyond her understanding, going again and again over a mathematical problem that threatened to defeat her until at last she defeated it; but mathematics and book learning had not been all he had taught her. He had taught her to use her brain to look logically at a problem, to search for its cause as well as its cure, and she had soaked up his teaching like a sponge soaks up water.

The only thing he could not teach her was how to walk, how to make her useless leg obey her, but he had refused to let it wither like a rotting tree branch. Every morning and every evening he had massaged her leg, matching the movements of his hands to little rhymes he'd made up to sing as he rubbed the wasted muscles.

'I have finished with books,
With slate and with chalk,
Now with Esther and Miri
I'll go for a walk . . .'

Esther's lips moved to the remembered words of her favourite rhyme, one she'd sung so often with John:

Swing your leg high,
Swing your leg low,
Just one more swing and off we will go.
Off through the garden,
Down to the brook.
I like that much better

Than reading a book.

John Butler. Esther looked away across the garden to where the green-clothed conifers halted her gaze. He had loved her, had been the father that man in Rowena House had never been, and John Butler had taught her more than he knew. He had taught her how to take revenge, and some day she knew with certainty, some day the opportunity would come for her to use that learning. Some day her father would pay for the pain he had caused her.

No Place of Angels

Meg Hutchinson

WH S

For my daughters, Lindsey and Kim,
who as children listened so patiently to
'Mother's stories', and who still listen with the
same loving patience

Chapter One

'I put you out of my way four years ago.'

Maria Beddows glared at the figure seated on the narrow wooden bench which ran around the walls of the third-class waiting room of Birmingham Snow Hill railway station.

'I put you where you could be no temptation and that is the way I intend matters shall remain. You thought to come out of that school and return to Holyhead House, to take up where you left off, but that is one thing you will never do.'

'But Holyhead House is my home!'

Maria's look was cold and hard as the brown-painted brickwork of the drab room. 'Holyhead House *was* your home, but not any longer. It ceased to be that the day you entered school.'

Her thin nostrils dilated, drawing in a deep draught of the room's cold air. 'Did you honestly think I would allow you to return, to enter my house again? Did you in truth believe you were sent away merely to finish your education?'

'But Father said . . .'

'It does not matter what your father said!' Maria snapped. 'Your father will not go against my decision when he hears what I have to tell him, and I say you shall not return home. You wanted to be out of that school, you were twenty-one and of an age to please yourself, to do what *you* wanted to do. You wanted your freedom. Well, now you have it.'

Maria glanced quickly around the dim room but the sharpness of her voice had elicited no reaction from the people seated around the damp walls, huddled into their coats, heads down against the cold that filtered its way inside them. Smoothing her grey corded skirts as if to brush away any possible contact with the shabbily dressed travellers she stood up, her cold eyes sweeping the girl who posed a threat to the life she had so long desired, waited so long to enjoy – a life she had no intention of losing. Bending, she brought her face close to the thin pale cheek of the girl, seeming to any onlooker to be bestowing a farewell kiss.

'Take your freedom,' she hissed. 'But use it wisely. Stay away from Moxley, and stay away from me!'

'But I must come home to Holyhead House!' The girl reached out, clutching at Maria's skirts, her eyes wide and frightened. 'Where else would I go?'

Maria twitched her skirts free, her own eyes cold as the walls that surrounded them.

'I don't care where you go so long as you stay clear of Moxley.'

'But I have no money.'

'You should have thought of that sooner!' Maria's tone was acid. 'You had the opportunity to stay in that school, to become a teacher there. But you said no, turned up your nose at that. As a job and a place to live they were not good enough for you, were they? Not fitting for Meshac Beddows's daughter!'

'But I did not want to become a teacher, I wanted to come home . . .'

'I know what you want!' Maria said viciously. 'The same as I knew what you wanted before you were sent away to school. Oh, I knew what you were about – the coy little smiles, the lowered lashes every time he looked at you. Yes, I was on to your game and I put a stop to it. You can forget what is in your mind, forget all thoughts of returning to Holyhead House and taking up where you left off – forget Ryder Tempal, you will never have him!'

'You are wrong!' The carpet bag that held her few possessions clutched in her hand, Carys ran after the older woman, already half way out of the door of the waiting room. 'I do not want Ryder Tempal, I never wanted him.'

'Oh, no?' Maria's brown eyes gleamed with menace. 'If you never wanted him, why is it that each time you came home for the holidays you hung on to him like a limpet, clung to him every moment he was in the house? Why, if you didn't want him, did you follow wherever he went, hanging on to his coat tails, embarrassing him with your attentions?'

It had not been like that. Carys followed her along the platform, aware of the watchful eyes of the uniformed station master. She had not followed on Ryder Tempal's heels; the reverse was true. He had dogged her footsteps wherever she went with his fawning smiles and lingering hands, followed her until she was forced to withdraw to her bedroom, the only place she could escape his unwanted attentions – her bedroom or her secret place.

'Please, I have no interest in Ryder Tempal.' She looked at the other woman but the face was cold and closed against her.

'Then that is as well for you, and it would be well to keep things that way. For should you try to return to Holyhead House or contact him in any way, I will see you dead!'

'Be you wanting this train, miss?'

Carys looked at the railway porter who touched his peaked cap to her despite the glare of the station master watching them from the doorway to his office. He had kept an eye on this girl dressed in a faded blue coat that had obviously been made to serve more years than it should. From midday she had stood at the end of the platform, an old carpet bag clutched in her hand, making no attempt to board any of the trains that had passed through. Now this was the last of the day. 'Get rid of her,' the station master had ordered the porter, 'tell her she has to leave. We can't have folk in the station overnight, much less a woman on her own.'

'Be you wanting this train, miss?' the porter asked again.

'I . . . I . . .' Carys turned to him, her amber eyes blank.

'Where do you be wanting to go?'

'Moxley, but . . .'

'You want this train then,' the porter said, relieved. The station master having taken several steps along a platform now almost empty of travellers, stared a silent command to the porter who added nervously 'C'mon, let's get you on board, train'll be pulling out in a little while.'

'No!' Carys hung back as the man made to take her bag. 'I can't – I can't go to Moxley.'

'But you said that was where you was wanting to get?' The porter cast a wary eye towards his superior.

'I know, that is where I thought to go, but now . . . now I can't.'

'Look, miss, this is the last train. There'll be no more till mornin' so it be this one or none at all, an' you can't go stopping on the station all night. So come on, there's a good wench, let's get you aboard.'

'But . . .' she said.

Carys's protests broke off as the station master, resplendent in brass-buttoned uniform, strode importantly up to where she stood with the porter whose eyes already spoke of his fear of the sack.

'Now then, young woman.' He did not touch his peaked cap; this was a third-class passenger and one who seemed barely able to afford that. 'If this be the train you be waiting on then you best be getting on now. It'll be pulling out in a few minutes.'

'No, I can't . . . it isn't.'

''Er said as 'er wanted Moxley an' I told 'er this was the train to be getting an' there'd be none other tonight,' the porter almost gabbled as the station master's irate gaze settled on him.

'Was it Moxley you was a-wanting?'

A respectful 'miss' glaringly absent, the station master turned his stare to Carys. He was having nobody, young or old, male or otherwise, on his station overnight. It was the train or the street and no messing about on the way.

'Yes, it was,' Carys answered quietly, feeling the man's antagonism almost touching her. She shivered. She knew that touch well enough, had lived with it for the past four years.

'Well then!'

The station master fingered his well-waxed moustache, aware of the inquisitive stares of passengers already seated on the train.

'I . . . I find I can no longer go to Moxley.' Carys saw the impatience in the man's eyes and almost cringed in expectation of the blow that usually followed such a look.

'Well, you'll not be going anywheres else tonight.' Stubby fingers worried one end of the stiffened moustache. 'Least not on a train, that is, so you best be getting along. Take your ticket to the ticket office an' change it when you makes up your mind where you wants to be.'

He glanced at the porter hovering nervously at his elbow and gave a slight hitch of his head, which clearly said, 'That's if a woman can ever make up her mind about anything.'

'I do not have a ticket to change.'

Carys watched the man's look of incredulity turn to one of anger.

'You don't 'ave no ticket!' he burst out. 'Then what the 'ell be you playing at? You've been standin' on this platform nigh on seven hours an' all that time you ain't had no ticket? That means you either had no intention of going anywheres or else you 'oped to slip on to a train without paying and . . .'

'I had no such intention!' Beneath the anaemic flare of the

gas lights that punctured the shadows of the platform Carys's cheeks flushed hotly.

'Then why stand 'ere all day? Hollings, see 'er off.'

The station master strode away, his hand coming up smartly to his bottle green cap as he scurried to open the door of a first-class carriage for a late arrival.

Along the platform Carys shrank against the wall, seeking the protection of the gloom. She recognised the man climbing into the train: the tall muscular build even under the dark velour overcoat, the sure confident step. Yes, she recognised him as she would anywhere, but he must not see her.

'You best be getting along, miss,' the porter said kindly. 'You don't want no trouble and the gaffer there, well, 'e will send for the bobbies if you don't go.'

'I . . . I'm sorry, I did not mean to cause you bother.'

Lowering her head against the yellow gleam of the gas lamps and the possibility that the man who had just boarded the train might see and recognise her, Carys began to follow the porter towards the arched entrance that gave on to the street. A possible confrontation with the police would be more than she could take right now.

'Eh up, you mad-brained bugger!'

Knocked almost off his feet by the figure hurtling into the station, the porter reeled and automatically reached out for something to arrest his fall. His hand fastening on Carys's arm, she stumbled on to her knees, the shabby carpet bag flying off across the platform.

'What the bloody hell d'you think you be about!'

Scrambling to his feet, the porter glared at the young woman who had cannoned into him, at the same time helping Carys to her feet.

'Ain't you got no more sense than to go running wild around a railway station?'

'Eh, I be right sorry, truly, but that there be my train and if I don't catch it then missis will be on to me summat rotten.'

'Being sorry don't butter no parsnips.' The porter glared. 'You young uns think you can go round doing just as you like an' sod the rest of we . . .'

'I said I be sorry.' The girl turned to Carys. 'Eh, luv, I hope as you ain't hurt none?'

'No, no, I am not hurt.' Carys dusted her shabby coat with both hands.

'That be as it might.' The porter glanced behind in the direction of the first-class carriages and visibly wilted as he saw the station master hurrying across to them.

'What be all the to do?' The station master's moustache bristled at his underling.

'It be nothing, Mr Robins, sir.' The porter retrieved the carpet bag, shoving it into Carys's hand. 'This young woman bumped into we, that's all.'

'But that ain't all!' The station master sucked in his cheeks importantly. There had been an accident on his station and that was something he did not like, something he did not like at all. His moustache, so stiff with wax it stood out from each side of his face like a couple of malacca canes, bobbed up and down with the angry workings of his mouth. 'That ain't all at all! This 'ere young woman has been knocked down. In short, there has been a haccident . . .'

'Nobody ain't hurt.' The girl who had raced into the station threw an anxious glance towards the steaming train.

'Nevertheless a haccident is a haccident and must be reported,' said the station master, bristling anew.

'There is really no need for that.' Carys took the bag, her back to the train, aware of faces turned towards the little drama being played out on the platform.

'There be every need.' The moustache rose and fell importantly. 'It be the policy of the L.M.S. railway to report every haccident caused to a passenger, no matter how trivial. An' this has been a haccident.'

'But I'll miss my train if you keeps me hanging about while you writes out whatever it is you haves to write out. Tell him you ain't hurt, miss?' The girl looked pleadingly at Carys. 'Tell 'im you don't want him making no report?'

'It don't matter what 'er says,' the station master returned pompously. 'There has been a haccident involving a passenger and as station master I haves to report it.'

'But there has not been an accident involving a passenger.'

Carys gave a last flick to her coat as she met the station master's intimidating glare.

'Of course there has!' he rapped at her. 'This here young 'ooligan knocked you down.'

'No, she did not.' Carys met the angry stare full on. 'She bumped into the porter who, as he lost his balance, accidentally caused me to stumble.'

'As I said, a haccident!' The station master wore his triumph like a medal.

'As you said, an accident,' Carys concurred quietly. 'But not an accident caused to a passenger. If you recall, I told you I had not purchased a ticket and that I was not intending to take a journey on any train. To be a passenger one must have a ticket and I do not have one, therefore I cannot be said to be a passenger, so it follows there is no need for you to write out a report.'

The station master's mouth worked fiercely, jerking the moustache up and down as he tried to come to terms with what he knew to be logical yet loath to relinquish his authority, seeing the girl's argument as in some way challenging the power he wielded.

''Er be right.' The second girl grinned. 'If 'er ain't bought a ticket then 'er ain't no passenger – so you can clear off out of my way afore I reports you for hobstructing the travelling of a young lady who has got a ticket, bought and paid for.'

'Just you makes sure as you have . . .'

'Oh, I have a ticket all right.' She fished in the pocket of her coat, drawing out a slip of white card. The black lettering and the neat hole punched in one corner showed clearly in the sickly yellow gas light as she waved it only inches below the dancing moustache.

A few yards away the engine belched noisily as a guard somewhere in the shadows blew his whistle.

'Blimey, I'm gonna miss me train!'

Grabbing Carys by her free hand, she ran for the train, oblivious to the calls of both porter and station master.

'Hold it, hold it!' she screeched, sprinting along to where the third-class carriages stood at the far end of the platform. 'Give a girl a chance to get on.'

Dragging Carys behind her, she jumped into a carriage, its door swung open by a passenger seeing them charge along the platform, and sank laughing on to the wooden seat as the guard blew three short blasts and the train steamed slowly forward.

'That was close.' The girl touched a hand to the bonnet that had come slightly askew in their race for the train. 'The missis would have my guts for garters if I didn't get back tonight.' She sank against the wooden back rest, her eyes closed. 'Eh, that was clever, the way you handled that la-di-dah station master. I would never have thought to pretend I hadn't got a ticket.'

'I was not pretending. I do not have a ticket.'

'Eh!' The girl's eyes opened and even in the dim light of the single candle enclosed in a glass shade held by a wall bracket, Carys could see consternation fill them. 'But you have to have a ticket! You can be prosecuted for tryin' to diddle the railway company.'

'I was not trying to cheat the railway company. In fact, I was not about to travel on this train.'

'Eh!' The girl's eyes widened still further. 'But . . . but you was on the platform.'

'Yes, but I was not about to board the train. I was just about to leave the station.'

'Oh, lor'!' The girl slumped back in her seat again. 'Oh, lor'. Now what do we do?'

Carys glanced across the carriage to the opposite seat where a woman fumbled her breast into the mouth of a screaming infant. What could she do? The best thing would be to get off at the first station and try to explain to the attendants there what had happened. And then what? Would the police be called and she arrested?

'Had you just got off this train at Snow Hill?' The girl shifted in her seat to look at Carys, ignoring the grumbles of a man wedged into the seat beside her as he pulled his flat cap over his eyes and settled to sleep.

'No,' Carys answered, seeing the woman feeding the baby look at her with interest.

'Well, if you wasn't getting on and you hadn't got off, what was you doing? I mean, it don't make no sense you being on the station if you wasn't coming or going.'

'Might be 'er was meeting somebody off the train.' The woman suckling the child eased her nipple from its mouth allowing it to burp noisily before pushing it back.

'Was that what you was there for, to meet somebody?' the girl asked. 'Lor', what will they do when they finds there you be, gone?'

In the narrow, half-dark compartment Carys smiled to herself. It had been four years since she had heard the peculiarly contradictory manner of speech that was the nearest Black Country people came to the King's English, a manner of speech that warmed her with memories.

They had spoken that way, the men and women employed in her father's enamelling works, but for all the roughness of their speech they had been kind to a small child lonely for companionship, unlike some of the teachers at that place her mother still referred to as a school who, for all their correct usage and polite speech, had made her life there a hell.

'Well, don't matter 'ow much they looks for 'er, they won't find 'er cos 'er be on this train.' The woman fastened her blouse across the breast she took from the now sleeping baby, adjusting the heavy woollen shawl about the child, then proceeded to peer across the narrow gap between the wooden seats.

'Eh, what we going to do?'

'Well, whatever it be, you better do it quick.' This time it was the man with the cap over his eyes who spoke. 'The conductor'll be here afore long and if 'e cops 'er without a ticket, it'll be the bobbies fer sure.'

'P'raps if we tell him what happened, he might turn a blind eye?' the girl suggested hopefully. 'If we tell him what with rushing for the last train, we hadn't time to go to the ticket office, he might let you off.'

'Arrh, and pigs might fly – only don't go holdin' your breath till you sees 'em go over,' the man answered drily. 'From what I hear, the railway be clamping down on fare dodgers. They be prosecutin' everyone they gets 'old of and that means six months down the line.'

Prison! Carys felt her heart leap in her chest. Would they really send a woman to prison for the sake of a few pence? She didn't ask the question aloud for she already knew the answer.

'P'raps if whoever you was supposed to meet said what you was at Snow Hill for, it would be all right?'

Carys heard the hope in the voice of the girl who had dragged her on to the train and hesitated, hating to destroy it.

'I was not there to meet anyone.' She had to say it at last.

'This is getting to be like one o' them there Sherlock Holmes stories.' The man sat up, pushing his flat cap back from his eyes. ''Er wasn't at the station to be going anywhere an' 'er wasn't there to be coming back, neither was 'er there to be meeting anybody – so what the 'ell *was* 'er there for? Best get your answer ready, wench, 'cos that magistrate is going to want to hear it.'

''E might not have to.' The woman lifted the hiccuping baby to her shoulder, patting it none too gently on the back. 'You could just pay the price of a ticket to the conductor when 'e comes round.'

''Course, that's right.' The girl heaved a long sigh of relief. 'I hadn't thought of that. Just pay to where you want to get off an' there'll be no trouble, that's the answer.'

Across from her the baby burped again and, crooning her approval, the woman rocked it in her arms. It would be the answer, Carys thought, except for the fact she had been left without a single farthing.

'No trouble?' The man shifted in his seat, a surly disgruntled movement as if this apparent solving of the problem had stolen his limelight. 'You drag 'er on to a train 'er didn't want to be on in the first place then tell 'er, all airy-fairy like, to cough up 'er own fare to pay for a journey 'er 'ad no need of – *then* you tell 'er it's no trouble! Huh! I know what I'd be telling you if it was me.'

'Well, it ain't you, is it?' the girl replied tartly. 'And I don't remember nobody asking you to stick your big nose into a private conversation.'

'Like that, is it?' The man slouched back in his seat, once more pulling the cap low over his eyes. 'Well, don't ask me to stick it in when that conductor asks for 'er ticket 'cos you'll ask in vain.'

'We won't have to ask.' The girl pushed herself more squarely on to the slatted wooden seat, shoving the man farther into the corner as a token of her annoyance. ''Er will pay for a ticket and there'll be no bother. That be right, don't it?'

Carys felt rather than saw the smile in the girl's eyes and had to force out the words that would drive it away. It had been done in the spirit of kindness, her being hauled on to this train; the girl had obviously thought she had intended boarding it.

'I can't pay for a ticket,' she said, 'I have no money.'

For a long minute the silence was broken only by the regular click of the train wheels passing over the points in the track, then from beneath the cap came a satisfied grunt.

'Like I said, best have an answer ready for the magistrate, 'cos sure as hell be hot 'e is going to want to hear it.'

'You mean, you ain't got no money at all?'

'Not so much as a penny,' Carys answered the other girl's question.

'Look, I don't understand this.' It took several seconds for her to speak. 'You was on a railway station but you had no intention of getting on a train, and you had no money to pay for a journey you didn't intend to take?'

'I told you it was like a Sherlock Holmes story,' came the voice from beneath the cap.

'Arrh, you did,' the girl replied acidly, 'but you ain't no Doctor Watson judging by the help you've come up with so far, so do we all a favour and keep quiet.' She turned to Carys, squinting at her by the dim light of the candle. 'Well, whatever you were about on that station it be my fault you find yourself on this train, so least I can do is pay your fare.' She hesitated, realising she had no idea where the other girl was headed. 'Where do you be going?' she asked. 'Where do you live?'

The answer was simple enough. Carys felt a tug in her chest. She was going nowhere, she had nowhere to live.

'My home is in Moxley,' she said, knowing she had to reply.

The girl rummaged in her bag then held out her hand, running a finger over the coins gleaming in her palm.

'I'm sorry but I've only got enough to get you to the station at Wednesbury,' she apologised. 'I ain't got the price of the cab you will need to take you on up to Moxley.'

'Wednesbury will do, I can walk from there.'

She would not walk to Moxley, Carys thought, she would not walk anywhere tonight except maybe a shop doorway somewhere. Then tomorrow . . . but what of tomorrow? It would bring no answer to her problem. Tomorrow would not bring her a home.

Chapter Two

Without a word to the maid who opened the door to her, Maria passed quickly up the broad staircase of Holyhead House, closing the door of her bedroom behind her.

Removing her feathered bonnet, she threw it on the bed, at the same time drawing a long slow breath. She had done it! She had prevented the girl's return to this house, prevented her from taking up with Ryder Tempal. There would be no more coy smiles and whispers, no more walks alone with him in the garden, and she, Maria, need no longer fear competition from a girl more than twenty years her junior.

'She shall not have him!'

Crossing the room, Maria Beddows stared with satisfaction at her own reflection in the long cheval mirror. At almost forty she still made an imposing picture. Her figure was good and set off to advantage in tasteful claret-coloured velvet, the dark hair dressed high on her head crowning a face that was almost beautiful.

Almost beautiful . . . Anger flared like fresh-lit coals in her brown eyes, drawing down her brows and marring her good looks. She had been aware of the girl's growing beauty, aware of the interest she commanded whenever guests were in the house, aware of the competition.

'But I put a stop to that,' she whispered to the image staring back at her. 'I have waited too long to let her take him from me, let her take what should be mine – what *will* be mine. She will not have him, she will *never* have him.'

Touching one hand to her head, she patted a non-existent stray hair into place, her well-shaped mouth curving into a triumphant smile. Her little trip to Birmingham had been successful; she had got rid of one thorn from her side and there would be no argument from the other. Meshac would make no effort to bring the girl home once he had heard what his wife had to tell him.

Meshac!

Dropping her hand to her breast, she smoothed it down to her tightly corseted waist, her mind busily weaving the threads of imagination. If only Meshac were to die, the rest would be so easy. If he were to die she would be free. The barrier to her happiness with Ryder Tempal finally removed, she would be free to lead the life she wanted, with the man she wanted.

A tap at her door interrupting the thought, Maria turned impatiently, calling her permission for the maid to enter.

'A messenger from the Bilston works, mum.' The girl bobbed a curtsy.

Message? Maria's mind whirled for a moment. Could it be that Meshac had met with an accident? Could he be dead? Seeing the girl look at her, knowing that for one unguarded moment she had let the light of hope shine in her eyes, Maria turned towards the bed, picking up her bonnet.

'Yes, Mary, what is it?' she asked, her voice more controlled than her thoughts.

'A message from the master, mum. He sent a man from the works to say as 'ow 'e will be bringing a guest to supper and to tell you they would be 'ome around eight.'

'Did the master say who his guest was?'

'No, mum, just that 'e was bringin' somebody to supper. Shall I tell Mrs Coates to come up, mum?'

'No.' Maria tossed the bonnet aside once more and turned back to face the maid. 'Mrs Coates will manage very well as she always does. Tell her I leave everything in her capable hands.'

Maria unbuttoned the claret velvet as the maid withdrew. Having a guest this particular evening suited her; it would delay any explanation of the girl's absence and give her more time to plan just what she would say as the reason for Carys's not returning home. Catching sight of herself in the mirror, Maria smiled.

Things were working out better than she could have hoped. Tonight with a guest to entertain Meshac would be certain to take more than a little of the wine and more than one glass of the brandy his doctor had advised against. Tonight he would have more than alcohol to lull him to sleep; tonight she would take steps to bring about her dream.

'It be a fair walk to Moxley . . .'

The girl who had paid Carys's fare to the none-too-pleasant conductor on the train turned to look at her as they left the L.M.S. station at Wednesbury.

'. . . and I don't feel too easy about your headin' off there all by yourself. It'll be black as pitch when you come to cross the 'eath.'

'I will be all right.' Carys clutched the carpet bag closer to her as though the paltry contents somehow gave her comfort. 'I am sorry to have taken the last of your money to pay my fare here.'

'Couldn't do no other seeing as it were my fault you was on that train in the first place.'

'But having no money left means you also will have to walk home,' Carys said as they trudged away from the dimly lit station.

'That won't hurt me none.' The other girl grinned. 'I'm used to walking home, ain't nothing new for me. But it is fcr you, ain't it?' Her grin gone, the girl looked at Carys more shrewdly. The shabby, seen-better-days coat did not hide the girl's innate look of gentility though the hands that clutched the carpet bag were those of someone used to manual labour. Wherever this girl had come from she had been worked hard, but even more puzzling was where she was headed and how she had planned to get there without money.

'You ain't never walked to Moxley afore, have you?' she asked again.

Carys shook her head, turning her face away so the other girl would not see the tears that suddenly threatened to spill.

'I thought not.' The girl stopped abruptly. 'What's more, it be my guess you ain't going to walk there tonight neither. You ain't got a home in Moxley, 'ave you? In fact, it strikes me you ain't got a place nowhere.'

Across the street the last few women hurried homeward from the street market. They had waited for the nine o'clock bargains from Tedd's fish stall and Harry Stokes's meat stall, sold off cheap as the day's business came to an end. Soon the town centre would be deserted except for men coming and going between Wednesbury's many public houses.

'Well, I knows one thing for sure.' The girl tucked her arm through that of Carys. 'You ain't sleeping under no hedge. You best come with me. Mrs B. ain't so hard as to see a young wench out of a place to spend the night.'

'Mrs B.? Is she your mother?'

The girl's laughter rippled through the gathering night. 'Lor', that 'er ain't! Mrs Bates be the cook and housekeeper up at Ridge House – that be where I'm in service. I be the parlour maid-cum-everything else. Chief cook an' bottle washer me mom calls it, but it be better than nowt.'

Carys hung back as the girl made to pull her along. 'I can't just turn up there, whatever would they think?'

'Well, you can't stop out on the streets all night neither. What if the bobbies sees you and takes you in for vagrancy? That would mean three months down the line. I tell you, it be better you come to Ridge House with me for tonight and you can sort yourself out in the morning.'

She was right, of course. It was not wise to stay the night under a hedge. Though she knew it would be no different tomorrow, Carys allowed herself to be pulled along.

'Say, I don't know your name? I can't very well introduce you to Mrs Bates as the girl I pulled on to the train, can I?'

'It would not sound very good.' Carys gave an uncertain smile. She still wasn't sure that turning up on a stranger's doorstep and asking for a night's shelter was the right thing to do.

'So what shall I call you?' The girl elbowed her way past a group of women, their baskets about their feet as they waited for the tram that would take them up Holloway Bank.

'Carys – my name is Carys Beddows.'

The name obviously meant nothing to the girl leading the way along Bridge Street and Carys added no more as she followed.

'Was that where you had your last place then, in Brummagem?'

'Where?'

'Brummagem. You was on the station there and you says you wasn't goin' anywheres nor comin' from nowheres so strikes me you must have been there from the start.'

'Yes . . . my last place was in Birmingham.'

It was the truth, Carys told herself. The only home she had known for the past four years had been that convent in Birmingham.

'And they give you the push, did they, the nobs you worked for? Hey!' The girl stopped suddenly, peering at Carys through the gathering darkness. 'You wasn't kicked out for nicking, was you? 'Cos I ain't taking nobody to Ridge House whose fingers be too light for their hands. The missis there be a good employer and I ain't repaying 'er by taking a thief into 'er house.'

'I am not a thief!' Carys flashed, indignation at the accusation flooding her with heat. 'I . . . I left my last place of my own accord. I no longer felt any satisfaction in . . . in being there.'

'I knows what you means.' The girl carried on walking. 'I feels that way meself sometimes. I feels I'd like to up and get meself off to pastures new, but I ain't never quite had the nerve.'

Behind them a tram rattled and shook as it came on, already groaning at the prospect of climbing the steeply rising ground. Carys watched as it passed, hearing the conductor calling out the next stopping point.

'So, Miss Carys Beddows, may I hintroduce Miss Alice Withers?' The girl giggled as she dropped an exaggerated curtsey.

'I am honoured to make your acquaintance, Miss Withers.'

Carys returned an equally affected curtsey, causing both of them to break into laughter.

'Well now, ladies, how would it be if a fine handsome strapping bloke was to join in the joke?'

A candle in a jar suspended from a hook cast a weak glow over a wooden sign announcing the building the man was leaving to be The Globe public house.

Instinctively clutching her carpet bag, Carys stepped closer to Alice as the man swayed forward, the stink of his breath carried before him.

'Well, I'd say as how that would be a fair treat.' Alice faced him squarely. 'If there *was* a fine handsome fellow in the vicinity, which there ain't. There be only you, and you ain't so much strapping as strapped, I'd say, and the only joke you can be joining is the one on you if you thinks otherwise!'

'I bet you thinks that be clever?'

The man's hands went to the leather belt about his waist, its buckle gleaming in the dim light of the candle, and Carys felt her heart jolt sickeningly as he began to ease it loose.

'I think it be a lot cleverer than your taking that off.' Alice stood her ground, staring at the whiskered face just a yard from her own. 'The men in there be hot from ale, and the waters of the Tame be cold. Both can be foul, as you will find out when we scream, mister. Men hereabouts don't take kindly to wenches being apprehended on their way home o' nights. One squeal from me and you be like not to see morning.'

For several moments the man's hands fingered the buckle then dropped to his sides, his shoulder deliberately driving into Alice as he lurched away. 'Bugger off!' he called thickly, voice mingling with a burst of laughter coming from the public house. 'Anyway, who wants to put their 'ands on shit?'

'I doubt 'e would have said no, given half a chance,' said Alice. But relief he had given up so easily told in her voice. She turned to where Carys had slumped against the wall. 'Don't you pay no thought to that little performance.'

'But he . . . he was about to strike you!' Carys had lived seventeen of her years in Moxley and well knew what it meant when a man unbuckled his belt. Though it had never happened to her she had seen the marks of the buckle on many a lad's back when visiting the Bilston enamelling works with her father.

''E would have got more than 'e bargained for if 'e had.' Alice caught her arm, tucking it beneath her own as she set off again, following the road that now began to rise fairly steeply. 'Thank God 'e had the sense to realise it.'

'Does that sort of thing happen often?' Carys flinched as a figure scuttled from the darkness only to disappear fast, swallowed up by the blackness of an alleyway that separated one row of small mean houses from the next. They had been built close to the edge of the cutting made to lay the road and tram rails.

'Not to me it don't,' Alice chuckled. 'Seeing as I'm usually with me brothers if I have to be out at night. And woe betide any bloke who tries any funny business with them around!'

'But your brothers are not with you tonight?'

'No, and don't you never tell 'em I've been out on me own at night. That would give me mother a heart attack. It only be that the mistress had this brooch 'er wanted special to wear at some do 'er has been invited to and the pin broke so 'er asked me to take it to be mended.'

Along the dark ribbon of houses a dog barked, the short staccato sounds raking Carys's nerves. Her arm tensed beneath that of the girl walking beside her. 'Is that why you were in Birmingham today?'

In the darkness Alice nodded. 'What a grand day it's been an' all! I ain't never been there afore. It were quite flummoxin' findin' me way among all them streets – it were like a maze. But you'll know that from living in the place. I enjoyed the visiting of it but I don't know as how I would like to live there.'

'But why go all the way to Birmingham just to get a new pin put on a brooch? There is surely a jeweller closer?'

Alice puffed from the effort of the long climb, dragging air into her lungs only to force it out between her teeth. 'Mr Josephs along Hydes Road be a watchmaker, I don't know whether you would call that being a jeweller, but the mistress always gets 'er trinkets seen to by them in the jewellery quarter and that be in Brummagem.'

Carys remembered her one visit to that part of Birmingham some called 'the jewellery quarter', while others referred to the narrow twisting streets and warren of tiny workshops as 'the gold quarter'. Her father had told her, when taking her with him to deliver a specially commissioned set of enamelled cameos she herself had designed, that the men who worked here in these small cramped rooms handled some of the rarest gems in the world and produced the most fabulous pieces of gold jewellery.

'Phew!' Alice stood for a moment, catching her breath, as they crested the rise. 'Not much further now. Ridge House be just across the 'eath to the left there.'

She pointed into the darkness but Carys did not follow the direction with her eyes. She had turned to look back the way they had come. There at the foot of the hill Wednesbury spread a carpet of tiny pinpricks of light; the flames of candles set in jars and the odd gas lamp all danced like the Jack-o'-Lanterns her father used to take her to watch, flitting in and out of the branches of the trees growing around the pool in a flooded mine shaft. And beyond those pinpricks of light, in the outer ring of darkness, lay Moxley and her home.

Her home! Carys felt hurt and despair sear through her. From now on she had no home. She had thought earlier, standing on the station platform, that her father would not believe what was told him of her not wanting to return home, wanting instead to lead her life away from him, but even as she had thought it, she'd known her father would believe anything his wife told him.

'C'mon.' Alice took her arm again. 'Mrs B. will be getting nervous at me being out so long. And watch your step – the ground be pretty bumpy this way, but by cutting across the 'eath we save time. We would follow the road on to Hill Top and branch off there to go along the drive straight up to the house, but like I says, that puts another ten minutes on the journey. Me, I always cuts across the 'eath.'

Feeling the heels of her side-buttoned boots sink into the soft earth, Carys stumbled in the wake of a hurrying Alice, expecting every step to throw her flat on her face so that it was with decided relief that she eventually saw the great solid black mass of Ridge House loom out of the darkness.

'Stranded, you says?'

Martha Bates's eyes took in the figure standing just inside the door to the kitchen. The coat she wore had seen better days but her face was well-scrubbed and her boots were polished; the carpet bag was shabby but the fingernails of the hands that clenched it held no line of dirt beneath them. This girl, whoever she was, kept herself clean though her clothes were old and she didn't have gloves.

'Yes, mam.' Carys bobbed a polite curtsey.

And she had manners, Martha noted, her anxiety that Alice

had brought some undesirable back with her fading a little more. And the girl's manner of speech was pleasant, not the usual careless dialect of the Black Country.

'Well, get you in by the fire, wench, there be time to tell all about that after supper. And you . . .' She turned to where Alice sat beside the range, unbuttoning her boots. 'Did you do the mistress's errand?'

'Yes, Mrs Bates.'

In the warm light of the kitchen the girl smiled as she eased her feet from her boots, stretching her stockinged toes to the fire glowing behind the steel bars of the grate.

'And the brooch, you 'ave it safe?'

'Safe as houses.' Alice nodded.

'Well, let's be having it, wench?' The housekeeper held out an impatient hand.

Standing up from the chair she had taken beside the range, Alice gathered up her skirts and petticoats, bundling them beneath her chin then pushing her bloomers several inches down from her waist and beginning to unhook her corset.

'Alice!' Martha Bates's eyes rounded. 'What in the world be you doing, wench?'

'It's the mistress's brooch. I put it under me corset for safe-keeping.' The smile became a grin as she fished beneath the half-open corset, coming out with a small brown suede bag.

'Well, I never!' Martha took it, her mouth widening into a surprised smile. 'Whoever would think of putting it there?'

'That's what I thought.' Letting her skirts fall, Alice plonked herself back on her chair, wriggling her toes against the heat of the fire. 'You did keep tellin' me to take care and keep it safe, and you did keep going' on about them pocket pickers, so I put it in the safest place I could think of . . . weren't no pocket pickers going to get their hands under my stays!'

'Mistress will have herself a good laugh when I tells 'er where 'er brooch has been this last few hours. And speaking of hours, what took you so long gettin' back here?'

'Ooh, Mrs Bates, you wouldn't ask that if you had seen that

there jewellery quarter. Talk about finding your way out of a maze! I reckon that would be child's play compared to getting yourself out of that place. You no sooner finds your way out of one back alley than you be in another. Them narrow little streets all weave in and out of each other like threads on a loom. I got meself lost a time or two an' by the time I did get to Snow Hill station I'd missed the afternoon train and the evening one was just about to pull out. I was lucky to catch it, what with that bloomin' station master.'

'Well, you be home now, and seeing as you am, you best get that girl out of her coat and then see to making a pot of tea. I think we could all do with a drink and a bite of supper.'

Slipping the suede bag into the pocket of her starched white apron, Martha glanced at Carys still standing uncertainly by the door. 'Take off your coat, girl, and get you to the fire. I know the mistress would not have you turned out into the night. Though comes the morning . . .'

Slipping out of her coat, Carys watched while Alice hung it in a tall wooden cupboard set at the farthest end of the large kitchen then accepted the chair the girl had vacated.

'What will you do tomorrow?' Alice busied herself with cups and plates. 'I mean, you ain't got no money, so you says, an' you can't live off air so you have to get yourself a place somewheres.'

'It's true I have no money, none at all.' Carys felt the warmth of the fire sink into her bones. She had not realised she had been so cold. 'But don't worry that I will impose upon your mistress's hospitality, I will leave first thing in the morning.'

'And go where?' Alice fetched bread and a haunch of cold beef from the larder, returning to bring out butter, cheese, and a large jar of pickled onions which she set on the table.

'And do what?' The second question was asked as she poured boiling water into an enamel tea pot.

'I . . .' Carys hesitated, trying to judge whether her next words were such a terrible lie. They were not the truth, she had not thought of finding a job or a place to live, she had thought only of those words she had heard on the station platform: *'Stay away from Moxley . . . try to return to Holyhead House . . . I will see you dead . . .'*

'I thought perhaps I might find something in Wednesbury.'

'You might find work.' Taking a large knife from a drawer set in the wooden table that occupied the centre of the kitchen, Alice proceeded to slice several pieces of bread then went on to carve thick slices of the cold beef. 'Though I doubt very much it will be the sort of work you be used to. Your hands be red but I'd say you ain't never done no really hard work – well, scrubbing floors ain't what I would call work, and they only have my sort in Wednesbury. Try down there an' you're like to finish up gleaning coal from the pit heaps to sell for a tanner a hundredweight. Lor', you'd be better off in the workhouse!'

'I told you the mistress would laugh when 'er heard where you had gone and put 'er brooch.' Martha Bates bustled back into the kitchen, immediately taking charge of filling each of the plates with slices of beef.

'Was 'er brooch mended suitable?'

''Er was very pleased with it, Alice, though 'er was concerned when 'er heard you had been and gone and got yourself lost in that there jewellery quarter.'

'No need for the mistress to go worrying.' Relieved of carving the beef, Alice fetched the enamel pot from the hob, filling each of the three cups with hot strong tea. 'I did get lost but I soon found meself again.'

'Arrh, you be a sensible wench when you uses your head.' Martha smiled benignly before turning her glance to Carys, beckoning her to take a seat at the table.

'I told 'er about you and how you have no place you can be getting to tonight, and as I said 'er gives permission for you to stay here.'

'Thank you, it's very kind of you all.'

'Yes, well, they says kindness is a virtue. Besides, there might be a time we shall all need a bit of the same.' Martha glanced at Alice, the teapot still in her hands. 'Don't stand there nursing the pot wench, come along and eat your supper.

'Mistress says, if you have no objection, 'er would like a word with you afore you leaves in the morning.'

'Oh!' Carys looked up from her plate, concern adding to the shadows already underlining her eyes.

'There be nothing for you to fret over.' Martha noted the fear rising like a tide on the girl's face. 'Mistress is just wanting reassurance that you will be all right travelling about on your own like, but 'er said as if you don't have no wish to talk with 'er then we was to see you well fed afore you left.'

'Carys thinks 'er will p'raps find a job and a place to stay in Wednesbury.' Alice sliced a piece of beef, placing it in her mouth, and continued shortly, 'but I told 'er there be nothing likely to suit 'er in that town. It's nobbut iron and steel mills, and 'er wouldn't last two minutes in that lot.'

'Don't speak with your mouth full!' Martha reprimanded then. 'So Carys be your name, eh? I told the mistress you'd not spoken it.'

'I beg your pardon.' A faint touch of pink blending with the pallor of her cheeks, Carys immediately apologised. 'I am afraid the events of the day have driven all the manners from me. My name is Carys Beddows and I live . . . used to live . . . at Moxley.'

Used to live at Moxley. Again Martha Bates saw the shadow of pain flit across that pale face. So what had happened to take away that home? How had this girl come to be stranded in a railway station, and who was responsible?

One by one the questions rose in Martha's mind but they would remain unasked, at least until morning. This girl had taken all she could for one day. Much more and she would break.

'We all forget our manners once in a while.' She smiled. 'Now you finish your meal and then Alice can take you upstairs. There be a room next to hers you can have. It be only small but it will serve, and there be sheets and blankets in the linen cupboard.'

'Mrs B. likes you,' Alice said later as she finished helping Carys make up the small bed in a room on the top floor of the house. 'I think 'er would take you on as kitchen maid like a shot with the mistress's say so. If you decides to go and talk to 'er in the morning, why not ask if 'er will give you a position here in this house? You'd be better off here than down in the town. And besides, I likes you an' all.'

'And I like you too, Alice.' Carys smiled across the width of the narrow bed. 'And I am very grateful to you for helping me. I shall of course speak to Mrs . . .'

'Mountford,' Alice said as Carys hesitated. 'The mistress be Mrs Virginia Mountford.'

'. . . to Mrs Mountford,' Carys went on, 'but as for asking for a position in her household, I couldn't. I wouldn't feel . . . I've never . . .'

'. . . You have done the work of a kitchen maid before.' Alice finished the sentence for her. 'I can see that, and this place ain't too bad once you learns the routine and I could help with the heavier chores. Mrs B. ain't too much of a slave driver, neither. Believe me, girl, you could do a damn' sight worse than take a post at Ridge House.'

Yes, she could do worse than take a post at Ridge House. Carys washed her hands and face with cold water from a jug set on a wooden wash stand. Taking one of the two cambric night gowns that had had to serve her since entering that convent from her carpet bag, she slipped it over her head, smoothing the cold fabric over her body.

She could do worse than take a post at Ridge House – like going home to Moxley.

Chapter Three

The evening had gone much as Maria had thought it would. Meshac had eaten a great deal and drunk more while talking endlessly of enamelling. For once she had not allowed this to irritate her; it served her purpose to have him absorbed in talking business which kept his thoughts from the daughter he had expected to see home. He had asked about her once when their visitor had remarked upon the beautiful designs of the boxes and caskets he had ordered. Meshac had told him proudly of his daughter's skills as a designer and her proficiency with a pencil.

'Quite a good little artist, my wench,' he had proclaimed. 'Could have been an asset to the business had her been a lad, but a wench . . .' He'd shrugged, drinking deeply from his favourite Madeira. 'Wenches be good for naught but the marriage bed.'

That had been when he'd glanced along the exquisitely furnished dinner table to Maria sitting at its foot and asked why Carys was not present. But she had been prepared for the question. Smiling directly at her husband, she had spoken the lie without flickering an eyelash.

'She asked if she might have a few days with a friend who will be returning to her parents in India at the end of next week, after which the girls will probably never meet again. My dear, how could I say no? She looked so tragic at the prospect of losing her friend, and it will be only for a few days.'

Her lovely mouth drooping becomingly, Maria listened with satisfaction as her husband reassured her that allowing Carys to remain with her friend had been the right thing to do. Meshac . . . She watched him now, smiling at her with those faded eyes. He loved his child but he loved his wife more. She almost laughed. It was so easy! Each time he had asked why the girl did not visit her home, the touch of Maria's mouth on his had wiped the questions away. Poor Meshac, he was besotted, so much so he believed her every word, and that was all to the good . . . her good.

In the darkness of her soul, Maria smiled. But when she turned that smile upon their visitor it had been all grace and charm.

'Young girls do so enjoy tragedy, do you not think, Mr Fereday?'

Maria remembered the look he had given her from eyes so dark they might be chippings of the coal Moxley was built on; eyes that held none of the admiration she was accustomed to encountering in men.

Tying the ribbons that fastened her lace-edged silk nightgown about her throat, she crossed her bedroom, taking up a hair brush from a dressing table liberally strewn with creams and cosmetics. No, the eyes of Reuben Fereday had not glinted with the desire she loved to evoke.

It made him more interesting.

Stepping to the cheval mirror, she stared at her reflection. Beneath the silken nightgown her body was firm and slender. Dark hair released from the constraint of pins fell around her shoulders, framing a face that was beautiful – almost as beautiful as that of Meshac's child.

Meshac's child! Maria pulled the brush through her hair savagely. Born to be beautiful and raised in every comfort, the only child of a wealthy industrialist, she had claimed everyone's heart with her gentle ways and happy laughter. She had claimed the attention of Ryder Tempal. Maria wielded the brush with long angry strokes. But Carys would not finally claim that man, she herself had made certain of that today. The girl would not return to Moxley, would not be here to tempt Ryder Tempal, to draw his attention where Maria could not allow it to stray.

In the six months since she had first met the tall fair-haired handsome nephew of Colly Moreton she had come to realise he was everything she wanted, to realise it with a cold conviction. She was more certain about this than she had ever been about anything in her life before. He was everything she had dreamed of in a husband, in all the long dreary years she had been tied to Meshac Beddows, and somehow or other that was what he would become: her husband.

Meanwhile . . . Maria ceased to drag at her hair, holding the brush in her hand, her eyes glittering back at her from the mirror like bronze pools, her well-shaped mouth touched by the merest smile. Meanwhile . . . it might be interesting to test the seeming indifference of Reuben Fereday!

Alone in the small room set under the eaves of Ridge House, Carys lay staring into the darkness. Had the events of today really happened or were they simply a nightmare that had not yet ended? Had it been only this morning she had left that school; only hours since she had been abandoned penniless at that railway station? But her nightmare had begun long before that. It had begun over four years ago, when she first met Ryder Tempal.

Maria had known him for several weeks before his first visit to Holyhead House, having met him at the home of Colly Moreton, a friend and business associate of Carys's father.

She had just been to her secret place.

Carys stared at the shadows painting the walls of the tiny room. It had been the summer of her seventeenth year. Outside her window a cloud passed in front of the moon, leaving a wake of darkness, as that summer had left a wake of darkness – four years of darkness that had seemed like four lifetimes.

Ryder Tempal had been in the drawing room when Carys had arrived home and from their first meeting his eyes had devoured her. Tall and broad-shouldered beneath aubergine coloured topcoat, he had taken her hand, holding it too long while he gazed at her with eyes the colour of a cat's.

Carys turned her head on the pillow as if in some way the movement would dispel the image of the handsome fair-haired man who'd stared at her from strange feline eyes. But the image persisted as the man had persisted, calling so often at Holyhead House as to be almost impolite.

That had been when Maria's attitude to her had deteriorated. Theirs had never been a close relationship, not one of real friendship or love, more a matter of mutual toleration. But that had given way the night Maria had come upon them in the garden.

The Moretons had been visiting for dinner when Zelda Moreton had suggested her nephew take Carys for a turn about the garden. It had been an exceptionally warm night and her father had supported the idea, claiming the air would do her good.

They had been in the garden only a few minutes when Ryder had grabbed her arm, almost dragging her into the summerhouse. Swinging her into his arms, he kissed her violently.

'Carys.' He whispered her name as his mouth left hers. 'Carys.'

Shock robbing her limbs of strength, she had stood limply in his arms as he rained kiss after kiss on her mouth.

'We will be married in a month.'

She remembered hearing the words but they had passed over her head, floating about her like motes in a sunbeam.

'Your father will agree, I am sure. I shall tell him of our

intentions when we return to the house and in one month you will be Mrs Ryder Tempal.'

Carys squeezed her lids hard down over her eyes, trying to dispel the memory as she had tried to so often over the past four years. But as always it remained, playing out its lurid drama in her mind.

'We will be man and wife and I will have more than your delectable mouth to kiss. This lovely body will be mine to admire, to enjoy . . .'

His hand had closed over her breast, squeezing the soft flesh, his wet lips searching for her mouth again.

'And I will enjoy it, so many times, and so will you . . .'

Her eyes open wide, Carys pressed the back of one hand to her mouth and sickness rose in her as she seemed to feel again his hands on her body.

His voice, hoarse and strained as his fingers kneaded her breast, at last penetrated the cocoon of shock that had enveloped her at the first touch of his mouth. She pushed against him but his arms held her.

'I . . . I don't want to be your wife . . .'

The feline eyes glittered down at her. His grip tightened as she struggled to free herself.

'I know this might seem a little sudden to you, but you knew from that first meeting I intended you to be my wife.'

'No, I don't wish to marry you. I will never marry you!'

In the darkness of her room at Ridge House Carys heard again his soft mocking laughter.

'Your intentions and mine may be different, but it is mine alone that matter. To fulfil those intentions I need money, and if the only way of getting it is to marry it then I shall do so. You have no say in the matter.'

'My father has!' She had twisted free from his arms but he stood in front of the door to the summerhouse, barring her escape. 'He will not agree to a marriage for which he can see I have no desire. He would never force me to marry you.'

'He will when he finds out his daughter has enjoyed the bed without the marriage!'

Ryder had launched himself at her then, the weight of him tumbling her to the ground, knocking the breath from her body. She had heard the tearing sound as he had snatched at her bloomers and the sound of her own cry muffled by the pressure of his mouth as he rolled on top of her.

That had been when Maria had lashed her foot hard into his ribs.

Carys had heard nothing of what she had said to Ryder. Scrambling to her feet, she had run for the house, entering through a side door and gaining her room via the back stairs.

The following day Maria had dropped her bombshell.

'Mrs Bates said you wished to see me, ma'am?' Carys bobbed a curtsey to the woman seated beneath a high rectangular window.

Virginia Mountford, iron grey hair complemented by the deep plum-purple shade of her gown, looked at the girl who had sought shelter beneath her roof. Her dress of brown calico was shaded in patches, the paler colour a testament to its long service, but though old it was brushed and well-pressed, and the boots that peeped from beneath it bore no evidence of clay, though having come here with Alice, she would have arrived by way of the heath.

'Sit down, my dear.'

Virginia watched as Carys took the chair placed opposite her own. The girl did not stare open-mouthed at the quiet elegance of the room which meant she was accustomed to such surroundings, or at least had been.

'My name is Virginia Mountford, but no doubt Alice has already told you that?'

'Yes, she did, ma'am,' Carys replied as the woman smiled.

'And do you have a name?'

'I beg your pardon.' Carys blushed at this repetition of the night before when she had forgotten to introduce herself. 'My name is Carys Beddows.'

'Of where?'

The woman's keen eyes on her face, Carys hesitated. Hill Top was only a few miles from Moxley. Would this woman know Meshac Beddows? Would she guess the girl in her house was his daughter?

'I . . . I come from Birmingham.'

The grey head nodded. 'The wise men came to Bethlehem from the palace of Herod, my dear, but that was not their home.'

The tinge of pink in Carys's cheeks deepened. Virginia Mountford was a shrewd woman.

'I came here from Birmingham where I have been at school for four years.' Carys swallowed hard on the word. 'Before that I . . . I lived at Moxley.'

'Moxley!' The grey head bobbed again. 'I have been there on occasions – a small place with a few houses and a church. Much like here at Hill Top except we have no church. We have to go into Wednesbury for that.'

She had visited Moxley! Carys let her glance rest on her own hands, clenched together in her lap. Chances were she knew of Meshac Beddows's child, but did they know of her mother's lies?

'Alice bull rushed you on to a train last evening, so I hear?'

If this woman knew of her history it seemed she was not about to refer to it. Carys felt weak with relief.

'It was not meant, ma'am. Alice did rush me into the train but thought she was doing me a kindness.'

'That is the one fault with Alice.' A quick smile curved the older woman's mouth. 'She does not think. She acts first, leaving the thinking until later. But she is a good girl and one I can trust. What she did, she did from the best of intentions so you must allow me to see you get where you wanted to go before meeting her.'

'There is no need! I . . . I can manage alone, thank you.'

Like she had managed yesterday? So lost and confused she had been, capable of going nowhere. Virginia thought over the scanty bits of information her housekeeper had gleaned from Alice whilst this girl had been dressing.

'My dear.' She spoke gently but there was a firmness in her voice. 'It is not easy managing alone, especially when you are young and straight out of school. Take the advice of one older than yourself and accept help when you know it to be offered in true friendship.'

Carys looked at the woman who had taken her unquestioningly into her house, sheltered her when there had been no need for her to do so, fed her, and was now offering yet more help. And suddenly she knew that help *was* indeed being offered out of a sense of friendship, and one that deserved to meet with the truth. Slowly, her fingers clenched together against the pain of it, she told of the events on the platform of Snow Hill railway station.

'Did you not think of returning to your school? They would surely have given you shelter until you had time to sort yourself out,' Virginia said when Carys finished speaking.

'To be honest, I did not think of that. I was so dumbfounded my brain did not seem to function.'

'That is not surprising! You were left there without money and without a home, but there must be a reason for such an action?' Virginia Mountford's eyes, grey as her hair, were fixed on Carys. 'Though I do not ask you to tell me of it.'

Carys did not want to tell this woman of the unreasonable and totally unfounded jealousy that had led her to be interned for four years in a hell only the cynical would call a school, and which had now robbed her of the home she loved. But she felt that the kindness already shown to her deserved a full answer.

'There is a reason, though it was no more than an imaginary one,' she answered softly. 'Maria thought the attentions Ryder Tempal paid me were welcomed by me, when in reality I found them detestable. Whenever I knew he was to be a guest at Holyhead House, I would try to invent some reason to be absent, the more so as his visits increased, but my attempts to avoid meeting him were not always successful. Then one night he came as a dinner guest with his aunt and uncle, the Moretons of Mesty Croft, and when he suggested a turn in the garden my father agreed. It . . . it was while we were there that he pulled me into the summerhouse and when I refused to marry him, he tried . . . he tried . . .'

'To rape you?' Virginia asked. 'Is that what he tried to do to you?'

'Maria must have known he was forcing himself upon me but she refused to accept it. So far as she is concerned, I was the one to blame,' Carys said against the tightness of her throat.

'That, I presume, is when you were sent away to school?'

'Yes.' It was a whisper redolent with the misery of four years. 'Except it was not a school, it was a convent – Maria entered me as a novice in the Convent of the Holy Child. As such I was to undergo three years' training then take the vows that would keep me there forever.'

'You had no idea what she had planned?'

'No, and neither had my father, of that I am sure. She must have told him some dreadful lie to keep him from searching for me.'

'I doubt he would have found you, incarcerated as you were in a nunnery. Many poor girls are lost that way.'

'It was my fourth year, the year of my final vows, when I became twenty-one. Sister Mary Immaculata, the Mother Superior, sent for me and asked if becoming a nun was my true vocation. Was I ready to give my life in the honour and service of God? I told her I hoped always to honour God and to serve him but not in the ways of a nun. She then told me I was free to leave if that was what I wanted. That she had only agreed to my entering the convent on condition the final decision of whether or not to take the veil should be mine alone.'

'Obviously Maria thought that after three years you would no longer wish to leave?'

Carys nodded. 'Mother Superior also returned my sketches.'

'Sketches?' Virginia Mountford's brows rose questioningly.

'It seems Maria had shown them to her as proof of my lasciviousness, of the danger I was in of becoming a woman of loose virtue. They apparently showed I was a child in need of strict moral training, for my own good, and I have no doubt she told the same to my father. She had brought the sketches with her so that Mother Superior could judge for herself the truth of what she had been told and then counteract such wickedness.'

'But Mother Superior did not destroy them?'

'No.' Carys shook her head. 'She said that such work could only be a gift from God, that great artists like Michelangelo and Raphael had made such sketches, and that I should use my talent to His glory and to enrich the lives of others.'

'These sketches, did Maria destroy them when she came to collect you from the convent?'

'I . . . I did not tell her I had them, nor did Mother Superior.'

'So you have them still?'

'They are in my carpet bag.'

'May I see them?'

Virginia watched the girl as she asked the question. There was no swift rush of colour to that beautiful face, no guilty lowering of the eyelids, yet there was something: a slight set to that fine mouth, a tilt to the head. Whatever she had sketched there'd been no intention of wickedness, no evil except in the minds of those who wished to see it.

'My bag is in the kitchen. I will fetch it.'

'No.' The older woman pulled a bell rope beside the fireplace. 'Alice can bring it.'

'My dear,' she began again, having instructed Alice to bring the carpet bag to the drawing room, 'I am going to claim the privilege of an old woman and use your given name, which by the way is a very pretty one.'

'It was my father's grandmother's name.' Carys smiled.

'Ah, the old names. So much nicer than the airy-fairy ones young parents seem so fond of these days. Well, Carys, to continue with what it was I intended to say! In short, child, you have nowhere to go and I have no one to talk to. If you will consent to stay here in Ridge House, I shall be pleased to have you.'

She had not waited to see the sketches first, to judge from them the girl's suitability to be in her house; she would not base her judgement on a few pencil lines scratched over a piece of paper. Virginia Mountford had accepted Carys at face value, accepted the girl on her own judgement and not that of others. Feeling the tears begin to trickle, Carys spoke softly.

'I thank you for your kind offer, ma'am, but perhaps you should see my sketches before offering me a place in your home?'

'I don't need to see any sketches to know you, child.' Virginia waited as Alice entered the room, handing Carys the carpet bag and bobbing a curtsey to her mistress before leaving. 'I asked to see the sketches merely from an interest in art. My husband, God rest him, had quite a passion for paintings. He collected many throughout the years and I too enjoy them, though I have to guard them from my nephew who would have them in a public gallery.'

'Your nephew is an artist?'

'No, though he seems to have inherited his uncle's passion for works of art. But Reuben is one of the new breed. "Art belongs to the public" is his motto. The beauty of it should not be a privilege held only by the wealthy few . . .'

'I think I agree with him, ma'am.' Carys's face coloured slightly as she voiced her opinion.

'Maybe I do too.' The old face wrinkled in a conspiratorial smile. 'But I will not give the young rogue the pleasure of knowing it. He can do what he will with this house and all it contains after I am gone, but in the meantime he will continue to think whatever it is he thinks of his old aunt. Now, Carys girl.' She held out her hands. 'Let us see these oh-so-terrible sketches of yours.'

'Sister Mary Immaculata was a wise woman!' Virginia Mountford held the last of the sketches in her hand. 'There is more than beauty in this work, there is strength – the strength of man glorying in life, praising the God who created him. They are hymns whose words cannot be written; songs in which only the true artist may join.'

Carefully rolling the parchment, she handed it back to Carys. 'You have a great talent, child. I hope you use it well.'

Taking the rolled up sketch, Carys replaced it in the carpet bag, covering it with her one extra petticoat and pair of bloomers.

'Well now, girl.' The older woman leaned back, her grey hair glinting with the sheen of gunmetal caught in the sun. 'I have seen what it was Maria thought the work of the devil. Now I await your answer to my proposal: will you stay here at Ridge House?'

'*Stay away from Moxley!*' Carys heard the words in her mind. Would Ridge House be far enough away? Hill Top was some four, maybe five, miles from Moxley and Wednesbury lay between. Would that span be enough to separate her from Maria or was the danger of their meeting too great a risk to take? But where would refusing this woman's offer lead her? 'You could do a damn' sight worse than take a post at Ridge House,' Alice had said. Remembering the convent and that awful interlude at Snow Hill station, Carys knew she was right. Ridge House, even with the possibility of meeting Maria, was the safest place to be.

'Thank you, ma'am.' Carys met Virginia's grey eyes frankly. 'I should be grateful for a position in this house. I can scrub and clean, and am well acquainted with the laundry room and the preparation and cooking of food. I can use a needle and was taught the skills of using herbs for healing. I was also taught to keep household accounts.'

'All this by the convent?'

Carys nodded, a thousand memories screaming in her silence.

'They did well, the Convent of the Holy Child, but did their teaching include none of the arts?'

'None apart from the music required for services. Not dance or drama and certainly not drawing. Even though Mother Superior acknowledged the skills of the artists of the past, she did not encourage their practices in any of the sisters or novices.'

'Well, that will not be the case at Ridge House.' Virginia smiled. 'You must take up sketching again, though I doubt you will find much of beauty beyond the garden. This Black Country of ours is well named for its feet stand in coal and its head is crowned with the chimney stacks of iron and steel foundries. In truth, a depressing picture. But its people have hearts as strong as the steel they work, they are among the finest and hardest working people this country has. Treat them fairly and they will treat you the same. And, remember, they are not all Marias!'

No, they were not all Marias. First Alice and now her mistress had proved that. Carys stood up, the carpet bag in her hand. 'Will I tell Mrs Bates that you have given me a position here or would you have me tell her to come and see you?'

'We have not yet decided upon what you are to do.' Virginia Mountford's eyes took in every aspect of the girl facing her though they never once strayed from her face. 'As I said, I have no one here I can really talk to and could do with a companion. But you look uncomfortable with the idea. Does it not suit you?'

A flush of warm blood rising to her cheeks, Carys lifted the gaze that had fallen to her feet at this proposal. To appear to be throwing the offer back in her face was the last thing she wanted, but to become companion to Virginia Mountford would be to come into contact with her friends . . . friends who would talk, friends who might also be acquaintances of Maria.

'Forgive me if I seem rude, ma'am.' She swallowed hard. The answer she was about to give could dash the offer of a home, it could put her back on the streets without money or hope, yet it had to be said. 'I . . . I would rather be in the kitchen with Alice and Mrs Bates. It . . . it isn't that I have no wish to be a companion to you, believe me, but . . .'

'But you see that as possibly bringing you to the attention of Maria?' Virginia pulled the embroidered bell cord. 'I should have thought of that. Hill Top is a small hamlet but gossip travels far. You are right, my dear, a housemaid will raise less speculation than a companion, though perhaps we two might chat together from time to time?'

'That would give me a great deal of pleasure.' Carys smiled, relieved that her refusal had caused no animosity.

'My dear . . .' Virginia Mountford hesitated slightly then went on, 'Forgive an old woman's curiosity, and of course you must not answer my question if you feel it intrudes upon your privacy, but this Maria you speak of – is she perhaps an elder sister or maybe your step-mother?'

'No.' Carys felt the room close about her. 'She is neither of those. Maria is my mother.'

Maria slipped off the jacket of her cerise velvet travelling suit and sent her feathered bonnet swinging across the hotel room. The journey to Birmingham had long ceased to be a pleasure; the train was far quicker and less obvious than her own carriage but the fear of being seen by someone who knew her increased with each trip. Not that there would be many more. She loosened the buttons of her skirt, letting it fall in heavy folds about her feet. Soon there would be no need for her to come to this dreary hotel hidden away in a maze of streets behind the Bull Ring; soon she would have the life she yearned – a life that did not include Meshac or Meshac's child.

She had never thought of the girl as her own. There had been no rush of mother love twenty-one years ago when she had given birth to her and no depth of love had developed in her as the years had passed.

She had kept their relationship more on what could be construed as sisterly terms, though in her case the elder sister felt nothing for the younger; in fact she had felt no emotion at all until Ryder Tempal had made an appearance, bringing in his wake something Maria had not experienced before, bringing jealousy, jealousy of a girl whose beauty was fast approaching her own . . .

Maria kicked away the froth of petticoats with an impatient thrust of her foot; pushed off her frilled bloomers. She had not seen him for a month, one which she had tried to pass in gaining the attention of Reuben Fereday – but his response to her advances had been so restrained as barely to be polite.

Snatching off her lace-edged chemise, she twisted it viciously in her fingers. Reuben Fereday had been to the house several times and on each occasion had enquired after the girl, eliciting fresh queries from Meshac too. Fereday showed no interest in Maria. But he *would* show an interest! She threw the chemise from her. He would show an interest as all of Meshac's friends showed an interest in his attractive wife.

Attractive! Crossing to the square mirror set above a small dressing table, Maria stared into it, seeing the dark hair fashionably dressed in thick glistening coils, the cool alabaster swell of her breasts, the trim waist and the face men found so appealing. Yes, she was attractive, but not beautiful. Not as her daughter was beautiful!

And how much longer would it last, this attractiveness? Not long enough. Maria loosened the pins from her hair, letting it tumble over her creamy shoulders as she stared into the mirror. Not long enough to waste further time married to Meshac Beddows.

'Now that is the way a woman *should* wait for a man!'

Maria looked to the door reflected in the mirror then turned, holding out her arms to the man standing just inside.

'Isn't this the way you would want your wife to wait for you?'

He smiled, walking into her arms and drawing her nakedness hard against him while pressing his face to her throat.

'Just this way,' he breathed thickly. 'And when you are my wife this is the way you will always wait for me.'

'Which is what I have been doing for a month now!'

Pushing him from her, Maria stared at him, an accusatory light in her brown eyes.

'A month and not a single word from you! Where have you been? Or, more to the point, what girl have you been chasing this time?'

'I have been with no girl,' Ryder Tempal said easily. What Maria did not know would not hurt her. 'I have been to Liverpool on business for my uncle.'

Maria allowed herself to be drawn back into his arms. Colly Moreton had talked of having business in Liverpool.

'But now I am back here with you.' He bent his head, kissing the tip of her breast. 'The only place I want to be, with the only woman I want.' Dropping to his knees, he drew his hands over the lines of her body, following with his tongue from her navel down over her stomach. 'Maria.' He pressed his mouth against the dark mound between her thighs. 'Oh, Maria, my love! If only you were my wife.'

She would be soon. Maria watched him from the bed as he threw off his clothes; watched the muscles ripple in his strong body and felt the blood quicken in her veins, felt the desire for him surge through her like a rip tide and knew it was just as dangerous. He was like a drug to her, robbing her of any sense but that of wanting him, and she had waited long enough for what she wanted. Her daughter was gone out of her life for good. Soon it would be the turn of her husband.

Chapter Four

'I bet you be fagged out?' Alice poked the fire in the kitchen range, clearing dead ash from between the bars.

'Of course 'er be tired, 'er as worked like a good one all day.' Martha Bates smiled at the girl her mistress had taken in out of the night. She had not said much of where she had come from or to whom she belonged, but so long as she worked well and kept her tongue civil then Martha reckoned her business was her own. Spooning liberal amounts of sugar into the large cups of cocoa she had just made, she handed one to Carys then turned to Alice, still working ash from beneath the embers of the fire. 'Just throw a bucket of sleck on that then come and drink your cocoa afore it be cold.'

'I'll get it.' Carys rose quickly, bringing the bucket filled with small fragments of coal from the scullery.

'It don't go on like that.'

Alice took the bucket as Carys prepared to empty it on to the fire.

'You have to damp it down first otherwise it will burn through afore morning and that'll mean havin' to light the range all over again. Here, let me show you.'

Filling a small pan with water from the pump over the sink,

she tipped it a little at a time into the bucket, mixing the chippings and coal dust into a thick paste.

'That be the way to damp a fire for the night.'

She grinned as the last of the paste was scraped from the bucket and on to the quietly hissing fire.

'Last all night, will that, and still be alight in the morning.'

'Arrh, that will keep the kitchen warm enough through the night, and you will be glad of that come winter mornings.' Martha nodded as Alice disappeared to wash her hands in the scullery. 'This house can get cold as a barn, stuck up here atop of the hill. I often wonders why the mistress don't go some place else. I know for a fact 'er as a fine house in Evesham 'cos I've been there with 'er a time or two.'

'Ee, I wish I'd been to Evesham . . .'

Alice returned to the kitchen, her hands red from their scrubbing in cold water. She knew that one hint of coal dust left on them would have her back in the scullery scrubbing them over again.

'I ain't never been nowhere 'ceptin' Wednesbury . . . oh, an' Brummagem.' Alice tilted her head to one side, remembering. 'But I don't like Brummagem. Did you like living in Brummagem, Carys?'

Had she liked living in Birmingham? Carys stared into her cup. Truth was she knew almost nothing of the place. One visit to the jewellery quarter with her father had afforded her very little insight, and on that journey to the convent she had seen nothing but a blur of tall buildings set so close together along the streets they seemed melded into one other. And once inside the convent she had seen nothing beyond its high curtain wall.

'You won't like getting up in the morning, Alice Withers, so cut the cackle and get yourself off to bed. And don't go chattering once you be upstairs. Carys be near tired out, 'er won't want to be listening to you prattling all night.'

* * *

'When I be wed I shall have my husband take me to Evesham and to . . . to lots of places.'

White calico nightgown tucked over her feet, knees drawn up to her chin, Alice perched on the end of Carys's bed, her eyes as dreamy as her thoughts.

Pulling a brush through her hair, Carys smiled to herself. Mrs Bates's intervention downstairs had cut short Alice's questions but had not dispensed with them. Tying her plaits with pieces of ribbon she turned to the girl, who was momentarily lost in a pink cloud of imagination. Carys liked Alice and knew her questions were just a young girl's harmless curiosity.

'Wouldn't you like to travel, to see places, ride in a carriage with your husband?' Alice asked dreamily.

'I would have to get a husband first.'

'Have you got anybody . . . I mean, was you walking out with a lad when you was at Brummagem?'

'No.' Carys's smile faded as thoughts of the convent returned. 'I was not being called upon by a man . . . in fact, I had not one visitor during the whole time I was there.'

'What, never!' Alice's eyes rounded. 'Not even your mam or your dad?'

Carys shook her head and when she answered her voice trembled. 'It . . . it was not allowed.'

'Ec, I don't rightly see as how a school can stop your parents coming to see you.' Alice frowned. 'Specially if they be paying a deal o' money for the teaching.'

'It was not a school,' Carys said, her trembling still visible. 'It was a convent, the Convent of the Holy Child, and I was entered as a novice.'

'A nunnery!' Alice breathed. 'They put you in a nunnery?'

'My mother did. I believe my father thought I was in some exclusive finishing school, possibly even on the Continent somewhere. That can be the only reason why he accepted my not going home for holidays.'

'But why should your mam stick you in a nunnery? I mean,

what had you done . . . you didn't go in 'cos you wanted to, did you?'

'No, I did not enter the convent from choice. As for my mother's reasons, she must have had them though I don't know what they were.'

Maybe no words of Maria's had told her the reason she was to be locked away from the world but her actions had spoken loudly enough, especially that night in the summerhouse.

'Anyway, you be out now and of an age where 'er can't push you anywheres you ain't of a mind to be, so forget about 'er. But truly, ain't you never had a fancy for a boy?'

Carys climbed on to the bed too, her own knees tucked beneath her chin, and smiled at the girl whose questions flitted from one subject to another with the ease of a butterfly exchanging one resting place for another. She had never had a fancy, as Alice put it, not for a boy, but would the same be true of a man? She felt traces of warmth steal into her face. Would it be true of the man she had seen in her secret place?

'There must have been somebody?' Alice warmed to her theme. 'You said you was seventeen when you was put into that nunnery. You must have had an eye to some lad in that time. Ain't no wench reaches seventeen years without some bloke taking her fancy.'

'Well, I did.' And Carys laughed, glad the light of the one candle was not strong enough to show the bloom of pink on her cheeks.

'Lor'!' Alice looked almost stricken. 'What on earth did you do with your time?'

'Sketched.'

'Sketched!' Alice's face lost none of its stricken look. 'You mean, drawring? With a pencil and paper?'

'Yes, drawing with a pencil and paper. Or sometimes with charcoal.'

'Lor', how boring!' Alice threw herself flat across the narrow bed. 'Catch me with a pencil and paper.'

'It wasn't boring.' Carys glimpsed the sun on water, caught

a breath of the perfume of wild flowers and heard the faint hum of insects in the grass. Her secret place had never been boring.

'These sketches what you drawed, have you still got them?' Alice sat up once more, her curiosity rekindled.

'A few.' Carys admitted. 'Just the ones Maria . . . my mother . . . took to show to Sister Mary Immaculata.'

'Sister Mary who?' Alice blew out her cheeks, letting the breath escape her mouth expressively. 'That be a mouthful of a name. Fancy landing a babby with a label like that! Immac . . . Immac . . . Lor', I can't even say it.'

'Immaculata.' Carys laughed again as Alice pulled a face. 'It was the name she took when she entered the convent.'

'Did you have to have another name?'

'Yes.' Carys's smile faded. 'I was known as Sister Michaela.'

'Michaela.' Alice rolled the name over her tongue. 'Michaela . . . hmm, I like it. It sounds better than that Immac . . . whatever it was. It be more real, if you knows what I mean. Who chose it, you or your mother?'

'Neither.' Her mother had already left when the name had been allotted to her. In the dimness she recalled the gentleness of the old nun who had given her her name in Christ – so different from the Mistress of Novices whose voice was hard and whose hand was harder. 'The name was chosen by Sister Mary Immaculata. She said my drawings held some of the beauty of those of Michelangelo, so perhaps it would be fitting to bear a form of his name.'

'You've lost me.' Alice drew up her knees, closing her arms about them. 'I ain't got a clue who this Michael Angelo bloke is.'

'Never mind.' Carys stood up. 'It's time you were off to your own room. If Mrs Bates hears us still talking she won't be any too pleased.'

'Give us a look at them there sketches first, the ones you copied off that Michael bloke?'

'I did not copy his work, nor anyone else's for that matter.'

'All right, so you didn't copy nobody.' Alice grinned. 'So let's be having a look.'

Carys guessed the easiest way to get Alice away to her own bed would be to show her the sketches. Taking her carpet bag from beneath the bed, she drew out the several rolls of stiff yellowy parchment.

'Hey!' Holding them one by one, Alice stared at them by the waxy light of the candle. 'These be bostin', they am, they be real good. Stick these in a fancy frame and they could hang in a posh house. You should show these to somebody who knows about drawrings and such.'

She twisted the sheet of paper, trying to angle the light more fully on to the charcoal lines drawn across it. 'This one be *great*, Carys. No coddin', I thinks it's lovely.'

She meant it, Carys realised, watching the appreciation on the other girl's face, she really wasn't pretending.

'Who is he?' Alice peered at her, screwing up her eyes to pierce the semi-gloom beyond the reach of the candlelight. 'Do you know him, did he pose for you?'

'No, I do not know him.' Carys retrieved the sketch and, rolling it, replaced it with the others in the carpet bag. 'And no, he did not pose for me.'

'But he is real? I mean, he ain't somebody you just made up. He ain't no wotsit of the imagination?'

Carys pushed the carpet bag back under the bed. 'No, he is not a figment of my imagination, Miss Alice Withers, he is real as . . . as Mrs Bates's anger will be if she finds you still here when she comes upstairs. Now go to bed!'

'I'm going.' Alice slid from the bed, padding on bare feet to the door. 'Lor', I wish I'd met a bloke like the one in that drawring.' She giggled impishly before opening the door a crack and checking the corridor for the housekeeper. 'You can bet your birthday five bob piece we wouldn't have parted strangers!'

Climbing into bed Carys blew out the candle but the image of the man she had drawn still blazed vividly in her mind.

She had been in her secret place, in the hollow set into the rising ground that surrounded the Cracker – the name given by the folk of Moxley to a flooded cavern in the earth that had once been a mine shaft. She remembered the light breeze that had blown across the open heath, how it had touched a fern to her cheek. Sketching had been the one real interest in her life, and this pool with its surround of softly rising ground was a favourite location. In the darkness of her room she saw it now in her mind: the sun glinting like a million golden sequins on the dark surface of the water. She remembered thinking how cross they would have been at home had they known where she was but she had told no one of her secret: of the hollow just deep enough to seat her, allowing the ferns to camouflage her presence, and keep her safe from prying eyes. It had been so peaceful there.

She had closed her eyes, lying back among the cool greenery. So quiet. Here she could be alone, shut away in her own tiny kingdom. Warm and comfortable, she lay cradled in her green world until an inquisitive insect landed on her nose. Brushing it away, she sat up, surprised to see the sun was considerably lower in the sky. She must have been asleep. There might be concern over her long absence.

Gathering the sketch pad and pencil she had laid beside her among the ferns, she made to stand up then fell back as a movement in the water, near the far bank, caught her eye.

She had not seen what it was that had caused the widening ring of ripples now spreading over its glassy surface but it was not a fish, of that she was certain.

Hidden by the curtain of ferns she had watched the water, waiting for whatever it was to break the surface.

Then it came. In one glorious surge, arms lifted to the sky, tiny drops of water showering like a cloud of diamonds from dark hair, the man's figure rose from the black depths.

Below her the crash of water echoed on the still summer air and Carys sucked in her breath, watching, as the figure launched itself into the air, landing almost flat on the surface and momentarily displaying a long muscular body before it was lost again beneath the water.

Warmth touched her cheeks with pink. Carys turned her head on the pillow, embarrassed to remember the way she didn't turn away. Instead she had sat transfixed, waiting for the figure to rise again like Neptune from the deep.

For several minutes she sat watching him sport, churning the silken water as he dived and rose then dived again.

She knew very well she should not be there, much less watching a man bathe. But the thought did not spur her to leave. Aware of the pencil gripped tightly in her hand, she began instead to sketch – marking every line with movements as fluid as the bather below her; capturing the litheness of his movements, the sheer joy of his communion with the water, the perfect beauty of his body as it emerged, arms raised, head slightly turned towards her.

Carys felt again that catch in her throat as the head stayed turned to her for a long second, and the ripple of fear that sang along her nerves at the thought of being discovered.

But he had dived again, pushing himself upward then curving that strong body into a surface dive that carried him from her sight down into the black satiny waters.

Held almost as in some unseen trap she had waited for the figure to rise once more.

But it did not.

Carys turned her face to the window, seeing the moon hanging like a great yellow lantern in a sky as dark as those waters, and her eyes probed its blackness as she had the depths of the Cracker.

But still the figure did not rise.

Anxiety stifling her breath, she had stared at the still dark water, its glassy surface unbroken by even the tiniest ripple.

She remembered how moments had ticked into seconds and seconds into eternity and still the air had remained in her lungs, held there almost as if, by sheer will-power, her suspended breath had filled the man's body, holding him safe from the encroaching waters.

'Hey!'

The remembered shout caused her to release her breath, as it had then, forcing it from between her tight lips, leaving her head reeling and her lungs aching as on that day.

'Hey, you!'

The second shout, angry this time, had cleared her head instantly. Without realising, she had risen to her feet while watching for him to surface and now from the opposite side of the pool he watched her. Before she could prevent it her eyes had swept the length of him, standing naked as Adam must have stood at his creation. Then, embarrassment flooding her, she grabbed her bonnet and fled.

Regaining the path that would lead her home, she pushed her drawing pad between her knees, holding it secure, while with her pencil between her teeth she tied on her bonnet, smoothing the curls that had blown awry in her mad dash from the pool.

Who was he? Who was the man who had swum the width of the Cracker underwater? Alone on the narrow path that led from the village across the open stretch of countryside to Holyhead House, Carys released her sketch pad and pencil then hitched her skirts calf-high. He could be any one of the Moxley men. Many of them used the flooded mine shaft as a place to wash and swim during summer. But, more importantly, did *he* know her? The Cracker was wide and the sun had been behind her, casting her face into shadow, but had light and distance been enough . . . or in spite of both had he recognised her for Meshac Beddows's daughter?

The dull thud of a horse's hoofs on the grass broke in on her thoughts: her father coming from the workshops. He used this path whenever he went there on horseback. She had hitched her skirts a little higher, breaking into a run towards the sound – that at least would furnish an excuse for her unusually red cheeks. Then she had stopped. The sight of the huge black horse, its rider sitting easily in the saddle, pulled her up sharply. The rider was most definitely not her father.

'So.' Tall even in the saddle, the man had brought down his crop against his gloved hand, eyes insolently roving over her. 'You didn't stay to thank me.'

'Thank you?' Carys answered, letting her skirts drop. 'I am unaware of any need to thank you for anything, sir.'

'No?' His glance had lifted to meet hers. Carys turned her face from the window, suddenly remembering the feeling his eyes had aroused in her.

'Do you always take what you want then leave without thanks or payment?'

'Payment?' She had looked up at the face way above her own, a face without a trace of friendship, as hard as it was handsome. 'I am at a loss to understand you. Now, if you will excuse me, I am expected at Holyhead House.' If the mention of Meshac Beddows's large red-brick house sprawled along the top of Moxley Hill was meant to make him move aside and allow her to pass, it failed miserably. The great black horse had stood like a living wall in her way.

'So you work at the House, do you?' The rays of the sinking sun touched his dark hair with a ring of red-gold. 'And your afternoon off is spent watching naked men swim. Then you run away without thanking them for entertaining you – or do you pay for your amusement?'

Something in those dark eyes had warned of danger. Carys remembered looking quickly across the rough uneven landscape. Even if her father were already home, surely some of the pitmen would be making their way to the cottages on the far side of the heath? But as she looked she knew it was too far for any shout of hers to be heard. She had stepped aside then, beginning to run, leaving the path to cut across the heath towards home, her skirts flattened against her legs. But she had gone only yards before the horse once again cut across her path.

'So you do leave without payment!' In her memory she saw

again the huge black horse and heard its whinny of complaint as its rider jerked the reins. 'Has no one ever told you that is bad manners?'

Lifting a hand to her throat, Carys rubbed at it. Fear seemed once more to hold her in its grip.

'And . . . has no one ever told you that to harass a woman is more than bad manners? It . . . it's criminal.'

'Harass!' He had laughed low in his throat. 'Is requiring payment for one's services harassment?'

'I . . . I was not watching you.' A fleck of foam from the horse's mouth drifted on to Carys's cheek. 'Not in the way you appear to think,' she added, brushing away the spittle.

Her sudden movement had caused the horse to shy but the man had it back under control before she could take advantage of the diversion.

'And in what way do I appear to be thinking?'

Beneath the shadowed eaves of the room Carys's face flamed as the man's slightly cynical smile had caused it to flame there on Moxley Heath.

'I . . . not . . . not in a manner becoming to a gentleman!' She had been angry at the insolent way he stared at her.

'Maybe I am not a gentleman, and you are no lady. After all, clothes do not make the man, if I have remembered the saying correctly.'

In her mind Carys saw again the slight curve of his mouth, the proud set of his body as with one hand he held the huge horse to his will. The fine lawn shirt thrown on with too much haste to fasten across the chest, the corded fawn trousers and coffee-coloured coat, masking him with the trappings of civility, masking yet not hiding man.

'You remember correctly.' Her answer had been sharp, made to cover the fear that had risen in her as he barred her way. 'The clothes you wear have quality and refinement. The man, I think, has none.'

She had seen amusement gleam in eyes black as night as he leaned towards her, his short riding crop lifting the collar of her dress.

'And these trappings?' His voice was low, with the texture of velvet. 'Does not their quality belie the woman beneath them? A woman who hides herself in the grass to watch a man bathe naked in a pool?'

Carys closed her eyes against the picture in her mind but it refused to fade. He had let the crop trail from her throat down to her breast, halting there as his devil's eyes had stared into her own.

'I was not hiding.' She had slapped the crop away at the same time, stepping backward on the rough uneven path that skirted the pool.

'No!' He straightened in the saddle but his eyes still held hers. 'But you were not exactly proclaiming your presence on the hillside. Not, that is, as long as you thought you might be seen. If not hiding, what am I supposed to think you were doing?'

'I don't care what you think!'

She had turned then, determined to go back the way she had come; she could skirt the Cracker and come out of the hollow on the opposite side. From there it was just a short way to Bull Lane. There were sure to be people about the Fever Hospital or the few houses grouped around the old coal mines at Cock Heath.

But quick as she had been, he had been quicker, guiding the horse to cut off her escape.

'Then I think you *were* watching me.' The black eyes swept over her from her head to her feet then rose again with slow insolence to her face. 'And what is sauce for your goose must equally be sauce for my gander. You have seen me naked, now I must see you in that same delightful state . . . so, miss, off with these.'

He had reached forward with the crop, hooking it in her skirts and lifting them above her knees. Stepping back and slapping at the crop all at the same time, she lost her balance and fell sprawling on to her back.

'Now that is most enticing to any man.' His smile had faded as he stared down at her, sprawled open-legged, her petticoats bunched about her waist. 'And with any other man you may not escape so lightly next time, young miss, so my advice is: stay away from that pool!'

Then he had gone. Carys opened her eyes. Beyond her window the moon slipped behind a bank of cloud, hiding its image in grey softness, disappearing as he had disappeared. But his image had refused to be hidden; it had stayed, stubbornly clear, in her heart.

For four years those coal black eyes had stared at her from the depths of her soul.

'So you be in the business of selling enamels? Then you could do no better than come to Bilston. Make the finest enamels in the world do the folk of Bilston, and the ones that work for Meshac Beddows makes the finest of them all. You'll do no better, and you can take that from me.'

Reuben Fereday looked at the faces of the guests seated about the dining table at Holyhead House. Each time he came to Bilston, Meshac invited him back here to this house, and each time he accepted the invitation. But why did he come so often? He could place larger orders with Meshac Beddows's works, orders that would reduce the need for his visits to one a year instead of one a month. So why didn't he? He smiled at a pale-faced guest whose yellow hair hung like tallow candles about her neck, and from the corner of his eye saw her mother beam from her to Meshac's wife. But there was no answering smile on that woman's attractive face. So why did he come? He felt brown eyes fix on him. Maria Beddows would think it was for her. She had tried hard enough to gather him into her net, as he supposed she gathered every man who came into her circle. The woman had looks, in fact most would call her beautiful, but for him that fine-boned face and those inviting eyes held no attraction other than as the wife of a friend.

No, it was not this woman who caused him to return to Bilston so regularly or to haunt Moxley Heath with every visit. It was the memory of a young girl with the wind in her hair and defiance in her eyes. A girl he guessed to be no more than twenty who had watched him as he swam in that pool, and then denied it. It was to find her, to see her again, that he came with such regularity. She had said she was returning to Holyhead House, this house, yet on no visit here had he seen her. That in itself would not be surprising if the girl were one of the lesser maids, but her bearing, the way she had carried herself, the way she had stared boldly into his face, the answers she'd snapped out with no trace of the hesitation or servility that could be expected in a servant, all made him doubt it. Besides which she'd carried pencil and sketching block and Meshac Beddows had spoken proudly of a daughter whose drawings he had adapted for use on many of the boxes he manufactured. But if the girl was his daughter, and if he did have the pride in her he seemed to have, why was she never present in this house? And even more of a mystery, why had Maria never spoken of having a daughter?

'Like I says, Fereday, you won't never buy finer work than can be got from Meshac Beddows.'

'I know that, Mr Turner.' Reuben drew his mind back to the conversation. 'I have only the best in my gallery in Birmingham. That is why I buy Bilston enamels, Meshac Beddows's enamels in particular.'

'You makes a good choice and all. Be a shame you don't deal in iron and steel, we could have done business happen you did.'

'What *do* you have in that gallery of yours, Mr Fereday?' Reuben felt the delicate probing of Amy Turner's question. She wanted to know the depth of the pockets of the man she saw as a husband for her daughter, a man she seemed to prefer above the one seated beside the girl, the one introduced to him as Ryder Tempal.

'I have many beautiful things, Mrs Turner, mine is a gallery of fine art. I have paintings, wonderful glassware, fine jewellery . . . but they are all insignificant against the beauty of the ladies seated at this table. I would deem it an honour were you to pay a visit there.'

'Well said, lad.'

Maria watched her husband drain his glass of Madeira then sign for it to be refilled. Let him drink, despite the doctor's warning. The more he drank, the easier would be the task she had set herself.

'You should go, Maria.' Meshac picked up his refilled glass. 'You could buy yourself a trinket, only make sure it don't be no enamel. I can get them doo-dads for free.'

Maria allowed herself to smile with her guests but her eyes were as calculating as her thoughts. This could be a perfect excuse for going to Birmingham. God knows, she found it hard enough to think them up any more.

'I should like nothing more.' Maria deliberately kept her gaze on her husband. 'But you so rarely seem to have the time to spare, my dear, you are kept so busy at the works and I could not go alone. I would be terrified at the thought. Why, I fear going alone to my dressmaker and she is only on the borders of the city.'

'Then perhaps you would allow me to escort you, Mrs Beddows?'

'Arrh, that be it, you take 'er for me, Ryder lad. Only make sure 'er don't give all my money to young Fereday.'

He had taken her bait as she'd known he would. Maria felt a warm glow of satisfaction. Meshac had given her the opportunity to be with Ryder, an opportunity she would not waste on visiting any fine art gallery for more than an hour, though that much would have to be spent there to avoid questions.

'And you, Miss Turner?' Ryder smiled at the girl beside him. 'Will you come with us?'

'I will take my daughter with me,' Amy Turner answered quickly. 'I too shall be accepting Mr Fereday's invitation . . . before very long, I hope.'

Reuben smiled inwardly. An inventory of his assets? It was as clear a signal to him as her rejection of his offer should be to Ryder Tempal. But why was she averse to the man paying attention to her daughter? Unless . . . He caught the glance that passed between Maria and her guest. He need ponder that question no longer, the answer was clear. Ryder Tempal was Maria Beddows's preserve.

'I look forward to it,' Reuben answered. 'I look forward to both of you visiting the gallery, but for now I must ask you to excuse me? I promised my aunt I would be back for ten. She retires early these days and it is not often I get to see her.'

'Your aunt be the widow of Oliver Mountford? Had the making of nails and screws along Carters Green and a house up at Hill Top, if I remembers.'

'There is nothing amiss with your memory, Mr Turner.' Reuben placed his napkin alongside his untouched glass. 'My uncle was Oliver Mountford and my aunt still has the running of Mountford Nail and Screw at Carters Green, and still lives at Hill Top.'

'Ee, lad, I clean forgot!' Meshac tipped Madeira into his mouth before rising from the table. 'Noah, get yourself a cigar and a brandy while I show Fereday the paintings he come to look at.'

'Why don't you relax with Noah and our guests, my dear?' Maria rose as quickly as her husband. 'I can show Mr Fereday the paintings, and I am certain Mr Tempal would take Edwina for a turn in the garden though he must not keep her too long in the summerhouse.' Maria's eyes gleamed as they met those of Ryder Tempal. He would not try his tricks on Noah Turner's daughter; his sights were set on other quarry.

'I'll do that if you have no objection, Fereday? The wife can show you all you wish to see.' Meshac shuffled from the table.

And that I hold no wish to see. Reuben followed the others from the dining room then turned towards the library as Maria led the way.

'Meshac had the paintings brought in here.' She opened the doors that gave on to a large room, its walls lined with books. 'He thought it would be more practical for you to view them in one room rather than trail through several.'

Reuben crossed to a long mahogany side table set in the one windowed alcove of the room where a dozen or so miniature oil paintings, each mounted in matching frames, had been set out for his inspection.

'These are exquisite!' He picked up one that was obviously a portrait of Maria, hair and eyes dark against the cream of her shoulders, the line of her amber gown just showing at the base of the frame. 'Who was the artist? A member of the Royal Academy?'

'No, no one of such distinction.' Maria picked up another of the miniatures, this of a woman with a flat straw bonnet over greying hair that escaped the hat in straggly tendrils, while the eyes retained a thousand secrets. 'This one is the flower seller that sits at the gate of St Leonard's church in Bilston.'

She handed him the miniature, taking the first one from him and replacing it on the table.

'Whoever painted these deserves that distinction.' Reuben held the miniature closer to the light of the gasolier. 'I swear Turner himself has no more delicate touch or finer appreciation of colour.' He glanced along the table, hungry to see the beauty of each small picture. 'Just look at this one!' He took up a painting of a pool set in a hollow below rising ground thick with ferns. He had seen that pool, bathed in its waters the day he had returned hot and dusty from Meshac Beddows's workshops. This was the pool where the girl he was searching for had sat watching him, and where he had caught up with her. Suddenly everything seemed to fall into place in his mind. The girl was returning to Holyhead House, the home of Meshac Beddows. She carried a sketch pad and pencils. Meshac had once boasted of his daughter's skills as an artist. These paintings had not been done by an accredited artist. It all pointed one way . . . Reuben's hand shook slightly as he replaced the painting with the others. The artist had to be the daughter Meshac spoke of, she had to be Meshac's child.

Forcing his voice to remain easy, he looked at Maria. 'These are exactly what I am looking for. They will make beautiful cameos mounted in a gold setting – that is, if your husband's enamellers are capable of reproducing the same quality as the originals? I take it the artist will have no objection to his work being so reproduced?'

'She won't have . . .' Maria stopped herself quickly. She had not meant to give any clue as to the painter's identity. 'The . . . the designs belong to my husband. They were done by one of the men in the workshop, I don't remember which one.'

She could be referring to any of the buildings referred to as workshops. Reuben thought of the warren of tumbledown dwellings whose outhouses had all become workshops complete with bellows and furnace; the women hammering lumps of metal-bearing rock into powder, hour after soul-destroying hour; their children sitting on the floor cleaning plates of tin or bronze before carrying them to their father who applied the powdered oxides mixed with water as a paste to the metal, then placed them in the furnace where oxide and metal would fuse. Maria was trying to tell him this work came from one of the dark, vermin-infested places those people called home and workshop, but Reuben knew it did not. The painter of these miniatures was not one of Meshac Beddows's workmen, it was Meshac Beddows's daughter.

He faced the woman who had brought him into the library, seeing apprehension in her deep brown eyes, and knew his suppositions to be correct.

'Meshac told me his daughter was a very talented artist. In fact, he said she was responsible for several of the designs I have bought from him, and you say this artist is female?'

Reuben saw the flicker of alarm shadow Maria's eyes and the slight tightening of her mouth before she turned to the table holding the miniatures. He was right. These paintings were the work of her daughter, so why deny it? And why had she not once, during any of his visits here, mentioned the existence of the girl?

'Could these also be her work?'

'Possibly.' Maria turned towards the door. It would be a mistake to deny what he asked, he would simply go to Meshac and that would spark off more of her husband's doubts and queries as to why the girl had never returned home after being sent away to school. School . . . Maria felt a twinge of guilt then pushed it away. It had to be a convent, it had to be a place of no return. Though the girl *had* left, she *had* returned to the world. But she would never return to Moxley, that much at least Maria had achieved.

'But you are not sure?' Reuben's glance followed her.

'No, Mr Fereday, I am not sure.' Maria's cool voice was a warning for him to question her no further.

'Then might I perhaps meet your daughter, ask her myself if this is her work?' He ignored the message in her voice.

The door already open, Maria turned to look back at him, a triumphant smile touching her mouth. 'I am afraid that will not be possible, Mr Fereday. Our daughter has taken Holy Orders.'

Chapter Five

'Be sure you be back here by the time it be six o'clock, my wench, or you will be hearing from me. And be sure to keep an eye on Carys. That Portway Road be hardly a fit place for young women to walk on their own, what with Irish navvies and Gypsy Fields none too far off.'

'We'll be fine, Mrs Bates.'

'Arrh, I knows *you* will, Alice Withers,' Martha Bates murmured, watching the two young women run across the yard and past the carriage house towards the heath. 'Ain't you I be so concerned for. A bevy of brothers taught you to look out for yourself, but the other one . . . that wench don't have the appearance of being able to fight off unwelcome hands.'

'You'll like me mother.' Clear of the grounds of Ridge House, Alice slowed to a walk. 'Her rattles on a bit, and her tongue gets the better of her at times, like Mrs B. reckons mine do.' Alice grinned, showing strong even teeth. 'But her don't mean no harm by her gossip, and after all, that be the only thing women in these parts can indulge theirselves in. Ain't never money to spare for anything else.'

'That is the very reason I think I ought not to visit your home.' Carys had been unsure from the first about imposing upon Alice's mother. Money in the Withers household was too hard come by to spend any of it on entertaining her. 'I do not want to put your mother to any trouble.' It was not really what she wanted to say but to put it more bluntly could give offence to Alice and that was the last thing she wanted.

'You won't be puttin' her to no trouble.' Alice bent to pick a daisy, twisting the fragile stem between her fingers as she walked. 'But you will put her out good and proper if her hears you talk like that. We ain't got much but what we do have me mother gives willing. Her likes having folk to call, 'specially somebody posh like yourself.'

'But I'm not posh!' Carys laughed, something that came more easily as the days at Ridge House went by, giving her a sense of being wanted, a sense she had not known for so long.

'Oh, but you am,' Alice insisted. 'You talks so lah-di-dah. But in a nice way,' she hastened to add. 'I wishes I could talk like you do.'

'There is nothing wrong with the way you speak.'

'Suppose not.' Alice twirled the tiny flower. 'Be strange if I talked any different, coming from the Black Country, but I still thinks it would be nice if I could talk all pound-noteish now and again.'

'Pound-noteish?' Carys laughed again. 'What on earth does that mean?'

'You knows. Pound-noteish . . . bay-windowed . . . lah-di- . . . posh . . . like gentry. Fancy being able to talk to a lad like that!' Stopping, she turned to Carys, the daisy held in an affected pose, her mouth pulled into a prim line. 'Ho, thah you be, my deah. Do come and sit dahn. Take the weight orff while I rings the maid for tea.' She paused. 'What do you think?'

'I think perhaps not.' Carys's laugh floated over the silent heath. 'I much prefer the Alice Withers we have. Besides, talking as posh as that would have the lads thinking you too grand for them to come courting.'

'Ain't none come yet, posh talk or not.' Her smile fading, Alice walked on. 'Seems I don't have any lad's eye.'

'I wouldn't see that as being the truth.' Carys caught the other girl's arm, tucking her own beneath it. 'More like there are several just waiting for the right moment to approach you.'

'Well, I wish one of them would shift his shins. I already be more'n one an' twenty. That would be an old maid in me mother's times.'

'But these are not her times.' Carys squeezed the girl's arm. 'In a few months it will be nineteen hundred, a new century, a new beginning, that will bring more for women than marriage following on the cradle. Twenty-one will not be the end for a woman still unmarried.'

'Try telling me mother that.' Alice sounded gloomy. 'Every time I goes home her asks if there be a lad calling on me yet, and her face gets as long as a fourpenny hock when I says there be nobody.'

'Then don't tell her that.'

'What! Tell me mother a lie?' Alice dropped the flower, her brown skirts brushing it aside as it fell to the earth. 'Ee, Carys, I couldn't! Her would know the minute I tried it. You can't pull the wool over me mother's eyes. Well, not for long you can't.'

'I did not say lie to her.'

Ahead of them a skylark rose from the ground, the sound of its call spreading over the stillness, and Carys followed its ascent towards the soft powder-puff clouds.

'I just said, do not tell her there is no one calling on you . . . yet.'

'Yet?' Alice turned a puzzled look on the girl walking beside her. 'But that be meaning there is somebody wanting to, and that be a lie.'

'It is only a lie if you say it,' Carys answered. 'But you would not be saying it, you would merely be implying it and therefore you would not be telling your mother a lie.'

'Well, if her starts on me today, might be as I'll just try that what you said . . . imp . . . imp . . .'

'Implying.' Carys smiled.

'Arrh, that!' Alice scooped up a fresh daisy. 'Might be it'll bring me a lad an' all.' Her smile returning, she plucked a petal from the flower, watching it float gently downward as she released it. 'He loves me . . . he loves me not . . .'

Their arms interlocked, they walked on, laughter echoing behind them.

'We won't 'ave long to spend at me mother's,' Alice said as they left Holloway Bank, following a left fork that took them into Potters Lane. 'It be a fair step to Brick Kiln Lane an' we be only halfway yet.'

Carys kept up with her friend's quickened pace as they passed the somewhat dilapidated Railway Hotel then picked their way gingerly over the tram rails before branching into Portway Road.

'I never comes back along here on me own, specially if it be dark,' Alice confided, glancing covertly at the long rows of small houses separated at intervals by uninviting alleys. 'This be a rough area, mostly Irish brought in when the Birmingham Navigation was being built. It was thought they would take theirselves back off to their own country once the canal was finished, but they still be here an' that has led to more than one lot of trouble in the town. The men here see the navvies as taking jobs that should rightly go to them, and when they don't there's trouble.'

A woman with a shawl pulled tight about her head stepped from the shadow of an alley, flinging a bowl of greasy water on to the narrow street. She stood, one hand on her hip, staring after the hurrying girls.

'That be one o' their women,' Alice said, pulling Carys closer to her. 'They be handy with their fists just like their men, it wouldn't pay to argue with the like o' that one.'

'If you never go home this way alone, how will we return to Hill Top?' Carys asked, hoping Alice would have an answer that would not include the Portway Road.

'Well, none of me brothers will be home, they'll be working

till seven, but not to fret. For a halfpenny we can ride the tram up from the market place to Hill Top.'

'Ride the tram!' Carys would have stood still but Alice pulled her on. 'Then why didn't we take it coming down?'

Alice giggled. 'What, and have you miss the thrill of walking the Portway!'

'Alice.' Carys followed her friend, taking the right-hand turning that led them past the black looming mass that was the church of Saint James, bringing them into Brick Kiln Lane. 'Next time, will you ask whether I want thrilling?'

'I knowed me mother would like you.'

Later they sat side by side, the wooden slatted seats of the steam tram jarring their bones as it grumbled its way up the slope.

Alice's mother had welcomed her, Carys thought, and had talked endlessly as Alice said she would, but her eyes had been sharp enough, taking in Carys's shabby coat and worn boots though she had asked no question as to her background. No, she had asked nothing. Carys watched the line of houses break off, giving way to open heath. But that did not mean she had none to ask.

''Tis a pity me dad and brothers were still at the brick yard,' Alice went on. 'But p'raps Mrs B. will give we a Sunday afternoon afore long and then you can meet the whole bloomin' family of Witherses.'

'Tickets, please!'

Carys glanced at the blue-uniformed conductor, his generous moustache twitching as he smiled down at them. She was glad his interruption had put a timely end to her need to reply.

'So where do you two pretty young ladies be goin' then?'

'Hill Top.' Alice fumbled in her pocket, taking out a small purse. 'Two halfpennies to Hill Top.'

Taking the penny from her, the conductor dropped it into the leather bag at his waist. Then giving the handle of his ticket machine two brisk turns, he punched out their tickets.

'There you be, me wench.' He handed both tickets to Alice, his moustache wiggling as he smiled. 'It be a pity you wasn't riding on further, give we a chance to get us selves acquainted.'

'You'll be getting yourself acquainted all right,' a woman almost buried beneath her hessian shopping bag and a large wicker basket covered with a blue cloth, called from the rear. 'Acquainted with your missis's foot if 'er catches you chattin' to the wenches!'

'You wouldn't tell 'er though, would you, Dolly?' Beneath the shiny peak of his cap the man's eyebrows were raised. 'Not with you an' me being lovers all these years.'

'Lovers!' The woman's jowls shook as her laughter rang out. 'I'd rather go to bed with a half pint of old ale any day.'

'Is that right?' The conductor raised a hand, fastening his fingers on the leather cord that ran the length of the tram. 'And here's me thinkin' you rode this tram every day all on account of my charm.'

'That bloomin' hill be the reason I rides this tram every day.' The woman gathered the bag from the seat beside her. 'Charm I can get without the paying of a penny.'

'Go on with you, Dolly!' He pulled the cord and at the front of the tram a bell jangled. 'You know you wouldn't miss my smile for a shilling, let alone a penny.'

At the touch of the brakes the tram shuddered to a halt and the woman hauled herself along the confined space between its double row of benches, dragging the well-filled hessian bag behind her.

'I wouldn't pay a shilling to ride with the King himself,' she puffed, easing herself and her bag from the tram to the roadway, 'and he could smile all the way from here to Buckingham Palace.'

Handing both girls from the tram in the wake of the woman and her bags, the smiling conductor hopped back on to the platform, giving the cord a double pull and holding on to the handrail as the driver released the brake and the tram lurched forward. He raised his free hand in a wave as the tram pulled away.

'Was the conductors as friendly as that on them Birmingham trams?' Alice asked, returning the wave with a grin before she began to follow the faint track across the heath that would lead them to Ridge House.

Carys glanced to the left, seeing the ground slope away to where the town lay, its grimed buildings smothered beneath the pall of black smoke that seemed to issue from every part of it. She carried her glance further to where Moxley lay beyond the limits of her vision. 'Keep away,' Maria had told her, and she had done so, not daring to defy the mother who had locked her away for four long years, a mother who in all that time had not once come to see her.

'I don't know.' She turned away, feeling the pull of her home across the dividing heath and knowing she could not yield to it. 'I never rode on any of them. That day we met on the railway station was my first day out of the convent and I came there with my mother in a horse cab.'

'Of course, I was forgetting about you being in a convent.' Stubbing her toe on a stone protruding from the ground, Alice stumbled, laughing as she regained her footing only to frown when she looked at the scuff mark the stone had scratched across the toe cap of her boot.

'Bugger it!' Spitting on her fingers, she bent and rubbed them across the offending mark. 'These be my best boots an' all!' Catching the look on Carys's face, she burst into laughter. 'Ee, they wouldn't have me in no nunnery, not if they heard me choice of language!'

'Mrs Bates will have you in the coal cellar if *she* hears it.' Carys smiled, finding the other girl's grin too infectious to resist.

'Oh, I minds my Ps and Qs when I knows Mrs B. is around. But, seriously, what was it like never getting outside that convent? I mean, didn't it drive you mad?'

'I thought at first it would,' Carys answered. 'But after a while I got used to it.'

'Lor', I'm sure I never could.' Satisfied she had done the best she could to cover the damage to her boot, Alice continued to walk in the direction of the house. 'They must all be saints who live in them places?'

Not all of them. In her mind Carys saw those eyes . . . the passion in them changing instantly to fear and then more slowly to hatred, a hatred that had turned four years of Carys's life into a living nightmare.

It had been only the second month after her entry to the Convent of the Holy Child. One of the nuns had sent her from the infirmary, where she had been set to scrubbing floors, to bring the Mistress of Novices to the bed of one of the sisters who had contracted tuberculosis and was on the point of death.

'Oh, this is the time it would choose to happen, with Sister Mary Immaculata away to the Mother House for three days.' The harassed nun had looked up from tending the sick woman, her eye falling on Carys. 'Leave that, child,' she ordered. 'Go you to the room of Sister Veronica. Father Hawthorne from Saint Saviour's church will be with her arranging the service in the chapel. Tell them Sister Thérèse is making to leave this world and ask the Father if he will come and give her the Last Rites. Quick, child, don't gawp like an idiot . . . go!'

And she had gone, running through the silent corridors breaking the rule that forbade it, ignoring the admonitions of the nuns she passed until she came to the room the Mistress of Novices used as an office and without thinking to knock, opened the door.

Sister Veronica was there as she had been told but she was not seated at the large plain oak desk. Instead she stood against the far wall, both arms stretched in a wide angle over her head, naked except for the wimple that still covered her hair. Eyes closed, her head arched slightly backward, she moaned with each thrust of her body, thrusts that matched those of the priest, naked as herself, who lunged into her.

Carys remembered the catch of her own breath, loud in her throat, and over the priest's shoulder saw that Sister Veronica's eyes had opened.

That had been the start of the torment. A constant hounding that had kept at her from the beginning to the end of every long day, days of work almost without cease from getting up at four in the morning until the evening meditation when she was allowed to sit for an hour to read the Bible before Compline, the last service of the day. As it ended at ten she was released to drop exhausted into her bed.

It had only been on leaving the convent that she had come to understand Sister Veronica's hatred of her, or rather to realise it was not so much hatred as fear; fear that Carys would speak of what she had witnessed, that the life the woman had forged for herself within the security of those walls would be snatched away. That fear had eaten away at her until she could think of nothing other than reducing Carys's own life to a state where she could no longer endure it; she had known only that to be utterly safe she must drive away the girl who had seen her fornication, seen the breaking of her vows.

'Well, I'm no saint.' Alice caught her hand, pulling Carys after her as she broke into a run. 'And if you have to live in one of them places to qualify for a halo, then you can keep it.'

If only she were free they would marry. Those had been Ryder Tempal's words to her as they had lain in that hotel bed together just a week ago. He loved her, he had said as he rolled her beneath him, and had kept on saying it as they made love again and again.

Ryder loved her.

But did he? Wouldn't it be nearer the truth to say Ryder loved money, any man's money, and would take any man's wife or daughter to get it?

She had been right to suppose there had been more to the attentions he had paid Meshac's child than simple flattery, and the same could be said of his performance tonight; he had played the game right up to his armpits, almost charming the bloomers off that mealy-faced girl of the Turners right there at the dinner table.

Maria pulled the pins from her hair, letting the silken weight of it tumble about her shoulders.

Ryder Tempal was looking for a wife, one who would bring him money. But that girl on whom he had danced attendance tonight would not be that wife, nor would the one he had tried to rape four years ago. He had set his sights on Meshac Beddows's money and that he could have, but not Meshac Beddows's daughter. The money would come only with Meshac Beddows's wife.

Behind Maria her husband coughed the lung-rattling cough of a man who had spent too many years in the dust of frit being pounded into powder for the painting of enamels, breathing in the oxides and silica until his lungs were half filled with the noxious black dust.

Twenty years she had listened to that cough; twenty years in which every moment she had wanted to silence it forever, to rid herself of the man almost twice her age to whom her parents had married her, despite the fact they knew she had no love for him.

Maria watched him now in the mirror of her dressing table, his domed head balanced like a huge pink egg on a stumpy neck. His shoulders were stooped from endless hours spent bent over a table carefully mixing the precise balance of powdered frit and metallic oxides or poring over designs for enamelled boxes and caskets. He had given her all the comfort his wealth could buy but still she had not loved him. And her daughter? Maria's hand closed over the beautifully enamelled hairbrush but she did not pick it up.

Did she love the child this man had fathered on her? Had she ever loved her? The answer, if she had to make it, was no. There had never been any love in her for the child she had felt had been forced upon her, a child expected of the union, her side of the bargain! Maria's gaze moved from the man standing behind her, coming again to her own face and body. She had never wanted a child, never wanted anything that would threaten the beauty of her body. Motherhood! Eyes on eyes, Maria smiled at herself. They could keep it!

But the child had been pretty, right from birth she had held the promise of beauty, and now that promise was being fulfilled. Day by day the girl came nearer to being a beautiful woman, a beautiful chestnut-haired, amber-eyed woman. One to rival Maria herself.

Her hand tightened on the hairbrush. That was the thought that had consumed her like fire each time Ryder Tempal had smiled at her daughter, each time he took her arm or suggested a turn about the garden. A beauty that would rival her own, detract from the attention that had always been hers. That was what would happen should her daughter return to this house. In the mirror Maria watched the shadows take her eyes, watched the rise of that emotion that bit into her with the strength of a ravening beast . . .

Behind her Meshac coughed again and Maria's hand tightened about the hairbrush.

She knew what that emotion was. If she were honest with herself she could put a name to the feeling which flared each time Ryder Tempal looked at another woman, any woman, the feeling that made her wish them dead.

Was that what she wanted for her own daughter? To see her dead! Maria's eyes shifted, fastening on the slim column of darkness in the gap between the heavy drapes pulled across the windows, the thought hammering in her mind, demanding an answer. Was that the measure of her love for Ryder Tempal? Did she desire him so much she would be prepared to kill for him?

Her glance sliding back to her own mirrored reflection,

Maria lifted the brush to her hair, the answer already stamped on her brain.

Yes, she would kill for him . . . if she had to.

'I'll be away to my room.'

Maria watched her husband weave uncertainly through the door that connected her bedroom with his.

'I will come to say goodnight, dear.'

In the mirror her reflection smiled. Meshac had taken to sleeping in a separate bedroom since that evening some two months ago when he and Reuben Fereday had sat for several hours discussing enamels, during which time Meshac had paid a great deal of attention to the brandy decanter. That night she had taken a step toward achieving her dream.

Meshac's heart was not strong. They had known that for some time but it had not stopped Maria; in fact that weakness was the weapon she had used, that and Meshac's other weakness.

She had waited until she guessed he would be undressed and then had gone into his room. He had been standing with his nightshirt in his hand and she had apologised sweetly for coming upon him that way, but at the same time had released the strings of her silk négligée, letting it slip from her shoulders to display her own nakedness.

'I just wanted to say goodnight, dear,' she had murmured, standing still as his eyes had fixed on her. 'But I will leave if you wish?'

'No, I don't bloody wish!' Meshac's voice had been thick with his desire for her, a desire he could never deny himself.

Gathering up the silken folds she had held them across her breasts, eyelids lowered in a supposed shyness that even after more than twenty years could still hoodwink Meshac.

Dropping the nightshirt he had lumbered forward, catching her in his arms and bringing his mouth down hard against her own.

Maria lifted a hand to her mouth, wiping her fingers across the fullness of her lips as if to wipe away the memory.

She had stood there while one hand had squeezed her breast, the other kneading her naked bottom, and then she had taken his hands, drawing each slowly over her body before placing them at his sides. Then, with a quiet shushing of his protests, she leaned into him, her body brushing against his as she slid slowly to her knees.

Passing a hand about each of his thighs she had brought her mouth to a point just below his navel. She could hear the noise of his breathing, a ragged gasping that each kiss accentuated. Sliding her hands to the front of his thighs she moved them slowly, intimately, matching the movement to each kiss. upward toward the flesh jerking below her mouth.

She had felt him trembling, the noise of his breathing gradually becoming a fight for air. Then he had fallen, crashing heavily against the bed.

Snatching up her fallen robe, she had run back to her room then, being careful to close the door that connected it to Meshac's. Pulling repeatedly on the cord that rang for the housekeeper, she waited, using the minutes to fasten her night clothes, hiding the nakedness beneath.

Now, taking her hand from the hairbrush, Maria stood up. Releasing the ties of her turquoise silk night coat she stared at her body in the mirror. Two months ago the touch of that body had almost finished Meshac. He must not get excited, the doctor had said when he had been summoned. It was fortunate for her husband she had been awake and heard him fall and understandable that she had been too afraid of what she might find to go into his room herself. There must be no exertion, the doctor had explained tactfully, his heart would not stand up to any stress. Rest and quiet must be the order of the day for Meshac Beddows.

Touching a hand to her breast, Maria watched it slide slowly over her shapely waist – but the hand she felt was Ryder Tempal's.

Ryder! Maria's eyes lifted to their own reflection. Had tonight's performance with the Turner girl been a way of showing her he would not wait much longer? Was he showing her that if she were not free soon he would play elsewhere?

But there was Meshac!

Maria slid her hand sensually over her flat stomach.

He stood between her and Ryder.

The soft light of the oil lamp beside her bed bathed the room in mauve shadows and in the shadows Maria's eyes gleamed.

But Meshac had a weak heart. Meshac would not stand there much longer.

Chapter Six

'Eh, Mrs Bates, is he handsome?' Alice's eyes gleamed with interest across the supper table.

'Handsome as he ever was,' the older woman answered, a touch of affection in her voice. 'But then, he always was a nice-looking lad, right from being a babby, and always knew his manners. There was always a "thank you, Mrs Bates" from him whenever he was here, just the same as today. Popped his head round that door he did just afore he left this afternoon. "Thank you for tea, Mrs Bates," he said, just the same as always, arrh! A right well-mannered lad be the mistress's nephew, there be no airs and graces about him. Not like some as has been to this house.'

'Oh, I wish I'd been here!' Alice breathed.

'Would have made no odds if you had. Be no use you setting your sights on the like of Reuben Fereday, my wench, he be far above we. But like I says, he don't have no bob on hisself.'

'Don't you wish you had seen him?' Alice turned a dreamy look on Carys.

'Why would I want to see the mistress's nephew?' Carys sliced her cold beef into squares, popping one into her mouth.

'Why not?' Alice returned. 'You never knows? Might be he would take a shine to you. Lord knows you be pretty enough for any man to take his hat off for.'

'I doubt that, but it is nice of you to say so.'

'Now then, Alice Withers, don't you go putting ideas where they have no call to be.' Martha Bates set her knife and fork noisily on her plate. 'Don't do for young wenches to go around with their heads full of nonsense, and your head be fuller than most. Reuben Fereday won't have no interest in either of you two except for the interest any lad has for a pretty face and a trim waist, and that sort of interest brings nothing but trouble. So mark my words and no more talk of catching his eye. That way you will catch the mistress's eye and be out of a position. Think on that when you be dreaming your dreams!'

'All the same,' Alice whispered, grinning at Carys as they carried plates to the scullery sink, 'I still wishes I'd been here when he was. Ee, right good-looking is Reuben Fereday.'

'Don't be talking all night over the washing of them plates, there be the mistress's tray to bring down from her room.'

'Mrs Mountford is not unwell, is she?' Carys asked, returning to the kitchen, concern furrowing her brow. Virginia Mountford took each of her meals in the dining room despite living alone; this was the first time Carys had known the routine to be broken.

Untying her voluminous white apron and folding it ready for laundering, Martha settled herself into her favourite chair to the left of the kitchen range.

'No, the mistress be herself. Just said as she wanted nothing more to eat tonight. Now, Alice,' she glanced at the girl coming in from the scullery, drying the last of the water from her hands on her own apron, 'you bank up the fire while Carys fetches that tray downstairs, then you can tell me all about your afternoon.'

Carys had not remembered Virginia Mountford had a nephew. She skipped lightly up the imposing staircase of Ridge House, her steps soundless on the thick carpeting. But then, why should she? There had been no reason for her to do so. But even so, she wondered, was he handsome, this Reuben Fereday? And would he perhaps have 'taken a shine to her', as Alice had said?

Stepping along the landing, by the dim glow of the gas lamps that burned at each end, Carys glanced at the portrait that hung on the wall: a face framed with dark hair, and eyes of almost the same shade gazing out with a strong piercing stare that seemed alive. Virginia Mountford's father had had a strong handsome face, as strong and handsome as the man she had met that day on Moxley Heath. Carys had never seen him after that day but had not forgotten even the smallest line of his body as it broke from the water, or the exasperating curve of his mouth as he had lifted the collar of her gown with his whip; she had not forgotten the man whose similarity to the portrait hanging in this corridor was so striking. Could they be from the same family? Carys lifted her eyes, almost expecting to see the same faint line of a scar above the right eyebrow that the man on the heath had borne. Had the man she had spoken to been Reuben Fereday, nephew to Virginia Mountford? Surely no mere accident of nature could account for such a striking similarity of feature?

Moving on towards the door to her mistress's room, Carys's thoughts raced. If the man who had been to Ridge House this afternoon were the man she had sketched, would he have recognised her? Did he remember as she did? And if he did, what then? She had told him she was returning to Holyhead House so would he want to know how she came to be here? Lifting her hand, Carys tapped on the door.

It was as well she had not been present at Ridge House this afternoon.

In the soft shadowy light of her bedroom Maria stood listening to the silence. She had dismissed the staff, giving them permission to retire as soon as the last of the guests had left, the Turner girl simpering up at Ryder as he fawned over her.

But he would not fawn so much after tonight. After tonight his attention would be all for her.

She listened again. There was no sound of movement. She would not be disturbed.

Almost on tiptoe she crossed the room, her hand fastening on the door that separated her from Meshac. He had almost died that night two months ago when she had pretended her need of him – almost died of the lust she could so easily rouse in him. Tonight there would be no almost, tonight would see her freed.

Turning the handle, she pushed open the door. Beside the huge oak bed burned a single lamp, casting a pool of sallow light over the face of the man who lay there.

'Meshac,' she called, her voice husky with promise. 'Are you asleep, my dear?'

On the white pillow his head turned, and across the dimness of the space that separated them Maria saw the leap of desire in his eyes. He had courted the wine and brandy decanter all evening yet still the urge to make love to her sprang readily, and as on that other occasion this suited Maria's purpose to perfection; the stronger his desire for her, the easier it would be to achieve her objective.

Crossing slowly to the bed, she stood with the pale light playing across the ivory swell of her breasts beneath the parted turquoise silk.

'I could not sleep.' She bent over him, brushing his mouth with her own. 'Did I do wrong to come to you, Meshac?'

'You never do wrong for me.' He threw off the covers, his speech slurred as he made to rise from the bed.

'Don't get up, dear.' Maria touched her fingers to the remaining fasteners on her night coat, pulling the ribbons with excruciating slowness, eyes watching the changing emotions play across her husband's face, seeing his fingers open and close with the promise of stroking the nakedness revealed as her gown fell fully open.

'Maria, you be so beautiful.' Meshac's mouth hung open,

his stare devouring her from head to toe as he held out his arms to her.

'Is this what you want, Meshac?' She cupped both breasts in her hands, lifting their fullness as she smiled again. 'Do you want them in your mouth? Do you want to pull on the nipples like you used to?'

His breathing sharp and ragged, Meshac reached up but she stepped back, just clear of his hands.

'Or do you prefer this?' She let her hands slide down over the slender column of her body, touching her fingertips to the mound of dark silken hair at the base of her stomach. 'This is what you wanted every night, remember, Meshac? Remember how you pushed yourself into me, night after night?'

Air rasping in his throat Meshac pushed himself to his feet, eyes bulging from the passion surging through him. 'Yeah,' he slurred, 'that be what I want, Maria.'

'Are you sure, Meshac?' Her fingertips playing among the dark bush, she laughed throatily. 'Are you sure you can still do it? Are you the man you think yourself to be? Remember last time, the heart attack you suffered? But don't worry, my dear, Ryder Tempal can do all you cannot. He sucks my breasts as you once did. He pushes between my legs just as often as you used to do.'

A low gurgle rising in his throat, Meshac swayed as he stared at her.

'Oh, yes, he has been carrying out your husbandly duties for some time now.' Maria trailed her hands back along her stomach to her breasts. 'He enjoys doing it.' She let her head tilt back slightly on her neck. 'He enjoys stroking my breasts, enjoys lying naked on top of me, pushing deep inside, and I enjoy it too, Meshac, as I enjoyed it tonight.'

The cry that came as he fell across the bed, his hand clutching convulsively at his chest, gave way to a rattle, a terrible rasping sound that splintered the silence of the room.

Crossing to the bedside, Maria looked down at the face twisted with the strain of breathing but whose eyes were not yet glazed with death. They stared back at her, unreadable in their pain.

She had thought her tormenting of him would surely kill him, but Meshac was alive. Maria felt the cold touch of fear. She had told him about herself and Ryder, he knew now they were lovers, and tomorrow . . . She thought quickly. There must be no tomorrow for Meshac.

'Yes, I enjoyed it, Meshac.' Despite her fear she bent slightly towards him, cupping one full breast to his mouth. 'Just as your daughter enjoyed it.'

Beneath her a hand clawed weakly at her arm but Maria slapped it away.

'Oh, yes, my dear,' she murmured, watching the changing emotions on his twisted face. 'Did you think I put her in some distinguished academy to finish her education? Oh, no, Meshac, I only told you that so you would raise no objection to her being sent away. The truth is I sent our daughter from this house to put an end to the education Ryder Tempal found so much pleasure in giving her. For one lesson I found them engaged upon in the summerhouse, they were both naked, Meshac.' She brushed her nipple across his mouth. 'Naked as I am now. Picture it, my dear, your child and Ryder Tempal. Her soft little moans as he drove into her, her hard little nipple in his mouth . . .'

Beneath her the rattle gave way to a long shuddering moan. Straightening Maria took the lamp in her hand, holding it close to the man sprawled backward across the bed. His eyes were still open but no sight remained in their glazed depths. Maria bent close, holding her free hand against the slack lips, feeling for breath on her fingertips, watching for any lifting of the chest.

For several long seconds she remained bent over the unmoving body then straightened up. Replacing the lamp on the bedside table, she made to ease the clawing hand away from the chest then hesitated. It would look more natural left there; a man suffering a massive heart attack would naturally claw at his chest. Lifting Meshac's legs back into the bed, she pulled the covers across him, leaving them awry about his waist as though he had pushed them down in his fight for life.

Satisfied that nothing looked out of place or suspicious, she picked up the turquoise gown. 'It was true what I said about Ryder and me, Meshac.' She laughed softly, looking into those sightless eyes. 'We *are* lovers and I do enjoy it, but it was not true what I told you about your daughter. Your precious child and he were not lovers, though that was no fault of his. I arrived at the summerhouse in time to prevent his seducing her, and it was no exclusive finishing school I entered her in, it was a convent. I put your daughter in a nunnery, which was why she made no visits home. But you would never have agreed to her going to such a place had I not told you her carryings on with Tempal were not the first I had caught her at, told you she was too free with her favours, that she required a hand stronger than ours if her morals were to be saved. And you believed me, Meshac, oh how easily you believed me! But then you believed anything I told you when I came to you like this!' She spread her arms wide, displaying her magnificent body, the smile widening on her lips. 'You always *were* a fool, Meshac!' She dropped her arms but the smile remained fixed to her mouth. 'You believed me each time I told you I was visiting her, yet each time I was making love with Ryder Tempal . . . But Carys renounced the convent life six months ago, she is no longer locked away behind its walls. She could be anywhere, doing anything, perhaps whoring to make a living. But you will never know that now, will you, Meshac? You will never know that.'

'I told me brother I would ask you, Mrs Bates. He will be outside now, waiting on your answer.'

'The Wakes, you say?'

'Yes, they be setting up on the heath across from St John's church yard.'

'Well, that be the quickest twelve month . . . where be that year gone to?'

'It is that long since the Wakes was here last. They only comes once in a twelve month, Mrs Bates.'

'Arrh, wench, I knows that.' Martha Bates looked at the housemaid, her plain face almost pretty with the excitement that lit it. Martha had loved the Wakes in her turn; going there had been an excuse to preen before the lads of the town and she had preened along with the rest of the village girls. The yearly visit to the Wakes had brought many of them a husband, her own dear dead Samuel among them. 'Right you are then, Alice.' She nodded. 'Go tell your brother he can come for you at six tomorrow night.'

'Mrs Bates . . .' Alice hesitated, glancing quickly to where Carys sat, a cloth spread across her lap as she cleaned the downstairs cutlery with a mixture of salt and vinegar. 'Mrs Bates, me mother said to ask, will you be allowing Carys to go an' all?'

'Oh, did 'er!' Martha looked sharply from one girl to the other. 'You be sure it was your mother said to ask that question, Alice Withers, and not that brother of yours waiting out there in the yard?'

'No, Mrs Bates, it weren't me brother, it were me mother, honest it were. Her said if two wenches was to be going then it needed two lads to look after them. Me mother said that going to the Wakes wasn't like a Sunday stroll in Brunswick Park. Her said a wench could get shoved and pushed unless a strong lad was there to see her didn't.'

That was right enough, Martha thought, once more remembering her girlhood days, and many a young man would take advantage.

'Your mother has the truth of it.' She nodded again. 'But I can't be letting you two girls out together. What if the mistress should have callers? I couldn't be answering the door and seeing to things in the kitchen, now could I? Stands to reason a body can't be in two places together.'

'There would be no need, Mrs Bates.' Carys looked up from the fork she was cleaning. 'I have no wish to go to the Wakes.'

'Ee, Carys!' Alice's eyes widened. 'You don't know what you'll be missing. The Wakes be a fair treat – all them side shows and hoop-la stalls.'

'Have you ever been to the Wakes, Carys?' Martha Bates turned her attention to the girl who had been at Ridge House these six months and of whom she knew little more than she had on that first night. There was something about her, a sadness deep inside that clouded her lovely eyes and showed occasionally on that pretty face.

'Have you, Carys . . . did your brother take you to the Wakes, or your parents?'

Dropping her glance to the cloth in her hand, she rubbed it across the fork but the action did not register in her mind.

'I have no brother, and no, my parents never took me to visit the Wakes.' The words were soft, suffered with silent tears. 'My father was always busy with his work, and my mother . . .' She swallowed hard as cloth and fork blurred together in her vision. 'My mother . . .'

'Well then, young woman, I think it be high time you took your first look at Mr Pat Collins's Wakes,' said, Martha sensing the unhappiness that stole the last of Carys's words. 'And this seems to be the perfect opportunity.' She glanced back to Alice, still standing just inside the kitchen door. 'You go tell that brother of yours we will be needing two escorts tomorrow night . . . Oh, and tell him . . .' she called as Alice whirled away before she might change her mind '. . . tell him to give my regards to your mother.'

'I would really rather stay here.' Carys swallowed the hurt speaking of her parents had caused, though her throat still felt tight with tears.

'You stay tied to the house too much altogether.' Martha rose from her chair. Balancing on one foot, she lifted the catch that held the door of the lower oven with the toe of her boot. Bending to peer at the pie inside, she murmured her approval of the golden-brown pastry crust before swinging the oven door closed again. 'A trip out once in a while will do you no harm.' She straightened up. What she really wanted to say was that whatever was troubling Carys needed to be faced; hiding herself away would provide no cure. Instead she smiled. 'For once in her life young Alice be right, a trip to the Wakes *do* be a fair treat. And who knows? You might even win a coconut.'

'Ee, I would rather save my pennies for a ride on the King and Queen boats!' Alice joined in as she came back into the kitchen. 'They fair bring your heart to a stop when they swings right over.'

'I don't go along with them newfangled contraptions.' Martha reached for the apron she had folded over the airing line strung above the range, tying it about her ample figure. 'What be wrong with the old swing boats?'

'There be nothing wrong with them,' Alice said, wriggling out of her coat. 'That is, if you have a lad with you to pull on the ropes enough to keep them swinging. But with the new King and Queen boats you don't have to do no pulling, they be worked by a steam engine.'

'I still says the old ways be best.' Martha smoothed the apron over her black skirts. 'Where there be steam there be noise, just like that there railway station down there in the town – great noisy engines! They be like something the devil dreamed up.'

'It's progress, Mrs Bates.' Alice winked at Carys. 'You don't never have progress without noise.'

'We will in *my* kitchen.' Martha placed her hands on her plump hips. 'Starting with you, Alice Withers, so stop your noise and start progressing with laying the table in the dining room. There be less than an hour to the mistress's suppertime and nothing done towards the making of it. And you, Carys, you get that cutlery swilled and put away then come and give me a hand with the salad.'

'What were the Wakes like when you was a young girl, Mrs Bates?' Her work in the dining room finished, Alice slipped off her frilly white cap and apron, folding them ready for the laundry woman who came in every Monday to do the washing and Tuesday to see to the ironing.

'You don't have to make it sound like that was a hundred years ago. I might not be as young as you but I ain't no fossil neither. First off, like I said earlier, there were not the racket that you young uns seem to think absolutely necessary to have a good time. We enjoyed ourselves without all the din of music you hears coming from that there steam organ. You could hear folk talk when I were a girl. There would be stalls selling pies of every kind, sweet sellers walking round with great trays hanging from their shoulders, every kind of sweet you could think of laid out on them. Ee! When I think of them great fat lollipops me dad would buy for us kids to take home, and me sat up on his shoulders sucking mine, dribbling sugar juice all down me chin . . .'

'What else was there, Mrs Bates, apart from hawkers, I mean?' Alice settled herself, drawing a stool closer to the range.

'Oh, there was all sorts of wonders.' Martha stared into the red heart of the fire, seeing her yesterdays in its flickering glow. 'And didn't us kids think they were wonders, even when we knew what we were shown were nowt but fakes? But the pretence didn't matter, it were the Wakes and the Wakes were magic.'

'It sounds wonderful even now,' said Carys, seeing the reminiscent smile playing about the older woman's mouth.

'It *were* wonderful, me wench,' Martha went on, seeing once more the childhood spent and lost. 'Least to we children it were. There was a roundabout with little wooden horses to ride, I remember. That were worked by two men turning a sort of double handle. Then there was swingle boats – least, that's what we called them. You sat one at each end and worked them by each pulling on a rope.'

'Them be much the same as now.' Alice looked up from her seat at Martha's feet.

'I dare say they be.' She nodded. 'Mr Pat Collins ain't fool enough to throw 'em out. Could be they'll still be working long after them steam-driven rides be gone to the knacker's yard. Arrh, the rides was a delight, not to mention the cake walk. Many a lad found the excuse to put his arm around a girl as her was shook off her feet on that thing.'

'Did you have a lad put his arm around your waist, Mrs Bates?'

'Arrh, Carys, I did.' Martha laughed. 'But it were a sight smaller in them days. That were where I met my Samuel. I were on the cake walk and I got shook right off my feet, accidentally on a purpose.' She laughed again, savouring the memory. 'Sam, he were right behind me. I'd noticed he seemed to turn up wherever me and my sister happened to be. Well, like I said, he was right behind me and catched me as I lost me balance and kept his arm round me all the while till we got off at the other end. We was married three years later. I was just eighteen.'

'Me mother seems to doubt I'll ever be married,' Alice said gloomily. 'Her be forever asking if there be a lad calling on me.'

'You sets too much store by not being courted yet. I've told you often enough, a man don't pick gold from the surface, my wench, he has to dig for it. Sooner or later one will dig down to you and you'll be wed right enough.'

'Hey, p'raps I'll find my true love on the cake walk!'

'As long as you don't find him in the two-headed man's tent!' Martha's laughter rang out again. 'A fella with one mouth be enough for any woman.'

'*Was* there a two-headed man?' Alice asked, forgetting her problem of having no sweetheart.

'Oh, arrh, Alice. Well, that's what the sign above the booth said, though whether both heads were real was something else again. That were where the wonder was, though, in them side shows. There was the bearded lady and the strong man . . . He sat me and my sister on his one arm and lifted us both up high, and we weren't little babbies neither. Then there was the snake woman. Her sat in a glass cage with at least a dozen of them horrors sliding all over her. Or for a halfpenny you could visit the world's tiniest man – ee, that were something to see! He was perfectly formed, hands, feet . . . and handsome! He had a face would charm ducks out of the water, but he were no more than thirty inches high. Then there were jugglers and tumblers, dancing bears and performing dogs, and of course there was always a woman to tell your fortune. Nearly every young wench paid her tuppence to hear what the future held for her. Ee!' Martha sighed. 'I tell you, the Wakes was really something then.'

'Did you pay your tuppence to hear your future, Mrs Bates?' Carys asked, thoroughly enjoying hearing of days past. Her own mother had never talked to her this way, never told her of her childhood, never shared with her a memory of the past. But then, Maria had never had much time for her daughter, leaving the care of her to a nanny then a tutor, and the loving of her to her father.

'Arrh, I was no different from the rest.' Martha returned her gaze to the fire but her eyes were fixed on a world where she was young. 'I paid my pennies, wanting to be told I would be swept up by a man rich as a prince, who would marry me then take me to live in a house as big as the one Queen Victoria has up there in London.'

'So you wasted your money?'

'I wouldn't go so far as to say that, Alice.' Martha smiled, her eyes still on her long-gone world. 'I lived on that dream many a month – at least I did till I realised Sam Bates were the only man I wanted. The fact that he had neither riches nor a house that would cover a couple of hundred football pitches didn't happen to worry me after that.'

'Ee, I hopes there'll be a fortune teller with the Wakes this year,' breathed Alice, 'I'd love to know what my future be holding.'

'I can tell you that.' Martha stirred in her chair, the memories of her youth sliding away. 'It holds a tired head and a slow hand unless you get yourself up to bed, and *that* means the sharp edge of my tongue. Now get that fire stoked up and off you go, the pair of you.'

'I hope the fortune teller tells me of a tall handsome fella who be coming to sweep me off me feet.' Alice heaved the heavy bucket of coal chippings on to the fire then damped it down with water from the kettle.

'You'd far better be hoping the mistress don't go having any unexpected callers.' Martha's eyes followed as Carys took the kettle to the scullery to refill it. 'If her does then it will be no Wakes for either of you.'

Did *she* want to know the future? In her own small bedroom Carys slipped the calico nightgown over her head, shivering against its cold touch. Did she want to be told of a future that could only hold more of the same? Her mother had held little love for her as a child, but from finding her being almost ravaged by Ryder Tempal had seemed to hold none at all. Why? She sat down on the edge of the iron-framed bed, staring into the light of the candle on the small chest beside it. Why had her mother blamed her, why had the blame been put squarely on her shoulders and none on his? Maria had not even wanted to listen to any explanation. *She* was the one in the wrong, Maria had told her. *She* had been responsible for what had happened. *She* had teased and flirted with Tempal, leading him on until he didn't know what he was doing. *She*, Carys, had acted the trollop.

But she had not. Carys stared into the candle flame. She had repeatedly done her best to avoid being in Ryder Tempal's company, making any excuse that would take her out of a room he was in. And why had she? Carys sat bolt upright as for the first time the question asked itself.

Why *had* she gone to such pains to avoid Ryder Tempal?

Was he ill-mannered? Was his manner of speech rough and uncultivated? Was he a braggart? Was his appearance or mode of dress not all it should have been? Carys knew the answer to each of these questions to be no. So why had she held such an aversion to the man?

With the last question came the answer.

Her body trembling with the force of her realisation, she let it flood into her mind, let the whole horrid truth of it flare like a beacon.

Maria was in love with Ryder Tempal!

Held there by the enormity of what had stared her in the face so often when she had come across them unexpectedly, Carys thought back across the twelve months before she had been sent away from Holyhead House.

His arm so often about Maria's waist, her hand pressed a moment too long to his mouth. Then had come the intimate whispering and sidelong glances across the dinner table, the invitations to the house that had grown more numerous with every month, the visits always timed to take place when her father would be at the enamelling works.

And her supposed trips to the dressmaker!

Carys swallowed the sickness that threatened, clenching her fingers, driving nails into palms in an effort to use one pain to drive out another. But the thought came on, driving into her consciousness, subduing any resistance until it was uppermost in her mind.

Were those visits purely what they were supposed to be? Had her mother really gone so many times to a dressmaker she had visited so rarely before knowing Ryder Tempal? Or were they an excuse to cover meetings of a very different kind? Lovers' meetings?

Maria and Ryder Tempal lovers!

Carys's fingernails cut deeper into her palms but the sharp sting was not enough to stem the flow of her thoughts.

Was it true? Was Maria that man's lover? Was that the reason she had incarcerated her own daughter in a nunnery, and why she had decried her as a virtual prostitute to the Mother Superior there? Was it the same reason that had caused her to label that sketch as lewd?

Almost without realising it, Carys slipped to the floor, drawing the carpet bag from beneath the bed. Opening it, she drew out the sketches Sister Mary Immaculata had returned to her. Climbing back on to the bed, she spread the sheets of paper around her. A likeness of her father at a work-bench, the light from a small window centring on an enamelled box held in his hand; one of the foundry men, sweat glistening on bare arms and shoulders as he bent before a furnace; and the sketch of the man rising up out of the waters.

'All men, only men!' Maria had told the Mother Superior, as if emphasising Carys's need to be cleansed of some disease. But these were the only sketches Maria had chosen to take with them to the convent, the rest she had ordered to be burned.

Carys remembered the look on the young maid's face as the sketches had been thrust into her arms, a look that said she would keep them safe. But for what? Carys's glance rested on her father's face, the charcoal lines of the sketch seeming to move in the flickering candlelight. Did the maid intend to give them to him? If she had it had not succeeded in softening his heart towards Carys, it had not moved him into recalling her from the convent.

'Why?' Tears clouding her vision, she touched a finger to the charcoal face. 'What did Maria tell you, Father? Was it something so dreadful you could not bring yourself to see me? Was it so awful to you that it made you want me out of your life for good? But I did none of the things she accused me of.'

A tear fell on to a corner of the sketch and Carys wiped it away, her finger smudging the black charcoal line into a softer grey shadow.

'I did none of them, Father,' she whispered brokenly. 'I did none of them.'

Gathering the sketches together, she paused, letting her

gaze rest on the one of the unknown man. Maria had called it obscene, Sister Mary Immaculata had likened it to Michelangelo's David, and Virginia Mountford had pronounced it worthy of the Royal Academy.

And she herself? Why had she kept it? Why, even now, did she not destroy it? Why, in the one sketch she had made since leaving the convent, had she drawn the remembered face of this man, a face so like that of Virginia Mountford's father?

Taking up the last of the drawings she held it for a moment, the light of the candle imbuing it with life, seeming to bring a taunting curve to the lips, a sensuous gleam to the black velvet eyes, and almost to lift the eyebrow topped by the faint line of a scar.

She should tear them up and in the morning put them on the kitchen fire, rid herself of these sketches, then perhaps she would be rid of the memories they invoked, of the unhappiness they recalled, of the pain that stirred afresh each time she looked at them. But already her hands had rolled them together and she was reaching for the carpet bag.

Settled beneath the sheets, the candle blown out, plunging the room into blackness, Carys closed her eyes. She had not answered her own questions. She had not told herself why she did not destroy her sketches. She had not told herself the reason behind her drawing of that handsome face.

Behind her closed eyes a strong athletic body leaned down from the saddle of a great horse, a man whose mouth curved in a mocking smile as he lifted the collar of her dress with a riding crop.

No, she had not told herself why. She turned into the pillow, pressing her face into its softness. But she knew the answer.

Chapter Seven

Caine Lazic paused in his task of filling the wooden water bucket, stretching his tall spare frame, easing away the strain of scooping water from the dark slow-moving brook. It was well named, he thought, staring down into its black depths. The Tame, the name the Saxons had given it, meant Dark River. The water, not much wider than a brook here as it cut its way across the flat plateau of ground, was dark but did not deserve the filth sent to despoil it from the numerous iron and steel works that disfigured the landscape, from every tiny back alley workshop that scarred the land like the marks of the pox leaving it little more than heaving sludge.

He glanced towards the wagon standing only yards away, then to the horse tethered to a nearby gorse bush, its yellow blossom defying the touch of the soot-laden air that hung over this town, marring plant and building alike with its black fingers.

Why bring the wagon here? his mother grumbled every year. And in reality there was no reason, no reason to return to this place that seemed to carry the curse of his name, no need to come, year upon year, to a part of the country that gasped in the fumes of smoke and dust of furnaces when he could as easily have driven the wagon to places of such beauty it seemed the Lord must have made them as homes for his angels.

But this was no place of angels. He turned his gaze, letting it wander over the jagged black scars of surface mining, the great grey slag heaps rising like weeping pustules from their edges, at the pitted holes that were gin pits: shafts stabbed into the earth, the coal ripped from its belly and the wound left open and gaping while another was sunk beside it.

No, this was no place of angels. This place held the devil. His devil. The one that brought him back here every year. The devil whose pitchfork of hatred and revenge prodded until he returned to the place where he had been blinded, to the place where he must seek recompense.

Every year they had come, he and his mother. Always at the same time of the year, always in the early spring, keeping faith with the time it had happened, when that one blow had torn out the eye of a ten-year-old gypsy boy.

Every year for sixteen years they had come.

Caine glanced over to where his mother sat on the steps of the painted bow-topped caravan. She was old, too old to face many more winters. And when she was gone? He let his gaze travel across the heath to where the road sliced through it. When she was gone, how would he travel? How then would he follow the gypsy ways? The ways that decreed his mother's wagon and all she owned would be burned at her death. He should take a wife, she was forever telling him, take a wife and build a wagon for himself. But Caine knew there could be no wife for him, no bringing children into the world, no family that would need his caring, until the devil he carried inside him was gone; until the need that brought him to this town was assuaged, that same need which for sixteen years had drawn him, guiding the wagon to this spot as though unseen hands held the old piebald's reins.

Every year they had come and every year that same inner voice had told him this was not the time, an innate knowledge that was the true legacy of his Romany blood telling him the moment was not yet come; that same inborn certainty that was telling him now, telling him this year he would taste revenge.

Picking up the water bucket, he carried it across to the wagon, emptying it into the large wooden barrel roped to its side.

This year . . . next year, whichever it was, he would be here. And be it with the help of God or devil, Caine Lazic would take his revenge.

'You two be minding yourselves!' Martha Bates tugged at the side of her all-enveloping white apron, smoothing away imaginary creases in the way she always did when wanting to emphasise a word or a feeling. 'And you lads,' she called to Alice's brothers, waiting over against the corner of the stables and carriage house, 'make sure and keep your eyes on these wenches and not go staring after others.'

'We'll watch them, Mrs Bates.' The taller of the two, a man well into his mid-twenties, stepped forward, flat cap held in his hand.

'Arrh, well, you makes sure as you do. And, mind, I want them back here at nine on the dot. Ain't no call for young folk to be out later than that!' Martha called, feeling the last word should be hers.

'Nine o'clock, huh! Her must think you two still be babbies!' Alice's second eldest brother, Edward, shoved his own flat cap back on short-cropped fair curls.

'No more a babby than you, our Eddie.' She tossed him a sharp look. 'You grumbles about everything you be asked to do lessen it be asked by that Peggy Rogers you be sweet on. If her was to ask for the moon, you'd be daft enough to go looking for a pair of sky hooks to haul yourself after it.'

'I ain't sweet on Peggy Rogers.' But Eddie's face flushed a deep plum red.

'Then if you ain't, you don't have the sense you was born

with,' his elder brother replied, 'cos that girl be taken with you, though for the life of me I can't see why.'

'Davey be right.' Alice fell into step beside her brother, tucking her arm into his. 'Peggy Rogers be a real nice wench, and if you don't have sense enough to say something to her soon then you can be sure some other fella will.'

'I'm sorry if having to escort two of us to the Wakes has meant your brother giving up time he wished to spend with someone else.' Carys looked up at the face of the man who now fell into step beside her. 'We are not very far from Ridge House. If I return now he could leave Alice with you and go wherever it was he wished to be.'

'That be a right nice way of thinking on your part, Miss Beddows.' Davey's smile curled the side of his mouth, giving his face a boyish appearance. 'But Eddie Withers has to learn there are others in this world beside himself; he must learn that once given a promise is to be kept.'

'A promise?'

'Arrh, miss, a promise. He told our mother he would look out for Alice and yourself and that is what he be going to do.'

'Mind!' He glanced ahead to where brother and sister, arms still linked, skipped across the heath like two children let loose to play. 'He don't never take no forcing into keeping his word, he's a great chap really, it's just a habit of his to grumble. I think it's a leftover from when we was kids and I was forever telling him what he could or couldn't do. Ordering him about, was what he called it. But seeing the size of him now, I wouldn't like to risk doing it again.'

Carys caught the smile that accompanied the words and heard the affection in the tone of Davey's voice. There was a strong bond between the brothers, a family feeling that she had witnessed on her visits to Alice's home, a love that bound them together and which had been painfully absent from her own life.

'I missed you when you didn't come with Alice on Sunday,' he said, breaking the small silence that had begun to build between them.

'Mrs Bates cannot easily manage with both Alice and myself gone from the house,' she answered. 'And seeing I have no family, it makes sense for Alice to have Sunday afternoon to go home.'

'But that leaves you no time at all for yourself!'

'Not quite.' Carys widened her stride, stepping over a small hollow in the path. 'I get an afternoon once a week.'

'And that be all?' Davey pointed to a stone jutting from the ground, alerting Carys to the danger of stubbing her toe against it.

'It's enough.' She skirted the obstruction. 'And Alice tells me we are fortunate in our free time. She says she knows several girls who get only one afternoon free a month.'

'Still it be little enough, though my father be always saying how well off we be compared to his father's time. He often tells of how me granddad, an eight-year-old lad, was woken for his shift in the coal pits at three in the morning, walking three miles over the heath in bare feet, come hail, rain or snow; and how, with only a couple of slices of bread and cheese and a can of water, he worked till seven at night then fell asleep, still underground, till his father finished his own shift at nine and they walked the three miles home. Compared to that my own shift of six in the morning to seven at night be not so bad.'

'And you have to work that number of hours every day?' Carys asked. She had known the workers employed by her father had worked many hours but had they really been as long as the ones these brothers of Alice worked?

'I know what you be thinking.' Davey laughed. 'You be thinking that if I works till seven every night, barring Sundays, of course, then how come I could be up at Ridge House for six o'clock?'

'Well, I had not thought that.' Carys answered his laugh with a smile that lit a twinkle of dancing lights in her lovely amber eyes. 'But since you mention it . . .'

'Since I've mentioned it . . .' Davey glanced down at her then quickly looked away, feeling his heart lurch at the beauty of the girl beside him.

'Since you have mentioned it?' Carys urged, unaware of the effect her smiling mouth was having on the man beside her.

'Arrh, well now!' He tried to keep his voice steady, to curb the flow of emotion that had his pulse going like the Great Western Railway's 'Zulu' express train that passed through Wednesbury station twice a week. 'Things be different this week.'

A squeal from ahead drew Carys's glance to where Eddie had his sister by the waist, lifting her off her feet and swinging her round.

'Why this week?' she asked, smiling as Alice squealed again, demanding to be set down.

Davey watched the antics of his brother and sister, taking advantage of the few moments their cavorting gave him to calm himself. Carys Beddows had had this effect on him from his first setting eyes on her seated at his mother's table. Since that time a few weeks ago he had thought of little save the girl with hair the colour of ripe chestnuts and amber eyes that glowed like the evening sky in summer.

''Cos this be Wakes week.' He forced himself to look ahead when all he wanted to look at was the sweet loveliness of her face. 'And Wakes week be special. The men at the brick yard be allowed to knock off one hour early during that week so as to visit the Wakes. That be one up on me granddad's time, eh?'

'Is it just the brick yard allows its workers an hour off their shift, or does everyone get it?'

'I reckon just about every man in Wednesbury will be treated the same. Them as works in the iron and steel foundries do, I knows that 'cos I've got mates as works there, and I reckon any other employer would follow suit. Could be he would have trouble should he try to put a stop to the Wakes hour.'

'So the people set great store by the Wakes?' Carys said as Alice broke free from her brother's grasp, swinging a friendly punch at his shoulder as he danced away from her.

'It be the highlight of the year, that and Christmas. They be the only times folk here seem to forget work, though I reckon most of them work just as hard at play.'

'That is a very deep piece of philosophy, Davey Withers.'

'I don't know about philosophy.' He caught her hand as her boot tangled in a clump of gorse, steadying her as she pitched forward. 'But I do know you and Alice would walk a lot easier if we left the heath and followed the road.'

Calling for Eddie and his sister to do just that, he released Carys's hand, embarrassed at the grin that flashed across his brother's face as he turned.

'Ee, Carys, we be going to have such a grand evening!' Alice's excitement shone in her eyes. 'I am going to have a go at everything there be on that fairground.'

'You'll need a shilling or two to do that!' Eddie laughed as his sister caught the other girl's arm, skipping her off. 'Have you suddenly been left a fortune by some rich lord as has been secretly in love with you for years?'

'Could be I have.' Alice tossed her head at her brother's teasing. 'And maybe I married him, secret like, and maybe now I be a very rich widow.'

'And maybe water don't run out of a bucket with a hole in the bottom of it!' Eddie laughed again. 'But somehow I don't think so.'

'You'll see,' Alice retorted. 'You might sing your song to a different tune when you sees how much I'll be spending.' Lowering her voice to a whisper, she squeezed Carys's arm. 'He don't know I've been saving every penny since Christmas turned.'

'But that can't be much?' She whispered back. 'Mrs Bates says you take your wages home to your mother every week.'

'Arrh, I do.' Alice glanced at the tram rumbling past as they left the heath to follow the road down to Bridge Street. 'But her gives me two shillings pocket money back and I don't have to spend much on clothes. Wearing me uniform every day saves a deal of wear on me own things, and I ain't keeping a bottom drawer, so what with me birthday five bob piece I have enough to see the both of us has a lovely time.'

'Alice, what is this birthday five bob piece?' Carys glanced to the opposite side of the road to where a man and a woman followed two children from a dark alleyway set between the long oppressive ribbon of houses.

'You'll be getting one on your birthday. The mistress gives each of the staff a gift of five shillings on their birthday. I told you she was a good sort.'

Yes, Alice had told her that. Carys watched the small girl on the far side of the road, pink ribbons trailing from a straw boater set on blonde ringlets, flounced pink skirts touching the top of shiny button boots, a maroon coat reaching just below the knee. The boy, taller and obviously older, also dressed in Sunday best, caught her hand as excitement sent her running in front of her parents. That child could have been her. She could have danced along, caught in the joy of an outing to the Wakes with her parents. But she never had. She had never known the kind of happiness that bubbled in that child. She had never been given the mother love that showed now on that woman's face.

'When is your birthday?'

'It is in August, the fourth of August.' Carys's mind flew back to the last birthday she had spent at Holyhead House – a birthday made special by her father's gift of an amethyst pendant, and even more so by the pride in his voice when he had said her designs were accounting for many sales of his enamels. There had been no more birthday gifts after that. But it was not the lack of gifts that brought the swell of tears to her throat, it was the loss of her father's love.

'That be still nearly six months.' Alice flicked her fingers as she counted the weeks. 'So you will have to wait before you will be getting your five bob. Still, not to mind, you will get it . . . if you live that long!'

She grasped Carys with both hands, dragging her away from the wheels of a carriage that had swept from the yard of the White Horse Hotel, careering around the corner into Mounts Road at the very moment Carys made to cross.

'Bloody mad-brained bugger!' Davey stepped quickly up to the girls, his eyes blazing fury as he looked after the carriage, turning now on to the heath where torches flared, lighting up the fairground. 'I'd like to kick his arse into his earholes!'

'That could prove quite painful . . . for both of you,' Carys smiled, hoping to relieve Davey's obvious concern for her.

'I bet it would bring tears to his eyes afore it would fetch them to mine, just the same,' he growled.

'Well, there's been no harm done,' Alice said, her enthusiasm for the evening ahead quenching the anger she would normally have displayed. 'C'mon, I don't want to waste a single minute.'

Her brothers close behind, they walked to where the flaring torches beckoned and Alice squealed her delight as the steam organ began to boom its strident music across the heath.

'Ee, Carys, do you think her will be here?' Alice shouted over the noise of the organ, the wooden figures adorning it clashing cymbals and beating drums.

'Who?' Carys called, feeling herself deafened by the blasts of music. 'Will who be here?'

'Her.' Eyes sparkling, Alice plunged into the crowds already milling about the sideshows, children's eyes feasting on the promised wonders. 'The fortune teller.'

Blushing as a ball was shoved into Davey's hands, with the stall holder inviting him to win his pretty sweetheart a fairing, Carys moved on.

'Ee, I hopes her is!' Alice said, as they paused before a booth boasting it housed: 'The living Cyclops, the only genuine three-eyed man'.

'Well, if she is not, we could always come back here,' Carys giggled. 'He is bound to see more with three eyes than we can with two.'

'Ee, you be getting a right cheeky monkey, Carys Beddows!'

Grasping Carys's arm more firmly beneath her own, Alice led the way between coconut shies and sideshows, breathing her delight and wonder as they came upon the majestic steam boats. Set a little apart from the rest, giving clearance for their boat-shaped bulk, sides painted with a central crown from which red, white and blue garlands stretched in loops and swirls from fore to aft, encircling the names William and Mary, they swung to and fro, gathering height with every swing, halting for seconds at the apex of each ascent before falling back to climb the other way.

'Watch!' Alice quivered as the riders, locked inside the metal restraints, screamed in delighted fear as the great boats rose and fell. 'Watch, they'll go right over . . . there, I told you!'

Carys felt the other girl tremble as the huge steam-driven boats reached the critical point, their occupants screaming as they swung right over in a complete arc.

'C'mon!' Alice fumbled two coins from a purse tucked inside her coat. 'Let's go on them first.'

'Mother said not to let you go on anything that might be dangerous.' Eddie stepped in front of her, barring her way to the tiny wooden platform on which a man stood selling tickets.

'That ain't dangerous!' Alice snapped, seeing the promise of a ride being snatched away.

'You don't think so.' Eddie refused to move. 'But then that be you all over, you never did see danger in nothing.'

'Well, there ain't none in them there boats,' she returned sharply. 'The folk be fastened in tighter than a pea in its pod. How can you reckon it be dangerous?'

'Be you takin' a ride or ain't you?' The man on the platform called, jingling coins in his hand. ''Cos if you ain't, then shift outta the way so other folk can get on.'

''Cos it'll be me and Davey will get Mother's tongue and Father's boot if you gets yourself hurt.'

Seeing the disappointment on her friend's face, Carys turned to Davey. 'It would not be *so* dangerous if you and Eddie were there to hold her, would it?'

'Reckon not.' Davey smiled down at her. 'But then, one of us would be holding *you*.'

'No,' Carys lied quickly. 'I have never been able to stomach being swung back and forth, please don't ask me to ride on one of those things. And please,' she turned her sweetest smile on him, 'don't let Alice be disappointed.'

He could not refuse her. Looking into her glowing amber eyes, Davey knew he would never be able to refuse this girl anything.

'C'mon then.' He swung away, taking his sister by the arm. 'Let's you, me and Eddie ride the King and Queen boats.'

From the edge of a crowd intent on the blood-spattered challenger being beaten senseless in a bare-knuckle contest a man stared at Carys, her head thrown back as she watched the giant boats ride the air.

Tall, his body muscular beneath a fashionable three-quarter-cut coat, his blond hair free of a hat, his yellow cat like eyes were fixed on her face. Across the ground separating them he could not be sure. The flickering light of the flaring torches cast shadows across the features that seemed so like . . . but that was all it could be, a similarity to a girl he had last seen four years ago.

Ignoring the demand they should move on from the woman clinging on to his arm, he watched the girl who clapped delightedly as she was joined by two men and another girl of about her own age.

It could not be her. Maria had said her daughter had chosen to remain in that convent. Carys Beddows had taken Holy Orders. All the same, Ryder Tempal's glance followed the slender young woman as she moved off.

* * *

'You've been on just about every ride there be to ride on and seen every sideshow that be decent. It be time we got you back home. No doubt it be getting well past eight,' Davey warned as Alice danced towards the bare-knuckle fighters. 'And there be no way you be going to watch men beat the life out of one another, so you can come along . . . and no arguing.'

'I don't want to watch no fighting,' she called over her shoulder, her step quickening. The crowds were thinning as families began to wend their way home.

'It must be getting late,' Carys said as Alice pulled her along. 'Mrs Bates said we must be back by nine.'

'We will.' Alice was almost running now. 'But I just have to get me fortune told first. There be a booth over against the one that holds the "Wolf Boy". There! There it is!'

Dragging Carys behind her, her brothers trailing in their wake, Alice dashed up to the small booth, dashing inside before Davey could grab her.

'I should have known her wouldn't go home without going in there.' He shook his head despairingly. 'And I suppose you will want your fortune told besides?'

'Of course.' Carys had held no intention of consulting the fortune teller but neither did she intend to let Alice take all the blame should they be late back to Ridge House.

'I give up!' Davey shook his head. 'But at least I have the consolation of being able to make a quick escape from Mrs Bates's tongue. You two will have to bear it . . . on your own heads be it.'

'But I thought your mother's instructions were to keep your sister free from anything you thought dangerous?'

'That they were, but there be dangers a man shouldn't be called upon to face, and a furious Martha Bates be one of them!'

One foot on the step of a horse-drawn carriage, Ryder Tempal watched a girl laughing up into the face of the man beside her, a girl he was almost certain he knew well. A girl Maria thought locked away in a convent.

* * *

'Ee, her was great!' Seated on Carys's bed, her feet tucked in her nightgown, Alice's face took on a dreamy look. 'Madam Rosa, Fortune Teller to Royalty.'

'So you keep saying,' Carys answered, her voice low so as not to be heard by Mrs Bates. She was cross enough at their arriving home ten minutes late without adding fuel to the flames by letting her know they were still not in bed.

'No, but her was, Carys. Her told me all about me family: about me dad hurting his arm that time in the brick yard, and her said me mother thought that when our Eddie were a babby he had got the TB from somewhere and how her pinched a orange every day from Gascoyn's fruit stall in the market 'cos the doctor said fruit were good for him and me mother hadn't the money to buy it. Ee!' Her eyes registering surprise and concern, Alice looked across the cramped room to where Carys was tying her hair with a ribbon. 'Do you think that were true, Carys? Do you really think me mother would steal oranges?'

'Do you think so?'

'I don't know what to think.' Alice frowned. 'I've never known me mother do anything down in her life, her's always been too open-handed, too ready to give to anybody what asked. I've never known her take even a farthing that wasn't due to her.'

'Then why think so now?'

''Cos Madam Rosa . . .'

Carys threw the long rope of her hair back across her shoulder. 'Alice, if Madam Rosa told you the moon was made of green cheese, would you believe it?'

The concern in Alice's eyes faded and they took on a look of wide-eyed innocence. 'But it is, isn't it?'

'Alice Withers, you . . .!' Holding a hand over her mouth, Carys stifled the laughter bubbling in her throat.

'Well, if me mother did pinch them oranges, I reckon as her has more than paid for them since, what with the price old Solly Gascoyn charges for his stuff!'

Their laughter subsiding Alice sat up, bedcovers tangled about her where she had rolled like a puppy, her face solemn once more.

'What do you reckon as to what Madam Rosa said about me brothers?'

Trying to straighten her covers, Carys sighed. 'Why not go to bed? We can talk about Madam Rosa's predictions tomorrow if Mrs Bates . . .'

'Her said as our Eddie will be married within a twelve month and that the girl would make him a good, sensible wife.' Alice ignored both plea and warning. 'I guess that'll be Peggy Rogers, and a good thing an' all. Our Eddie needs a wench that'll keep his head out of the clouds. But what her said about our Davey didn't sound too good.'

One thing Carys had learned since coming to Ridge House was that once Alice got started on something it was best to let her get it out of her system. Only along that path lay the promise of peace. So Carys climbed up on to the bed, hunching her knees under her chin and wrapping both arms around them.

'Her said our Davey wouldn't know a smooth life,' Alice went on as Carys settled herself on the narrow bed. 'Seems how he will love a woman, but that same woman will love another. Our Davey will watch her wed and his heart will break. He will not take a wife till he be near enough forty and by that time will have made money. But that money will not mend his heart nor take his thoughts from his one true love.'

'Alice Withers, you are making this up!'

Grabbing a pillow in her arms, Alice held it to her face, laughing into it.

'I know,' she gurgled, 'but it sounds good.'

'It does *not* sound good.' Carys smiled despite her determination not to. 'It sounds like those penny dreadfuls you have in the box under your bed.'

Alice pretended to drop the pillow, striking a melodramatic

pose, holding the back of one hand to her forehead and the other with palm flat against her heart. 'I am undone,' she sobbed, 'you know my wicked secret.'

'I know you should be on the halls!' Carys laughed, then clapped a hand across her mouth, glancing towards the door.

'Don't worry,' Alice whispered, dropping her pose. 'Mrs B. went to her bed half an hour ago.'

'And you should be in yours!' Carys whispered back. 'We will both be too tired for anything in the morning.'

'I did make up the bit about the money, but the rest, that about our Davey not getting the woman he really loved and not being wed till he be nigh on forty, that were just as Madam Rosa told it to me.' Alice chose not to hear Carys's whisper. 'Ee, poor Davey! I wonder who the wench is he be sweet on?'

'I am sure you will know sooner or later,' Carys answered, hoping deep inside the foretelling would not come true. She had met Davey Withers only twice but that was enough to tell her he was a gentle, caring man, one too good and kind to be hurt.

'So what did her tell you?' Alice switched easily from one question to another. 'You said you would tell when we got back.'

'It's too late . . .'

'No, it ain't.' Alice shuffled into a more comfortable position, tucking her night-gown over her feet. 'I told you my fortune. I told you her said there was a man in the shadows: a tall, well-built man with hair golden as sunlight, a man whose clothing spoke of wealth, and that he was looking at me, and giving a love token to a young lad and pointing to me. Then her said the token would be in my hand before the spring of the new year. You said p'raps things would change come the turning of the century, *you* said that an' all, so that bit must be true.'

Carys shook her head. 'I am not a teller of fortunes, Alice, I don't know what your future holds.'

'No, but you knows what *yours* holds,' she retorted. 'Or leastways what Madam Rosa says it holds. So come on, Carys, a promise is a promise.'

'I think the woman invented a future for me, just as you have invented wealth for Davey . . .'

'It ain't impossible our Davey could come to be rich,' Alice interrupted.

'No, it is not impossible, and I sincerely hope he may . . .'

'Look, forget what was said about him.' Alice fidgeted, wriggling the covers of the bed into an even more crumpled pile. 'I want to know what was said to you.'

Knowing it would be useless to resist, Carys rested her chin on her hands, eyes gazing into the shadows of the room. 'She said a woman had done me great harm though the cause of it was not of my doing. She had struck at me from a jealous heart in the hope of keeping a man, one who would play her false. She said this woman was well known to me and would strike again after the year had turned. That due to her I would know great fear, and that she would try to take my life but would take another's instead.'

'Go on!' Alice urged as she stopped speaking.

'She said that soon I would learn of the death of someone dear to me.'

'And?' said Alice, squirming.

'She said that in the distance a man stands beside a brook, a man whose face bears a mark of Cain, a man who holds a heart in his hand and vengeance in his soul.'

'My God!' Alice loosed a long pent-up breath. 'Didn't her have anything good at all to say? What you tell me sounds too awful for my worst nightmare. Be you sure that was all?'

Drawing her gaze back from the shadowed corner, Carys drew a steadying breath. 'She said that the efforts of the woman who wished me harm would come to nothing, and also the one who had found me a home would remain close for the rest of my life.'

'That be the mistress,' Alice murmured. 'I did say you

would be best off staying at Ridge House. I did say that, Carys.'

'You did, and that at least was a sensible prediction.' She jumped from the bed. 'And now I am going to make another, and that is you get off my bed and leave me to get to sleep or you will find yourself on the floor.'

'All right, I'm going!' Alice scrambled from the bed as Carys made a determined grab at the rumpled quilt. 'Carys,' she called softly, the bedroom door ajar, 'this time I don't hold no truth to that fortune teller. I reckon her was making the whole thing up, so don't you go worrying over what her said.'

The bed straightened, Carys settled beneath the sheets. One short breath had extinguished the candle, plunging the room into darkness. Alice held that no truth was contained in the words Carys had heard in that booth at the fairground.

Gradually the darkness retreated before the moonlight from the room's small window, collecting itself into shadows that hovered about the walls.

But Alice had not been told all Madam Rosa's words, she had not heard everything.

In the blackness Carys heard again the words she had chosen not to tell her friend.

'I see a man whose hair and eyes be black, black as the inside of the devil's mouth. A man who searches beside a pond, searches for a woman, one who carries pencil and paper in her hands. He has searched this long time, and though he be far, still he be near. There be long months to go before he finds what he be seeking but find it he surely will, for his will be the claiming of you, 'tis him will have the taking of you.'

Searches beside a pond . . . Carys covered her eyes with her hand, shutting out the limpid light of the moon. But though she dismissed the light she could not rid her inner eye of the image of a strong handsome face, one whose hell-dark eyes mocked her, the face from the sketch which lay beneath her bed.

Chapter Eight

'Mistress says her wants to see Carys. Says to ask you to send her to the drawing room at eleven.'

Alice placed the last of the dining-room crockery on the large table that occupied the centre of the kitchen at Ridge House, her gaze troubled.

'Do you think the mistress be annoyed at Carys and me for being late back last night?'

'Did her say to send you upstairs as well?' Martha Bates looked up from the pastry she was mixing in a large earthenware bowl.

'No.' Alice rested the tray on the table but her hands kept hold of it. 'Her just said to ask you to send Carys to her at eleven.'

'Well, if her doesn't want to see the pair of you then it isn't you coming in ten minutes late that be the trouble. And in any case the mistress would not be seeing you for that unless I had complained to her about you, and I haven't done that.'

'Then what do you think it is, Mrs Bates? Could it be Carys don't be doing her job proper?'

'Mistress wouldn't be sending to see her about that neither, least not until I'd been spoken to first. Truth be I don't know what her's being sent for.'

'Ee, I hope her won't be given the sack!' Alice turned as Carys came from the scullery. 'Mistress wants to see you in the drawing room, Carys. I hope you don't be in no trouble.'

Halfway into the kitchen she stopped dead. Around her the familiar range and dresser merged with whitewashed walls before dissolving into spindrift mists that melted into emptiness.

In a fraction of time one world had faded and she stood in another, a world of silently moving figures robed in black, a world of cold, high-ceilinged rooms and closed doors. 'The Mistress of Novices wishes to see you. You will go to her room at eleven.' In the shrouded, fear-ridden mists of her mind the words became twisted. She was to go again to that room where she had seen . . . the room where she was beaten.

'Carys!'

'Yes, Sister . . .'

It was a low, frightened reply as memory carried her down a long soundless corridor lined with closed doors that each gave on to a tiny cell holding a narrow iron bed and single cupboard. One by one they slid past until she came to one bearing the sign 'Mistress of Novices'. Tapping at this door, she entered, head bent and eyes on the floor.

'Your work is unsatisfactory.' The voice ringing in her mind did not even give her her name. 'You dawdled over scrubbing the floors in the Chapel of Our Lady.' A thin cane whistled through the air, slicing across her arms and hands, stinging through the thin cloth of her novice's robe. 'And you were talking while working in the vegetable garden.' The cane rose again, the force of its blow almost knocking her off her feet. 'What were you talking about?' The voice became a hiss. 'Perhaps you were talking about what you saw here, were you?' The cane sliced close to her face, striking hard on her shoulder. 'Were you? Were you!'

'No, Sister Veronica. No, I was not . . . no . . . no . . .'

'Carys . . . Carys wench, it's all right, it's all right. You be here with Alice and Mrs Bates. Shh . . . shh . . . there ain't no Sister Veronica here.'

Grabbing the tray of freshly washed dishes from Carys's trembling hands, Alice set them beside the dining-room crockery she had brought from upstairs.

'Ee, Carys!' she said, as Martha led the girl to a chair. 'I didn't mean to scare you.'

'You have a mouth as big as a parish oven, Alice Withers,' the housekeeper snapped, 'and you don't know when to close the door.'

'I'm sorry, Mrs Bates, I didn't think Carys would take on like that.'

'That be another of your faults, you don't think!' Martha's plump face was wreathed in anger. 'You come barging into the kitchen, talking about trouble and folk getting the sack, with never a thought for the consequences.'

'Ee, I am sorry.' Alice's mouth drooped. 'Last thing I would want would be to give Carys cause for worry.'

'I know, me wench.' Martha's anger faded as rapidly as it had risen. 'You wasn't to know the girl would take on. Go brew a pot of tea, a cup will help pull her together.'

Yes, it might, thought Martha, holding Carys, feeling her tremble. But it would not banish fear which could drain a face to the colour of milk and reduce the girl to a quivering wreck, nor heal a pain that went deeper still. That would take time and love, both of which, God in His mercy, she would have at Ridge House.

Carrying the enamel tea pot to the table, Alice looked towards Martha and at her nod filled three cups.

'Here you be, Carys.' Martha pushed a cup into the girl's hands, noting the tremors that still shook her fingers. 'And you sit yourself down an' all, Alice. Five minutes will do no harm, we can all catch up later.

'Come on, Carys, drink up.' Martha smiled, though it was forced. She was concerned for this girl who had turned up out of nowhere with no place to go. Surely the mistress had no complaint? Surely she was not about to dismiss her? It was true they had been told almost nothing of her background and less of her parentage but her very demeanour told she could not be from the slums.

'Carys, I be real sorry for mouthing off. I didn't mean . . . I wouldn't . . .'

'It was not your fault, Alice.' Carys looked across at the girl seated on the opposite side of the table.

'Weren't nobody else's.' Alice's eyes brimmed with tears. 'Me and my big mouth.'

'You are not to blame.' Reaching out, Carys pressed a hand to her friend's arm. 'It was just a memory.'

'Some memory!' Alice blurted out the very words Martha Bates was thinking. If what they had just witnessed was due to a memory then just what were the memories locked in this young girl's mind, and who or what was responsible for them?

Pulling back her hand, Carys cradled both of them about her cup.

'I don't think it be anything serious the mistress wants to see you about,' Martha said, as Alice drew a handkerchief from beneath her apron and wiped her eyes. 'So both of you be putting your fears away. Were anything amiss, Martha Bates would have heard of it first.'

'You thought it was somebody called Sister Veronica was sending for you.' Alice held the handkerchief to her mouth as Martha's glance told her once more her mouth was running ahead of her brain.

'Sister Veronica was the Mistress of Novices,' Carys said, knowing the time had come for explanations and suddenly feeling relief on realising she could tell these two kind people what had happened to her. 'I was placed under her supervision when my mother enrolled me in the Convent of the Holy Child. She was strict but not unkind. Not at first. It seemed she understood the loneliness of newcomers to the convent. Then one afternoon it was just before Exposition of the Blessed Sacrament, I was scrubbing the floor of the infirmary when one of the Sisters sent me to fetch the visiting priest to an old nun dying of tuberculosis. I ran all the way to the office of the Mistress of Novices, though I knew running was forbidden. When I got there I knocked and rushed right in, without waiting to be given leave to enter.' Carys paused, a flush of colour staining cheeks that had been chalk white. 'Sister Veronica was there.' She forced herself to go on. 'And so was the priest. They were . . . they were . . .'

She hesitated, finding the words painful to say, feeling that to speak of what she had seen was a betrayal of trust, a breaking of her word, a promise made in her heart long before the nun's cane had beaten it from her mouth.

'Carys, wench.' Understanding her hesitation yet knowing too that there would be no healing until she spoke what was in her mind, Martha softly encouraged her. 'Carys, there is that inside you that would be best shared with others. It may be you have promised not to speak of it and don't care to break your promise. So maybe it's best if I speak the words for you. Your promise will not be violated but p'raps your heart will be eased.'

Taking the cup from Carys, she laid it on the table then folded the girl's hand in both her own. 'It be my belief,' she went on as softly as before, 'that you came on that priest and that nun doing what should be done only between man and wife.'

For fully half a minute silence hung like a stifling shroud over the kitchen. Alice, holding her breath in the prison of her lungs, stared at the housekeeper. What she had just said . . . it couldn't be the truth. Nuns and priests, they didn't do such things . . . Beside the long dresser the clock on the wall ticked away the seconds but Alice would not breathe, would not fracture the silence by proclaiming the truth.

'That be it then.' Giving Carys's hand a final comforting pat Martha pushed back her chair. 'There will be no more said on that subject in this kitchen, or beyond it.' She cast a meaningful glance at Alice who only now was releasing her breath. 'You, Alice, get them crocks put away then see to the dusting of the front parlour.' She glanced over at the clock which showed ten minutes to eleven. 'And you, Carys girl, get yourself up to your bedroom. Wash your hands and face and put on a fresh apron before you go to the mistress. And remember,' she added as Carys walked to the door that gave on to the back stairs, 'you can't be in no trouble 'cos if you was I would know about it. And anyway, you know yourself by now the mistress be no ogre.'

But why should Virginia Mountford want to see her?

Carys tied on a freshly laundered apron, smoothing its starched expanse over her skirts.

Was she to be dismissed? She felt her heart thud in her chest. Would she have to return to that convent?

Virginia Mountford sat in a high-backed brocade chair beneath a wide window overlooking a part of the garden that was filled with roses – ones that had been bred and named for her. Her husband had been a keen gardener while he lived, and developing a new strain of rose each year had been his delight. Shifting her glance to a beautiful long-legged table she smiled wistfully at the huge bowl of 'Ginny's Beauty' at its centre, the wonderful golden-bronze of the petals of her favourite rose reflected in a huge oblong silver-framed mirror.

Oliver had never once spoken of his sadness at their having no child but she knew that the sadness was there. How she had wanted to give him a son, but the years had passed and none had come to them. She swept her glance over the rest of the room: the walls panelled in oak, the beautiful French tapestries, graceful Regency chairs and sofa. They had been given wealth in plenty, she thought, but the richest gift of all had been denied.

A tap at the door pulled her back from the realm of memory. Touching one hand to the single rope of pearls about her throat then smoothing her deep blue skirts, before folding both hands together in her lap she called permission to enter.

Carys, face still pale from the episode in the kitchen, bobbed a brief curtsey.

'You asked to see me, ma'am?'

Virginia looked at the girl. If she and Oliver had been given a daughter she would have been about this age and she too would have been lovely, she would have had her father's laughing eyes and . . . Pushing the thought away, she tightened her mouth with the effort and for several seconds found it too difficult to speak.

'Yes.' She spoke at last but the words were thick with tears. 'There is a matter I wish to speak to you about.'

Carys felt her stomach muscles twist but lifted her head proudly. If she was to be dismissed, then whatever the reason she would face it full on.

'Sit down, Carys.'

The chair nearest her was a few feet to her right and on moving across to it she caught sight of a box, its beautiful enamelled sides and lid edged with a delicate filigree of silver. Without thinking what she was doing, she picked it up, turning it in her hands, knowing each of the lovely scenes painted on it before even looking at them.

'It is very beautiful, do you not think so?'

At Virginia's softly spoken question Carys looked up, sadness and longing stirring the depths of her amber eyes.

'Yes, it is very beautiful. Forgive me, ma'am, I should not have touched it.'

'Bring it to me.'

Taking the box Carys handed to her, Virginia touched one finger to its smooth surface.

'My husband bought me this box many years ago,' she said, her voice taking on the tone only a cherished memory can bring. 'It was an anniversary gift, the tenth year we had spent together. I remember he said he had bought it while on a business trip to Bilston. I have never been there but I imagine it must be a very pretty place to produce such beautiful objects as my box.'

Pretty? Carys remembered the times her father had taken her there with him. The cramped, huddled together houses, each of them giving part of their tiny space over to a workshop where every member of the family old enough or strong enough to work pounded metal ores into frit, or sat in the sallow light of tiny smoke-filmed windows coating tin and brass with white lead. Above all she recalled the fierce heat of the coal-fired kilns.

'You seemed surprised when you saw this, almost as if you knew it?' Virginia Mountford looked up. 'Is that so, Carys? Do you know this box?'

'I,' she answered softly. 'I have seen something like it before. 'I . . . I am familiar with the design.'

'Hmm!' Placing it on a rosewood table set near her chair, Virginia nodded. 'Bring your chair over here to the window and sit beside me.' Then with Carys seated, she went on: 'Would you tell me how you come to recognise the design on my box?'

'Only my father's enamels have that depth of brilliant blue. He . . .' Carys hesitated. She had not meant to speak of her father, the words had just tumbled from her out of pride in his work.

'It is a wonderful blue, so very vibrant.' Virginia ignored her hesitation. 'I have often wondered what gives it such a magnificent depth. It always reminds me of the blue of the Madonna's robes in the religious paintings of Raphael and Botticelli.'

'That is because my father shared their secrets. He added a tiny amount of powdered lapis lazuli to the oxide, then fired at over eight hundred degrees centigrade.'

'Lapis lazuli.' Virginia nodded again. 'The favoured stone of the Pharaohs of Ancient Egypt.'

'My father thought them among the greatest artists the world has known. He said they understood colour better than any Renaissance painter.'

'Your father sounds a very perceptive man?'

Was he perceptive enough to see what his wife had done to his daughter? Virginia watched the girl who sat looking at the box. Perceptive enough to realise that to face his wife with the truth was to lose her. Was that too much for him? Was living without his child preferable to living without his wife? Was that the real reason he had not found her?

'Was it only by the depth of blue you recognised that box as your father's work?' Virginia probed gently.

She had already told this woman of Maria and her jealousy; it could do no harm now to tell her the rest. Carys drew a long breath.

'That box is one of a set of six. Their design and painting I recognise from my childhood. My father encouraged me to draw, he used many of my designs in his products and often took me on visits to his enamelling works in Bilston. He preferred his employees to give up the practice of using their homes as workshops and gave them every encouragement to do so by building foundries that were roomy and light, though not everyone would give up their old ways. But my father treated his workers fairly. He paid them a decent wage, unlike some others in his trade, even though this caused him to be ostracised by some of the masters.'

'So you are familiar with the trade of enamelling?'

Carys nodded. 'Yes, ma'am.'

'One more question,' Virginia said as the girl looked from the box to her. 'Is your father's name Meshac Beddows?'

For a moment Carys did not answer. How had her mistress come by that information? She had told her of Maria, the morning after being brought to Ridge House, but she had not mentioned her father's name. But she *had* mentioned Moxley and Holyhead House. It would be simple for Virginia Mountford to discover the name of its owner.

From her chair beneath the spacious window Virginia

waited for the answer to her question and felt pity well in her when it came, a simple yes.

'Forgive my bluntness, my dear, but I think you will soon understand the reason for it. I had to be sure, you see. I had to be positive there could be no mistake. Now that I am, I feel I should show you this.'

Reaching for the newspaper, she handed it to Carys.

Puzzled, her eyes scanned the page. What could there be in a newspaper that Virginia Mountford felt she should see? It was then, halfway down the third column, that she saw the blacker, bolder print of a headline:

TRAGIC DEMISE OF PROMINENT INDUSTRIALIST.

A sudden awful fear squeezing her heart, she read the underlying report, the cold impersonality of it ripping at her heart.

> Meshac Beddows, proprietor of Beddows Enamels of Bilston, who died of a heart attack one week ago, was today laid to rest in the cemetery of the Church of All Saints, Moxley. Mr Beddows, whose home was Holyhead House, was a great benefactor to Bilston and to Moxley. He will be greatly missed by family, associates and employees.

Bethesda Lazic sat on the small wooden stool set close to the wood fire over which swung a smoke-blackened pot. She had come here to this same spot with her son for sixteen years. Sixteen years in which he had searched in vain for the only cure for the trouble that ailed him: revenge.

Would that cure be found this year, or would his hope fade as the summer would fade? Yet if it did, it would flourish once more as surely as the buds of spring would break, and with it the journey would begin all over again.

Did she resent their coming? She stared into the fire, seeing among its dancing flames a tall boy, trousers ragged below the knee, a laughing, handsome, black-haired boy whose strong limbs and sparkling eyes seemed fashioned by the gods.

No! She pulled hard on the yellowed stem of a clay pipe breathing out smoke from between teeth equally discoloured. If Caine were to die she would come alone; she would come until she took the life of the woman who had blinded her son, or the Lord took Bethesda Lazic from the earth.

True she grumbled at their returning here every year, but that was a shield, a pretence, to keep her son from knowing the depth of her own pain, and the longing in her heart to see that woman die.

She watched him through the smoke of her pipe. He was tall as his youth had foretold he would be and strength rippled through every cord and sinew of his body, but the pride had gone from him, marring him as that whip had marred his face. He should have had a wife by now, and children to carry his Romany blood, children she could sing the old songs to as she had sung them to him. But the blood that ran in his veins ran also in hers and with it the same desire that burned away all others. Bethesda Lazic would nurse no child of her son and that struck her to her heart but as surely as the sun rose in the heavens she would see that woman pay.

'Take what you be wanting from the pot.' Caine came up to the fire. 'Then see that all is ready in the wagon, I want to be away within the hour.'

'Be it Bromwich you be heading to?' Bethesda removed the pipe from her mouth, tapping out the remains of burned tobacco against the stool.

Caine glanced across the wide emptiness of the heath. They had spent sixteen of the springs and summers of his life up along West Bromwich. They had taken the wagon across the lyng fields scattered about with tiny purple flowers, massive oak trees spreading branches so wide they seemed to cover the earth, then down into the wooded hollow of the pretty Sandwell Valley which, long ago, had sheltered a Benedictine monastery but now held a beautiful mansion owned by a lord.

Each year they had been given permission to set the wagon at the edge of a copse of sycamore trees that bordered Swan Pool. There the estate workers, and even some of the people of the town, would come seeking his mother's herbal cures, and many a woman asking for her palm to be read while she was there. It brought money to keep them in food, the money he himself earned from odd jobs being kept against the winter months.

But this year he would not go to the Sandwell Valley. This year he would turn to the north.

'I was thinking to go in the opposite direction.' He looked back at his mother. 'I thought to go along of Bilston then on to Wolverhampton, making up into Shropshire for the winter.'

Bethesda made no reply, showed no surprise at this change to the route they had followed so many years, accepting the inner knowledge that was telling her son the time was now.

'I'll make we both some tay then put the fire out.' Placing the empty pipe in her mouth, she rose from her stool and went into the wagon.

Would it be this year? Was the quickening in his veins a sign that the reckoning had come at last? Murmuring softly to the old piebald mare, he fastened the harness to the collar about her neck then slipped a halter and lead reins over her head. Guiding the horse the few yards to where the caravan rested, he gently and slowly backed it between the shafts. Then, his movements quickening, he fastened straps and buckles, securing the harness about her back and tying the traces to the shafts of the wagon.

'Tay be ready,' Bethesda called from the fire, as yet still burning. 'Come drink it while it be hot. 'Twill be some hours afore you get the next.'

His hand resting a moment on the mare's soft flank, Caine glanced to where the Holyhead Road cut a narrow trail across the heath, letting his eyes follow the figure of a woman dressed in a coat that had once been blue but was now faded almost to grey. She was bareheaded but the spring sun glowing on her hair seemed to turn it into a cap of bronze. She walked slowly, head held low to her chest, hiding her face, but around one arm he saw a velvet band, the circlet of black that spoke of bereavement.

Bethesda too had seen the woman, and as she watched her pass the nerves in her own body jangled and a sixth sense, passed from mother to daughter in her family for as long as could be remembered, and so strong in herself as never to have played her false, told her that in some way the path of that woman would cross with her own; that in the future their lives would intertwine. Watching the figure slowly following the line of the road, Bethesda felt that here was a woman who would be the key to the revenge her son had sought so long, though that revenge would ultimately come through Bethesda Lazic.

The two tin cups washed and stored in the cupboard inside the wagon and her stool safely wedged beside the stove, Bethesda emptied the last of the water from the pot, dousing the small cooking fire before kicking earth over it. The woman had passed from her sight along the road but deep inside her every nerve still sang. This was the reason her son had changed their route of sixteen years. Whether he knew it or not, the fates were ready to play their part.

Chapter Nine

. . . Was laid to rest . . . died a week ago . . .

The words she had read in the newspaper danced in Carys's mind.

Her father was dead!

The numbness that had overtaken her in the drawing room of Ridge House gripped her still.

Her father was dead. She would not see him again. She would never be able to put her arms about him, to tell him the truth he would never know she was not what her mother had surely claimed. That she had done none of the things that had been told to the Mother Superior of the convent.

Behind her on the road a horse clopped loud on the rough surface, the rumble of a wagon's wheels rumbling in the quiet afternoon, but Carys heard no sound other than the crying of her own heart.

'You were not to know,' Virginia Mountford had told her kindly. 'And heart attacks happen so quickly, they can take a life and give no warning of their coming. The Lord took your father swiftly and that was a blessing. Accept it as such, my dear. Forget now about the past, forget Holyhead House, there is nothing for you there.'

There was nothing for her there.

The cold chill of truth added to the numbness that held her. There was nothing for her in her father's house, nothing except trouble and perhaps danger should Maria find her there.

'*Stay away from Moxley, and stay away from me!*'

Those had been her words that day on Snow Hill railway station. Well, she would stay away from Maria, and as for her father's house, there was nothing she wished for there, but she would not stay away from Moxley, away from the churchyard that held her father's body. She would pay her respects from love for him, a last service Maria would deny if consulted.

'Could you be doing with a ride, missy?'

Alongside her a gypsy wagon came to a halt.

'The road be rough, missy, and you have a look of weariness about you.'

Carys looked up at the wagon painted with bright flowers, its window hung with yellow curtains.

'The offer be kindly meant, you need have no fear.'

Carys's glance switched to the woman on the driving seat sitting beside a man who held his head turned slightly away. The woman's face was heavily lined, bearing the marks of her years. Her hair, grey as morning mist, escaped in straggling wisps from beneath a red head kerchief fastened at the nape of her neck. A black shawl, splashed liberally with a pattern of full-blown roses, was draped about her shoulders, the knot which held it resting where breasts had once jutted firm and proud, though they were now indistinguishable beneath layers of clothing that ended in dark layered skirts sweeping to her boots.

'Or be it you have no liking for gypsies? In that case, we will be on our way.'

'I have no dislike of gypsies.' The woman's voice clearing some of the fog from her brain, Carys realised the rudeness her failure to answer had implied.

'Then think on the length of the road that lies ahead. Your feet be aching now, if I be not mistaken, and they will ache a deal more before you get where you be heading. I know this way well, there be no dwelling atwixt here and Moxley and that be a step of two miles or more.'

Already the air was cooling, the sun losing the weak warmth of spring. Carys realised the sense of accepting a lift. The horse hardly looked capable of speed but its pace would still outmatch her own and her strength would be saved for the homeward journey. Squinting up at the old woman, back resting against the closed bottom half of the wagon's stable-type door, her shoulder touching that of the man beside her, Carys thanked her, catching hold of the hand held out to help her on to the wagon.

'You be telling us where it is you want to be set down?' The woman hitched herself along the wooden seat, allowing Carys to sit without their bodies touching. 'We be bound for Bilston though we might not get the whole way before the light goes. The days still fade quickly this early in the year. Mayhap my son will camp up for the night some way from that town, but we will take you as far as we go.'

'I am going to Moxley,' Carys answered. 'I want to visit the church there.'

'That be the church of All Saints.' The gypsy woman nodded, her gold hoop earrings glinting in the pale sunlight. 'I know it, though I have never been inside.'

Bethesda waited for the girl to respond, wondering, if an answer came, if it would be the same as that her sixth sense had already placed in her mind. This girl's home had been in Moxley, though it was there no longer. She had been taken from it while still little more than a girl by Gorgio reckoning, and put in a place that had brought fear to her heart and labour to her back. The girl would not know, for Bethesda guessed she did not have the gift of the sight, but this day would bring a new fear.

'Moxley was once my home . . .'

Bethesda listened to what she knew.

' . . . but I . . . I left when I was seventeen and have

not been back since then. I am going to visit my father's grave.'

'It is good to see respect for the old given by the young. Your father has been long gone?'

'Last week.' Carys felt the tears catch in her throat. 'He died last week.'

And he was placed in the ground but yesterday. Bethesda could have added but did not. The girl was grieving and had no kin of her own to share her pain. Suddenly feeling the familiar surge in her stomach, the old gypsy clamped her lips tight together. It always came to her like this, almost as if her veins had widened, allowing a rush of blood that was followed by a fierce heat, a burning that seemed to reach from her very soul into her mind, searing away her thoughts, clearing her brain, removing all else in preparation for the coming of the sight. Then it was with her. Clearly as watching actors upon a stage she saw a woman rolling naked beneath a golden-haired man, then the same woman handing a younger woman to a nun. The picture in her mind changed to a large house, to a bedroom in that house, a bedroom where that same woman flaunted her body before a different, much older man, a man who grasped his chest before falling dead across the bed. The woman turned and Bethesda saw her face. It was the face of the woman she and her son had searched for these sixteen years.

'I'll pull off the road here and take to the heath.'

Caine spoke for the first time as he guided the piebald left on to the rough surface of untilled ground. Over to the right fields of corn waved their shoots like small green flags. 'I tell you so you will have no worry that we don't be going where my mother said. I know the tales Gorgios tell about gypsy folk making off with their children.'

At Carys's side Bethesda relaxed as the sight left her, but the uneasiness that remained puzzled her. This was not how it usually was. Once the sight had revealed itself, shown her what it was she had to know, then it cleared, leaving no trace of having been. But this time . . . this time she felt its purpose unfulfilled, unfinished. This time she had not been given the whole of it. Sometime in the future it would come again, and she must watch and wait.

'Arrh.' Bethesda nodded. 'Lies told to frighten young uns into behaving, filling little hearts with fear and little heads with untruths. Gorgios call that love . . . pah! I wouldn't give that sort of love to a pig in the wild.'

'We leave the road here 'cos beyond that rise lies the toll house.'

Caine resumed his explanation and Carys turned to look at him, past the figure of his mother, but still he kept his face turned slightly away.

'We pay no toll to travel God's good earth.' Bethesda again took the conversation to herself. 'It was given to all men, for all to walk freely. It was given to Adam who was father to us all, and the Almighty did not tell him to parcel it up and give parts to some, telling them to make others pay to cross it. No, that was the idea of graspers, men who batten on the backs of others. But they'll not batten on the gypsy folk, they won't take our money for things that be the God-given right of every man.'

Cresting the rise, Caine pointed ahead to where a double-storied octagonal building, an added gable to one side giving a lop-sided effect, stood close to the side of the road.

'Carts have to pay threepence to pass that,' he said, 'and a packman pays a penny.'

'I have threepence.' Carys reached a hand to her pocket. 'I will pay for you to pass the toll.'

Catching her hand as Carys made to pass the coins to Caine, Bethesda almost gasped. With an intensity that threatened to spill her from her seat, the feeling came that this girl and the woman who had blinded her son were close kin.

'We'll take nothing from you, missy.' The words were said slowly, giving time for the feeling to fade away. 'It be a kindness you offer and we be grateful for it, but we won't take it. A Romany takes no reward from those he offers his wagon to, but we will remember all the same.'

And she would remember, Bethesda thought, as the wagon skirted past the toll house, its keeper standing beside the crudely built dry stone wall that sheltered a vegetable patch from the gorse and grass of the heath. She would remember, and would return a kindness with a kindness.

They drove on in silence, the landscape beginning to grow more familiar to Carys. Over in the distance a curtain of trees she knew shielded the hospital where fever patients were cared for, the thread of Bull Lane leading to it across the heath, and moments later she caught the glint of light reflecting from the waters of the Cracker.

'That be where we'll set the wagon.' Caine pointed a brown finger towards the pool. 'There be shelter and water enough and none so close as to be troubled by the presence of a gypsy.'

Calling a soft 'whoah' to the mare, he let the reins fall slack across her back.

'This be where you will be leaving, miss.' He jumped from the driving seat, coming to where Carys was beginning to climb down. Putting his hands to her waist, he steadied her.

'Thank you.' Turning quickly as he released her, Carys caught her breath. One side of his face was drawn together in a long puckered scar, and the socket of one eye was empty.

Without reply he returned to the wagon, swinging himself up into his seat and taking the reins into his hands. With a quiet word to the horse, he set off for the pool.

Watching as the caravan dipped into the hollow that held the swimming hole, Carys remembered a different scene. One where a young girl sat among screening ferns, pencil and paper forgotten as she watched the figure of a man rise from glistening black water, the gem-like droplets showering into the sun as he shook water from his dark hair.

It had been a lifetime ago.

Turning away, she pressed on over the heath, slanting

her steps towards the road she must cross to get to the church.

Glad that it was Wednesday, and the middle of the week would almost certainly mean the churchyard would be empty of people, Carys crossed the road, pausing by the gate beyond which headstones loomed like skeletal fingers, the Sunday flowers shedding the last of their colour over the grass-topped graves. Sunday afternoon was the time the village folk brought their tokens of love and remembrance to their departed loved ones, this being their only free time. Even their burials were usually made as late in the day as could be arranged, she knew from hearing his workers talk with her father. That way they lost less time from their work and less of the money they needed to feed the living.

But she had brought no token of her own love. Carys looked at the flowers, mostly yellow gorse cut from the bushes that littered the heath, with a sprinkling of blue periwinkle and the pinkish-mauve of lungwort found among the hedgerows. She had not thought even to bring these wild flowers, she had nothing to lay on her father's grave. For a moment she thought to turn back, to come again when she would have flowers. But it was not flowers she wanted to give her father, it was her love. To tell him, though he could not hear, of the love that had never faltered in her, the love of him that she would hold in her heart forever.

Keeping to the path of scree stones she walked around the side of the church, its red sandstone colour already veiled by soot drifting from the foundry chimneys of Bilston and Wednesbury. She came to where other headstones, more generously spaced than the rest, were enclosed by a boundary wall. In one corner, beneath a large oak, a mound of flowers more colourful and plentiful than the rest was heaped beneath a stone of blue-grey marble.

Slowly, Carys walked up to it, her eyes blurring at the words carved in the headstone:

Sacred to the memory of Meshac Beddows
Born sixth day of June 1840
Died fourth day of April 1899
Husband of Maria Ann Beddows
Father of Carys Margaret Beddows
He rests with God

'Father! Oh, Father!' Tears blinding her, she sank to her knees on the damp earth. 'I'm sorry,' she sobbed, 'I'm sorry for the hurt I must have caused you, I'm sorry for the pain I must have given you.'

'Was on no account of you the master suffered pain, and you was not the one gave him worry.'

Tears still blurring her vision, Carys saw that a woman was on her knees beside her, a posy of wild flowers in her hands.

'Mary?' Carys brushed a hand across her eyes, clearing the tears from them. 'It is Mary, isn't it?'

'Arrh, miss, it is me, Mary Bartlett. But what brings you here?'

'I came to visit my father's grave.'

'I could guess that for meself, miss. What I means is, how come you could get leave to come here today and not yesterday when your father was buried? I mean to say, it be a bit strange them letting you out after the service was done with.'

'Them?' Carys's voice held a question.

'Arrh, miss, you know, them nuns in that convent you have joined. I know it don't be often they'll let you out after the taking of Holy Orders, but for the burying of your father . . .'

So that was what Maria had told them, and her father too no doubt: that she had chosen to take the veil, that it was her own decision not to return home.

'I am here now,' Carys answered, choosing not to deny what had obviously been said.

'Arrh, here you be, and in the clothes you went away in four years since.' Mary Bartlett looked squarely at the girl beside her. 'Truth is you be no nun, you have taken no Holy Orders, you have given no vow. That be the truth of it, don't it, miss? Permission to go outside a convent might be given and given late, but a nun would not change her habit for any other clothes. The mistress has told us one thing but your presence here tells another. You were left behind all right, but it weren't in no convent, you tell me if I be wrong?'

Mary laid the flowers among the others.

'I was in the room when that lie were told to your father. It was his wife caused his pain, not you, and I can guess why it was done. The mistress isn't one to lose what her sees to be her own, and Ryder Tempal comes in to that category.'

'Does . . . does he still come to the house?'

'That he does, miss.' Mary pushed herself to her feet, brushing moss from the skirts of her green coat. 'He's been a regular visitor, mostly during the day when the master was away at the works. We below stairs used to wonder how he made his living, always gadding about like he does, but then we reckon as we know how. His sort lives off the women they dance attendance on, and Ryder Tempal isn't one to dish out flattery and get nothing in return.'

'Was Mr Tempal present when . . . when my father suffered his heart attack?' Carys touched a hand to the soft earth that covered her father's coffin.

'No, miss.' Mary watched the caress, the last tiny gesture of love. 'It happened sometime after your father had gone to bed. The doctor didn't say exactly when, or if he did we got no word of it below stairs. It were Mr Wilkins, you know, the butler, who found him when he took his hot shaving water to his dressing room and the master was not there. Mr Wilkins says he went into the bedroom and the master was lying in bed, all peaceful like, with the covers pulled over him. He must have died in his sleep and you can be sure that way he would have no pain.'

'I didn't even bring him flowers,' Carys whispered.

'C'mon, miss.' Maria's housemaid lifted Carys to her feet and held her while she sobbed. 'Try not to take on. Your father wouldn't want you to shed tears, though we all know it be best at times. Come sit in the church for a while, just till you feel more eased.'

Sitting in a pew at the back of the dimly lit church, the maid waited until Carys's tears abated.

'Where do you be living, miss?' Quiet as the whisper was, it seemed loud in the silence of the church. 'You're not on the streets, are you?'

Carys twisted her damp handkerchief in her fingers.

'No, Mary, I am not on the streets. I have a position with Virginia Mountford. She owns Ridge House at Hill Top.'

'A position!' Mary was dumbfounded. 'You mean, you are a servant?'

'A housemaid.' Carys smiled fleetingly. 'Like yourself, Mary. There is nothing wrong in being a housemaid.'

'No, miss, no, there isn't, for the likes of me that is. But you – you be the daughter of Meshac Beddows. You shouldn't be housemaid to anybody. Why not come home, miss? Come home with me.'

'I don't think that would be wise, Mary.'

'Why, miss? On account of your mother? I don't see how her could do you mischief once everybody in the house knows you be back.'

'*Come back to Moxley and I'll see you dead!*'

Mary had not heard those words, she had not heard all that Maria Beddows had said.

'I do not think my mother would want to do me mischief, but I prefer to stay at Ridge House, at least . . . at least until the shock of my father's death has worn off a little.'

Mary watched the afternoon light strike the stained glass windows and burst into a glory of colour, showering the altar standing at the end of the long aisle. She knew the girl was defending her mother when she said the woman would not want to do her mischief: Maria would do any woman mischief if she thought Ryder Tempal were paying them a mite too much attention. Or was her daughter waiting for Tempal to disappear from the scene? Mary felt a cynical laugh in her throat. Much chance there was of that while Maria Beddows had a penny left! And even should he take himself off there would be another to take his place; the mistress was too fond of a young man's company to remain alone for long.

'You know your own way best, miss,' she said, deciding to say no more on the subject. 'But you knows you have friends at the house, so if ever you feel . . .'

'I know, Mary.' Carys touched the other girl's hand. 'Thank you.'

'Ee, Miss Carys.' Mary folded the hand between both her own. 'I hates to think of you being a housemaid.'

For several moments they sat together, hands entwined, their figures almost lost among the heavy shadows at the rear of the church, hiding from the light.

'I have to be going.' It was Mary who spoke, standing as she did so. 'I only get an hour off today and that be almost spent.'

Leaving the pew, they both curtsied acknowledgement towards the altar before leaving the church.

'You sure you will be all right, going back on your own, miss?' Mary squinted against the bright light. 'I don't rightly know where this Hill Top be that you spoke of. P'raps you should wait here and I'll get Mr Wilkins to send one of the men to take you there?'

'That will not be necessary, Mary, I shall be perfectly all right.' Carys hesitated, wanting to return to her father's grave.

'Then let me see you on your way.' Mary guessed at the reason for her hesitation, but further grieving would do no good. 'I don't want to think of you here all day by yourself.'

Allowing herself to be steered down the pebble path and beyond the gate, Carys returned Mary's friendly hug, fresh tears rising to her throat as the girl waved her along the road.

She had said goodbye to her father. And her mother? Her mother had said her own goodbyes four years ago.

'I tell you, it was her!'

Coming from her bedroom, Maria paused as voices drifted up to her from the hallway below.

'Couldn't have been.'

The answer came clearly. Whoever it was had not thought to lower their voice.

'I tell you, it was!'

Recognising the voice as that of the housemaid, Mary, Maria waited. It was surprising how much could be learned from servants who did not know you were listening.

'But it couldn't have been, the mistress said . . .'

'Oh, we know what the mistress said!' Mary's voice became tart. 'And we all know what a liar her can be when it suits her.'

Maria allowed a cold smile to curve her mouth. Mary Bartlett could speak of her as she wished . . . until Maria had heard all she had to say.

'I tell you, it was her I was talking to. There her was, kneeling by that grave and sobbing something awful. It fair pulled me to pieces hearing it. And when I spoke to her, I was recognised straight off. Ee, poor wench! Her clothes were that shabby – they were the very same ones as her left the house in. I tell you, Amy, my heart fair bled for her.'

'But if it *were* who you say it were, why hasn't her come back here?'

'I asked that,' Mary replied. 'Her told me her preferred to be with that woman, said her wanted to stay in her house till her was over the shock of her father's passing.'

'But a servant? That wench never ought to be no servant, Mary.'

Mary's voice carried clearly to Maria. 'I told her that an'

all and her answered that there be nothing wrong in being a housemaid. Nor there isn't, I said, not for such as meself, but you should be grafting for nobody.'

'Ee, it ain't right, Mary. That girl should be in her own home.'

'Reckon her should, and I also reckons we all know why her isn't.'

Above them Maria waited. Fear was telling her who the subject of the two maids' conversation was, but her brain was telling her to hold back, hear everything before moving.

'It be jealousy,' Mary went on after a moment of silence. 'The mistress be jealous of her own child. It be that and nothing else caused her to say that girl had taken the veil.'

'Her child!' Amy's voice was suddenly scornful. 'More like Meshac's child. He had far more feeling for that girl than ever her mother had . . .'

It *was* Carys! Maria felt her brain swirl. The maids were talking of Carys, of seeing her beside a grave. That could only mean her father's grave. Maria's hands tightened. That meant Carys was here, in Moxley.

'. . . but I never thought a mother could be jealous of her own.'

'That one could if her thought to lose her playmate. Maria Beddows would scratch the eyes from any woman's head if her thought Ryder Tempal had looked at them with a passing fancy.'

'Ee, Mary, do you think the mistress has been playing away?'

'Don't you?' Mary laughed. 'I not only think it, I be willing to wager a year's pay I'm not wrong. That one be mad about Tempal, anybody but a blind man could see that. And you ain't blind, Amy Fletcher.'

'So who be this woman the girl be housemaid to?'

Maria caught her breath, every part of her focused on the answer.

'Said her name was Virginia Mountford.'

'Don't ring no bell, can't say I've heard that name before.'

'It's not surprising . . .'

Mary's voice was fainter now, as if she had moved across to the far side of the hall. Maria took a careful step nearer to the head of the stairs, mindful to remain out of sight should either of the girls glance upward.

'. . . seems her don't live in Moxley but somewhere called Hill Top.'

'Where do that be?'

Amy's voice was even fainter than Mary's. They were moving away. Maria clenched her teeth, willing herself to listen. She must hear the rest.

'Blowed if I know.' Mary was only just within hearing range. 'All I know is what I was told. Miss Carys said her was housemaid to a Virginia Mountford who had a place called Ridge House and that it were somewhere along a place called Hill Top.'

Slowly, quietly, Maria released her breath. Carys had not taken her warning. She was living only a few miles away. She turned to her bedroom and pulled the cord that would summon her maid.

It had been a week since she had learned where her daughter was living; a week in which Mary Bartlett had been dismissed from her post as housemaid.

Leaning against the upholstery of her carriage, Maria gazed at the passing heath, at its interchange between tilled field and fallow, between hedged corn and wheat field, then the giving way to gaping black stretches of worked out surface mining and high heaps of shale and spoil that erupted like huge grey boils on the skin of the earth.

But she was not interested in the beauty or the deformity. Her mind was engaged only upon her own errand. She had waited a week, not wanting to return the calls of condolence to Holyhead House nor to reply to those arriving by post without leaving a suitable time between.

A widow must not be seen to be making the effort too soon.

Opening the bag that hung about her wrist she drew out a card, the edges of which were black. A card that bore the name 'Virginia Mountford' and a message of sympathy in her loss. Maria smiled. How fortunate that the woman's husband and Meshac had sometimes done business together.

'If you would wait in here, ma'am, I will tell the mistress you be calling.'

Opening the door to the library, Alice bobbed a curtsey as the woman, dressed entirely in black, a fine tulle veil covering her face and shoulders, passed inside.

Maria glanced around the room. Bookcases of light elmwood lined the walls on three sides, each filled with expensively bound books, while the fourth was taken up by an elegant fireplace, its carved lines clean and tasteful. It seemed Virginia Mountford's preferences were much the same as her own, with none of the heavy ornate furniture so beloved of forty years ago and still markedly present in many of the houses Maria visited.

'Mrs Mountford asks if you will join her in her sitting room, ma'am.' Alice bobbed a second curtsey as she returned, then led the way upstairs to a room adjoining Virginia's bedroom, one which she kept as her private sitting room.

'My sympathies, Mrs Beddows. How very kind of you to call.'

Accepting the chair Virginia indicated, Maria swept a rapid glance around the room, again noting the graceful Regency furniture, the tapestries and carpet that spoke so strongly of France. In taste at least she and the grey-haired woman seated opposite her had a lot in common, it seemed.

'I wished to return your own kindness.' Maria folded the delicate black tulle back over her head, revealing her face. 'It was very thoughtful of you to send your condolences on my bereavement.'

'Will you take some tea?' Virginia's hand went out to a tapestry bell pull beside the fireplace.

'Thank you, but no.' Maria gave a faint smile. 'I still am not ready for social calls.'

'I understand.' Virginia withdrew her hand.

'However, I felt I must call on you right away upon hearing . . .'

'Upon hearing?' Virginia looked at her visitor, not liking what she saw. But no, that was not so. It was more what she felt, a feeling she could not define, yet one she most definitely did not like. 'What is it that you heard, Mrs Beddows? And now think I should hear?'

Maria dropped her glance to the black velvet bag resting in her lap, hoping it would give the impression she was not entirely happy with what she was doing.

'It was something I overheard two of my housemaids talking about. That was a week ago and I have wrestled with my conscience all that time as to whether to speak of it to you or whether to forget the whole thing.'

'But in the end you thought you should speak?' Virginia's eyes stayed on her face. Maria Beddows was a very attractive woman but Virginia felt it was an attraction that existed only on the surface; that the woman had no trace of inner beauty, a beauty of the spirit that could shine through even the plainest individual, and knew she would have had much the same feeling had she not known what the woman had done to her daughter.

'Yes.' Maria took her time raising her eyes. 'I was afraid that not to speak would be to do you a disservice.'

'I appreciate your thought for me. Perhaps you will tell me what it is you have to say?'

Maria drew a deep breath, holding it for a few seconds before letting it sigh slowly from her parted lips, making it seem as if what she was about to say was causing her grief.

'As I explained, I overheard my maids talking. They were discussing a meeting one of them had had with a young woman they said was a housemaid in your employ – a young woman named Carys.'

'I do have a housemaid of that name.' Virginia nodded.

'May I ask, did she come with references?'

Virginia felt her dislike of this woman increasing but stilled a desire to ask her to leave. 'No, Mrs Beddows, she did not. In point of fact she came with another of my housemaids. They met in Birmingham.'

'And, forgive my asking, do you know her background?'

'Only the little she told me.'

'I see.' Maria paused again then quickly, and for effect added, 'Of course, there is every possibility I may be wrong and that the girl you employ is not the one I dismissed four years ago.'

'I agree the possibility exists,' Virginia said coldly. 'But tell me, if you will, the reason for that dismissal?'

Maria allowed her glance to falter and her fingers to twitch nervously on the bag in her lap.

'It . . . it was a rather delicate matter. I spoke to her one day as she returned from her afternoon off. She had what appeared to be a sketch pad in her hand. She said she had been drawing, and was most reticent when I asked to see her work. She became rather agitated when I repeated my request, and when she eventually showed the sketches to me I saw why. Some were quite pretty, good depictions of the area, but others . . .' Maria drew another long breath. 'Well . . . others were obscene.'

'Obscene?' Virginia repeated the description. 'That is a serious, not to say distressing, statement.'

'It was my fear that, given those drawings, she might be engaged in doings of an even more unwholesome nature during her time away from the house, therefore I dismissed her.'

'As I shall myself most certainly do if I arrive at the same conclusion.' Virginia reached for the bell pull, this time giving it a sharp tug.

'Alice,' she said when the girl presented herself. 'Has Carys returned from her errand?'

'No, ma'am.' Alice darted a glance at the woman in black.

'Alice,' Virginia asked again, 'has Carys ever shown you any sketches?'

'If you mean drawrings, ma'am, yes, her has.'

'Does she still have them, do you know?'

'They be in her room, under her bed.'

'I want you to bring them here.' Virginia caught the girl's look. 'It will be all right, Alice. I will speak to Carys when she returns.'

'Very good, ma'am.'

Turning to her visitor as Alice left to fetch the sketches, Virginia's face showed none of her feelings. This woman had not come here out of solicitude but from spite. She wanted only to do more harm to a girl who had done her none, and that girl her own daughter!

'Take out what is inside,' Virginia instructed, when Alice returned with the carpet bag belonging to Carys. 'And, Alice, I want you to tell me truthfully if those are the sketches that were shown to you.'

Unrolling the sheets of paper, Alice looked at each one. 'Yes, ma'am, these be the same.'

Virginia nodded. 'Try to remember, Alice. Were there any shown to you that are not here now?'

'No.' Alice looked again at the sheaf of drawings. 'This be all of them. I remember 'cos I counted them when they was spread out on the bed. Well, I say all of them, but there be one new one – Carys drawed it two or three weeks since. I know, ma'am, 'cos I kept a listen out in case Mrs Bates took it into her head to come upstairs to bed early like. Her would have got mad to find we was not in our beds.'

'Will you show us the one you mean?'

Fumbling nervously, the maid drew out one paper from among the rest, handing it to her mistress. Looking at it, Virginia Mountford felt a wave of pleasure spread through her. The sketch was a likeness of her father, taken no doubt from the portrait in the corridor, though the girl had shown him as much younger. Handing it to Maria, she indicated that Alice should do the same with the remainder.

'Are those the drawings to which you refer?'

Maria's nostrils widened, evincing disapproval. 'They are. It would appear the girl I dismissed has found her way into your house, Mrs Mountford.'

Taking back the sketches, Virginia glanced again at the drawing of a man, his powerful body surging up out of a pool of water, every charcoal stroke shouting his pleasure at the feel of it, every line perfect. But it was the face that held her breath. Half turned away, it was shown only in profile. The sketch drawn long before being brought into this house and the one so recently drawn had the same face, she realised, a face almost identical with her father's portrait though in fact it was a face she had seen much more recently: the face of her nephew.

Forcing herself to hand the drawings to Alice, she dismissed the girl, telling her to return the bag to Carys's room.

'I am sorry if the reason for my call has distressed you.'

'On the contrary, Mrs Beddows.' Virginia's back was ramrod straight and her eyes icy, but her voice was steady as she answered, 'It has afforded me the pleasure of seeing those drawings once again. Oh, yes,' she saw the surprise spring to Maria's eyes, 'I have seen them before. They were shown to me the morning after the girl came to this house.'

'But how does she . . .'

'How does she still come to have them? Is that what you were going to ask? She has them because the woman who was asked to destroy them saw them not as obscene but, as I do, as things of beauty. That woman was Sister Mary Immaculata, Mother Superior of the Convent of the Holy Child, and it was you who handed those sketches to her, you who told her the same lies you have just told me. You did not turn a housemaid out of your home, Mrs Beddows, you turned away your own daughter!'

Virginia's knuckles whitened as she pulled the cord beside the fireplace and her top lip turned inward with suppressed anger. 'Was attempting to confine a girl to a life behind walls your way of showing concern for her moral welfare, or was it rather your way of disposing of a threat to your own sordid affair? Yes, Mrs Beddows, I know a little of Ryder Tempal's part in all of this. And as for the rest, I can guess. It is my opinion you got rid of that girl because you were afraid – afraid he would come to prefer her over you. Just what sort of a mother do you call yourself? I call you none at all!'

'How dare you!' Maria's face blanched with temper. 'How dare you speak to me like that? I will . . .'

'What?' Virginia did not blink an eyelid. 'What will you do? Take me to court for slander? Do it, Mrs Beddows. I am too old for that to worry me but not too old to enjoy it – enjoy hearing what you have to say to a magistrate regarding your entering your daughter into a convent then abandoning her, penniless, on a railway station when she refused to take the vows that would keep her locked away for life. And certainly not too old to enjoy hearing what your friends will say afterwards.'

Virginia smiled. A light tap on the door brought Maria to her feet.

'You will no doubt have your solicitor contact me? I look forward to it.'

Watching Maria sweep out of the room followed by an obviously curious Alice, Virginia Mountford felt a cold touch in her stomach, a feeling that warned she had not seen the last of Maria Beddows.

Chapter Ten

Reuben Fereday looked at the beautifully enamelled boxes laid out for his inspection. In the dim light of the tiny workroom the colours seemed to glow, vibrant and alive, and he found himself marvelling, as he always did on his visits here, that so drab and smoke-heavy a town as Bilston, with its narrow streets and viciously cramped houses, could produce something so exquisite.

'These are excellent.' Taking one of the boxes in his hands, he turned to the man at his side whose shoulders were hunched from bending over a workbench almost every waking hour.

'Thank you, sir.'

'Who is responsible for the designs?' He turned the box in his hand, a memory stirring in the back of his mind.

'I don't rightly be knowin' that, sir.' The workman pushed his flat cap back on his head. 'They be some the master brought along of 'isself.'

Reuben continued to examine the box. The garden he saw painted there, a summerhouse boxed in by a hedge of white roses . . . He had seen that same summerhouse, admired those same roses.

'Do you have more like these?'

'Arrh, sir, but I ain't got them 'ere.' The man pulled his cap back on to the front of his head, drawing the peak low over his brow.

'Where are they?' Reuben replaced the box on the bench that ran the length of the narrow ten-foot-long room.

'They be along of the master's room. 'E kept them there, said as 'ow they was not to be sold, but since . . . well, mistress 'as the running of the business now and 'er says to sell. That be 'ow I comes to have put that one out with the others, though it come 'ard, having to go against master's wishes.'

'Did Mr Beddows give you any reason for not wanting this particular box to be sold?'

'No, sir.' The man touched a finger to the box, its jewel-bright colours aflame against his dirt-streaked skin. 'But they was special to 'im, that much I does know. Though just between me and yourself sir, begging your pardon, it be my guess that there box, and the five others in the master's room, were drawed by his little wench. 'Er were mighty fond of drawring, as I remembers.'

Drawn by his daughter! Reuben felt his heartbeat quicken. The design on that box seemed likely to have been drawn by the daughter of Meshac Beddows as it was a picture of the garden at Holyhead House. And the girl . . . the girl he had confronted that day above the pool at Moxley, she had carried a sketch pad, and had claimed she was returning to that same house. The girl he had looked for each time he passed through. The girl who had taken Holy Orders and was now lost to him forever.

'The others . . . I would like to see them. Take me along to Mr Beddows's room.'

'Don't know as I can do that, Mr Fereday, sir.' The man pushed at his cap again. 'Mr Beddows, 'e didn't like nobody goin' into his room lessen 'e was there.'

Taking out his watch, Reuben glanced at it then replaced it in his waistcoat pocket. He had several more calls to make in Bilston. He could return here later in the day.

'What time will Mr Beddows be here?' he asked.

''E won't be comin', sir.' The man shook his head. 'Not no more 'e won't.'

Reuben glanced at the man, noticing for the first time the look of sadness and worry on his face.

'You said a moment ago that the mistress now has the running of the business. Is that mistress Mrs Beddows?'

'Arrh, that be 'er, sir.'

Reuben's brows drew together. 'Has Mr Beddows sustained some accident?'

'No, sir, 'e ain't had no accident.'

'Then why will he not be coming here again? You *did* say he would not be coming any more, did you not?'

'Arrh, I did, sir.'

Reuben glanced the length of the confined workroom. At the far end a woman hammered a large lump of frit, pounding the metal-bearing stone into powder. Her dust-covered skirts were held about by an apron of rough dark cloth, her hair beneath a scrap of the same material. Nearer to him, two boys of about eight years old each painted metal boxes with a coating of white paste-like substance, before placing them beside a brick-built furnace that belched the heat of hell into the room whenever it was opened. Lastly a young girl of around fourteen held a box to the grimy light of a window set high in the wall, then dipped a fine paintbrush into liquid oxides mixed in a cracked saucer, painting each with a steady hand on to the white-glazed metal. Reuben glanced again at the selection of beautifully decorated boxes set out along the bench. The skills of these people were astounding, their artistry and knowledge of oxides producing artefacts of a beauty that could match any in the world. And mostly, he knew from his visits, not all from workshops such as this, but from tiny, dark back to back places that were part of a family's living quarters.

Glancing toward him, the girl halted in her task, her eyes enquiring.

'Perhaps I should call to see Mr Beddows on my next visit.' Reuben returned his attention to the stoop-shouldered man hovering beside him.

'Won't do no good.' The man turned as the door to the furnace was raised and the two boys began to fill its red hot interior with freshly glazed boxes. 'You won't see no more of Meshac Beddows 'cept you goes to Moxley cemetery. That be where the master is now, six feet under.'

'Mr Beddows is dead?' The slow rise of irritation that had sharpened Reuben's last words gave way to surprise.

'Arrh, sir.' The man's eyes followed the loading of the furnace. 'Been gone this last month or more. Mistress be the one has the running of this and all the rest of the master's interests in the town. But how long before . . .'

'How long before . . . ? Go on, man, say it. How long before what?'

Pushing his cap completely back from his head, the workman ran a hand through his thinning hair.

'I knows I shouldn't be saying so, sir, but the worry of it all has me and the missis there awake nights. Y'see, since the master was took there ain't been much come our way. No orders, I means. The mistress, 'er says to sell whatever be asked for, but 'er didn't say anything about customers' orders. And the master, 'e always seen to it we 'ad fresh supplies of frit to work with, but there's been none of that since his wife took over. We be wonderin', the missis and me, what be going to 'appen. Does the mistress's intention be to close down the enamellin'?'

Reuben could see now the cause of the worry on the man's face. Should that happen, this and many another family in Bilston would know the misery of empty stomachs.

'The five other boxes you spoke of, can you fetch them from Mr Beddows's room? I am interested in purchasing the set.'

Reuben watched the crestfallen way the tired-looking man pulled his cap back over his head. It must seem that his own response was heartless but Reuben could give no answer to the man's question. He had no knowledge of Maria Beddows's intent.

'If you'll pardon the sayin' of it, sir, I don't know as I can. The master, 'e never let nobody into that room 'less 'e was with them.' He nodded to where a small, low-windowed brick building stood across the yard from the workroom, a building Reuben knew had served as Meshac's office. 'That box there, one of them six, that was fetched out by the mistress 'erself, and 'er 'olds the key.'

'I see. Thank you.' Reuben made his way to the door, the eyes of the man's family following him. 'Will you see to it my boxes are dispatched to Birmingham on the morning train?' he asked as they stepped into the yard. 'As for the others we spoke of, I will contact Mrs Beddows, today if possible. Should it happen that anyone else enquires after their purchase, then do not sell them until you hear from her or myself.'

Closing his hand over the florin Reuben dropped into his palm following every visit to the workshop, the man touched his cap with a lead-stained forefinger.

'I'll do that, Mr Fereday. Won't nobody see them boxes, least not with my showing of 'em they won't.'

Why did he want those boxes so much?

Reuben glanced sideways as the driver of his hired carriage shouted a loud uncomplimentary caution to the carter cutting across the path of the hansom, causing the horse to veer too close to a passing dray, then fell back into the dark well of the thoughts that had plagued him throughout the rest of the day. He had visited each of the enamelling firms with which he did business. The articles they produced were of a surpassing degree of workmanship, the colours being of a clear brilliance or a muted softness that seemed to whisper, their beautifully executed designs sometimes breathtaking.

But it was more than that. He did not want those boxes purely for the beauty he was sure each would have.

Passing along Pipes Meadow, Reuben watched the sad little

buildings that clung to the edge of the road as though to a lifeline, watched them string into Temple Street, cluster round the Mission Hall. Such a dreary, work-laden maze of narrow streets. So many tiny houses that had half the living space given over to a workshop where women and small children must help with tasks that hardly paid for their bread.

The cab driver called softly to the horse as he guided it left into Lester Street, then half turning to Reuben called, 'We be coming up to The First and the Last. It be a decent ale house, sir, if you be feelin' in need of something to wash the smell of the enamellin' from your throat.'

'The First and the Last?' Reuben glanced at the man.

'Arrh.' He nodded. 'It be first ale house in Bilston if you be coming in from Moxley end, and last one when you be coming out again.'

Reuben smiled, admitting to himself the logic of the name, though guessing from his knowledge of the humour of this town that it bore little resemblance to the original.

''Course that don't be its proper name,' the driver added, as though divining Reuben's thoughts. 'Proper name be The Bush, but it's always gone as The First and the Last to the folk round about.'

Consulting his pocket watch, Reuben saw he had more than enough time until the last train to Birmingham. A stop might be welcome, if only to clear his head of thoughts he knew to be hopeless.

Across from the inn a smithy rang to the sound of hammer on anvil, while away behind it Bradley Heath lay like a grey-green carpet, spreading away to the black hill mounds of waste from the Fiery Holes and Bradley Rowe coal pits. All around the loveliness of nature was being scarred by coal mining and the making of iron and steel.

But that was the burden of these little towns that had been so aptly named the Black Country. He turned, glancing back the way they had just driven. Overhead the sky was dark with the smoke of a thousand tall chimneys, while from the ground as many black drifts spiralled upward, adding their tribute.

'There be a fire in the snug, sir.' The cab driver hitched a feed bag over the horse's head, his tone hopeful.

Reuben gave a brief nod. 'Thank you. But I will take a glass here in the open. I have had more than enough of being indoors today.'

'I'll send Caggy out to you then, sir, and if you have no objection to me having a mug of the best meself . . .'

'No objection.' Reuben walked several steps in the direction of the smithy, somehow finding the tiny green that fronted the ale house a peaceful spot despite the noise of hammer on iron.

'Afternoon to you, sir.'

Returning the inn keeper's pleasant address, Reuben waited for the ale he ordered.

'There you be, sir.'

The landlord laid a tankard on a table constructed of roughly planed planks then, still using his left hand, took the coins held out to him.

Reuben smiled to himself. The man was left-handed; that explained his being called Caggy.

Taking up the tankard, he sipped the cool liquid, the smell of hops and barley pungent in his nostrils.

Why had he told Meshac Beddows's workman to sell those boxes to no one else? Gazing out over the bare heathland, the thoughts he had hoped to banish returned full strength. True, they were beautiful, but he could get boxes of equal beauty. The artistry rife within the smoke-filled confines of Bilston was nothing short of startling, so why insist on having these?

From the heath a light breeze fanned his face. In his mind he saw again tendrils of softly curling chestnut hair being lifted by that same breeze then falling gently about a lovely young face. The face of the girl on the heath. *She* was the reason he wanted those boxes, because *she* might have painted them. He wanted them because of her. He wanted her!

* * *

'Good afternoon, Mr Fereday.'

Maria Beddows, dressed entirely in black, held out her hand.

'My condolences, Mrs Beddows.' He touched her fingers briefly. 'I did not hear of your loss until today or I would have paid my respects sooner.'

'It . . . it was a very private funeral, I could not bear . . .' She touched a lace-edged handkerchief to her nose.

'Forgive me. I should not intrude upon your grief.' Reuben half turned to where a housemaid was placing his gloves and cane upon a side table.

'No, Mr Fereday. I must get used to seeing people again, accustom myself to life without Meshac. Please, stay.' Maria gave him a wan smile.

The silk of her skirts rustling, she led the way into her sitting room.

'Mrs Beddows.' Reuben had waited until the business of taking tea was over. 'I visited Meshac's workrooms today in order to ascertain if my order for caskets had been completed.' He paused, looking at the woman opposite him. Even in widow's weeds she made a striking picture. 'I beg your pardon for speaking so directly to you but I must ask – will the agreement I had with your husband still stand or do you consider a signed contract to be preferable?'

'I had not thought . . .' She made a suitable show of touching the handkerchief to her eyes again.

'Of course not,' he apologised. 'It was clumsy of me to speak of business so soon.'

'Yet it must be spoken of.' She raised long lashes touched with the silver of tears. 'But it is all so foreign to me. I have no idea where to begin. Meshac did not make a practice of discussing his business with me.'

That much he could believe, but as for her not having any idea what to do, that was something else. It was his bet Maria Beddows knew exactly what she was going to do. Watching her turn her glance to a photograph, its heavy silver frame draped with black tulle, then dab again at her eyes, he felt certain this was all a show put on for his benefit.

'If only Meshac had acquainted me with the running of his business.' She traced a finger over the sepia-coloured print of her husband. 'But he always maintained it was not for a woman to worry her head over such things. That being so I find myself unsure in which direction to proceed. Should I try to carry on with the enamelling business or should I sell it? One thing Meshac did tell me was that the trade was dying out. The call for enamelled products was almost gone. If that is so, then I think perhaps I should sell up while there is still a chance.'

Sell up while there is still a chance *of profit*, she meant. Reuben glanced away, to the elegant furniture and beautiful carpets. Enamelling had brought Meshac and his wife wealth and all that went with it; to the people who produced the wares it had brought little more than a bare living, and now even this was to be taken from them.

He brought his glance back to Maria. 'At the workroom I asked to buy a set of boxes, only one of which had been set out for my approval. I was told you had authorised the sale along with anything else a prospective buyer might wish to purchase. However, it turned out the other five boxes were locked in the office to which only you have the key. Would it be possible for you to arrange that I might see them? With a view to their purchase, of course.'

So that was why he was here. Maria glanced at the handkerchief held between her fingers. She had guessed Reuben had some other motive for calling at Holyhead House than to see her. But to ask specifically for a few boxes . . . Why? Why that particular set when there were so many others to choose from? What was it that set them apart? It was surely not the standard of the painting; all Meshac's workers were the best the town had, he had always been careful to select *only* the best. So what was it that lay behind Reuben Fereday's request?

'I think you must be referring to the workshop in Vine Street.

Meshac did his testing of new oxides there.' Maria looked up. 'He was quite strict about the room he used being kept locked. I believe he would allow no one but himself in there. He took me with him only once, just after our marriage, but I have to admit I understood nothing of his talk of metals and oxides. The man you spoke to will be . . .' Her voice tailed off as though she was searching her memory for a name. '. . . Blakeway, Thomas Blakeway. Yes, his family occupy the rest of the building.'

Reuben thought of the house-cum-workshop, one of many such he had seen in that town.

'I cannot say I know the boxes of which you speak, Mr Fereday.' Maria gave him the benefit of her practised smile. 'But I will send word to Blakeway to have them brought out for your inspection when next you are in Bilston. I trust he knows the ones in which you are interested?'

'Yes.' Reuben nodded. 'Though I am not sure when my next visit will be. It could be several months. Perhaps you might allow them to be sent to my gallery in Birmingham?'

'Of course. I will have word sent today.'

'That is most kind.' He got to his feet.

'It has meant your coming out of your way to visit me here. I hope that does not mean you will miss your train to Birmingham,' she continued.

'No.' Reuben consulted his pocket watch. 'I have ample time.'

Marie followed him towards the door of the sitting room, the few feet separating them allowing her to admire his broad shoulders and tight hips; to imagine them, as she had on several nights when sleep had evaded her, without the concealment of clothing.

'Your gallery,' she said as he opened the door, 'you once invited me to see it. Does the invitation still stand?'

'Certainly.' He stood aside, allowing her to pass in front of him. 'Whenever you feel you are ready to do so.'

'Then I shall visit you. I shall also endeavour to keep our

business relationship going. I only wish Meshac had prepared me for such a task . . .'

'Your husband did what he felt was right. He thought to protect you from such mundane matters.'

'Yes, of course you are right, Mr Fereday.' Maria's well-practised wan look was once more directed at Reuben. 'But I find it all so confusing without him.'

'Might I suggest, a relative . . . someone who could take on the management for you?'

She shook her head, the handkerchief once more in operation. 'There are none,' she murmured. 'I have no one on whom I can rely for advice or comfort.'

You have a daughter. The thought brought a sudden anger he could not explain. A daughter who had taken Holy Orders. She may have been unable to give advice on the running of the business but she could have given comfort. Why? He found himself wondering. Why had a girl so young and so beautiful given herself to a life of seclusion from the world? Was it truly a vocation, or had there been some other reason?

Trying to keep the sudden unreasonable coldness he felt from showing in his voice, he went on, 'Then I urge you to employ a manager, Mrs Beddows.'

Following him across the hall Maria waved away the housemaid coming to hand him his gloves and cane. 'I would find dealing with a manager a very daunting prospect, Mr Fereday.' She dropped her lashes appealingly. 'I would be much happier were a friend to help me.'

'Then perhaps you will allow me . . .' He smiled into the eyes lifted quickly to his own '. . . allow me to suggest Mr Ryder Tempal. He, I feel sure, would be very willing to assist.'

Closing the door behind him, Maria let her hand rest on it, anger hot inside her. She had hoped to draw him into acting as her manager, hoped in that way to bring him close to her, but he had not succumbed to her portrayal of a helpless widow.

She had thought this her chance to find just out to what extent Reuben Fereday's seeming indifference stretched.

She had failed today. But she had a great many tomorrows.

'Back to Bilston, sir?'

Behind him Reuben heard the thud of the door of Holyhead House as it closed. A thud that was just a little too loud. Almost smiling, he stepped into the hansom. Maria Beddows had thought to secure him as her manager . . . and what else? Settling into the seat, Reuben laid his cane across his knees. Whatever else it was the woman had planned, he wanted neither.

'No.' He glanced at the man awaiting an answer to his question. 'No, not Bilston. Take me to the railway station in Wednesbury.'

He wanted time to think, to decide whether to continue to buy from Beddows Enamels. He could buy anywhere in Bilston, there was no need for him to have any more to do with Meshac's widow, yet Reuben knew he had to maintain that link, however tenuous, however hopeless, the one link he had with the girl on the heath.

Picking up the road that ran past the gates of Holyhead House, the driver turned the horse to the left, taking the carriage in the direction of Wednesbury. Bilston had a railway station, and it was some two or three miles nearer than the one he had been told to go to. He gave a flick to the reins, calling encouragingly to the horse. It wasn't his place to point that out. Besides, it was all money in his pocket. He could ask at least twice what he would ask for the run back to Bilston.

Hands resting idly on his cane, Reuben watched the final scattering of poky buildings give way to the heath that separated them from the tall spired church that seemed to stand sentinel over the huddled village.

Maria Beddows had mentioned the probable selling of the business that now belonged to her. And his daughter? Had

Meshac made any provision for her should she forego the life of a nun, or had he written her out of his life completely?

The rumbling of a cart on the other side of the road drew his attention but as it passed by his eyes remained on the glint of water just visible in the hollow that fell away from the road. That was the pool where he had swum. The place where he had met a girl who had haunted his thoughts ever since.

Was she Meshac Beddows's daughter?

Yes. His mind and his reason told him that she was.

And had she taken Holy Orders?

His reason told him she had. So why did his heart tell him otherwise?

His gaze lifting from the expanse of water, he caught sight of the caravan nestled at the tree line. It had not been there that day, but then gypsies drifted in and out of places like mist on a morning sky.

Seated on her stool beside a fire of sticks, Bethesda puffed on her old pipe. This would be the year of her avenging. The taking of retribution would be hers alone, it would not fall to Caine. The sight had told her so and the sight never told her wrong. Her son had waited long to take revenge for the spoiling of his face. She had heard him many nights get up from his bed, and watched those same nights as he had walked round and about their camp in lonely torment. He deserved to take payment in kind, to take full toll for what had been done to him, to taste the sweet fruit of vengeance that he had yearned half a lifetime for. His would be the tasting. Bethesda sucked on the stem of the briar pipe. Hers would be the plucking.

Her eyes on the hansom, she let her gaze travel with it along the road that cut like a knife across the pitted heath. Within that cab sat a young woman's happiness. It would be long yet in reaching her, but the arrival was predestined, as it was ordained that her son Caine would be the instrument of the girl's salvation.

Chapter Eleven

'You say the mistress sent you to get the girl's things?'

'Just her bag.' Alice watched her mother peel potatoes. 'It was just the bag I 'ad to fetch.'

'Still don't seem right to me somehow. Mistress of Ridge 'Ouse 'er might be, but to go lookin' into a young woman's private effects behind 'er back! All I can say is that gentry should be better brought up than they seems to be. You wouldn't find no child of mine prying into folk's private things, no, by God you wouldn't! Try that and I'd 'ave the skin off their arse, no matter how old they be.'

'I didn't open the bag, Mother, not until I gave it to the mistress.'

'I should 'ope not neither.' Letty Withers looked up sharply. 'You've always been taught to respect other people, and their property an' all.'

Letty selected another potato and set to paring it thinly. 'Dressed in black, you say?'

Alice nodded. 'From head to foot, with a veil pulled down over her face so it couldn't be told who it were 'cept you heard her name.'

'Beddows, you says?' Letty sliced through the skin of the potato, letting it drop in one continuous coil into the enamelled basin held on her lap. 'Maria Beddows . . . Can't say as that name rings a bell. Ain't nobody of that name in Wednesbury, not as I knows of anyway, and I knows most.'

'Her don't belong of Wednesbury.' The last of a pound of peas shelled, Alice gathered the empty pods and set them to one side. Her mother would use them later to make pea pod wine. 'Seems her comes from Moxley.'

'Moxley, is it?' Letty dropped the peeled potato into a large cast-iron pot before setting aside the knife. 'I ain't never been there so it don't be surprising I don't know the name.' She looked over to where Alice was now scalding tea in the tea pot. 'But it be a bit strange, 'er bein' called Beddows. That be the same name as that young wench you brought visitin', don't it?'

Taking the heavy pot of potatoes to the fire, Alice hung it on the hook from which she had taken the kettle moments before.

'Arrh,' she said, gathering the peelings from her mother and carrying them into the scullery where they would be boiled down for pig food. 'Carys be named Beddows.'

Letty followed her to the scullery carrying the basin of water in which she had rinsed each potato. Going out into the yard, she flung the contents into the shallow runnel that drained between the houses, mouth clamped tight against the smell that rose from it.

'What be even more strange,' Alice continued as her mother returned to the house, 'is Carys said as how her home was in Moxley afore her was taken to Birmingham.'

'And what did this woman in black want with the wench's bag?' Letty cleared a space on the table, setting two heavy platter cups beside the jug of milk her daughter had fetched in from the scullery.

'Seems as her asked to see the drawrings Carys had in it.' Alice filled the cups from the teapot. 'Anyroad up, when I fetches it from the bedroom the mistress tells me to open it and give them there drawrings to her visitor. Then her asked me to say if they was the self-same ones as Carys had with her the night I brought her to Ridge House. And when I said they was, all saving the one her drawed since, well, then mistress said I was to put them back where I got them from. That was all I heard.'

'So the woman didn't take any of them drawrings?' Letty asked.

'No.' Alice handed her mother one of the teacups, taking the other herself and sitting beside the fireplace. 'Seems her just wanted to look at them. Her didn't find them much to her liking neither, not judging by the way her nose screwed up when her looked at them.'

'There ain't nothin' filthy about them, I 'opes, not with you lookin' at them an' all?'

Alice knew her mother's Chapel upbringing and her views on anything she thought unfit for the sight of God. 'No, there were nothing like that. They was pictures of an open heath, and a pool with ferns and trees all round.' She sipped at her tea. What her mother was not told about the figure of a man rising naked from the water of that same pool would not give her sleepless nights!

'So, if her didn't take any of them drawrings, why did her ask to see them? And if, as you said, the woman had not visited Ridge House in all the time you 'ave served there, why did her come that day?'

Alice continued to sip her tea. She had asked herself the same questions but had come up with no answers save one: Maria Beddows was up to no good. One way or another she meant to harm Carys.

'And what did the wench 'ave to say when you told her of this visit?' Letty refilled her cup.

'That was the strangest thing of all,' Alice answered. 'I told you of how Carys told Mrs Bates and meself about how her come to be in that convent and how her had been left on Snow Hill station without a penny piece? Well, it turns out that the woman who left her there and the mistress's visitor be one and the same!'

Letty Withers looked at her daughter, disbelief bright in her eyes. 'Be you telling me . . . ?'

'Arrh, Mother.' Alice nodded. 'I be telling you Maria Beddows be Carys's mother.'

'God love me!' Letty dropped her cup heavily on to the table. 'Her knows her own flesh and blood be servant to another when all the while it seems there be money enough to keep her at home?'

'That be the nub of it though, don't it, Mother? Carys ain't wanted at home, and though I can't be rightly explaining why, I feel that mother of hers don't want her to be at Ridge House neither. In fact, I sometimes think her would rather Carys was nowhere at all.'

'Ee, wench, don't be lettin' your imagination run wi'out a rein!'

'Well, if her meant Carys any good, why not take her home to Moxley?'

'And why not take her there if her intention was to do the wench more hurt?' Letty gathered the cups in one hand, the cream-coloured enamel tea pot in the other. 'Surely it would be easier to do in her own place with no outsiders lookin' on?'

Alice followed her to the scullery sink, drying the crockery her mother washed.

'Anyroad,' Letty enquired, 'why should her want that young wench out of the way?'

'I can only think that the man who tried it on with Carys in that summerhouse figures in it somewhere. I bet her mother be more than friends with that one, otherwise why not tell Carys's father what happened? But her didn't. And it seems he still visits the house from what was said to Carys in that church.'

'Do you mean that her mother and . . . who did you say he was?'

'Ryder Tempal,' Alice supplied the answer.

'Well, whoever he be, do you be saying that them two be great together?'

'I say there be the possibility.' Alice laid the drying cloth over the airing line strung across the black-leaded grate of the tiny sitting room-cum-kitchen. 'I can't think why else a mother would want her daughter out of the house.'

'Wouldn't be the first woman to lose her head over a younger man,' Letty mused.

'Then you think her mother be jealous of Carys as well?'

'I don't think nothing of the kind,' Letty snapped. 'And don't you go making presumptions either. You keep your thoughts to yourself, Alice Withers. What you don't say you can't be blamed for. A still tongue be a wise tongue, just you remember that.'

But what her daughter had said made some sense, Letty thought as Alice hugged her goodbye. There was nothing so quick as desire for a man to set one woman against another.

'Was it your daughter the maids were speaking of?'

Ryder Tempal sat in the drawing room of Holyhead House, legs stretched out comfortably in front of him, very much at home.

Maria glanced down the long sinuous length of him, feeling the twitch again in the base of her stomach. She wanted him. Wanted to feel the nakedness of him press against her. It had been a couple of weeks since that last quick visit to a hotel in the Bull Ring and as yet he had not suggested another.

'Yes, it was her,' she answered. 'I called on Virginia Mountford last week. It appears Carys is serving as a housemaid at Ridge House, just as I heard.'

'Then it *was* her I saw!'

'You saw her?' Maria asked sharply. 'You saw Carys?'

Pale sunlight danced on his fair hair as he nodded.

'When? When did you see her?' Maria's voice was harsh.

'Oh, a couple of weeks or so.' He smiled languidly but his yellow eyes were watchful. 'I saw her at the Wakes. At least at the time I merely thought it could have been her, but you said she had chosen to take her final vows, didn't you, my dear? And that she would spend the rest of her life behind the walls of that convent, so how could it have been Carys that I saw? Now, it seems, it was.'

'Why did you not mention this before?'

'For the same reason, Maria. How could I possibly be seeing a girl who was cloistered in a nunnery?'

'Well, she is not cloistered any more.' Maria moved about the room in her agitation.

'So it appears.' Ryder Tempal drew in his legs, straightening himself in his chair. 'So you, my dear, must bring her home.'

'Oh, must I?' Maria swung on him, her eyes glittering with temper. 'You would like that, wouldn't you? It would suit you just fine having her here under this roof. Perhaps this time you might succeed in tumbling her. That is it, isn't it, my darling? You could have your cake and eat it at the same time.'

Ryder glanced at the woman he knew wanted to be his wife, his languid smile hiding the thoughts firing his brain. If Carys were out of that nunnery, as it seemed she was, what were his chances of marrying her? Meshac must have made provision for just such a thing as her renouncing her vows; if Ryder had the daughter for a wife he would no longer have to pander to Maria. True, the woman was attractive, but she was also possessive, too possessive. Carys had not been responsive that night in the garden, but that had been his fault. He had rushed his fences and she had taken fright. Next time it would be different.

'Well, you can hardly leave her there as Virginia Mountford's paid help.'

'You're right.' Maria's anger seemed to melt into a dazzling smile. 'You are so very sensible, Ryder. Of course she must come home, though it will mean some very great changes in my own life, and maybe a few in yours.'

Ryder drew in his breath, holding it against what was still to come.

'You see, my dear . . .' Maria paused, letting her words hang on the silence. 'Under the terms of Meshac's will every last penny of his was to go to his daughter in the event of her leaving the religious life and re-entering the world. Every stick and stone of his business, together with this house, would revert to her.'

'But you?' Ryder's brow furrowed. 'What of you? Meshac could not have meant you to have nothing.'

'Oh, he didn't.' She laughed hollowly. 'He said he left me that same comfort he suspected I had enjoyed for the last two years before his death.'

'Comfort?' Ryder watched her sink gracefully into a chair, smoothing the folds of her black taffeta skirts. 'I don't understand.'

'Don't you, Ryder? Don't you really?' Maria's smile faded. 'He meant you. You were the comfort he was leaving me. Don't you see? He knew although he never admitted as much. Meshac knew about us! But to admit it would have meant losing me, and that my poor deluded husband could never bring himself to face.'

So everything he coveted belonged not to Maria but to her daughter. Ryder almost smiled. And it could still be his, and with it he would no longer have to hang on to the skirts of any woman who had more than ten shillings to her name, and thanks to the fates would not have to marry Meshac's widow to get it. He would marry Meshac's child.

Maria turned the key in the lock of the office door, closing it carefully behind her. Moving to the window, she stared through the dust-covered pane to the low-roofed workshop that stood opposite. Thomas Blakeway was not in the doorway.

Satisfied she was not being observed, Maria crossed to a locked cupboard against the far wall. She had seen inside that cupboard once only but had never forgotten the jar Meshac had pointed out to her.

Opening the cupboard, she ran her glance quickly over

the line of jars on its top shelf then across the brushes ranged below. These were Meshac's oxides, kept for his own experimentation. He'd had a real feel for colour and had often stayed late here, mixing and firing new blends.

Reaching into the very back of the shelf, she drew out a small glass jar, lid fastened down securely. She read the label written in her husband's flowing copperplate hand, then glancing towards the window, slipped it into her bag.

'Is everything all right, ma'am?'

Thomas Blakeway watched the wife of his late employer as she prepared to climb into her carriage.

'I am afraid I cannot truly say.' Maria smiled sweetly. 'You see, Mr Blakeway, I would not know, especially with regard to my husband's office, this being the only time I have ever been inside it.' She turned as if to return to that building. 'You must be familiar with it, however. Perhaps you can tell me something of its contents, of what use my husband had for it, for I can see no papers there that correspond with customers' requirements?'

'I be sorry, ma'am.' Thomas shook his head. 'I ain't never been in the place meself. Master, he let nobody in there. Place were kept locked and he held the only key.'

'Then I can only leave it to be sorted along with the rest of Mr Beddows's business interests.' She sighed affectedly. 'It is all so very difficult.'

'Arrh, ma'am, that I can understand.' Thomas twisted his flat cap nervously in hands stained black by the constant handling of metals. 'But, beggin' your pardon, I 'ave to ask if you be goin' to keep on with the enamelling?'

'Keep on?' Maria made a pretence of not knowing to what the man was referring.

'Yes, ma'am. Be you goin' to carry on with the making of enamels, boxes and such? I know I shouldn't be botherin' you with it, not with you having no knowledge of such, but the family . . .' he glanced behind him to where his wife and children were working on the last of the materials. 'We only has what we earns here and we be almost out of frit, and the last of the metal was used yesterday.'

'Do you know where Mr Beddows obtained his supplies?'

'Arrh, ma'am, I do.'

'Then order enough for another month of working.' Maria climbed into the carriage. 'That will last until I can install a manager.'

'An' what will we be making?' Thomas looked at the carriage, head jutting out from between stooping shoulders.

He looks like a tortoise, Maria thought, distaste for the man and the workshop thick in her throat.

'What sells best?'

'Jewellery boxes, ma'am,' he replied. 'Boxes and caskets be about all we 'ave call for these days.'

'Then you had best make boxes.'

'And the design?'

Maria felt irritation with the man seep into her. What did she care what he painted on them?

'Repeat the work of last month.' She gave a peremptory tap on the door of the carriage then as quickly called for it to halt. 'Speaking of boxes,' she said as Thomas drew level with the door, 'Mr Reuben Fereday enquired of me concerning five that, I understand, are in my husband's office?'

'Arrh, that be so. They be in there still, far as I knows. Least that's where the master put them.'

Reaching into her bag, Maria handed him a key. 'Fetch those boxes to me, I will have them sent on.'

The boxes lined up on the seat beside her, she watched the smoke-blackened houses thin away, replaced by open heath. She would see that the boxes reached Reuben Fereday, but would not dispatch them to his gallery in Birmingham. She would take them there herself. When it suited her.

Bethesda squatted beside the edge of the pool, her flounced skirts taking on a darker hue where they rested on the damp ground. Leaning out over the water she washed the rabbit she had just skinned and emptied of its innards. It would make a good meal with the onions and potatoes she had earned that morning.

They had soon learned of her potions, the folk of the village, and had begun to visit her in their twos and threes as did the folk of West Bromwich whenever they camped in that part of the country.

Why had they not gone there this spring?

She swished the rabbit carcass in the water, brown eddies of blood swirling away in circles.

Why had Caine broken with his usual practice and come to Moxley instead? He had said nothing to her, but she had seen him glance after the girl they had dropped off near to the church that was just a little way further on. Did he know what the sight had told her? Did her son feel, as she did, that the girl had a part to play in the vengeance that drew ever closer?

Pushing herself to her feet, Bethesda felt the pain that none of her herbal remedies eased shoot through her hips. Soon she would be unable to travel with her son. She would have to set up a camp that would not move with the seasons, would no longer see the finger of God move across the broad fields of England or see his wondrous mountains.

'But Bethesda Lazic will not stay tied to that camp for long,' she muttered, swinging the rabbit in the air shaking away droplets of water. 'When the time comes, I holds that which will end all pain and sorrow, that which brings freedom to the spirit and gives it licence to roam the stars.'

Her steps uneven with pain, she limped across the open ground to where the caravan rested beneath the fringing trees. Taking the stick Caine had sharpened to a point, she skewered the rabbit then placed it across the fire, resting each end on tripods of branches built to each side. Holding a hand to her hip, as though to charm away the pain, she gazed towards the pall of grey that lay like a blanket across the distant sky, knowing it was the darkness of smoke from the chimneys of the myriad workshops of Bilston. How could people live like that? she thought. Breathe that filth when they could breathe God's clean air? To live in a few feet of dark cramped space when they could roam the beautiful countryside . . . She smiled, showing gapped teeth stained brown from tobacco. And these were people who thought gypsies were fools!

Taking an iron pot that was strung along the side of the caravan, she half filled it from the barrel Caine had filled the night before. Settling it on the glowing heart of the fire, she dropped in the onions and potatoes she had cut into rough cubes, adding a handful of dried herbs she always gathered from the wayside.

The meal prepared, she fished out the briar pipe from a pocket deep in the folds of her skirts and lowered herself painfully to the stool set in the lee of the painted wagon. Tonight she might taste the juice of the poppy, but not now. The pain had not yet beaten Bethesda Lazic.

Squinting against the pallid sun, the pipe held unlit between her teeth, she watched the approach of a woman, a child swaddled beneath the chequered shawl that draped her thin shoulders, three more of less than five years holding to her skirts.

'Good day to you,' Bethesda said, the pipe still in her mouth.

Just beyond the fire the woman halted. From where she sat Bethesda could see the tiredness in her eyes, and lines she guessed to be premature coursing her face. Beside her the children pressed their faces to her patched skirts.

A mended skirt. The fact was not lost on the gypsy. And the children. Their clothes were worn and obviously passed down one to the other but they were clean. But while each of them was barefoot their faces were scrubbed. The woman was poorer than a church mouse but she cared for her children.

'Good day to you.'

The woman dropped a hand to the head of the small boy as he began to cough, holding it there, comforting him with her touch until he wheezed to a stop.

'That be a dreadful hack of a cough.' Bethesda removed the pipe, resisting the urge to spit tobacco-tainted saliva on to the ground. Children of the Gorgio were frightened enough of gypsies and these poor mites could do without the adding of more.

'It be getting worse.' The woman lifted her hand from the boy's head. 'Nothing I do seems to 'elp.'

'And why be you here?'

Her face threatening to crumple as the boy was once more siezed by a fit of coughing, the woman looked at Bethesda.

'I 'eard about your ointment healing the open wound on Joseph Bartrum's leg, and the mixture you gave Hannah Lacy for when 'er stomach be bad, and I thought as how you might have a potion that would help my lad?'

Replacing the pipe in her pocket, Bethesda looked towards the boy clinging to his mother's skirts and again felt the breath being snatched from her body and the blood tumbling through her veins like a torrent let loose from the hills. She sat unmoving as the sight claimed her. There would be naught she could give would save that child nor the woman who had given him life. The cough that wracked him was devil given, the sickness that had eaten her lungs eating his. With the eyes of her mind she watched two bodies wrapped in one winding sheet, the mother holding the son in her arms as they were lowered into the ground.

Stirring as the sight left her, Bethesda rose to her feet and mounted the steps of the caravan. Inside she pulled a battered wooden box from beneath her narrow bed. Lifting the lid, she smelled the sweet scent of herbs that had instilled itself into the wood. Selecting a linen bag, she loosed the drawstring and took out a handful of dried yellow flowers of meadowsweet. Then opening a cupboard she drew out a small jar, a snippet of cloth secured over its open top with a string.

'These will do the lad no harm.' Coming from the wagon she held out the jar and the herbs she had placed in a piece of cloth.

'Cover a pinch of the herb with water fresh boiled. The jar be honey from bees collecting their nectar from the sweet flowers of the fields. Take as much as would cover a farthing and add it to the cup then leave it to cool. When this be done, sieve the mix through a cloth and give it to the lad to drink, once at his rising, once at noon, and once with the setting of the sun.'

'Will it cure him?' The woman's tired eyes were lit with a beam of hope.

'Curing be with the Lord,' Bethesda replied as the cough now took the woman. 'I be just another of His instruments.' She would not add that if it were God's will the child would recover for she knew already that would not be, that the boy would not know health in his life.

Hitching the child she carried in her arms higher on to her breast, the woman fumbled in a pocket of her skirt then held out her hand to the gypsy woman.

'I'll not . . . take . . . all from you,' she said, her breathing shallow and ragged as the cough subsided. 'I don't be having the money to pay for that which you offer. If you would measure a portion of the herbs it will be enough.'

Bethesda looked at the coin lying in the woman's open palm. One bronze penny. It would buy the herbs if not the honey; it would also buy a pennorth of scrag end of mutton from any butcher and that would mean a meal of broth for them all.

Wincing at the pain catching her hips, she bent towards the lad, placing the jar of honey in his hand and giving the cloth-wrapped flowers of meadowsweet to the taller of the two girls.

'I will be taking no money for things the Almighty gives freely,' she said, straightening. 'The flowers of the field be His gifts along of the bees, as my knowledge of their benefits be also His gift.' She had needed no church or chapel, nor the teaching of any priest, to learn compassion and the idea of charity never entered her head. 'Help thy neighbour and the Lord will help thee.' That had been the all of her

Romany upbringing and she had followed it well through the years.

'Thank you.' The woman's hand closed over the coin but her dark-ringed eyes were wide with gratitude. 'The Lord bless you, as I do.'

Once more taking her pipe from her pocket, Bethesda placed it in her mouth then sat watching the woman lead her children away. A woman on whose shoulder the Angel of Death already rested his hand.

Chapter Twelve

'I told him, I told our Davey you wouldn't be wanting to walk with him.' Alice looked apologetically at Carys. 'But he would insist. Said he would call about three.'

'I really don't want to go out.' Carys picked up a china Staffordshire dog, dusting it carefully. 'Not that I don't like your brother, I do, I like them both, it's just that I don't feel I want to go walking.'

'It would do you good though, Carys.' Alice picked up the second dog of the pair, giving it a thorough rub with her duster. 'You hardly ever goes out. You might just as well still be in that convent for all you do with your spare time.'

'I go with you to your mother's house.' Replacing the ornament, Carys crossed the room and began carefully to dust the dainty porcelain figurines grouped on a graceful long-legged table.

'Huh!' Alice retorted, setting viciously about dusting the silver-framed photographs grouped along the mantel-shelf above the fireplace. 'Twice. You've been to me mother's twice. I 'ardly calls that visitin'.'

'What would you call it then?' Carys laughed.

'You knows what I mean.' Alice turned to look at her. 'Every time it be your turn for an afternoon off, you refuses, and though I be grateful for the taking of it, it don't be right. You *should* get yourself out. Won't do no good living your life inside four walls. Ee! Be you worrying over that visit? The one your mother made to the mistress . . . you ain't frightened of her?'

Carys replaced a figurine, her hand resting on the delicate piece.

''Er won't hurt you.' Alice came to stand beside her. ''Er just tried to get you throwed out so as to make you leave Hill Top. 'Er still be jealous of you but 'er can't do anything, not now mistress knows everything.'

'No, I am not worrying over Maria's visit.' Carys picked up another ornament, feeling a need to avoid the other girl's eyes. 'And as for being afraid . . . Maria might prefer me not to live here but she would never harm me.'

'Well then!' Alice said firmly. 'If nothing be worrying you, why not go out for a couple of hours? Our Davey, well, I know he's not handsome, but he be a nice chap and he thinks the world of you.'

'Alice, I . . .'

'Look, don't say anything now,' she interrupted. 'Wait and see 'ow you feel come three o'clock.'

She would still feel the same, Carys thought as Alice went back to her dusting. David Withers had called at Ridge House several times, always with the excuse of a message for his sister but they both knew it was Carys he hoped to see. But though she liked him a lot there was no feeling deeper than that. She would always want him as a friend, but as a husband, a man to whom she could give her heart and her love . . .

Taking up the box that held dusting cloths and polish, Carys carried it out into the corridor that led to the kitchen and replaced it in the boot cupboard in the scullery.

She could not give her heart to Davey Withers. It was given already. Given to a man she had seen only once, a man who swam naked in a pool on Moxley Heath.

* * *

'I think as Alice be right.' Martha Bates relaxed into her usual chair. Sunday lunch served and cleared, she watched as Alice and Carys collected plates and dishes for washing. 'You should go out for a while, get some fresh air into your lungs, you be looking right pale.'

'You need only be out half an hour or so,' Alice whispered as they carried crockery into the scullery. 'Would keep Mrs B. quiet an' all.'

'Very well.' Carys gave in. She did not want to go over the whole argument again. She would walk with Davey but must make it plain to him there could not be anything between them. It would be unfair to allow him to think otherwise.

In her bedroom Carys removed her apron, folding it neatly and laying it on her bed against her return, doing the same with the dress provided as uniform. Noticing a spot on the hem of her petticoat, she fetched her only other one from the chest beside the door. Taking off the one that was marked from polishing the hall floor earlier, she slipped the fresh one over her head, feeling the cloth catch on the pins that held her hair. Glancing into the mirror as she lifted her hands to free it, she caught her breath sharply. Draped about her head, hiding her hair completely, the white petticoat fell like a wimple about her shoulders like the headdress she had worn for almost four years.

'You will not be so quick to spy again.' The voice of the Mistress of Novices whispered against her ears and she flinched as she seemed to feel again the sharp sting of the slap to her face. 'Remember who has charge of you here. So long as you wear the robe of a novice it is I who order your life.' Carys flinched again as memory brought another slap to her face. 'You will say nothing of what you saw in that room, do you hear? You will say nothing!' The slap had come again, hard and vicious, to her mouth. 'Remember why you are here. To cleanse you of the lust that drove you to draw a naked man, to set his body on paper so you could look at it in your room after you had fornicated with him in some field.

Don't deny it!' The voice in her mind cracked with an anger driven by something Carys had not then understood. 'I have seen the drawings Mother Superior thought hidden, I know what you are, and if you breathe a word about what you saw I will make sure the whole convent knows it too. They will not believe the word of a slut against that of their own sister!'

The weight of the petticoat pulling against a hairpin released it and the garment slid down over her shoulders, wiping the vision from her mind. Trembling, Carys fastened the cloth-covered buttons that held it to her waist. She had thought the memories of those years buried and as good as forgotten but she had been wrong; it had taken only the fall of a petticoat to bring them flooding back.

Her hands still shaking, she slipped on the same brown dress she had worn when her mother had taken her to the Convent of the Holy Child, and had worn again only when she had left it. She had thought, when at last that day had come, that she would be returning home to Holyhead House to be with her father again. But she had been wrong.

Would it have been so much worse for her, life behind the convent walls? The other sisters had been so kind; only the fear and shame of what she had done with the priest had driven the Mistress of Novices to treat her as she had. But for all her harsh treatment Carys had not sought the help of any of them; she had told no one of Sister Veronica's cruelty to her. Young as she had been, she'd sensed the woman's unhappiness and would not have added to it.

Doing up the last of the buttons that fastened the bodice of her dress, she turned from the mirror. Taking a ribbon from the same drawer that had held the petticoat, she tied it about her hair, catching the silken chestnut strands within its bright yellow.

Ready to go back downstairs, she bent to smooth the covers of her bed and as she did so, caught her foot against the bag pushed beneath it. Lifting it out, she sat with it beside her. Had Virginia Mountford noticed the similarity between the two faces she had drawn, one so long ago, the other recently? Had she wondered at the likeness of one man to another as Carys herself had done? Drawing out the sketches, Carys looked from one charcoal drawing to the other. It was remarkable: the same bone structure, the same colouring, the same eyes and mouth. They might be sketches of the same man save for the fact one had been young and virile, a man who had dived and swum in a pool on a heath, and the other was Virginia Mountford's father.

Staring down at the sketches Carys seemed to hear again the voice of the Mistress of Novices. '. . . You set it down on paper so you could lust over it . . .'

Was it true? Was that the reason she had kept the drawing Mother Superior had returned to her, the same drawing her mother had used to blacken her character?

Touching a finger to the paper she traced the lines of the face, remembering the mocking look the man on the heath had played over her, remembering his mouth, his dark slumbrous eyes that seemed even now to draw her down into their velvet depths. Was thinking of him each night as she lay in bed, lust? Was conjuring the memory of his words and the timbre of his voice, lust? Was wanting to see that handsome face just one more time, lust?

She should destroy these sketches, get rid of them, and then perhaps the phantom of memory would leave her. Her hand curling the edge of the paper, she felt her heart twist. To destroy her sketch would not destroy her memories. She would never forget. She had met him only once, but that would last forever. Rolling the sketches together she replaced them in her carpet bag, pushing it back beneath her bed. Halfway along the corridor that gave on to the stairs she glanced at the portrait of Virginia Mountford's father. Even should she destroy her drawing of an unknown man she would be faced with his likeness so long as she remained in this house. But here or anywhere, she would need no portrait to remind her. A far more enduring one was drawn upon her heart.

'Our Eddie and Peggy Rogers have put a date to their marriage.' Davey Withers plucked several bright yellow flowers from a clump of gorse.

'That's wonderful.' Carys smiled. 'When is their wedding to be?'

'In the summer. They asked the priest for July the sixteenth, that be our mother's birthday.'

'So it will be a double celebration?'

He nodded, breaking several more strands of the brilliant flowers from the bush.

'Does Alice know yet?'

'Not yet. I expect Mother will tell her when next she gets to come home.'

'Then I shall not tell her. To do so would spoil your mother's pleasure. She is pleased for them, isn't she, Davey?'

'Oh, arrh!' He stared at the flowers, twisting their tough stalks together to hold them into a bunch. 'It's what my mother has been wanting long since. Her would like to see all of her brood married and settled.'

'So Alice has told me.' Carys watched him twine the stems of the gorse. 'She says every time she visits, your mother asks if she is walking out with a man yet, and she does not seem too pleased with the answer always being no.'

'That I can believe.' He looked up from the flowers to stare out across the heath. 'Like I said, Mother will only be truly satisfied when each of her children be wed, but I reckon not all of us will go as easy as our Eddie has.'

Meaning himself, Carys thought, feeling almost guilty as she glanced at him. She ought not to have come walking with him, it would only serve to give him the wrong impression and that could well cause him pain when she had to tell him of her feelings, tell him she could only ever feel friendship for him.

'Alice would like to be married, I am sure of it,' she said, feeling the awkwardness of the silence that had settled between them. 'And I don't think it will be long before some man asks for her. Then your mother will have the pleasure of planning a second wedding.'

'Arrh, she will have the pleasure of them two . . .'

As he turned to face her, Carys saw the sadness in his eyes and knew she would not have to tell him of her own feelings. He already knew!

'. . . and that will have to be enough for her, for I have no notion of wedding any girl.'

In the quiet of her mind Carys heard the whispered words: '*Seems how he will love a woman, but that same woman will love another.*' Despite herself she had to acknowledge the truth. Whether spoken by Madam Rosa or invented by Alice, they had been right. Davey Withers was in love with her. And she? Was she in love with another, and if so was he the man on the heath?

'You may think that now, Davey.' She tried to sound light-hearted. 'But given a year or two you will feel differently.'

'I will never feel differently.' Savagely he threw the tiny knot of flowers to the ground. 'I love *you*, I will never feel the same for any woman.'

'Davey, I . . . I . . .' Carys looked at the broken posy lying like a pool of sunlight on the bare earth.

'You don't have to say anything.' He turned to look at her, his eyes swimming with misery. 'I know you don't return my feelings, but at least you have never pretended otherwise. You have never tried to lead me up the garden path.'

'I would never do that, Davey. I would not deceive you, in that or in anything else.'

'I don't know who the chap is as holds your heart,' he said softly, 'but I do know he be the luckiest man on God's earth. But *you* know this. Should I ever hear of his harming you in any way – in any way, Carys – then I'll break his back.'

Feeling his fingers tight on hers as he helped her over a

stile that separated heathland from tilled ground, Carys felt a surge of warmth towards the tall, gentle man, but at the same time a twinge of pain that twisted her heart. The man who held her heart was the luckiest on God's earth . . . What would Davey say if she told him she was in love with a man she had met only once, a man she would never meet again?

'It is so good to see you, Reuben, but should you leave your business to come calling on me?'

'Since when has business, or anything else, come before my favourite aunt?'

Reuben Fereday tossed the parcel he was carrying on to a wide-seated Hepplewhite chair, pulling Virginia Mountford into his arms and hugging her.

'Your only aunt, young man.' She freed herself, the look she gave her nephew as warm as his hug.

'Of course.' He grinned at her. 'But still my favourite nevertheless, the woman of my heart.'

'Sit down, you rogue,' Virginia laughed. 'And tell me all your news. What have you been doing with yourself?'

'Oh, the usual.' The grin remained, showing white even teeth. 'Drinking, debauching . . .'

Virginia laughed again. 'Your usual behaviour, as you say. Rape and pillage. It's a miracle you have time to visit your aunt.'

'I interrupt those fascinating activities only for you.' He took up the parcel he had thrown on to the chair and handed it to her. 'Happy birthday, Aunt.'

'It's almost too pretty to open,' she said, admiring the swathe of pale peach-coloured ribbon expertly ruched and tied into a bow.

'Then shall I place it on a table somewhere where you can admire its packaging?'

'Age has not improved you,' she returned, attempting to put a note of reproof into her voice yet failing dismally. 'You are still the cheeky imp you always were.'

Looking up as a tap on the door answered her earlier order for tea, Virginia watched Alice try to settle the tray on the table without taking her eyes from Reuben's face.

'Thank you, Alice,' she said as the maid hovered, a moon-struck look on her own face, then as the door closed behind her, asked, 'Rape?'

Reuben's wicked smile flashed. 'I think I will stick to pillage, if you don't mind?'

Her own smile mischievous, Virginia pulled the swathe of ribbon, releasing it from the package.

'Oh!' she breathed, lifting a pair of beautifully painted cameo portraits from a velvet-lined box. 'These are absolutely beautiful, Reuben. Thank you, my dear, thank you so very much.'

'I knew you would like them.'

'How could I not? They are truly exquisite. Who is the artist?'

'A fellow called Edward Emslie. He has already been noticed by the Royal Academy. I think he is set to become a great painter.'

Virginia tilted the miniatures in their oval frames, using the light from the window to release the depths of their colours. 'Well, if this is a sample of his work, then I agree with you.'

Placing the paintings on a table beyond the rays of sunlight, she returned to her chair and poured tea for them both.

'The library might be the place for my lovely present,' she said, handing Reuben his cup, 'but I don't go into that room very often so I would not be able to look at them as much as I would wish.'

'Then why not in your bedroom?'

'Such beautiful faces should not be hidden away in an old woman's bedroom. No, I shall have them here, in my sitting room.'

'The same as you have the charcoal sketch of Uncle Robert?' Reuben lifted his glance to where the black and white sketch in a plain lightwood frame hung over a small writing desk, moved to the private sitting room for his aunt's convenience. A dark-haired, somewhat heavy-browed face stared back at him, a half smile hovering at the back of his eyes, echoing the line of the mouth.

'It is an exceptionally good likeness.' He rose, crossing the room to where the portrait he had not seen before hung. 'Did the artist know Uncle Robert?'

Virginia sipped her tea, her eyes too on the sketch of her late husband. The artist had not known Robert, the startling accuracy had been caught from a treasured photograph and drawn by the same hand that had copied the oil painting of her father. Watching her nephew as he examined the sketch, she thought back to when Carys had brought the sketch to her, with a shy smile and half apologetic words. 'I hope you do not mind . . .' Virginia had not minded, but had cried out with pure pleasure as she had unrolled the paper and looked down into those smiling eyes.

'The artist and your uncle never met,' she said at last.

'You could almost swear they had not only met but had known each other for a long time.' He leaned across the desk, bringing his face closer to the sketch, examining the lines of it as though searching for some unseen signature. It had the same sureness, the same character, as the painting on the box he had bought from Beddows Enamels, and *she* had sketched with charcoal! But it could not be by the same hand, it could not be by the girl he had surprised on the heath so long ago; that girl had given her life to a convent.

He turned swiftly, refusing to let memory fill his mind, refusing to allow it to plague him as it had done so many times before. Why was it he thought so often of a slip of a girl he had met just once? Why couldn't he forget her?

'So, Aunt, what have you planned for your birthday?'

Virginia caught the look on his face as her nephew turned away from the sketch, caught the frustration and unhappiness before he banished the last vestiges to smile at her. Did he recognise the style of the artist? Had he and Carys Beddows met somewhere? Realisation dawned. The drawing of the younger man . . . the one she had thought to be her father in his earlier days . . . the faces that were so alike, one drawn years before the girl had set foot in this house. It was not a representation of Virginia's father that Carys had drawn, it was her nephew!

Virginia replaced the cup she was holding on to the silver tray, using the movement to shield her eyes from Reuben, not wanting him to see what she knew to be reflected there. Was the girl now working as a maid in her kitchen the cause of what she had seen on Reuben's face? Had he met her, and if so what had happened between them to produce such a look as she had caught in his eyes? Had he done something terrible to the girl, something so awful that even now he could not face up to the truth of it without pain? Had he forced himself upon her? No! Virginia thrust the thought away. She could not, would not think such a thing of him. Reuben would never treat any girl so.

'I shall spend it here at Ridge House, probably with a book and a cup of Mrs Bates's hot cinnamon milk,' Virginia answered his question, relieved that it had turned from the subject of who had drawn the sketch of her husband. She would not tell him of the presence of the artist in her house. If he had met Carys Beddows almost five years ago and that meeting was the cause of the worm eating away at his heart, or maybe his conscience, then she would not feed it. Best let the past lie.

'Do you honestly mean you prefer a book and cup of hot cinnamon milk to dinner and the theatre with a very eligible young man?'

Virginia answered the smile that now veiled the sadness she had seen a moment ago. Yet she knew it was merely below the surface. For a moment she thought to recant her decision not to speak of Carys, but to do so and be wrong in her assumptions would be to cause embarrassment to them both.

'I might reconsider if that eligible young man were quite handsome.'

'You are a flighty piece, Virginia Mountford.' Laughing, he pulled her into his arms. 'Lucky for you I am here to keep you on the straight and narrow. I shall be back for you at six tomorrow. And be sure, woman, I will take a shot-gun to any other young beau I see hovering around!'

'I will be sure to have them safely hidden in the cupboard by five minutes to six.'

Smiling, she held her face up for his kiss. Her brother's child had the looks and the charm of his grandfather, so why, at the age of thirty-two, was he still unmarried?

Guiding the horse he had hired from the stables in Great Western Street away across the heath towards Wednesbury, Reuben did not see the couple crest the rise that backed Ridge House, the late-afternoon sun glinting on the girl's chestnut hair.

Clutching the posy of wild flowers Davey had picked for her, Carys watched the horse and rider canter down the hill and into the distance. He had sat a horse with the same ease, tall in the saddle as the rider she watched, and with the same dark hair unfettered by a hat. She remembered the wide shoulders and strong body, one she had sketched rising from the diamond-strewn water, and the sensuous mouth that had mocked her on the heath. Perhaps . . . But she turned away. The man who had waylaid her on Moxley Heath was no more than a memory, a phantom who came to haunt her nights. For Carys Beddows he might never have been.

For her there could be no perhaps.

Chapter Thirteen

Eyes half closed, Maria watched the tall, agile figure come towards her where she lay on the bed, light from the window catching his fair hair in a halo of light.

A halo! Maria could have laughed at the thought. That was one thing Ryder Tempal would never wear. Nor would she! Lifting her arms to him, she felt the heat of desire flare through her, and as his body covered hers she felt she did not care. Having a halo came a poor second to having Ryder Tempal.

It had been too long. Maria moaned softly as he drove into her. It had been three months since Meshac's death, three months since she had tasted the pleasure now ripping through her almost painfully. Observing the rules of society she should not entertain for at least a year, more if she wished to be well thought of. But to hell with society! She gasped as he took her nipple in his mouth, teasing it with the tip of his tongue. It had been too long, too many nights spent lying awake thinking while her body yearned. She would not wait so long again. Regardless of what people thought, she would marry Ryder Tempal, and that marriage would be soon.

How many times had he done this? Maria turned her head on the pillow, watching the breath heaving in his chest. How often in those three months had he lain with a woman, and which one?

Outside in the street the shouts of tradesmen mingled with the rumble of cart wheels. Maria glanced around the room they had taken for the afternoon and her nose wrinkled with distaste. It was not distaste solely for her surroundings but for the fact that they must meet here at all. But soon that need would be over.

Propping herself on one arm, she touched a hand to the fine golden hairs spread like mist across Ryder's chest. Soon they would lie like this in her own bed at Holyhead House. Meshac had left her the comfort she had enjoyed for two years before his death: the comfort of Ryder Tempal's body. It was one she meant to enjoy, and one she would not share. There would be no other women for him. He would enter Holyhead House as its master but she would be mistress of it, and of him!

'I think we should marry.'

The movement of his chest eased but his eyes remained closed.

'I want us to marry.'

She traced a finger down the line of his chest, losing its tip among the golden hair at the base of his stomach.

Slowly he breathed again, a measured sound that hid the sudden onset of apprehension. He wanted Maria Beddows's money, but not Maria herself.

'We will marry,' he answered, still not opening his eyes. 'As soon as is decently possible.'

'Decent!' She laughed softly. 'Since when did decency enter into your mode of thinking, my dear? You have always taken what you wanted, whether the taking were decent or not.'

'But we must think of your position.' His eyelids lifted.

'This is the only position I care about.'

Her fingers busy in his crotch, she leaned over him, breasts brushing his chest as she closed her mouth over his.

She had said she wanted to marry. Ryder's thoughts moved

quickly. Did that mean now, within a few weeks? He had planned on having at least a year in which to part her from her money, or at least enough of it to tide him over until the next rich widow came along, or a mother desperate enough to pay well for him to marry her daughter. But instinct told him Maria would not wait a year. If he did not give her what she wanted she would find someone who would. And where would he be then? There were precious few heiresses in Bilston.

'But perhaps you do not wish to marry me?'

Maria moved her fingers teasingly and smiled inwardly as his penis jerked.

'Maybe you have set your sights in another direction?' She trailed her tongue over his chest, tasting the salt tang of sweat, searching his navel with the moist tip. 'In which case . . .'

'There is no other direction.' Reacting to the warning of his brain, he grasped the hand that, despite the trend of his thoughts, had his body intoxicated. He lifted it above her head, pushing her on to her back. 'There is only you, my darling, I want no other woman but you.'

Parting her legs, feeling the hard fire of him inside her, Maria knew that what he said was a lie. He would take a woman tomorrow and not even bother to wave her goodbye, supposing the woman were young and wealthy. A woman like Carys.

Later, fastening a pale blue cravat at his throat, Ryder went over the thoughts that had troubled him since leaving the bed. What guarantee had he that Meshac's daughter would not claim her inheritance? She was no longer enclosed in a religious order, and Hill Top was just a few miles from Moxley. How long would it be before she enquired after her father's will, and could Maria prevent her from finding out about its terms? And if Carys did learn of the whole of her father's wealth belonging to her, where then would *he* stand? To be married to Maria Beddows was one thing; to be married to her without her money was another altogether, and one he definitely did not relish.

'What of your daughter?' His back to Maria, he felt the tension quicken in the room.

Taking her time, threading each button of her black jacket slowly through the relevant button hole, she watched her own reflection in the fly-spotted mirror. She had known the question would come, known the thoughts being so carefully analysed in his mind.

'What of her?' she asked, slipping the last of the buttons into place.

'You know perfectly well!' His desire sated, Ryder was in no mood for prevarication. 'What if she returns? What if she claims that which is hers once we are married?'

Reaching for her hat, Maria set it on her head, securing it with a pearl-topped hat pin before drawing the veil of black tulle over her face. 'Then you, my dear Ryder, will be married to the wrong woman, but married none the less.'

Taking up his gloves, he glanced across the room at the woman who only minutes before had lain moaning beneath him, the meaning implicit in her words rankling in his mind. Was it worth the risk? Could he marry her, knowing the threat of losing Meshac's money hung over them like a cloud?

Maria smoothed a black lace glove over her hand, easing it over each finger with separate, deliberate movements. Both gloves fitted to her satisfaction, she raised her glance to his. 'Of course,' she said softly, 'there could be no question of Meshac's child claiming her inheritance were she not here to claim it.'

'But she *is* here!' Ryder spoke irritably.

'Yes, she is here.' Behind the tulle Maria's mouth thinned. 'And so long as she is we are under threat. So, my dear, *we* must do something about it.'

'What do you mean?'

'I mean, if we are to enjoy our marriage, the girl must be got rid of.'

A shiver of unease touched Ryder's spine. Maria was a determined woman, there was no telling to what lengths she was prepared to go to get what she wanted.

'You tried that once before without success!'

The touch of sarcasm in his answer did nothing to endear him to her.

'Then this time we must have the benefit of a man's superior intellect.'

'Meaning?'

From behind the softness of her veil, Maria surveyed his handsome features. Ryder Tempal was a good-looking young man, both in face and body, but there his appeal ended; his morals and his backbone were neither of them worth a thought. But it wasn't his morals she was interested in, and this once at least she would see to it he found the backbone to do as she wanted. For her to be sure of him, he must be as much a part of getting rid of her daughter as she herself.

'You, my darling,' she answered his curtly spoken question, 'must help me dispose of our problem.'

Tracing his lips with the tip of his tongue, Ryder felt the same unease ride higher up his spine. 'How?' he asked.

'Tomorrow!' Maria swept to the door of the shabby room, the swish of her heavy silken skirts raising a cloud of dust from the worn carpet. 'Come to Holyhead House tomorrow afternoon. I will tell you then how we will make certain Meshac's money will never go to his child.'

'I have had a most enjoyable few days, Reuben. The theatre was a most refreshing change and I so enjoyed seeing your gallery. Thank you, my dear.'

Virginia Mountford smiled at her nephew. He was the last of her line and had always been dear both to her husband and herself, taking the place of the child they had never had.

'The more enjoyable for me, Aunt. Having the most beautiful woman in the room on his arm does wonders for a man's ego.'

'Yours needs little bolstering,' she laughed, 'but flattery lifts mine.'

'Who is flattering?' Reuben's dark eyes smiled beneath his finely marked brows. 'You were the most beautiful woman at the theatre, and at the hotel where we dined I could feel every man's envy.'

Virginia played a glance over his face. Apart from the small white scar high on his eyebrow he was the image of his grandfather. She remembered the accident that had resulted in that scar. He had played all morning in one of the outhouses behind Ridge House. Then, in the afternoon, she and Oliver had been taking tea in the rear garden when Reuben had called to them. They had not seen him at first, then when he called a second time they spotted him on the roof of the stables, standing with arms outstretched, a contraption of webbing and feathers strapped to his back and buckled about his wrists.

Virginia closed her eyes for a second as the fear of that moment returned to her. Oliver had shouted for Reuben to climb down but he had only laughed. 'I am going to fly.' His child's voice had rung with the confidence of ignorance. 'I shall fly like Daedalus.' Scrambling over the roof, his foot had dislodged a slate, sending it hurtling to the cobbled yard, the sound of its landing sickeningly loud in the hot afternoon.

'Reuben, stay where you are!' Oliver had risen to his feet and was already halfway to the stables. 'Don't move, we will get you down.'

'No need!' Reuben's laughter floated to her on the still air. 'I can fly down. Watch, Uncle Oliver, watch me fly!'

Virginia had stared, seeing the figure of her husband seem to move in slow motion, seeing her nephew raise his arms, and vaguely, as though it were simply a shadow moving along the base of the stable wall, seen the figure of Ned Jeavons, one of the stable hands.

'Stay still, Reuben!' Oliver's shouted command had mixed

with the child's delighted laughter – and then he had jumped!

Virginia never knew if the scream remained imprisoned in her throat. She remembered only the small body as it launched itself into the air, arms flailing wildly as it fell, tumbling head over heels, and Oliver coming to a standstill, unable to move as the child's figure hurtled towards the ground.

His boyish laughter turning into a frightened cry, the boy had called her name and Virginia's blood had turned to ice. Then he had landed, his head lost beneath a jumble of webbing and chicken feathers – landed in the arms of Ned Jeavons! Virginia released the breath in her throat. Ned had fallen from the weight of his catch and the boy's head had struck the cobbled yard. She had run to them as Oliver had taken their nephew into his own arms, thanking Ned profusely while she dabbed Reuben's bleeding face with her handkerchief.

'Reuben.' Virginia felt all the love she had for him surge upward. 'Reuben, are you happy . . . I mean, truly happy?'

His mouth moved as if to answer, then catching the look in her eyes, he hesitated. He had never been able to fool his aunt. Oh, sometimes as a child she had allowed him to think he had hoodwinked her but it had never been truly so. And now? He knew it was useless even to try.

'I am as happy as I ever expect to be, Aunt.'

He had told her the truth. Virginia climbed into the hansom. There was something in Reuben's life that was causing him pain, keeping him from happiness, and she could not ask what. He was no longer the child who confided his secrets in her, he was a man who would keep his own counsel. She leaned from the cab, touching a finger to the tiny scar white against the bronze of his skin.

'Take care, my dear.' Her caution was for more than his physical welfare. She could almost feel the pent-up emotions inside him, emotions that might tip him into the arms of a woman he did not love. 'Take care, Reuben, don't go flying in the wind.'

In the sitting room of Holyhead House Maria glared angrily at Ryder Tempal. He wanted to have jam on both sides of his bread. He wanted Meshac's money but wanted none of the risk that would accompany the getting of it.

'If you really think the girl will give you so much as a second look, you are sadly mistaken!' she rasped. 'You destroyed any chance you might have had with her when you attempted to treat her like one of your whores.'

'Like I treat you, you mean!' Ryder saw her flinch against the sting of his reply. The sight pleased him.

'Like I allow you to treat me . . . so long as it pleases me.' Maria's voice was soft, dangerous as a serpent, and her wide brown eyes sparked a warning. 'But then, my dear, I can pay for my little foibles, *I* have the money. Take care yours do not cost you what little you have!'

Ryder moved uncomfortably beneath that fixed stare. She could well be right when she said her daughter would not countenance him as a husband, and if so he would be out without a penny after servicing this bitch for over two years!

'It most probably would make very little difference to my life should she return and take what her father left her.' Maria could not resist driving the nail home. 'I am, after all, her mother. She would understand my sending her away – I was just trying to keep her from the likes of you until she had gained a little more experience of life.'

'And she was to get that experience in a convent?' His smile was acid but Maria let it slide over her; he was fighting a losing battle, she could allow him one small triumph.

'Do you really think I could not give a plausible reason for that?' She laughed. 'Meshac is dead, he cannot deny it was his doing together with the leaving of her on that railway station. A few tears, Ryder, a few tears and she will believe all I wish her to believe. Then I shall be in comfort for life. But *you*, my dear, where will you be? With Colly Moreton's daughter, perhaps? I don't think so. Nor with any other girl whose parents know about you. Face it, Ryder. You either do things my way or you have seen the last of Meshac Beddows's money.'

'What do you suggest?' He knew he was beaten.

'A love letter.'

'A love letter!' His eyebrows rose. 'How will a love letter dispose of your daughter?'

'We could call it a poison pen letter, if you prefer.'

'I would prefer to know what the hell you are talking about!' Irritation bubbled in him. 'Yesterday, in that hotel, you said to come here and you would outline your idea, but so far all you have done is talk about yourself, how you will come out of this. That, frankly, is highly irritating, so say what you have to say or I am leaving.'

'Frankly . . .' Maria's eyes burned with an almost intense savagery '. . . Your being highly irritated does not bother me one bit. As for your leaving, then do so . . . if you can afford to.'

Ryder clenched his jaw. She had won again. Always it came down to his having no money, and always that gave her the upper hand. But it would not be that way forever. One day he would have every halfpenny she now called hers, and that would not constitute the only change in Maria Beddows's life. When that day dawned, *his* would be the upper hand, and he would bring it down . . . hard!

'How do you propose a love letter will get her to leave Hill Top?' he asked, tasting the bitterness of new defeat with every word.

'Oh, I do not propose Carys should merely leave Hill Top.' Maria allowed her smile of triumph to remain just a shadow about her mouth. 'That would keep matters much as they are now. She could return whenever the mood took her. You, I am sure, my dear, do not want to live under such a constant threat. Therefore I propose she should depart permanently. In other words, I propose we kill her.'

'Kill her!' Ryder's face blanched. 'For God's sake!'

'No, not for God's sake, Ryder,' she returned smoothly, 'for yours.'

Silence settled over the room. Maria smoothed her black taffeta skirts and waited. He would agree. He would see the sense of what she had said. He would help her to get rid of Carys and of these trailing widow's weeds she hated so much. And he? He would become her husband . . . should she still want him.

'Could it be done?' he asked at last. 'Could it be done without our being found out?'

'Yes.' Maria felt her blood begin to race. She had gone over it in her mind again and again, testing her idea for faults, altering and refining until it was perfect. 'I have a way that will be totally undetectable.'

Drawing a linen bag from a pocket in her skirt, she held it in her hand. 'This is an oxide from Meshac's private supply. He showed it to me once just after our marriage. When I made to touch it he pulled it away, telling me it was quite deadly. It was kept locked in a cupboard in his room at one of the workshops, to which no one but himself held a key.'

'What did he use that stuff for?'

'In his experiments with enamelling colours, Meshac liked to try for unusual shades. I took it from his room when I paid the workshop a visit a couple of weeks ago.'

'Won't it be missed?'

'The man in charge told me he had never been in that room, nor had anyone other than Meshac, at least not in the time he had worked there. He said Meshac took great care to keep the place locked. He guarded his secrets well. If no other person goes in there then no one knows what the cupboard held.'

'Did he see you take it, the man in charge?'

'No.' Maria shook her head. 'I was careful to watch for

that. Rest assured, no one knows of the existence of this jar other than you and me.'

'But if that stuff is as lethal as you say, why did Meshac hold on to it?'

'How do I know?' Maria snapped. 'He did, that is all I need to know.'

'What exactly is it?'

Stretching the neck of the bag, she folded the linen back upon itself, disclosing a jar half filled with a white powder. Across the body of the jar a label read: 'Thallium'.

'I've never heard of it,' Ryder said, leaning forward to read the spidery copperplate scrawl.

'That is not surprising.' Maria replaced the cover, drawing the strings of the bag tight. 'Though I would be surprised if anyone in Bilston has. Meshac got it from a chemist in London. He told me his name was Crookes, and he had recommended the salts for use as a dye or in paint. But Meshac was warned that they were highly dangerous. They could be absorbed into the body by the mucous membranes in the mouth and also through the skin. Thallium was, he said, odourless, colourless and tasteless, one of the most toxic of all metal Mr Crookes had encountered, and once it has entered the system a man can be dead in twenty-four hours.'

'Phew!' Ryder eased back into his chair. 'Lethal is the word. But how can you get her to take it? She will hardly open her mouth while you spoon it in.'

'Agreed.' Maria half smiled. 'But then she will not have to open her mouth and I will not have to spoon it in. You, my love, will be the one to give it to her.'

'Me! But how? She will hardly take a spoonful of that or anything else from me.'

'But it will not be given from a spoon, it will be given in the letter I spoke of. Thallium dissolves in water. Paint that water on to an object and the water evaporates while the toxic salts remain. If that object is then handled before the oxides are burned in the furnace, they can kill. So you will mix the salts with water and soak a sheet of writing paper. When it dries it will show no trace of the powder. Then you can mix a little more in a bottle of ink and write a love note with it.' Maria's eyes took on a scathing gleam. 'For that you should not need my assistance. Then all you need do is address an envelope with an ink that does not contain thallium and deliver it to her at Hill Top.'

'Deliver it personally!' He frowned his displeasure. 'There is surely no need for that? It can go through the post.'

'And thus be the more traceable.' Maria scowled. 'The fewer people see or know of the letter, the better.'

'But it is bound to be seen by someone other than your daughter when I hand it in at Ridge House.'

In irritation Maria went on: 'That is exactly why I said you were to deliver it personally. It is to be given to no one but Carys. And, remember, no name is to appear on the letter or the envelope, not yours or hers. It must remain impossible to trace its sender.'

'But why must *I* write it?' he asked suspiciously. 'Why not you? She cannot be too familiar with your hand.'

'Perhaps not, but that is not my reason. You stand to share most handsomely in the profits, therefore you must share the risk. With you as deeply entrenched in this as I am, I can be more sure of your continued complicity.'

Rising to her feet, Maria handed the linen bag to Ryder. 'Be careful when you are handling that sheet of writing paper,' she said with acid sweetness. 'Wear gloves when you write on it and a fresh pair when you address the envelope. Remember how very lethal is the powder you are dealing with, I would hate to lose you under such circumstances.'

'I'm sure you would.' He matched her sarcasm with his own. Theirs was no love match. This marriage would be one of convenience, and the convenience would be all his.

'One more thing,' Maria said as his hand fastened on the handle of the sitting-room door. 'Once the letter is written, take everything you have used – gloves, ink, pen, everything – and bury them somewhere lonely and deep, *very* deep.'

As the door closed behind him Maria sank into her chair. He would do as she had instructed. He would deliver the letter to Meshac's child and the poison would enter her body through the skin of her fingers as she held it, then she, Maria, would have all she wanted. She would own Meshac's property. She would own Ryder Tempal.

Chapter Fourteen

Carys looked at the little heap of withered brown leaves and stalks, the colourless flower heads, all that was left of the floral tribute Mary Bartlett had laid on Meshac's grave. No one had been to tend it since that day.

Kneeling on the soft earth she felt the tears rise in her throat. He had loved her so much and she had loved him, always so happy to see him home, wildly delighted whenever he said she could accompany him to the workshops.

'What happened, Father?' she whispered. 'What went wrong? We were so happy until . . .'

Her words hung on the silence. She had been happy until *he* made an appearance; until day after day she found herself making excuses to be away from the house in case *he* should call, in case she had to meet Ryder Tempal.

But her mother had always been so ready to welcome the man into their home, and even when she had discovered him trying to rape her daughter, it had not been him she had blamed, not Ryder Tempal who had been sent away, enclosed in a religious order, not visited once in four years!

'You could not have known, Father.' She touched a hand to the moist earth warmed by the sun. 'I am sure you knew nothing of where I was. You would not have left me there, you would have come for me.'

Beyond the wall surrounding the church Bethesda Lazic watched the kneeling girl lay a posy of blue cornflowers and scarlet poppies on a grass-covered grave. She did not need to read the headstone to know who lay buried there, even had she the skill of letters, which she had not; nor did she need to see the face of the girl to know it was the same one who had ridden with her and her son on the wagon.

The girl had not spurned the hand of the gypsy, she had not turned her back on them as did most folk, she had not treated them worse than a man would treat his animals. Her own hand brown and gnarled as a dead twig, Bethesda gripped the shawl she had half filled with wild herbs and plants as the sight rushed in upon her, pushing the blood through her veins, pounding into her head, washing her mind clear until no other thought stood in its path and she was left staring at pictures no mortal eye could see.

A brick-built house stood tall and square atop a rise in the ground. To one side the heath was pocked with the marks of coal pits; to the other it fused with fields of waving corn, the gold rippling to the edge of a town sprawled at the foot of the hill. As she watched, a man with hair the colour of the corn called to a young ragged boy, taking something from his pocket, holding it towards the child, smiling as he enticed the lad to him. With her inner eyes Bethesda peered at the man's outstretched hand, at what he held towards the boy. It was a letter. She was looking at a letter. Then the boy was running away up the hill like a startled hare and Bethesda saw a girl, in the dress of a servant maid, come from the house towards him.

She leaned heavily against the curtain wall of the church, almost drained of strength as the sight left her. It had been stronger this season, stronger than at any time since the blinding of her son. The time was near and drawing ever nearer, the time of vengeance, and in her soul of souls she knew the girl kneeling at that graveside would play a part in it.

Taking the withered flowers, Carys carried them around to the back of the building, to where she knew from childhood the groundsman kept his compost heap. Returning, she stood a moment more beside her father's grave then turned for the gate. Seeing Bethesda, she smiled and quickened her step.

'You be paying your respects.' Bethesda nodded as Carys came to her. 'That be good. The young should respect the old, whether they be living or dead. That one there,' she flicked a sideways glance in the direction of Meshac's grave, 'be it the same one you spoke of when you rode the wagon?'

Carys glanced behind her to where the blue and scarlet posy nestled in the green grass. 'Yes,' she said softly, 'my father.' When she turned back her eyes were filmed with tears.

'It be 'ard.' Bethesda saw the grief in the girl's eyes and knew they must hold more yet. 'Losin' the ones you love never be easy, and them you love most hurts worst of all. But we gets over it, we lives on.'

But there were some griefs you never got over. Bethesda turned away from the church, crossing the road to reach the heath on the far side. There were some griefs too powerful to forget, too powerful to heal. Grief like the losing of an eye, like the losing of grandchildren who were never to be born.

'Is your son well, ma'am?'

Beneath her bony frame Bethesda's heart warmed. She had never been addressed as 'ma'am', not once in all her life. Not even by the villagers who came to her with their ailments of body or heart, asking for her cures and potions. They paid her in kind or with a penny but never with the word this young woman had chosen to speak.

''E be well.' She smiled, exposing a gapped line of tobacco-browned teeth. 'Be you tied to returning 'ome straightaways?'

'I have until six this evening, then I must be back at Ridge House.'

'Be that a tall square house atop the rise as you leaves Wednesbury, on t'other side from this?'

'Hill Top,' Carys answered. 'Ridge House stands just on the crest.'

'We ain't never camped thereabouts, but I knows it.'

Bethesda remembered the house the sight had shown her.

'I work as a housemaid there.'

The sight had not shown her wrong. Bethesda felt her pulse quicken. This was the girl she had seen, in white cap and apron over dark skirts: the uniform of a servant girl.

'And would a housemaid take a drink o' tay with a gypsy woman, or be 'er too grand for that?'

'I can't speak for any housemaid,' Carys smiled, 'but for myself I would enjoy a cup of tea.'

'Come you with me then, and welcome.' She looked sharply at Carys as the girl took the shawl from her but said no word. Theirs would be a binding, a coming together in a friendship that would need no words. Theirs were lives that had been linked together by powers stronger than theirs.

Reaching the caravan set beneath the fringe of trees, Bethesda saw the younger woman's eyes turn towards the pool of dark shining water. It held memories, she knew, and a promise she did not yet understand.

Taking the shawl from Carys, she carried it up the steps into the caravan, emerging with a small wooden box held in her hands. Setting it beside the stool, she reached for the tin kettle, black from the smoke of many fires.

'Settle yourself, girl.' She nodded towards a log Caine had placed beside the ring of ash that marked the cooking fire. 'I'll fill this from the barrel and set it to boil. Won't take not five minutes to brew a dish o' tay.'

'Let me do it.' Carys reached for the kettle.

'Nay, girl.' Bethesda shook her head. 'Though you can be fetching pots from the wagon, should you have a mind.'

She turned away, leaving Carys to climb the few steps into the caravan. Inside she stared at the neatness of it. At the far end was a narrow bed, the base of it a line of beautifully carved cupboards. The bed, covered with a quilt of bright yellow that was echoed by the curtains of the bowed window, its tiny alcove set around with deeply carved edge, folded back from which was a pair of painted wooden doors. From the wooden roof a candle lamp hung on a length of chain, while along the sides were more cupboards and a huge, heavily carved chest.

Carys stared around her, feeling herself almost clothed in warmth and light. The little room was sparkling clean and bathed in colour, a place that shouted a welcome.

'Cups be in the cupboard a'side of the stove,' Bethesda's voice floated in to her.

'I never dreamed a gypsy caravan would be so pretty. Are they all as beautiful as this?'

Bethesda took the cups from Carys, pursing her lips and blowing into each to chase away imaginary specks of dust. 'What thought you they would be like?'

'I really had no idea.' Carys's cheeks took on a pinkish tinge as she met the piercing gleam of the gypsy woman's eyes. 'I sometimes saw gypsy caravans pass across the heath when I went with my father to Bilston and I wondered what the insides were like, but I never imagined them to be as beautiful as this.'

'Arrh, they be beautiful.' Bethesda placed the cups on a flat stone. 'And every one be different.'

'Different, how?'

'They all be built each by their own man, and each man holds his own ideas as to the decorating of what he makes.'

'You mean every gypsy builds their own caravan!' Carys asked, surprised.

'Every gypsy man do, and it be painted by his own hand. Together with the making of the bed and all it holds, 'cept for curtains and bedding. That be the charge of the woman he takes to wife.'

'Did your husband build this one?'

''Ave I not said already that that be so?'

'But surely your son will have no need of doing so? Your caravan will be his after you.'

Spooning tea into the cups from the box beside the stool, Bethesda poured boiling water over it. Then from the caravan she fetched a china jug covered with a linen cover, and a tiny matching lidded dish.

'My son will not be taking the wagon when I die. No true Romany takes the wagon of another. When I pass from this world, the wagon and all that is mine will pass along of me.'

'Do you mean the caravan will be broken up and buried?'

Adding milk to the cups, the gypsy woman handed one to Carys, pointing to the lidded dish.

'There be sugar for the taking.' And as Carys spooned some into her own cup, added: 'The wagon will not be buried and nor will I. It will be burned to ashes with my body inside it.'

Carys looked at the prettily painted wagon. So much artistry and care, so many years of love, to be burned away. Finishing her tea, she thanked Bethesda for her hospitality then set off, following the line of the Holyhead Road where it led towards Hill Top.

Cramming tobacco into her briar pipe, Bethesda held a burning stick to the bowl, sucking hard on the stem, coaxing the cheap tobacco to burn. Throwing the stick back into the flames, she stared through the lavender haze of smoke, watching the young woman growing smaller with distance and feeling a knot of apprehension, almost of fear, tighten her stomach.

'You be in danger, child,' she whispered. 'You be in mortal danger.'

In the parlour of the little house he rented, Ryder Tempal fumed over having to write that letter. Why him? he had wondered as he rode from Holyhead House. Why could not Maria have written it? But he knew her insistence had been because to have him write it would increase her hold over him. Brandishing her money in his face at every opportunity was not enough for Maria; she wanted him bound to her with stronger fetters, wanted him tied by fear of the hangman's rope. Well, they would play things her way, but not forever. One day the tide would turn in his favour, then Maria Beddows would dance to his tune.

Laying the gloves he had fetched from his dressing room beside ink, pen and paper he had already arranged on the small writing desk, he turned and locked the door. His cleaning woman had left but he would take no risk of anyone walking in on him.

Next he took a small piece of newspaper and rolled it to a cone. Slipping on a pair of the gloves, he held the cone over the bottle and tipped a little of the white powder into it, watching it trickle into the ink. Laying the cone aside on a piece of cloth torn from a shirt, he recorked the ink, shaking the bottle to absorb the powder. Maria had been right when she said it left no trace. He had soaked some into a sheet of writing paper and it had dried without stain or odour.

Reaching now for the sheet of notepaper set aside on the cloth, he uncorked the ink and began to write. He had thought long over the wording. It would be better were it to appear to have been written by some boy overcome by infatuation, someone who lacked the finer skills of writing.

'*To the most beu . . .*'

He crossed the last word through with a thin line as though unsure of its spelling and carried on.

. . . lovely Girl I knOw,

I see Your smile in the Morning sunlight and Hear Your sigh on the eVening breeze. I feel the touch of your hair in the Mists from the HeaTh and hear the sounD of Your voice in the Song of the skyLark. My heArt is happY when I see you but When you do not come it is a Stone, heavy in my Chest. I Watch for You in the Town and When you come Your smile fills mY daY with happiness.

your adMirer

Folding the letter, he removed the gloves, putting them aside on the cloth and slipping on the fresh pair. Looking at the folded note, he hesitated. Were this oxide as powerful as Maria seemed to think, then a little extra precaution would not go amiss. Tearing another small piece from the shirt, he used it to pick up the folded letter and place it in the envelope. Pressing the same scrap of shirt on to the wet sponge he used for sealing letters, he applied it to the envelope. Then using his usual pen and ink he wrote upon it:

To the Girl wiTh prEtty haiR

That would be enough. It must seem her admirer did not even know her name. Leaving his regular pen and ink in their usual place on the writing desk, he gathered all the rest into the torn shirt, glancing around several times in order to ensure that nothing had fallen to the floor or been forgotten in any way. Satisfied he had overlooked nothing, he placed the letter in his pocket. The rest would fit easily into a saddle-bag which would not give rise to speculation should anyone see him riding on the heath.

Clearing Paul Street, leaving behind the last of the straggle of cottages, he guided his mount past the Blue Fly coalmine, crossing over newly constructed Hydes Lane on to the heath. He kept to the trackways worn into the earth, knowing the fields about Mesty Croft to be riddled with worked out mines, not all of their shafts having the precaution of a cover.

The saddle-bag containing the deadly powder and materials he had used to write the letter jogged against his knee with the movement of the horse. Ryder glanced at it. He would feel more comfortable once he had disposed of it, but could not risk doing so here. To do so would be to risk being seen by men coming and going from the mine. He would wait. Five minutes further across the heath he would pass Burr's Cottage and beyond there the disused Traveller's Rest pit. He smiled at the irony of the name.

There would have been no rest for any man there, traveller or otherwise.

Urging the animal forward, he followed the way towards Ridge-House. In a few months a new century, would begin and with it a new life for Ryder Tempal.

From the vantage point of horseback he stared across acres of flat heathland. Satisfied he was alone, he dismounted, taking the saddle-bag. The ground about him was littered with black patches marking the earth like open sores, the scars of endless numbers of gin pits each discarded for a new one when the coal seam ran too deep for a man to work alone.

Watching the ground carefully, he picked his way to where a hole gaped in the covering scrub. Peering into it, he could see no bottom. That would be sunk at least a hundred feet into the earth, and if he dropped a few clumps of gorse into it no one would guess a saddle-bag lay hidden underneath.

Giving a swift, cautionary glance all around, he dropped the bag into the shaft. Then pulling up several small bushes of gorse and fern he sent them following after.

The evidence was gone, lost altogether. Soon it would be the same for Carys Beddows.

Riding on, skirting the hedges where the heath gave way to fields of corn, he came to a hump-backed bridge that crossed the Tame Valley canal. A little way beyond a boy sat on the towpath dangling a stick with a string attached into the water. Halting the horse Ryder watched the boy for several moments before calling to him. The lad turned his head but did not move.

'Would you like to earn sixpence?' Ryder smiled pleasantly.

'Depends on what I 'aves to do for it?'

'Take a message to Hill Top. Do you know Hill Top?'

'Arrh, mister.' The boy watched Ryder through wide, intelligent eyes. 'I knows it.'

'Then perhaps you know Ridge House?'

The boy nodded. 'Big house. On the crest.'

'That is the one.' Ryder smiled again. 'I have a letter I wish to be delivered there but I find myself late for an appointment. Take it for me and I will pay you sixpence.'

Maria had said he was to take the letter personally, but then how was she to know he had not? If he were not the one to give it to Carys then there was even less chance of his being implicated in her death, should the cause ever be discovered.

'Do I get the tanner now, or do I 'ave to fetch it from you later?'

'I shall not be at home for several days.' Ryder congratulated himself on the ease with which the lies tripped from his tongue. But then, he had always been peculiarly well accomplished in that art. 'That being so, I shall pay you the sixpence now.'

Reaching into the pocket of his velvet waistcoat, he drew out a small silver coin, tossing it in the air, letting the sunlight glint enticingly on the metal before catching it in his palm.

'Well, lad, do you take my letter or not?'

'Arrh, mister.' The boy scrambled to his feet, stick and string forgotten. 'I'll take it for yer.'

Removing the letter from the side pocket of his coat, Ryder held it as the boy came up to him.

'I do not want this delivered to the front door. You are to ask for the housemaid and give this letter to her. It is very private and must be given to no one else, do you understand?'

''Course I does, mister, I ain't no fool. You wants that there letter given into the 'ands of the 'ousemaid and nobody else. Ain't nothing to understand in that.'

'Then see to it you give it to her and her only,' Ryder cautioned again.

'Be it for your lady friend?'

'That is none of your business.'

'I thought as much.' The lad grinned cheekily. 'A love letter. In that case, mister, I shall carry it next to my 'eart.'

'And my hand next to your ear, if you go on like that.' Ryder remained good-humoured; he did not want the boy to back out, leaving him with the distasteful task of carrying a letter to the servants' entrance of Ridge House.

'Only pulling your leg, mister.' The boy held out a hand for the letter.

'Now you are certain you know the house?'

'Ridge House,' the boy said, emphasising the words. 'A red-brick house. It stands on the crest of Hill Top. I am to give your letter to the 'ousemaid there and to 'er only. Satisfied, mister?'

Giving the boy the letter, Ryder watched as he stuffed it beneath a shirt that lacked several buttons.

'My tanner, mister.' The letter tucked away, the boy held out his hand for payment.

'I shall expect an answer to that letter tomorrow.' Tossing the sixpence, Ryder watched the boy's grubby fist close over it. 'So make sure you deliver it or it will be much the worse for you.'

'Billy Aston be no thief, mister.' The grin that had transformed the young face faded, replaced by a look as hard and challenging as any fully grown man might assume. 'If you ain't got no trust in me, then yer takes yer money back now.' He held his open palm towards Ryder, the sixpenny piece gleaming in the sunlight. 'A bargain be a bargain, and once made Billy Aston don't be the one to break it.'

'Then we have a bargain, Billy Aston.'

Touching his heels to the sides of the horse, Ryder turned in the direction he had come. How long? he thought spurring his mount to a canter. How long would it take that powder to do its work? How long before Meshac Beddows's child departed this earth and how long before her money became his?

Chapter Fifteen

'Carys.' Alice glanced behind her to where Mrs Bates sat reading yesterday's newspaper sent down from the mistress's sitting room. 'When you goes to that cemetery to visit your father's grave, you goes through Wednesbury, don't you?'

'Of course.' Carys selected another of the carrots she had washed in the scullery and began to slice it into thin narrow strips.

'Do you go straight up along the Holyhead Road or do you follow the old Bilston Road?'

'The Holyhead, it's more direct. Why do you ask?'

'No reason.' Alice shrugged.

'There be a basket of early potatoes beside the sink in the scullery.' Mrs Bates turned the page, shaking the newspaper into manageable folds. 'The mistress will enjoy them with a little parsley butter. You can scrape them when you be finished doin' them green beans.'

'I'll get them now. Beans be finished.'

''Ave you got all the strings off them?'

'Yes, Mrs Bates.'

'You certain, Alice? You knows how mistress detests gettin' a piece of it hanging from one of them.'

'I took good care, Mrs Bates.' Alice flicked a smiling glance to Carys. 'I told you 'er would ask,' she mouthed silently, then coughed to cover the laughter that bubbled in her throat.

'I will help you carry them.' Her own mouth twitching with a suppressed giggle, Carys followed her friend into the scullery.

'Shh!' She touched a finger to her mouth as Alice laughed aloud.

'I told you.' Words and laughter muffled together behind her hand, Alice made a charade of peering over a newspaper. ''Ave you got all the strings off them beans?' she mimicked.

'We had better take those potatoes into the kitchen before Mrs Bates comes and catches you impersonating her.' The smile still around her mouth, Carys caught one of the handles of a round wicker basket.

''Ang on.' Alice rested a hand on the other handle but did not lift. 'Carys, can I ask you something.' She paused, the laughter gone. 'It be something personal.'

Looking into her face, Carys saw the faint blush gathering in the other girl's cheeks.

'I have no secrets I would not want to share with you, Alice. Ask me whatever you wish.'

At the word 'secret', Alice's blush deepened. Carys would share any with her but she had kept one from Carys. Only for a few hours but the length of time did not matter. She had kept it to herself and now the guilt of it weighed heavy. She should have told her the minute she returned from the cemetery.

'Carys,' she whispered, 'when you goes down into Wednesbury, do . . . do you meet an admirer?'

'A what?' Carys's eyes widened with surprise.

'You know, a man. Be there a man you think be sweet on you?'

'Alice, what on earth makes you think that?'

'I ain't just being nosy, Carys, honest I ain't, but I just had to ask. Believe me, I 'ave me reason.'

Releasing the handle of the basket, Carys straightened. 'I hardly ever go into the town,' she whispered. 'Once a month I go to Moxley, to the cemetery, but as for going to Wednesbury town, well, I am always with you. If there were a man sweet on me, you would know it as well as I. There is no one.'

No one other than Davey. She kept the thought to herself.

'Then it had to be for me.' Alice let out a long breath of relief.

'What did?'

'The letter.' She grinned, her guilt suddenly alleviated. 'A young lad brought it while you was out, said it were from a man and that he had to give it to the 'ousemaid at Ridge 'Ouse and to her alone. Nobody else were to get it. Brought it the back way, he did. I seen him over by the line of bushes farthest end of the garden and went to find out what he was doin', trespassing where he weren't supposed to be. That was when he give me the letter.'

'Did he not say who it was sent it?'

Alice shook her head, her fair curls bobbing beneath her starched cap. 'Just said it were from a man, then legged it as fast as if his backside was on fire.'

'What makes you think it might have been meant for me? The name on the envelope . . .'

'That be it,' Alice interrupted, 'there were no name on the envelope.'

Carys's brows drew together, a puzzled look evident in her eyes. 'Then if the envelope bore no name, how could you know it was intended for either of us?'

'That takes no reasoning.' The grin returned, wide and cheeky, to Alice's face. 'There be only two women in this 'ouse beside you and me, and I wouldn't describe either of them as being a girl.'

'Be you two going to take all afternoon on the fetching of a basket of potatoes?' Martha Bates called from the kitchen.

'Coming now, Mrs Bates.' Alice grabbed one handle of the basket. 'Tell you later,' she whispered as Carys took the other.

* * *

Draped in black tulle, Maria ignored the polite 'good day, ma'am' of the station porter holding the carriage door open for her to alight from the train. She had thought not to make this journey again, not to frequent another of the seedy back-street hotels of Birmingham, but as yet there was no other way of meeting Ryder Tempal. It was too risky having him in her bed at Holyhead House, so for the present it was this or nothing, and she was definitely not ready to accept it be nothing.

Emerging from Snow Hill station she signalled a hansom, holding out a slip of paper to the driver.

'I knows where that be.' Alighting, the man held a hand to Maria's elbow, assisting her into the cab. 'Be no more'n a five-minute ride, ma'am.'

Maria nodded as the door closed on her and the man resumed his position, clucking to the horse to set away.

Following along the busy Colmore Row, Maria looked out at the imposing Regency buildings of the Great Western and the Union Hotels, with their uniformed doormen and chandeliered reception halls, and her resolve hardened. As soon as was possible she would frequent those places, do the things Meshac had never wanted to do. Meet as many young men as she liked, and have her pleasures wherever the fancy took her.

''Ere we be, ma'am. Queen's 'otel.' The cabman waited while Maria took a florin from her purse. 'Place be named for its keeper,' he grinned, showing grimy teeth. 'Queenie Meers. Ain't no palace 'er be runnin' 'ere, though. Be you sure it be this place you be wanting? A lady like yourself would be better off in the Great Western, if you don't mind me saying so like. There can be some unpleasant characters gets to Needless Alley.'

'I shall be here less than half an hour.' Maria held out the florin.

'Then p'raps you will be wanting me to wait?'

'No.' She turned towards the doorway of the rundown building. She had no wish to stand here where she might be seen, though the chance of anyone she knew being in this Godforsaken part of the city were thankfully slight. 'I shall not require you to wait.'

'Your change, ma'am.' The man selected a coin from a handful drawn from the pocket of his greasy coat. 'It be a shilling ride from Snow Hill.'

'You may keep it.' Gathering her skirts, Maria swept into the hotel. Needless Alley! She glanced at the drab walls and faded carpet. Only when a man was dead could he need less than this place furnished.

'Did you *have* to choose such a down and out dump!' She stared angrily about the room Ryder had booked.

'Perhaps you would prefer me to take a room at the Grand, or maybe the Excelsior?' He smiled scathingly. 'You would have stood an excellent chance of being recognised by any number of your late husband's acquaintances in either of those places, they are very popular with businessmen.'

Snatching off her hat and veil, Maria threw them on to a marble-topped dressing table. To stay here would only increase his hold over her but to leave would be to add to the frustration that nights spent alone had built in her. She would take what she wanted quickly and then go. At least, she thought, turning toward him, there would not be the awful smell drifting across from the fish market – a smell that had perfumed the hotel behind the Bull Ring.

'Why waste time talking about the hotel?' He came to her, his mouth descending on hers, fingers already loosening the buttons of her jacket. He had to make this good if he hoped to get the money he needed. 'There are many things I would rather do with you than talk.'

Shrugging out of her jacket, Maria parted her lips as it fell to the floor, her blood already rising as his tongue probed her mouth. One by one he removed her clothes, each movement of his hands accompanied by kisses to her lips and eyelids. Then, as she stood naked, he slipped agilely out of his own.

Maria let her eyes rove over his body: the tight thighs and waist rising to a well-muscled chest. Ryder Tempal kept himself in good condition.

Standing for a few moments he saw the approval flash in her eyes and her lips part in anticipation. Maria Beddows liked what he had so let her view the goods. He intended she should pay for them. Stepping close, he pulled the pins that held the thick swathes of her dark hair, letting it tumble like black velvet about her shoulders. Holding her face between his hands, he stared into eyes already smouldering with desire. Yes, Maria would pay.

'Soon we will spend every afternoon like this.'

Beneath him she sucked in her breath as he pushed into her. 'We will make love as often as we wish. And that will be often, my love, very often.'

Waves of desire riding high in her, Maria could only moan as she clamped both hands to his buttocks, drawing him further into her as she lifted her body to his, riding each thrust of his hips.

Twisting his hands in her hair, he dragged upward, forcing himself further into her. Then his breath became a long agonised gasp as desire spent itself. But her own body exploding with his, Maria was oblivious to the pain inflicted by him.

'Did you write that letter?'

Passion spent she lay beside him, her eyes on the smoke-stained ceiling.

Ryder kept his eyes closed. He could so easily prevent what he knew to be coming. He had only to roll his body on to hers and she would forget the letter. But what was not answered now would have to be answered later, and later he could give her his body to more effect, to satisfy both her need and his wants.

'Yes, I wrote it.'

'And you delivered it yourself?'

Reaching for his coat, Ryder took out a slim gold case, a

present from a former paramour. There would be others, he thought, extracting a slim brown cheroot, both presents and lovers. Maria was merely one of a line, and even when she became his wife that line would continue. Choosing a match from a box thoughtfully placed beside the bed, the one convenience other than the saucer presumably put to serve as an ashtray which the room offered, he lit the cigar, inhaling deeply before answering drily: 'I delivered it myself.'

Allowing smoke to trickle from between his lips, he folded one arm beneath his head.

'Did she say anything?'

'I gave her no time.' He drew on the cheroot, expelling the smoke in a grey stream that spread like a veil before floating upward.

'But she recognised you?' Maria propped herself on her elbow, looking down at his face. 'She must have done.'

'People change in four years,' he answered.

'You have not.' Maria thought of the possibility of his having been seen on his way to Hill Top. He was not unknown in Wednesbury, a number of people could have recognised him. One of them just might wonder what had taken him to the home of Virginia Mountford.

'I made pretence of wiping my face with my handkerchief. I threw the letter to the ground as she came towards me, and was gone before she had a chance to get a proper look at me.'

He blew a fresh stream of smoke. She would never know the story was a lie, and he would never enlighten her.

'You are sure it was Carys? It could not have been anyone else?'

Laying the cheroot in the saucer that stood beside the match box, he turned to Maria, pushing her gently back to the mattress.

'There was no one else in sight. I watched from a safe distance. She picked up the letter and put it in her pocket.'

Lifting her arms to his shoulders, Maria smiled. It should

be over within days. The amount of thallium the paper had absorbed was not as great as that which could have been added to food or drink. That being so it would take longer to achieve its results, but those results would be equally deadly. In a few days the threat of losing Meshac's money and Ryder Tempal would be gone.

'What did you write in the letter?'

'Never you mind.' He bent his head, pressing his mouth to her throat. 'It was nothing like this.' Trailing his mouth to her breast, he tongued her nipple, drawing it erect. 'Or this.' Coursing his mouth languidly over her body, he pressed a line of kisses down over her stomach to the crop of dark hair at its base. 'Or this.' Pushing her legs apart, he rolled on to her.

Feeling the hardness of him drive into her, Maria gave herself up completely to the pleasure of the moment. From now on there would be nothing but pleasure for Maria Beddows.

'Be you feeling poorly, girl?' Martha Bates cast a glance at Alice's untouched plate. 'It don't be like you to leave your food.'

'I'm all right, just a bit tired.'

'That ain't like you neither, you ain't never said you was tired afore. I 'opes you two ain't been sitting up nattering half the night?'

Carys met the housekeeper's accusing stare. 'No, Mrs Bates, we did not talk at all last night, Alice went straight to her own room.'

'Hmm!' Martha rose from the table, touching a hand to Alice's brow. 'Don't seem to have no fever,' she said after a moment, 'skin be cool enough. Be there a pain anywhere?'

'Some.' Alice touched a hand to her stomach.

''Ave you been at them gooseberries?' Martha crossed to a cupboard, unlocking it with a key taken from the drawer of a chest that stood beneath it.

'I ain't never touched a single one.' Alice groaned as a fresh twinge of pain caught her.

'Then what could 'ave given you the gripe? Can't be nothing I've cooked or we would all be feeling bad.'

'Alice was in the town yesterday.' Carys went to stand beside the other girl. 'Do you think she could have picked something up from there?'

Taking a spoon from the drawer of the kitchen table, Martha measured a dose of rich-looking brown liquid from the bottle she had extracted from the cupboard.

'It wouldn't surprise me. There always seems to be some illness or another rife in that place. Ain't been but a few years since the cholera took half the town.'

Carys's eyes widened with fear. She remembered the sisters at the convent, how they had worked constantly throughout the cholera epidemic that had swept the surrounding area of Bordesly, tending the sick and comforting the dying. But most of all she remembered the fear in each woman's eyes – fear that she might be the next to be touched by the sickness. And then Sister Luke had fallen sick. For almost a week she lay quarantined in the infirmary tended by two of the sisters, each of them excused attendance at services. The novices had been told this was due to the long hours of nursing but they had known it was a way of reducing risk to the convent. But all the nursing, and all the long hours of prayer, had not saved Sister Luke, nor one of the nuns who had cared for her.

'Don't look so frightened, wench.' Martha held the spoonful of liquid to Alice's mouth. 'There don't be nothing serious amiss. Like as not it be coming up to that time of the month. Some girls suffers quite a bit of pain before the flow starts. You get this drop of Indian Brandy into you and then get you up to bed. Come morning you'll be right as ninepence.'

Alice's chair scraped on the quarry tiles, her shoulder sending spoon and medicine flying from Martha's hand as she fled out through the scullery.

'I ain't never known the wench's time to cause her to be

sick, not never once.' Reaching for a cloth draped over the drying line above the range, Martha dabbed at the drops of brown liquid splashed across the front of her apron. 'We best get her to bed and if 'er be no better come the morning, I'll ask the mistress to send for the doctor.'

An hour later Carys looked at the girl whose face was almost as white as the pillow she lay on. 'Where did you call yesterday when you went into town?'

'Just to the butcher.' Alice smiled wanly. 'I didn't 'ave the time to go visiting nowhere else, not even me mother's. And don't go saying I picked up something nasty from Frank White's butcher's shop, not unless you wants to be the next lump of meat laid out on his block!'

'And you were telling the truth when you said you had not been eating gooseberries from the garden?'

'I hates goosegogs!' Alice grimaced. ''Ave done ever since I was a little kid, ask me mother.'

'Then what?' Carys sat on the side of the bed, the concern she felt still obvious on her face. 'What is causing a pain in your stomach and making you feel sick?'

'Whatever it was, I feels better now. Carys,' Alice glanced towards the door Martha Bates had closed when leaving the bedroom, 'about the letter . . .'

'Letter?' She had forgotten.

'Yes, you remember, the letter that young lad brought this afternoon. I told you about it, in the scullery.'

The tiny frown that had gathered between her eyes cleared as memory brought their conversation flooding back and Carys nodded. 'I remember. But you don't want to talk about that now.'

'Oh, but I do!' Alice loosed the top button of her nightgown, taking out the folded sheet of paper she had worn next to her breast since first reading it. 'You remember I said there was no name on the envelope?'

'Not now, Alice. You should get some sleep. We can talk about your letter tomorrow.'

'Carys Beddows, you be getting as bossy as Martha Bates, telling me what I should and shouldn't be doing!' Alice snapped as a spasm of pain shot through her stomach.

'I'm sorry. Concern caused me to forget my manners.' Carys felt it deepen at the uncharacteristic behaviour of her friend.

'I . . . I'm sorry an' all.' Alice gritted her teeth against the pain. 'But I . . . I 'ave to tell you.'

'I will only listen if you promise to go straight to sleep afterwards?'

'Promise.' The semblance of a grin passed over the girl's mouth. 'That envelope,' the smile faded, 'it bore no name. It had the words "To the girl with the pretty hair" wrote across it, and the lad said quite definite 'e had been told to give it into the hands of the 'ousemaid.'

'I see no mystery there. You are a housemaid and you do have very pretty hair.'

'But I ain't the only one. *You* be a 'ousemaid and *you* 'ave lovely hair. Don't you see? That letter could be for you same as it could be for me. I shouldn't 'ave opened it the way I did, I should 'ave waited and shown it to you first.'

'Nonsense.' Carys touched the other girl's hand. 'I have no one who would write me a letter. It was intended for you, there can be no doubt of that. Now what about keeping your promise and going to sleep?'

'I did promise, didn't I?' Alice's eyes gleamed briefly. 'But you said to do it when I had finished talking about the letter and I ain't got to that yet. I've only spoken about the envelope.'

'Alice Withers, you are a crafty madam.' Carys smiled at the return of Alice's humour.

'So me mother is always telling me. 'Er says that one day me tongue will be so sharp it'll cut me own throat.'

'Then why not give it a rest, at least until morning?'

'Cos if it don't get some exercise it'll flap about in me head all night. Here.' She thrust the paper toward Carys. 'Read it and see if you recognises who might 'ave wrote that.'

'I most certainly will not read it!' Carys withdrew the hand covering Alice's. 'That letter was written to you. Whoever has sent it does not want its contents divulged to another.'

'It be a love letter.' Alice pressed the paper to her throat.

'All the more reason for it to remain private. The words are for you Alice, no one else.'

'It be the first I've ever had, the very first in my whole life, but I don't know who sent it. Why do you think there be no name signed to it? If a man truly feels for a woman, so much that he writes 'er a love letter, then why don't he put his name to it? Why do you think that be, Carys?'

'A man can sometimes be as shy as a woman. He does not know if you will welcome his attentions or be annoyed by them. If you spurn him then it is obvious he would be as embarrassed as he was sad. Leaving his letter unsigned could be his way of protecting his pride.'

'How can I welcome his attentions or otherwise when I don't be knowing who he is?'

'You will.' Carys stood up. 'He will write again, I am sure of it, and next time he will sign his name.'

'Ee, I wonder who it be! Maybe it's Albie Fletcher, I caught him staring in church last Sunday. He turned red right up to his ears when I smiled at him.'

'I should think so too, you saucy thing!' Carys bent to kiss the girl's brow. 'Now if you wish to be in church this Sunday, I suggest you keep your promise and get to sleep.'

'Leave the candle,' Alice said as Carys made to blow it out.

'You've got the pain again?' The worry that had not left Carys since her friend ran from the house to be sick in the privy deepened. 'I shall stay with you tonight.'

'There be no need of that.' Alice smiled weakly. 'I ain't got that pain, I just wants to read my letter one more time.'

'One more time and then sleep. Mrs Bates is sure to look in on you before she retires, and if she catches you reading then your letter will finish up in the fire.' At the door Carys turned to look at the girl in the bed, the girl who had befriended her when her own mother had turned her back. And suddenly a finger of cold fear touched her spine.

Watching the door close, Alice opened the letter, pressing its words to her lips.

'You say the girl was taken poorly yesterday?'

Virginia Mountford looked at her housekeeper. Martha Bates was not one to worry unduly. 'Have you dosed her?'

'I tried to, ma'am. 'Er didn't touch her supper and when 'er showed signs of the gripe, I tried to give her a spoonful of Indian Brandy but 'er vomited afore I could get it into 'er.'

'And you say she is no better this morning?'

'Alice ain't no better, ma'am. In fact, it be my opinion the girl be worse.'

'I will come at once.'

'Begging your pardon, I don't think as that be wise. There be signs of sweating. It . . . it could be fever. I thinks it would be best for you not to go near.'

'The girl is my responsibility.' Virginia Mountford's mouth set in a determined line. 'So long as she is under my roof she will remain so. But what of the other, does she display any symptoms?'

'No, ma'am.' Martha shook her head. 'Carys don't be showing no sign of sickness.'

'And you?'

'No, nor Enoch Fletcher nor the lad who helps out with the gardens neither. Seems to be only Alice be poorly.'

'Then it is likely nothing she has eaten, unless of course she has been in the fruit garden.'

'Says 'er ain't, and Alice be no girl to lie.'

'Then why the pain? You said she was griped?'

'So 'er was, and still be.' Martha followed her mistress along the servants' landing. 'But that could most likely be the girl's monthly, it can sometimes be painful. What be most worrying is 'er asking to be sent home.'

'Sent home!' Virginia's hand halted on the door knob of Alice's room.

'Yes, ma'am.' Martha's face held a worried look. 'When I went in to her this morning, 'er asked to go 'ome. Seems the girl wants her mother.'

'Please, ma'am.' Alice's eyes were ringed by dark pools, their pupils dilated, and her face was bathed in perspiration. 'If it be all right with you, I would like to go 'ome to me mother.'

'I think we should first have the doctor to examine you, Alice.'

'I don't want no doctor, thanking you all the same.' She clamped her teeth, waiting for the spasm of pain that twisted her insides to pass. 'Me mother will know what to do. Me mother always knows what to do.'

'I really think we should keep her here.' Virginia turned to her housekeeper. 'I fear, as you do, she could have a touch of fever. To allow her to leave could worsen things. She needs a doctor and I doubt she will get the proper attention at home.'

'You need 'ave no fears on that score. Letty Withers be a good mother and caring of 'er children. The doctor will be sent for and 'e will go, even if them sons of 'ers 'ave to carry him there.'

Virginia glanced again at the girl. Her eyes, dark with pain, seemed to fill her pale face, and hair damp with perspiration clung to her face. 'Alice, my dear,' she said gently, 'do you really wish to go home today? Would it not be better for you to stay here . . .'

'I want to be with me mother,' Alice intervened, eyes brimming with tears. 'Me mother will get me well, I know 'er will.'

'Very well, my child. If you wish to return home then of course you must go, but I shall insist the doctor be called.' She turned to Martha. 'Make sure she wraps up warmly. I will give instructions to Enoch to drive her to her mother's house. Call me, please, when she is ready to leave.'

'Will she be all right?' Carys shaded her eyes, watching the carriage with Alice inside it, round the bend of the drive and out of sight.

''Course 'er will.' Martha turned back indoors. 'The mistress give me two sovereigns to send to her mother, enough to pay a doctor's bill and more beside. 'Er said there was more should it be needed, and that I was to keep 'er well informed of Alice's progress.'

'Can I go to visit her this evening?'

'Best give the wench time.' Martha gave a negative shake of her head. 'A couple of days will be soon enough for that. Letty Withers has enough bodies under her feet in that house without you adding another. Leave Alice to her mother, that be the best help we can give. A mother's love be the strongest cure of all. Two days, that be all it'll take, two days and it'll all be over.'

Following Martha into the house, Carys once more felt the icy touch of fear upon her spine.

Chapter Sixteen

Caine took a rabbit from the snare then reset it, covering it loosely with bracken and ferns. The rabbit had died quick and clean, he thought, picking it up and fastening it on a string about his waist. Not for animals in the wild the agony of living a half life, a life with half a face. Not like him, Caine Lazic, scarred and blinded by a woman.

He had been so sure. It was a short time only since the blood in him had told him this would be the year he would drink the sweet wine of revenge. And now? He walked to the edge of the flooded mine shaft and stood staring into the ebony water. Now he was not sure. The certainty had left him, leaving his mind like an open sore, festering with thoughts of what might be, what should be.

Had his Romany blood told him wrong? Was this to be another year of frustration, one more year he would leave Wednesbury with the aloes of disappointment bitter on his tongue?

On the surface of the black water a woman dressed in velvet the colour of moss rushed towards a boy who stroked his hand along the soft brown flank of her mare. The woman's arm was raised, and as the boy turned it came down, bringing a whip hard across his face.

Kicking viciously at the loose earth, Caine sent a shower of earth into the pool and the picture dispersed with the ripples. Turning away, he stared into the distance. He had dispersed the vision memory had recreated, but he had not destroyed it. It was there still, deep within him, waiting to rise again, to torment him as it had for sixteen years. No, it was not destroyed, nor would it be until that woman was destroyed. An eye for an eye? For Caine Lazic that would not be enough. He wanted more, much more.

From the steps of the caravan, sheltered by the fringe of trees, Bethesda watched her son turn away from the pool and knew the thoughts that twisted his mind, as that woman's whip had twisted his face.

'Was the snare full?' Removing the briar pipe from between her teeth, she spat on the ground, spitting in the face of the evil that dogged her son.

'It was full.' Caine removed the rabbit from the string, dropping it at his mother's feet. 'It will feed the two of us well.'

She descended the two remaining steps of the caravan and picked up the plump rabbit. 'That it will, and some left for the morrow.'

'We move on tomorrow.'

Bethesda showed no surprise. Placing the rabbit in a box strung to the side of the wagon, she returned to the fire. 'There be tay should you be ready, and a bit o' bacon I got for a mixture o' herbs.'

'Bacon will be well.' Taking a large enamel cup, Caine carried it to the log, nursing it between his hands as his mother cooked bacon in a smoke-blackened pan.

'I'd thought to camp here through the summer,' he said, accepting the tin plate criss-crossed with strips of well-fried bacon. 'But the rabbiting be poor and the stream holds few fish.'

'Where be you thinking to make for?' Bethesda refilled the ancient pipe.

'We will go the old way, up along the Sandwell Valley where we will camp for some days, and then down to Worcester for the winter.'

'Why come up 'ere along of Moxley then?'

Caine put the last of the bacon in his mouth, chewing and swallowing before he answered.

'I had thought to spend the winter out along Shrewsbury way, but it seems more practical to go where you be known. Not all villages welcome gypsies.'

'True.' Bethesda held a burning stick to the bowl of her pipe, sucking hard on the stem. 'There be many only too ready to set the dogs on the like o' we.'

'We'll have little trouble if we keep to our regular route.' Caine laid aside the tin plate, picking up the mug of tea. He was no coward. Taking new routes held no fear for him but Bethesda was getting old, she could do without the worry of snarling dogs and men set on breaking bones.

'There be many along of Smethwick and Netherton as well as Lickey End welcome my medicines.'

'That be so.' Caine drank from the mug. 'You saves folk a deal of pennies in doctor's takings, and your herbs often do them a sight more good. And the waters of Droitwich great pool will ease your own bones.'

'Arrh, they be good, the waters.' Bethesda blew a stream of smoke. 'But they will keep, and my bones will take no harm from the waiting of a week or two.'

'No sense in waiting!' Caine flung away the dregs of his tea, setting the mug down hard on the log. 'There be nothing for we here.'

'There be nothing here?' Bethesda watched him through the haze of tobacco smoke. 'Nothing but what you desire most, what your heart be crying out for, and that which will leave you no peace till it be settled. You don't be wanting to leave here for reasons of rabbiting or fish, you be wanting to be away because of what your mind be telling you.

'It says that this year will be the same as all the others, that you will not taste vengeance. You are feared the blood that runs in your veins has told you wrong when it said this was the year. But that blood is of the Romany, it has surged in the veins of your family for generations past and it speaks truth to them as knows how to listen. My mother and hers afore her had the sight that is given to few, and I carry the same sight. It has never told me false, and it does not lie when it says that before summer fades, you will make your reckoning. The debt will be paid in full.'

Maria glanced at the packages beside her on the seat of the small governess cart. She had enjoyed the choosing of the materials they held: taffeta and chiffon, silk and lace, whose colours had glowed like jewels against her skin. Wearing black irritated her, it was a colour that gave her no pleasure. She would have the beautiful cloth made into gowns and the minute the mourning period was over she would burn every stitch of black she possessed.

Stretching out a hand, she fondled the paper-wrapped cloth. If only that time were now! And why not? Why not take the materials to her dressmaker today? That way they would be ready for her the moment she could wear them.

Guiding the cart along Union Street, she hesitated. The house that Ryder rented was only a few minutes from here. She could so easily call. Who was to guess the identity of a woman sheathed so heavily in her mourning dress, and who would guess the reason for her visit?

Calling softly to the horse she crossed the Five Ways and on along Church Street. The Hawthorns stood a little way below the parish church of Wednesbury.

Touching her hand to the door, her first tap sent it moving. Ryder must speak to his staff! Maria stepped into the hall. So this was what her money was paying for! She glanced around. Well brushed carpet, furniture that gleamed. The Hawthorns, it seemed, was not the drab little house Ryder had said it was.

He had asked her for two hundred pounds before they had left that hotel in Needless Alley. The annual rent had to be paid, he said, or he would lose his tenancy. Two hundred! Maria glanced towards the staircase; a huge newel post carved and crowned with a miniature hawthorn bush stood at its base. Seemingly the place was worth the price.

About to cross to what she guessed would be a sitting room, Maria halted. Ryder's laughter rang out from a room above. She could call out to him, or go in search of a servant to announce her.

The laughter came again, lower this time, coming from the back of his throat in the way she had come to know so well. Gathering her skirts in her hands, she climbed the stairs, her tread soundless on thick Axminster. Following the sound of his voice, she turned along a corridor. Whoever he had with him he could get rid of. An hour or so of his love making would be an added fillip to her day.

'But, Ryder darling . . .'

Maria stood perfectly still. Ryder darling! Who would address him in such terms? He had no female kin; in fact, if he were to be believed, he had no relatives at all. If he were to be believed . . . Maria forced herself to remain calm even as once more the high-pitched voice floated to her.

'. . . we shouldn't, your housekeeper . . .'

'I have given her the day off,' Ryder's deeper tones answered. 'We are alone, my sweet.'

Alone! Maria moved in the direction of the sound. His housekeeper dismissed for the day. The front door not secured on the latch. The signs of the hasty admittance of someone whom he wished to remain unseen. Must the visitor remain unknown to any but Ryder? Why? Cold anger rose in her. There could be only one answer.

Now keeping her steps deliberately light, she moved to where she knew them to be, Ryder and his friend.

'Ryder, be patient, only naughty boys grab.' A high-pitched feminine laugh emanated through a doorway a little along the corridor. The door, Maria saw, had again been left open. Careless, she thought, walking quietly towards it.

'Open your mouth.' The voice, half laughing, half commanding, was followed by a moan, the sort of pleasured sound Maria was so very used to hearing.

'That's enough.' The laughter held a domineering tone. 'You must share. You will have more later but now it is my turn.'

Stepping to the open doorway, Maria looked in then stood immediately to one side, using the wall to hide her presence.

It was as she'd thought. The softer voice *was* that of a woman. Anger turning to bile in her throat, she peered around the edge of the door, seeing the rounded buttocks and narrow waist of the figure astride the naked body of Ryder.

So this was what he needed money for! Maria bit back the scream of anger pushing against her teeth. He was playing her for a fool. No wonder he could not find so much time for visits to Birmingham any more. She listened to the soft moans, to the creaking of the bed. How long? How long had he been playing his double game? One year . . . two? Had he known the woman before knowing Maria or was it only since her money had become available that he could afford this pleasure?

Was it someone she knew? Someone who knew her? Did the two of them laugh together at her gullibility, or was that strictly Ryder's preserve? Anger sat, hard and cold, in her chest. Perhaps it had been, and it could go on being so, but not for long.

Carefully, she peeped again into the bedroom. She must see the woman's face, she had to know if Ryder's whore was an acquaintance of hers.

Ryder lay spread-eagled across blue silk sheets, his blond hair tousled across his brow, his eyes closed. The figure now beside him was lying at an angle, auburn head pressed to his crotch.

Maria watched his body jerk in time with his moans, the movement of a puppet in the hands of a master. Then, as he gasped like a drowning man, the head lifted from him and Maria caught a glimpse of smooth creamy skin, the line of a finely curved eyebrow over a straight nose, and along the chin a neatly clipped auburn beard . . .

He was indeed playing a double game! Maria snatched at the reins, slapping them across the horse's flank, sending the cart back down the road towards the town. He was playing it in every sense of the word. What a fool he must think her! How clever to have his cake and eat it too! But that could not go on. Maria Beddows was not a woman to be fooled with. Ryder Tempal would not laugh for long.

'I have decided to take Reuben Fereday up on his offer, I have a fancy to see that gallery of his.'

Maria's smile held none of the anger of yesterday as she looked at her lover.

'That is, of course, if you will accompany me, my dear? It would not be fitting for me to visit alone.'

'I shall be happy to take you there,' Ryder's answering smile was wide. 'When do you have in mind?'

Maria tugged the embroidered bell pull that hung beside the graceful Adam fireplace. 'Now, at once. Unless you have something else to do?'

Ryder glanced sharply at the woman whose goodwill he depended upon, catching a hint of something in her voice. Maria had acted pleasantly enough since his arrival at Holyhead House, but he had sensed a change in her, an underlying ambiguity, a tone in her voice that sounded almost like menace.

'I never have anything to do I would not willingly put aside for you.'

How willing would you be to put aside your interesting diversions? Maria continued to smile despite the thought. The infidelity she had seen yesterday in his house had not been so much of a surprise, but the fact that his companion had been a man had disgusted her. To think he had done those same things with her!

'Then we will go. There is a train at noon.' Maria turned as a maid answered her summons, ordering her carriage.

'Oh!' Swaying as she stepped down from the carriage, Maria leaned heavily on Ryder's arm.

'What is it?' He was aware of heads turning towards them in the street. 'Are you unwell?'

'Will I be taking you back to the 'ouse, ma'am?'

'No! No, thank you, Simms.' Maria glanced at her coachman who had jumped from the driving seat on seeing her sway against Ryder's arm. 'It was just a touch of dizziness, nothing more. I will be perfectly all right.'

'We can easily visit Fereday's gallery another day. Perhaps you should return home?'

Return so you may enjoy another afternoon in the manner of yesterday? Maria smiled beneath the tulle veil. She had left that house as silently as she had entered; he had no idea she had seen him, no idea she knew of his making love with someone else, and that someone a man.

What would happen to him if she let it be known, not only to him but to others in his circle? Tongues wagged in Bilston, wagged long and loud. One word from her and Ryder Tempal would be finished in the Midlands. And it would be worth the risk to her own reputation – worth it had she not something else in mind for her handsome consort.

'I won't hear of it.' Maria too was aware of the interested stares of passers-by. 'Perhaps I might rest in the waiting room until the train arrives.'

Resting her hand on Ryder's arm, she walked into the station.

'There be folk in the waiting room.' The station master, his green uniform resplendent with brass buttons and yellow braid, touched a finger to his peaked cap. 'The lady might be more at ease in private, sir. If I might suggest my office?'

'That is most kind.' Maria swayed again and the portly railway official stepped quickly to the other side of her.

'If you will allow me, ma'am?' Tentatively taking her other arm, he led the way to a room at the end of the platform. 'Sit her in there, sir.' He looked up at Ryder. 'I'll go and get a glass of water.'

'I still think you should return home, Maria,' Ryder said after the station master had brought the water and left them alone in his office. 'It is foolish to continue on to Birmingham when you are obviously feeling unwell.'

'Why let a small dizzy spell spoil a whole day?' She handed him the glass of water, leaning back in a horsehair sofa.

'The Birmingham train is due in two minutes, sir.' The station master tapped politely before entering the office.

Ryder nodded, holding out his arm as Maria rose from the sofa, following the man on to the platform.

A little way from its furthest end the approaching train emitted the piercing shriek of a steam whistle. Uttering a small frightened cry, she shrank a little closer to Ryder. 'I do so fear these dreadful machines,' she said to the station master, still hovering in their vicinity. 'They are so frightening to a woman.'

'They be all right, ma'am, supposing you stands back from the edge of the platform.'

Beneath her veil, Maria smiled at his slightly superior tone.

'If I might suggest your wife stand behind you, sir?'

Ryder nodded, puzzled by Maria's professed fear of trains. She had travelled on them before, and alone. But he stepped in front of her.

'Not too close, Ryder,' Maria cautioned in a small faint voice.

Reaching the start of the short wooden platform, the train emitted a second screech of its whistle while grey-black smoke belched out in regular blasts, shrouding its carriages, the engine appearing like some nightmare monster from among the mist.

Beneath the shelter of her veil, Maria watched the train lumbering onward

Ryder really should have remembered, he really should have thought of the depth of truth contained in the adage: 'Hell hath no fury like a woman scorned.' Nor did it have that which Maria still felt at finding him making love to a man: a cold determined desire for revenge. A woman she might just have accepted, but a man . . . Ryder should have remembered how closely akin was love to hate. She had been so enamoured of him, so filled with a desire that she had mistaken for love. But that had been last week! She would make no more mistakes.

Two short sharp blasts of the whistle signalled the train's drawing to a halt, wheels adding to the screeching sounds as they ground against the brake.

One second. Maria smiled. Ryder really *should* have known. Love and hate. How quickly one turned to the other. Two seconds. He really should have known. Mistakes were so easily rectified for a woman as beautiful as she, and lovers so easily replaced.

From the fog of coal smoke and steam a spine-tingling blare erupted.

'Ohhh!' Giving a startled cry, Maria lifted a hand to her brow, her legs folding beneath her, her body falling against Ryder, sending him toppling to the ground. She heard one piercing scream as his body hit the platform then rolled over the edge, disappearing beneath the engine's huge iron wheels.

Hidden by her veil, the smile deepened. Poor Ryder, he really should have known.

Two hours later Maria lay in her own bed, eyes closed as they had been for most of the drive home, a doctor beside her in the hansom.

'She must be kept very quiet.' Maria listened to the man's voice. 'I fear the losses you have told me of can wreak havoc on the feminine nervous system. Your mistress parting with her only child and then the sudden death of her husband have proved too much. A woman can hide sorrow from her neighbour but she cannot hide it from her body. Your mistress's illness is a result of that sorrow. You will admit no visitor for a week. I will call tomorrow morning.'

The rest of what he said was lost to Maria as together with her housekeeper he left the room.

Ryder had got what he deserved. Her eyes remained closed. He had thought to play her for a fool, but he had lost. I told you, my love, I told you I would share your body with no woman. Bitterness sharp in her throat, she saw painted on her mind's eye two figures sprawled on blue silk sheets.

'No woman, Ryder,' she whispered. 'And no man either.'

Chapter Seventeen

Virginia read once more through the letter she had received from her nephew. Why had he made such a request? Was it truly for the sake of art, or was it something deeper?

She glanced across her sitting room to where the charcoal drawing of her husband hung on the wall.

Reuben had paid more than passing attention to the sketch. He had examined it in detail and when he had turned back to her his face had held a sadness she could not define.

He wanted to mount an exhibition of unknown artists, his letter said. To bring hitherto unknown talent to the notice of the art world. But how many of those words were true? She folded the letter, replacing it in its envelope. Was his motive truly one of enriching the world of art? Was it the talent of many unknown artists that he was interested in, or would it be more honest to say it was only one? She thought again of the look on his face at seeing that sketch. This was only one unknown artist her nephew wished to discover, she was sure.

Virginia pulled the cord that would summon Carys to her.

'You visited Alice yesterday evening?' she asked as the girl entered the room.

'Yes, ma'am.'

'Did you find her any more recovered?'

Carys shook her head, feeling tears prick her eyelids.

'Try not to be sad, child. Mrs Bates tells me the doctor is certain it is not the cholera. We must thank the Lord for sparing us that.'

'Alice is so pale, and she is constantly soaked in perspiration. Her mother is afraid it could be fever of another kind.'

'Letty Withers is a sensible woman,' Virginia replied. 'But when a beloved child is sick much of our common sense flies out of the window. Rest assured, my dear, if the doctor feared that Alice had fever of any kind he would have had her admitted to the isolation hospital. We must trust to his judgement.' And pray God it is sound, she added silently.

'May I ask if I might visit Alice again this evening? I don't think Mrs Bates has anything special she requires to be done. I could be there and back in little more than an hour or so if I take the tram both ways.'

Virginia looked at the girl who had insisted on serving as a maid in her household – at the lovely face, taut with worry, the amber eyes dark with fear – and her own heart twisted. She had hesitated after reading the letter from her nephew; now she knew she had made the right decision. If Reuben and this child of Meshac Beddows *had* met before then, instinct told her, he had not abused her.

'Of course you may visit Alice, and tell Letty I will go myself after church on Sunday. And now, child, I have a request to make of you. My nephew has written to ask for the loan of the drawing you made of my husband. He wishes to give an exhibition of the work of unknown artists and feels that sketch would be a considerable addition.'

'The drawing is yours, ma'am.' Carys maintained the polite form of address she had adopted from their first meeting. Her birth made her the social equal of this woman, but circumstances made her Virginia's employee and as such she would address her. 'You have no need to ask me what you may do with it.'

Virginia's neatly dressed grey hair took on a silver sheen as a beam of sunlight swept through the high window at her back.

'As you say, Carys, that drawing is mine to do with as I wish, but my request is not for that drawing, it is for those you have in your room.' Virginia caught the look that flashed rapidly over the girl's face. 'You have not destroyed them, have you?'

Carys's thoughts ran wildly through her mind. She could not lie, she could not say she no longer had her sketches, yet how could she let them be seen by others? Her mother had called them obscene and labelled her lustful and wicked for drawing them. How would other people think of her?

'Have you destroyed them?' Virginia repeated her question when Carys did not answer.

'No.' She shook her head, a faint trace of pink rising to her cheeks. 'I have not destroyed them.'

'Then would you allow my nephew to borrow them? I give you my word they will be returned to you, and none but myself shall know the name of the artist unless you wish it.'

'I will fetch them for you.' Carys turned towards the door.

'One thing more, my dear,' Virginia called. 'Would you agree to my having them framed before sending them to Birmingham?' She smiled as Carys nodded. 'And try not to worry over Alice. God holds the girl in His hands.'

Closing the door of the sitting room, Carys pressed her hands to her mouth. Yes, God held Alice in His hands, but would He let her go?

Maria fastened the buttons of her black taffeta dress, this time exulting in its colour. She had paid Ryder two hundred pounds . . . how much of that had gone on his fancy man? She had supplied him so often with money, which he had probably spent on deceiving her. Thirty pieces of silver! Ryder Tempal had taken all of that. 'Ryder!' She spat the word. 'Judas would be a better name.'

Now she had paid him in full. She glanced at her reflection in the long walnut-framed dressing-mirror, admiring what she saw. She was cured of her infatuation with her lover. Maria Beddows would enjoy new conquests.

'Do you really ought to be going, ma'am? A funeral, even in early summer, be a dismal affair, and the doctor said you was to be kept in bed a week or two more yet.'

'How can I not go?' Maria turned to the plain girl whose tap on her bedroom door had warned her to wipe the smile of triumph from her face. 'Mr Tempal was a friend of my husband's. I must pay my respects.'

He was even more of a friend to you! Chrissy Williams knew as much of her mistress's carryings on as the dismissed Mary Bartlett. She turned to a drawer, selecting a pair of heavy lace gloves which she handed to Maria. Yes, that handsome Ryder Tempal had been more than a friend to this woman, much more.

'The wreath you ordered be ready in the kitchen, ma'am.'

Maria drew on the gloves, smoothing them slowly down each finger. 'Have it placed in the carriage,' she said, lowering her veil over her face.

Seated in her carriage as the cortège of mourners filed into Woodgreen Cemetery, Maria instructed her coachman to add her own tribute of white Madonna lilies to the carpet of flowers surrounding the newly dug grave. Then, as the priest began his long peroration, she signalled she should be driven away.

She had given Ryder all the respect he deserved, she was well rid of him. As she was rid of Meshac's daughter.

She smiled behind the veil.

There was one good thing Ryder had done: he had ensured she was now sole inheritor of all her husband's wealth. He, Ryder, had mixed the poison. His was the hand that had written the letter, and he the one who had delivered it. Carys had died by his hand. The evidence lay at the bottom of some mine shaft. There was no way in which she could be linked with that death, no blame could be attached to her as could none for Ryder's death.

Maria leaned back in the comfort of her carriage. It had been an accident. So many observers had seen the spells of dizziness attack her in the street – she had taken care they should. And the station master had given her the privacy of his office, even fetching her a glass of water. It had worked exactly as she had planned. A sick and frightened woman fainting on a station platform. Who could lay any blame on her for that? Who could say Ryder's falling beneath a train was anything other than a tragic accident?

A few more months was all that was needed to bring her mourning to a suitable conclusion. A few months only and then she would be able to dress in the jewel-bright colours that so suited her colouring; could dispense with the misery of her widow's garb and be free to enjoy her wealth.

And who would she choose to enjoy along with it? Which young man would share her money and her bed? For a brief moment she thought of Reuben Fereday and the smile returned to her mouth. He had not yet succumbed to her charm, but then she had not as yet fully exerted it. She would visit his gallery alone, and who could tell? Perhaps the handsome Mr Fereday would be the next thing she would buy.

The smile still on her face, Maria watched the drab line of shops and even drabber houses, each packed tight against the other, each as dreary as its neighbour. The Black Country deserved the title its workshops and steel mills had earned, their smoke covering every brick and stone with soot. Maybe she would sell Holyhead House, maybe she would move to Birmingham or London.

Happy with the dream of a fine house set far enough away from the dirt of smelting steel and the smell of factories and workshops, Maria gave only a passing glance at the figure of a young girl turning left off the main highway towards a square of shabby houses.

A faded blue coat, too tight for comfort . . . Subconsciously memory stirred. A brown dress, equally faded, short of her feet by several inches . . . Suddenly the floodgates of memory opened. Those were the clothes Carys had worn the day Maria had taken her to the convent; the same ones she had worn the day she had left it.

Her attention caught, Maria leaned forward, watching the girl walking along a narrow alley that disappeared into the warren of houses. She had the same rich chestnut hair. Then the girl turned to look behind her and Maria gasped. Even from this distance there could be no mistake: the girl she watched was her daughter, the daughter she had thought dead.

Hearing the clip of horses' hooves and the rumble of carriage wheels, Bethesda looked towards the road. Squinting against the sun she watched it come and with it came the quickening. Low in her stomach a surging heat began to throb and blood pounded like a tidal wave, threatening to burst her very veins. Behind her eyes a mist the colour of the setting sun began to swirl, lowering a veil across her sight, cutting off the picture of heath and carriage. Then it lifted, leaving Bethesda with the clearer pictures of her second sight.

From a small governess cart a figure wreathed in black called to Caine and as he answered the summons Bethesda saw a glint of gold move against the blackness. Like seeing figures on a stage, she watched Caine nod his head then point in the direction of the town they had left days before. Replying, the figure lifted one hand. Raising each black-clad finger slowly until all five stood erect the hand closed, then equally slowly repeated the action until each had lifted as many times as Bethesda had fingers on both hands. Caine nodded. Then the hand reached for the whip, and as it was lifted above the veiled head of the figure two uniformed men ran to Caine, seizing both of his arms. As he struggled for freedom, Bethesda again caught the gleam of gold on the breast of the driver of the carriage. But now the gold began to expand and to move, crowding in upon her, twisting and writhing like some living creature, filling the whole of her vision. Then it was gone.

Watching the carriage with her living eyes, Bethesda clenched her briar pipe between her teeth, the memory of the policemen seizing her son vivid still. Caine was in danger from the woman that carriage concealed – mortal danger. She watched the carriage disappear in the curve of the road. The sight did not lie. Tomorrow she would come. Staring into the fire, Bethesda knew the end had begun.

Carys turned into the square of houses. She had ridden the tram to the junction at Dudley Street then walked on along the Holyhead Road, not wanting to follow the Portway on her own. In the quiet streets grouped about St James' church silence seemed to hang heavy. Whenever she had come here with Alice there had been the laughter of children and the occasional greeting from a woman passer-by. But today there was nothing; no one watched her turn into Brick Kiln Street to enter the Witherses' house.

'Mrs Bates allowed me to leave early. She said it would be better to come while the sun was on the streets.'

'Martha Bates has sense.' Letty smiled at the girl who had visited each day since her daughter had returned home.

'Mrs Mountford sends her regards and asked me to tell you she will call to see Alice on Sunday after church. If you will permit it, of course?'

'Arrh, her can come and welcome, and pleased we'll be to see her. Alice always says what a good mistress Virginia Mountford be, though my Alice be a good wench and a hard worker. The mistress ain't never had no call . . .'

The words trailed away and Letty buried her face in her hands, her shoulders heaving as she sobbed.

'Oh, Mrs Withers, don't cry! Please don't cry!' Carys threw her arms about Alice's mother, holding her while the tears poured.

'My wench,' Letty sobbed, ''er don't seem to be getting any better.'

'She will,' Carys soothed. 'It is early days yet. We must give her time. The doctor has said it is not the cholera so you have nothing to fear.'

'I know.' Letty allowed herself to be seated, dabbing her eyes with the hem of her apron. 'But to see my girl just lying there, as pale as if the life had already left her.' She lifted the apron, holding it against her face. 'It fair breaks my heart.'

The months spent in the kitchen of Ridge House had taught Carys the salve for many ills. Unasked she set about making a pot of tea. If only Alice's illness could be cured so easily, she thought, when minutes later she handed the quietly sobbing Letty a cup of the strong sweet liquid.

'I be sorry to go on like that.' She tried to smile. 'You ain't come all that way to listen to me blarting.'

'You cry all you want to, Mrs Withers. Mrs Bates says it does us all good to cry sometimes.'

'I reckon her be right.' Letty smoothed the damp edges of her apron down over her skirts. 'But that don't give me leave to go upsetting visitors with my tears.'

'I am not upset,' Carys lied, feeling the sting of her own tears prick behind her eyelids.

'You be a good wench, Carys, same as my own.'

'How is Alice today?' she asked, having to fight hard against the emotion the other woman's words stirred in her.

Letty took the thick platter cup in her hands, staring into it. ''Er don't seem no better, for all the medicine the doctor says to dose 'er with. Not that her can keep it inside her. I no sooner holds the spoon against 'er mouth than 'er be heaving fit to bring up her stomach.'

'Has she eaten anything?'

'Not a crumb. Not a bite since entering this house. The doctor says not to worry too much on account of that, but how can a mother not worry?'

'I know how hard it must be for you, but Alice will recover, she will get well soon, I am sure of it.'

'Arrh, we must all think that.' Letty smiled through a film of tears. 'We must put our faith in the Lord. Now you drink up that tea and then I'll take you up to see her.'

Alice lay in a narrow iron-framed bed which despite its size almost filled the tiny bedroom. A two-paned window let in a stream of afternoon sunlight that played over a small table set beneath, and Alice's dress hung from a nail knocked into the wall, a dark smudge against the whitewash.

'You 'ave a visitor, me wench.' Letty bent over the bed, lifting her higher on the pillows. 'You two 'ave yourselves a natter. I'll be up later with some broth.'

'Hello.' Carys smiled at her friend as Letty left them. 'How are you?'

'I be all right.'

Alice's voice was little more than a whisper and her face creased with the strain of speaking.

'Mrs Bates sends her love, and Mrs Mountford said to tell you she will come to see you on Sunday, after church.'

Alice tried to smile. 'How be you managing up there? It must be awful hard on you, doing the work of two.'

'I am not doing the work of two.' Carys sat on the edge of the bed. 'Mrs Bates insists I do no more in a day than I did before. She says what does not get done today will bide until tomorrow.'

'Sounds like Mrs B.' Eyes that seemed to have lost their colour stared up from dark hollows. 'Carys, have . . . have there been any other letters?'

Her heart twisting at the hope she saw flare in those faded depths, Carys knew she could not bring herself to answer truthfully. If lies brought damnation to her soul then hers was damned, and she would give it gladly.

'There was no letter.' Carys smiled at the pallid face. 'But a man came yesterday to Ridge House. He stood beneath the trees that edge grounds to the rear, where you say the boy brought that letter a few days ago. He stood there several minutes but when I went towards him he left.'

'What did he look like?'

'He was tall.' Carys paused as if recalling the appearance of the invented figure. Trying desperately to sound convincing, she went on, 'He had fair hair and wore a brown jacket. He was very handsome and as I went towards him he smiled but once I got close turned away.'

'Did he say his name?'

Carys forced a smile to hover about her own lips though her throat felt tight. Was she merely storing up disappointment for her friend? Would her lies have to be faced, or would the man who had written to Alice come some day to speak to her? And if he did, would he in any way resemble the picture she was painting?

'No,' she said, holding the faded eyes with her own. 'He did not say his name. But when I called to him he said I was not the one he came to see, I was not Alice. I asked if he had a message I could give you and he said to tell you he would come again soon. That was as good as a letter, don't you think? This time he came himself, he did not send a boy to bring his message.'

'He come to see me.' The girl's voice was like the whisper of dry leaves. 'He truly came? To see me?'

'He truly came.' Carys pushed the lie past the barrier of her throat. 'It was clear I was not the one he wanted to see. "You don't be Alice", were the words he spoke, neither would he stay to talk. I was not the girl he had written a letter to and therefore he had nothing to say to me.'

'The letter.' The movement tired, almost listless, Alice reached beneath her nightgown to where the letter lay open on her breast. 'I read it often. I know every word that be written on it.' She pressed the paper to her lips before letting her hand fall across her chest. 'You says he was handsome?'

'Very handsome. I could not see the colour of his eyes but he had fair hair and his skin was bronzed by the sun.'

'He . . . he'll come again, won't he, Carys?'

'Yes.' She leaned forward, kissing the other girl's brow. 'He will come again, but now I think you ought to rest. I don't want to make your mother cross by tiring you.'

'Carys!' Her eyes suddenly enormous, Alice clutched at her hand. 'I . . . I don't think I'll be coming back to Ridge House.'

'So you plan to marry your handsome beau as soon as you are well!'

The answer was light but Carys felt a heaviness creep over her as she looked at the girl, lying now with closed eyes, the letter held once more to her mouth.

'She is sleeping.' Carys met the enquiring gaze of Alice's mother.

'She be doing more and more of that, but how did you find her?'

'She seemed little changed from yesterday.' Carys could lie no more but at the expression on Letty's face, added: 'But that will alter soon. Mrs Bates thinks it is too early to expect signs of recovery yet, but it will come.'

'That be what the doctor tells me, but I finds the wait all too worrying none the same.'

'Has he given any intimation of what is wrong with Alice?'

'Like I told you, he has ruled out the cholera. Says the sweating and the aching in her joints be down to something he calls the influenza. Says it seems like fever when it first starts and that we 'ave to guard against it turning to pneumonia. That be why I keep a fire burning in her room even though the days be warm.'

'May I please come again tomorrow?'

'Arrh, me wench.' Letty nodded, accompanying Carys to the door. 'Supposing the mistress allows it.'

Watching Carys until her slight figure turned the corner into St James's Street, Letty closed the door and went upstairs to Alice's room.

She had been reading that letter again. It was all she had done these past days, pressing the paper to her lips as if they touched the mouth of the sender then placing it beneath her nightgown, sleeping with it spread over her heart.

Letty smiled. She knew the thrill of the very first words said in love. Her girl had not heard those words from a man's lips but she had them from his hand, and the thrill they gave was the same.

Bending, she pressed her lips to the girl's brow, then to each of the closed eyes. Tears filling her own, she turned towards the window, towards the brightness spilling through. Slowly she walked across and stood staring out on to the maze of tiny houses, and across to where the spire of the church rose above them. Then, grasping a curtain in each hand, she drew them together. The room was dim now as she turned from the window but the bed could still be clearly seen. Letty crossed to it, staring down at the figure lying there, the letter held to her mouth.

'That be your letter,' she whispered. 'It will be seen by none but you.' Easing the paper from Alice's hand, she flung it into the fire, watching the edges brown and curl, seeing the blue and purple of the flames that consumed it. Then turning back to the bed, Letty Withers drew the sheet over her daughter's face.

Chapter Eighteen

'My mother asked me to come, ma'am.'

Davey Withers showed none of the discomfiture he felt at being in Virginia Mountford's elegantly furnished sitting room.

'I am happy to see you. Davey, isn't it?'

'That do be my name, ma'am.'

'Well.' Virginia's smile was pleasant and genuine. 'Please sit down, Davey. Would you take something to drink? Tea, or perhaps a glass of ale.'

'Thank you kindly, but no. This don't be . . .' He paused, mouth twitching as he sought to keep a hold on his emotions.

'Carys tells me your mother has been kind enough to agree to my calling to see Alice on Sunday.' Virginia covered the awkward moment. 'Please give her my thanks when you return home.'

Davey swallowed visibly, and his eyes as they met Virginia's were moist. 'That be what my mother sent me to tell you. It won't be any use your calling, not to see our Alice anyway. You see, ma'am, my sister died yesterday.'

'What!' Virginia was stunned by what he had said. 'But yesterday . . . Carys said she still looked quite poorly but that the doctor saw no reason to be overly concerned?'

'Miss Beddows told you right, the doctor did tell us that, but it seems he was wrong.'

'I . . . I can't believe it! Only a few days ago Alice was as chirpy as a sparrow.'

'We can't believe it neither.' Davey glanced at the carpet, unwilling for his brimming eyes to be seen.

'Your mother, Davey, how is your mother?'

'Taking it badly, ma'am, as you might expect. Her hasn't showed it by weeping and wailing, and her hasn't said much, but you can see in her face it has torn the heart from her.'

I know the feeling, Virginia thought, the anguish of never having a child could in no way match that of losing one yet the old agony rose in her as she thought of Alice's mother. The woman had been given heartache and sorrow that would be with her for the rest of her life; no amount of tears could wash them away, nor any number of years erase them.

'Give your mother my very deepest condolences,' she said gently. 'And if I may, I would like to be allowed to attend the service?'

'Arrh, ma'am.' Davey could not look up. 'I know my mother would like that you be with the following. I will come myself to tell you when the funeral is to be held.'

'Thank you, Davey.'

Virginia watched him leave. She had wanted to offer financial help but knew this was not the time. They were proud people and would prefer to take care of their own. But Virginia would not forget Alice or her family.

Below stairs, Martha Bates's eyes held the same incredulity as that of her mistress as Davey imparted his mother's message.

'But when?' She dropped heavily into her chair beside the range. 'Carys was only there yesterday and Alice were all right then.'

'It must have been just after she left.' Davey glanced at the girl standing beside the freshly scrubbed table, eyes huge with disbelief. 'Mother says her watched Carys turn the corner into

St James's Street then went straight back upstairs to Alice. Her were lying with her eyes closed and me mother thought as her was sleeping, until her kissed her, and then her knew it were more than sleep.'

'Oh my good God!' Martha murmured. 'Oh, your poor mother! How be her bearing up?'

'It has hit her badly, finding our Alice like that after the doctor saying there were no need for worry.'

Alice dead! Carys felt the breath desert her lungs. It was not true. It was all a lie. She had seen her only yesterday, held her hand, told her of an admirer come to call.

'No!' Her eyes dark with pain, she stared at Davey. 'It is not true, it is not! Alice is not dead, she is not . . . she is not!' Holding a hand to her mouth, she ran from the kitchen.

'Carys.' Davey came to where she stood, staring out across the open heath towards the town sprawled at the bottom of the hill. 'Carys, I be sorry to be the one to hurt you.'

'Oh, Davey.' Tears spilling down her cheeks, she turned to him, sobbing as he took her in his arms. 'Davey, why, why?' Her face buried against his shoulders she repeated the question again and again, grief shaking her slender body.

Holding her close against him, he pressed his lips to her head as he stroked the rich curls of her hair, even in his grief knowing another heavier sorrow. The sorrow of knowing the girl he held so close in his arms did not love him as he loved her. That her being in his arms was through grief and not through love. Above Carys's head his eyes swam with tears.

Reuben Fereday touched his heels to the flanks of the horse he had hired from the livery stables close to Wednesbury railway station. He had received the sketches he had sought to borrow from Virginia and others besides, unmistakably drawn in the same hand: the one that had painted the design on the box purchased from Meshac Beddows, the hand of his daughter. But how? That girl had entered a convent, had taken vows that would keep her apart from the world for the rest of her life.

But that sketch of Virginia's husband . . . there was no mistaking the style. He had examined it minutely, comparing it with one which Virginia assured him in her accompanying letter had been drawn five years ago; the sketch of a man rising from a pool, head thrown back, exultant in his superiority over the dark satiny water. A man he knew to be himself.

The wind playing through his dark hair, Reuben laughed from sheer happiness. It had to be her! It had to be the girl on the heath. God only knew how, but it had to be. The girl who had filled his thoughts for so long must have left her convent, and God willing he would find her.

Cresting the rise, he followed the track that led to the grounds of his aunt's house. He had chosen to come this way rather than drive up Holloway Bank even though riding across the heath meant his approaching Ridge House from the rear.

Still some yards from the wall that protected the gardens from the rough winds that could sometimes rise with devastating force from the flat heathland, he reined in the horse, his eyes on the two figures that stood in its lee.

A man, tall and broad-shouldered, held a girl in his arms, his fair head bent close to hers, hand stroking the rich chestnut of her hair.

The girl on Moxley Heath had had chestnut hair. Suddenly Reuben felt cold. She too had been of slender build, as was the girl in this man's arms. Tightening the reins as his mount tossed its head, the coldness turned to a kind of fear – fear of what he might see. He watched the girl release herself from the man's arms and as she lifted her face to his, Reuben saw clearly the one that had remained indelibly printed on his mind. The girl the man had been holding, the girl he had kissed, whose hair he had stroked, was the girl on the heath.

Disappointment striking him like a hammer blow, Reuben jerked on the rein, whipping the horse about, digging his heels sharply into its soft flesh as he raced back down the rise and across the heath.

He ought to have known. It was nothing short of idiocy to think she would even remember him, much less think she would harbour any love for a man she had spoken to just once, and then for moments only.

Drawing into the yard of the White Horse Hotel, he swung from the saddle. Giving a shilling to the ostler in charge who agreed to return the horse to its owner, Reuben strode into the building. Ordering a gill of brandy he strode into the smoking room.

From her stool beside the fire Bethesda watched the sky turn to crimson as the distant steel works opened their furnaces. She watched as the trails spread like blood oozing from some gigantic wound. Usually the sight so magnificent in its awesome majesty impressed her as did a beautiful sunset, but this evening she watched with eyes blind to its grandeur.

All day she had willed the sight to return, to show her again what she felt she had missed, to tell her what she needed to know. But it had not returned and in its absence cold fear had settled in her heart.

That carriage had held a figure robed in the colour of death, and the figure was a woman's. She had raised a whip. The carmine glow of the sky reflected on Bethesda's face, etching the wrinkles about her eyes and mouth, shadow filling them, showing minuscule ravines whose depths held the secrets of a thousand lifetimes.

Though the face was veiled, the sight told her that the woman was the same one. The same who once before had raised a whip that had cut the eye from a boy's face. That time she had blighted a life; this time she would destroy it. This time Caine would die.

'The Peel men come for him,' Bethesda muttered. 'That much the sight give me. 'Tis the Peel men will take Caine and the Gorgio will 'ang him.'

Overhead the brilliance of the sky muted into gold-fringed purple and then to pearl as the furnace flames were once more closed behind steel barriers, but their beauty was lost to Bethesda. Only the inner world of her mind was real and desperately she probed its corners for the answer she had sought all that day. An answer that would not come to her call.

Tomorrow would be too late. Wrapped in her shawl, she rocked endlessly on her stool. The sight had shown her the danger and her Romany blood told her just as clearly that danger would come with the new dawn, as it told her she, and she alone, could protect her son.

But how? Across the shadowed heath a roosting bird called to its mate whose wide black wings filled her vision as it swooped in answer across the sky.

Its answer was hers.

Pulling the shawl tighter, passing the corners around her back before knotting them beneath her flat breasts, Bethesda spat into the fire. The ways of the earth were ancient beyond time, their mysteries lost to those who had forgotten how to look and listen, how to read the signs. But she had not forgotten. She carried within her the wisdom of her grandmother and many grandmothers before her, taught to her through the years of her growing. A wisdom that surpassed the Gorgio's, a knowledge that caused them fear. But Bethesda did not fear it.

The black wings of the bird had told her, giving her the answer in its swoop to earth. She must seek among the old ways, travel the dark paths, ask the help of the old gods.

Going across to the caravan, she unhooked the tarred leather water jack, pouring a little of its contents into her tin cup before replacing it. Beneath the waistband of her dark flounced skirts a knife touched against her bones. Taking the tin cup in her hand, Bethesda left the camp and headed towards the trees.

Evening had already closed over the sky and as yet no moon rode its dark infinity. The soft sounds of moving animals and the rustling of breeze-touched leaves filled the darkness that closed about her as she entered the small wood. These were sounds that brought trepidation to those who did not have the knowledge, but to Bethesda they sang a song of welcome. Here she would be given what she asked, here the dark ones would answer.

Coming upon a small clearing she halted, listening to the call of her soul. This was the place. It was here she must honour the old ways. Waiting for the light she knew would come, she looked about the clearing, and as the moon broke cover, bathing it in clear silver, saw a flat-topped stone. Crossing to it, she knelt, placing the cup beside her on the ground together with the knife. Reaching beneath her shawl, she brought out the leaves of a rowan tree and tiny twigs of oak she had gathered that morning, grouping them in a heap on the stone.

'Let thy flesh be my flesh. Let thy bones be my bones.'

The words quivered on the silver-traced night as Bethesda picked up the knife. Holding her hand over the cup, she drew the blade across her palm.

'Let thy blood be my blood,' she intoned as droplets of red fell into the water. Then, holding her hand above the stone, dripped several spots on to the dried twigs. Setting the knife aside, she took her box of matches from the pocket of her skirt and struck one. Holding it to the piled leaves and twigs, waiting while smoke began to spiral upward, she leaned her head into it.

'Let thy wisdom be my wisdom. Give me that which the sight did not.'

Sitting back on her heels, Bethesda watched the smoke rise from the stone, drifting into two separate lines. Her mouth tight, old eyes sharp as a hawk's, she watched and waited. Above the stone smoke showed clear in the moonlight, the two columns curling and writhing like twin serpents, their grey bodies twisting in and out of each other, forming and melting only to form again until they hung in the air, two shapes, one interlocked with the other. A perfect 'M', its body joined to an equally perfect 'B'. Below them the last flames spewed from the leaves and sticks, bathing the letters in red-hued gold.

The old ways had revealed what the sight had kept hidden, but Bethesda was not yet finished. She had to know how her son was to be avenged.

Scraping up a handful of loose earth, she mixed it with a few drops of the water. Moulding it into the rough shape of a human figure, she laid it on the stone beside the ashes of the leaves. Then, taking up the cup, she held it between both hands.

'My blood mixes with thy blood,' she whispered, 'let thy wisdom be mixed with mine.' Pouring the water on the ground about the stone she felt her pulses quicken. From the trees circling the glade came a rustling. Like the sound of many voices it rushed towards her, circling the stone, the breath of its coming lifting the ashes of the dead fire, sucking them into itself.

Breath caught in her lungs, Bethesda waited. Then it was gone, leaving the mud figure speckled with dots of grey ash. Gathering cup, matches and knife, she rose to her feet, making a sign of gratitude. Leaving the remnants of her asking upon the stone, she turned away. The old ways had not failed her. Caine would not die. But the woman who had maimed him would often long for death.

Alice had been buried.

In her little bedroom on the top floor of Ridge House, Carys buried her face in the pink cotton of her friend's one walking out dress. She would never see her again, never huddle with her as they laughed over some silly happening.

It had all happened so very quickly, and now Alice was gone.

Sobs dry in her throat, Carys folded the pink-sprigged dress, putting it with the rest of Alice's things in the brown hessian bag Mrs Bates had supplied.

Everything must be returned to Alice's mother. Carys stared

at the few possessions, hardly filling the small bag. Was that all there was to show for a life? Was there no more remaining of the bright bubbly girl than a few clothes?

Bitterness and sorrow merged in Carys as she picked up the bag. Alice had been more like a sister than a friend, always laughing away a problem, always eager to share a confidence.

'Is that everything?' Martha Bates eyed the bag Carys set on a chair in the kitchen.

'Yes.' Her voice was choked. 'That is everything.'

'I be sorry over having to ask you to do what rightly be my duty. Perhaps we should send a message to Letty explaining that I be laid up with the rheumatics and that I will go to see her when they be gone?'

'I really do not mind taking Alice's belongings to her mother. In fact I want to go. Mrs Withers and her family were so very kind to me, and . . . and I feel somehow Alice would want me to be the one to be with her mother when her things are returned.'

Martha touched a hand to her hip in an attempt to ease the painful joint. 'If that be the way you feel then I won't be the one to tell you no. But be sure to explain to Letty. That woman be going through enough heartbreak without feeling I be turning me back on her now.'

'Mrs Withers will not think badly of you if return Alice's property. She knows you well enough to realise you would not forgo your duty lightly.'

'You be right.' Martha nodded. 'Tell her I'll be along just as quick as these 'ere rheumatics be cleared.'

The afternoon sun was warm as Carys followed the Holloway Road towards town, but she felt nothing but the bag in her hand that held so many memories: the beads bought from a pack man who had called at the house, cheap glass that Alice had worn with the pride of a queen bedecked in diamonds; the china shepherdess Eddie had won at the Wakes – sadly tawdry but all Letty had left of her daughter.

Turning into Brick Kiln Road, Carys glanced at the line of cramped houses, each so like the other in their drabness. The curtains that had been closed in respect on the day of the funeral were now open, except in Letty's house. There the merest fraction of a parting allowed in the light of day, a fraction that she knew would increase little by little over the next ten days.

'Sit you down, wench.' Letty Withers tried to smile as she opened the door to Carys but her eyes were averted from the bag. 'It was thoughtful of you to call,' she added, hearing Martha Bates's message.

Placing the bag in a corner alongside the dresser, Carys turned as Letty's sobs filled the little room. Her own eyes filling with tears, she cradled the woman in her arms, holding her while the grief poured out like a stream released from a dam.

Passing into St James's Street later, Carys glanced at a sky that was purple with evening. Letty Withers had cried until she could cry no more, and then she had talked – talked of her daughter, reliving memories of her childhood. And Carys had held her and listened, understanding her need, and though she had never been in the situation before, recognising the healing of the soul her speaking of Alice would bring. The whole of the afternoon had been spent comforting the girl's mother and now it was growing dark.

Drawing level with the church, Carys glanced into the churchyard. She ought to go straight back to Ridge House, she had promised Letty she would when declining the woman's suggestion that she wait for Davey to come in from work so he could see her home. But it would only take a moment to slip around the back of the church to where Alice lay and say a goodbye it had been too difficult to say on the day of her burial.

Glancing along the street, she saw it was deserted. If she went in no one would see and speak of it to Letty. In the gathering darkness her eyes searched for the still bright flowers that had been heaped upon the grave. Here there were few tombstones to mark a person's passing; the inhabitants of this part of Wednesbury did not boast the money to spend on stone.

Picking her way along the narrow paths worn among the grass, she knelt beside the new mound.

'I wanted to be with you once more, Alice,' she whispered, hot tears finding their way down her cheeks. 'I wanted to tell you so much but you were gone before I had the time. The letter came and you were so happy, and now . . . But you had that happiness, you knew the feeling of having a man love you. And you have my love, Alice. I will never forget your kindness to me. I love you, Alice, as much as I could love a sister. I won't ever forget, I will never . . .'

The rest of the sentence was lost as a heavy cloth fell over her head and a pair of strong arms hauled her roughly to her feet.

Chapter Nineteen

She had come that morning, the woman veiled in black. She had come as Bethesda had known she would, as the sight had shown.

'Do you know Ridge House at Hill Top?' she had enquired after calling Caine to the small trap in which she drove herself.

'There is a young woman serving there as housemaid, a girl with hair the colour of ripe chestnuts. A girl I would rather were not there, or any other place. Would you, for a price, be willing to see that she . . . leaves?'

'How much be you willing to pay the gypsies for doing what you ask?'

'A hundred guineas, in gold.'

Bethesda's heart had turned over when Caine had told her of the offer. It was more money than ever they could hope to see in a lifetime, but it was money her son would not live to spend should he accept it.

'What is it you be wanting done with this girl?'

Caine's question had caused no surprise but seemed expected.

'She would make a pretty companion for your bed.' Behind the black tulle Caine had seen the woman's mouth curve into a smile. 'Or if you have no fancy for her then a bed could easily be found in a ditch. I am sure you have enough knowledge of the country to know a suitable place, one where a body could easily be lost.'

'When do you want the girl taken?'

Bethesda had watched her son as he talked, seen the scar that ran along his cheek like a crucifix as he turned his head in the direction of the smoke-shrouded town, and in her heart she saw again the blow of the whip that had taken his eye.

'Today. I want her gone by morning.'

Caine had nodded, sunlight dancing on his hair.

'Do I be getting the guineas now?'

'I am not a fool!'

The woman had jerked in annoyance as she spoke and Bethesda's hand had closed over the knife at her waist. The woman would strike Caine no second blow.

'You will be paid when I have proof the job is done.'

She leaned forward then, the sun catching the gleam of the gold pendant at her breast.

He had told his mother all that the woman had said and listened as Bethesda in her turn related what the sight and the dark ones had shown. Caine was not a follower of the old ways but he respected them.

Slipping her hand into her pocket, she drew out a slender gold chain with its pendant holding an intertwined monogram. The letters of smoke had curved and twisted in just the same way, coiling and circling, joining until they formed the letters 'M' and 'B'. The letters that now glinted on the pendant in her hand.

This was what the dark ones had told her. This was the payment Caine must ask for doing the woman's bidding.

She had been reluctant to part with the trinket, but as Caine had made as if to turn away, had lifted it from her neck.

Returning the pendant to her pocket, Bethesda fetched a rabbit from the box strung against the caravan. Once more seated on her stool she sank the knife into the soft fur, stripping it away from the flesh.

Her son was not a follower of the old ways but he listened when they spoke, just as he listened to his mother. Taking the gutted rabbit to the pool, she bent to wash it in the water . . . Caine would do as she had told him.

He had watched the house from the shelter of the trees, waiting for a chance to strike, yet when the girl had left the house she had gone by the road. It had been too risky to approach her there, with passing carts and trams. But he had followed her along the heath, staying just out of sight, his Romany knowledge telling him always where she was.

It had been almost dark when she had turned into that churchyard. Even had she looked about her she would not have seen him follow. He had dropped the horse blanket over her head before she could utter a single cry, then half dragging, half carrying her, had disappeared into the black shadows of the surrounding heath.

She had struggled as she was struggling now. Caine tightened his grip, pulling the girl's slight body close against his own.

Fifty guineas in gold the woman had promised. Put into his hands this very night. He quickened his pace to a run as Bethesda's words returned to his mind, her warning not to go against the old ways. But he did not fear the old ways, and fifty guineas was fifty guineas.

'I be going to set you down.'

Beneath the rough blanket Carys heard the quietly spoken words. 'If you know what be good for you then you will raise no scream, do you understand?'

The cloth pressed tight against her mouth, Carys could only hope that whoever held her understood her muffled reply.

Still holding her with one arm he pulled the bandanna from his neck, then whipping away the blanket he quickly wrapped the scarf about Carys's eyes, knotting it at the back of her head.

'Why are you doing this?' Fear almost closing her throat,

Carys stood waiting for what might happen next. 'What do you hope to gain?' she asked again. 'I have no money I can give you, and no family who will pay for my release. Please,' she cried as a hand grabbed her arm, propelling her forward, 'please let me go.'

Silence answered her cry. Carys stumbled along, only a strong hand preventing her from falling as her feet caught against clumps of rough ground.

Why had this man attacked her? That it was a man she could tell from the deep quality of his voice when he had spoken. Where was he taking her? What was it he intended to do?

Terror pounding in her veins she could only stumble along beside him, hoping he would soon let her go. How long would Mrs Bates expect her to take visiting Alice's mother? How long before she sent someone to the house to enquire after her? However long, it would be too late. Carys whimpered at the thought and a hand clamped over her mouth.

'I told you not to raise a scream!' The hand pressed against her lips, adding painful emphasis to the words muttered against her ear. 'One more sound from you, just so much as a whisper, and I'll do for you right now. You hear what I be saying . . . you hear?'

Releasing her mouth, the hand grabbed the collar of her coat, shaking her with a violence that rattled her teeth then releasing her so she fell sprawling on to her knees.

'Mark me, my pretty one . . .'

The voice, close to her ear again, held more than a hint of a threat as she felt herself once more hauled savagely to her feet.

'. . . you be doing just like I say or I kill you right here. There be none as will see, ain't no moon to light up what I be about. Won't be none will find you for a long time, so just you stay quiet . . . very quiet.'

How long he dragged her with him Carys had no way of reckoning, nor in which direction they travelled. She knew only that they kept to the heath.

'Stand you still.'

The order came after what seemed to her to be hours of jolting and stumbling over uneven ground. Swaying from terror and fatigue, she obeyed. Unbuckling the belt from his trousers, Caine drew the length of it through his hands.

Swallowing the horror that spread through her, giving only a tiny sob of panic, Carys shuddered as her arms were pinioned behind her back, shivers of ice touching her spine as she felt the strip of leather fastened about her wrists. Then she was lifted bodily, slung face down over the man's shoulder.

Pain lancing through her ribs, shooting the breath from between her lips with every step he took, Carys tried to fathom the reason behind her abduction. She had no money, she had told him that, and even if he disbelieved her there could be no denying the truth of it illustrated in her worn out clothes. And if the motive were not the hope of gaining money, then what? If it were to kill her, why had he not done that already? Why drag her miles across the heath before fulfilling his threat?

Questions racing through her brain, Carys felt herself tipped from his shoulder and as her head hit something hard, fell away into unconsciousness.

'Where is she, Aunt?'

Reuben Fereday strode into Virginia's sitting room. He had unpacked the pictures she had loaned him for display in his gallery and among them had been another. A charcoal sketch, tastefully mounted in a simple frame that did not detract the eye from the subject: the body of a man rising through the surface of a fern-fringed pool, a man with his dark head thrown back lifting his face to the sky – a face that was Reuben's.

Virginia smiled, holding up her own face to be kissed. 'Where is who, dear?'

'Aunt, please!' Reuben paced to the window then back again, tension in every line of him. 'Don't torment me. I know it was a woman who drew that sketch of Uncle Oliver, and that the same woman drew the sketch of me swimming in that pool.'

'So it *was* you.' Virginia looked up into the face of her nephew. 'Have you no shame to go bathing in such a public place!'

'It was indiscreet of me.' He acknowledged the reproof. 'I can only say the day was warm and I could not resist the temptation.'

Virginia continued to watch him, seeing the play of emotions across his handsome face. She had ignored her better judgement in including that sketch in the ones she sent to him, telling herself that whatever demon haunted her nephew was best exorcised by facing up to it.

'Was that your only indiscretion that day?' she asked quietly. 'Was swimming the only pleasure you could not resist, or did you avail yourself of another?'

'Such as what?' Reuben stopped pacing.

'You may not forgive what I am about to ask, Reuben, but nevertheless I will ask. Believe me, my dear, when I say I ask it because of my love for you and because I am convinced of what the answer will be. That day you went swimming, did you force your attentions on a young girl?'

The blood drained from Reuben's face and his eyes hardened to black stone. If any man had asked that question he would have knocked him senseless.

'I have never forced myself on any woman, either that day or any other,' he said through clenched teeth.

Virginia felt relief sweep through her but allowed no trace of it to show on her face.

Too distracted to sit, Reuben walked about the room. 'I was returning from Bilston,' he said, 'and decided to bathe in a pool in an old mine shaft. It is somewhat sheltered from the roadway and I thought I would remain unseen, but then I saw a movement among the ferns. When I called out, a girl stood up. She had obviously been watching but on my seeing her she fled. I guessed if I were quick about it I would catch up with her before she reached her home, the nearest houses being some distance away.'

'And did you catch up with her?'

'Yes, I did. And from that day I have never stopped searching for her. I thought once that maybe I had found her. That was in Meshac Beddows's house. I admired several pieces he told me had been painted by his daughter, and the girl on the heath had said she was returning to Holyhead House. But when I asked Meshac's wife about her she told me her daughter had taken the veil. From then it seemed my search was over. Until, that is, saw the portrait of Uncle Oliver.'

'But why be so persistent in your search for this girl if you owe her nothing?'

Reuben sank at last in to a chair, cradling his head in his hands. 'I have asked myself the same question over and over again.'

'And the answer,' Virginia prodded gently, 'was that the same over and over again?'

For several moments silence hung between them. A silence in which neither of them moved. Then Reuben looked up.

'Always, right from the first, I searched for her because I had to know. I had to be certain of what I felt. I have not been free of her since that day.'

He looked up and Virginia felt a jolt in her heart at the look on his face: the sadness, the frustration, the not knowing.

'Aunt,' he asked, 'is it possible to love a woman you have spoken to only once?'

'I think perhaps it might be. But thinking you love a person is not enough, Reuben, you must be sure.'

'I know that.' He gave a half smile. 'I feel I would be sure if I spoke to her. I *must* talk to her, Aunt, before she marries.'

'Marries?' Virginia's brows met. 'Why do you suppose her to be getting married?'

'I saw her.' As if suddenly he could bear the inactivity no longer he got to his feet, resuming his pacing of the room.

'I was in Wednesbury last week and decided to call here at Ridge House. I hired a horse and rode by way of Millfield Heath. I was almost at the house when I saw her. I was not sure at first, many girls have chestnut-coloured hair, but then I saw her face.'

'So why did you not speak to her then?'

'I was about to but she was with a man, one who took her in his arms and held her. A girl only allows the man she is to marry to hold her so close.'

For the first time since his abruptly entering her sitting room, Virginia felt herself want to laugh. Stifling the desire, she simply smiled. 'It is not always love that drives a girl into a man's arms, Reuben. Sometimes it is sorrow and the need for comfort. It is my guess that you called the same day as Davey Withers brought us the news of his sister's death. Alice Withers had been my housemaid for several years. Carys and she were very close friends, and when she heard what had happened she was heartbroken. Davey tried to comfort her. Martha Bates told me of it. That does not mean to say that Carys is to marry the fellow.'

'Carys?'

Virginia nodded. 'The woman who drew the sketches I sent you is, I believe, the same one you have hoped so long to meet again. Her name is Carys Beddows, daughter of Meshac Beddows, and she is here in this house where she has been since leaving the Convent of the Holy Child a year ago.'

'Then it *was* her!' Sinking to his knees beside his aunt's chair, he took her hands, his eyes holding a brilliance she had thought lost. 'May I see her?'

'Not on your knees, my lad.'

Allowing her laughter to escape, Virginia pulled the embroidered bell cord, but when she returned her glance to her nephew her face was solemn once more.

'The girl is still very young and she has been hurt far more than any girl deserves. If it should be she does not wish to see you, or to speak to you, then I will not allow you to press her, Reuben. Carys is under my protection so long as she chooses to be in my house, and though you have always been as a son to me I will not see you, or anyone else, cause her more grief.'

She broke off as Martha Bates limped into the room and her voice took on a note of concern.

'Martha, you should not be hobbling around on that leg. Why are you not resting it as you were told to do?'

'You rang the bell, ma'am. Somebody had to answer it.'

'But that somebody did not have to be you!' Concern for the woman who had been part of her household since the first days of her marriage to Oliver gave Virginia's reply a sharp edge that was not intended.

'Well, somebody had to, begging your pardon, ma'am. There be only me and Carys in the 'ouse, and seeing her don't be back yet then it were me had to answer.'

'I'm sorry, Martha, I was not aware Carys had not returned or we would have come to you. I do not want you walking about the house while you are in pain.'

'The rheumatism be easing.' Martha touched her hip. 'I reckon it'll be well cleared by morning.'

'Then sit down.' Seeing the hesitation on her housekeeper's face, Virginia nodded to Reuben then waited while he helped Martha to a chair.

'That's better.' Virginia smiled. 'Martha, you say Carys is not yet returned from visiting Letty Withers?'

'No, ma'am, she ain't.'

'Is it usual for her to be gone so long?'

'Not usual at all, not for Carys. If her says her will be back by a certain time, then that be the time her keeps to.'

'So when are you expecting her return?'

'I thought her would be here some three hours since.' Martha glanced at the carriage clock on the mantelpiece. 'It don't be like her to be late.'

'She might have waited for Davey to get home from his work so he could escort her. The heath is not a place for a young woman to be alone in the dark, there are so many disused mine shafts dotted all over it.'

'That be worrying me, ma'am. I know Letty would have had the girl home hours ago if one of her lads had been sent along with her. I be feared something might be amiss.'

'We must send and enquire of Mrs Withers. Martha, will you see the trap is made ready?'

'No!' Reuben was on his feet. 'I will go. You cannot take a trap across the heath in the dark. Just tell me how I can find this house.'

'It be close to the church.'

'The one on the hill?'

'No.' Virginia shook her head. 'Martha does not mean the parish church. She is speaking of the church of St James. It is a quarter of a mile from The White Horse. Follow the Holyhead Road in a straight line and you will come to it. Letty Withers's house is opposite to the right.'

Back in the kitchen, Martha started as a heavy knock on the door was repeated several times.

'This be Ridge House?'

Martha stared at the powerfully built man. His hair reached to his collar; a white scar like a crucifix ran the length of his cheek, the empty eye socket staring like a black hole. 'I wants to speak to the mistress.'

'Well, 'er won't be wanting to talk to no gypsy!' Martha made to slam the door but the man moved quickly, the strength of his raised hand throwing the door from Martha's grasp banging it back against a large wall cupboard.

'You tell 'er, missis.' Caine Lazic brought his scarred face close to Martha's. 'You tell that mistress o' yourn, that if 'er be wanting to see that maid o' hers alive then 'er best talk to Caine Lazic.'

'Carys!' Martha gasped. 'You have Carys?'

'If that be the name o' the maid with chestnut hair and a pretty way o' talking, then yes, I've got her.'

'Oh, my good God!' Martha shrank against the door.

'You best be telling your mistress what I say, I don't be intending to stay all night.'

'Yes, the mistress. You come in. No . . . stay there!' Flustered by his sudden appearance and even more bothered by what he had said, Martha stared into his swarthy face.

'You need have no fear for your knick-knacks, missis.' He swept a cold look about the kitchen. 'Caine Lazic takes nothing he has not earned.'

'You've taken Carys!' Martha retorted sharply. 'Gypsies be all the same: liars, thieves and murderers. I wouldn't trust a gypsy no further than I could throw one.'

'That be your choice. But remember it were a gypsy came to tell you of a young woman's whereabouts; that it were a gypsy brought you news of her. Think on that if your mistress asks of her.'

'Wait!' The discomfort in her hip forgotten, Martha almost ran from the kitchen.

'What is it, Mrs Bates?'

Halfway across the hall, Reuben turned as the housekeeper hurried in from the kitchen.

'It . . . it be a gypsy, Reuben. He be in the kitchen, and says as 'ow he has Carys.'

'A gypsy has Carys?'

Virginia's startled exclamation followed instantly on her nephew's query but already he was disappearing through the door that led to the servants' quarters.

'Her be safe enough, but her won't be much longer lessen you come with me.'

Virginia heard the words as she preceded Martha into the kitchen.

'If you have harmed her in any way . . .'

'I done the girl no harm.' Caine did not flinch from the rage in the other man's face. 'Had I wanted I could have done that and been long gone, but I be here.'

'The man is right, Reuben.' Virginia stepped forward, placing a restraining hand on her nephew's arm. 'Had he intended doing Carys harm he would not be here to speak of his taking her.' Her eyes frank, mouth unsmiling, she looked at Caine. 'Forgive my forthrightness but yours is a face we would be unlikely to forget and one the police would have no great difficulty in locating. To me that is a strong reason for believing in what you have said. Now if you will tell us what ransom you are seeking, we can bring this matter to an end?'

'I want no money.' Caine looked from one face to the other, seeing rage on the young man's and calm common sense on the woman's.

'Then why take her?' Reuben's fists tightened ominously and anger sparked from his dark eyes, but again Caine did not flinch.

'I took her to keep her safe.'

'Safe?' Virginia held on to her nephew's arm, feeling the tremor of rage coursing through him. A display of fisticuffs would do no good, and should this man choose to leave . . . 'Are you saying Carys is in danger in my house?'

'Not while she be in your 'ouse, but every minute 'er be outside of it.' He spoke quietly, his tone, while polite, showing no deference to the wealthy gentry. 'Does a woman veiled in black, a woman whose initials be "M" and "B", mean anything to you?'

Virginia's hand dropped from Reuben's arm. '"M" and "B",' she murmured. 'Maria Beddows – Carys's mother!'

Chapter Twenty

Maria slid her arms into a silken négligée, drawing the soft eau-de-nil folds together across her breasts. She had thought to hear from that gypsy before retiring for the night – hear that he had done what she had asked, and promised to pay fifty guineas for.

Fifty guineas! Maria laughed, shaking her hair to fall loosely about her shoulders. The man had been a fool to believe her when she had said she would pay such a sum! He would get nothing. Oh, she knew why he had demanded the necklace that bore her initials. He would threaten to use it against her, threaten to show it to the police, claiming he took it in payment for doing away with her daughter.

Maria laughed again. Let him go to the police, let him say what he would! She would claim that she had lost the necklace weeks ago and that he must have found it. She had been grateful for its promised return, for it had been a present from her husband, but when she had refused to pay fifty guineas . . . She walked to the cheval mirror practising the disappointed, hurt expression she had used many times before and found it impossible for a man to ignore. Then, she would murmur, the gypsy had threatened to concoct the story he told now.

Reaching for her hair brush, she pulled it through her mass of brown curls, mouth curving in a confident smile. But he would not go to the police; gypsies and police did not accord well together. No, the man would cut his losses and leave, but not without returning her necklace. A distraught woman with a torn veil; a beautiful woman, sobbing out the story of her attack by a scar-faced gypsy!

Maria pulled the brush through her hair, smile widening on her mouth. Maria Beddows would not be the one to lose; hers would be the winning hand as it had been with Ryder Tempal.

Oh, he had played well. Making love to her and professing to love while at the same time playing the field. The one she had caught him with would not have been his only sideline. Ryder Tempal would always have had more than one lover. *They* might have been able to turn a blind eye, to accept his carryings on, but she would not.

Anger rising like a newly kindled flame burned in Maria and she threw the heavy silver-backed brush hard on to her dressing table, smashing a dainty painted porcelain powder bowl and a crystal bottle filled with French perfume.

She would have married him! Given him everything Meshac had acquired. She had thought herself in love with him. Then she had found him with his lover and the last of her self-delusion had vanished. Ryder Tempal was taking money from her, money he was spending not on rent or keeping his household as he'd told her, but on keeping his prostitutes. What he had been doing then he would have continued to do after marriage to her, only then he would have had no need to ask for her money.

'Poor Ryder.' Maria turned back to the mirror. 'Poor foolish Ryder. You should have known, you should have known Maria Beddows would be no second string to any man's bow. You could have had all of this.' Opening the silk night coat she stared at her own nakedness reflected in the glass, admiring the swell of her breasts, the curving waist above hips that swelled like a newly opening rose. 'All of this, Ryder,' she murmured, 'but you chose to gamble and you lost.'

Refastening the gown, she crossed to the bed and draped herself across its silken cover.

'And now, my dear . . .' She smiled up at the ceiling. 'Now you are gone and soon will be joined by my daughter.' That had been a shock, she thought, her good humour fading. Ryder was so adamant he had delivered that letter, placed it in Carys's own hands. But if so how come Maria had seen her walking along the street? And it *had* been her, of that at least Maria was certain.

Damn him!

She sat up sharply. Damn Ryder Tempal for a fool! She had thought at first he had lied about sending the letter, but then common sense told her he'd had nothing to gain by not doing so; nothing to gain and everything to lose. Yet she had *seen* the girl. Had the powder she had taken from the office at Bilston lost its potency? She had thought that must be the answer, until she had taken a little from the amount she had kept and fed it to one of the cats. No, the powder was as lethal as Meshac had claimed.

So how?

Staring into the shadows gathered beyond the reach of the lamp beside her bed, Maria twisted the ribbons of the night coat between restless fingers.

The cat had died almost at once, so why not the girl? Unless . . . that must be it! There were at least two housemaids at Ridge House. The one who had shown her in, and Carys. What if somehow the letter had gone to the wrong one? Ryder had said he had given it to Carys herself, but then he had lied before. But it made no difference now. *She* had taken matters into her own hands. It had been a puzzle at the beginning, wondering if it were necessary after all to dispose of the girl, now Ryder was dead.

She smiled again at the thought of how she had trembled and wept, almost fainting into the arms of an attentive constable as she had given evidence at the magistrates' enquiry into the accident. She had lifted her veil back from her face, showing it so pale and beautiful, her wide eyes brimming with tears as she blamed herself. But she must not blame herself, the magistrate had said. A sick woman who had fainted was in no way responsible for what had been a tragic accident.

Tragic? Yes, for Ryder Tempal. But accident? Maria laughed softly.

And now Ryder was dead. He could not blackmail her with threats of exposing that letter, so perhaps she had not needed to employ the gypsy to carry out what should already have been done. Then she remembered the way Ryder had looked at Carys, remembered the beauty that surpassed her own with its fresh softness. He had wanted that softness, and where he led others would follow, and that she could not face.

Rising from the bed, she slipped off the night coat and slid naked between the cool sheets.

The last time she had lain like this had been in that back street hotel. Beneath the sheets, she ran her hands over her breasts and down to her waist. She missed Ryder, missed his lovemaking, but what he had done for her many another man could do. Ryder Tempal had been amusing, but in no way irreplaceable.

Turning off the lamp, she stared into the darkness. Tomorrow he would come, the scar-faced gypsy. Tomorrow there would be no child of Meshac's left alive.

Her head throbbing, Carys tried to open her eyes but they were covered. Behind her back a cord bit into her wrists. She had been kneeling beside Alice's grave. The mists rolled away with blinding speed, the memory of what had happened washing in on her in sickening waves.

He had dropped a cloth over her head, the man with a deep voice, then had dragged her across the heath. To where? She tried to push herself into a sitting position but succeeded only in pressing the crown of her head against something hard. Where was she . . . why had he taken her . . . did he intend other things for her before killing her? Questions tormenting her, she tried again to move, to ease the aching that tortured her every bone.

Would she be missed yet? Was Martha wondering at her absence? How long before someone was sent to enquire of Letty?

She had asked herself these same questions as she was being dragged along by her abductor, and now, as then, the answers afforded her no comfort.

How long did he intend to keep her here, blindfolded, her hands fastened together? Perhaps he had already abandoned her, left her helpless to die in the dark!

Panic filling every part of her, Carys screamed.

'Stop that!'

The voice was not the same. This was softer, a hint of sympathy beneath its curtness, a voice Carys recognised. It was the voice of the old gypsy woman.

'You knows who I be!' Bethesda saw her recognition by the way the girl stopped shrinking and held her head up.

'Now listen to me carefully. I will remove your bindings if you give your word to sit quiet while I 'ave my say. Do you promise, wench?'

At Carys's nod Bethesda loosened first the scarf from her eyes then the belt that held her wrists.

'Why am I here?' Carys rubbed her wrists, her arms painful as the blood began to circulate more freely. 'Why have I been kidnapped? It was him, wasn't it, it was your son?'

'You promised you would listen. You promised to sit quiet while I had my say.'

Carys struggled to her feet, a little of her fear abating. This woman had shown her only kindness, they had sat together at her campfire; surely she would not harm her now?

'Then please tell me what it is has made your son bring me

here in the manner he has? I would have come willingly had he asked me.'

'Which is just what we both of us thought.' Bethesda pointed to the stool she had brought inside the wagon for the night, waiting until Carys was seated. 'We knowed you would come if you thought it was me who bade you, whether the message be brought by Caine or the mouth of another. Tell me, girl, know you this?' Dipping her hand into the pocket of her skirt, she drew out the gold pendant, holding it so Carys could see.

'That belongs to Maria!' She looked from the pendant to the eyes that watched her with the sharpness of a knife.

'Your mother.' Bethesda returned the pendant to her pocket.

'How do you know she is my mother?'

'Bethesda Lazic knows many things.' Placing the briar pipe between her darkened teeth, Bethesda held a fine sliver of wood to the fire burning in the stove. Holding the glowing twig to the pipe, she sucked it into life. 'Things like a young girl nigh on raped in her own garden; like the same girl entered into a convent then abandoned when 'er chose to leave it; like a young woman who even now be grievin' for a friend newly taken from this life.' Bethesda sucked on the pipe, watching the surprise on Carys's face. The sight had shown her this girl's past as clearly as pictures in a book. 'Believe you these things?' she puffed. 'Believe you when I tell you I know many things?'

Carys nodded. 'I believe you, though I do not understand.'

'A Gorgio does not know the ways of the Romany.' Bethesda blew out several tiny clouds of tobacco smoke that rose then hung suspended in the air like lavender baubles. 'He does not have the knowledge. He lost it long ago when he gave up the travelling and chose to live out his life in one place. But Bethesda Lazic knows.' A fresh stream of smoke joined that hovering over her head. 'She sees what others cannot, and she saw the hand of your mother raised against you.'

'You must be mistaken!'

Bethesda's bird-bright eyes peered through the dim light of the candle lamp suspended from the ceiling of the caravan. 'Did 'er not seek to harm you when 'er called at your place of work to tell your mistress of a drawing on a paper beneath the bed you sleep in? Arrh.' Bethesda nodded at Carys's gasp. 'Did I not tell you, wench, I knows many things? And this also do I know. Had my son not taken you then another would have been paid to do it, and it could have been one who would not baulk at the killing of a woman. Oh, yes!' Bethesda met her startled gaze. 'Caine was promised payment if he killed you, but he be no murderer, though there do be one he would do for and gladly, but that one don't be you. 'Twas me told him to take you, me who told him to handle you roughly but do you no real harm. Did my son listen to *all* I said?'

Recognising the meaning behind the question, Carys nodded.

'I said he was to frighten you,' Bethesda went on then. 'You was to learn what will surely happen, for that woman will strike and strike again till 'er be rid of you.'

'But I cannot be any threat to her!'

'While you live you be a threat to the woman who wore that pendant.' Bethesda drew heavily on the briar pipe. 'One day you will know why, but for now it is enough to know that what I and my son have done was for your own good. You must never answer a message that comes from that woman.'

'But could Caine not simply have told me?' Carys rubbed her stinging arms.

'And what attention would you have paid? Words be like leaves in winter, they fall away and are forgotten. But fear, real fear, lives on. It can be hidden in the mind but never truly dies. The fear we have caused you was meant as a lesson, one hard learned 'tis true, but a lesson you will not forget. One that could mean the difference between life and death.'

'But what do you intend to do with me now? You have proved you wish me no harm. Do you intend I should go with you?'

'The travelling be no life for you.' Bethesda shifted the pipe with her teeth. 'Caine be fetching your mistress to take you back. 'Er must see for 'erself how easy it be for that woman to strike at you, just as 'er must choose whether or not my son be given over to the Peelers for taking you. It be a chance he be taking by fetching 'er, but it be one he is prepared for if it means the woman who took his eye and laid that mark upon his face will be paid for the evil 'er has already wrought, and prevented from doing more. But this much I vow. The gaoling of my son will not keep that woman safe, for 'tis the mother of Caine will take vengeance in full!'

'You know the woman I be speaking of.' Caine caught the look that flashed across Virginia Mountford's eyes at his description of Maria Beddows. 'Then you will know I speak true when I say her be offering a hundred guineas for the death of that girl.'

'And you took it?' Reuben tried to shake off his aunt's restraining hand but Virginia clung on.

'I took no money from her as I'll take none from you.' Caine watched as fear and anger chased across the other man's face. He could be no brother to the girl, not dressed in the fine clothes he wore and her nobbut a serving maid in this house. Then what feeling, if not a brother's love, gave rise to the fury that burned in his eyes? 'I came here to ask the mistress to come with me, learn for herself the true extent of the danger that young woman be prey to.'

'My aunt will certainly not go anywhere. And you . . . You will be serving life along the line – that is, unless they hang you!'

'The thought of hanging 'olds no terrors for me.' Caine touched a finger to his scar, tracing the line that ran to his chin. 'I died sixteen years ago, the day Maria Beddows took a horsewhip to a young lad and left him like this.'

'I will go with you.' Virginia held up a hand, silencing her nephew's protest. 'Please wait until my carriage can be made ready then we will go. You, Reuben, may come if you wish.'

'Follow the Holyhead Road toward Bilston,' Caine said as Reuben helped his aunt into the carriage then hauled himself into the driving seat. 'You will see me when you get to the place you be going to.' Before Reuben could answer he'd slipped silently into the shadowed blackness of the garden, swallowed up by the night.

'I will see you in a place other than that,' Reuben murmured, picking up the reins, urging the horse to a sharp trot. 'I will see you in hell!'

She should have known Maria Beddows would not give up with just one attempt to have Carys dismissed her post. Virginia stared out into the darkness. But the girl could not be kept confined to the house, held inside its four walls for a lifetime. She might just as well have remained in the convent if she were to live like that. Nevertheless Virginia could not dismiss altogether the feeling that somehow the blame for Carys's abduction lay with her.

The lighted windows of the Globe Inn came and went, as did those of The White Horse. Then they were passing the constabulary house and a few moments later the spire of St James's church stood like a sentinel against the night sky. Then the huddled shapes of the houses of the Portway, seeming to cower beneath the dark threat of night, were slipping away and no landmark alleviated the black emptiness of the heathland. How far must they travel? Just where had that gypsy taken Carys? To the left of the road the toll house reared darkly but no voice demanded they should halt and the carriage rolled on, the horse's hooves loud in the silent stillness.

Was the girl harmed? Had the man spoken the truth when he said he had not hurt her? Impatient with herself, Virginia forced the thoughts away. It would do no good to harbour doubt.

The sudden halting of the carriage threw her forward in her seat and when she pushed herself upright it was to hear a voice command them to follow: 'But slowly, the heath be rough just above the pool.'

Looking out through the window she caught her breath at the silver beauty of moon-bathed water nestling in a hollow at the foot of a gently sloping rise, trees and ferns etched in black silhouette about its edge.

Was this the pool where her nephew had bathed, and this the place where Carys had made that sketch?

'This be where you'll find the girl.' Caine made to open the door of the carriage but Reuben was there, pushing him aside.

Alighting from the carriage, Virginia looked over to where the caravan stood beneath the sheltering trees. Its colours were lost in the darkness but its bowed roof stood clear and proud against the sky.

'You brought Carys here?' Reuben's voice was strangled with an unnamed fear.

'I brought 'er here.' In the moonlight Caine's face held a cold challenge but in his heart he could understand what it was the other man felt, for kin or not he held a deep love for the girl they had come to fetch. ''Er be in the wagon with my mother. There be only room for one more,' he added as Reuben turned toward it.

'I know your feelings, Reuben, you don't hide them very well.' Virginia looked up at his taut face. 'But *I* must be the one to go inside. Carys could well be in shock, she should first see someone she knows well.'

'Of course, Aunt.' He continued to stare at the caravan. 'I will wait here beside the carriage. You have only to call if you need me.'

Escorting Virginia to the steps of the caravan, Caine waited till she had entered then crossed the clearing to where the horse stood tethered. Tomorrow he would confront the woman who had hired him for a killer. Tomorrow he would tell her that her plan had failed. After that the Peelers could take him, for in the eyes of the law he was guilty of abduction.

Across the clearing the two animals whickered to each other in the soft darkness.

Inside the caravan Virginia sat with Carys's hands held between her own as she listened to all that Bethesda had to say.

'Your motives were good,' she said as the gypsy woman finished speaking, 'though the implementation of them was less so.'

'If by them fancy words you means my son and me acted wrongly then that be your opinion, though I says again, who learns by words alone? Doing is understanding. Only by experience, by living through the fear, would that wench truly come to appreciate the danger that follows 'er. A thing half learned be not learned at all. For all the good it does it might just as well not be done. What I 'ad done this night was meant for a girl's well-being but if you sees it any other way then you send him that come with you along to get the Peelers. Me and my son will still be here when they come.'

'There will be no policemen called,' Carys said quickly. 'I am unhurt. Had the intention been otherwise then there has been ample opportunity for it to have been done before tonight.' She glanced at Virginia. 'This is not the first time we have met. I rode on the caravan the day I came to visit my father's grave, and afterward Bethesda was kind enough to give me tea. So, you see, there *was* opportunity had that been what was intended.'

'I do see, my dear.' Virginia rose to her feet but her hands still held Carys's protectively. 'It shall be as you wish, we shall not involve the constables. Now I think we should get you home to Ridge House.'

'And what of that woman?' Bethesda stood with her back to the door of the caravan, her thin body partly blocking the exit. 'What be 'er reward? What be you going to do about her?'

'There will be time to think about that tomorrow,' Virginia answered. Even in the sallow light of the lamp she saw Carys's mouth quiver and felt the shudder that coursed through the girl's body.

'No, not tomorrow! There 'ave already been too many tomorrows for that one.' Bethesda pulled the patterned shawl more closely across her flat breasts, her eyes glittering with determination. 'There must be a reckoning!'

'She did not mean me real harm.' Carys still tried to block the truth from her mind. Tears she had managed to subdue now streaming down her cheeks, Carys sobbed against Virginia's shoulder. 'She didn't . . . I know she didn't. We were happy until . . . until *he* came. Maria was kind to me in . . . in her way. It was only when Ryder Tempal came along that . . . that she changed. She seemed to think I wanted him, but it was not true. I disliked the man though she did not seem to believe that.'

'That is sometimes the way of things, child,' Virginia said gently. 'A woman can become so infatuated with a man she can see no wrong in him. For her he does right in all things, even when she knows the opposite is true. One day Maria Beddows will see it was so with her, she will know the full depth of her own foolishness. But she must be made to realise that her behaviour towards you has been abominable. She must be brought to justice.'

'No!' Carys pushed away from the older woman, wiping the tears from her cheeks with the flat of her palms. 'No. I will not have her brought before the justice. That will not right the wrong she has done, and she . . . she is my mother, she did what she has because of her feelings for Ryder Tempal. I cannot take vengeance on her. Promise me you will take no action against her?'

'Very well, my dear. It shall be as you wish.' Glancing past the still tearful girl, Virginia saw the tightening of the gypsy woman's mouth.

'And what about this?' Bethesda drew the chain from her

pocket, dangling its pendant from her fingers. 'Will you be wanting to take it with you for proof of what you've been told this night?'

Wiping the remaining tears from her face, Carys glanced at the golden letters. 'Will you ask Caine to return it, please?'

'That 'e'll do.' Bethesda stood aside.

'I must thank you for what you have done, both for Carys and for myself. I know the wisdom behind your actions. It is true when I say that though I myself would have listened to a warning, I would not have treated it with the seriousness it so obviously deserved.' Virginia met the gipsy woman's eyes. 'I would like to repay your kindness to my friend.'

Bethesda's mouth stretched into a smile that showed black gaps between her yellowed teeth. 'Your words be payment enough for Bethesda Lazic.'

'Thank you, Bethesda.'

Beneath Carys's kiss Bethesda's arms ached to hold her as she might have done a grandchild, though she knew that now one would never come.

At the edge of the clearing Caine watched the little group of women come down the steps of the caravan. Would they send for the Peelers tonight, or would they wait for morning? Either way would not bother him were it not for his mother. He would only be arrested after he had taken his revenge.

'Caine!' Her eyes accustomed to the night, Carys ran over to where he stood, his hand still gentling the horse. 'Caine, I know now what my mother did to you and I'm sorry, I am so very sorry.'

Looking into her upturned face, seeing the moonlight reflecting in her eyes, Caine's heart swelled with pain. He had felt something of the kind before when seeing a gypsy girl laugh up at her man, or caught the quiet look of companionship that passed between a man and his wife, but here, looking into those brilliant eyes, he knew for the first time the real extent of what Maria Beddows had robbed him of.

'Thank you, Caine. Thank you for helping me.' Reaching one hand to his cheek, Carys traced a fingertip over the livid scar, then pulling his head towards her, kissed him.

Standing beside the carriage Reuben saw the caress, and though his mind told him it was the caress of a woman for a friend, his heart lurched. Was there someone for whom such a touch would be made from love rather than gratitude? Had the girl he had searched for so long given her heart to a man? He would know soon enough. He watched the slight figure turn and walk back to his aunt then together they came to the carriage.

He would know soon enough. But did he *want* to know?

In the shadows of the carriage he watched his aunt place a protective arm about the younger woman, coming with her towards the place where he stood.

This was the moment he had thought of constantly for five years. At last he was to meet her again, to speak to her, the girl who had captured not just his likeness but his heart.

'Are you all right, Miss Beddows?'

His mouth dry with tension, he strode the last few yards that separated them, the shadowed light etching the planes of his face in gaunt lines.

Carys gasped as he grabbed her hand, but it was a sound of pleasure. She had wondered so many times whether she would recognise him again, but even in the half light there could be no mistake. This was the man she had seen swimming in the pool; the man who had accosted her, his mouth and eyes mocking; the man who had lived on in her mind and heart from that day.

'Oh, my dear, I should have told you someone waited outside for us.' Virginia misconstrued the gasp as one of fear. 'Allow me to introduce my nephew, Reuben Fereday.'

Murmuring a reply, Carys tried to withdraw her hand but he held it fast, staring at her face which moonlight seemed to have turned to white marble.

Urged by Virginia to assist Carys into the carriage, Reuben

reluctantly let go of her, but as he closed the door he looked again into the face of the girl he had wanted to find so badly.

'You will never be in danger again,' he said softly. 'Never, so long as I live.'

Chapter Twenty-one

'Promise me, promise me, you will take no action against her!' The words echoing in her mind, Bethesda lay in her narrow bed, eyes staring out at the patch of dark sky that showed through the bowed window.

The Gorgio woman had promised but Bethesda Lazic had given no such promise. Her tongue had stayed still, shaping no reply to the girl's request. Maybe *she* wanted no retribution, felt no burning inside her for revenge, maybe the girl could forgive, but Bethseda could not, and neither would her son. 'An eye for an eye,' she whispered. 'A life for a life. As you stole from my son so will I take from you. Payment in kind be the Romany way, and you will pay, Maria Beddows. *You will pay in full!*'

Caine had been hard to convince. He wanted the woman arrested, brought before a magistrate to answer for what she had done. But Bethesda knew that without the word of the girl and her mistress they had no real case. The word of the wife of a wealthy man, albeit a dead one, would carry far more weight than the word of a gypsy. No, Caine's way was not the right one. Maria Beddows would answer to a far higher power than any magistrate. But how long could his mother hold back the hand of Caine? He had listened to her tonight, had gone quietly to his blanket beneath the wagon, but the same Romany blood coursed in his veins as coursed in her own. It made the same demand, uttered the same cry for vengeance. A cry that would not be stilled until he had what he sought.

As the sky lightened to a pearly pink dawn Bethesda rose from her bed. She had followed the old ways there in the heart of those trees, followed the ways practised by countless generations of her kind, and the dark ones had answered. They had told her the meaning of the sight, given her what had been left unshown. They would give her the way, but she must wait, wait until all was ready. But could she hold back her son?

Caine was gone. Bethesda picked up the folded blanket laid on the top step of the wagon and placed it inside on a chest. She would lay it across a bush when heat was in the sun. Laying thin sticks in a criss-cross pattern she set light to them before filling the kettle from the water barrel.

'He must not strike,' she muttered, eyes straying towards the copse, words directed to the forces she had conjured there. 'Stay the hand of my son.'

Sipping from her third brew of the day, Bethesda watched a figure advance across the heath, coming out of the midday sun. Putting the tin mug on the ground beside her stool, she replaced the pipe between her teeth.

It was not her son who came towards her. With a swiftness that snatched the breath from her throat, her blood turned to flame in her veins, burning with a fierceness that rocked her, cleansing her mind with the purity of fire. Then came the quiet, almost tranquil state, the less becalming of her mind that preceded the coming of the sight.

With inward eyes Bethesda watched a figure approach, halting a little way from the fire. Turning back a corner of the shawl that wrapped its upper body it revealed a child lying in its arms, a child with hair that lay like a halo about its head, a child that wore the mark of death.

As suddenly as it came so the sight left her. Drawing in a deep breath Bethesda remembered the tiny figure fashioned from mud and water into which she had dripped her own blood, remembered the rush of wind that had scooped up ash from the tiny fire of leaves, scattering silver spots over the effigy. The dark ones had sent her her answer.

The briar pipe gripped between her teeth, she stared at the approaching figure. It was not Caine who came towards her out of the sun. It was the vengeance of Caine.

'They told me you would help my babby.' The woman halted a little beyond the fire. 'The folk over along Bull Lane said as you 'ave a way with herbs, that you would cure my boy.'

Bethesda rose, laying her pipe behind her on the stool. 'I don't be the one to cure, you must ask the Almighty for that blessing, though if I can bring comfort I will.'

Stepping closer she watched the woman turn back her shawl to reveal a golden-haired child of about two years. The eyes were closed and the pale face marked with small florid spots.

This was the sprinkling of the ash. The spots covering the figure of mud. This was the way of revenge.

'The child has been poorly these many days.'

It was not a question. Silently the woman nodded.

''E be sick, very sick.' Bethesda glanced again at the sleeping child. ''T'would be wrong to tell you other. I 'ave herbs that will ease his body, take away some of the heat that burns in him, but the curing of him lies not in my hands. Maybe you should take him to a doctor.' She turned back towards her stool. The woman could take the child to a doctor but it would not save him. She had seen the smallpox too many times not to recognise what it was lay on this woman's son; she had nursed her own child through it, but no medicine or care, however loving, would save this boy.

'Parish won't pay a doctor for one that don't be its own. I

don't be of this parish. They will help only if I go into the workhouse.'

The woman's voice was toneless, stripped of all hope. Bethesda turned again, her glance taking in the ragged clothing, the thin face and arms that held the child with a fierce protectiveness.

'I will make you a potion.'

'No.' The woman covered the child again with her shawl. 'Tell me what plants to gather and I will make it myself.'

Bethesda saw the brief flash of pride in the tired eyes. ''Tis a skill must be learned,' she said. 'A body must know the right amounts to balance one with the other, what will poison and what will not. It don't be a thing you can turn your hand to lightly.'

'Please.' The woman bent her face to the child as it began to whimper, then looked again at Bethesda. 'I 'ave to try. I . . . I 'ave no money to pay.'

'A gypsy seeks no payment for the helping of a child.'

'But I can't be taking from you and give nothing back for it.'

Bethesda slid her hand into the pocket of her skirts, feeling the pendant, winding the chain about her fingers. 'You can pay me if that be your choice.' At the woman's nod she went on, 'There be a place a bit further along the road, a house that carries the name Holyhead. Take a package there for me. Give it into the hands of the mistress, only into her hands and no other. That will be payment enough.'

'I'll go straight away.'

The sad empty eyes pulled at Bethesda. If only it were within her skill to cure the child, but she knew it was not. He would not live beyond a week.

Going into the caravan, she took the knife from her belt. Cutting a snippet of the precious white linen she stored as dressings for wounds, she wrapped the pendant in it.

'Take you good care of this.' Outside once more she held the tiny parcel towards the woman.

Taking it in her hand, the woman made to slip it into her skirt then paused. 'I'll let the babby take care of it.' She flashed Bethesda a weary smile. 'That way he can thank you same as me.' Turning back the shawl, she slid the small package beneath the child's clothing, tucking it against his skin.

'The potion be best made fresh.' Bethesda watched the woman close the shawl about the child. 'It be taking near two hours to bring it ready for drinking.'

'I can be back in that time.'

'Should it be the mistress be not home then bring that packet back to me. Leave it with nobody other than her.'

Watching the woman walk in the direction she had pointed Bethesda felt no regret for what she had done. The disease the child carried would be taken by Maria Beddows, a disease Bethesda knew in her heart would not kill her but would take from her as she had taken from Caine.

Maria Beddows would rise from her sick-bed to find her beauty gone. A face pitted with the mark of the pox would stare back at her every time she looked into a mirror. Payment in kind was the Romany way. This then was Bethesda Lazic's vengeance. The reckoning was made. The taking of it was hers.

'I still can't believe it! It still seems unreal.'

In the garden of Ridge House, Reuben smiled at the girl he loved. He had not lived a fantasy for five years. He had searched for the seemingly impossible, not truly knowing what drove him, then he had found it. Looking at her now, so soft and radiant, he knew his heart had not misled him. He loved this girl with a depth he had not believed possible and a passion he longed to share.

'What seems so unreal?' Carys smiled.

'You.' His black eyes deepened as emotions he had to fight to control swept over him. 'Your not being a figment of my imagination, my finding you after so long. God, there were times when I thought I would go mad! I went back to Moxley on any pretence, hoping I might see you by that pool. Then I saw a box at your father's Bilston works. The foreman there told me it had been painted by you.'

'Thomas Blakeway?' Carys's glance strayed shyly to a bed of full-blown roses. 'He was always so kind to me. He would find time to help me get a design right or to blend oxides to give the colour I wanted, no matter how busy he was. He was an extremely good enameller. My father always had plenty of demand for Mr Blakeway's work.'

'He is a very good artist. I have asked him to work for me once your mother has sold up.'

'My mother is selling the business?' Carys returned her glance from the roses to him.

'I went to see her after buying your box. Thomas Blakeway said it was one of six and I wished to purchase the other five. He told me the business was being wound up, everything sold off, and I was afraid that someone else might buy those boxes so I went to Holyhead House. Maria promised to have them sent to my gallery in Birmingham but they never arrived. But that does not matter now. I have found the artist. Carys!'

Taking her shoulders in his hands, he turned her to face him. 'There were times I thought I would never find you, times I almost gave up hope – as when Maria said you had taken final vows and would never leave the convent. But even then something drove me on, forced me to keep searching. Carys, these weeks since finding you in the gypsy caravan, I have wanted to tell you: I love you. I love you so much it's killing me.'

Looking up at him, her lovely amber eyes sparkling mischievously, Carys smiled. 'Don't die yet, Reuben,' she murmured. 'Not until I tell you I love you too.'

Holding her in his arms, his mouth finding hers, Reuben felt the first sweet touch of content settle in his heart.

'I knew it was not his old aunt brought him here from Birmingham every day.' Virginia smiled on hearing Carys had consented to become Reuben's wife. 'But nothing can give me greater pleasure than your news. Now I absolutely insist you take your proper place in this house. I will no longer suffer your being a housemaid, and if you protest I will dismiss you without a reference!'

'Then where would I find a position?' Carys joined in the laughter.

'There is only one position you are ever going to hold.' Reuben took her hand, pressing it to his lips, his eyes melting. 'The position of Mrs Reuben Fereday.'

Carys stared at the little houses grouped in squares about a communal yard. Alice had lived in one of these. The sadness that filled her each time she thought of the smiling, good-natured girl welled up again. Alice had never found out who her admirer had been, who it was had written her that letter. It had given her so much pleasure, Carys thought, remembering the last time she had seen her friend, remembering how she'd pressed the sheet of paper to her lips, how she had held it against her breast as if the very feel of it somehow brought the sender to life before her eyes. Why had everything been snatched so cruelly away? Why could Alice never know the sort of love she and Reuben shared?

Blinking away the tears that misted her eyes, Carys watched the houses until they disappeared. Reuben loved her. The wonder of it, of their coming together after so long, still left her breathless. In two months she would be his wife, the loneliness of her life a part of the past.

'Be this the place, miss?'

It still felt strange, riding in Virginia Mountford's carriage, and Carys smiled shyly as the coachman helped her alight.

'I'll be close by, miss, should you 'ave need of me.'

Her thanks as shy as her smile, Carys turned into the little cemetery skirting Moxley Church of All Saints. Going to her father's grave she stared at the two tiny posies of wild flowers. Mary Bartlett still placed offerings beside those Carys left.

'I came to tell you, Father,' she whispered, replacing her

wilted posy with the spray of summer flowers Virginia had asked her to take from the garden of Ridge House. 'I am going to be married. You knew the man, and liked him. His name is Reuben Fereday.' Carys lifted her glance to the marble headstone, tears stinging her eyes, her whisper barely disturbing the silence of the warm afternoon. 'If only you could have been here to share my happiness. I love you, Father, I love you very much.'

'I thought it would be you.'

Startled, Carys turned from placing the dead flowers on the compost heap behind the church.

'When I saw them fresh flowers on the grave I knew it 'ad to be you as put them there. Ee, Miss Carys! But you look different to the last time I seen you 'ere, all them lovely clothes an' all.'

'Mary! Oh, how wonderful to see you.' Carys smiled, the pleasure clear in her eyes. 'I see your flowers whenever I come here but I have not seen you since . . .'

'No, miss.' Mary Bartlett threw her own wilted posy on to the heap. 'I don't get to visit Mr Beddows's grave as often since I don't work at the 'ouse no more, but I comes when I can.'

'You have left Holyhead House?'

'Not so much left as been chucked out.' Mary's grin was rueful. 'I was given me ticket the day after seeing you 'ere. The mistress up and told me she no longer required my services and that I was to get meself out of 'er 'ouse that same day.'

'But why?' Carys asked astonished.

'Didn't say, miss. Just said "out" and I *was* out. Maria Beddows ain't one for giving reasons. 'Er says jump and the likes of me jumps, we don't ask how high. But 'er ain't telling folk to jump now. Like as not 'er won't tell anybody anything ever again.'

'What do you mean!' Carys felt a sudden fear cold against her spine.

'You ain't heard? No, you wouldn't 'ave, living away over

at Hill Top. Maria Beddows be sick of the pox. It's said by Chrissy Williams that 'er won't live, 'specially seeing as there be nobody to look after 'er except the cook.'

'No one to look after her!'

Mary turned as Carys came to a halt.

'Like I say, there be just Kate Walker – everybody else left when they found out it was the smallpox. Chrissy Williams, the girl who took my place as maid, said the doctor didn't hold out much hope.'

'How long has she been ill?' Carys's voice trembled.

'Can't say for sure. Must 'ave been a couple of weeks, could be longer, Chrissy didn't say. All 'er did say was the medicine they was giving 'er didn't seem to be doing much good, but then 'er didn't really wait long enough to find out.'

'Thank you, Mary.' Carys walked swiftly to the carriage waiting beyond the churchyard. 'Tell Mrs Mountford I have gone to my mother's house,' she instructed the coachman. 'Tell her I say she is not to call there and neither is her nephew.'

'Eh, miss! You can't go to that house,' Mary intervened. 'Smallpox be a terrible thing, it be an awful risk. More often than not folk die of it.'

'I can't not go there,' Carys answered. 'She is my mother, I cannot leave her to the care of just one woman.'

'Well, you know my view, miss, but if you must go then I'll come with you.'

'No.' Carys shook her head. 'Thank you, Mary, but I can't take the risk of your taking the sickness. I will manage.' She turned again to the coachman, repeating her instruction, and as the carriage rolled away her glance wandered to the hollow that sheltered the pool where Reuben had bathed, then to the fringe of trees that had sheltered the gypsy camp. The caravan was gone.

'Ee, Miss Carys, I be glad they found you.' Kate Walker's round face broke into a smile that showed more than a little relief.

'You are glad who found me, Mrs Walker?'

'Why, them solicitors, o' course!'

'I have spoken to no solicitor.'

Kate's smile faded. 'I . . . I thought you be 'ere because of them solicitors?'

'No, Mrs Walker.' Carys shook her head, a little perplexed by the woman's greeting. Why should Kate think she had been in contact with solicitors? 'I am here to see my mother.'

'Then you don't know?' Kate stared at the young woman she had known from birth.

'If you mean I did not know of my mother's sickness then you are correct, at least I did not know until a little while ago. I met Mary Bartlett in the cemetery.'

'A good wench is Mary.' Kate shuffled her feet, fingers twitching a corner of her wide apron. 'It were a shame when her was given the sack from this 'ouse, but her tongue were loose in the wrong place. Gossip be best left unsaid if you don't want it to come back at you. Just what was it 'er told you, Miss Carys?'

Carys glanced about her, at a house she had known so well and which now seemed almost foreign in its quietness. Was it the same house where her father's laughter had rung out as he scooped her into his arms? Had the quiet stillness that now lay over everything always been there? Had she simply imagined Maria's bright, elegant presence, the sound of people talking?

'What did Mary Bartlett tell you, miss?'

Carys looked back at the cook, remembering how the woman had ruled the kitchen, how at a look from that round face maids would scatter like wind-blown leaves, yet at the same time she had been kind and caring, especially to a little girl.

'She told me my mother had taken the smallpox, and that you were nursing her here alone.'

'That be right.' Kate nodded. 'Be that all?'

'Yes, Mrs Walker, that is all that Mary told me. Now, I will go up to my mother's room.'

'Won't do no good. Your mother don't be in that room, nor any other in this 'ouse.'

Her brow creasing, Carys glanced at the well-polished staircase. 'Then where is she?'

'Mary Bartlett didn't tell you the all of it.' Kate led the way to the sitting room. 'Sit you in here while I brew you some tea and I'll tell you what I know.'

'No,' Carys said as the woman's hand fastened on the door knob. 'I . . . I would prefer to sit in the kitchen. That is, if you don't mind?'

'I never minded you being there when you was a child, and I've no objection now you be growed.'

'Mrs Walker, if my mother is not here, then where is she?' Carys had held the question while the other woman had bustled about her task of making tea. Now, seated at the large table with its blue cloth, a cup of tea untouched in front of her, she broke her silence.

'Best I start at the front end.' Kate twisted her own cup in her plump hands. 'Were not long after the funeral of that Mr Tempal . . .'

'Ryder Tempal is dead?' Carys asked, astounded at what she heard.

'Some weeks since.' Kate did not look up. She had said before that gossip was best left unsaid and there was gossip enough about Ryder Tempal's going under that train, and how Maria had shown no sign of any fainting turns afore going off to Bilston station that morning.

'Did . . . did he have the pox?'

'No, miss.' Kate answered the query without meeting Carys's eyes. ''E died of an accident. Then, like I say, your mother were took sick some time after. At first we thought it were nothing more than a chill, but when 'er got worse we sent for the doctor. When he said it were the smallpox the others panicked and left. It be a vicious thing the smallpox, nearly always it kills, and if not that then chances be that them who gets it be marked by it for life, so you can't blame folk for getting out.'

'But you?' Carys asked. 'Why did you not go with them?'

Kate twisted her teacup. 'There be a few who somehow be safe from the pox, don't ask me how for I don't be knowing. All I know is I be one of them, though my father and my two brothers didn't be.'

'I'm sorry, Mrs Walker.'

'Arrh, well, miss, that time be long past.' Kate took a sip from her cup, using the moment to subdue the sorrow that still rose whenever she thought of that period of her life.

'But how did my mother contract the illness?'

'Who knows?' Kate's head moved in a slow shake. 'It strikes at whoever it wishes, comes out of the blue, smallpox. It don't send no visiting card.'

'If I had only known!' Carys breathed.

'Thank God you didn't.' Kate Walker's glance shot upward. 'That at least be one blessing to come out of all this. Anyway there were little to do once the doctor had her moved to the fever 'ospital.'

Of course. Carys remembered the small isolation hospital in Bull Lane. All cases of infectious disease were sent there.

'Be no use your going to that 'ospital neither,' Kate said as Carys made to rise. 'Truth be, Miss Carys, your mother died a week gone yesterday.'

'Died!' She stared disbelievingly. 'But . . . but Mary said she was here?'

'I told you Mary Bartlett didn't know it all.' Kate's tone held sombre sympathy. 'Maria did come 'ome, but in a couple of days she was sick again, this time of the pneumonia. Seems 'er didn't 'ave the strength left to fight off another illness and 'er went. It were quick, wench, you 'ave that consolation at least. There were no suffering the second time.'

It was not true. Kate inwardly sought her maker's forgiveness for the lie. But 'Sufficient unto the day was the evil thereof' was the motto she lived by, and this girl had had enough sorrow for one day. Kate Walker would not be the one to add to it. She would not tell her of the screams that had rent this house when Maria Beddows had looked in her mirror and seen the marks that pitted her face like tiny craters. She wouldn't tell this girl of hearing her mother pace her bedroom day and night, nor would she mention a tiny pouch that held white powder or finding the woman who had swallowed some of it dead on her bed. She had burned the pouch and washed Maria's scarred face, leaving no visible sign of what had happened. She alone knew, the doctor saying Maria's lungs had collapsed and she had died of the new infection. But her suicide had come as no surprise to Kate. Maria Beddows had been a woman too proud of her own beauty to live with scarring, and though she had also been bitter and spiteful in her dealings with her own daughter, the Lord would inflict His own punishment for that. Kate would not have it known she had died by her own hand.

'I be sorry, Miss Carys.' She watched the girl push the cup about the saucer. 'I would 'ave sent word but I had no idea where to send to. Besides, I was told everything would be handled by the solicitors, that's why I thought they had told you.'

'No.' Carys forced the words past the tears welling in her throat. 'I had no word.'

Walking slowly through the silent rooms she let the tears fall unhindered. Both her father and her mother were dead and she had not been there to comfort either of them.

Chapter Twenty-two

Why had Virginia not sent for him? It had been a week since Carys had gone to visit her father's grave. A week since his aunt had received that message to say she had gone to her mother's house. Clearing the busy area around The White Horse, Reuben urged the carriage on, feeling the same panic that had swept over him when he had at last wrung the truth from Virginia.

Smallpox! The word rang like a death knell in his brain. Maria Beddows was ill of the smallpox and Carys had gone to her. Virginia had not sent him word, knowing he would go to that house; she had wanted to protect him from possible contagion. He could not be angry with her for that, but what use was his life if Carys should lose hers? If he had found her only to lose her now?

'*You will never be in danger again. Never, so long as I live.*' Those were the words he had said to her that night at the gypsies' camp. But what use had they proved? Why had he not been with her, to put actions to those words?

Flinging a coin to the keeper of the toll house, Reuben kept the carriage moving. Maybe he would be in time. Please God, let him be in time! He would bring Carys from that house even if he had to carry her out.

Kate answered the insistent ringing of the doorbell, almost falling backward as Reuben rushed into the hall, blinking at his curt, 'Where is she?'

'The mistress be . . .'

'I do not mean your mistress.' Strain showed deep on his face. 'I refer to her daughter, to Miss Beddows, where is she?'

'Miss Carys be outside, sir, in the garden.'

'Is she all right . . . is she ill?'

'No, sir.' Kate watched relief flood his face. 'Miss Carys isn't sick. Who will I tell 'er be calling?'

Reuben released the fear that had held him, letting it drift away in a long, slow, silent breath.

'I will tell her myself.'

Following the way the plump woman pointed, Reuben stepped into the garden, immediately recognising anew the scenes he had seen painted on boxes bought from Meshac and sold in his gallery. A shaded walk overhung with jasmine, a small water garden where a Grecian goddess poured water from one urn on to a surface studded with deep pink water lilies, but it was for a white-painted summerhouse his eyes searched.

Locating it deep with in the garden, it took every vestige of his will-power to walk quietly towards it. He wanted only to rush up to her, to take her in his arms, to kiss away her fears and his.

'Carys.' He called her name softly, then spoke it again louder as she ran into his arms. The questions he wanted to ask became lost; fear he thought had left him caused him to hold her in a fierce embrace.

'Reuben.' Carys tried to speak but the repeated pressure of his mouth on hers prevented her doing so and she lifted her arms to him, giving herself up to the joy of having him hold her.

'Why, my darling?' Lifting his head just enough to see into her eyes, Reuben at last asked the questions that had plagued him all the way from Ridge House. 'Why did you come here? Why put yourself in so much danger?'

Laying her head against his chest, Carys answered softly: 'Because she was my mother, Reuben. Would you not have done the same had it been Virginia who was sick?'

Reuben held her silently, knowing he had no argument against what she said, and only too thankful she had taken no harm in coming to this house.

'My mother is dead.' Carys released herself from his arms. Lifting a face wet with tears, she added: 'I came too late to speak to her, to tell her I did not blame her for what happened between us. Oh, Reuben, can't you see? It was her feeling for Ryder Tempal that caused her to act as she did.'

The sob in her throat catching at his heart, Reuben drew her again into his arms, holding her tight against him as she sobbed out her beliefs – beliefs that would be her comfort in the days to come.

'Love can do strange things to a woman and she was in love with Ryder Tempal. That can be the only reason for her placing me in that convent and then refusing to allow me to return to Holyhead House.'

Was it the only reason? Reuben touched her hair gently with his lips. Maria might once have thought herself in love with Tempal, but would it not be nearer the truth to say Maria Beddows's one true love was herself? That she would have suffered no rival even though the opposition be her own daughter.

'If only I could have been with her, Reuben, told her I understood. Told my mother I knew what drove her to do the things she did.'

From the garden the perfume of full-blown roses drifted across the golden afternoon. The girl he loved had risked her life in coming to this house, but in doing so had eased her heart, had found a kind of peace. Tilting her face with his hand, he looked into her lovely eyes, his own melting with love, and as his mouth closed over hers Reuben knew his own happiness was complete.

He had found his girl on the heath.

If you enjoyed NO PLACE OF ANGELS, here's a foretaste of Meg Hutchinson's new novel, A PROMISE GIVEN:

Chapter One

'You killed him. You killed my son!'

Hannah Cade glared fixedly at her step-daughter.

'You drowned my child . . . my baby. You killed him!'

'The wench wouldn't do that, Hannah Cade. Her wouldn't do the lad harm.'

Hannah swung round, eyes rapidly surveying the faces of the crowd that had gathered, the gleam of madness deepening as they settled on the stick-thin figure of Ginny Marshall.

'No, p'raps her wouldn't, not without help from another.' Hannah's voice rose to a screech. 'Maybe that other one be you, Ginny Marshall! We all know you be partial to Richie Cade's daughter, like we all knows you be partial to anything female. What did her give you, Ginny? What did her give you for helping her to kill my son . . . what did Rachel Cade let you do to her?'

'I never helped her.' Ginny's crow-bright eyes met her accuser's squarely but already the seeds of suspicion had sprouted. The listening women sensed a lynching in the offing and were ripe for the entertainment. 'I never helped her 'cos her didn't do it. Rachel loved the lad, ain't nobody 'ere can say other. As for what you say, 'tis a lie, Hannah Cade. I never killed for no woman!'

'Mebbe not.' A second voice rose from the centre of the crowd. 'But you've fumbled more than a few.'

'That be true, the dirty bastard!'

'Wenches don't be safe where her be!'

'Chuck her in the lock – it be the best place for the likes of her.'

The cries came from all sides now, feeding on each other, threats flying thick and fast.

'Throw her in. P'raps the cut will wash the filth from her black soul!'

The latest cry adding fuel to the flames, the group of women closed tighter about Ginny and the terrified girl.

'And her!' Hannah Cade's body twitched and jigged to the tune of madness playing within her, her crazed eyes gleaming and her finger pointing at her step-daughter. 'Let that one feel the water an' all. Let her know the touch of it in her nostrils, let it fill her lungs as it filled my babby's, let it fill her mouth while it carries her deep. Do to her what was done to my son!'

'Yes, do it, do what the madness inside Hannah Cade be wanting you to do.' Ginny Marshall stepped to the side of the young girl. 'C'mon,' she goaded. 'Where be your spirit? Which of you will be the first to cross Ginny Marshall?'

Almost as one the advancing women halted as Ginny, her clothes hanging like rags on her skinny frame, lifted a warning hand. 'You all know the things Ginny Marshall can do. All but two or three of you 'as sought her out to shift an unwanted child from the womb. If that be the fumbling you speak of then, yes, I fumbled you, but it was of your own asking. And how many of you 'ave come for potions? Like you come, Hannah Cade.' Her glance, black and piercing, swung to her accuser. 'You came to seek a potion that would bring Richie Cade to your bed when your own plain face and scrawny body could not. You got what you asked – but you forgot to ask for one that would hold him there. He came to you once only and when you told him the result of his lying with you, he married you. But never since that one night has he slept beside you, never but that one time has his body covered your own, and *that* be your bitterness, *that* be the root of the jealousy and spite that grows like hemlock inside you, sending its poison into your veins, nourishing its fruit of bitterness and deceit.'

'That be lies!' Hannah's demented scream rang out over the heads of the now silent women. 'Richie Cade loves me. He married me out of love.'

'Did he?' Ginny's thin face held a mocking sneer. 'Ask *them*. Ask who believes it was love and not Ginny Marshall's potion brought him to your bed?'

The watching women shuffled uneasily and their glances fell before Ginny's fierce stare.

'Richie Cade lives in the same house as you for one reason only, and she be standing 'ere beside me. It be his daughter. The child you loathe with all the strength that be in you – a hatred born of jealousy for the love he holds for her and the one who birthed her, a love you know he never had for you nor never will. That be the canker that be eating you away, Hannah Cade, the rot that will see you in your grave.'

'My grave waits for me same as yours waits for you.' Hannah stared at the silent onlookers, eyes rolling like a terrified horse's. 'Will you go to it in peace knowing the murder of a five-year-old boy went unavenged? Will your spirit lie quiet in the knowledge you let a murderer go unpunished, left her free to roam God's earth, maybe to commit the same foulness, again and again? Who knows how many more mothers' children that girl will kill?'

'Ar, your graves be waiting on you.' Ginny lifted her head, her thin hair blowing like dust before the breeze. ''Ow many of you will go to them with blood on your hands? The blood of a young wench, guilty of no more than loving a half-brother, and 'ow many be willing to risk the words of Ginny Marshall? For I tell you this: any woman who lays hands on the daughter of Richie Cade will know *my* vengeance. Any woman raising her hand against this wench raises it against me and in the raising condemns her own, for no child of her body will live.

Each, whether 'tis born or yet to come, will go before her into the ground.'

'Your words hold no fear for me.' Hannah's manic laughter rang out. 'My child was taken from the canal, the life already gone from him, and my body will carry no more. But my spirit will lie in peace, the peace of knowing I repaid the death of my boy, knowing I took the life of her that robbed him of his.'

Before anyone could move, she grabbed a brick that had fallen from the half-demolished wall at her back, lunging with it towards the trembling girl.

'Your words won't save her, Ginny Marshall, you shan't keep me from paying her out. You shan't keep me from killing her!'

The words screaming from her Hannah threw herself forward, the brick raised in her hand.

'Her has to die, as my lad has died.'

Swinging the brick in an arc about her head, she brought it slashing downward as Ginny stepped in front of the girl. The same instant the brick caught her full in the face, smashing her skull instantly.

Rachel Cade opened her mouth but there was no scream, only blackness as her body crumpled to the ground.

'You are charged with murder.'

The sound of Isaiah Bedworth's voice echoed in the high-ceilinged upstairs room of The Jolly Collier.

'You are accused of deliberately throwing a five-year-old boy into the canal at Toll End Locks. How do you plead, guilty or not guilty?'

'I didn't.' Rachel's mouth trembled. 'I would never hurt Robbie, he was my brother and I loved him.'

'That is no answer!' The magistrate brought his fist down hard on the table before him. 'How do you plead, guilty or not guilty?'

Her fingers twisting tightly together, her voice little more than a whisper, Rachel gave her reply. 'Not guilty.'

Isaiah looked closer at the girl the constable had brought before him. Hair the colour of wild wheat framed a face that already held a remarkable beauty before tumbling over breasts that looked firm and pert beneath the simple brown dress. Beneath the cover of the table he felt a stiffening in his groin. This girl was pretty, very pretty. He had not had one like her for a long time.

''Tis a lie! 'Er killed him, 'er killed my Robbie!'

Hannah's wild cry rang through the room of the tavern that served the small community of Horseley as courtroom, interrupting Isaiah's anticipation of what he was sure was to come.

'Silence!' He slapped the palm of his hand against the table as he glanced at Hannah. 'I recognise the pain you are suffering, but this room is now a court of law and will be observed as such. Any disturbance and I will have the constable remove the lot of you.'

Turning his attention once more to Rachel, the constable standing at her side, Isaiah quenched the lust that flared in him.

'Now,' he said, small eyes roving over her, 'tell me exactly what happened?'

'We . . . we were out for a walk.' Rachel's quiet voice trembled as much as her mouth. 'I . . . I always took him out for a walk on the heath when . . . whenever my stepmother allowed.'

'And you took him on the heath this morning?' Isaiah fingered the generous moustache that spread over his cheeks joining bushy sideburns, effectively framing the upper half of his podgy face.

Rachel looked over to where her father sat, his head in his hands, among the folk crowded into the room to watch the spectacle. Someone had fetched him from the mine and he had come running just as Ginny Marshall had fallen dead, her face smashed in. He had held Robbie a long time, cradling the small body in his arms while tears marked long white channels through the black coal dust that covered his face.

Then, after laying the small form on the kitchen table, he had kissed his son and come to see his daughter brought before the magistrate.

'Yes, sir.' Rachel tried to stem her own tears but they refused to be stopped. 'Hannah . . . my stepmother . . . wanted groceries from Tipton Green and when Robbie begged to go with me, she said he could. We were on the way home when Robbie asked to see the barges that tie up in the basin at Workhouse Lane. I . . . I know I should have said no,' she glanced up at the magistrate, her wide violet eyes swimming with tears, 'but I never could refuse Robbie anything. I loved him . . . I loved him.'

Glancing sternly towards the murmuring villagers the magistrate waited a few moments, allowing Rachel's sobs to subside, then asked: 'Did you take your half-brother to the basin at Workhouse Lane?'

Wiping away tears with her fingers, she nodded. 'Yes,' she whispered. 'We didn't stay very long. I knew his mother would be angry if we were late.'

'And what happened then?' Isaiah asked, her tears affecting his groin more than his mind.

'We made our way home, following the heath along the canal. Robbie was hoping to see a barge being towed. He liked to stroke the horses and the bargees were always very kind. They would lift him on to a horse's back and let him ride a little way along the towpath, or sometimes they even let him ride on the barge. We were about to branch off across the heath back to Horseley when he shouted that the lock was being filled. He darted away before I could prevent him. I ran after him but the basket of groceries was heavy. I saw him jumping up and down on the edge of the lock, and then he . . . he was gone.'

'Are you saying the child fell in?'

'Yes.'

''Tis lies!' Hannah screeched, drowning Rachel's whispered response. 'He didn't fall in, her pushed him in! Her pushed my Robbie in the lock.'

'Hannah Cade!' The magistrate's eyes glared from between bushy eyebrows and encompassing whiskers. 'You also are under indictment and will in turn answer to this court. Until then you will remain silent or be taken to a place of security until you are called.' Turning back to Rachel he asked in a milder tone, mindful of more pleasurable events to come, 'Go on, tell us what happened then.'

Glancing first towards her father, Rachel saw he had not lifted his head but sat slumped as he had from the moment of her being brought into this room, the constable's hand about her elbow.

'I shouted for Robbie to step away from the edge but he called out there was a barge being lifted. He . . . he half turned towards me. I saw his face, full of excitement, and then he began to lean over the lock. He . . . he seemed to hang in the air, and then he fell in.'

Somewhere among the people she had known from childhood, Rachel heard her stepmother's keening stifled as a sympathetic hand was clapped over her mouth. In the murmurings that accompanied the action she heard no sympathy for herself. It was as if the folk of Horseley had already condemned her.

'I ran to the edge of the lock but there was no sign of Robbie. All I could see was the barge with the water churning around it.'

'Was there anyone on the barge at the time?' The magistrate's question was aimed at the constable.

'Just a lad, your worship.'

'Just a lad! Do you mean that barge was being handled by a boy?'

'It be usual practice, your worship. Ain't much a bargee can do while the boat be in the lock, 'cept wait. It be usual for 'im to turn the horse loose to graze and take 'isself into the nearest hostelry, leaving a lad or a wife with the barge.'

'And in this case?'

'A ten-year-old lad was with the barge, your worship, while

his father was in The Navigation – that be a public house set near the wharf. There weren't no wife.'

'I see.' The plump face enveloped in iron grey whiskers turned back to the young girl whose fingers twisted incessantly, but the next question was still directed at the constable. 'Did this boy make any attempt to save the child?'

'Weren't no chance o' that, sir.' The constable shook his head solemnly. 'Lock be just big enough to take a barge. Ain't but a few inches between the boat and the sides. Anything that gets sucked under a boat once it be shut inside of a lock has no chance of surfacing till the operation be over. Weren't nobody could have gone in after that child.'

'O' course not!' Hannah struggled free of the hands that held her, madness born of grief lending her strength, propelling her towards the table. 'O' course nobody could have got him out. Locks be twenty-foot deep and their sides be covered in slime. There be little chance of saving a body when no barge be in there, but given it holds a boat, that chance be gone – and 'er knowed that!' She turned a wild glance on Rachel. ''Er knowed my little babby would drown. 'Er knowed it . . . 'er knowed it!'

Picking up the wooden gavel that had lain unused on the table, the magistrate brought it down with a bang.

'Remove that woman from the court,' he ordered. 'She will be heard tomorrow.'

''Er was always jealous!' Hannah screamed as two of the watching men grabbed her arms and began to haul her from the room. ''Er were jealous of her father's marrying me, her were resentful right from the start.' Twisting her head to the side, she sank her teeth into a hand that restrained her. As the man released her, yelping from the sting of her teeth, she pointed to Rachel. 'You killed my babby,' she said, voice now low with hatred. 'You killed him and you'll pay. If I 'ave to dance with the devil for all eternity because of it, I'll see you pay!'

* * *

Tibbington workhouse smelled powerfully of soda, carbolic and misery.

'*You will be lodged at the workhouse until this day week.*'

The magistrate's closing words had turned Rachel's blood to ice in her veins. The workhouse! A week there would seem an eternity. She had passed the low, dark, tiny paned building with its heavy wooden doors many times when going along Church or Workhouse Lane, and each time had felt a sense of foreboding. Once in there, the women of the village said, you only got to come out in a wooden box.

Now a grim-faced woman escorted her inside. Dressed in heavy grey serge, unrelieved by anything other than a bunch of keys to the left side of a black leather belt and a short thick-ended truncheon on the right, the wardress was a fearsome sight.

'You be treated special.' She grinned, showing several blackened stumps among yellow teeth. 'You be given this nice room all to yourself. Magistrate said you was to be made comfortable until you was sent for, and that's what you'll be – if you know what's good for you!' The woman's large hand fondled the stick at her side, the meaning behind her words made clearer by the threat in her cold eyes. 'Now, you got two minutes to change into that nightgown and get yourself to bed.'

Dazed by the swiftness of it all, Rachel glanced about the tiny room. Light from the single candle flickered over brick walls painted brown. Against one, a table not much bigger than a stool held a plain jug and bowl, a square of rough calico draped over its edge. Beyond this the room held nothing but a narrow iron-framed bed.

'Well, what you waiting for!' The wardress's hand tapped against the stick. 'P'raps you be wanting me to help you?'

'No!' Rachel's hands flew to the buttons at her throat, remembering the feel of the woman's rough hands propelling her through the dimly lit corridors of the workhouse.

Trembling beneath the cold gaze, pressing dry sobs back

in her throat, she removed dress and petticoats, folding each garment before laying it on the foot of the bed.

'And the rest!'

The order was sharp as Rachel reached for the calico nightgown.

'I . . .' She felt the word catch in her throat as she looked at the wardress. 'I would like to be left alone.'

'Oh, you would like to be left alone!' The woman's harsh laughter rang against the painted walls seeking a way of escape from the nauseating enclosure of the tiny room. 'And just who do you think you are? Lady muck!' She stepped forward, her hard face half lit by the candle flame bore a menacing gleam. 'Just you get one thing clear,' she hissed, 'you ain't in no fancy house and you ain't no honoured guest – you be in the workhouse. You be here until you goes to the gibbet for child murder, and while you am here you'll do as Sadie Buckley tells you. Now I be telling you to strip or else you'll be going back to face the magistrate in naught but your skin, and that marked nicely with a "P".'

'Marked!' The fear already clouding Rachel's violet eyes deepened.

'O' course.' Pleasure at instilling terror into another person throbbed in Sadie Buckley's voice. This was her one consolation in working as wardress where she had once thought to be governess. Thought to be until that cow upstairs had smarmed like butter over the Appointments Board! 'Like I said, you be in the workhouse, and like everybody else who eats at the expense of the parish, you'll be branded.'

In a sudden swift movement she lunged forward, knocking Rachel's hands free of her throat and at the same time snatching at her thin cotton chemise, ripping it open to the waist.

'I wonder where you'll feel the iron?' She smiled sadistically, eyes roving over the trembling girl. 'Here?' She touched one shoulder. 'Or maybe here.' The smile widened as she touched a finger to the pale brow. 'Though it be my bet the brand will go here.' Cold eyes glittering like those of a serpent, Sadie Buckley trailed her hand slowly down Rachel's face, then over her neck and throat, down to the soft flesh of her breast.

'Yes!' She breathed faster, the noise of it rasping in the silence. 'That be the spot the brander likes best to press the iron. He likes to leave his mark on a woman's tits, 'specially young tits like these.'

The cry she had tried so desperately to hold back burst from Rachel as she shrank away from the hand fondling her breast.

'Don't touch me!' she gasped. 'Don't touch me.'

Sadie's hand dropped but the malicious smile remained. 'There'll be time enough for me to stroke them. I prefers to do it while the flesh be festering from the iron – you squirms even more that way. Think on that while you be waiting for morning to come.'

Swaying in the blackness she felt descending upon her, Rachel heard the slam of the door and the rasp of a bolt being shot into place.

Branded! The word rang in her brain. She would be branded with the mark of the workhouse. But wasn't she already branded with a far worse mark? Wasn't she branded her brother's killer?

Humiliation and revulsion at the wardress's treatment mixing with the fear already potent within her, she sank to the bed.

'I did not kill Robbie,' she sobbed into the darkness. 'I did not kill my brother.'

A small square of light played on the wall above the jug and basin, telling her it was morning. Rachel pushed herself from the bed, her body stiff with cold. Somewhere in the silent building a door banged. Grabbing her clothes, she struggled into them, anxiety making her fingers clumsy as she raced to be dressed before the odious wardress made an appearance. Having no comb, she smoothed her hair with her hands, dropping them as the bolt on her door scraped back.

She had passed no one when Sadie Buckley had escorted her last night but now, as they entered a room at the end of a corridor, Rachel saw three long trestle tables, the benches to either side of them filled with women, each wearing the same dun-coloured uniform, each head cropped to within an inch of the scalp.

Following the wardress's barked instructions, Rachel collected a tin bowl and spoon from a table alongside the door, taking it to a crop-headed woman standing behind a second table at the farther side of the room. On the stone flags stood a large two-handled pan from which she served porridge.

Following a brief nod of direction Rachel seated herself on the nearest bench, but no head lifted towards her and no one spoke.

'Room one will be in the wash house.' Sadie Buckley's strident voice overrode the rattle of spoons against bowls. 'Room two, in the kitchen. Three, the corridors and stairs. Four, the floors. And you . . .' She poked a sharp finger between Rachel's shoulder blades. '*You* will take the privies.'

'Why has her put you doin' the privies?'

A thin stringy woman, her scalp showing pink through her close cropped mousy hair, whispered to Rachel as she led the way from the dining hall to the yard behind the workhouse.

'Did you hit her? God, I 'ope you fetched the bastard a wallop that knocked her senseless! Though by the look of you, I doubt you have the strength.'

'No, I did not strike her,' Rachel whispered back, feeling the wardress's eyes following them as she stood in the doorway that gave on to the huge wash house.

'Pity!' The thin woman stopped before a pile of large rectangular metal trays, each about a foot deep, and beside them several short-handled shovels. 'I only be waiting for the chance to have another go at the hard-faced bitch, I swear I'll do for her then. But if you ain't tried landing her one, 'ow come you be put cleaning out privies?'

'Is it unusual?' Rachel took the tray and shovel handed to her.

'Ar.' Taking a second tray and shovel, the woman set off in the direction of a row of low-roofed narrow buildings, each barely faced with a narrow door that left a wide gap to top and bottom. 'I be the only one for six month or more been put to shovelling shit. It be her way of paying me out.'

'Paying you out for what?' Rachel glanced back across her shoulder to where the wardress still stood watching them.

'For hitting her in the face with a jug!' Kicking open the first of the doors, the woman glanced at Rachel, a smile creasing her thin face. 'It weren't so much the breaking of the governess's platter jug that bastard minded, as all the women laughing to see the gravy it held running down 'er face. Ever since then 'er's had me emptying the privies. So what did you do to upset her?'

'I . . . I haven't done anything.'

'I see.' The woman's smile slipped away. 'That be another of Sadie Buckley's dislikes. 'Er don't like a woman as don't respond to her petting, and that be what you done, ain't it?'

'I . . . I did not care for her watching me undress.'

'Nor for where 'er put her hands?' the woman said, seeing the colour rise high in the girl's pale face. 'One of these days that woman will have no hands with which to maul a wench. One day 'er will find them chopped off!'

'Cleaning privies not fit work for you this morning, Paget? Is it the bending and scraping you dislike . . . or perhaps the smell is not to your liking? Maybe we should sprinkle a little cologne in each privy so as not to offend your delicate nose.' The wardress's smile was vicious as she crossed the yard to them.

Squatting on her haunches in the first privy, the thin woman drew out a metal tray from beneath a bench-like seat with a hole in it. Bringing it out into the yard, she stood with it resting against the hessian apron that covered her down to her feet.

Rachel stepped away, stomach heaving at the sight of the evil-smelling mass that filled the tray.

'It ain't the smell of the privies be offending my nose,' Paget said, staring into the wardress's mocking eyes, 'it be the smell of a shit hawk – the stink of *you*, Sadie Buckley. You've had shit in your mouth ever since you learned to speak, now see 'ow it feels to swallow it!'

Lifting the tray she had taken from the privy, she heaved it full in the face of the wardress. Then, snatching off the hessian apron, she was over the surrounding wall and gone.

In the bath house Rachel had scrubbed her whole body until the skin burned but still the smell of the privies remained thick in her nostrils. All around the giggles of the women bore testimony to a delight that had lightened their soul-weary day: the delight of seeing Sadie Buckley covered from head to toe in excrement.

'Be Rachel Cade in here?'

Rachel stiffened as she heard her name called.

'You be Rachel Cade?'

A wardress she had not previously seen marched into the cubicle that housed one of the tin baths, and suddenly Rachel felt cold.

'Hurry up and get dressed,' the wardress continued as the girl nodded. 'You be wanted. There be a man waiting to see you.'

She had wondered when he would come. Now he was here, and it was to be done. She was to be branded.